The Diary of Andy Angus

The Lost Year

Joe Brewer-Lennon

ISBN: 9781086312249

For Oliver:
Your unwavering faith, love and support
has got me to this point.
My life is richer, warmer, sillier
and more fun with you in it.

About The Author

Joe Brewer-Lennon grew up on a Scottish council scheme that no longer exists. When he wasn't playing Kick the Can with friends, he would spend rainy days creating adventures with his limited supply of Doctor Who figures and his sister's Sindy dolls; the humble beginnings of his fictional creativity. In the mid-nineties, he somehow qualified as a nurse and has spent most of his adult life under a tedious mountain of paperwork convincing people to have unpleasant things done to them for their own good. After studying Sexual Health at Stirling University, he decided to turn some of this insight into the work of fiction you are about to read. He currently lives in Glasgow with his husband and two cats: two of which have no choice but to dress in black and white; one of which is smugly tortoiseshell.

Thanks to Anna:
The first to read this book and pour on the pride.
You pushed me to finish this story while
the clock was ticking loudly for you;
I'm glad you did.
You are missed.

Also, many thanks to Mike & Lindsay:
Your enthusiasm, feedback and
corrections gave me the confidence
to press on past the shy, awkward stage
of publishing.
I'm eternally indebted to your second-
born for keeping you up at night.

The Diary of Andy Angus

The Lost Year

Joe Brewer-Lennon

New Year Resolutions:

- I will wash out all recycling before popping it in the recycling bin (must find out what effect using more hot water and detergent has on the environment beforehand).
- I will clean out the grill pan after every use and not leave it for the next day.
- I will finally create a flawless dinner party on New Year's Day that will impress my family and seal my status as a Domestic God.
- I will make new friends and grow socially to inspire me to cook impressive dinner parties that people will gasp at when I present a table groaning under the weight of hearty, home-cooked deliciousness. (Sadly the postman is not really a friend; I should stop experimenting on him and chasing him down the garden with prepped tubs of food, but he is the only regular visitor to our cottage. Work colleagues are out as they are work colleagues, and I NEVER mix business with pleasure. And they all have weird children.)
- Spend more time in local cafes to meet decent people.
- Buy more classic Hornsea pottery to add to my collection, as it pleases my homemaker heart to see it on the shelf in all its vintage glory.
- Have more sex with Thomas than just once a fortnight (if that) and stop nagging him so much about minor domestic issues (such as window cleaning) as this is probably influencing the urge for him to have fun.
- Clean windows inside and out weekly.
- Dust skirtings weekly.
- Change bed sheets weekly (may inspire more sex).
- Stop worrying about getting old and enjoy finally being sorted in life.
- Visit my parents more often, maybe even stay over, and learn to like Mum more.
- Propose to the most handsome love of my life and draw up an action plan, with achievable but time-limited goals, for the big day.
- Stop feeling like a failure by setting unrealistic goals.

Monday 28th December 2009

Little Troll Cottage, Ewes Water

My mother, father and batty Aunt Moira have arrived today, staying through Hogmanay and hopefully not too long after. It will be a test for us all. Why do we self-harm like this? I could see the tension in my boyfriend Thomas' hands as he attempted to open a packet of HobNobs. He reduced the first five chocolate and hazelnut biscuits to dust. I tried not to worry about the crumbs on the laminate floor, but my eyes were drawn to them for the next ten minutes as he brewed some tealeaves poorly (he never warms the damn pot). I love him dearly, but it bugs the hell out of me that he tends to leave domestic matters to the last minute. Often that last minute involves me mopping, vacuuming, rinsing and crushing recycling, dusting, wiping, scooping or polishing. Is it asking too much of a gay man to be a little stereotypically house proud?

Aunt Moira took me to one side as I was Dust Busting and thrust this diary into my hand. She whispered with crazy, concerned eyes, 'People find it a comfort to write it all down when disaster strikes.' She then proceeded to break into an emphysemic rattle that could frighten the wolves from the woods and lumbered off with her oedema laden calves to get one of her many inhalers. She's a far cry from the blue-eyed brunette who turned heads when she sang professionally on cruise ships. Mum says Aunt Moira had a beautiful voice that could bring the angels down from heaven, but decades of neat vodka and cigarettes have taken their toll. When ill-health took hold, and she was decommissioned, Moira turned to the DSS and has earned cash on the side as a clairvoyant ever since. The wild-haired quack honestly believes she has some mystical power of prediction. No one needs a prophet of doom four days before the new year, so I threw the diary away as soon as she left the kitchen, but Mum excavated said diary later as she discarded her 20th Tetley teabag of the day. I was chastised like a seven-year-old boy who'd been caught kicking his ball against the neighbour's wall.

'You know fine well Moira's just had a colostomy fitted in November,' she stated bluntly as if it were a new en-suite bathroom. 'If she learns what a thankless little shit you've turned out to be, the disappointment could increase the anxiety of an already highly-strung pensioner, which in turn could inflame her innards, over-inflate her bag and cause all kind of odours, not to mention the strain on her fragile heart.' There followed an awkward silence as she gritted stained teeth that a Tanzanian tea tycoon would be proud of and tapped her foot in a manner I've known ever since I accidentally snapped the leg off my sister's new Sindy doll, circa Christmas 1982.

I conceded in this season of goodwill. As I peeled the soggy teabag off the cover, I informed her that the pound shop in Galashiels is currently doing 'buy-one-get-one-free' on Colgate Whitening.

'Your father and I aren't short of cash!' she snapped. 'We don't need to wander amongst the downtrodden of society to buy something as simple as toothpaste!' She has delusions of grandeur: they've lived in a Right to Buy council house since I was born and still have a polythene hothouse in their front garden.

11p.m. It's evident to me now that Aunt Moira's gloomy prophecy has un-nerved me; otherwise, why would I have written in this diary? She does have some powers of prediction: she was adamant that Betamax wouldn't last, even when half of Petersburn had invested their insurance money in the now-defunct video recorders after they fell off the back of a rather large lorry. My mother didn't heed her warnings of, 'You always end up paying for knockoff goods.' The only tapes that were supplied by later lorries were VHS, rendering the recorder useless as my folks couldn't afford to purchase tapes legally. Mum spent the next five months cowering under the lounge window every time the insurance man called to collect the payments she'd blown on the Betamax as it collected dust. She claims to have housemaid's knee, but I know how and when her problems really started.

Tuesday 29th December

I had to get out of the house this morning, Thomas was called into work for a boiler emergency (he's a plumber for Borders Gas), and I was left with the rabble. Dad was bemoaning the quality of our digital signal, Aunt Moira was bothered continuously by an itchy arse and bosom, and Mum was continually dropping, what she calls, 'advice' into my menu for New Year's Day. It is nothing but interference from a woman who believes cooking is as simple as reconstituting dry noodles.

'Nigella's a tart with no filling,' she said, 'It's all tits and pouting lips with her as she licks whipped cream off a spoon in slow motion. I don't know why you idolise her so much. Now Fanny Cradock, there was a cook.'

'If you like every course served with a large dose of vinegar,' I bit back, slamming Nigella's book shut. I scarpered for the tranquillity of the Ewes Water, but Mother Dearest followed declaring she needed fresh air as she picked at the inner lining of her parka and pulled out a pack of twenty Richmond Superkings (she *supposedly* gave up years ago).

'Don't look at me with your grandmother's eyes, God rest her soul,' she scowled in frustration as her hands shakily guided a tiny flame towards the cancer stick that was wobbling precariously on her ruby red lips in anticipation.

I tutted my disapproval.

'For Christ's sake, Andy,' she snapped, 'I gave up when we got married, raised two children through the miners' strike, nursed your Gran through a recession, watched your sister give birth on our kitchen linoleum as the Twin Towers fell, and coped when you decided the school nativity was the perfect time to come out of the closet without so much as a draw on a menthol.' Mum has never forgiven me for straying from the usual characterisation of Joseph by declaring that Jesus was most definitely the son of God and nothing to do with me as I was only interested in boys. I was ten at the time, very sure of my sexuality, and had no filter or insight into the consequences. She continued, 'But nothing has prepared me for the early retirement of your father and the tedium of being home alone, day after day, with no distractions but Phil and Fern and Hugh Fearnley-bloody-Whittingstall.'

Turns out Mum's upped her hours at the Post Office to:

a) Escape Dad's new passion for tropical fish.
b) Be able to smoke away from home without the risk of being caught.
c) Afford cigarettes.
d) Avoid Dad's monthly prescription of Viagra.

Sweet Jesus!

'I don't know how you and Thomas do it,' she muttered

through a shroud of smoke, 'just the two of you out here, in a windswept old cottage, surrounded by nothing but shrubs, sheep and shit.'

She made it sound as if we're living in a mountain shack in Mongolia. We have a village shop twenty minutes away and a local church for refuge in floods. I assured her that we are very, very happy. We love each other dearly and have the company of our cat, the Colonel, most evenings. After all, if there's a warm, stable home, a devoted man who puts food on the table, love and understanding, what more do you need?

Mum stared pensively as the discarded carcass of her sly fag floated tumultuously down the river. I was just about to mention the Country Code when she turned to me and said: 'He's sold my knitting machine on eBay and transformed your sister's bedroom into an aquarium. He's becoming more insular and selfish by the day. Marriage can be a total cock sometimes,' before retracing her frosty footprints back to the cottage.

I watched her stomp in her furry boots and parka until her hunched frame disappeared through the back door. I visualised how Mum used to be, back when I was small, all flowing red locks of curly hair that would bounce in unison with her confident stride as she dragged my sister and me down the market. She had such poise, speed and buoyancy that we had trouble keeping up with her. Now her hair, red though it still is, is restricted by a scrunchie and the only thing buoyant about her life is a room full of tropical fish. It seems a lifetime of cooking, cleaning and caring for a small family wears you down.

Little does she know I intend to propose to Thomas just after the bells. Ten years on and I am still deeply in love with my man. Not a single shot of cynicism can change that.

Wednesday 30th December

Aunt Moira choked on a small plastic fortune-telling fish this morning. She had been pulling a Christmas cracker covertly with my mother while the rest us were beginning to stir (I had been saving the last five crackers for my Grand New Year's Day Dinner). Said plastic fish had been inside the stolen cracker. I heard Moira's gasps of desperation and my mother's useless attempts at resuscitation from the comfort of our bed while reading an article on the current craze for dogging in the U.K. I flew through to find my mother smacking her sister on the back with a rolling pin on top of the kitchen table. I feared for their safety as our table is only IKEA and won't withstand the weight of two post-menopausal female wresters cavorting around on top of it. I pushed Mum to the side and proceeded to perform the Heimlich Manoeuvre on Aunt Moira's ample frame. It took four attempts, but she coughed the fish up with such ferocity it flew out of her mouth and landed on the table with some accidental sick.

'Oh, look, Moira,' Mum said casually as she examined the curled up piece of red cellophane, 'it says you're honest and caring.'

'Aw, that's nice,' replied Aunt Moira without a hint of oxygen starvation.

I cannot believe my family, they go from the ridiculous to the sublime within milliseconds! Thomas and Dad are just as bad. Both men staggered through bleary-eyed in boxer shorts, examined the scene and asked if anyone would like coffee.

I went back to bed after bleaching the table to find the newspaper I'd been reading gone. I bet Mum binned it in disgust. Now I'll never gain insight into dogging.

Thursday 31st December

Tomorrow's festive feast is Carrot and Orange Soup to start with, followed by Vodka Beef, with Heaven and Earth Mash, lentils braised in red wine, and a side of bitter chicory salad. Dessert is Nigella's Chocolate Guinness Cake, with Irish coffees to finish. The beef is marinating, and the cake is waiting to be iced. It's only 11 a.m., and I am in total control.

3.35 p.m. Shit! I have no Irish cream or double cream! It's New Year's Eve, and this part of the country is a ghost town during the holidays. My heart is racing! This is the first meal of 2010, and it has to to be flawless. I've demanded Dad drive me to Hawick as Thomas is busy at work and my car is stuck in our driveway under a weight of snow.

Mum was no help at all. 'Honestly, you're such a drama queen,' she quipped. 'Can't you just use Jack Daniels and Angel delight?' It's comments like this that makes me wonder if we are related. Perhaps Delia Smith has a secret lovechild from 1974; you can conceal anything under a gingham maxi dress.

5 p.m. Thanks to J Sainsbury's a colossal disaster has been averted. On the way back home I caught sight of Thomas' steamed up van in a lay-by off the A7. He must be exhausted from all the overtime he's doing. I almost asked Dad to stop the car to say a quick hello but figured my man would be having a fly kip between jobs, so I let him rest instead.

8 p.m. Seeing Mum and Dad getting on so well and sitting almost on top of each other on the sofa this evening has convinced me that they're still very much in love, no matter how stubborn she is to admit it. On the surface she's calloused, but deep down inside there's a candy floss heart. She possibly even enjoys the quiet company of tropical fish. There can be something steadfast and reassuring about a regular partial water change.

It's ten years to the day since Thomas and I met. It was at a millennium party in Edinburgh that I'd been harassed into attending by the anxious host: my long-lost friend Ryan. I remember his bitter tone when I called to say that I'd maybe skip his party and do CC Blooms instead (desperate to pull someone before midnight and have one final bout of sex before the millennium bug caused the world to implode).

'Well, thank you very much, Andy. I've spent the past three hours making one-hundred pralines. You had better show up, or else I'll stuff every last one of them into every one of your orifices the very next time I see you.' Ryan always had such a charming way of convincing people to do the right thing, for him. Like a good friend, I attended and clocked Thomas straight away. He was socially awkward, and I was bored stiff: we were the only two not smoking pot. It was only a matter of time before one part of this equation would extract its digits from the party, find the other and multiply. And so, in the quiet kitchen of Leith Street, over a bottle of red and many pralines later, we got friendly enough to share a nutty kiss by the time the millennium bug had failed to cause a major catastrophe around the globe. We were in bed within the first three hours of the

21st century and in love before the buses started running a normal service. Bliss! It's long overdue that we make it official. I intend to remedy this at midnight in front of my folks. I even have a ring to slip on his finger until I can replace it with a proper wedding band. I'm a little apprehensive but excited at the same time. I'm sure he'll say yes as we know each other inside and out and both enjoy hill walking in matching anoraks. There's no risk of public humiliation.

Friday 1st January 2010

10 a.m. My head is killing me. I have to cook, and all I can think about is sticking my noggin in a bucket of ice-cold water for the next five hours. It was all okay until Dad opened a bottle of Highland Park I had been keeping for after today's dinner. I was inebriated and comatose on the sofa before Jools Holland's Hootenanny had finished with the ring still tucked safely in my sporran. I'll do it at the meal tonight. Everyone should be feeling brighter by then, including myself.

10 p.m. Disaster! It was going so well until I served the Vodka Marinated Beef. Everyone attempted to eat it without too much fuss, but I was well aware that the water jugs were being passed around as if they held the elixir of life.

'It's nice,' said Mum, masticating quickly, 'if not a tad salty.'

A tad salty? It was as if I'd swallowed the entire Sahara Desert.

Within thirty minutes, we were all taking it in turns to vomit in the downstairs loo. I note that my family are incapable of vomiting quietly, becoming more vocal as the lavatory rotation carried on. The convulsions of my diaphragm were just easing when Aunt Moira sweated profusely, became incoherent, scurried out to the back garden (I assume for air) and collapsed headfirst into the snow.

You can't help but feel a failure when you watch your family being carted away in an ambulance on New Year's Day. Thomas must have a stomach of steel as he was fit enough to drive me to the hospital to join them. I waited for five whole hours before being seen as I wasn't a 'priority'. Aunt Moira, who is the sickest of us all, is being kept in overnight for close observation. Mum and Dad are fine now and have been released. Mum is in a mood and shut herself in their bedroom. She hasn't spoken to Thomas or me since we returned. I'm sure it's not all down to me. Aunt Moira is mostly responsible through her debauch lifestyle and choosing not to live in a 2-up-2-down with 2.4 children. A tiny salty slice of rump can't cause major complications, I'm sure.

In other news, I've lost the damn ring. It was definitely in my sporran when I was stripped off for bed by Thomas in the early hours of New Year's Day, as I had all the coordination of a man who had just had a CVA. I fumbled around for it after the main course and began to lead into my proposal, but by the time I'd released it was lost, the bile started to bite and gagged me, sending me headlong to the toilet bowl first. Thomas stayed by my side while I was most unattractive. He is a good man. He stroked my sweating forehead throughout, which was reassuring and romantic, but it did seem inappropriate to hint at a civil union between fluid chunks of chicory and chokes of chardonnay. I'll ask him tomorrow when I'm sure the family will all be back together in good health.

Saturday 2nd January

1.25 a.m. I'm on the sofa after a muted row with Thomas. I hinted it was strange he was the only one not affected by the beef incident. He admitted he had been reluctant to touch my carefully prepared dinner and had spent the first few minutes disguising the beef under his mash. After all the time, energy and money it cost me! I found myself unable to stop ranting for the next half hour. His pretence that he was settling into a comfortable sleep was a genuine irritation. I cast up his lack of help around the cottage, his inability to cook, or even try, his ignorance of an overflowing recycling bin and his total refusal to pick poo out of the Colonel's litter tray.

'Why do we even have a litter tray?' he asked. 'That dumb cat is outdoors most of the time anyway.'

'Don't call him dumb,' I said, softening my voice from Mum's prying ears by tucking my nose under the duvet. 'I know you've never really wanted him.'

Thomas sat bolt upright and growled, 'Well, it was you who took him in. And I'm not apologising for leaving your poison to one side yet again.'

'Poison? Yet again?'

'Aye, yet again. After one lick I knew it was inedible, just like your cardamon curry, Tunisian meatballs, yellow split pea and frankfurter soup, and the Yorkshire puddings you manage to burn to a crisp that are only fit to wedge doors open with. Aunt Moira's lucky to be alive. You've never been that great a cook. Give it up! You spend your days searching the web for ridiculous recipes and criticising my every move around the house. God forbid I leave skid-marks on your pristine toilet bowl, or an unwashed mug in the sink, or a tiny crumb on the kitchen table. You've never been a Domestic

God, and *this* most definitely is *not* domestic bliss! This kind of shit doesn't actually matter, don't you get that? Can't you see the bigger picture?'

What the hell was that supposed to mean? I had no idea I should be looking for some colossal portrait of our life together encased in a frame of dissolution and sarcasm. I thought we were good. Not only good but great.

With his words ringing in my ears, I left our bed without a word and took the duvet with me. He can bloody freeze as far as I'm concerned! After a decade of, what I assumed to be bliss, the truth is out. What else has he been lying about? Am I going to find he doesn't like the way I iron his underpants? Or the way I fold the toilet roll into a point every night before we go to bed so that it's perfectly presented for his buttocks in the morning? Am I going to learn that, during the days I'm at work, he's resting his filthy boots on top of our coffee table while drinking milk from the carton?

What a bloody fabulous way to start the year. It couldn't get any worse.

1.25 p.m. I was wrong. It did. Aunt Moira died of a heart attack. Mum got a call at eight this morning saying she was fading fast and urging her to come quickly. Dad rushed her into their car and drove like a lunatic to the Borders General. Thomas and I followed, but we were all too late. My mother was informed of Aunt Moira's passing in the relatives' room of Ward 5 still wearing the nightdress she'd borrowed from her sister the night before.

There's something terrible about seeing your mother weak and crying truly inconsolable, unstoppable tears. She clung on to my dad, the pain causing her to buckle at the knees, asking, 'Why?' over and over again. Dad hung on to her as tight as he could and asked us to go. I've never seen her in such a state. Thomas and I drove back home in a stunned silence mixed with post-argument awkwardness. This silence followed us through the front porch, down the hall and into the kitchen. The Colonel purred hungrily between my legs, unaware that part of our small pack had just been lost forever. But life has to go on, and so I fed him. Thomas opened the fridge door and saw the leftover beef, sedentary and shamefully dehydrated on the shelf.

'I'll just throw this out,' his voice cracked as he tossed the whole joint into the bin and slowly filled the dish with water to soak for what seemed like an eternity. The pain was killing me.

'It wasn't poison,' I whimpered.

'No, it wasn't.'

'I didn't just poison my Aunt, did I?' The words hung in the air as tears filled my eyes.

'Of course not,' he said, leaving the dish to soak in the sink. Bubbles of Fairy Liquid dispersed around his head as he grasped the bottle from the draining board. The suds popped playfully against the greasy slick that floated on the top of the hot water that the dish was drowning in. He picked up the sponge scourer (useless at absorbing any fluids) and said, 'The doctors said this had been brewing for a while. She'd already had minor twinges, which she'd ignored.' He wiped down the draining board rather carelessly I thought, leaving dirt in the edges and streaks throughout. 'Besides, if they couldn't save her there ... I don't know ... there was no hope.'

Tears flowed down my cheeks, I'm not sure if they were out of mourning for my aunt or just relief that the person who matters to me most believes I wasn't entirely responsible for her passing. Even though we both know, I was most definitely a catalyst.

That was the time we should've hugged and made up, but he just whispered, 'Better start calling the family,' and left me and the dish steeping in the kitchen.

It's 1.30 p.m., and we are still hugless.

Sunday 3rd January

Mum and Dad have left for home. Aunt Moira will follow tomorrow. She's going to the undertakers in the High Street, the one with the garish looking gravestones in the window. The same pile of plastic flowers have laid at the foot of each headstone for decades. I informed Mum that they offer a Groupon deal every so often and a 25% discount off your next funeral if you choose to use their services again within the year.

'Every cloud ...' said Mum, sarcastically.

A death right at the beginning of the year. This is not a good omen. I feel totally drained. This is *not* how expected 2010 to begin.

10.30 p.m. We're still hugless. There's a yawning chasm between us now when we sleep. The ring is lost. Proposal postponed until we're both better equipped to work through this.

Monday 4th January

Called Mum in the afternoon, Moira's funeral is on Saturday morning, with a light spread afterwards at the wake. Beef is not on the menu. Life returns slowly back to normal. I fixed Thomas' breakfast and packed lunch. We ate together between bouts of stilted conversation. He dropped me at Tesco Galashiels at the usual time (7.45 a.m.) and sped off to his typical day stripping boilers and hobs. I offered a kiss, aiming for his lovely lips, but he turned his cheek, and I misplaced it desperately, kissing him on his ear. I guess my suggestion that he trim his ear hair was poorly timed. He skidded off with a face like thunder.

Clocked in, shelves stacked, fifteen-minute break had, more shelves stacked, clocked out. Part-time hours put in once again. With the shift done, I text Thomas. No reply, so I untethered my bike from the trolly barrier and set off home along an icy, breezy road. I guess any journey in his van would've been just as frigid.

I text him to say I was home safe, again no answer, and then realised we had no milk or bread, so off I pedalled again to the local shop. While cycling back, I spied his van in the same lay-by on the A7. It was getting dark. I couldn't see him in the driver's seat, but I know his numberplate well. He must've been dozing for some time as the windows were all steamed up. There were several cars and vans parked-up there in the same condition; poorly air-conditioned tin cans of condensation.

He arrived back home just in time for dinner and Coronation Street. Weatherfield proved a happy distraction, but there is a lump in my throat that makes eating or talking difficult. I feel I could burst into tears at any second. While making small-talk over apple crumble and custard, I just happened to mention spotting his van earlier. He became all shirty and barked, 'If I choose to have a snooze between jobs, it's nobody's business but mine. You've no idea the pressure I'm under. It's winter, and everyone's suddenly pushing their ancient heating systems to the limit. My boss wants me to do as many home visits as possible in the day. The company needs all the jobs it can get. It's struggling to climb out of the pit of debt it was in before this recession started.'

I emphasised I didn't have a problem with him getting his head down, I'm just concerned he's taking on too much work. He's covering more hours than before, and he's hardly at home. He also wakes frequently through the night as if something is preying on his mind and seems to laugh so little these days. I'm happy for him to rest when he can, as long as he doesn't get caught by his boss.

When did he stop laughing at my silly jokes? I never expected to win the Edinburgh Comedy Festival, but I had hoped I would stay interesting enough for my lover to crack a smile now and then and look at me with adoration.

Tuesday 5th January

I have backdated the proposal to a more exciting time in our lives as this is not a good patch. Judging by his current mood, I can't be sure he'd commit to a weekend away at Alton Towers, never mind a lifetime legally tethered to a Doctor Who fan. What I wouldn't give for a blue Police Box to materialise and fast-forward me towards our happy ever after.

Wednesday 6th January

Today, while I cycled home from my late shift, I passed the previously mentioned lay-by, which I will curse forever. Thomas' van was parked there yet again. Something inside me told me to backtrack and have a look. Instinct, maybe. There he was, my life-partner, in the back of his van, going down on a *woman!* Maybe it was the shock of discovering he's been lying to me all these years or the fact that the girl beckoned me to join in, I'm not sure, but I started to cycle away in a daze. Thomas had no idea I'd seen anything as his face was busily engrossed in vaginal fluids. It took almost being hit by a passing truck to throw me to my senses and turnabout.

'Thomas? What the fuck?' I yelled into the back of his open van.

'Andy!' he yelped as he fumbled to pull the jeans from around his ankles and struggled off his knees. 'Now, hold on a sec. It's not how it looks.'

Not how it looks? How else *could* it look? It's a pretty sure thing your other half has made a shift in sexual orientation when you find him diving headlong into some tart's crotch! 'How long have you been cruising lay-bys?' I asked, the anger boiling from my head to my fists.

'Well, technically speaking, it's not cruising. It's *dogging* ...'

And with this, this one stupid, fastidious sentence, I lost it. My fist bounced off his top lip, and he lost an incisor. *He* dared to call *me* a bastard as he clutched his face and searched for his tooth in the bloodstained snow.

'*I'm* the bastard? I cook, I cleaning, I run around after you and do my best to fulfil your every need. And for what? Thanks for showing me the bigger fucking picture. Now I see everything very clearly.'

I jumped on my bike and cycled as fast as I could home. The cold air ripped at my panting lungs, but I didn't care as the pain in my sobbing heart was far worse.

Midnight. He hasn't come after me. I am alone for the first time in ten years. Ten years!

Shit!

Thursday 7th January

I've texted him, I've tried calling, I have even left voicemails. Nothing. I should be raging, throwing his crap into bin bags and tossing all of it onto the front lawn, but I'm lost. I can't function on my own. Who am I if I'm not with him?

This is bullshit! I should be the one ignoring his calls for mercy, and yet I'm hanging on to my phone as an asthmatic hangs on to an inhaler during flu season.

I hope he's ok. He could be dead or anything. Is it possible to bleed to death from a burst lip and violently removed tooth? Maybe I should call A&E. No, that's just ludicrous. He'll turn up soon. If he ever loved me, he will.

Oh, God! It's Aunt Moira's funeral on Saturday. How the hell can I explain this to Mum and Dad, not to mention the rest of the mob? I know I'm pathetic, but I just can't bring myself to tell my family we're over.

Friday 8th January

'Thomas is dealing with a major gas leak in Hawick today,' I lied casually as Mum inspected Aunt Moira's corpse in her coffin. She's on full display in the front room of the tiny bungalow she's lived in for most of her solo retirement. Mum had attempted to tidy the lounge a bit, but there are still the signs of an old eccentric jutting out awkwardly from every corner. Decade-old copies of The Stage, half-knitted sweaters and tickets to theatre shows were strewn all over the place, some dating back as far as 1963. A chocolate digestive was stuck down the side of Aunt Moira's easy-rise chair. I struggled to ignore it. The usual pictures hung on the wall, many from her time as a singer on the Caribbean line before her career ended and she was sent back to Petersburn under the overbearing eyes of her younger sister.

'That's not Midnight Blue eye-shadow,' Mum tutted in distaste. 'I know our Moira, and she never wore that shade.' She tutted several times more in succession. 'I told them specifically Midnight Blue.' Her nose sniffed as keenly as a bloodhound's, 'Can you smell her Charley?' she asked.

I leaned forward and waved my nose reluctantly over the gap in the coffin lid. There she lay, looking as colourful as an elderly member of Pan's People on pause. Ironically, I'd never seen her so full of life. Practically Technicolor. I sniffed some more, moving southwards with a grimace. I pulled back. I just couldn't. 'Look, Mum, I thought they took care of these issues of ... um ...' I mouthed, ' "personal hygiene", at the undertakers.'

'Not that, you filthy buggar! Her *Charley*! Her favourite perfume.' Mum slapped me on the shoulder and shook her head in disbelief. 'Honestly, do you really think I'd ask that?' She turned back to Moira – I swear I could see my aunt smile – and continued, 'Well, I can't smell Charley. I'll get some from her handbag and give her a few squirts.'

When Mum came back, carrying the bottle of perfume upfront with some urgency, she maced Moira head to toe and pinned a small, gold and silver hummingbird brooch on my aunt's lapel. 'I can't find her favourite, so this will have to do. There, that's much better, eh, Sis?' Mum calmed and stared pensively towards Aunt Moira as she poked her cheek and chewed on the flesh inside as she does when in deep contemplation, 'Oh, she's left you her assorted collection of carpet samples.'

'What? Why?'

'I don't feckin' know. She said you'd need them someday. You were always flicking through them with your sister when you were young. God knows why.'

'Well, I suppose it saves me having to lay on the floor to get carpet burns,' I joked.

Mum spun towards me in disgust, almost knocking Aunt Moira to the floor, 'Please, Andy, don't mention anal sex on a day like today, do me that one favour.'

I find it irritating that my mum still associates homosexuality with anal sex. There's so much more to being gay than being on your knees; however, I bit my tongue and cast my eyes over a copy of The Daily Mail from 1972. Peering suspiciously at my aunt over the yellowed pages, I would say, from that angle, she was positively smirking.

Saturday 9th January

Aunt Moira's Funeral

To Mum's annoyance, Dad stuck by her side constantly. She must've been craving a cigarette, but she kept a brave face on it all as she greeted a never-ending line of Aunt Moira's friends from the local operatic society and psychic college. I could see her occasionally reassure herself by stroking a lump – distinctly the shape and size of a packet of Richmond Superkings – that jutted through her parka lining.

It was just after the local church had played *Climb Every Mountain* from The Sound of Music (Moira's favourite musical) that it went pear-shaped. Thomas appeared beside me on the creaky bench with his front tooth temporarily superglued in place, attempting to look angelic while holding a copy of the New Testament. He opened the Bible and held it close to his face, murmuring over the spine into my ear, 'Andy, we need to talk.'

Susurrations of, 'What the hell are you doing here?' from me, and, 'I told you to get lost!' were met with muted replies from him of, 'Look, I need to tell you something. Besides, she was my Aunt too.' And, most irritatingly, 'You owe me this moment to say goodbye to her.' Mum hushed us as the priest began his final eulogy.

'I owe you?' I turned on Thomas before Mum spun around briskly, reaching as far as she could to smack both of us on the head with the skill that can only be learned from raising two troublesome children.

'Will you two show some respect?' she grunted.

A begrudged calm fell over us as the reality of the situation crept in. The sentiments of the priest cut through me like an icy blade: 'Moira, in her career, had plenty of rehearsals, but life is not a rehearsal. We only get one chance of happiness ...'

I mouthed his words back to Thomas, 'One chance.' He turned his attention to the priest, listening as intently as a nun does to the pope. I pretended to do the same. We remained this way throughout the rest of the service.

To my displeasure, Mum insisted on having Thomas join us in the family limo as it followed the hearse. 'What was that all about back there?' she snapped. 'Whatever has happened between the two of you can be put aside for one day, by God.' She smiled reassuringly at Thomas and, knowing Dad was safely out of view in Marie's car, seized the moment to light up a cigarette. The limo driver informed my mum that it was a non-smoking car. She snarled, 'Aye, well, I'm having a bit of a shit day, Sonny Jim, in case you hadn't noticed. And don't think I've not spotted the dog hairs in the back here.' She vigorously wound down her window and slammed the glass partition shut on the driver. I shook my head in despair. 'What?' was her aloof reply as she forced wisps of smoke from cocked, tight lips towards the heavens.

****

I could feel my blood reaching boiling point as Aunt Moira was lowered into the sodding grave. Mum's grief inspired some pent-up emotion deep inside me to bubble to the surface, and my eyes began to sting. But it wasn't the death of my dotty old aunt that caused the dam to burst, it was Thomas' careless statement as we got out of the car, 'I need the cottage. It is mine, after all. You'll have to move out.' Was he testing me? Trying to see how upset I was and how far I'd throw us? 'We can work out the direct debits later,' he added. Ten years and that's all we boiled down to – finances. As my aunt was lowered deeper into the earth, something else was dying and being buried with her. It was my hope and faith in humanity.

Mum stepped forward and took a handful of dirt to be the first person to sprinkle it over her sister's coffin, and I felt a hand clasp mine. A hand that before would have been warm, loving and reassuring, but now felt icy cold. 'No!' I yelled as I tore free! 'No! No! No!' Mum paused over the grave, her bloodshot eyes bulging towards me. Her mind slowly ticking over. 'Don't you *dare,*' I bellowed as I pushed Thomas away. 'Don't you dare manipulate me when I'm broken. You've taken everything I thought was good and decent about us and shit all over it with your lies and your deceitful, detestable antics!'

Mum cut in and whispered with fire in her lungs, 'What the *hell* is going on?'

'He's been fucking around, Mum.' I nodded to the priest, 'Sorry, Father.' 'He's been screwing a *woman!* Sorry, Father. Not just one woman, but loads of sluts! Apologies again, Father.'

'But ... but ... you're gay,' Mum said through a red mist as she strode towards my ex.

'Turns out that's not so, he's bi and been *dogging,*' I assured her.

My sister flapped around her kids like a panicked chicken in an attempt to cover five pairs of ears. Realising this was impossible, and that the conversation was heading lower than Aunt Moira's coffin, she opted out and took to locking them in the hearse.

Mum stumbled closer, high heels sliding in the sodden ground, 'Dogging?'

The priest cut in, 'I believe it's an activity in which men and women drive to a public area to ...'

'I know what dogging is, thank you, Father,' Mum snapped, 'I do watch Channel 4.' There was a breathless pause between us all. Mum's knuckles whitened as she squeezed the dirt in her palm. And then she let rip. Handful after handful of mud was taken from the box and thrown at Thomas.

'Go on! Piss off, you dirty piece of filth! Don't you ever come to my house again. That's the last time I make pea and ham soup for you – boiling a bloody pig's bone for hours – what a waste of my precious time. And keep your cheating paws off my son.'

My pride soared as Mum chased Thomas the length of the graveyard, weaving in and out the headstones skilfully as the mourners watched, some horrified, some cheering her on until Thomas careered out of the gates to be seen no more.

She returned to a little more respectable level of silence, a tad out of breath, shoes muddy and a wet-wipe at the ready to clean her soiled hands. I burst out laughing. Not appropriate at a funeral, I know, but I couldn't stop.

'What?' she asked, a little dumbfounded.

'Nothing,' I said. 'It's just, you're bloody outrageous some times.'

Mum's face became stone-like, 'Andrew, please. God is present. Mind your language.' She gave me the tiniest crack of a smile and then pointed to the mourners, who were chuckling to themselves, and said, 'And that goes for the rest of you. Save the joviality for the wake. Then anything goes.' They nodded eagerly, desperate for a drop of alcohol. Once her hands were spotless, she gripped mine, held her head high and whispered to me, 'Well, I'm saying goodbye to my sister, but I got my son back.'

Sunday 10th January

Hangover number two of 2010. The old dears from Aunt Moira's Psychic College can most certainly hold their own. I've been woken by my dishevelled mother in a pink, faux-silk housecoat, red and white polka dot cat-eye sunglasses and fluffy flip-flops. Her usual curly locks were matted to one side of her head as a result of passing out on the sofa at 2 a.m. Her voice reverberated like a Dalek with laryngitis as she bid me a half-hearted, 'Good morning,' and slid a bacon roll on my old bedside cabinet which is still adorned with Dr Who transfers. It was nice to be looked after. I'm normally the one running around, organising a grown man, a cat and myself, but for now, I'll be taking it easy. The simplicity of childhood leaves us without a whisper of goodbye, and we never give it a second thought once it's gone, because being older and wiser is supposedly better.

Mum and Dad say I can stay with them as long as I need, but to tell you the truth, I don't think I can face living with semi-retired parents whose idea of a fun weekend is wandering around B&Q lusting after new garden furniture. It's time to head home and face the music. I've no idea what's going to happen. Where the hell do I go from here? Can I pack up my whole life in a 2001 Vauxhall Astra? Can the suspension take almost ten years worth of baggage? Will Thomas even be at home, or is he preoccupied living the life of a swinger?

9.25 p.m. I got back to find the cottage deserted. I knew Thomas would be finishing work soon, so I made a quick job of it after I'd ensured the coast was clear. His Datsun was in the driveway, but his van wasn't. I've climbed the steps to that front door easily thousands of times, but this time it was like a mountain. I turned the lock and crept cautiously into the hall. Our blissful milestones were dotted within frames along the walls, eyeballing and mocking me as I crept through our home. I progressed towards the bedroom, in which I'd been told repeatedly we'd had the 'best sex ever'. Passing the kitchen, I noticed a pile of dirty dishes overflowing from the sink and sliding slowly, with help from the scum and grease, across the draining board. Used pots were congealed to the hob. A futile attempt at washing clothes had been made, idle in the drum of the machine, probably musty from days before. A pile of dirty laundry was perched on the dining table in need of rescue. I continued along the hall: dirty towels laid on the bathroom floor; dirt from his boots coated the carpet all the way to the bedroom; the bed was a tumultuous sea of used linen; the curtains were still drawn, and drawers were yawning open.

I should've been satisfied that he couldn't cope without me, not even for a few days, but it disgusted me. I've been used as a domestic for years, with little payment but for the odd hug and appreciative comment. I was so keen to please. So gullible.

Next to the bed, I found a small pile of clothing, purple in colour, and a killer pair of heels. I could almost admire the wearer for being able to walk in them, but I knew they were rarely used for walking: these were fuck-me-pumps. A female had been here who was comfortable enough to leave her shit lying around. I picked up the clothing by the flimsy straps. It was delicate and smelt of woman; entirely foreign to me. There were stains on the front and back. The pungent smell of sex clung to it like a desperate whore to a new pimp. I began to feel sick. I dropped the offending item and picked up the pace.

Finding my way through the crap, I stuffed a few cases and bin-bags quickly with clothes. I started by folding everything neatly but gave up on neatness as the clock ticked faster. Clothes packed, I filled a small box with sentimental relics from a life now lost. I piled them by the door and quickly carried each item to the car, unaware of the weight I was carrying until it came to my most prized possessions: my full collection of Doctor Who magazines and DVDs. They almost broke my back, but I wasn't leaving them to be sold by some harpy on eBay.

During my last sweep around, I heard the familiar meow of the Colonel hungrily demanding his dinner in the kitchen, ignorant of the impending loss of a parent. I wondered if he sensed this would be the last time I'd feed him as I placed his bowl in its usual spot and tried to stop myself from crying. Just a quick burst of emotion and then there was the familiar sound of Thomas' key turning in the lock and his boots scraping laboriously on the mat. He caught sight of me and paused as if in preparation for a battle. There we were, feet away from one another, but miles apart. Teetering on the edge of our past before stepping off into the unknown. 'Oh, it's you,' he said.

'Don't act surprised, Thomas,' I said, 'there's an Astra out there that I can barely shut the doors on.'

'True,' he muttered as he slid off his high viz coat and hung it neatly on the hook by the door. *Why be so tidy about that?* I remember thinking. *The rest of the place is in as much turmoil as our lives.*

'I'm not staying, but then even your pea-brain could work that out. But as you're here, answer me this: did you ever love me?'

He sighed, tucked his hands into the back pockets of his jeans, and said, 'I did. For a while. Before it all became about the house, and work, and bills, and upsetting perfectly placed coasters.'

'Fair do's.' I went to leave, but before I did, I said, 'Just for the record, not that it matters much now, but I loved you with all my heart, and I honestly thought we were doing just fine. What a fool, eh?'

'You're no fool.'

'Yeah, well, you could've fooled me. And you have.' I threw my keys towards him. They bounced off his chest and landed at his feet. Before I shut the door behind me, I gave one parting shot, 'Oh, and Thomas?'

'Aye?'

'A man who has such low self-esteem and who asserts his sexual prowess in lay-bys should never fuck with a pair of heels that are twice the length of his cock.' Low, I know, but it's all I had.

I was gone.

It saddens me to say it, but he looked relieved. For a relationship that lasted a decade, it ended swiftly. He owns a three-bedroom cottage with extensive gardens, a cat, and my potential happiness locked within. I own a car, two suitcases and four bin-bags of clothes, a pile of Doctor Who magazines and DVDs, a Hornsea pottery collection and a whole lot of emotional baggage. Not to forget a useless engagement ring that is mocking me from inside its box, which I found tucked at the back of Thomas' sock drawer. He must've seen it in my sporran when I passed out at Hogmanay and sabotaged my plan. It seems he was determined that I would never find the perfect moment to propose.

It hasn't been easy to drive through the dense, relentless snow with glazed eyes while I ponder the past and endeavour to find clues to his deceit within the parameters of our tiny life together, so I've pulled over at Thornilee Picnic Park to clear my thoughts. I've been here for an hour, scribbling in this diary by the tiny light above the rear-view mirror. I would've left ages ago, but my stupid car is stuck in thick snow. I have no mobile signal and have already eaten the emergency Yorkie I keep tucked in the seat pocket. I have no fluids of any sort. The fuel is low, therefore, I can't leave the engine running, so that means no heater. Bloody fantastic. At this rate, they'll find my blood-drenched trail in the snow after I've been dragged to the woods to be eaten alive by wolves. I have the distinct feeling someone is shitting on me from a great height.

Half a freezing hour later. Through the Dark, by KT Tunstall, which I've listened to a hundred times before, rolled on the CD player and caused uncontrollable tears. Such big sobs. It's never affected me before. I've always liked the song, the melody is well known to me, but the words came through loud and clear tonight and hit me like a baseball bat in the gut. For the first time in ten years, I'm alone. What the hell am I going to do now? The snow is the heaviest I've ever seen. I'm literally lost in a blizzard and confusion and despair is at every turn. My mind is blank. A total white-out, you might say.

Monday 11th January

Where did I turn? I fell on the mercy of a stranger in a big way. A forty-year-old businessman helped me out of the snow with a towrope, a can of petrol and the brute force of his 4X4. He appeared like a knight in a smart Armani suit and helped me free my car with the aid of Aunt Moira's carpet cuts wedged under the wheels. His idea, not mine, proving that my psychic, giddy aunt was right to gift them.

It only took a few minutes of wheel spinning, and then I was free to go. The blizzard had passed, and delicate white flakes danced around his beautiful head. If I wanted to set off with a clear view of the road, now was the time. But I didn't. He didn't rush off either. I felt un-expectantly at peace in his presence as he described the history of the landscape illuminated by moonlight. He moved so close to me that I could smell his beautiful, manly frame was pleasantly sprayed with a cologne that drew me in. Aware I was playing with fire, I invaded his personal space. To my joy, he didn't back off. His sweet muskiness enveloped me. Mutual arousal ensued. Within seconds, we were at it like animals in the freezing air as snow crystals dropped all around our naked frames. It was downright risky but bloody liberating. The second I came, I felt guilty: I'd just gone through a breakup, what the hell was I doing? I was desperate to leave, but he seemed to want to stay and chat.

So we chatted about the shocking weather conditions, travel chaos, cars, the history of the Scottish Borders and the constellations above our heads. It became a kind of therapy. Deceiving ourselves into believing that, if we could establish some connection, no matter how small, then it would be a less sordid encounter. Hell, I have nothing to feel remorseful about. I'm a free agent. And even though he was some random bit of stuff, he was decent, educated and kind. We swapped numbers, just in case I needed his help further down the road, of course. No names. Why would we? It was just meaningless sex. My first piece of meaningless sex in ten years. Quite liberating, actually. He's stored as '4X4 Guy', that's all. Keep it simple. I don't need complication in my life.

Tuesday 12th January

222 Mull, Petersburn

I woke this morning with my feet hard pressed against the footboard of my teenage bed. My Spider-Man quilt was wrapped around me at least twice after a restless night reliving the lay-by incident over and over in my dreams. This bed is where I spent many hours of adolescent exploration, discreetly poised under the duvet with the sports section of the Daily Record clutched in my quivered hand as I edged towards climax several times a day. My attraction to men didn't just creep in the room, at puberty it kicked the door down, injected a hefty dose of testosterone directly into the pleasure centres of my brain and never lost its potency. Thrilling as those days/nights/afternoons were, I don't expect to be revisiting them as a thirty-five-year-old. I've outgrown not only this bed but this room and this house too. I'm a giant trapped in a place that's so much bigger in the childish recesses of my mind. Yes, I've been back before, but never with the intention of staying, not even for a night.

I slid up the pillows easily by way of pushing off the irritating footboard with my socked feet. The bed creaked, unaccustomed to the weight of an adult male and all the woes that are now piled upon his shoulders. I took time to think. I'm fortunate to have my folks to rely on, but this feels like a huge step back. Faces of 90's pop stars stared back at me from sun-bleached posters cut from *Smash Hits*. Did we really look all that different in the 90s? That bad? It wasn't *that* long ago. Jeez, the 90s: when I had a centre-parting and was desperate to escape Airdrie after that god-awful train journey. I didn't suddenly grow up with a first taste of beer in the local club, or with some misdirected fumble with a girl in a bus shelter, I had maturity kicked into me. Ten minutes of my life that changed me forever.

A collection of toys, ranging from the main cast of Star Wars, the Fourth Doctor made by Denys Fisher (with both legs repaired by Mum several times due to many a leap from our staircase), two Daleks (one blue, one red, vocalisation immobilised by bathwater), three battle-scarred Action Men and my sister's damaged Sindy doll (with yellowing sellotaped leg), stand on the shelves pretty much as I'd left them. A pile of astronomy books for kids fill the bookcase alongside original Doctor Who Target novels. On the sideboard sits my ghettoblaster, surrounded by neatly stacked and alphabetically arranged cassette tapes and CDs. The poster above of Dolph Lundgern, shirtless and in red boxing gloves, poised ready to pummel Sylvester Stallone in Rocky IV, still attracts me. I tore my attention away from his amazing pecs and glanced at the alarm clock. It was 10 a.m.

I stumbled out of bed with the duvet wrapped around me and staggered towards the window, which is still flanked by the curtains that have hung since we got our first GPO telephone. My eyes flinched as they registered the brightness of the fabric; orange, yellow and grey warped circles that spin in every direction. I could hear Mum giggling away to Radio 2's Ken Bruce as he poked fun at Sally Traffic in the kitchen below. 'Is that you up, Andy?' she called, her parental sonar picking up my footsteps with ease.

'Aye,' I yelled, aware there was no real need to answer. Her ears have been trained to my movements since I started kicking her womb.

'Kettle's on,' was her cheery reply. She then joined Elkie Brooks singing *Pearl's a Singer.*

I pulled back the net curtain. Spring Fresh wafted as they parted, defying the weather. *Freshly laundered,* I thought, *Mum may not be a cook, but she does the laundry every day.* I peered out of the window and down the street I'd skinned my knees on as a child. The neighbours' gardens are as much the same shape as the template burned onto my mind's eye. Mrs White's 1987 entry to the Beechgrove Garden's Best Presented Garden competition is still evidently being maintained, even though it's smothered under a thick rug of snow, it's obviously the most orderly of gardens in the scheme. The McGregor's garden was patchy with thin strips of snow and large lines of muddy grass and weeds; the byproduct of tiny feet pushing balls of snow to build a healthy snowman in the middle. This tells me the McGregors are still as fertile as ever. The Doyle's rusting Ford Cortina is still stranded on bricks in the tyre-worn trench of their garden. They've never had a proper driveway; instead, they've chosen to fashion their own through the persistent parking of cars on their grass until it finally gave up and slopped either side to grant space for their old bangers. Every child in their family has risen to the dizzy heights of boy or girl racer.

Our house is preserved in much the same style as the brutalist architect intended: concrete, flat-roofed and boxy. A few alterations have been made after my folks bought it from Thatcher's Britain, like roughcasting, the conservatory strapped to the back door and a PVC front door, which Mum fastidiously washes down weekly just to catch the gossip from passing neighbours. Inside, the old hatch between the kitchen and lounge has been plastered over and the time-worn metal framed single glazing has been torn free and replaced by more energy-efficient double glazing. Oh, those windows would have caused so much condensation on a day like today and ice would've formed inside and out, distorting the view of the somber flats that crowd the horizon. Towels would've been laid on the sill to protect the wood from warping, but it was futile as the gloss would still flake, and the carpet would stain. Every wall has been freshly decorated in my mother's unique taste; not quite minimalist, but not quite Laura Ashley either, with blank walls interrupted by the occasional clump of stencilled flowers.

My room is pasted with the same red and blue wallpaper dotted with random triangles. The carpet, a practical dark blue, hasn't been changed either. Interestingly, it's only now I realise that pretty much every room in my folks' house has been altered and updated in some way, apart from mine. My room looks as if three decades have converged at one point on this planet – the 70s, 80s and 90s – and have refused to budge.

Wednesday 13th January

Mum tossed an envelope towards me at breakfast with my name on it. It'd been stuck on the fridge for over a month to remind her to forward it quickly. She would've been as well dropping it behind the fridge. It's typical! Her poor organisational skills were responsible for my tardiness at school. I was often found wearing odd socks and without the tobacco tin used for storing my spelling words, which was always forgotten on top of the kitchen fridge if *I* didn't remind *her*.

Anyway, the envelope. It's a blast from the past; a Save the Date from Ryan, my old buddy from Edinburgh who's, as it turns out, getting hitched in December. Sadly, the guy he's getting tied to (Tony) is a total tosser. Ryan and I were inseparable. We lost touch soon after I moved to the Borders to live with Thomas. I'd no driving licence, and he was a city dweller that didn't do the provinces. The hour-and-a-half bus journey became a pain in the arse, if I'm honest. Facebook and Twitter were nonexistent, as they pretty much still are to me today, so it's not surprising we let our friendship slide.

The Save the Date said:

'Mr Andrew Angus.
You Are Invited to the Wedding of
ANTONY MATHEWS & RYAN LEADBETTER.
Saturday 18th December, 2010.
Venue TBC.
SAVE THE DATE!'

I would be excited to see Ryan again after all these years if he wasn't signing a legal contract to spend the rest of his life with a sarcastic, patronising G.P. receptionist who smiles as often as a pug and spits just as much drivel.

'That's great news,' said Mum, trying desperately to push me out of my blackness.

'Is it?' I asked, tossing the invite onto the table. 'Marriage isn't everything, Mum. Remember? You said as much just a few weeks ago. The poofs are getting married. Woo-hoo! Let's all celebrate that the gay scene will never be the same again. Goodbye Boyfriend; hello Civil Partner. Ta-ta, promiscuity; bonjour, mind-numbing fidelity, routine, weekends at IKEA, evenings in front of the telly hardly talking and the same knob in your hand night after night.'

Mum clipped me on the ear and said, '*This* is why you need to go to confession, you cheeky bugger. And don't bloody swear in front of your nephew.'

Zack, three-years-old, then proceeded to repeat the word 'poofs' for the next thirty minutes, despite warnings from his gran.

'See!' she said, bitterly, after he was distracted by sitting him down in front of QVC with a dud mobile phone. 'You've succeeded in turning your own nephew into a homophobe. You've probably set the Gay Rights Movement back fifty years, you ungrateful little shit.' She mouthed the last word so as not to encourage Zack to new lows.

'Good! And don't be daft, Mum. The Gay Rights Movement hasn't hit Petersburn yet!' I said as I stomped up the stairs to bed.

Safely shut in my room, a little calmer and more optimistic, I can't help but wonder how much Ryan's changed in the ten years since we last shared a drink. Are we level in the ageing process? Are we at uniform greyness in the hair department? Is he fat? Will he think I'm fat? Will he still laugh at my jokes, or has a decade of the quiet life stunted my witty repartee? Am I now and forevermore, God forbid, boring?

I can't bring myself to see him right now. I can't even call him as I know I'm flat in tone and sepia in colour. I'm pretty much a wreck. I'd only rain on his parade by telling him the cold, hard facts: love makes fools of us all and, mostly, we end up on our own.

I guess I'm not so optimistic after all.

Thursday 14th January

I found Dad in his 'aquarium' this morning tending to shoals of tropical fish. Mum's right, every inch of my sister's presence has been deleted and replaced by the smell of fungating water, wall-to-wall tanks and the sound of filters droning through The Eagles.

'Why this room?' I asked. Dad seemed a bit surprised that the threshold of his sanctuary had been breached.

'It's bigger than yours,' came the reply.

'No, it's not.'

Dad sighed, 'Your mother wouldn't let me use yours as she felt you'd need it someday. Your sister's pretty much been married for five years now, so it was a natural choice.'

I was annoyed, 'But I was with Thomas for ten years.'

'Aye, and look how that's turned out.' I felt hurt over Dad's lack of confidence in my choice of partner, however justified that may be now. He said delicately, 'Look, you never seemed settled. You always appeared to be trying so hard to make it work. Far too hard, in fact.' He tapped a little green net on my shoulder as an attempt to comfort me. I glanced at it quickly to be sure it wasn't wet or housing a dead fish. 'You were always running after the big shit, dropping down to part-time hours to be there for him at the end of his day, cooking, cleaning, putting him first and yourself last. He never really was there for you as much as you were for him. You were desperate for his approval.'

'Dad, relationships aren't a scorecard.'

'No, but they should be balanced with equal respect,' he assured me as he wandered towards a tank that had a small fish listing to one side. 'He'd swan in after a day's work and drop his shit everywhere, and you'd pick up after him. I've never done that to your mother.' He chuckled, 'Hell, I'd never get the ruddy chance! My head would've been off my shoulders within the first week of our marriage.'

I noticed his bald patch is now the size of a beer mat as it reflected the glow from the lights in the tanks. I felt the back of my head as I briefly pondered my own follicle fate.

'Don't get me wrong,' he said, 'I liked Thomas, but it's hard to love someone who doesn't give your own flesh and blood the respect they deserve. You didn't have a spine, Son, not with him. Maybe this will be the making of you.'

'Sorry to be such a disappointment,' I croaked.

'Don't be silly, Andy. You never have been. Your mother and I just want you to be happy, whether that's with someone or not. That's what matters to us.' He scrutinised the listing fish, mumbled something about fin rot, then cut himself off with, 'Look at this wee lad. All he wants is to survive, gills panting away, trying to keep afloat, and he will. With a little help, we all survive. You will too. I know your life feels like it's ending right now, but you'll soon see the world still turns.'

I laughed briefly and said, 'You know, all I wanted to be is like you and Mum: happy, settled and in love.'

Dad laughed, 'I wanted to be George Best but look how that turned out. Mind you, I think I got a far better deal, the poor sod.' He peered over his glasses and dropped some fluid into the tank from a little dispenser. Blue clouds dispersed in the water and enveloped the ill fish. He watched with care in his eyes. Then he turned those caring eyes to me, 'Life never goes how you planned it. There's always a redundancy, a traffic jam on a day-trip to Saltcoats, the death of a friend or a prostate problem to contend with. It's the good and bad in life that shapes us and makes us who we are. It's having the balls to take what's dealt and learning from it, that's the real challenge. You've made me and your mother so proud, she might not admit that, but both you and your sister have, and you will again.'

At that very moment, I felt so much love for my dad that I couldn't hold back from hugging the man for what must be the second time in my adult life. He laughed it off and gave me a quick manly pat on the back. Our hug time was up. But as far as hugs are concerned, quality is always outweighed by quantity. It's probably the most genuine hug I've had in a decade.

I left him doting on the sick fish with a small dose of hope running through my veins. Not bad for a working man with depression.

Friday 15th January

The snow has eased off. The roads are beginning to become murky with slush, muck and the useless grit that the council spread days ago with zero effect. It took the turning of the planet and the change of a weather front to do any good, both items free and untaxed, as yet. Even so, I'm not inspired to venture out. I can't bear the smarmy Spanish Inquisition from the neighbours. God forbid I bump into an old school mate. I'm sure the local town crier has notified everyone of my return, i.e., my own mother. I heard her blatantly discussing my past mishaps and current woes between the trimming and pruning of the variegated foliage that is failing to keep her segregated from our know-it-all-neighbour Mrs White. I'm feeling low again, have decided to give up, switch off from the real world and watch Mum's stockpile of *Come Dine With Me* on Sky Plus. This may be how agoraphobia starts.

Saturday 16th January

Today Sarah Brightman & Hot Gossip have decided to haunt me. *(I've Lost My Heart To A) Starship Trooper* has been rattling around my head on repeat all afternoon as I've shuffled between the kettle, bed, loo and couch in my rather short Empire Strikes Back housecoat and Simpsons slippers. Why? What part of my useless brain has banked this 70's travesty and saved it for a random day like today? I suspect the curtains in my bedroom are beginning to warp my mind. Is this what living as a single man in your parents' house can do to you? How many others have gone insane in this predicament?

Sunday 17th January

Mum distracted my gaze from the TV to ask if I wanted to go to confession with her this morning. 'Why?' I asked as I choked on my third Curly Wurly of the day. 'I'm sure the church walls will collapse in on me, being gay and all that. There would either be a stoning, an exorcism, or a full-on Benny Hill-style chase out of Airdrie by the entire congregation.'

Mum tied her clear plastic headscarf around her well-bundled locks and pursed her red, wrinkled lips tightly. 'It would get you out from under our feet and give you an excuse to take a bloody bath for a start,' she cracked like a whip. 'God help you!' she added, a little judgementally for a woman who carries a fake Gucci bag on her shoulder that was 'acquired' from Dodgy Dave's car boot in the depths of his very shady garage. 'The immersion is on. Wash your hair at least for Christ's sake! You're beginning to look like bloody Worzel Gummidge.' The lounge door slammed behind her as she muttered something about the world revolving around me and the disregard I have for the labour pains I inflicted on her, describing them weirdly as 'birth shakes' and adding something about 'hating me' as the front door was dragged shut in her time-honoured way by one brisk pull of the letterbox flap.

The TV screen went dark, and the titles to another *Come Dine With Me* melded into focus. I caught sight of myself surrounded by used mugs and chocolate wrappers, my hair's tatty and in desperate need of a trim, greasier than a seabird after the Exxon-Valdez oil spill. I'm letting myself go to the dogs, it seems, and I only care a tiny bit. At any rate, only my family see me. I'll come out of my cocoon in my own sweet time.

7 p.m. Jon Pertwee's *Worzel's Song* has been rattling around my head all day thanks to Mum. It's bloody irritating.

Monday 18th January

My last payslip (minus the cost of two unreturned uniforms and two weeks absent from stacking shelves) and a P45 from Tesco Superstores arrived today (redirected by Thomas). I've lost my job. Fair enough. I omitted to phone in sick and have been ignoring their calls.

Mum hit the roof when I told her. What did she expect? Did she really imagine I'd drive the 1hr 30mins every day to a job in Galashiels? She turned off the telly, leaving me sitting in the dark in the lounge, and stomped out the back for another fag. Dad still has no idea she's a lapsed non-smoker as she disguises the stale stink well with whatever scent is at hand, be that Dior, Lynx or Dettol Sparkling Lemon & Lime kitchen wipes. To be honest, I feel pretty numb to any kind of stimulus these days, good or bad, so her drama didn't really smart at all. I sat in the dark until she returned coughing her lungs up and flicked on the dazzling overhead light with a swipe of her palm, coming at me like an aggravated bull terrier. 'Get your lazy arse down that dole office tomorrow, or I'll be booting it all the way there!' she yelped as she headed out the door to the local darts match.

I've never claimed the dole. I don't know how it works really. I wonder if I'm entitled to incapacity benefit, as I am most definitely incapacitated by depression caused by an inane future and a fruitless past.

Tuesday 19th January

'If you think you're depressed, you should see your G.P.; mental health isn't my department. I'm here to sort out your employment, or rather, lack of,' Lynda stated from behind the copious pages of my application for Job Seekers Allowance. She must be barely out of school, and here she is with my life in her hands. She knows nothing of the hardships to follow. How can she truly show me the right path when she's just learnt to walk?

'Hmmmm ...' she droned as she stretched her well-waxed fringe that acted like a naturally grown eyepatch and mulled over my previous history. 'Giving your current age, *thirty-five*,' she seemed to exaggerate the volume on the last word, 'you may be entitled to £67.50 per week.'

'Super!' I said but was stopped by the palm of her hand pressed flat to the air in front of me.

'Buuuuuut!' she droned again. 'This would be on our,' she raised her fingers to illustrated quotation marks, ' "Contribution Based Benefit", which may not apply to someone such as yourself that has more than likely *not worked hard enough to make that gain*.' Her last few words echoed as I shifted uncomfortably in the orange plastic, and might I add, far-too-small-for-a-grown-man chair.

'You've only been a part-time worker for the past ten years? I'm not sure your tax contributions even qualify it as "part-time".' She mimicked quotation marks again and allowed an unprofessional laugh to escape.

I failed to see the amusement.

'Sorry,' she said, composing herself. 'We find some of our clients' frankly exorbitant requests here most amusing – it can be a thankless job with very little joy. Any-hoo, that coupled with the fact that you have no dependents and are now *living with your mother* may drastically reduce your entitlement further.'

'How much less are we talking here?'

'To the point of nonexistent,' she smiled with clenched teeth as she handed me an appointment card and a little book.

'What's this?'

'It's your Job Seekers Diary, which you must complete every time you apply for new employment and are more than likely *rejected*. A Seeker, such as yourself, with minimal experience in these times of austerity, may need several diaries. But don't let that dishearten you. You can still do it. Against the odds. At your age.'

Cheeky cow, I thought.

She continued rattling off orders at speed, 'You must attend here fortnightly on a Thursday at 0916hrs, with your diary, any job applications and letters of *rejection* you have received over that period. There will be many, so try to keep them in order of date. Your benefit amount will be calculated in due course. Failure to comply with these requests *will* result in your benefits being stopped with *immediate effect*. Understood?' she grinned.

'Every other Thursday at 9.16?' I asked dumbfounded. Why not 9.15? It's as if they deliberately want to trip me up on timekeeping alone. 'You can't be serious,' I laughed.

Lynda gave me a deathly stare. 'Mr. Angus, I'm *deadly* serious.'

'But what if I go on holiday?'

Lynda stopped stretching her fringe, leant over the desk just a few inches from my nose, which I may add, was almost touching the veneer of the table, and probed superciliously, 'But, Mr Angus, where *exactly* would you *be* on holiday?' Suddenly I felt my old school blazer chaffing the back of my neck and my brown leather satchel cutting into my shoulders as I shrivelled up smaller and smaller behind the desk.

I thanked her and left immediately. I think I even called her 'Miss'. I'm glad I told Lynda nothing of the £3000 savings I have stashed away in the Airdrie Savings Bank, just a few meters down the High Street from her specialised lumbar support chair.

Wednesday 20th January

Midday. There's been a catastrophic earthquake in Haiti? It happened on the 12th of January. The death toll is said to be well into 100,000! How could I've been so oblivious to these terrible events? I've been so ignorant. Not my fault as I've been depressed (despite what Lynda says) and suffering from mild agoraphobia. However, this must change. I have been maudlin and melancholy for too long. If I allow this to continue, I'll soon believe the world extends only as far as our whirligig. Indeed, when Mum left in a rather un-holy rage the other day, she didn't mention *birth-quakes* and *hating me* but rather the *earthquakes* in *Haiti*. This explains why she ranted briefly about my problem being insignificant with respect to the rest of the world's.

I've immediately sent £200 from my savings to the disaster appeal and a text to Ryan thanking him for the invite and a request to meet sometime next week. I've been impatient for a reply since. I've even offered to help Mum with Dad's retirement party at the Workman's Club next Saturday. If she hadn't been resting on their bed, I think she would have fallen flat on her face-mask. She whipped away cold teabags from her eyes and gawped at me perplexed. 'Oh, that would be lovely,' she said, as her neck craned around the door to follow me out of their room in disbelief.

I've been so self-centred. I'm not the only person forced to start over again (Liz Taylor did it on eight occasions with great ease). There are more significant disasters out there than a failed relationship. I am, however, the only man in his thirties to be living with his parents in our street, so I best get my arse in gear.

5.30 p.m. Joy of joys! Ryan has replied, and we are now in free flow of texts. We're meeting next Friday in Edinburgh, at Starbucks on Princes Street. The hardest part of our chat was breaking the news that Thomas and I are no more. This is becoming more real by the day. It'll be common knowledge on the gay scene, if I know Ryan's partner at all, by this evening. However, Ryan's been very tender and sent his condolences and support. Every cloud has a silver lining, it seems, as we're both ecstatic about our reconciliation.

Thursday 21st January

I have a sore throat. So much for vitamin C. Is it any wonder I'm run down with the torturous mill I've been dragged through? Lynda was oblivious to my illness as she informed me during my appointment at *precisely* 9.16 a.m. that I'll receive the grand sum of £35.83 per week. Measly, considering the mountains of tax I've been robbed of over the years. She noticed the look of disgust on my face and said, 'On the positive, Mr Angus, we'll pay it directly into your account, which takes the pressure off you having to come in and queue.'

'I will, however, still have to walk over half an hour here every fortnight, as I can no longer afford to run a car, thanks to your limited generosity, and wait in line with the rest of the disheartened faces whilst listening to washed-out pop songs sung poorly by cheap cover artists, who are most likely on the dole and living on the breadline too.'

'Uh-uh, Mr Angus. It's "Job Seekers Allowance", remember?' She used those damn inverted commas again.

'And all just to show you my "job seeking" homework,' inverted commas used pointedly on my part, 'which will be stuffed to the gunnels with rejection letters, as you so dearly assured me; thanks so much for pointing that out to me and annihilating my hope.' I said, sarcastically.

She flicked her new, blond dreadlocks and said, with all the authority a High Court judge, 'A *car?* But what do you *need* one for, Mr Angus? You're going nowhere, judging by the limited applications you've made since we last met.' She flicked through my paperwork with some dramatic pretence and chuckled. 'I say limited applications; I really mean zero.'

I panted a futile sigh, was thankful I didn't live in Haiti and accepted that £35.83 is better than nothing. My life has come full circle: I'm now earning the same as I did on my YTS training scheme back in the '90s. It's just a shame Mars Bars aren't as big and cheap as they were back then.

11.30 p.m. Sore throat worse. Gargled on soluble paracetamol found in the back of the bathroom cabinet. Choked mid-gargle when I checked the packet and saw they expired in 2003. Practically coughed up Adam's apple. Cleaned bathroom mirror of spit. Sprayed glass cleaner in my eye while checking blocked nozzle. Eye now as red as the throat.

Friday 22nd January

The bright winter's sunshine radiated on the frost-coated headstones, causing the whole graveyard to glisten with an ethereal optimism as Mum laid fresh roses on Aunt Moira's grave. My aunt's memorial was installed this morning and, as family tradition states, we were making the usual trip to inspect all was as it should be. I figured the undertakers had very little to do this month, judging by the speed at which it had been made, but Mum said Moira was super-prepared for the inevitable. The only task she'd left for the etcher to do was an end date; the epitaph had been written and purchased twenty years ago.

'Fortunate for us the firm didn't go bust in the recession, or we'd all be out of pocket,' I said.

'There will always be a market for incontinence, haircuts and the dead, Andrew,' assured Mum.

I leant forward to read the verse below Aunt Moira's name. Mum noticed my puzzlement and explained, 'It's from Loretta Lynn's *Who Say's God Is Dead?* She was a big fan. Wanted to be her. She was a big inspiration for her country nights on the cruises.'

I felt a chill run down my spine as my death phobia crept up behind me and breathed down my neck. I glanced over my shoulder to be sure the Grim Reaper wasn't giving me a flirtatious wink. A solitary thick cloud muted the sun and, just for a few seconds, the marble, sandstone, dirt and greenery around us became typically drab. The space behind me defied the goosebumps all over my body. *Not yet,* I thought as the sun returned, and I felt discreetly for a radial pulse.

As headstones go, my aunt's chosen a pretty touching one: a large, imperfectly shaped grey marble heart (I imagine all hearts are imperfect these days), being hugged by a kneeling angel in white marble casting a tender gaze upon the ground when Moira lies. I felt my eyes sting with tears as I watched my mother's stooped figure fuss around the stone as she polished it with a duster and some Pledge, muttering to her sister's corpse even though many meters of soil separate them now and forever. Then something in the distance caught her eye.

'Oh, the poor dear,' she whispered as she nodded behind me towards a stumpy, rotund woman in a French beret and charcoal fur coat. It was Mrs Hammond, a neighbour that has lived in the scheme since it was built. She was on her knees, sweeping away at a well-established grave with a plastic dustpan and brush.

'When did Mr Hammond die?' I asked, rapidly becoming aware of my parents' mortality.

'He hasn't, although I think death would be a relief as he's quietly rotting away in a terrible care home after three strokes, the poor sod,' replied Mum, pensively. 'It's George, their son.'

'But George was the same age as me,' I flinched.

Mum's eyes glazed over as her face become as stony as the monuments around us, 'The poor woman hasn't been the same since that day. You remember George? Good old, sweet George, who wouldn't hurt a fly?' I nodded as Mum continued, 'He married that Lisa McKenzie from just up the road. She was in your class at primary school. Remember her?'

'Aye, she peed in my paddling pool one summer.' (This may be the point at which I became obsessed with cleanliness.) My mind rattled through images of a toothy girl in pigtails running ahead of me down the glen, wading through the rank stream, tethering ropes to trees to make swings so dangerous it'd give some parents a heart attack, stoking fires and building dens. Lisa was a bit of a tomboy and able to handle herself if anyone picked on her because of her skin colour.

Mum continued in full morbid flow, 'They were married for years. Lived in one of the maisonettes in Iona.'

I was taken aback. 'What? Lisa came back? When?'

'Oh, about nine years ago. Turns out she'd been down in London studying and working as a nurse after alcohol got the better of her mother. She'd got in touch with George on some friends website and, Bob's your uncle, she's biding with him.'

'And you never thought to tell me she'd come back?' I asked

irritated.

'Och, it must've slipped my mind,' she said slyly. 'Besides, she was always getting you in trouble.' She looked at me incredulously and raised her hands to plead, 'What? Don't look at me with your father's eyes. You'd moved away. What would've been the point?' Then she muttered, 'Anyway, the real point is: George worked hard on the baker's van, out all hours, up and down the country at times. No kids, but they seemed happy. Then one morning, about three years ago, he just stopped the van on the Old Monklands Bridge, right in the middle of rush-hour traffic, and without warning, rushed out of the van and leapt off the bridge to meet his maker. He'd only done one delivery that day. Died instantly, they said, but part of me wonders if they just say that to give families some comfort in those Godforsaken circumstances. Poor soul, I used to love his Danish Swirls. The ones at the shop haven't been the same since.'

I couldn't be sure now if her glazed eyes were induced by sorrow or the want of a sticky bun.

'Why'd he do it?'

'No one knows. Some say he just went mad, some say he'd been depressed for years, others say that Lisa drove him to it. She was hanging off all kinds of men down the club and had been seen arriving back on the early morning train from Glasgow as others went to work. Dirty stop-out.'

Mum gave Moira's grave one final rub and hooked her arm into mine, leading the way through the endless line of lonely sodden souls towards Mrs Hammond. 'As God is my witness, there was something more going on,' she whispered towards me, keeping her chin and voice low. 'Me and the rest of the scheme know it as that Lisa McKenzie disappeared soon after, never to be seen again. Selfish bitch. No consideration for the mourning of a mother.' She'd become almost inaudible, mouthing part of the last sentence as we approached Mrs Hammond.

Lisa had been a friend. We became friends from an early age. So early, I can't remember the first time we met. She was my closest friend when I was a kid. I figured we could share anything and take on the world, but I was wrong. She moved away with her mother and missed my fourteenth birthday party. She didn't even have the decency to tell me they were going – a moonlight flit. I was lost for the next few years. Out and lost. I felt cheated.

Mum hastily muttered, 'She was always trouble.'

Mum pulled an aching expression – kind of a cross between constipation and heartburn – and asked Mrs Hammond, 'How are you, dear?' There then followed a conversation punctuated by, 'Awws', 'Naws', and loud, sympathetic tuts on both parts. Mum commiserated with a good dose of her traumas, including, rather irritatingly, the use of my predicament as her latest. More clucking and pity nods followed, this time from Mrs Hammond directed towards me. I kept my mouth shut and found myself subversively playing the role of the wounded son. Why? I don't know. I was just following the script. I'm the typical jilted lover who's come home with his tail between his legs to recover emotionally and financially.

We said our goodbyes and strolled away. Mum pulled me closer in a display of PR that would impress any spin-doctors working for the Royal Family. As we made our way across the red gravel path, I noticed that, even though she's the same age as Mum, Mrs Hammond looks terribly withered. She struggled to her knees, using George's headstone as support, whipped out a Dust Buster from her matted fur coat and sucked up the crisp, dead rose petals that littered her son's grave.

Mum asked me, 'You and that Lisa were quite close, weren't you?'

'Aye, for a while.' I hastened a change of subject, 'Do you want to visit Luke?'

'No, sweetheart, I think it'll be too much for one day. Maybe next week. I'll wave to him quickly on the way out.'

Luke was my older brother. His cot-death, as it was called back then, broke my parents' hearts. I don't think they ever fully recovered.

Saturday 23rd January

I woke this morning with *(I Lost My Heart To A) Starship Trooper* sweeping through my brain yet again. It's become more animated now. My overactive imagination has transformed it into a Vaseline-coated dream of the Top of the Pops dance troupe Hot Gossip prancing in their usual camp 80's style. I could've coped with this if it wasn't for my parents sweeping in, decked in scanty silver space garb, with heavily lacquered 80's hair, and thick makeup. Mum with Farrah Fawcett flicks and Dad with a massive handlebar moustache. My head shot from the pillow when Dad's button mushroom protruded disgracefully through his Barbarella hot-pants. When he appeared for breakfast, I watched him with suspicion, expecting his housecoat to slip open and reveal this travesty. I asked him, 'Has Mum ever owned a pair of hot-pants?'

'Don't be daft, Son,' he laughed as he cleared up the cold teabags my mother had carelessly left on the draining board the night before. 'It took me six months after we met to get her to unbutton her duffle coat, and that was only because we had a heatwave. Her stupid uptight mother – and don't you repeat a word of this to anyone – told her she'd get breast cancer if she allowed sunlight to grace even the cleft of her bosom. When I finally got to see them, they were so white they looked like two ostrich eggs in a net shopping bag. I'd never seen such anaemic nipples.'

I was relieved and disgusted all at once.

Sunday 24th January

I spent the early morning shivering from door to door through the sleepy Petersburn schemes, dropping off hastily sealed envelopes with my mum's spit frosting over the edges. I wandered around the streets that used to be my playground. My teeth chattered intermittently like a tiny machine gun. I delivered thirty-two invites for Dad's retirement party on Saturday. Why was I posting these by hand? Simple, my mother is tighter than a nun's snatch when it comes to spending, which is ridiculous as she works in the Post Office. Surely a discount on stamps is part of the deal? With less than a week to go, she's cutting it fine. They'll be lucky to have anyone other than close family there.

This place is bursting with childhood memories. My old playmate James' house is now coated in garish cladding, in shades of mauve and salmon, and the garden is fully landscaped, but it still has the same front door I'd chap on daily. James has moved on to better things: a Bachelor in Science, one wife, two kids and a detached Victorian house in Stirling.

Down the main road, I could see the old fallen tree at the top of the glen that was our usual haunt away from the rest of the scheme.

It still bears the charcoal scars from the day Lisa stole a box of matches from the corner shop and started a fire inside the hollow of the trunk to bake potatoes. The fire brigade arrived before a forest fire could spread, and we scarpered full of nerves and giggles.

I passed the house that Lisa McKenzie once lived. It brought back a gush of happy, carefree memories to a time when pogo sticks and clackers were free to use without a risk assessment, and Sofi Ellis Bexter's mum did magical things with 'sticky-back plastic' on Monday and Thursday afternoons. I touched the wall. The concrete felt reassuringly familiar, just as it did when I lent on it as I waited on Lisa escaping for the day, usually when her mum was unconscious on the sofa with a bottle of cider tucked under her arm.

Lisa didn't mind her mum's drinking as it ensured some relief from her overbearing personality for a short time. Until she'd waken, become volatile, apologise, and then the cycle would start over again. Mum described Miss McKenzie as 'ill' on her drunken days. I once peeked through the letterbox to find Lisa's mum facedown on the floor of their hall, with her wig hanging by a determined kirby grip. Despite an ambulance being called and several neighbours being involved, Lisa denied any knowledge of the event.

But on her 'ill' days we'd escape down the glen and swing on rope suspended from trees, climb up hills that seemed like cliffs to our young minds, crawl into caves and cross the North Calder Water to investigate the farmland on the other side. We were living in our own Indiana Jones movie.

I wish I could turn back time and live it all again.

Monday 25th January

I made the mistake of being enticed out with Mum again and fell for a fraudulent 'spontaneous' visit to Mr Borkowski's corner shop. She wasn't desperate for a half-pound of cola cubes after all: there was a hidden agenda. I was, in fact, being pimped out by my mother as a possible successor to Caroline, Mr Borkowski's former sales assistant who has now left to study Graphic Design.

'Oh, *really*?' said the flame-haired illusionist, rather over-dramatically, 'I'd no idea you're looking for a replacement so soon.' She nodded to me suggestively with such eyebrow acting it wouldn't have gone amiss in one of those dreadful Mexican telenovelas. She completely forgets that she'd mentioned it to Dad over mince and tatties last week while I was scraping the back of the freezer in an attempt to free a strawberry Cornetto from the clutches of the glacier within.

I played along with her am-dram and listened to the job description: part-time; early starts; £5.93 an hour; 5.6 weeks annual leave (pro-rata); under no obligation to cover shifts but it would be helpful. The bare minimum wage really, apart from a free bag of boiled sweets once a week and all the magazines you can read.

Mum chirped up, 'Andy, isn't this the perfect solution for you? And you'd be just next door to me so we could have coffee and lunch breaks together. And I could pop in and see you any time I wanted. We could even walk to work together.' She was grinning so much it scared me. Then her face dropped, 'You need a job, Andy, desperately. Your father and I can't afford to keep you indefinitely.' She tapped her foot again, her patience at breaking point, I had to make a decision there and then. And then the blow to the gut, 'You're turning into one of those sad adult men who live with their parents and never work, Sonny Jim.'

I start a week on Wednesday, references permitting. I've no other option, and my savings are not going to last forever. I'm now living in a cul-de-sac and have been backed into one metaphorically by my own flesh and blood. I've gone from a successful supermarket chain to a struggling corner shop. This isn't the change I'd hoped for. Why won't people leave me alone? I should be the protagonist of my own life, God damn it!

Tuesday 26th January

Woken this morning by a text: 'R u free?' It was the 4X4 Guy.

I replied immediately, of course. No denying it, I am free. I've no job until next week, and I could do with a good shag to brighten up my days.

'Can we meet in next hour???? I'm in your area and really need to see you!!!' came the reply.

I arranged to meet him at the other end of the Glen, under the Old Monklands Bridge, as far out of Mum's radar signal as possible. I felt my neck prickle when I pulled up in my car and gawped at the height that George leapt from. It must've taken a pile of faith that the next life is better than this. I put myself in his place and became dizzy. My thoughts were interrupted by a silver 4X4 pulling up beside me. My silver-haired hunk grinned and beckoned me into the passenger side. He looked as amazing as he did the night he pulled me from the snow. I slipped inside; the car was filled with the unmistakable scent of him. *This is what heaven smells like*, I thought.

'Hello,' he said cheerily. 'How are you?'

I had the urge to kiss him there and then and leaned forward over the gearstick to plant one on him, but he backed away, eyes darting around under a furrowed brow to see if anyone was around. I'd gone too far perhaps. It was broad daylight, after all. However, to my surprise, he said, 'What the hell,' and gave me such a passionate and manly kiss that blew me away.

'Man, I'm so glad you text me,' I said as I planted my hand on his crotch.

'Hold your horses,' he laughed as he lifted my hand and plopped it back in my lap.

'Sorry, want to go somewhere quieter?'

'No,' he answered disappointingly.

'Oh.'

'Andy, have you been okay?'

'I've been fine. Well, apart from having to move back in with my folks, which has been slightly depressing, but I'll be out of there soon as I can and then we can get down to some real fun.'

'No, *well,* I mean? Have you been *well?*'

'Aye,' was my quick answer as I reached for the inner of his meaty thigh. Again his hand grasped mine and stopped my horny motives dead.

'I mean, *healthy* well?' he said in all seriousness.

'Well, apart from this mild throat infection, but that's all.'

'Ah,' he leaned back in his seat and gazed out of the window, 'I think you may have given me the clap.'

I said nothing, suddenly finding my hardon deflating faster than the current economy.

He continued, 'Gonorrhoea, to be exact. You'll have to head to your local GUM clinic and have a check. You may not have anything, but it's best to be safe than sorry.'

I was dumbfounded. This was awful news. I've never, in all my years that I've been sexually active, caught anything. I couldn't possibly have Gonorrhoea. It's a filthy thing. I'd know. I stammered, 'But ... but ... I have no real symptoms ...'

'Oh, they tell me that's possible. Some guys have none but can still pass it on, especially if it's just in your throat.' His eyes flooded with kindness as he grasped my knee and reassured me, 'It's okay, big man. I wouldn't blame you if you did give it to me. I could so easily have given it to you. Just get it checked out, eh?'

I agreed to get the first available appointment. Surely these kinds of infections are reserved for the young and promiscuous? Not someone like me: old and starved of any shenanigans. He sent me websites to several GUM clinics and left soon after. So that's that, not only am I at the lowest I've ever been, but fate seems to want to hit me where it really hurts: repeatedly in the balls with a baseball bat dripping in Neisseria Gonorrhoeae.

Wednesday 27th January

'And where have you been all day, sunshine?' was Mum's impatient inquisition as I attempted to close the front door quietly on my return late afternoon.

I was relieved when Dad chirped up from behind his copy of Camping & Caravanning, 'Oh, leave the lad be, Beth. His ears will be bleeding with your bloody nagging. He's a grown man, not a teenager.'

I'd no intention of filling in the blanks and leapt through that window of opportunity briskly upstairs to the refuge of my adolescent boudoir. The truth was, I'd just returned from a GUM clinic in far-off Glasgow, as anonymity is nonexistent in this community. It was my first experience at a drop-in clinic, and sadly I'd no idea about the card system in operation and only twigged when a couple in their twenties wandered in hugging and muttered in disgust on how far back they were in the queue. I reached into the box marked 'Males' and found I was 'M 18'! How could this be? The doors to the actual clinic were locked, and hardly anyone was waiting in the corridor when I arrived earlier. I soon found that there were indeed seventeen males in front of me when the doors were unlocked to the unit at precisely 9 a.m. People poured from adjacent stairwells like ants scurrying into a nest. I followed everyone's lead and attempted to sit matter-of-factly in the partitioned off areas, endeavouring to ignore the posters on HIV testing and the comeback of Syphilis.

One frantically filled out contact form later, three copies of *The List*, one copy of *Hello*, and a bored scan through *Golf!*, and I was taken into a wee room with a trolley bed, one-way-window, a desk covered in blood forms, two plastic chairs and a trolley overflowing with empty blood tubes and assorted fear-inducing instruments that made me cross my legs.

'So, Andrew,' said the frightfully posh Doctor Kettlewell – a lady in her mid-forties with messy hair pinned to the top of her head and legs confidently splayed in red culottes– 'what can we do for you today?'

'Well, I'm here because I've been told I may have passed Gonorrhoea to someone. He's been treated, but I haven't. Well, I'm not even sure I have it. Highly unlikely as I've only been with one man for the past ten years, and I haven't got a single symptom apart from the slightest of sore throats, and that's probably due to singing *(I Lost My Heart To A) Starship Trooper* loudly in the shower.' I listened to myself ramble on nervously, the verbal equivalent to a bumper car speeding out of control down a long, tight alley, 'You know the song? No? It's by Sarah Brightman. I'm not really a fan, but it's been rattling around my head on and off for days. My Aunt Moira used to be troubled by with Doris Day, you know? Drove her nuts one Christmas, but que sera, sera ...' I let out a goofy laugh.

'Andrew!' clipped Kettlewell concisely, 'The clock is ticking. I'll need your sexual history, and then I'll take a swab from your throat. When was the last time you had a sexual M.O.T.?'

'Um, not for ten years. That's how long I was with Thomas, my ex.'

'Then I'll do a full screening, swab your throat, the inside of your penis, anus and also take bloods. Would you like an HIV test today?' she asked without glancing up from my notes.

I felt my buttocks clench against the unforgiving chair, 'Can I pass on that today?' I squirmed.

'It's entirely your decision, but I would recommend it very soon if you have been having unprotected sex. Early diagnosis could prolong your life.' I very much doubt that, as I surmise, I'll end it swiftly if it's a bad result. The questions came thick and fast from then on, and the Slut-o-Meter in my head was activated:

'How many men in the last three months?'

'Two.' Yellow: Safe Zone.

'In the past year?'

'Two.' Still Yellow.

'Oral sex?'

'Yes.' Yellow.

'Anal sex?'

'Yes.' Edging out of yellow into orange.

'Both giving and receiving?'

'Yes, but only with my long-term ex.' Way down low in Yellow.

'Protected?'

My heart sank, 'No.' The Slut-o-Meter's arrow swung from the safe Yellow Zone to the slightly dodgy Orange Zone.

'This last encounter, was it casual?'

'Yes, very much so. And brief.' Further into Orange!

'Do you know his name?'

'No.' Aaaaaand ... straight into Red!

'Okay, it just would be helpful in contact tracing,' she muttered as she scribbled. I craned my neck to see what awful comments she was putting permanently in my record, but I couldn't read a thing. Damn you, illegible doctors handwriting!

'I do have his mobile number.' Good recovery: back to a less slutty Orange again.

After a few more probing questions, I was asked to hop up on the bed and take my trousers down. Then it felt like it was a free-for-all as I was literally probed from every angle, the worst being my pee-hole as it felt as if she was positively punting with the gusto of a gondolier. Blood was taken (she reassured me just for Hepatitis immunisation response levels) and I was sent into a small lavvy to discreetly pee into a container, which seemed odd as she'd just viewed the best and worst angles of every orifice I house, learning more about me in a few minutes than my mother has in my lifetime.

While I was peeing, Dr Kettlewell nipped out of the room. Once my frightened willy was safely back inside my jeans, she returned with a few boxes of pills and said, 'It'll be two weeks before your results are ready.' She handed me a small white card. 'Here's the number to call and your patient I.D. Number, but as you could have been exposed to Gonorrhoea, I'll treat you for that today. Any allergies?'

Thankfully I was able to say I had none and popped six antibiotics in total, two for Gonorrhoea and four for Chlamydia, which I learned today, can also be present during such infections. By the time I left the clinic, after arranging a follow-up appointment in a week for something called a 'Test For Cure', it was 1 p.m. and I was convinced I was nothing but a wild and wicked slut who shouldn't be allowed out, day or night, without a chastity belt and gag.

I drifted along with the flow of a bustling, damp Glasgow in a daze. On autopilot really. Stopping at red traffic lights without thinking, crossing at green and window-shopping without intent, until I stumbled upon a blue Police Box in Buchanan Street. It was familiar to me. A forgotten old friend from day trips to Glasgow with the family. I walked all around the box that fascinated me as a kid. I attempted to ignore the colossal stomach cramps the petite pills were mercilessly inflicted on me, and the pressing issue Doctor Kettlewell had raised as I left the clinic: if I tested positive for anything at all, Thomas would need to be contacted and informed immediately. I'd hoped I'd seen the last of him. But more worrying than that was the fear of being HIV positive. My heart filled with dread as I touched the TARDIS for luck. I wished I could feel some warmth or vibration that told me it was alive. That it was unreal enough for me to step inside and dematerialise away from reality. But all I felt was cold, dead concrete, and my stomach in knots.

Thursday 28th January

Hallelujah! Confirmation from Ryan this morning, as I scarpered from my room for the quickest evacuation of my life thanks to yesterday's pills. We're meeting tomorrow at 5 p.m., then moving on somewhere else for grub.

Anxious to look my best, I decided it was high time tame the unruly grey hairs on my temples and took myself off to a local barbershop. As per usual, I failed miserably in small-talk with the blokey barber as he continually ranted, rather loudly I thought, about football, cars, golf and the infertility issues he's having with his girlfriend. It's a sad moment when the barber is more stimulated by waiting customers, becoming ignorant of you and removes most of your scalp. I grew concerned at crucial stages of the cut, i.e., fringe and sideburns, but he failed to read my mind.

'That do you?' he asked, remembering there was a reflection in the mirror of something other than his ego.

'Aye, perfect,' I lied, as I smiled kindly, gave him £10 of my pittance from the state and left with an itchy neck and something that would only need the tiniest droplet of styling gel.

I immediately fixed it when I got home as best I could, but styling is limited when you have nothing to play with. I stopped fudging up my head for a moment to examine my thirty-five-year-old appearance. The years have not been kind. Too many wrinkles to count. My DNA has recently decided that I'm in some way related to a fawn as my ears and nose are sprinkled with hairs, three of which on my right ear are thick and dark, and there's a blonder criminal on my left. It seems Mother Nature is a comedian, not even giving me an equal proportion. The odd long eyebrow hair can distract me for days, causing painful tears and a runny nose when plucked. And yet the same damn follicle sprouts back with a vengeance within days, and I'm back in front of the mirror, tweezers in hand, ready to waste another ten minutes of my ever-shortening life. I've been on a plucking frenzy.

I always believed that, once the wrinkles came, the spots would go. Not so. My back not only cultivates a fine sprinkling of hair but the occasional pluke too. This irritates the shit out of me. I almost sprained my neck while painstakingly ensuring all offending items were eliminated. The odd, almost indiscernible to the ageing eye, grey body hair is prevalent too. I should be thankful that such hairs are almost camouflaged, but dread the day it spreads south, and my pubes give up the ghost, becoming spectral white, scaring off anyone under forty from entertaining the idea of giving me oral. I'll have to shave them off completely the day that horror manifests its ugly head.

Hey-ho, life goes on, not how we intend it, but it does. The alternative doesn't bear thinking about.

Friday 29th January

2 p.m. I'm washed, scrubbed, plucked, shaved, clipped, trimmed, moisturised, suited and booted. After many a wardrobe disaster, I've plumped for a favourite NYPD T-shirt, my usual boot-cut jeans and Caterpillar boots. Said T-shirt is a little tighter than I remember but still looks impressive around the chest and shoulders. I'll just have to keep my arms low and crossed to camouflage my pot belly.

Edinburgh, you beauty, here I come!

Saturday 30th January

3.30 a.m. (The latest I've been up in years!) I sat in Starbucks as nervous as a prostitute at confession while attempting to sip my caramel macchiato as indifferently as I could. The place was bustling with tourists who seem to have been unaffected by the global downturn as they continually dripped coins into the ravenous till. Ryan was half an hour late (traditional), so I managed to work my way from an uncomfortable wooden chair to a nice, soft and fluffy couch as people vacated. I sank into the well-ridden cushion with smug satisfaction and admired the view. Edinburgh Castle hadn't lost her beauty.

I was feeling the effects of the caffeine and becoming quite sentimental when Ryan swept in with the energy of an excited teen. His long, hairy, green and brown overcoat swept open from the speed of his entrance. He recognised me immediately and waved, beaming a Hollywood smile that would outshine any showgirl. Sadly, Tony (a.k.a. 'Biffo', the derogatory name given to him justifiably by harsh queens on the scene) was in tow. I stopped slouching and tensed up my stomach in a vain attempt to engage my rarely used abs.

Ryan's hardly changed. He has no grey flecks, unlike me, and seems to have been living in Tupperware for the past decade as there's not a crease on any part of his well-presented façade. I'd go so far as to say he looks youthful. You'd hope, after losing a boyfriend, the stress of it all would mean you'd instantly burn all that unnecessary fat, but no, my body screams for comfort food, slowly topping up the levels like a barrel attached to a drainpipe.

Ryan yelped in excitement and hugged me like a long-lost brother. 'Andy, you look amazing!' he said and then paused expectantly for a compliment in return.

I shushed him bashfully and said, 'No way, but you do.'

'I know I do,' said my confident friend.

I neglected to compliment Tony as I just can't lie convincingly. He's spray-tanned so much he's on the verge of becoming a fat satsuma. However, as we were throwing hugs around, I was obligated to give him one too, but as half-hearted as I could possibly make it (hugging Biffo is akin to embracing a turd in a wig).

I immediately wanted to trade that hug for a slap the second Tony pulled back, gawped at my face and cried, 'Goodness, life has been rough on you, my dear. Haven't you collected a lot of wrinkles!' and laughed as shrill as a mad banshee.

I countermanded by saying, 'Wrinkles? No, they're the trademark Angus laughter lines.'

Whereupon Tony sniggered and threw another verbal grenade, 'Well, what a family of comedians you must be.'

Cue fixed grin and stunned silence on my part.

I visualised dropkicking him through that bay window until his mangled body was tangled in the castle's craggy rocks, but I knew this wouldn't be a great start to rekindling a relationship I'd let slide a long time ago. Even if one of the reasons I'd let it slip was still very much the monkey on Ryan's back. A monkey that will be backbreaking to carry as Tony has gained several pounds and is struggling to fit into his *Fat Face* jeans. His thinning brown hair, jug-ears, snooty nose and jutting incisors certainly fit his insulting nickname *Biffo the Bear*. And his lips ... I don't remember them being *that* big. Collagen injections, by the look of it.

'*Moving on*,' I said. 'Coffee?'

'Oh, not here, cupcake. I can't abide coffee beans that have been raped by a multimillion tax-dodging company,' said Ryan. 'I hope nobody saw us come in, Tony. Well, nobody that counts. We know a delightful independent place on Broughton Street that you'll adore. Cosy and they do the best tasting Americano this side of the country. I hope no one sees us leave, either.' He turned to a busy server filling a large tray with sloppy cups and sticky plates and asked, 'Is there a fire escape we can use?'

'The owner can be a bit of a cow, though,' interrupted Tony, tartly.

I was sold. Anyone who's a cow to Tony is a friend of mine. A bit of a walk, but I figured my potbelly and bashed ego needed a stroll.

'Let's go then,' I insisted.

'Oh, hang on,' said Ryan, whipping out his mobile. 'A quick celebratory selfie. Stand over there away from the branding. I *won't* be tagging our location.' The boys struck a well-rehearsed pose as he snapped the picture before I'd the chance to focus. I was gawping, my eyes half shut and I noticed a coffee drip on my shirt. It was online quicker than the time it takes to drink one shot of espresso. We left via the fire exit.

******

Café Jamaica, a slither of a place that you'd miss if you weren't looking for it, is green and black on the shop front with swirly yellow flower power style lettering above the door. Cavernous inside, it gets more extensive the deeper you delve, opening out to an ample space at the rear. On the far wall, beyond a decorative fireplace, sits an intimate stage flanked with purple felt curtains. An eclectic mix of local art hangs on the walls, from picturesque scenes of Edinburgh to the abstract brushstrokes of an aggressive mind. Rainbow coloured paper lanterns hang from the ceiling, softly lighting the chilled ambience, enhanced by grand ornate mirrors dotted around the area. The whole café has a feel of homely, lived-in chaos. Not a single table or chair match in colour or style. Nag champa snaked lethargically through the space and Nina Simone's voice echoed from somewhere deep within the shadows. It felt reassuringly geek-friendly.

As I squished comfortably into a sofa, a tall, slender, middle-aged black woman with a tower of thickly piled hair emerged from the back of the café and made her way towards us as she flirtatiously dipped into the depths of her ample bosom to remove a small notepad and pen from its clutches. Her hourglass figure was tightly caressed by a green dress that groped her in all the right places and caused her breasts to spill forward like two large, shiny chestnuts. She oozed sexual confidence. Phenomenal. If it weren't for her sincere smile and gentle Jamaican accent, I would've felt intimidated.

'Ryan, you old hound. So good to see you, what can I get you?' she grinned. 'And I see you've brought a handsome young man with you,' she said, nodding to me and ignoring Tony. I warmed to her more.

'This is my good friend from the West, Andy,' said Ryan, which melted my heart instantaneously as it became apparent all those years I'd neglected our friendship seemed to bother him not one jot.

'Andy?' She smiled wider, 'Andy, who?'

'Andy Angus,' I added, hand stretched to shake hers.

'Oh, Andy,' she muttered as her eyes glinted in the lamplight and gazed deep into mine. Well-manicured scarlet nails flickered as she cupped my hand in both of hers and shook it intensely, 'It's so good to meet such a fine, handsome, mature man.' She raised her head proudly and announced, 'I'm Miss Molasses Brown, queen of this fabulous establishment, where all friends, freaks and lost souls are welcome to linger.' It felt as if I'd known her for years, such was her warmth.

'Drinks!' she shouted, 'Mojitos on the house, for my dear friends. Back in three shakes.'

'We should take you out more often,' said Tony, glaring at Molasses as she wiggled away, 'the old hag has never given us so much as a free after-dinner mint.'

'Oh! Selfie!' said Ryan, mobile at the ready.

Goggle-eyed, I said, 'Really? But we've only just taken one twenty min ...'

Snap and post!

We sampled delicious home-cooked recipes that blew my mind, several non-alcoholic cocktails and Molasses's very own Rum Truffle Cake. A sober evening for me, but a most enjoyable one. We talked about their wedding, and I brushed over my defunct relationship with Thomas briefly. I imagine Tony was keen to perform a detailed autopsy, but I preoccupied the evening with them. Ryan is a window dresser for Jenners and Tony works in a G.P. surgery as a receptionist. They still live at their old flat on Leith Street, but now, instead of renting, they own it. I got most of this information from a very animated Tony. Ryan was hardly given room to breathe, so I was relieved when an early start pulled Tony out of the door around midnight. Even if I had to witness repeated, heavy petting for the next ten minutes until Ryan loosened his leash and the door shut on his saggy arse.

I could relax for the first time all evening. With Biffo gone, we were free to chat over old times, when I lived just a stone's throw away from Ryan on London Road. Life seemed more relaxed and less complicated. I had more of the pink pound in my pocket, and the scene was new, exciting and risky. He talked about some of the older queens still doing the rounds, the ones who'd since moved on (or worse, died), and the colourful new characters he's met since I left.

Then he asked, 'Do you ever think of Steve?'

My heart suddenly ached. I shared the flat on London Road with Steve. He was older than us, experienced, wealthy, butch and bitchy, cheeky and damn handsome. He'd say, 'When you hit forty, boys, there is a certain clientele that finds you fascinating. Twinks don't turn my head, but I seem to turn theirs, and if the chap is on the right side of his twenties, then I'm willing to entertain the notion for nothing more than a night. Anything more than that is some form of relationship, and that is definitely not my china cup of tea. What would I want with a twink, anyway? They haven't lived. They use moisturiser, for fuck's sake, bathe in aftershave and have no idea how to fix a stop-cock. I just want a real man to rodger and take the bin bag out in the morning, is that asking for the world?' Riotous laughter would follow, and others would turn their heads towards our usual corner of the bar. We must've looked like witches around a cauldron, but we were having a blast.

How could Ryan dare to bring him up? Steve was taboo. Our gang fell to pieces after he died – forty-four and cold on a slab looking a shadow of his former self. His good looks eaten away. Such a jovial, glorious mind ruined by something that could've been, should've been, treated sooner.

I hesitated some and said, 'I think of him every day. I still blame myself; after all these years, I still do. I knew he wasn't right. Six weeks later, he was gone. No more Friday night drinks that turned into Saturday morning breakfasts. Gone was that shameless smile, those playful moves on the dance floor and that gorgeous set of blue eyes that excused him no matter how bitchy he became.'

Ryan nodded, 'He could charm the Crown Jewels off the Queen.'

That rock that we had clung to was now far away in the middle of a foreboding sea that could never be crossed. At least, not in this lifetime. This marked the beginning of our separation. We met through Steve, and we only knew how to function around Steve. So we clung to new rocks as quickly as we could and lost sight of each other behind the solidity of what we'd found. His funeral came fast and left us with little time to think. And before we knew it, we were toasting the man and, with a tear in our eyes and dregs in our glasses, it was time to move on. And boy, move on we did. Swiftly. Ryan to Tony, and me to Thomas. But even tonight, after all that water has flown under all those bridges, the events leading up to why we lost touch hurt.

'Not your fault,' consoled Ryan with a hand clasping mine. 'Hell, I would've told him to shut up with his moaning, but then, I've never had much patience with the sick.'

'I remember,' I jibed. 'When I snapped a tendon falling off the stage at Vibe, you quickly asked me to leave as I was embarrassing you. I limped towards the exit, and you continued to dance as if nothing was wrong.'

'Oh, dear. Did I? I'm sorry about that. I must've been on something.'

I laughed. 'You were on everything back then!'

Ryan chuckled, 'Yes, I suppose you're right. I don't nowadays. Too old to deal with the comedowns. And who wants to have the teeth of a medieval pauper? I miss him,' he said with his smile gone and his eyes glistening, 'and I miss you too.'

It felt so good to be wanted again. Wanted by *him*. I squeezed his hand tight and told him what I should've told him a long time ago, 'I miss you too. I've always missed you.' It was good to feel as if someone cared once again. I didn't want to lose that moment. God, I really have missed him. How could I have been so stupid?

'Are the two of you hypnotised or something?' came a familiar Jamaican accent. 'Anyone would think you kids were in love.'

This snapped us out of our bubble.

'Don't be daft,' I spluttered between breathy laughs.

As the doors to Café Jamaica were locked behind us, we wandered along the cobbles reflecting the streetlights' pale yellow glow. Arriving at my car, we said a reluctant farewell. Ryan hugged me tightly. It was great to be close to his beating heart once more.

'It's fabulous to have you back in my life, my friend,' were his parting words.

As I drove along Gorgie Road, I realised I'd finally found an old piece of me that has been forgotten, buried beneath the chaff of domesticity for far too long. Maybe, just maybe, it is possible to go back in time and start over.

The twenty-five-year-old Andy inside me had woken. He yawned and blinked at the moon as it hung large and low before me on the drive to Mum and Dad's. I could see the silhouette of Edinburgh's skyline in my rearview mirror, and even though I was heading in the opposite direction, Ryan, Steve and my twenty-five-year-old self were travelling alongside me and having a whale of a time.

4.35 p.m. It's Dad's retirement do tonight, and I'm feeling more than a little tired from my late night.

Sunday 31st January

Hangover number three of 2010.

It was a grand night. The DJ was excellent, choosing an eclectic playlist which even got me on the dance floor after my 6th gin to the beat of Black Box's *Ride On Time*. Mum did the bump to *Nutbush City Limits* with my sister, Marie, and momentarily recaptured her youth. Later, Dad made a very touching speech that flipped my intoxicated brain maudlin side down. I took myself to the bar and sipped on a whisky while surveying the scene: everyone happy, tipsy, friendly. The nicest people you could ever meet. Retired friends of my folks, neighbours and familiar faces from school who now have kids of their own. Good people, salt of the earth kinda people, and yet, I don't feel I belong here. Not at all.

My brother-in-law, Dodge, confirmed this when he reared his ugly head at the bar. 'Hey, Andy-pansy (his nickname for me that I hate), why so glum?'

'Well, I've just been through a pretty shitty time of it recently, or has that headline not hit the rolling news banners on the betting shop screens yet?' I said, dryly – he's always blowing his wages on the gee-gees; it's partly why my sister is stuck in a three-bedroom house with too many kids and not enough bunkbeds.

'Oooooh, who's a touchy lad then?' I ignored this and turned to watch the dance floor. He put his arm around me and gave me excessively, masculine squeezes that made me spill what little of my Jura I had left. 'Come on, Andy, it's a party,' he punctuated with further squeezes. 'You're free. Enjoy it. Your lot don't hang around for long anyway, do they?' More squeezes. More spilt whisky.

As if I wasn't already pissed off through ever depleting whisky. 'My lot? What lot would that be?' I challenged.

'Come on, ya' ken what I mean. I mean, you lot practically invented promiscuity.' He leant in and muttered in my ear, to be sure no one heard and mistook him for one of *our lot*. 'Bet it's a heck of a lot easier to get yer leg over and get over a breakup than it is us men. Women are highly strung, high maintenance and highly overrated, if you ask me. If I only could, I'd try it just to get me some more action. But I'm a man through and through.'

'And by "us men" I take it you mean *real men* who can build walls, wear high visibility vests with no T-shirt in the winter and down a pint in seconds?'

He threw his arms wide, splashing his Stella over the stool next to me, and gave a moronic grin, 'Well, I am talented, I'll give you that.'

I picked up a napkin and mopped up his carelessness. 'Oh, Dodge, you don't have to do any of that to prove to me you're a real man. Downing pints is nothing compared to a guy who can keep going all night long.'

'Well, you're right there. I have fathered a load of sprogs to your good sister. I can stay solid and drill a' night long if needed, and I'm no' talking about a night shift on the M8, ya' ken?'

'Oh, I know you can, as I discovered when you wandered into the wrong hotel room at Cousin Mary's wedding and fell into a drunken slumber next to me at three in the morning.'

'Eh?'

'By the way, I'd no idea you were a spooner. Your little willy poked and prodded my back until dawn, and you didn't even have to think about it to get hard. Damn annoying for me, so much so I left before you woke and enjoyed an early, peaceful breakfast. I've meant to tell you about that.'

Dodge became less bolshy and laughed nervously, 'Y'er talkin' crap.'

I looked down at his beer-stained crotch and grinned. 'Shaved, tattoo of a Tasmanian Devil on the left, and I'd say, four inches, at a push. Maybe four and a half, if it's warm and I'm being kind.'

Dodge went scarlet and soon lived up to his nickname, dodging through the room to get away from the homo he'd once dry humped in a drunken misadventure.

I called after him, 'Cheers, Dodge, you know how to cheer *my lot* up. I feel better already.'

Monday 1st February

Pushed by Mum's nagging over my porridge, I reluctantly called the Job Centre and informed them I'd be starting at Mr Borkowski's shop in less than two days and was no longer needing their pittance. I'm dreading this move to corner shop consumerism as I'm aware St Dominic's and Petersburn primary schools are a stone's throw away, literally, as I've seen them throwing stones towards the shop from the playground. My lunchtimes will be tied up serving droves of whinging youths. Is there a name for a collection of youths? An ASBO of youths? A dread of youths? It'll be hectic and soul-destroying.

Tuesday 2nd February

My results have come back early from the GUM Clinic. The automated voice at the end of the line confirmed I'd gonorrhoea in the throat and the rectum. This means my 4x4 Guy definitely did not infect me as we didn't have anal sex: Thomas is the culprit. I'm not surprised. This has serious implications for him and his bit of stuff. This could be the end of them. If she has any sense, she'll pull the plug on their sordid fun and become a nun. Good! I get some pleasure from that thought.

After picking up my mobile and putting it back down many times, I finally let the call go through. I was a bit startled when it was answered quickly as I'd been hoping to leave a simple, uncomplicated, drop the bomb voicemail.

'Yup, what do you want?' cut Thomas, rather flippantly for someone who has stomped all over my heart and given me the clap.

I stammered at first, unsure how to deliver words like *infection* and *discharge*, but eventually settled on a straight forward, 'I have Gonorrhoea.'

'Uh-huh,' came the careless reply, 'and what do you want me to do about it?'

'Nothing. I've sorted it. But I need to let you know as you may've infected me.'

'Aye, I had it, but I've got rid,' he replied tersely.

I felt my blood bubble with rage, 'What? When? And when were you going to tell me?'

'Andy, you've pretty much cut me out of your life,' he said bitterly.

'Don't give me the wounded soldier crap. I was gonna tell you on the day of your Aunt's funeral, but you and your maw saw to it that I was bounced off the graveyard. I figured you'd soon show a symptom or two, pop a few pills, and get over it. It's just a wee bug. You're not the first to get the clap, and you won't be the last.'

'Aye, but one with serious consequences if left untreated,' I argued, pacing around my room. 'So it wasn't just about settling our estate, it was also about the consequences of your risky behaviour.'

'I was trying to do the right thing, ass-hole!'

'Maybe the right thing would've been to keep your dick in your pants, instead of waving it around local lay-bys for any Tom, Dick or Fanny to ride. Go fuck yourself, Thomas, and see how it feels to be at the sticky end of your knob!' I hung up the phone, threw it on the bed and punched one of Milli Vanilli in the face, forgetting there's a solid supporting wall behind their poster. It hurt like hell, but it was therapy.

All other results came back clear, which I suppose is something. All barring the HIV test. This has to be done. At some point. Soon. Soonish. In the future. The distant future. At some point.

Bugger, bugger, bollocks! What if?

Wednesday 3rd February

I'm knackered. When did kids get the bank balance to afford a vast variety of E Numbers disguised in sugar, cocoa, salt and fat? They obviously fleece their parents to buy as many magazines, mobile phone charms, fake tattoos and energy drinks as they want. I had Steve's voice in my head saying, 'It's a want, not a need.'

Even if the kids hadn't been there, I would've been run off my feet. 'Move this box.' 'Shift that shelf.' 'Arrange those magazines.' 'Don't slouch behind the counter.' 'Stock that fridge.' 'Push those almost out of date tins to the front.' 'Take that delivery through the back.' 'Keep smiling.' 'It's right to lead the customer into thinking they are always right, but use it as an opportunity to get a sale.' 'Let the customer browse; it allows them to think they have the upper hand, but always promote the most expensive brand if they're unsure,' and so on. I would be convinced I was slogging my guts out in some labour camp if Mr Borkowski wasn't called Mr Borkowski.

The lunchtime rush was hideous. An army of Protestant and

Catholic kids collided in the shop and proceeded to push and shove to get served, screeching at a pitch that only dogs could hear, chattering on their phones or goading the children from the opposing school. One of them even had the cheek to call me old. I could've jammed his head repeatedly in the till drawer, however, I avoided any such charges of manslaughter and maintained a strained-but-friendly grin under the autocratic mentorship of Mr Borkowski.

Don't get me wrong, they're not all bad. Some of them are my distant relations, and others fit into the bracket of lonely misfits, just as I did at school. As the droves of juveniles left in a cloud of bad language and sweetie rappers, a wee pale ginger kid in an oversized black bomber jacket covered in NASA badges sidled up to the counter and slid a copy of Doctor Who Magazine towards me. Matt Smith, the new Doctor, graced the cover. I marvelled at it for a few seconds. I have a copy at home, which I've read cover to cover already.

'Just this, Mr,' he uttered in a committed attempt to lower his voice to manly depths. My heart fluttered in recognition of the awkwardness in his small frame, and I took his money with my first genuine smile of the day. Here I was as an adult, serving a younger version of myself, both awkward in our own skin and unable to fit in. 'Cheers!' he called as he quickly scurried towards the door, hungrily scanning the pages as he went.

'Next month's got an exclusive interview with Steven Moffat and is packed with new series news,' I bellowed as he ran out the door. He gave me a thumbs-up as the bell jingled behind him. He was a little ray of sunshine in a generally grey day.

Thursday 4th February

It's inhumane to be rising at 6 a.m. in these freezing conditions. I'm up way before my own tight-fisted mother and, therefore, have to brave the house in sub-zero temperatures as I munch on my cornflakes cocooned in my p.j.'s, housecoat and the Tom Baker scarf that Aunt Moira knitted me when I was six.

Mum came downstairs and rolled her eyes at me. 'Why on Earth are you wearing that moth-eaten thing?' she remarked as she briskly flicked on the boiler switch.

‘Because it’s bloody baltic in here,’ I grunted.

‘Don’t swear, Andy. And don’t swear with your mouth full either,’ she said before heading back up the stairs to fulfil her morning ritual of loitering in bed until the bathroom and the bathroom alone warms up enough to shower. My bowl was empty at this point. I guess she mistook the chattering of my teeth for mastication.

Now that Dad’s retired from being a field service engineer, they’re cutting costs all over the house. The first to go was the automatic timer on the central heating. ‘Heating is to be used only as and when required and not as dictated by a clock,’ she informed me the other night. ‘The timer has no idea if it’s minus five or plus ten outside.’ Easy to say when you have two hot water bottles hidden inside the top of your housecoat.

‘No, but winter is pretty much a dead cert in this country and lasts for several months. At this rate I won’t be seeing my testicles ‘till the end of May,’ I argued.

‘Well, you’re not using them anyway, I hope,’ she said. ‘And don’t be so damn crude.’

I plopped my bowl in cold water and stuck the kettle on to have a second cup of coffee just to spite her. After breakfast, I quickly threw my clothes over the bathroom radiator and showered as the icicles slowly melted from the taps. I was tempted to wrap the scarf back around me on the fifteen-minute journey to Mr Borkowski’s but decided against it as that would make me not just the only gay in our scheme, but a crazy one too. I arrived at the shop to find one of the papergirls, Debora, impatiently kicking a lamppost and tapping purposefully at the clock on her mobile. She’s a bit of a bruiser of a girl, only 12 years old and already has the attitude of a premenstrual lesbian abstaining from chocolate. She’s only five-foot-two but still manages to look down her nose at me.

The usual rabble of kids at lunch and the gossip worshipers throughout the day kept me busy until I could smile and serve no more. No wee ginger boy was to be seen. I hope he’s okay. I finished my shift at 7 p.m., dragging my worn carcass back up the frozen cul-de-sack, and flopped on the couch in the igloo that is number 222. Mum switched the heating off at 6 p.m. sharp as, thanks to their double glazing, ‘the house keeps its warmth until bedtime’ allegedly. I was in bed by 8 p.m. When I’m fortunate enough to earn a decent wage I'll have my own place with under-floor heating *and* radiators throughout, cavity wall insulation injected into every crevice, three layers of loft insulation and triple glazing installed. The heating will run 24/7, and I'll dance around naked to Kylie while drinking mojitos packed with crushed ice.

Friday 5th February

I asked Mum about her winter fuel allowance, which she received this quarter. She flippantly said it had been spent on a new jacket and boots and that it was keeping her 'nice and cosy indeed, thank you.' Selfish is a word that immediately fell into my mouth, but I was cut short as she moaned about my use of the microwave to warm the milk for my cornflakes. What does she want me to do, use flint and sticks from the garden?

I said two words to her, 'Imelda Marcos,' and made for the safety of my bedroom. She spent the next thirty minutes blow-drying and styling her hair, which is the equivalent of at least thirty bowls of cornflakes brimming with scalding milk.

Saturday 6th February

A wee bit of a lay in this morning – 6.30 a.m. to be precise – as the shop opens later on a Saturday. I finally get a day off tomorrow, even though Mr Borkowski is pulling up the graffiti-covered shutters for a few hours on the Sabbath.

'We're constantly being punched in the gonads by the green fist of the supermarkets, Andy,' he keeps reminding me with fear in his eyes. 'We have to keep floating like a butterfly and stinging like a bee.' Sadly I believe Mr Borkowski's a featherweight under the heavy-weight fist of Tesco Tyson and could be K.O.ed at any second.

A text came through in the afternoon from 4x4 Guy asking, 'R U OK?'

I replied reluctantly, 'Aye, I'm OK. Sorry, but as it turns out, I was the one who gave you the clap.'

He came back with, 'No probs, buddy-boy! Them's the breaks! Let me know if you want to talk???'

I held back from saying: 'Yes! Yes! I do want to talk!' I want to talk to someone, anyone, who will listen. To tell them I'm miserable living in a frosty coop with a hen-pecking mother. That I miss having someone to hold me at night. I want to say that I've taken to lining pillows at my back to give the illusion I'm not alone, as I struggled to fall asleep in a tiny bed, in a teenager's room, in a cul-de-sac that I thought I was destined never to live in again. But instead, I said, 'OK.' It saved on time as I was being called on to restock the tights, tampons and Tena shelf.

Sunday 7th February

A glorious day off with no intention of stepping outside as the *Daily Record* headline said, 'Scotland To Be Hit By -12 Degrees As Big Freeze Returns'. That was until my mobile rang.

'Good Sunday afternoon to you, daaaaahling!' said the chirpy voice at the other end of the transmitter. 'What you up to?'

It was Ryan: suddenly things were looking up. I confessed, 'I'm doing sod all, and I'm on the verge of killing my mother.'

'Come to Edinburgh. You won't suit prison orange with your complexion, anyway.'

'I can't, I've got to serve burgeoning sectarians in Mr Borkowski's empire first thing in the morning,' I grumbled.

'Sectarians? Oh, how seventies. What's occurring, cupcake?'

'I'm being forced to work in the local corner shop by my parents, and I have to serve school children from the local primary schools.'

'Ugh! How grey. Why?'

'Because I have to be a sensible grown-up, apparently, and knuckle down for my own future.'

'How noble and very Eastenders of you. I don't envy your predicament. When are you next off? I have a bottle of Armand De Brignac that has accidentally been chilled and needs to be consumed soon. It'll be a tragedy if it dies on its own while festering next to an M&S ready meal.'

'Wednesday,' I said, ignorant of what Armand De Brignac actually was, but knowing Ryan, I figured it wasn't your average bottle of Buckfast. (I Googled it later; it's champagne.)

'Come over on Tuesday evening, just you and me, we'll grab a bite at Café Jamaica, have a few drinks and then hit the bars properly,' he said as I imagined his bright, broad grin on the other end of the line. 'And, before you gurn about not being able to drink and the late drive home, you can stay over. We've got a very comfy bed and one heck of a bathroom to use in the morning.' He put on a plummy accent and added, 'I have two continental showers now, you know?'

'Are they warmer than your average, run-of-the-mill showers?' I quipped.

Ryan laughed. 'A done deal then, no excuses. Besides, I may have an offer that could be the beacon of light you need to guide you away from those jagged rocks you appear to be pitifully sailing towards. Oh, the tragedy of it all!'

How could I refuse? 'Well, it sure beats miming to Pulp's *Disco 2000* in front of my bedroom mirror of an evening.'

'Good man, what time?'

'Around eight?'

'Perfect, bye.'

I hung up and stumbled bleary-eyed from the darkness of my little pod towards our Icelandic shower cubicle. I almost changed my mind when I found the towel I'd used yesterday morning was still damp and hanging like death above a decommissioned radiator, but I know that allowing one's personal hygiene to lag is a slippery slope to becoming a social outcast. I showered for a good twenty minutes, using far more hot water than my dig money covers and relishing every drop. After Ryan's call, my mood has lifted more than I expected. I even went for a walk, Tom Baker scarf included.

Monday 8th February

Back to the grind. If I'm not stocking-up or stock-taking, I'm sweeping up or washing down. Mr Borkowski is continually on my back and watching my every toilet trip and tea break. He seems to think I'm in this for the long haul and is keen for me to become his prodigy and maybe even build an empire for myself. The only empire I want is a box of Empire Biscuits free off the shelf to go with the teabags I've had to purchase from his shop for my break as the skinflint doesn't supply tea, coffee, milk or sugar.

The wee ginger-haired lad – Willy, as I've learned – popped in on his way home from school and asked for me especially. I was busy in the back returning the unwanted soft porn and fitness magazines (unsurprisingly there were far less of the soft porn variety to return) when Mr Borkowski called me through the front. All wee Willy wanted to do was show me his new sonic screwdriver, which really touched me. His uncle deals with the licensing of all Dr Who merchandise and has ensured Willy gets masses of pre-released toys. I was jealous. Sad, I know, but I am a fanboy after all.

I'm warming to this wee loner. He brings out a protective paternal instinct that I never knew I had. Usually, I believe all children should be gagged and bound in public for my own protection; such is their unpredictable and brutally honest nature it makes me nervous.

Tuesday 9th February

'Edinburgh? Again?'

'Yep,' I said, as I swung out of the lounge, quickly shutting Mum in. 'Don't wait up, I'm staying over at Ryan's,' I called as I jumped out of the front door. I couldn't get down our steps quick enough, aware she was peeling back the net curtains as I leapt into my car. She opened the window and called after me like a banshee, but my CD player kicked in, and Aretha Franklin's *Respect* drowned her out at the turn of the key.

Free!

Ryan and I spent the day walking around Edinburgh, taking in the Royal Mile, dipping into a few museums and generally clowning about. It feels so good to be back, not only with my buddy but within this beautiful city. Edinburgh has a vibe that I lost sight of a long time ago, and no matter the time of year, her glorious landscape seems to wear any season well.

We returned to Café Jamaica, whereupon Ryan enlightened me to his whole plan: I could move in with them and rent their spare room, and Molasses Brown is looking for a new server at the Café. Then, by sheer coincidence (not), Molasses appeared at the table and said, 'Oh, my dear boys, I'm so tired. We're short-staffed again. If only I could find a young man to fill the gap here at Café Jamaica. Do you know of anyone?'

I was being set up yet again, but this time, I was going to grab the opportunity by the bollocks and not let go. 'I'm free to work,' I lied. Just the small detail of my job at the corner shop that needs to be fixed.

Molasses announced, 'I have to tell you, I only hire pretties, Mr

Angus. I know it isn't very PC to do so, but frankly, tough titties. The customers like beautiful food *and* service, you understand? What I offer them on a plate is important. I'm sure with your good looks and charm my investment will continue to grow.'

'Are you really offering me a job?' I chuckled in disbelief.

'I most definitely am, Mr Angus, or my name is not Miss Molasses Brown.

'But you hardly know me.'

She leaned towards me over the plumes of steam from our fondu, her big dark eyes widened, appearing as some kind of Voodoo priestess as she uttered in a thick Jamaican accent, 'I have a sixth sense; I know a good person when I seen dem.' She pulled back, swept up a few of our empty beer glasses and wiggled off towards the bar, 'I'll give you a week to think about it, but I know what your answer will be,' she beamed and nodded purposefully. 'All lost souls need a home.'

******

Ryan and I have returned to his flat on Leith Street and started on that bottle of fizz. I sipped it delicately as I didn't want Tony, who was at home sadly, to think Ryan was throwing the pearl before the swine. Their old apartment has been entirely revamped and now boasts one of those wet-rooms and multi-jet showers that I've only seen on TV shows such as *Grand Designs*. Ryan used to rent the place when the walls were coated in emerald green paint and fertile patches of mould. He had a windfall from a dead grandparent during the economic downturn and bought the flat at a knockdown price, just after his elderly live-in landlord fell down two flights of stairs, breaking his neck as a result and conveniently dying without any inheritors. These boys could land in shit and still come out smelling of Paco Rabanne.

'It was a terrible shock arriving home and finding him there, all broken like a discarded mannequin, but time and money heals all,' explained a smug Tony. I'm sure he took one glance at the crumpled body and saw the investment potential. He probably called his lawyer before he called the ambulance.

Anyway, credit where credit's due, they've ripped the flat's rotten carcass open and performed open-heart surgery that's given the place a new lease of life. It's modern, with clean lines, minimalist and yet warm. The room I could be renting pleases me. The mood lighting is perfect as it makes me look a few years younger. There are wall-to-wall built-in wardrobes with mirrored sliding doors that could be fun to have sexual encounters in front of. My weak bladder is pleased too as it's a very short trip to the ensuite, which is clad in black and white tiles and has under-floor heating. It would undoubtedly be no chore to shower here in contrast to the iceberg that is 222 Mull. The sound of cracking beechwood from the log burner in the lounge can be heard between Ryan's annihilation of Cher's *Believe*. He's in their vast bedroom changing for a second time today as he now chooses to dress in day-wear and evening-wear. I'm obviously going to have to up my game in the fashion department if I do move in with them. But I wouldn't know fashion if it slapped me in the face with a Yves Saint Laurent belt, if she makes belts. However, tonight I'm very excited as it's my first night out on the gay scene after an absence of ten years. Can't wait!

Wednesday 10th February

Recognisable faces paraded before me, worn down by a tumultuous decade of drink and drugs in search of 'the one'. They hovered above the youth of today expectantly. And when I say youth, I do mean *youth*.

'How old are some of these kids?' I asked Ryan as he returned from CC's bar.

'It's the knock-on effect from the equalisation of the age of consent, my friend. This place can seem like a damn Tolkien novel sometimes. Out of my way hobbits!' he nipped as he pushed past a group of teenagers to gain the perfect vantage point of the dance floor.

I can't really blame the boys and girls for feeling free and liberated by the change in the law, it's what we fought for after all. Thanks to this, there's a now a pile of support available that wasn't when I came out. And it allows sexual health education more freedom too. I just wish they didn't make me feel so *ancient*.

'Some things have changed for the better though,' added Tony, who had just elbowed a guy in the ribs to get through the crowd. 'The lesbians have got prettier.'

'Who's the drag on the pole?' I asked, pointing towards three pole-dancers on podiums. Two fit lads wearing nothing but white pants and boots cavorted and contorted either side of a girl kitted out in a black corset and fishnets as she moved slickly to *Mein Herr* from Cabaret.

Ryan laughed, almost choking on his pint, 'That isn't a drag queen. *That* is Ms Sally Knowles, all-round entertainer and close friend of Miss Molasses Brown. A bit of an enigma, if you ask me. Appeared on the scene a few years ago. She causes quite a stir with her performances.

'Even though she's obviously getting on a bit, the poor thing,' chirped in Tony.

Ryan continued, 'The jury's still out if she swings both ways or is just a boring straight. She doesn't give much away, but the girls and boys love her, and *she* most definitely *is* a *she!* Just wait and see, she'll be popping her tits out soon enough for you. One of those new girls that do a stint of fake drag, which takes some balls, if you ask me. You'll meet the biggest fag hag in town sooner or later if you take the job at the café.'

'She waits on tables there to subsidise her waning career,' added Tony, as if he'd just swallowed vinegar.

Her toned frame glistened with beads of sweat as the lights reflected on her mocha coloured skin. Slight in frame, she sported a black bobbed wig, wide eyes caked in thick dark makeup, and knee-high, kinky boots that Emma Peel would be proud of. I watched her routine, mesmerised by her total command of the crowd and flexibility, ignoring the muscular boys next to her. Within minutes, the show was over, and she was gone. I thought it was a damn fine performance and suspect Tony is a tad envious. Even so, could I really work in a place that employs a stripper? What kind of establishment would do that? A place that isn't as boring as a corner shop, I imagine. You know what? I think I really could.

Beer after beer, cocktail after cocktail: the night danced on. Before long, I lost myself in the entity of the seething masses while alcohol coursed through my blood and detached my brain from the complications in life, sliding me towards the dawn through a smoky haze and the rhythm of the night.

Sheer bliss.

******

Later, after at least ten selfies in which I looked consistently drunk, we returned home hungrily forking our chips and buzzing from a great night. Ryan suggested taking a walk after Tony decided to head to bed. I figured that an early morning stroll would be just the tonic. I needed to sober up a little. So, at 4 a.m., we climbed Calton Hill and gazed down on Edinburgh as she ebbed and flowed. As any city, she's a feisty creature that sings her own lullaby but is never able to fall asleep. Ryan chose to sit on the north edge of the hill and asked, 'Do you remember when we'd come up here together at the end of the night if neither of us had pulled?'

'I remember. Which was pretty often, as we rarely pulled,' I laughed.

'I didn't mind,' he said. He turned to face me and smiled that beautiful toothy grin. He held my gaze and bit his lower lip. It was as if he'd rattled some old emotions and was fighting to keep them boxed in. He looked away. 'I sometimes forfeited a shag just to come up here with you. I needed our time together. There's a stillness about you, Mr, that I've always loved. Your calmness at the end of the night helped me wind down.'

'Thanks. That calmness didn't stop Steve pulling every single night,' I joked. I sat next to him, the ground was cold and damp, but that didn't bother me now we were alone again.

'No, it didn't. But then, there were nights he'd take anything.'

We chuckled and then went quiet for a time. In our own thoughts. Faint traffic could be heard making its way down Leith Walk. The occasional ladette's drunken yelps echoed through the night as the amber lamps twinkled along the streets. Lights of the tenements on Leith Walk randomly glimmered into life for a short time and then died. Below our feet, just along the steps, the last pieces of trade wandered up and down the gravel steps in the safe anonymity of darkness, occasionally stopping to inspect a possible opportunity or to rest against the wall and wait on something better coming along.

'Cruising doesn't turn me on,' I interjected. 'I like the chase. The intimacy and sheer bliss of unhurried sex in the comfort of a potential lover's home. Learning who they are by scanning their CD collection and bookshelves. Where's the fun in cruising?'

'But cruising's a part of life that's always existed. It demands to be included.'

'True,' I agreed. And here it was, keeping our feet firmly on the grit and dirt of this fairytale city. 'Steve never had a problem with it.'

'Totally!' nodded Ryan. 'Brazen hussy, that he was.' We laughed, and then he asked, 'Hey, do you remember, when he was really drunk, he'd shout loud over the dance floor, "Ryan! Andy! I just want ma' hole! Is that too much to ask? *I want ma' hole!*" ?'

I cringed, 'Oh, yeah. I forgot about that. Bloody outrageous.'

'Totally inappropriate,' agreed Ryan.

'And he'd leave us high and dry if an opportunity caught his eye. Do you know, he once left me on a train to Glasgow?

'No way!'

Yes, way! We were heading for a night out. He buggered off to shag a ticket collector in the station toilets? There I was, doors closed, train moving, thinking he'd just nipped to the loo in the carriage, and I only realised when I was well out of the city. I got off at Croy and turned about. I was the only queen at Croy. In a bloody glittery Kylie tee-shirt, damn it.'

'He was a selfish idiot at times, but great fun.'

We burst out laughing. A guy called from the steps, 'Hey! Keep the noise down! Some of us are trying to get some down here.'

'Sorry!' we called back, toning down to a giggle. We fell silent and huddled together to keep warm. Ryan rested his lovely head on mine. It was perfection. We didn't really need to talk about the gap years, we just needed to start again – a second chance. I'm bloody thankful for that. Sat there with him, watching tiny lives stumbling around before dawn. Stumbling through life like the rest of us. Getting up and going at it again, just as Ryan and I could. It felt like it was us against the world once more. I basked in the tranquillity of the moment. A little pocket of time and space just for us. Ships sailed quietly on the Firth of Forth as lighthouses pulsated their reassuring beacons. The water melded with the star-speckled sky. So much darkness and yet, reassuringly, tiny glimmers of hope, guiding us safely through the dark.

'Look at this,' he said. 'Where in the world do you get all of this? A city, with a castle, built on a volcano, with bridges buried under buildings, with a loch that's now a park, *and* a palace, *and* all sitting on this gorgeous coastline. It's a sort of fairytale.' A rush of pride came over me, and I nodded in agreement. I felt his hand grip my arm through the thickness of my coat as he pulled me even closer. His eyes were steadfast. 'Come back,' he whispered.

Forget the dancing, the men, the city ... that was all I really needed. With two little words, he'd managed to turn back time.

Thursday 11th February

Whatever dreamlike state I've been in for the past few days was eradicated after my shift at Borkowski's. I crash-landed and skidded to planet Earth when I returned home this evening. My mother waited expectantly at the kitchen table like she'd been sucking lemons. A letter from the GUM Clinic was laid squarely before her.

'Have you got something to tell me?' she asked as pot lids rattled and spat boiling water behind her, annihilating the veg and murdering any vitamins they once offered. I'd clean forgotten about my 'Test for Cure' appointment at GUM and quickly realised they'd sent me a letter, rightly so, asking why I hadn't attended.

'Have you been reading my mail?' I asked, attempting to act nonchalant as I unpacked the small bag of shopping I'd brought her.

My mother, on the other hand, has been trained by the Gestapo in every possible interrogation technique, so I knew I was only delaying the inevitable thunderclap. 'Of course, I've bloody opened it! How else could I've read it?' she snapped, rising from the table and stalking my every move around the kitchen as I put the shopping away. 'What the hell have you been up to?'

I explained I had to go for a little treatment as I had an infection last week, and it really wasn't any of her business.

At that point, Dad arrived back from the local match to ear-piercing caterwauling from a wild banshee. 'Treatment? *Treeeeatment*! What kind of treatment?' she echoed as the door swung open and Dad stumbled in drunkenly.

'What the hell's happened now?' he asked, exasperated.

'Treatment for gonorrhoea, Mother Dearest,' I blurted out, ignoring Dad as I slammed the fridge door shut.

Mum flinched, 'Did you hear that, Charlie? The lads caught the clap from staying out all night! And to think I was giving him the best towels as well. I'm glad I washed your sheets while you were away. I knew something was up when I saw the stains on the inside of your pants.'

'Jesus! Are you inspecting my clothing at every wash? I'm sure you'd fit in quite well working covertly for the News of the World,' I spat.

Dad tried to calm the situation, but she continued to pace the linoleum and clattered pot, after dish, after pot. And then the straw that broke the camel's already weary back: 'Or did you get it from your "4x4 Guy" ?'

I saw red immediately. The gloves were off. It was time for this camel to kick back! 'Have you been reading my diary?' Mum became a little more demure realising she'd said too much. I let rip, 'Jesus! You've done nothing but suffocate me since I came back! Pushing me into a job that I hate, gossiping to the neighbours about my failures, living vicariously through my own misfortune, and generally sticking your nose where it doesn't bloody, buggery belong. If you had bothered to read further, you would've found it was Thomas in fact who'd given me gonorrhoea, not some random guy on a country lane when I was at my lowest.'

She was a bit more subdued now, sitting back in the chair that she had most probably been rocking furiously in since she read the letter. 'Thomas?'

I didn't care or listen and continued on, 'And if we're talking about truth here, I've been offered a job in Edinburgh and a place to stay, with under-floor heating and a continental shower, so you won't have to waste your time inspecting my boxers any more as I've accepted both.' I strode towards the hall with my head high. 'And one more truth before I go. Dad, did you know your wife's smoking again? Twenty a day, I'd say. Check the compost heap for dabs.' I swung the door shut on my mother's flabbergasted expression.

It seems fate and my rather large mouth have done the deed for me; I'm leaving home again, and this time most definitely not coming back.

Friday 12th February

Despite being busy at the shop from 6.30 a.m. onwards, I managed to see a few tasks through to fruition:

1. Miss Molasses Brown contacted and job offer accepted. Start a week today at 12 p.m.
2. Text sent to Ryan requesting the use of his spare room for the

foreseeable future until I can afford a flat of my own. New tenancy accepted immediately.

3. GUM appointment rescheduled to Monday the 15th for my Test for Cure. Rather cross receptionist berated me over the line for being AWOL on my previous appointment. Totally justified.
4. Mother has been successfully avoided all day due to strategic toilet stops and covert staircase operations.
5. Takeaway delivered by 8 p.m. and eaten out of tubs with a small plastic fork while watching back-to-back episodes of *Genesis of The Daleks* in my bedroom.
6. One celebratory masturbatory session completed (quietly as parents can be heard sniping at each other through the wall) and I'm now entirely spent.

Night, night.

Saturday 13th February

I heard yelling from the shop's backyard this afternoon. When I jumped out to see what was going on, I found wee Willy pinned to the wall by three, much taller, older boys. A sudden wave of fatherly protectiveness washed over me, and I found myself shouting abuse at the goby wee shits and, thanks to inheriting my mother's lungs and determination, all three scarpered within seconds. Wee Willy took flight too, I imagine out of embarrassment as he didn't even look me in the eye. Seconds later, I noticed his sonic screwdriver crushed to pieces on the ground. When I was Willie's age, I was bullied by a sadistic lad called Gary Roberts every day for a year. I'll never forget his name or the humiliation he put me through. I know how miserable life can become and how dreaded a walk to and from school can be. I feel for this wee kid. I really do. I need to do something to help him. He needs to know he's not alone.

Sunday 14th February

Valentines Day (So what!)

I finally got round to giving Mr Borkowski my notice. He seemed a little crestfallen and scooted into the back of the shop. I served six people in the time it took him to re-surface. I think I've broken his little retail heart. I feel so bad, but it's my future here, damn it!

When I got home, Mum was sweeping the front path just to intercept me. Our path only gets a good brush and bleaching when there's juicy gossip slopping around the scheme. Mum doesn't feel satisfied until she can listen, digest and embellish the rumour to at least ten passers-by. I imagine the slabs haven't had such a vigorous scouring since Lisa McKenzie disappeared. She leant on her broomstick purposefully, eyeballing me as I strode past, and called to Mrs White over the hedge, 'Aye, Edinburgh, of all godforsaken places. He's got a job in a fancy café serving cup-o-chinos and Bedoing Chicken to posh students that don't know one end of a razor to the other.' I hopped in the house with a smug grin. Everyone but her knows it's *Bedouin* Chicken, surely?

Later, as I headed to the kitchen to re-fill my hot-water bottle, we met at the kettle. She crept up on me under the tinny cacophony of boiling water. 'You're not still wearing that shoddy old thing?' As usual, Mum plumped for a jibe rather than a kind word to start communication. If she were around at the Malta Summit in 1989, the Cold War would be firmly frozen and impassable on either side of the iron curtain today.

She was talking about my Tom Baker scarf, which had been thrown around my neck again to defrost my windpipe as the house is still only heated in the 'necessary rooms', my bedroom not being necessary apparently. I think she's been hell-bent on freezing me out to the more pleasant climates of the lounge and kitchen. I opted for nostalgia to encourage a pleasing end to the now tiresome standoff, so I asked, 'Remember when Aunt Moira knitted this?'

Mum broke a smile for the first time in a week, 'I do,' she said as she stirred a delicious pot of Dad's broth. 'She spent ages trying to get the right wool, the right colour, even had me and your dad traipsing in every shop on Sauchiehall Street trying to find the perfect match.' She stopped to taste the broth, added more salt and then continued, 'And there was that night she came round for a knit and a natter when it was almost finished, just before Christmas, casting off furiously in the small hours. You had a sleepwalking fit and appearing like an apparition at the living room door. Scared the living daylights out of us. I've never seen a sofa stuffed so quickly with wool in all my life.' She clicked open the washing machine door and scooped out a pile of freshly laundered clothes that fought to counteract the oniony stench from the pot. 'You won't remember that as I managed to coax you back upstairs with a promise of a bedtime story and a hug.'

Mum hugging me. I forgot she used to do that. When did she stop? Why did she stop? I asked her if she remembered the other boys picking on me for wearing it to school.

'That Gary Roberts?' she asked, flapping my jeans out straight, 'I remember the wee shit. Butter wouldn't bloody melt! I would've loved to have slapped him *and* his mother within an inch their lives, but you begged me not to. The silly cow couldn't keep him under control. Turned out I didn't have to, that Lisa McKenzie did it for me. She wasn't all bad, I suppose,' She stared out of the window and poked her cheek with her index finger, chewing on the inner flesh in contemplation.

'Lisa stood up for me loads.'

'And led you astray many times.' This I couldn't deny, but it was always good fun.

It was then I told mum about my dilemma with wee Willy, and she listened objectively, only adding, 'It's changed days since you were young, when you could give a bunch of lads a good clout round the lugs and a warning that their mothers would've approved of. With wee Willie, you could go through the proper channels, but you know as well as I do that that takes time and he may say no to any help anyway, just as you did back then. At any rate, you give them a slapping, and the police and social services would be round here before your hand has left their faces.'

'It's changed days now, Mum, thankfully.'

'It's overkill, that's what it is. You can't look at a kid the wrong way now without getting sued. I may have clipped you round the ear a few times, but you always deserved it, and it was done with love. You never needed it often. You weren't a bad kid at all. You're not a bad lad now either.'

I can't imagine anyone smacking with affection, but a problem shared is a truce made, it seems.

Monday 15th February

It doesn't get any more comfortable going to the GUM clinic. I didn't warrant a doctor this time, just a nurse and a round of swabs that I swear could remove paint off a blackboard. The nurse reassured me that it was more common than not to pick up some kind of sexual disease if you're single and sexually active.

When I reminded her that I'd actually contracted it from a long-term partner, 'Ah, okay, that's not uncommon too,' was her less-than-reassuring reply. 'Have you thought any more about taking an HIV test?' she asked with a weighted stare.

'I have,' I said, shifting uncomfortably as my buttocks clenched. 'I've decided to wait until life becomes more normal. Right now is not the best time for bad news. I'm living with my parents in Airdrie, you see, and have no friends close by.' The second I said it I knew I was just throwing excuses to stall for more time. More time as the man I've always been: Andy Angus, sexually active and uncomplicated.

She looked pitifully at me, possibly because I'm living with my folks, maybe because I'm friendless in Airdrie, or perhaps because I was the twentieth person that day obviously bargaining with themselves. 'Okay, but it would be best to get it diagnosed sooner rather than later, as your chances of a better quality of life will increase dramatically through early treatment.' I left untested and more pensive than before. It's going to be another two weeks before I get these results. On my way home, I noticed a text from 4x4 Guy asking to meet. I feel so sick, tired and unattractive that I've chosen to ignore him.

Tuesday 16th February

While rubbing the expiry dates off countless tins of peas with a Nitromors soaked cotton bud, Mr Borkowski told me that wee Willy had come looking for me yesterday. It's the first time I've actually regretted not being at the shop since I started. Mum came in and popped one of the expired tins of peas in her basket. I quickly retrieved it and drew daggers at Mr Borkowski for almost fooling Mum into purchasing peas that had been grown when ABBA had their last number-one single. 'I'll cook tonight,' I said. 'My treat. You know, to say thank you for putting up with me.'

'Oh,' she stepped back, a little unsteady on her feet, 'Alright, but nothing too spicy. I'm not flapping a duvet all night trying to get rid of your father's farts. And none of that crap mince from that cheap

German supermarket down the road either. Get decent stuff.'

'Okay,' I smiled.

'What are you grinning at?'

'Nothing,' I lied, unable to keep a straight face.

She paid for a bag of Cola Bottles and added before she left, 'And we eat at six, remember? Any later and I'll have heartburn from now until the cows come home.'

This, in Mum's terms, is a thank you.

Wednesday 17th February

Another text message from 4x4 Guy asking to meet as soon as I'm clear for another session. Remarkable, as I thought the idea of being infected by another would put anyone off. He seems keen, but I can most definitely say I am *not* in the mood for sex and probably will never be again.

Thursday 18th February

Oh, my God, I am so HORNY! So much for remorse. I called the GUM hotline in the hope that my results have been fast-tracked by some kind lab technician who understands the potency of testosterone. After I gave my I.D. Code to the automated voice in assorted different accents (my exasperated Transylvanian accent at the 6th attempt got me through, weirdly enough) the pretend woman, who sounded suspiciously like Johanna Lumley (is she really that hard up to do a sexual health phone line?) itemised a list of my previous positive and negative results. The Slut-o-Meter started ringing in my head again. No new results, so it seems I have to wait a further 12 days after all.

I have needs, damn it!

Friday 19th February

I arrived at the shop this morning uncharacteristically early to find it was already open and being swept by the papergirl, Debora. When I asked her where Mr Borkowski was, she said, 'He's trusting me with opening the shop from now on as you've been late every morning for the past week.' My face must've said it all as I raised my eyes to the cracked ceiling and threw on my green tabard. She added, rather sarcastically I thought, 'He wants to invest his time in someone who actually cares about the community and who has a keen eye and business model in mind. You, apparently, are a bit shit at that.'

I was a tad gobsmacked by her cheek and foul language. She wants to be the next Dragon in the Den and has aspirations way beyond her years. I informed her, 'It's true, I've no intention of working in a shop for the rest of my life. I've grander schemes planned.'

She guffawed and said, 'And that's why you're moving to Edinburgh to work in a café? Say what you like, but it's still a shop. The only difference is the goods are cooked.'

Run a shop? She can't even push a broom properly. I found two humbugs behind the fridge moments later.

Saturday 20th February

Wee Willy showed face today, so I took him out the back of the shop where his bullying incident happened and tried to give him a pep talk on the insignificance of bullies and how, as an adult, you grow and become stronger with every knock you take.

'I too was jibed in and out of school for being skinny and loving Dr Who, but look at me now and how much I've grown,' I reassured him.

He replied, 'But I don't want to live with my mum when I'm old, sulking around in my housecoat after being dumped, and eating my bodyweight in Curly Wurlies.'

I must admit that I was taken aback by his direct and well-informed, if slightly warped, insight. When I asked him where he'd got this information, he told me, 'Yer Maw!'

'Well, technically, I wasn't "dumped", and thirty-five isn't old either. And it wasn't just Curly Wurlies; there has been the occasional Yorkie bar too.'

'If y'er no' old, then why do you wear slippers at work?'

I looked down at my feet and blushed. 'Um. Because they're comfy,' I whimpered as I quietly accepted my comfort needs have superseded my style.

That woman can't hold her own water. Leaving their freezing cul-de-sac can't come soon enough as she is beginning to rip my knitting. I wished I'd never cooked such a delicious, if I might say so myself, shepherd's pie for her the other evening. I should've made her bedouin chicken and have her eat it at eight o'clock in the evening.

Sunday 21st February

I asked Mr Borkowski if it was legal for a twelve-year-old schoolgirl to be opening a corner shop at six in the morning. He kept his head buried in the sports page of the Airdrie & Coatbridge Advertiser and mumbled, 'Perfectly legal.' Debora continued to stack the shelves with a smug grin on her face. She's now slotted into my part-time spot regularly at weekends and is firmly positioned under Mr Borkowski's nurturing wing.

Wee Willy popped in again, this time a little more downtrodden than I've seen him in the past. I asked him if he was getting more stick, but he wasn't forthcoming. I know he has been; he has several bruises on his right arm. He's the only reason I feel uncomfortable leaving this town. As today was my last day at work, I brought in a small gift for him in the odd chance he'd show up. His little face light up the second he saw the Tom Baker scarf my aunt made me. I figure I won't be needing it where I'm heading, not with double glazing and under-floor heating throughout. I hope, like me, it'll give him a lifetime of adventures.

As soon as Debora saw it, she said, 'Is that an exact replica of the fourth Doctor's scarf from 1974?' I was stunned that such a brutish imbecile could know such facts.

Willy draped it over his neck, hopped around excitedly, and said, 'Aye! You want a shot?'

'I wouldnae mind,' she said eagerly.

I interjected that Willy probably shouldn't wear it around town with all the hassle he's been getting, but Debora swept her arm around him as they walked out of the shop. 'Don't you worry about them, kiddo, I'll look after you. Us Whovians need to stick together.'

As my old scarf trailed out the door, I was transported back to the day Lisa McKenzie first stood up for me. I was being threatened by a group of thugs lead by that nasty element, Gary Roberts. He had me pressed against a wall by the throat and was trying to force me to say Chips was better than Dr Who. He was just about to throw a blow right to my gut when a fist came from nowhere and cracked him right on the jaw. When his grasp loosened and the oxygen returned to my brain, I saw Lisa standing over Gary's cowered frame. 'Go on, piss off ya spotty faced wanker!' she called as his tail disappeared around the corner in fear. 'Come on, kiddo,' she said calmly, holding out a scuffed hand to help me up, 'Us Whovians need to stick together.' Debora is the new Lisa. How could I not see it before? I think Willy might be okay.

Monday 22nd February

Every time I mention Edinburgh, Mum leaves the room. This is ridiculous.

Tuesday 23rd February

Time to pack.

Mum came straight up the stairs when she got home from work and almost caught me stuffing a bottle of lube in my rucksack. 'You could stay,' she muttered as she inspected a pile of my t-shirts, tutted and flapped them open purposefully to fold them *better*.

'I can't.'

'You bloody well could, Andy Angus! I'm sure Mr Borkowski would give you that job back. That Debora is pretty useless and nothing but trouble if you ask me. She once pushed Jesus, Mary and Joseph off the stage in a rage at the local nativity just because Mary was carrying the baby Jesus by the leg: he was only a doll, after all. And I guess, if we're getting dig-money from you, we can turn on the immersion a little bit more.'

'I can't. I don't belong here.'

'Nonsense, your whole family is here.'

I stopped her frantic folding and sat with her on my bed. I decided to tell her something that I've never mentioned to anyone before.

'Listen, Mum, when Lisa moved away, and I was left more or less friendless, something awful happened to me. One day I got the train from Drumgelloch to Coatbridge, I think I was fifteen at the time, and a bunch of lads got on a stop later and sat all around me. They knew who I was. They knew what I was. They all started kicking me repeatedly and laughing. Sat opposite, methodically taking a turn at bruising my shins. I could feel the skin tearing. It was torture.

'Other people on the train did nothing. The carriage was half-full, and they saw it and did nothing. These boys chose me because they knew I was *different*, weak in their eyes and easy fodder. Not a soul did a thing. I spent the next year fearing that every stranger in this town could tell I was gay and hated me for it, and from then on it stopped being home.'

'But times have changed; we have a lesbian couple running the butchers.'

'Aye, but they're together. I'm on my own.'

'You're not on your own. I told you, you've got me, your dad and your sister.'

'No Mum, I can't put myself through this. I'll never really relax here because that memory is there every time I take a train, a bus, or every time I walk past a bunch of lads hanging on a street corner. I can't shift it. This place is tainted to me.'

'Edinburgh isn't the answer.'

'It may or may not be, but it's the only place I've felt free enough to be me. I need your support in this. You won't believe me, but it makes all the difference, it really does.' I paused. Reluctant to tell her the ugliest part of the story. But I had to make her understand why. 'That day on the train, when they were done kicking me, they got up to leave, and I began to feel some relief. But it didn't last as, before they left, they stopped to snort and spit on me. Right in my face. Every one of them. And boy did I cry. I really did. In that carriage. In front of all those people. I was meeting you at the next stop, and I couldn't let you see how upset I was, how weak I'd been, so I wiped the tears and spit off my face best I could, got off and carried on as if nothing had happened. You had no idea. My shins bled for the rest of the day, so much that my socks were stuck to my wounds by bedtime. Bruises and cuts heal, but that fear lasts a lifetime.'

'Oh, my boy. I'm so sorry.' She looked like she was going to cry. She paused to think, perhaps reluctant to give me her blessing in light of my honest vulnerability, but she nodded and added, 'Okay. Understood. Go be with your friends. But if anything like that ever happens to you again, you tell me right away. Okay?'

I nodded in agreement, unable to speak.

'And I'll send Big Bob the bouncer from the Four Isles to sort them out.'

I couldn't help but laugh through the tears. And then, relief. That awful moment was out of me at last. And as a result, for the first time in a long time, Mum became *my* mum and hugged me and held me. And by God, I felt loved.

Wednesday 24th February

21 Leith Street, Edinburgh.

20:00hrs. I've moved again! As I left my Mum and Dad's, I couldn't help but notice that their house was the warmest it's ever been. I'm sure I heard the boiler sparking away, but decided one more confrontation would have soured an optimistic bon voyage.

Ryan was brimming with joy when he opened the door to my luggage-laden frame, but he soon grimaced when he saw the bloated Iceland carrier bags (my frozen food supplies from Mum) that were swinging from my forearms, 'Quick,' he flapped, 'get inside before the neighbours see you!' He led me down the hall, calling to Tony as he did so, 'He's here, and it seems it's not just mums that shop at Iceland, but destitute gay men too.' As I dropped the bags on the kitchen floor, he added, 'I have some Harvey Nichols tote bags that I insist you use from now on. We may be on Leith Street, but we are not actually living *in* Leith. This is Edinburgh.'

'It's on the verge of Leith,' I said.

'Well, thank you very much for that reminder. The grand Balmoral Hotel is closer, and therefore, we are firmly on the good side of town,' he assured me.

He's still keeping up appearances. I couldn't help but smile.

My room is picture perfect. The bed sheets are white Egyptian cotton, a fresh pair of white flip-flop slippers (acquired from the Malmaison Hotel) are placed in suitable alignment to the foot of the bed, and the softest, maroon housecoat is hanging from the fitted wardrobe on a hanger, all ready for the new houseguest. Fresh towels are laid on well-plumped pillows of assorted sizes, and a gift box filled with Molton Brown toiletries accompanies these luscious marshmallows of comfort with a welcome card. Also, there's a selection of golden wrapped chocolate eggs presented on the nightstand. It's touching the effort Ryan's put in (I'm under no delusion Tony has done any of this), it feels as if I'm staying at a five-star hotel.

By the time I'd emptied my car, walked the distance back and forth from the only space I'd found within a ten minute radius, and carried my stuff up the two flights of stairs – Ryan excused himself from any heavy lifting by saying, 'I can walk, or I can hold, but I can't walk and hold things. I'm not built to work in the export industry, sorry, cupcake. I have dainty joints. This is why we should have staff.' – I was sweating like a glass blower's arse and happy to use the fantastic shower, shower gel, body scrub, moisturiser, body lotion, towels and bathrobe supplied by my new landlords. It may only be digs, I may just be a lodger, but I have arrived!

Thursday 25th February

I'd no problem fitting my frozen food into the boys' freezer as it's devoid of anything but a single bag of ice. They don't cook and use their oven for storage. Dinner was takeaway served on Versace plates (which Ryan Facebooked, of course). I apologised for holding the boys up from their usual mealtime, but Ryan was fine about it, saying, 'It's ok, we don't usually manage to eat until nine anyway.'

When I commented that eating late at night isn't really good for digestion and encourages weight gain, Tony interjected with a jolly insult. 'Hark at her with her little pot belly!' patronisingly patting my paunch en route towards the M&S pavlova I'd speedily swept off the shelves to compensate for my current shortcomings in gastronomy. I had to concede somewhat reluctantly to Ryan and his acerbic bitch of a boyfriend that I'd gained a few inches of contentment fat over the years as I pressed heavily on my tummy in a futile attempted to flatten the protrusion. 'Please,' spat Tony as pieces of meringue flew out the cold slit he calls a mouth, 'nobody has ever been *that* content.'

It didn't help when Ryan added, 'It is true; you are single now, and no one loves a paunchy poof, dear. It's so strange; I can eat cake and drink booze to my liver's content and still be exactly the same weight I was when I was twenty. It's a curse. I will never be a hit on the bear scene. You, my little friend, are ripe to be thrown to a throng of naked bears right now.'

I'd forgotten how humble Ryan actually could be. If humble means 'tactless' in the Oxford English Dictionary.

Friday 26th February

My first day on the job at Café Jamaica and I'm exhausted. I was supposed to be inducted by Sally Knowles, but she called in sick at the last minute, so it was in at the deep end and keep paddling frantically below the surface while maintaining a fixed grin atop. Molasses claims I'm a natural, but I beg to differ: I got three orders wrong and dropped a steaming hot cappuccino in the lap of an elderly gent. Luckily he'd kept his raincoat on, eliminating any risk of 3rd-degree burns.

I'm in bed now. I haven't showered since this morning. It's 1 a.m., and I'm exhausted. Goodnight!

Saturday 27th February

Another frantic day. I slept until midday and have been catching my tail since. I started my shift at 1 p.m. on the busiest day of the week for a café-cum-bar. Again, we were one server down as Sally called in sick one hour after her start time.

I heard Molasses give her short shrift from the telephone at the bar, which she calls her office. 'I mean it, missy,' she said in a thick Jamaican accent (it seems anger brings it out of her more), 'if you don't get your sorry fanny here tomorrow, you'll be losing a job and a shack to live in.'

I mentioned to Barry, the chef, that I most certainly don't want to get on the wrong side of Molasses. He laughed and said, 'Aah, the dance of Sally and Molasses? She goads Sally like that all the time, she has to, but there's a quality in Sally I've always admired: she doesn't seem to give a shit.' It seems this Sally is infamous. I am not looking forward to meeting her, let alone work with her.

On my return home, I found Ryan and Tony on the floor examining possible cuts of fabric for the inside lining of their 'wedding' suits. There must've been at least thirty different colours, patterns and types of material. Who cares? It's not as if anyone is going to see the inside. It was as if I'd walked in on a military strategy meeting involving Dolce & Gabbana, Gucci and Prada. They were engrossed in their plans and hardly noticed me as I swept in and grabbed a glass of milk before bed.

It feels as if I've hardly seen Ryan, what with my shifts and Tony being constantly by his side. I'm actually feeling a bit lonely. As I left them to it, Tony raised his head and said, 'Andy, can we have a chat tomorrow about the rent?'

'Sure thing, not a problem,' I lied. I've been dreading this awkward discussion. I'd hoped it would've been the soft option (Ryan), but no, I get stingy Tony. I may have to sign my life away in my own blood.

Sunday 28th February

£500 a month plus phone bills! And £500 deposit to be paid by tomorrow! Bloody hell! Tony reminded me that I've the use of all the communal rooms in the flat, a large bedroom, a spacious ensuite bathroom with tiled flooring and underfloor heating throughout.

'Aye, but it's not Holyrood Palace,' I laughed nervously, beginning to feel as if I'd made the same error as Hansel and Gretel, but unlike them, I'm not just visiting a gingerbread house, I'm signing a legal contract with the witch.

'Look,' explained a terse Tony, 'a large deposit is needed as we've rented the room before and, after that tenant did a moonlight flit, found unforeseen damage that required the carpet to be replaced and extensive redecoration. I'm sorry, Andy, but we're not willing to take that risk again. Even with a friend of Ryan's.'

Ah, 'a friend of Ryan's'? Now I know exactly where I stand, I thought.

It seems I'm being punished for the irresponsibility of a previous numpty. I reminded him it's actually an ensuite shower room, not a bathroom, I'm using and asked if it would be possible to soak in their bath occasionally as my legs ache from standing all day in the café.

'No,' came the reply. 'Ryan has chaetophobia and cannot stand pubic hairs on porcelain.'

I'm anally retentive when it comes to hygiene and manscaping. My pubic hairs are clipped weekly, minuscule to the naked eye when moulted and therefore insignificant unless you went hunting with a magnifying glass. But I wasn't about to give Tony this personal information, so I caved in and agreed. He has me over a barrel, bent over backwards and tugging at my short-and-not-so-curlies.

I looked up chaetophobia later and found it's a fear of all hair, attached or otherwise. I believe Tony is manipulating me; Ryan spends so much care and attention on his barnet (hours in fact), and the only hint of trauma is when he accidentally Maces himself on his own lacquer. I find Tony's story as hard to swallow as a matted, dry fur-ball.

Monday 1st March

I'm free from disease! Joanna Lumley has confirmed that I'm negative for the big G in every orifice! I text 4x4 Guy in anticipation. Sadly he can't make it today for a discreet romp on my Egyptian cotton sheets – which would have been perfect as I'm on a day off and the boys are busy at work – however, he can make it tomorrow morning before my shift. A bit rushed, but a result all the same.

I felt frustrated the rest of the day, so I cleaned the kitchen and took care of the pile of dishes that resembled a small scale model of Everest. For such image-conscious lads, they really don't treat their flash kitchen with respect. Tony arrived home later and didn't even acknowledge my hard graft. I tried not to be antagonised as he waltzed in from their bedroom and dumped a couple of stained wine glasses and waltzed out again, but I could hear the blood pulsing in my ears.

He returned seconds later to ask, 'Have you got the rent yet, Andy?' I pointed to the envelope that he'd just rested said glasses on. He immediately moved them, tossed them in the sink and tucked the envelope into the back pocket of his jeans with a sneer. 'Cheers, mate,' he added as he patted me on the head and buggered off out, probably to spend his winnings.

I'm not your mate. You made that perfectly clear yesterday, I thought. My first week in this place doesn't feel so warm and friendly. I'm a tenant in a flat that has underfloor heating throughout, and yet it feels as if I'm staying at Resolute Bay.

Tuesday 2nd March

What a fantastic sex session filled with warm kisses, quaking muscles and goosebumps. I arrived at work, entirely satisfied and jelly-legged. That man definitely knows how to use his tongue! I should be ashamed. Sordid, fast, no questions asked fumblings are not usually my thing, but I'm enjoying the casualness of the whole affair. It feels like my life with a lowdown dirty dogger is a long, distant memory now. I know nothing about this 4x4 Guy, and I'm happy for it to remain that way. No emotional attachment = zero complications and harm.

Wednesday 3rd March

I arrived at Café Jamaica to find that Molasses Brown had nipped out to a local supplier of Caribbean grub, leaving Barry in charge and me running the tables. My first customer of the day was challenging, to say the least. She was confident and curvaceous, with jet black impish hair, cocoa coloured skin, and breasts spilling out of a very tight white blouse and waistcoat combination.

She ordered a Jamaican Peanut Punch, then called me back within a second of being served her drink by tapping loudly on the glass with an emerald painted fingernail and hollering, 'Excuse me!' several times in an irritating whine. 'This is delicious, but the wrong order,' she complained in a confusing accent somewhere between New York and Glasgow. 'I asked for the Guinness Punch.'

I was sure she ordered the Peanut Punch, but the customer is always right.

'Don't you recognise me?' she asked with a mischievous grin.

'No, should I?' was my indifferent reply.

'Oh, it's just I'm a bit of a celebrity around these parts, darling!'

'For what?'

'Entertainment, of course. Don't you just see it in me? I'm destined for stardom.' She does have a certain air about her, but that was mostly sarcasm. I left to get her the *right* drink.

When I got back to her table, she was wading through a titanic Prada handbag, off-loading assorted items, such as: 2 packs of tissues; one red vibrator (still packaged, thankfully); condoms in various styles and sizes; a travel pack of Durex Intense Lubricant; 4 bottles of perfume; a pair of knickers (hopefully not used); a quarter bottle of vodka (half-empty); one pillbox; one wrench.

'Oh,' she nodded towards the fresh drink I'd almost dropped at the sight of all this filth in a dining area, 'Did I not say a large? That's a medium, surely. I wanted a large.'

I was getting a bit irritated at this point. She may not have known what she wanted, but I knew exactly what I wanted; I wanted to ram her red vibrator up her snooty nose, but instead, I gritted my teeth and smiled as I turned to get this pain in the arse of a customer what *she* thought *she* wanted.

It took all my strength to head back to her and remain remotely charming.

'Oh, you are a sweetie, thank you,' she said before taking a sip. I prayed it would either please her or choke her. Luckily, for her, it did the former. 'Deee-licious!' she drawled. She took several large gulps and added, 'That's probably the best Guinness Punch I've had in a long time. It's supposed to put a little lead in your pencil, don't you know? Not that I need that,' she winked at me suggestively. I winced and forced a smile. She continued, 'I don't suppose you do know, being new here and all that, but you'll soon get to know me. Molasses is right, by the way. You are good. Mastering this in such a short time.' She took another sip and licked her lips with intent.

Had my all-seeing boss and this floozy been talking about me already?

Just then, Molasses returned carrying a weighty box of veg with great ease. 'Ah, Andy! Just the strapping man I need,' she said. 'Could you be so kind and help me get the rest of the shit out of the car?' Then she turned to my *celebrity* customer and added, 'Sally, get off your lazy glutes and do some work for a change. I bet that dishwasher hasn't been emptied since I left, you lazy good-for-nothing girl,' and then disappeared into the kitchen.

Sally grasped a little compact from the bottom of her bag and chimed, 'Found it! A girl should never leave home without one.' She then swept the scattering of inappropriate items back in her bag, downed the remnants of her drink in one, stood blot up-right, wiped her hand on her skirt and then flopped it in front of my face as if waiting on a kiss on the knuckles. 'I'm Sally Knowles, your dazzling new friend and fabulous colleague.'

I was a little annoyed, to say the least. Who did she think she was to test the quality of my service? I left her hand hanging in the air. She dropped it and swung her bag on her shoulder.

'Sorry,' she said. 'I was sizing you up, darling. Very naughty of me. Just checking out the competition. Don't worry, you're good. With a bit of tweaking, you could be almost as great as me. Nice ass too; I wouldn't mind tweaking that too.'

I didn't know what to say, so I stumbled over, 'My ass and my service are not to be tweaked with.'

Sally pouted and said, 'Suit yourself, but I'm here if you need me,' adding in a husky drawl, 'for anything, darling'. She minced around the bar and purposefully tied on an apron.

So this is Sally Knowles. Celebrity? Celebrity my arse! She's just a waitress living on tips. This does not bode well for a happy working relationship. And how can I rely on a woman who's so disorganised she carries a vibrator and a monkey wrench in the same bag?

Thursday 4th March

Sally has no idea how to talk to customers, and I've no idea why Molasses lets her away with it. A woman arrived for lunch and complained that there was only one high chair, which was already occupied.

'I have a toddler here that refuses to sit still and tends to wander,' argued the haggard lady. 'I also have a telephone conference in ten minutes, and I can't be feeding her, myself *and* speaking to my advertising agent at the same time while holding her on my knee.'

Sally shrugged and said, 'Your fault for not keeping an eye on your cycle, love. Not mine.'

'How dare you: I had six bouts of IVF for this child!' spat the stressed customer as she swung her papoose towards the exit.

Sally called after her, 'Next time save your cash, darling, and buy a Porsche Panamera instead; they're less noisy and easier to park.' When the woman left, Sally brushed past the occupied high chair and said to me, without a hint of shame, 'I just cannot abide kids. They suck the life-force out of everyone in the room and drain your breasts until they're drooping like two used party balloons on the 3rd of January.' She glanced down at the family with the high chair and drew them a look that could curdle water.

I mouthed a 'Sorry' to the fathers of the little kid and added, 'PMT,' as a way of explanation.

Sally laughed as she walked away, 'Yes. Pretty Much Thankful I'm single and on my own.'

I despair. She's beginning to rip my knitting. All this and I have toothache. I need to register with an NHS dentist ASAP and step up my oral hygiene.

Friday 5th March

Bit of a shock when I got up and used the loo this morning. After a moment or two of effortless heaving, I glanced down, like you do, to have a brief inspection, and found a long tape-worm-like object bobbing around in the water. I felt the blood drain from me as I reached for my mobile and called NHS24. I'd a hard job navigating the automated selection with one hand desperately jabbing touch-tone numbers while using the other to scrutinise the nasty parasite by poking it with the loo brush.

Could this be why I've been so run down of late? Had this little pest been sucking the nutrients out of my body?

Bypassing the usual flu and diarrhoea options, I finally reached a call handler who took my details and, after what seemed like forever, I was eventually connected to an actual nurse. Ten minutes had dragged by, and I was convinced the head of the beast was still in me and inching its way through my intestinal tract, feasting on me slowly from the inside-out. I became quite weak and began to feel the warmth of the tiles as my face pressed on the floor with the phone still attached to my ear. The nurse asked me a multitude of questions, and I willingly gave my medical history, conjuring up more colourful symptoms by the second and relaying the minutiae of my daily bowel habits for the past week down the line.

I felt myself getting sicklier, sweatier and more nauseated as the details of my now life-threatening illness (my thoughts, not hers) unfolded. I clung on to the sink and pulled my face up towards the taps. If this thing was trying to kill me, I wasn't going down without a fight. Water would help. I turned on the cold and lapped at my palm like a racoon. Then I caught sight of a small blue carton I'd bought the day before. No, not a parasite, after all, just a combination of tired eyes, forgetfulness and mild hypochondriac hysteria.

'Oh, I'm so sorry for wasting your time.' I confessed to the nurse, 'It's just some dental tape I'd forgotten to flush away and accidentally pooped on.'

This is where her professionalism ended. Shrieks of laughter were only broken momentarily – and even that was a struggle for her – as she relayed my idiocy to her colleagues. I hung up the phone and flushed the toilet. I hope I don't become seriously ill any time soon and have to call them back. I'll have to put on a different accent and pretend to be a tourist.

******

Later this evening, in need of reassurance that my call was in some way justified, I replayed the 'tale of the tail' to Ryan and Tony. Ryan was very amused, but Tony winced and pushed his Cantonese noodle soup aside.

'You plonker. I can tell you the real reasons why you're run down,' advised Tony. 'It's because you're rapidly approaching forty, your metabolism is no longer a Ferrari and is now a Nissan Micra, and you do as much exercise as a paraplegic in a coma, our little paunchy poof.'

Pot calling the kettle black, methinks! He could do with losing several pounds, the cheeky little shit. His low-cut jeans are constantly locked way below his navel due to rolls of fat that I imagine harbour lost property such as TV remotes and soggy cornflakes. He can no longer get off the sofa without breaking a sweat. He's got this habit of rocking back and forth on the edge to gain some momentum. A wet seal clambering onto weather-beaten rocks in choppy seas has less difficulty.

Toothache lessened today: brushing teeth and flossing three times a day, followed by a good swirl of industrial-strength mouthwash seems to have done the trick.

Saturday 6th March

This tooth is killing me! Yesterday it lulled me into a false sense of security and gave me a mild molar mollification; today it's hell-bent on torturing me. It is a tooth Stasi! Sally offered me some of her painkillers during our shift, but I told her I've enough to get by until I get an emergency appointment.

'Suit yourself, but I have a good supplier,' she breathed and winked as she turned on her heels.

I think painkillers are painkillers, whether you get a fancy brand name or Tesco's own, the strength is still the same. I've no idea why she thinks hers are better.

11 p.m. A text from my 4x4 Guy asking if I'm free for a blowjob. I reluctantly declined, saying, 'I've got toothache at the moment. I'm finding it difficult to eat soup.'

His reply was speedy:

'U could fuck me instead.'

Gift horse and sore mouth. The throbbing became a different kind altogether within seconds. He's booked for Monday evening after my shift. The boys are out for the night. I'm such a whore! I'm in pain but have needs, damn it! Besides, I seem to remember reading an article that said sexual intercourse releases happy endorphins, therefore offering some form of anaesthetic relief.

Sunday 7th March

I asked Tony if it would be okay to pop some posters up on the walls of my room as it's very white and looks slightly like the luxurious lair of some mad scientist intent on taking over the world. He was probably not the best person to ask as he's always been very clinical himself.

'Posters? With Blu Tack? No way! It'll mark the walls. What are you, fourteen?' came his curt reply.

I proposed having them framed and mounted properly, which got an equally negative reaction. Today was not the best day to ask, I suppose; Tony's been hungover from a heavy night at MINGING (a pretty rough monthly club night). Drugs must've been involved if he says he was out till 4 a.m. 'enjoying' himself. No one our age can be out beyond 3 a.m. without some form of performance-enhancing drugs. And for Tony to actually 'enjoy' himself, he usually needs to take something.

Much later, I caught him pilfering from the pack of pills I've tucked in the cabinet of my ensuite. He left the room sheepishly with four of my ibuprofen in his hand, offering nothing close to an apology. He just said, 'What? I can't find Ryan's usual supply, and I think I have a migraine coming on. I'm sorry, but I need these more than you. Now, I need to lie down in a silent, darkened room. Keep the noise down, will you?'

I thought, *You perpetually have a migraine, judging by your resting bitch face. Thanks for pointing out to me that this time it's actually symptomatic.*

Monday 8th March

Total dose of painkillers swallowed yesterday: 4g of paracetamol; 1,200mg of ibuprofen. Pain moderate, but I need more this morning to get through my shift. I'll be a junkie by Friday at this rate.

Tuesday 9th March

3 p.m. I've lost a day of my life that I'll never get back. It started poorly yesterday when I arrived at the café with a pulsing, aching jaw. I'd found that my little pharmacy of analgesia had been gorged on by the 'pill daemon'. I headed to my shift on 400mg of ibuprofen only, which did nothing.

By 5 p.m., the dinner rush was about to start, and I was about to end it all. My lower mandible felt like it would explode at any second. I wanted to be fit for my 4x4 Guy, so I quickly asked Sally if she had anything remotely therapeutic. After popping two of her pills, my pain subsided instantly.

The walk up Broughton Street was the most holographic I've ever experienced. Technicolour to the extreme. It was as if I'd just landed in Oz, with dancing and singing munchkins all around me and a rainbow guiding me home. However, I did feel the most confident and aroused I've ever been my entire life, so I decided to hurry my evening along but stripping naked as I entered the main stair. I slightly remember passing someone on my way up.

By the time my 4x4 Guy arrived, my feet were mushing ankle-deep into the hall carpet as I thrust him towards the bedroom. The sex, from what I can remember, was messy and very verbal. I remember saying the most disgusting things to him and riding him practically to the speed of the Benny Hill theme. In fact, in my head, it was playing at full blast. My willy chased his prostate around every inch of his colon. No nook or cranny was left un-probed. I remember laughing like a madman on twenty cans of Red Bull when he asked, 'Wow, what's happened to the shy boy I found at the side of the road months ago?'

When it came to the point of ejaculation, I passed out.

I woke this morning on a trolley in the Admissions Unit of the Edinburgh Royal Infirmary in nothing more than my Aussie Bums, an IV line and an NHS blanket. A nurse, who was tending to an elderly lady with some facial injuries in the next bed, saw me stirring and quickly checked my observations.

He said, 'Careful, you have fluids plumbed in. What were you on?'

I told him, 'Nothing intentional, but I have my suspicions I've been spiked by an irresponsible pole dancing waitress.' I laid my head gingerly on the crisp pillow and felt the toothache bite once more. A temporary reprieve only. 'How did I get here?'

'Your friend, a tall man with grey hair, he brought you in and stayed with you for a few hours. He left late last night as he had to get back to his wife.'

Wife? Was I still hallucinating? I hoped so. I'm no better than Thomas if this is the case. Maybe the nurse misheard him. Perhaps he said, 'I have to get back to Fife.' Yes, that's probably more likely as I don't know where he's from.

When I got back to my digs, Tony asked me who the man was that carried me drunkenly down the stairs yesterday evening as they arrived home. Apparently, I was singing *You Are Sixteen Going On Seventeen* at the top of my voice.

I was too frazzled to create an excuse. 'A fuck-buddy, Tony. Who else?'

'But he had a wedding band on. Isn't that a bit immoral for someone who finished with his ex because he cheated?'

Bloody typical. 'Thanks for stating the obvious, Inspector Clouseau,' I mumbled while cupping my jaw with one hand and clutching my forehead with the other. I swung my bedroom door shut in his face.

9.35 p.m. A text from my possibly married knight in shining armour: 'R u ok??? U were very ill last night!!!'

A little ashamed, I asked if I could explain my erratic behaviour, but really I want to get to the bottom of this wife/Fife nonsense.

He said, as a married man that has to sneak around while having an affair would, 'I'm pretty tied up at the moment, but I'll see what I can do.'

Wednesday 10th March

It's two weeks before I can get an appointment at the Dental Hospital. This is ridiculous. The nation is heading towards a collective cavity at this rate. No wonder there are so many toothless people on the Jeremy Kyle Show. The receptionist, who incidentally had a bit of something green stuck blatantly on an incisor, had the cheek to berate me for not having a local dentist.

'Not a single one in my area is willing to take on a new NHS patient,' I argued.

She wasn't interested in the fact that I've recently been cheated on by a dirty dogger and, as a result, have been forced into some kind of modern-day hobo lifestyle with very little autonomy.

'Yes, yes,' she cut in, interrupting my rant. 'Your appointment is at ten-fifteen on Wednesday the twenty-fourth of March. And don't talk to me about autonomy, I have to take the Number 25 bus to work every morning, which is either late or early, but never on time, removing any hope of autonomy from my day right from the get-go. Have a good day, Mr Agnus.'

'It's *Angus*,' I corrected her as I left in a quiet but steaming rage. It's only five letters, how hard can it be to get it right?

****

I cornered Sally in the cellar of Café Jamaica and made it clear that I knew she'd given me anything but prescription meds on Monday afternoon, ruining a perfectly good shag and causing a blackout for at least fourteen hours. If I didn't know her better, I'd say she was genuinely concerned. She stopped shifting stock and said, 'Oh, dear! I'm so, so sorry. I must've got my little pill boxes mixed up. Tell me, who exactly were you planning on having a little frivolous fun with? I wonder if it's an acquaintance of mine? Is it a customer here?'

'That shall remain a mystery to you, Sally Knowles, because I get the feeling we'll never be close enough to bear our sexual souls to one another,' was my riposte.

'Suit yourself,' she said, which is her usual blasé response to rejection and oh-so bloody irritating.

Tooth Update: Continues to pulsate and keep me awake. Ryan offered some prescription-only Co-codamol, but I shied away for fear of a relapse and possible addiction. I'm not exactly sure how it starts, but I imagine shared prescription drugs and well-meaning friends are in the mix.

Thursday 11th March

I've been caught with my pants down, or rather, off. I thought as Ryan and Tony were at work all day, I'd grab a sneaky dip in their lovely jacuzzi bath before work. In my defence, I needed to chill for a while, this molar kept waking me overnight, and a nice therapeutic soak was just the ticket.

All was grand, the bubbles were tickling my toes, the room was candlelit and soft music was playing through their invisible sound system. The water was beginning to cool when disaster struck. I'd just surfaced from a deep, soothing plunge when my hips inadvertently suctioned to the glossy corner of the tub. After several minutes frenetic tugging in various directions – it felt as if my kidneys were about to be vacuumed out of my skin – I had to admit defeat. I was firmly stuck. I wasn't even going to reach my towel, never mind Café Jamaica. My mobile was out of range, but irritatingly, within view on top of the toilet. Nothing to do but hope and pray that, as the water chilled, my skin would become prune-like, and I'd somehow manage an amoeba-like slide up and out over the edge.

One hour later, with the music stopped and the water cold, I was more shrivelled than Mother Teresa and still sealed to the boys' tub as firmly as a Boeing 747's doors in flight. Enter Tony, unexpectedly home for lunch. After a quiet moment of panic and gentle but painful thrusting to gain some traction, I weighed up my options:

A. Lie in wait, settle in for the day, be late for work, lose my job and pray Tony has the bladder of a twenty-year-old woman who can manage long journeys on a convenience free bus around the Isle of Arran. Then find something that will act as lubrication and free myself before both of my landlords get back.
B. Hope he goes away and lay in wait for Ryan to come home, who will be very compassionate and free me instantly. Then I'll bribe him to keep his mouth shut with a slap-up meal and makeover of his choosing.
C. Accept my fate and call for help from Tony, from the bathroom that I was distinctly told never to use under any circumstances.

(C. would happen over my cold, dead, prune-like body only.)

My indecision lasted a good ten minutes. What's another ten when you've already been bound to a bathtub for over an hour? I heard him pacing around. Searching in their wardrobe, clunking a pair of shoes off, moaning over the strain of his belly (I assume, to bend over and tie a new pair), and then the reassuring sound of fabric sliding over fabric as he pulled on a coat just outside the bathroom door. I watched his shadow move about in the gap between the bottom of the door and the black glossy tiles and prayed that he'd be leaving without needing a pee.

The handle of the bathroom door creaked as he rested his hand on it, ready to enter any second now. I winced and closed my eyes. Why hadn't I locked it? If I couldn't see him, he couldn't see me, right?

Then his phone rang. 'I'm on my way,' I heard him say. 'You got my shit? Good. Okay, I'll come meet you.' Then more annoyed, 'I got held up, okay? I'm coming.' The door handle eased, and I breathed a sigh of relief. Light shone brightly in the gap at the bottom of the door and, with the jangle of keys, I assured myself that he'd be on his way down the hall and, thankfully, soon be out of that door.

Just then, my mobile rang. Loud. For ages. It seemed never to stop. I never thought that the Grange Hill theme was actually *that* long. Where was my bloody answerphone service? I threw a rubber duck in the direction of the funky seventies tune, only to miss and hit a cup containing half-used tubes of toothpaste. And then I watched as the glass toppled off the shelf and fell towards their precious flooring, shattering into a million pieces in what seemed like cinematic Dolby Surround Sound. Then I heard purposefully placed footsteps, which got louder and closer with every beat of my exasperated heart.

******

After the door was kicked open, and Tony had seen me almost totally naked (save for a rubber duck carefully shielding my modestly), Ryan was called. Then I'd the pleasure of two fussing queens bickering about the best method to crank me free. It was agreed that smothering my back in olive oil would do the job, or so we thought until Ryan exclaimed, 'I told you to get *olive oil*, Tony. That's fish oil!'

Tony apologised and said, 'But we're out of olive oil, Pookie. Besides, this is karma: we did explicitly say our bathroom was out of bounds to the lodger.'

If he reminds me I'm nothing more than a lodger one more time, I'll slap his teeth straight, I thought.

Moments later, after copious volumes of fish oil had been applied, I was freed by an unfeeling Tony levering the pointed end of a Royal Ascot umbrella between my delicate fishy flesh and the porcelain, yanking with such glee I'm convinced now that he is one of life's many sadists.

As I hurriedly left their precious bathroom, clutching a towel to my cold, frightened manhood, I heard him bitch to Ryan, 'Seems it's not just a paunch, but back blubber too.'

I'd no time to shower as I was way late for my shift, and I'd four missed calls from Molasses (the first of which had alerted Tony to my predicament; the last had fire in her throat). As the heat of the Café soaked through my skin, the whiff of fish oil intensified and I was asked by my boss, 'Could you please leave as soon as possible? Our customers are beginning to think the fish tank is rank.'

On the road home, I was dive-bombed by seagulls eager for a peck at my salmon scented skin, so much so, it felt as if I was in a Hitchcock sequel. Damn you corner bath! Damn you contentment blubber that has decided to squat in what used to be a very fit and tidy body! Tomorrow I'll join a gym, not for myself, but to wipe that smug grin off Tony's chops.

- Toothache: head pounding like I've been shouted at by Brian Blessed.
- Blubberache: like I've been rugby tackled by Brian Blessed.
- One bottle of olive oil found tucked suspiciously to the back of the cleaning cupboard, and therefore, one arch-nemesis of a landlord revealed.

Friday 12th March

Tooth continued to pulsate all day. With no chance of an appointment at a local dentist sooner than my hospital arrangement, I gave up on legal methods of attaining relief and have started taking Ryan's well-meaning box of prescription-only Co-codamol. He's now my landlord and drug pusher.

Saturday 13th March

My first Saturday off since I started at Café Jamaica. I decided to distract myself from my affliction and wandered the streets of this glorious city. There have been many changes since I left. Some buildings have been entirely deleted from the skyline, like the C&A building on Princes Street (which Ryan used to say stood for 'Crap &

Awful'). I can't even recall where it stood and which of the shiny new buildings replace it. Mind you, I'm highly dosed up on analgesia and therefore and bit foggy. Every corner throws a misplaced memory my way: many are good; few are bad. Princes Street is a building site for now. I say, for now, but the tram-works have been trundling along since 2008 and still have a way to go. At least the tracks are being laid at last.

I grabbed myself a takeaway cup of tepid soup for lunch and rested my tired ass on a park bench in Princes Street Gardens, soaking up the magnificent view of the castle before me. She really is an impressive sight to behold, sat proudly on her volcanic throne as the clouds drift past her crown. Weather-beaten, but all the prettier for it. *I love this city.*

Moments later, I noticed a familiar figure on the bench next to me ferociously munching on a pie and staring pensively into space. It was Ryan, so I seized the opportunity and plonked my arse next to him with a smile. It took him a few seconds to notice me, but he soon forced a smiled in return, spilling pie crust from his mouth. And so, for the first time since I moved here, we had a proper chinwag.

He's stressed about their civil partnership. 'It's overwhelming me, Andy,' he said pensively. 'I desperately want to marry Tony, but the road towards that day is filled with sniping and disputes as we collide over all the planning.'

'Well, I've never heard so much as a tut between the two of you. You always look like you're having a ball together.'

'We have to keep up a happy facade; being the Posh and Becks of the gay scene puts pressure on us to be the perfect couple at all times.'

I nodded in agreement, but in my head, I was saying, *Posh and Becks of the gay scene? Really?*

'We haven't even got a venue booked, and it's this year!' he said stuffing the last of the crust in his mouth. 'We can't agree on a reception venue, the cake, the waistcoats, the lapels, and don't get me started on the theme. He wants sci-fi and musicals for goodness sake! Dancing girls, top hats and phasers! And you know how much I hate Star Wars.'

About as much as Tony hates Doctor Who, I thought — he's

always slagged the classic show for its limited budget: another reason to dislike the man.

Ryan continued, 'Half of Edinburgh's exclusive gays will be our guests, and that means they all take part, which means at least fifty bodies that need to be choreographed. I want class, couture and close friends. Clean and simple, you see? I don't want a wedding dress that matches Princess Leia's frock from A New Hope. Every night all we do is talk about this bloody spectacle. It's less about us now and more about the show.'

I could see he had a large piece of pie filling stuck to his chin. I wiped it off gently with my napkin. Ryan's eyes filled with tears. I must admit, I selfishly seized my chance and suggested a night out to forget all about it. But if I'm sincere, I just miss him. I miss my friend, not the Ryan I know now, but the Ryan I knew way back when there were no civil partnerships and no other halves. Us, on the town, having a right laugh. He agreed to an exclusive night out. I could've leapt off that bench and hopped all the way up to the castle with joy, but instead, I heard these words fall from my mouth, 'If you need a hand with anything, I'm here.'

Shut your neck, Andy!

As soon as I uttered the words, I regretted them, but there they were. How could I possibly take them back? Ryan jumped at the chance with an enormous yelp and vigorous hug, 'You can help with the wedding planning!'

Shit! What does an unmarried failed Domestic God know about wedding planning? I only hope, somewhere along the line, he'll realise that this civil partnership is a huge mistake and I'll be there to help him move swiftly on. Maybe I can throw a few spanners in the works. No! Naughty! Perhaps just some banana skins. Soft, unobtrusive banana skins that wouldn't really hurt anyone. Just enough to show the real Tony in the pure light of day: a selfish arsehole.

'I'm sorry about the bath incident,' I said as I nudged him playfully with my shoulder.

'It's okay,' he smiled. 'I'm sorry about the fish oil. I'm not entirely sure Tony didn't do that on purpose. He's so highly strung over you just now.'

'Hmmm, I hadn't noticed,' I joked. But it really is no joke. I need to work on making Tony a friend of some sort. I believe it was The Godfather II that had the quote, 'Keep your friends close, and your enemies closer.' By hook or by crook, I'll find his dirt. I'd better suck it up and find something more endearing about the guy than his ability to leave a room.

Sunday 14th March

No reply from 4x4 Guy so far. I think he owes me some kind of explanation. I sent another text this morning asking when he'll be free to talk, no sex necessary. I checked my mobile all shift and nothing. I could feel Molasses scanning me every time I delved into my jacket pocket. I'm pretty sure she can read minds as she towered over my shoulder at one point and whispered, 'Whoever it is, honey, he ain't worth it.'

She could be right.

Monday 15th March

On the news today they said the collapse of investment bank Lehman Brothers has come to be viewed as the beginning of the financial crisis. I watched this revelation in our lounge, which is once again a tip. There are half-empty takeaway cartons strewn across the coffee table and piles of wedding, catering and fashion magazines dotted around the room. There's no hint of a recession here amid the drained champagne bottles and assorted designer carrier bags strewn on the floor.

On the sofa, I found: *In The Pink Magazine, Pink Weddings Monthly* and a *Pinky & Perky Annual* from 1969. I think the latter is a result of an online shopping typo.

Tuesday 16th March

Quiet day at Café Jamaica, the sun seems to be keeping people out of cafés and in parks. For a long period, we only had one customer, so I had time to chill at the bar with Molasses and flick through the paper. Usually, I'd be pulling my hair out due to boredom, this time, however, I was delighted to loiter so's to catch the eye of a hot guy, who was munching on a portion of Escovitch Lobster.

Who knew eating dead crustaceans could be so damn sexy?

I took a good ten minutes sizing him up over the top of the

horoscopes: mid-thirties, slender, with short, curly blond hair, piercing blue eyes and a tight wee body that I'm pretty sure, judging from what I could see through his clinging tee, is athletic.

Blond's not my usual type, but maybe it's time for a change, I thought.

When the guy came to pay, I practically kicked Molasses to the kerb, as I've found exchanging change with guys is a good indicator if they are attracted to you or not. I let my fingers linger with more contact than usual on his palm and, to my surprise, he did the same, almost gripping mine in return. Just at that moment, my toothache returned. I took a sharp intake of breath and grimaced.

'Sorry, I have terrible toothache just now,' I winced. 'I'm not scowling at you.'

'You getting it sorted?' he asked, his full lips bouncing steadily and seductively as life seemed to slip into slow motion.

'I've just moved to the city and don't have a dentist.'

'I could look at it for you. I'm a dentist.'

I was stunned. Beautiful, helpful and a professional? A bonus! I smiled and tried to find the right words, coming up with, 'You do oral? Hygiene! Oral hygiene, I mean.'

He smiled, 'Yes, and yes.'

Beautiful, helpful, professional and playful. Even better! I tried to ignore the innuendo rising in the room. 'Good, good,' I said, attempting to get the right balance of casual and interested, nervously gouging at my notepad all the while with my pen.

'Do you want me to look at it this afternoon? I have a cancellation.'

Music to my molars. 'Aye, that'd be great,' I said, both scared and aroused.

He gave me his card and smiled an ultra-bright grin:

G Bennett & Son Dental Practice
24 Belleview Terrace
Edinburgh.
New NHS Patients Welcome.

I sloped off around four, much to Molasses' relief. 'Anything to stop your wincing and mincing,' she said. By 5 p.m. I had a shiny new filling and sparkly, deep-cleaned teeth. Nothing major wrong with me after all, just a small crack in a filling. Is my pain level so low? I was confident I'd need a tooth pulled. But there's a bonus to all of this nonsense. As he was polishing, amid much flirtation, G Bennett (or Son) asked me what I was doing for the rest of the evening. I attempted to throw a significant hint by name-dropping a selection of gay bars my *friend* and I will be frequenting later, but between mentioning *CC's* and *Vibe* I choked on a mixture of water, toothpaste and my own saliva.

Raising his lovely thin eyebrows that frame those fantastic clear pools of blue, he said, 'Ah, I'll maybe see you out and about then.'

I can't be sure if he heard my, 'Hope so,' as the dental nurse dived in for such an intense suction, she nearly shredded my uvula to mince.

The damn mask was still covered his lovely lips as I said goodbye, but I was 90% certain he was giving me a cheeky grin as I went. I left cured, a little numb on the left side of my face and overstimulated in the nether regions. Here's hoping I stop drooling before I order my first pint.

9 p.m. I've been through the toughest two-hour prep for a night out I've ever experienced. It usually takes me ten minutes. Ryan decided that I needed a complete makeover if I was aiming to impress. I'm now wearing his skinny, tapered jeans that make my balls feel as if they're wedged in two garlic crushers every time I sit down. My size eleven feet look enormous in these ridiculous white plimsolls. If that wasn't bad enough, I'm decked in a red chequered shirt that's tucked into my ample waistline, which makes my skinny legs look as thin as a pink flamingo's. And it's all crowned off with a straw trilby that I haven't seen worn since 1985.

I suggested tossing the hat and just slapping some gel in my hair, but Ryan replied with, 'Puuu-leeze! There aren't enough hours in the day to rescue your hair from the neglect you've insulted it with over the years. What have you been using? Swarfega? Besides, I still have to do mine, which will take an hour tops. We have to get out there at the exact moment for optimal cruising – too early, and it's dead; too late, and there's nothing but dregs. It's Tuesday night; your options are limited to shift workers and students. And do *not* remove that hat from your pretty little head even once tonight or I'll be disowning you.'

I assured him I was quite capable of styling my own rug when he cackled, 'Good Lord! How can anyone apply so much product in such a short space of time?'

'What do you mean?' I asked a little hurt.

'Uh, cupcake?' he scoffed. 'There's product and then their's *by-product!* I dread to think how stained your pillows are already.'

So here I am, a lanky Lord of the Dance. A potbellied Prince. Perhaps I'm out of the loop as far as what's en vogue. Maybe this really is cutting edge. Perhaps G Bennett (or Son) will love it.

Ryan offered one more piece of advice, 'Don't make the dentist your only goal. He's just option one.'

'He's my only option,' I said, meaning I fancied him like mad.

'You shouldn't run yourself down like that, Andy, you have loads of options. There are plenty of middle-aged men looking for the companionship of a middle-aged queen who's been washed up on the shores of singledom through no fault of his own.'

Sometimes, just sometimes, he's so unaware of how offensive he can be when he channels all his energy into being caring. He asked for the dentist's name. I had to confess I've no idea if he's G Bennett the son, G Bennett the father, or even what the G stands for.

'You best pray he's not *Gordon Bennett*!' he snorted. 'I mean, I can't be introducing you to my friends as Andy and his *exclamation*, can I?'

'Of course, he isn't, that would be ridiculous,' I replied. 'Who would be so stupid as to name their child after a vociferation?'

'Oh! Hang on! Selfie time! Pull your chins in, thank you very much, Andy.'

Wednesday 17th March

11.10 a.m. Gordon Bennett flinched when he first saw me at the bar. 'Andy, is that you?' he asked, in disbelief. 'Bloody hell! What happened to you?' I believe he would have yelped, 'Gordon Bennett!' but that would've been ironic, I loath to report. I spun a yarn about spilling a large glass of red wine over my original outfit and having to, unfortunately, borrow this ensemble from a colourblind fashion victim of the New Romantic period. He didn't sound convinced when he asked, 'And the hat?'

'My hair was singed badly by one of the many scented candles my flatmate irresponsibly leaves burning around the flat,' was my swift reply, as I shot daggers at Ryan who was oblivious and having a whale of a time at the bar with his moocher friends. 'Drink?' I yelped, in an attempt to move away from fashion completely. Ryan winked at me as if to say, 'All going well so far.' I could've killed him. I was the fashion equivalent of Pricilla Presley's Botox job.

Despite this, the night got better. Let's face it, the only way was up. Ryan let his hair down and even got a bit of interest from a few students. 'I'm at that age when younger men find me fascinating and alluring,' he wailed over the music to Gordon. 'The experience of an older man is very enticing to the younger generation. This is no revelation to our Andy, mind you, as he's considerably older than me, Gordon Bennett!' I detested that he took every opportunity to say Gordon's full name with an exclamation.

'Sixteen months is not that much older,' I interjected.

Ryan flicked his hair sloppily, as he was well on his way to drunkenness, and ignored my protest. 'Of course, all this allure and youth is wasted on me as I just can't see past my gorgeous Tony,' he slurred.

I wanted to grab him and say, 'You fool! Tony is a tactless, egocentric streak of piss!' while shaking him feverishly by the shoulders and slapping him up and down the bar, but I could hardly shake a leg in my circulation constricting jeans. Instead, I opted for the slightly sarcastic and yet safe, 'Aww!'

Despite my awful attire, Gordon was keen to get close to me as the last track was played and T-shirts were pulled back over sweaty, youthful torsos. I was glad they turned up the lights as Gordon's teeth went neon every time the bar's UV strips caught his grin. It was like talking to a Cheshire cat. Still, only one minus so far, so not bad.

Gordon leant in and gave me a kiss with such passion I was delighted the anaesthetic had worn off. 'Sorry,' he said, pulling out of the kiss but still holding me close. 'Just checking my work.'

'All okay?' I asked, blatantly flirting.

'I'd better check again. You know, to be thorough. I need to get as far back as seventeen and thirty-two.'

'Is that far back?'

'Molars, baby, we're talking molars.'

What's a boy to do? 'Ah, okay.' I opened wide, and he slipped his tongue deep into my hungry mouth. He was that far in me, I could feel his breath in my lungs. My arousal was so apparent through the stretchy jeans I became embarrassed when we parted again, covering it up with my beer. Gordon, however, seemed amused and impressed at the now prominent silhouette. He pushed the bottle out of the way and squeezed the denim hard, causing me to pulsate in agreement.

Ryan slid his hands between us and pushed us apart. 'Ugh! Enough, girls. Get a room. Honestly, keep this up and I'll ...' He didn't manage to finish his words, but we soon got the gist when he took a mighty gasp and proceeded to projectile vomit at our feet.

'I think we'll call it a night there,' said Gordon, retching as he inched back in disgust from the diffusing pool of WKD, bile and M&S Chicken Tikka Marsala that had been served up between us.

'I think you're right,' I sighed as we watched Ryan crack and collapse like a condemned high-rise block that had just had a ton of explosives detonate at its feet.

It wasn't easy supporting Ryan on the road home. Even the taxi warden wouldn't allow us the short trip up the street, which says something as I watched her guide a raucous hen party into a hackney moments before.

'You know, I'm glad you came back. I really do love you, Andy,' sprayed Ryan as he slid down the front door. I fumbled for the key as quickly as I could. It doesn't come naturally to requite love when your mate's hair is matted with a mixture of Paul Smith, alcohol, bile and curry.

Tony wasn't best pleased to be woken by a drunk husband-to-be and his wedding planner, but I don't give a damn. It was well worth torturing him for a night after the bath incident. What's he going to do? Throw me out? I don't think so. Any-rate, I have a date with Gordon on Friday night. A lovely, single, sane, handsome, professional homosexual. Already I can see a lifetime of comfort and gleaming molars.

Result!

7.33 p.m. A text from 4x4 Guy: 'R U free tomorrow at 12?'

His timing is rubbish! And short notice. But I agreed. We're meeting at Joseph Pearson's on Elm Row. I'll be wearing my usual casual attire. I will most certainly *not* be making an effort for a married man. He's lucky I don't turn up in my TARDIS pyjamas.

Thursday 18th March

There he was, reading the Financial Times and looking every bit as dashing as when I first laid eyes on him. I spotted him instantly. His full head of grey hair illuminated in the beams of sunlight cast through the large windows. I tried desperately to ignore his broad, lickable, muscular frame ... *No, Andy! Focus!*

He stood up to welcome me. I reached out instinctively for a hug, but he caught my hand and shook it. *Ah, we're playing the 'just good mates' game, are we?* I thought as it dawned on me how public and exposed he must've felt meeting me in a busy bar. My instinctive act of affection surprised me, and his cold, almost business-like approach, caused me to berate myself for being so willing to forgive him for leading me along. *Okay, no PDA, I'll give you that.* I sat down.

When he brought my pint he asked, rather judgementally, I thought, for a man with such loose morals, 'So, have you recovered from your little trip on the Magic Roundabout?'

'Ah, sorry about that. I *never* do drugs.' Was I really apologising now too? How dare he wave the upper hand. But still, I continued, 'Unfortunately, that day, I'd been spiked by an irresponsible cow who doesn't know her aspirin from her acid.' I added, 'I don't usually do married men either, but it seems I've had a heavy dose of that too. And covertly it seems.' Yes! Back of the net! Upper hand achieved and within grasp of the trophy.

'Ah, yes,' he said bashfully as he slurped the froth off his pint. 'You have done now,' he joked. My face fell, which prompted a hasty, 'Sorry!'

'If I'd known you were married, I would never have started this. Whatever this is.'

'Come on, Andy,' he laughed nervously through his words, 'what kinda man did you think you'd pick at a cruising area?'

I was more than shocked. What could he mean, 'cruising area'?

He continued, 'Come on, you knew that place was a cruising area, right?'

'No, I did not!' I hastened. 'If I'd known that, I would never have stopped there.'

'Ah, well,' he whispered, 'I couldn't believe my luck bumping into someone like you there. You really are a stunning lad: manly, and you certainly know how to treat a guy.'

It was careless and clumsy of him. Now was not the time to give me compliments. Crude compliments, at that. I felt more a slut than ever before. I didn't deserve praise when some innocent woman was caught in the firing line of our fun.

'Okay! Stop!' I heard myself shout as I stood up from the table, disgusted. I was shaking. If this was true, I really was no better than Thomas: hanging around local cruising areas waiting on the next piece of meat, watching others having sex, reducing what should be something special between two people to nothing more than a means to an end. A function. 'If I knew that, I would never have seen you again, Mr ... what is your name anyway? What is the name that you've shared with your wife, the name that she's probably proud to write on her cheque books and that you're so desperate to hide?'

I could see him glance around quickly as some people shuffled past our table. He needn't have worried, the bar was a cacophony of chatter and my words just mingled with the rest to become the same wall of sound. They were totally disinterested in our predicament and moved on quickly, but I could see they unnerved him all the same.

'Andy, I never hid anything from you. You just never asked. You told me you were happy keeping it simple and casual, so you can't judge me on that.'

All of a sudden, I noticed his wedding band. There, plain as day, on the finger his wife had slid it on in the hope of a faithful life together. Had he always worn it? It seemed familiar. How could I've been so blind?

'Andy Angus,' he whispered. 'We met in a cruising area, I'm married, and we have great, no-strings sex where we've an understanding, and no one gets hurt. What's so wrong with that?'

Everything! I thought.

'I never hid it from you. I'm married. I thought everyone knew it was a cruising area. It's notorious down there. Come on, you're not *that* naïve?'

'The sad fact is, I think I am.'

I could feel my eyes tingling on the edge of tears, damn it. I had to get out. It's not as if I saw any potential in this guy. It's not as if he's given me the best sex I've ever had in my life. It's not as if I know him at all. Oh, sweet Lord, I really am *that* naïve. It was then I realised I'd fallen for the perfect man. A perfect stranger. One who could never disappoint because I didn't know him at all. No hopes, no dreams, no disappointment. Safe, until he shows you the truth about yourself: after all these years, you're still a fool.

He could see it too. I could feel the revelation pass between us. 'Oh, Andy, I'm sorry. I didn't expect it to get so complicated for you.'

And there it was, that awful word slid into my mind: unrequited. I had to go. And quickly. I ran from that moment. That needy, unrequited love. I could hear him calling after me, but the sudden gushing of blood that pulsed through my skull became raucous and began to drown him out. It felt thick and heavy, stifling my emotions as I imagined it coursing through my entire body until I turned into a cold, heartless stone.

Friday 19th March

'What you need is a good rebound shag!' butted in Sally as I was relaying my highly personal 4x4 Guy tale to Ryan. Like Miss Molasses Brown, Sally Knowles seems to have extrasensory perception when it comes to other peoples' business, able to hear the slightest syllable over the music echoing through the café.

'Thank you, Sally,' I called as her arse minced away, 'but I don't think diving headlong into another's crotch is the answer to my problems.'

'Suit yourself!' she shrugged as she swiped yet another small pile of tips off a neighbouring table. 'Works for me every time.'

I mouthed the word 'slut' to Ryan and said, 'This is coming from a girl who seems to be on a downward spiral of drink, drugs and sex.'

To my amazement, Ryan muttered, 'Well, we've all been there,' as he crammed his hungry aperture with an ambitious fork of Coconut Red Stripe Chicken.

How can *he* have been *there*? He's been with Tony for years, and I've never known him to be on the rebound.

'She may be right,' he continued. 'The dentist may be just what you need to extract this puss-filled abscess that this 4x4 Guy has left you with.'

I couldn't believe my ears. Did this old romantic really think that a casual night of sex would help me get over it? 'So you're saying I should sleep with him?'

'No, I'm saying you should be open to the possibility.' He raised his fork and prodded my sternum with it. 'You shouldn't let one bad experience get in the way of several greats.'

I reminded him that it'd actually been two disasters so far: Thomas and the 4x4 Guy.

'One, two, ten, whatever. Just do it. Get it out of the way, either with this guy or the next. Wham, bam, thank you, Tam! This city is full of attractive single men who are lovely, although none more so than my Tony.' At this point, Sally flitted by and mimicked self-induced vomiting. As much as she's pissed me off over the past few weeks, I couldn't quash a smirk. I regained my composure as Ryan looked up from his plate. 'Don't let fear starve the soul,' he concluded as he crammed his face with even more chicken.

I received an irritating slap on the back from Sally as she interposed, 'Yes. You go, girl! And if you actually do manage to get your leg over, drop by tomorrow and tell me all the yummy, cummy, frothy details.'

******

Later, once Ryan had headed to his yoga class — 'Tony likes me flexible enough to be taking it from the rear and still give full-on tongue.' Over-share! — Sally and I skirted around the subject of the sickeningly happy couple, the self-proclaimed gay equivalent to Posh and Becks. She guffawed and said, 'Tony? I can't stand the man.'

An alliance perhaps? I wondered as she packed up at the end of her shift.

She cheerfully waved goodbye with a, 'See you later, brotherfucker!' I found myself waving warmly back. Could we actually be political bedfellows in the war against Tony's acerbic tongue? She would be a formidable ally. Her ovaries are far bigger than most men's balls. I'm beginning to warm to her. A week is a long time in the politics of friends.

Saturday 20th March

Is it wrong to go off a guy because of the way he climaxes? Gordon and I chatted into the early hours of the morning at The Street, a bar on Picardy Place, which used to be OT's back when I was a lad. I chose this place as it's well lit and has no UV lights above the bar, therefore, no Cheshire Cat. He seemed a decent chap with nothing I could foresee that'd put me off. When he went to the loo, I did a quick checklist in my head:

- No fuck-buddies sniffing around.
- No crazy ex-boyfriends.
- No fag hags.
- No schizophrenia (that I can see so far).
- No debts.
- Owner of a massive house in Morningside.
- Drives a Porsche (not that I care about cars).
- Family orientated (both parents respected lawyers and a sister with learning difficulties that he adores).
- Friendly, attractive friends that said hello in the passing.
- Good looking.
- Not a fan of Ouzo, which proves he's sane.

All was well. Why wouldn't I go back home with this total ride? And boy, what a home! A four-bedroom sandstone job that stands in well-sculpted gardens with a large summerhouse to the rear. The kissing against the door frame didn't disappoint either. The sex was full of body contact and intense, just the way I like it. As he became close, he climbed on top of me, as he wanted to spurt his load all over my 'fit chest' (his words, not mine). Despite his compliments, my awkwardness ensued. The lights were on, and my belly wobbled far too much as the fit dentist gyrated astride my hips as he got closer and closer to the edge. Then, just when I was about to cum, as he was too, he turned into a wild banshee that caterwauled shrill laughter at every single spurt from his shaft. I don't mean just a snigger. It was full-on-creepy and totally took me by surprise. His eyes rolled around his head like one of those laughing policemen trapped in glass boxes that you see at fairgrounds. This, combined with his almost luminous teeth, spoilt my climax.

'Em, what just happened there?' I asked, catching my breath.

'Eh? Oh,' he laughed a tad calmer now as he leant forward for a kiss, our bodies sloppy and wet, 'sorry. I always laugh when I cum. I can't help myself. You got me so fired up.'

Off he leapt to grab me a towel. I was left thinking, *Laugh, please, but not in that 'Here's Jonny' kinda way.*

I was glad that he was running late for work by the time we woke this morning as that cancelled any chance of a second round of hysteria.

11 p.m. I've just relayed this story to Ryan and, under protest, Tony. Tony was most unhelpful and quipped, 'We have a ball gag you can borrow next time.'

Borrow? I'm sure I can keep it as it's been a while since they've used even the pillow to bite into. I know their sex-life has been put on pause since I arrived; I've heard Tony through their bedroom door muttering, 'No, not now, Boo-Boo. Not while the lodger's here.' The price some people pay for an extra household income, eh? I'd rather live on the breadline than forfeit sex.

Sunday 21st March

A text from Gordon Bennett asking if I was free this afternoon for lunch. I declined as I'm doing the hangover stint (non-stop fried breakfasts) at the café until 4 p.m. The texts then became a bit saucy on his part, but I'm afraid all I can see in my mind's eye is his ridiculous laughter and lightsaber teeth. I quickly changed the subject and text back that I'd an induction at Virgin Active gym booked from 5 p.m. onwards, which is a half-truth as I'm just enquiring tonight about joining.

11 p.m. I've been given a 'special deal' at the gym: three training sessions with a qualified instructor, unlimited access to all classes for a month and thirty hours worth of sun-bed tokens. Forget the Domestic God, at this rate, I'll look like a Greek God before May. Men shall fall at my feet and worship my pecs as women utter, 'What a waste!' and, 'Why can't he be straight?'

The gym looks well plush, with a pool, jacuzzi, free weights, resistance machines, steam room, sauna and plenty of clean showers. I'll be staying away from the free weights area, however, as I felt quite intimidated by all the sweating, muscular guys there, grunting and bursting blood vessels as my skinny legs and nonexistent shoulders skulked by. My first training session's on Friday.

Monday 22nd March

I chatted to Ryan about the dentist as he's still keen to hook-up. Sex is definitely on the cards, judging by the flirtatious text and winking, tongue panting emoticons. I've replied but kept it cool. My problem is, once I put-out, I feel obligated to keep putting-out.

'Seriously though,' asked Ryan as he massaged moisturiser into Tony's ugly feet, 'have you actually thought about gagging him, or at least covering his mouth with your hand at the point of ejaculation?'

'It's not just the laugh, my friend,' I replied. 'It's the weird thing he does with his eyes. It's like watching two lottery balls clanking around Guinevere on a Saturday draw. I'd have to cover his whole face with my hand.'

'Oh, dear. Flip him over and bugger the poor sod,' quipped Ryan. At this point, Tony flinched and told Ryan he was rubbing too hard. Ryan apologised.

'Oh, good Lord! Why are we still wasting time on this nonsense? Don't Tell The Bride is on,' interrupted Tony. 'Just tell him you don't like how he climaxes and move on. I don't put up with any nonsense during sex, do I, Ryan?'

'No, Tony, you don't,' replied Ryan. I could hear an element of dismay in his voice that Tony was oblivious to. They're obviously having problems. I'm driving Ryan around possible wedding venues on Monday. I'll get the truth out of him then.

Tuesday 23rd March

I must need my head read. I've agreed to meet Gordon Bennett for dinner this evening. I could hardly say no, he was eating lunch in the café at the time and had been dropping hints that he was finishing at 3 p.m. and would be free for the rest of the day.

'Your trouble is you are far too nice,' said Sally as the door closed behind him and I pulled an exasperated face. 'You won't get anywhere in this city unless you harden up. If you're not careful, you'll carry on with this dentist, and before you know it, you'll have met the parents and be moving in together. Harden up, kiddo! Life isn't all about finding love. If it were, I would've had zero fun by now.'

Wednesday 24th March

About last night ...

When the sex started, of which I felt I'd no real option to refuse, I was tanked up on several cocktails. I could hear the disembodied voices of Ryan, Tony and Sally fluctuating in my head:

'Have you thought about gagging him?'

'Harden up, kiddo!'

'Dump him!'

'Flip him over!'

I discovered a pulse-point at the side of my head that I've never felt before and started to wonder if my neck was swelling to the size and pressure of a Goodyear truck tyre. Copious amounts of alcohol, a throbbing head and the dread of what was literally to *cum* did not inspire my loins to catch fire. I was juggling with all of this as Gordon juggled with my balls, sat astride me in his favourite position.

I could see it coming, no mistaking it, I could hear it! He sounded like a Vespa revving up a steep hill as he got closer and closer to the edge. I pulled him forward to snog him in the hope this would keep him quiet, but he leant back and insisted on watching me.

It's a shame I'm having to 'enjoy' the view from here, I thought as his engine revved some more and his eyes began to spin, and cross, and spin again. I raised one hand to cover his mouth, but he just chewed and grunted on the flesh of my palm and became more feral, howling in the moonlight. *Both hands, try both hands, you fool.* I eventually cupped one behind his neck and the other firmly over the mouth of this foghorn, which, struggling for breath, caused his eyes to bulge and seem more insane. He became louder and louder, chuckles splitting his sides, saliva pooling in my palm.

'I'm close!' he yelped between barrels of laughter.

Don't I know it! Oh, sweet Jesus! The eyes! They're going into hyper-drive! Cover the eyes! No the mouth! No, the eyes!

I felt my hand clutching his whole face in a vain attempt to cover everything, but nothing was working. And then he began to shoot, and the cacophony of shrieks and laughter escalated, echoing around the room as the disembodied voices of my friends spiralled in my brain.

Until I felt my hand slap something fleshy and stubbly.

Hard and fast.

I've no idea where it came from. Drink and a boy with an unsettling reaction to an orgasm are a terrible combination it seems. I felt instant guilt. I hate violence and cruelty of any sort. I'd never seen a guy stop mid-climax and freeze in shock before this. The look of sheer bliss switched to disbelief and hurt within the flick of my wrist. I apologised, but Gordon wouldn't even look at me. His cheek facing me, becoming more scarlet by the second. 'Please leave,' he uttered like a small boy as he flopped off me and curled up, clutching the sheet over his naked body in fear. 'I think you've been most inappropriate.'

As a red handprint developed on his face like some sadistic polaroid, I picked up my clothes, edged sheepishly out of the bedroom and moved quickly down the broad staircase, getting dressed as I scurried through the huge house I would most definitely not be biding in with him. 'I think we should cancel your follow-up appointment,' he called from the bedroom.

'Aye, I think we should,' I agreed as I clicked the gorgeous ornate front door shut. If there's the slightest chance he'd hold a grudge and take revenge on my already fragile molars, I'd rather not take that risk. Oh, well, Morningside yummy mummies are inconsiderate, posh pains in the arse most of the time, anyway. Who, with any sanity, would actually choose to live amongst them?

Thursday 25th March

It's Mum's and Dad's wedding anniversary today. She called to remind me with a large slice of sarcasm chucked in. I totally forgot and lied that a card was in the post while hurriedly putting my shoes on to run to the shop as soon as we hung up.

To move on quickly, I asked her, 'What's Dad treating you to for your thirty-seventh year together?'

She sighed and said, 'A set of golf clubs.'

'I'd no idea you liked golf?'

'I don't, but he seems to think it'll bring us closer together. I'm part-retired now, have poor circulation and flyaway hair, why on Earth would I want to stand in the drab Scottish weather and whack great clumps of dirt out of the ground?'

'Come on, Mum, you might enjoy it. Do some research and give it a go. A lot of pensioners find it a grand way to keep moving.'

'Andy, I'm sixty-bloody-one, I could be drying up, but I'm not seizing up and pissing my support pants as of yet. He best pray I don't figure out which number iron will do the most damage to him and leave very little evidence.' Our conversation was cut short when she growled, 'Steven, come down from there! Look, I have to go, one of your sister's children is hanging upside-down from the top banister with a piece of Barbie furniture in his mouth.'

Again, she's delusional, she *is* a pensioner. The government says so. She's slowly shuffling her way towards bingo halls and irregular bowel habits.

Friday 26th March

Hot instructor at my gym, you've no idea how much I enjoyed every touch you gave me, every smile you flashed, every squat you performed in front of me with your muscular, hairy thighs, and every softly spoken Irish word you uttered to me. Nash, with your dark hair, tanned skin, big smile and huge biceps, I couldn't really decipher all of your words through that dreamy Irish accent, but it must be the norm for you to have vacant gazes come your way. With a body like yours, how could any red-blooded gay man focus on anything but those tight-fitting, ass-hugging, crotch-cupping shorts?

I prayed: *Please be gay! If not gay, bisexual. If not bisexual, curious! If not curious, drunk and coincidently in my bedroom (by accident) as I arrive home. Naked, naturally, too.*

Saturday 27th March

Nash! Nash! I curse your name! What the hell have you done to me? I can hardly lift my arms to wash my hair, let alone do Part B of my workout with you tomorrow. I gave up shampooing midway through my usual obsessive ritual as my arms ached so much. But I bet yours could do it for me. I could hardly stoop to wait on tables too. Molasses asked me if I'd shit myself and Sally's convinced I've experienced an S&M session that went awry. If only! Nash! Nash! I curse your name, but I love your frame! I'll forgive you as you are a wet dream come true. You're now my motivation and masturbation.

Sunday 28th March

'You're doing grand. Press it hard. Squeeze that butt. Feel it. Feel it! Good man!' No, this isn't sex talk, this is encouragement from Nash as I struggled with legs today. I find going to the gym is like being in a soft porn movie: all grunting hunks and bromance. A hard session in more ways than one. Boy, am I beat! Nash continues to give me a beasting, and I continue to take it willingly. I want to impress him no-end. It's nothing to do with the fact his bottom is a peach, and his nipples poke provocatively through his polo shirt under the pressure from his rock-like pecs. Not at all! Dark hair protrudes from the tempting opening below his Adam's apple, and his calves have contours that I never dreamt were possible. I feel like a teenager around him, of the blond, pigtailed, giggly variety.

It took me 30 minutes of Training Session B to establish he's single, has been in Edinburgh for 18 months and shares a flat on McDonald Road with three other PTs.

'Oh, that's just a short walk from mine,' I said casually.

He didn't bite. Is he straight? Gay? Bi? I need to know. He touches me like a man who's comfortable touching men, but I'm not sure if that's because he's comfortable touching everyone, male and female. It's so confusing. My willy has risen and fallen more often than a stack of weights on a pec deck machine.

The only unfortunate mishap was during my 3rd set of squats, as I was at the lowest point in the dip, I let out a lady-fart from my taut, parted buttocks. I'm no expert on dating, but I think this may influence his decision if he is actually open to the idea. Why such a feeble fart? Why not a manly ripper or a silent whoosh? At least you could've granted me that, God!

I spent the next few hours with my aching legs elevated on the couch and enjoyed peace until the boys arrived back at three o'clock. From then on it was civil partnership all the way, even through yet another takeaway, until I could fake-smile no more and retreated to my room by nine, after taking care of their filthy kitchen yet again.

Ryan has tomorrow so perfectly planned the Third Reich would be proud of his efficiency. We have eight venues to visit, and he has every part of the journey mapped out on Google Maps to the second. Eight! I was planning on giving up half of my precious morning, but it seems we're making a day of it. Joy to the world!

11 p.m. I've tried masturbating over Nash, but my calves are too sore to flinch their way towards an orgasm. Lactic acid is the nemesis of a horny soul.

Monday 29th March

Okay, it was idiotic for me to believe it would've just been Ryan and me on this little jaunt around Lothian. Very stupid of me to assume Tony would be at work. Why would I think the most controlling groom would be happy to sit back and watch his husband-to-be and his best mate narrow down where the most important day (so he says) of his life will be?

We went from registry office ('... too dark.'), to stately home ('... too musty.'), to parkland ('... too exposed to the elements.'), to riverside mansion ('... too close to the airport.'), to Edinburgh Castle ('... too small.'), to a barn ('... stinks of cow shit.'). By 3 p.m., my gut was well and truly self-digesting from hunger as the Terrible Twins quarrelled in the back of my car.

'If you two don't calm it down I'm going to clip both your ears!' I heard myself snap as the bickering became high-pitched. Flashbacks of day trips away with my folks in the back of their Austin Maxi came to mind, with my sister and me arguing within thirty minutes of leaving home and Mum's tongue lashing us within an inch of our lives. The Terrible Twins fell silent as I stopped the car irresponsibly in the middle of a country lane and made a sharp exit in a huff.

Tony wound down the window and said, 'Alright, dear. Keep your wig on!'

I paced back and forth for a time and eventually rested both hands on the bonnet of the car to confront them head-on through the windscreen. I delivered my ultimatum, 'I want the two of you to settle on at least two — that's TWO —' I raised two fingers to emphasise my point, 'of the venues we've seen today!'

'Well, I kinda liked the Atrium,' stammered Ryan.

'I liked that, too, sweetie,' agreed Tony. 'But prefer the Balmoral, as they have fantastic views over the city.'

'So does the Atrium. And it's modern,' argued Ryan.

'I love the Victorian style of the Turmeau Hall,' interjected Tony quickly.

My patience was still being tested, and my gut was running on empty. I swung the driver's door open and got in, 'Good! That's two and a bit. They'll do.'

'But there are the Caves in the Old Town,' added Ryan sheepishly.

I sighed and slowly strangled the steering wheel. 'So, you are telling me that there are two, maybe three, maybe four possibilities within the city? *The city*. The city we actually live in. Where we started from. And you're telling me this after a six-and-a-half-hour trip through the deepest, darkest countryside of Lothian?'

Ryan and Tony looked at each other collectively and murmured, 'Yes.'

I booted her into drive and skidded off, 'Right! Grand! Super! And now, lunch!' I drove in silence all the way to a drive-through McDonald's and forced both of them to eat common junk food. I'm a heartless bitch when hungry.

Tuesday 30th March

I couldn't finish my shift quick enough to get to my final training session with Nash. I've never been so keen to lift weights in all my life. I'm sure if every resident in the U.K. had a sexy, fit personal trainer beasting them (male or female, depending on preference) then obesity would be obliterated. I break a sweat and burn off calories just looking at him. I was chuffed when he suggested showing me the free weights section. And I'm beginning to become fluent in 'Nash' and gym terms. I understood every word until he said, 'I'll spot you.'

'Sorry, you'll do what?' I asked, laid flat and totally submissive on the bench, dreading the measly forty kilos I was going to struggle to shift.

'Grip the bar,' he said.

I did.

'No, too close together. Wider than your shoulders,' he said, cupping my fingers in his palms and moving my arms further apart. A pleasant electrical current was now buzzing through my body, my skin became sensitive, and every hair raised up from my sweaty skin. 'Okay, take the weight, and I'll spot you.'

'Sorry, you'll do what?' I asked after lifting the bar from the rack, my elbows quaking under the weight.

He stood close behind me and leant over the bar slightly, his hairy legs inches from my highly erogenous ears. Short shorts caressed his bulging thighs as his crotch blocking out the spotlight on the ceiling that'd previously been blinding me.

'Ah, I see. You're *spotting* me. Yes, I understand.'

'Don't talk, breathe,' he encouraged me.

I'm trying, but it's pretty impossible not to hyperventilate right now, I thought. I could see *everything*: every crease and every bulge.

'Down to the chest with the bar, and up again. Down and up for twelve at the very least,' he ordered.

I obeyed. What's a boy to do? I lowered and pushed the weight in unison as he cupped his hands just below the bar, protecting me from collapsing. He squatted slightly with every dip, his legs becoming more pumped every second. His packet shifted in the creases of his kit. Testosterone must've been rife through my muscles as I managed every rep and two more on top! Amazing what you can do when you have a clear view of your goal.

It was over far too quickly. All good things, and all that. 'So that's you inducted and educated, my fella,' he said cheerily with a satisfied look on his face.

My hand reached for my wallet to pay for more private sessions, but I stopped myself as the meagre wages of a waiter doesn't cover a year's worth of personal training sessions three times a week. Besides, how many would be enough?

'However, if you do need anything, anything at all, just give me a shout,' he added with a cheeky wink.

A wink can mean something, nothing or everything. What good is a wink when you need a wank? Damn it! I wish I were telepathic.

Wednesday 31st March

I arrived home to a major bitch-fight between the boys. They were in full swing arguing about the wedding venue, entertainment, food, theme and shoes. I quickly hid in my room just after I saw the first of three crystal glasses shatter against the hall wall. The assailant was unseen, but I surmise it was Tony as it's his style of drama; he's always idolised Sue Ellen from *Dallas*.

Their fight fizzled out at 1.15 a.m. when Ryan burst into tears. I could hear Tony comforting him, and within minutes I was subjected to *their* album – most people have a song, but no, *they* must have a whole bloody album! Even Céline Dion's powerful lungs couldn't drown out their stunted make-up sex. I heard every grunt through two pillows and a winter duvet. I don't pay a fortune in rent to come home to amateur productions of Hollyoaks and Sexcetera!

Thursday 1st April

All Fools' Day.

Ding-dong! Ding-dong! Went the doorbell at 7 a.m. on All Fools' Day and my cheating ex-boyfriend, Thomas, is the first fool I have to deal with.

'Oh, good lord! How the hell did you find me?' I asked exasperated.

'Your mum. Here!' he said, thrusting a basket in my arms. 'I need you to look after him as Constantine and me are heading to Gran Canaria for a break and nobody's daft enough to take him.'

'Who's Constantine when she's at home?' I asked.

'You've met,' he said, hinting with the flicking of an eyebrow.

'Oh, the woman in the van. Is this a thing the two of you do? No, don't tell me, I don't really want to know.' Changing the subject, I peered into the box; it was the Colonel, our only child. 'Thanks, but I live in a flat now, thanks to you, and can't take him. The Colonel was feral when he found us if you remember? Cooping him up in this place will drive him insane.'

'It's you or the wilderness, Andy,' protested Thomas. 'There's not a cat home in Scotland that will have him, and you know he doesn't take to my maw.' As far as I'm concerned, no one can take to his mother. He threw a bag of dry food in the hall and a cat bed, thick with moulted hairs. 'It's time you live up to your side of our bargain and look after the kid you decided to adopt. I'll be back in two weeks. I think you can handle the responsibility until then.'

'I suppose you were responsible while hanging around lay-bys at every turn of the steering wheel?' I shouted after him, but he was already halfway down the stair and not giving a damn. The main door banged shut. I resigned myself to the fact Tony would be throwing us out tonight, and I'd be sharing the Colonel's bed with him in some damp close. I've tucked him away in my bedroom, still in his basket, until I dare to drop this furry bombshell on my landlords' heads.

Constantine? What sort of name is that for a dirty dogger? Are the lay-bys of the U.K. littered with the upper-classes?

10 p.m. Ryan was uneasy about having a temporary new housemate, but Tony was surprisingly keen.

‘Come on, Pookie,’ uttered Tony in Ryan’s lug as he caressed him from behind, ‘it can be our practice for starting a family.’

‘Okay, but two weeks only,’ stressed Ryan as he frowned at me. Tony can get Ryan to do anything if he so wishes. They’re firmly back in love, it seems, and I’ll just have to cope with that. It’s sad but true, the longer they stay happy, the longer the Colonel and I will have a roof over our heads.

Friday 2nd April

I’ve blown £120 of my weekly wage on assorted cat paraphernalia. A new bed was needed, as the old one was torn to shreds overnight, and a variety of toys and scratch posts now clutter my room to keep the Colonel amused and away from any soft furnishings, or fashion items that the boys leave carelessly lying around the flat.

Saturday 3rd April

Joy of joys! The new series of Dr Who starts tonight! A new Doctor, a new companion, and a new production team. I’m chuffed that it’s in HD as I get the full benefit from watching it on the boys’ telly. Both of them are out with Ryan’s mother this evening. They’re about as interested in watching Doctor Who as Ann Widdecombe is in reading Vogue.

I was a bit shocked when Sally, after hearing me blabber on all things Who, asked if she could join me as she’s keen to see the new series and doesn’t have a television. I couldn’t believe that, in this day and age, a person could live like that. ‘But what do you do, of an evening?’ I asked.

‘I listen to my 78s, drink gin and read classic novels, darling. It’s retro living. Very refreshing. You should try it. See you about six?’

So we watched a thrilling episode of Who with the curtains drawn, lights low and a bottle of gin between us. The Colonel has taken to Sally so keenly it makes me a little envious. He brushed around her ankles as soon as she arrived and purred and padded her breasts as if she was his long lost mother. He rarely likes anyone.

Speaking of likes, I like the new Doctor, Matt Smith, and I’m weirdly warming to Sally Knowles too. She cooed like a little kid as the re-vamped opening titles flashed on the screen. This child-like amazement lasted until the closing credits when she announced she had to leave for work.

'But you're off tonight, no?' I asked.

'Oh, not the café, darling. I pole dance at Madam Yo-Yo's in the Pubic Triangle every now and then,' she added nonchalantly as she gathered her bottle of gin and fags and stuffed them in her large overcoat. 'Much more fun than waiting tables. Hedonism is an expensive pastime: oh, the booze, the pills, the dancing, the come-downs and yet more pills ... it's like having three jobs,' she added, giving me an affectionate peck on the cheek. 'It's been fun. Ciao, brotherfucker!'

The cooing child was gone, eradicated by the stiletto heels of a thirty-something pole-dancer teetering on the edge of addiction.

Sunday 4th April

Amid serving hangover recovery brunches, Sally and I shared a conversation while waltzing between tables, our arms balancing plates as skilfully as a well-established circus act — it's as if I've always been a waiter and we've worked together for years, knowing the other's rhythms and nuances instinctively.

'So it's tonight. TAKNO,' she hollered, sliding past me.

'Yup,' I said, clearing a table.

'You up for it?'

'Why not? Should be fun.'

'Super-cool! It's a monthly club that plays cheesy tunes from more decadent decades than the drab one we live in now, as I told you. Doors open at ten.'

'Okay.'

'But we don't want to get there too early.'

'No?'

'We'll arrive when there's a crowd; it's more interesting that way.'

'True.'

'I'll meet you at The Street's pre-party, and we'll aim to get to the club around midni ... no, that's how they come, Sonny Jim; they aren't burnt.'

'Super.'

'The theme this month is Sci-fi, so right up our street.'

'Wow! I'll be there.'

'But we're not dressing up, kiddo. Leave the tinfoil at home.'

'Check! Oh, and here's your cheque, Sir.'

******

Later, as I did final checks in the mirror, Ryan asked, 'Where are you heading all glammed up?'

'On a date with Sally.'

'Oh,' he said, with a tone of discontent. 'Well, have fun.' He forced a smile.

'Thanks, I will,' I said merrily, almost out the door.

'Andy,' he quickly called.

I popped my head back in, 'Aye?'

'Maybe we could go out next week. Just you and me?'

'Yeah, I'd like that,' I grinned. 'Gotta go, I'm already late.' I left confident that my newfound friendship with Sally is just the thing to bring Ryan a little bit closer to his old pal and a little further away from Biffo.

Monday 5th April

It's time to exorcise some demons, I surmised the second the intro to *(I Lost My Heart To A) Starship Trooper* echoed towards me at the bar. I explained to Sally the recurring nightmares I'd had while staying at my folks' and with due consideration, she said, 'Okay, down that mojito. It's time to dance the shit out of it.' She grabbed my arm and spun me towards the dance floor with the ferocity of an American wrestler. 'It's time you shook off the past and shimmy towards that bright, glittery mirror ball of a future, kiddo!' she bellowed.

She's right, naturally. I have to move on. I danced without a care for the rest of the night and thoroughly enjoyed her company. She seems so free. Like she's syphoned off the good parts of 60s free love, the sparkle of 70s disco, the decadence of the 80s and injected it into her veins. I think I could do with some of that in my life.

Tuesday 6th April

I must stop lusting after Nash's legs. I find myself following him around the gym floor whenever he's training clients and casually using the machine/bench/dumbbell/water fountain close by like some lustful, grunting shadow. I lose track of how many reps I've done and find myself pushing machines that are not part of my programme.

When Nash pointed out I was doing more than my fair share of his allotted plan, I said, through a haze of blurry eyes and a very flushed glow, 'Well, you know me, Nash. Health, health, health! Always pushing myself to my limits.' I berated myself internally for finishing my sentence with the goofiest of goofy laughs. I pushed the adductors for another set and promptly broke wind crucially when the background music had gone quiet. That's two public farts in one week. What's wrong with me? I think I may've blown it in more ways than one. Nash won't want to share a bed with an involuntary sphincter. I excused myself and went to the showers immediately.

When I got home, I found Tony Googling 'cats'. He seems to have taken to this adoption full throttle. Maybe I've got him wrong. Perhaps under all those green scales lives a warm-blooded human being.

The Colonel, on the other hand, has most definitely not taken to him. He sits at the far end of the room and watches Tony with suspicion.

Wednesday 7th April

Yet another surreal dream. I was in bed, dozing while watching the TV when the Colonel hopped up wearing a yellow dickey-bow and slowly curled his tail around himself to sit and eyeball me for a few seconds. Then a disembodied voice said, 'You have no concept how problematic it has become to curtail my prospects. I was free when I found you. Domestication is the side effect of a warm lap and that box of delicious crunchiness you kept aloft on the cold box in the food room, my two-legged friend. That was dandy, we had a pact, but now one has no shrubs to relieve himself in, let alone fields to hunt. You anticipate one will be content trapped within the few white boxes you share with the other highly-strung entwined two-legs? Forgive me if my talons caress and destroy inanimate objects as my senses sniff out a stiff breeze. It's therapy. You see, my dear friend, the demons of hunts of old will not let me be. Oh, for the brush of the Nepeta Cataria against my soul!' He then leapt off the bed and began to tap-dance to *Putting On The Ritz* on the top of the fireplace.

I woke to find my room in gloomy silence. It was 4 a.m., and I was in a cold sweat. What worried me most was the Colonel, who was sitting on the mantlepiece, staring at me through the darkness. One anxiety dream has been replaced by another. Great! I can't afford a psychologist. And why the hell is my cat channelling Noel Coward?

Thursday 8th April

We ran out of a particular wine at Café Jamaica this afternoon, so I was sent to the wine shop next door to get a few bottles. *Broughton Bin-ends* is run by a sweet Spanish lady called Christina, with dark, flowing locks, tanned skin, big brown eyes and a petite body that would compliment any tight-fitting flamenco dress. Friendly and courteous in manner and instantly likeable. She's the kind of woman I imagine I'd chase if I were straight. I'm not, but I am a little smitten by her beauty.

When I got home this evening, I found the Colonel tearing at my Converse boots. My old faithful reds have been destroyed by his razor-sharp talons. I squirted him with the water pistol I've been saving for such behavioural issues, but he just strutted away as cocky as an errant teenager.

Friday 9th April

It was full civil partnership planning at the flat from 4 p.m. onwards, with an assortment of Ryan and Tony's buddies roped in to provide advice and take on allocated roles. Their big day requires the services of a set designer, musical director, choreographer, costume designer and small orchestra. If they didn't have these connections, they couldn't afford this ridiculous extravagance. It's just a piece of paper, after all. It's not even a real wedding. They have enough people involved to put on an amateur production of Funny Girl.

By the time the clock had struck nine, I'd escaped for a long drive. I found myself heading towards the A1, and before I knew it, I was alone on Gullane Beach. The Firth of Forth twinkled before me. Vacant lighthouses still providing guidance and safety from those rocks. I'd give anything to have some guidance right now. I'm so lost it scares me. I sat on the car bonnet for a while, watching the fluttering reflection of the steadfast moon on the crashing waves and allowed my mind to drift.

The sudden cawing of a seagull close to my head snapped me out of my ruminative state. I was cold. It was time to warm up and drive home. I turned the engine over only to hear my old girl sputtering and choking at every injection of fuel. She died several times. *Maybe I should've listened to that warning light on the dashboard, after all*, I pondered. It'd been there a month, and she had driven just fine. After a further five attempts and no hint of another car around for a jumpstart, I called my breakdown recovery.

Little did I know what and who was to come.

Alistair, my mechanic, arrived within thirty minutes. He's a handy, working-class guy, who owns the business, but mucks in with the boys when they need a night off from salvaging idiots like me from creeping tides of despair.

Alistair, with his silvery hair, handsome chin, thick thighs and brooding eyes would be the perfect package if he wasn't supposedly straight and married. If he wasn't my 4x4 Guy. The guy I swore never to see again, let alone have sex with in the back of his truck, which I'm ashamed to say I did. In my defence, I resisted for some time. The time it took to drag my old car up the ramp, to be exact. It was wild, risky and exciting. With his oil-stained overalls unzipped to reveal just enough of that hairy chest, how could I resist?

'I'm sorry I'm married,' he said as we approached Leith Street and some sobriety.

'Don't worry about it,' I said. 'I'm not looking to break up a happy home.'

'It's not that happy.'

That statement hung in the air and clung to me. *Don't give me hope*, I thought. It was just a few steps from his truck to the boys' door, but it felt like a mile. I didn't say goodbye, I just said thanks. I can still smell the engine grease on me. I'm curled up in bed and lusting after him. I do feel some guilt, but the urge to do it again overpowers this. My car's in his garage. I've no option but to see him again, honestly.

Saturday 10th April

I thought I was going to burst over breakfast. My head and heart would've exploded in unison, I'm sure, had I not told Ryan what happened last night. I knew instantly I'd made a mistake as his cheery optimism on their looming civil partnership dropped and split like a sack of coal on their pristine parquet flooring.

'I was going to ask you to be my best man, but how can I offer you that honour if you don't appreciate the enormity of the commitment I'm about to make?' he said dryly as he left the table. 'Your relationship karma will be shot to shit, Andy, if it hasn't been already.' He left with a face like thunder.

'Bollocks to that!' said Sally, later at work. 'If it makes you happy and fulfils your needs, go for it. Marriage is jolly-well overrated, as Alistair's wife will find out someday. No one is a hundred per cent committed these days thanks to the internet and saunas. Do what you like; it's nobody's business but yours.'

I felt quite reassured but a tad anxious moments later: what happens when I want commitment again?

Sunday 11th April

The Colonel has spent the day obsessively scratching at strategic patches of the carpet in my room. It's irritating and of concern as these are classic signs of cat cabin fever. No matter how many treats I give him, or how often I dangle different toys in front of his nose, he continues to choose my quiet time to dig at the boys' expensive pile. I lost it and threw a Terry Pratchett at him, but this only relieved the situation for an hour.

Monday 12th April

It's 40 years to the day that the Apollo 13 mission blasted off for its harrowing flight to the moon. Sally and I are commemorating the moment by watching the Tom Hanks movie after work. It's her suggestion, not mine, but I'm chuffed to bits as, after all these years, I have a friend who digs Sci-fi and spacey stuff as much as I do. We're going to do a classic Who series double bill next week too.

Tuesday 13th April

The BBC have released internal memos from the 1960s revealing that the good Doctor's regenerations were modelled on LSD trips. I'm in shock. I asked Sally if it's possible that the show I've loved since I was tiny could have been influenced by drugs.

'How should I know? I've never done LSD. How old do you think I am?' If I didn't know her better, I'd say she walked off in a strop. I'll buy her a drink to soothe her ego later.

Wednesday 14th April

I'm becoming inherently hedonistic through my association with a pole-dancing waitress. I woke this morning with her on one side of my bed and a half bottle of gin on the other. We were both naked. In my rush to find some clothes, I slipped on the half-eaten, cold, fatty remains of a kebab pizza and fell on my bare arse, causing considerable bruising to my butt and riotous amusement from my female friend beneath the duvet. Why couldn't I've befriended a librarian or a headmistress, neither of them would be a sponge to alcohol and leer at men while failing to keep upright against the local chip shop's hot cabinet.

Later, fully dressed, I chummed Sally to work after she'd popped a concoction of 'herbal remedies' to clear her head and slapped a ton of makeup over the dark rings that somewhere, in the depths, housed her eyes. She said, 'That Tony's a bit weird.'

'You're telling me!' I scoffed, tucking heartily into a mince round (my late breakfast).

'Why must he Febreze your room in strange corners?'

'What do you mean?'

'Well, I saw him sneaking in when you went to shower while I was smothered by the duvet. He tiptoed around the corners of your room, squirting your carpet at every pitstop. Even the chest of drawers got a treatment. I don't think it smells that bad. Mind you, that lingering stink of Brut aftershave you slap on daily could strip the barnacles off a cargo ship's hull.'

'That *is* weird,' I pondered. 'And it's not Brut, but the way, it's English Leather.'

She laughed, 'He got quite a shock when I sat up. Honestly, darling, you would think the boy had never seen tits before. He legged it faster than a terrorised blond in a horror movie.'

'Aye, I've meant to talk to you about that,' I said as I held the door to the café wide, 'I think I need to invest in a pair of pyjamas for you if you're going to stay over.'

'Ha! Pyjamas? Me? You're very sweet, darling, but they're really not my style. Buy me a revealing black negligee, and we'll talk. And we need to work on your scent; it's not so good sharing a bed with a man who's wearing the very same bottle of aftershave he got his father for Christmas 1988.' She smiled, fluttered her eyelashes innocently, handed her hardly smoked cigarette to an appreciative passing tramp and slipped inside.

Thursday 15th April

Flights to and from the U.K. have been disrupted due to volcanic ash billowing out from Eyjafjallajökull on Iceland. A vast cloud hangs over our heads, apparently, but I see nothing. Ryan thinks it's a conspiracy to stop an imminent threat from Al-Qaeda crashing planes into prominent British landmarks. Sally believes the U.K. government are trading humans for weapon development with aliens hovering above our heads in a huge invisible spaceship. Tony couldn't give a damn.

'Why should I give a shit?' he told the TV. 'I'm not travelling this week. It doesn't affect me.' He apparently believes the news should be filtered for his needs alone and that television presenters can hear his pleas. He should be concerned, however, as it does affect him and his cosy soft furnishings. This nonsense may delay Thomas' return. I've sent Thomas a text but had no reply. I think the Colonel has all the makings of a cat on the edge of a nervous breakdown and may snap at any second if he isn't allowed to roam free in the wild. This morning he had the look of Jack Nicholson in *The Shining* on his face as he stared at me on the loo. It put me right off; I had to get up halfway through and shut the door.

Friday 16th April

This damn volcanic ash continues to cause significant trouble for the U.K. and parts of Europe, not to mention my nerves. The Colonel has decided he's bored with my room and has taken to sniffing around Ryan and Tony's instead. His frustration continues. His toys and scratching posts are now in shreds. It's like a soft toy slaughterhouse. I'm driven to distraction watching his every move. I'm as edgy as a store detective on Christmas Eve. He only relaxes when Sally pops in. I'm at my wit's end.

The news reports are full of posh Brits huddled together in family groups at airports being prompted to say words like 'ridiculous' or 'disgraceful' and tutting loudly into reporters' microphones for effect. One lady couldn't pronounce *ridiculous* correctly and said, 'This is redicillious,' at least six times.

I checked the bustling queues on every report for Thomas and a middle-class harpy, but couldn't see hide nor hair of the dirty doggers. I've sent another text but again no reply. I can feel Ryan getting edgy. He's giving the Colonel the same look my mother does when her brother-in-law overstays his welcome on a Friday night at theirs, drinking their homebrew dry.

Saturday 17th April

The National Air Traffic Service has re-imposed the ban on flights to cover the whole of the U.K., extending it until at least seven o'clock this evening. A volcanologist spoke on Radio 4 today and was asked to give his opinion on how long this inconvenience will last. The simple reply was: how long is a piece of string? So that's it. We could be in ATC Zero for a long time to come.

Sally called me and asked, 'Where are you, darling?'

'At home, keeping an eye on this damn cat,' came my frustrated reply.

'Boring! Come join me, right now,' she demanded. 'I'm in Princes Street Gardens.'

When I got there, she wasn't hard to find, laid on a sunflower blanket, her mustard coloured blouse tied in a knot at the waist to show off her toned stomach and amplify her globular breasts. Her kinky boots had been kicked off next to her. Her thighs must've been catching a chill as they were exposed up to the seam of her blue denim hot pants that reveal the crease of her peachy ass. She greeted me without a word, just by peering over her yellow mod sunglasses and patting the blanket firmly as an invitation. I sat beside her. She grinned as she thrust a glass of champagne into my hand.

'Wow! Champs? Thanks!' I said.

'Sssssssssh ...' she whispered as she raised an emerald fingernail to her ruby lips. 'We may not get another day like this.'

'What day?'

Sally pressed her sunglasses to the top of her nose and toasted the sky, 'No buses or taxis on Princes Street, no tram-works and no air traffic overhead. In this city, that's rare. And the sun is shining too. Enjoy it with me, Andy, darling.' She downed a full glass of fizz and flopped onto the blanket. 'Peace, Andy. Peace from life. If only the world could be perpetually like this.'

I lay down beside her. She took my hand, and we listened to the chatter of people passing by, the wind bristling the weeping ash trees and the stillness of a transport system that'd been forced by man and nature to stop in its tracks. I lay there for an immeasurable period and forgot about cats, missing ex-boyfriends, cleaning, lazy landlords, schedules and civil partnerships. It's good to pause and not think. It's even better with a friend by your side.

Sunday 18th April

Day 4 of the travel disruption and still no reply from Thomas. It's the only time since we parted that I've checked my phone morning, noon and night for his name to appear. I can't stay in this flat with the Colonel in tow. I fear Ryan is becoming less tolerant as the days go on. His lips are becoming so tight they're developing pressure sores. Tony, weirdly enough, seems only too happy to have a moggy tear at their soft furnishings. He practically giggled as Ryan kicked off over the corner of their sofa being shredded by the feline equivalent of a Gillette razor. I've promised to keep a closer eye on the Colonel, but it's difficult to control a cat that is as hyperactive as a child on eight cans of Red Bull a day.

Monday 19th April

Day 5: The International Air Transport Association is to hold a press conference on how European governments are dealing with the shutdown of Europe's airports, which it estimates is costing airlines $200m a day. Sod that! It's costing me a fortune in cat paraphernalia and compensation for sliced soft furnishings. If this continues, Ryan and Tony will be gaining an entirely new lounge at my expense. Thanks, Eyjafjallajökull! I now understand why madmen are seen in the streets shaking their fists skyward. I found myself taking a wrong turn on the way to work and muttering frustrated expletives to the supposedly ash-strewn blue haze. But I'm pretty sure I'm not mad. Yet.

Tuesday 20th April

The boys have finally set a place and time for the pantomime that will be their wedding day (Civil Partnership to anyone else who isn't delusional). It's to be held at 12 p.m. on the 18th Of December, 2010, in the ballroom of the Balmoral Hotel, Edinburgh. The pink world can collectively sigh in relief and begin to hold their breath again in anticipation of these two actually surviving the rest of the planning stage and making it down the aisle.

Their wedding suits have arrived. Thanks their photographer friend's connections with the world of fashion and victims thereof, we now have the most hideous purple and white velvet jackets from Christian Dior with frilly pink shirts and matching top-hats hanging in the lounge as conversation pieces. Ryan and Tony have spent the evening cooing and stroking them in between sickening bouts of snuggling on the sofa. They're the epitome of a smug couple that you just want to smash in the face with a chunk of stale wedding cake. I shut myself in my room as I was having major trouble hearing Dr Christian's talk on average penis size on Embarrassing Bodies over the smacking noise their wet lips made every time they clashed in romance.

I caught sight of my reflection in the wardrobe mirror as I cradled the Colonel on my lap and pondered perpetual single life. Fearful that spinsterhood is not far away, I picked up my mobile and called the garage to see how my car was doing. Inadvertently, of course, booking a session with Alistair in the process. My car is fixed and will be dropped off at my door on Thursday afternoon by the boss. I arranged this, you understand, just to be sure I'm not a total ogre and destined to be hidden under the shadow of a bridge for the rest of my life.

Wednesday 21st April

I fear I've been led a merry dance. I've sent twenty-two texts to Thomas and not had a single reply. There may be a valid reason for the delay, but I can't see how the dust cloud is affecting mobile reception. I might have no option but to call the British Embassy in Gran Canaria and tell them he's missing. Or take the more sensible option of driving down to *Little Troll Cottage* and check-in on the neighbours (some 3 miles away) to find out what exactly is going on.

Thursday 22nd April

9 a.m. European skies have fully re-opened and, coincidentally, I'll be flying high with Alistair this morning. The boys are mercifully at work. He's asked that I leave the door to the flat slightly ajar while I lay face down on the bed, ass exposed and ready for a good rimming. I swear, if it weren't for his now noticeable wedding ring, I'd be convinced he's an experienced gay man. I'm beginning to wonder who's the teacher and who's the student. I'm learning new things every time he touches me.

4.20 p.m. Alistair's departed with jelly legs, and I'm fired up and self-assured. I sent a bombardment of texts to Thomas, each one becoming progressively aggressive. He really is treating me like a fool and is, as I said in my last text, an ignorant and inconsiderate p**k.

Friday 23rd April

6.15 a.m. Mum called to announce she and Dad will be using their discounted-to-zero pensioners' passes to visit me tomorrow (Why God? Why?! All I ask is for a quiet life). They've decided to take me out for dinner and have invited the boys too. I suspect she's angling for an invite to their ceremony as it's all she asked about. I'm sure the Terrible Twins have far more exciting things to do than hang around with an indifferent couple in their sixties.

10 p.m. So it seems I'm wrong, Ryan and Tony both jumped at the chance to spend the evening with my folks. Saturday will be spent carting my mum and dad around Edinburgh. Crappers! I think Mum would've preferred Ryan as her son; she's always laughed hysterically at his jokes. She acts like he's the most successful man alive. It rips my knitting! She'll do the usual and will complain about the price of everything and the lack of proper supermarkets within the city.

Saturday 24th April

Ryan, the golden boy, made a significant blunder during dinner at the Phuket. He mentioned in passing he'd recently read that anal sex can stimulate the prostate and reduce its risk of cancer. Mum lost her doting eyes as quickly as she lost her appetite for her Chu Chi

Ped. An uncomfortable silence was followed by much back-pedalling on Ryan's part. If I wasn't there, I'm pretty sure he would've denied ever having seen a man's bottom. It's the first time I've witnessed him being stuck between his gay pride and his constant craving to be accepted.

Mum has always been fine about my homosexuality, but she's never been ecstatic over the thought her son might have his chimney swept occasionally. Dinner was brought to a swift end, pudding and coffees were skipped, and there was a sudden desire to catch the next train.

By the time we'd ditched the boys and got to the station, Mum was running out of small-talk. 'Well, this has been nice, hasn't it?' she kept repeating. 'Aren't the boys lovely. Absolutely lovely. Really nice boys.' She fumbled in her purse for the tickets and added, 'They look so happy and nice together. They must really be excited about their coming anal partnership ... *civil,* I mean civil partnership.'

Dad was most amused.

I pecked Mum on the cheek before she clumsily tripped through the turnstiles towards their train. Dad hugged me and parted with, 'Your mother, eh? I've been trying to convince her for years it adds an extra dimension to sex, but she remains very uptight over it, as does her sphincter.'

Maybe some things should remain between couples and kept strictly between the sheets, I thought as I grimaced and waved them off.

Sunday 25th April

I arrived at *Little Troll Cottage* to find two Land Rovers stationed in the drive and a kids trampoline dominating the front garden. By the time I'd stumbled through a swathe of toys and bikes on the short trip up the weed-infested path, I was pretty sure it wouldn't be Thomas and his tart answering the front door. Still, I couldn't abate my nerves as I rang the bell.

After much verbal abuse levelled at someone inside, a bedraggled woman in her mid-thirties opened the door and scanned me from top to toe. 'Yes?' she asked in an irritated tone.

I explained I was looking for Thomas, claimed I was an old friend and muttered a quick excuse about a lawnmower he'd borrowed that

I needed back desperately.

'Oh, Thomas and Constantine don't live here anymore,' she said between yelps of hush to little brats who seemed determined to rip apart my old home from the inside out. 'They've moved abroad. I'm Constantine's sister, Clarissa. I'm renting this place from them ...'

The rest of her chatter fell on deaf ears as the words *'moved abroad'* echoed in my head. It was clear to me I'd been taken for a total mug. My thoughts turned to my own fate. Ryan will not be happy to let a room to a violent Colonel indefinitely. I began to digest my future living in a urine-stained cardboard box under some rail bridge. An ogre after all.

Clarissa's voice trailed back into my consciousness, '... I'll have to check with him before I can give you it back, as the garden is pretty extensive and takes some tending.'

'Aye, I understand,' I said, subconsciously slapping myself awake. 'They are beautiful, the gardens. The whole place was ... is.' I began to walk away. 'I'll be in touch after you get in touch. So keep in touch. I have to go. I've a thing to do,' I stumbled over my words as I flopped into the car, 'I've loads of things to do. Busy, busy me!' I started the engine.

'Do you have a number I can call you on?' asked the tart's sister. I ignored her. Foot on the accelerator and off I went.

So everyone wins, apart from me: Thomas gets a new life in the sun, Constantine gets Thomas, her sister gets my dream home, and I get nothing but a cat and a bucket load of bitterness. I'm a total failure and entirely lost.

Monday 26th April

Of all the days for Ryan to hightail it to his mother's down south, he had to pick this one. Tony camouflaged his glee over my desperation by offering a very stunted olive branch, 'Of course you and the cat can stay,' he said through a wry grin as he paused from flossing his jagged fangs. 'Ryan and I have discussed this possibility. We also discussed the need to increase the rent.' He continued to floss, but his eyes were fixed on me in the mirror, anticipating my reaction and enjoying every second of it.

I felt my heart sink. I knew there would be a catch. 'Increase? By how much?'

'By £80.'

'Annually?'

He stopped flicking debris at the mirror (which I cleaned only two days ago) long enough to laugh and say, 'Monthly, of course. For cat hair, wear and tear, etcetera.'

This place is plush, but it isn't that plush, I thought. But I heard myself saying, 'Okay, I'll speak to Ryan when he gets back.'

'No need,' added Tony as he unleashed the floss from his twisted teeth and splattered some more spit on the mirror, 'it's effective from whenever the cat arrived. So I'd say you owe us about a month's worth already.

I could tell he was savouring this moment. I didn't want to give him an opportunity to see me crack, therefore, I airily agreed. As much as I hate this, moving is a pain in the ass and, even though rented accommodation is plentiful, flats that allow pets are not. I'm here for the duration.

Tuesday 27th April

Cat compensation paid to my tyrant of a landlord. Mood low. I need to get back to the gym. I feel I'm on a downward spiral of fatty hips and depression. I've eaten three Wispa bars within the hour, and my serotonin is still at zero per cent.

Wednesday 28th April

One weekly fumble with Alistair done and dusted. I thoroughly enjoyed every second of it, but know I called him up mostly to make myself feel better. The excitement of being mildly attractive to a guy who, quite honestly, could have anyone he wants, is an addictive drug. I find myself dismissing all the compliments he gives me, but secretly banking them at the same time.

Thursday 29th April

One week until the General Election and I feel nothing towards any of the party leaders. By their looks alone, I can trust no one: Clegg looks like a shifty lawyer; Cameron is a pink-faced, fat-headed public schoolboy; I've major issues regarding Gordon Brown's lack of personal hygiene; and as for the SNP's Alex Salmond, I can't respect any man in the public eye who can't find the correct collar size, appearing on TV like a strangulated turtle.

Friday 30th April

Disaster! There were two tortured wedding suits hanging in shreds in the boys' lounge and one highly satisfied feline fashion killer smugly cleaning threads from his claws as Ryan came home. I've never heard a man wail over Christian Dior, but wail he did as I stumbled from the bedroom to learn what the commotion was about. I found him on the floor, like a distraught Jane Hudson, his tears streaking the foundation that hides his real age. His fiancé was cradling him.

'Take your vile cat suit slayer and go!' ordered Tony. 'We're tired of putting up with your shit, your cat's shit, your pubic hairs in our bathroom and the filthy trade you bring home.'

It took me precisely thirty minutes to pack my meagre existence into an assortment of cases, rucksacks and bin bags (I've never unpacked my Hornsea collection; a sure sign I wasn't settled). Then a further twenty to stuff the Colonel into a cat box, claws flailing violently with every push of his torso until blood ran down my wrists and dripped on their pristine cream carpet. *All the money they've bloody-well robbed from me will more than cover the damage,* I thought as I threw their keys on the tidy-but-not-for-long-without-me-around breakfast-bar, and walked out of their door for the last time.

I've nowhere to go apart from Mum and Dad's, which is *not* an option. I'm lucky enough to have locked up the café tonight and still have the keys. So here I am, diary in hand, cat on my lap as if butter wouldn't melt, getting ready to curl up for the night on the sofa that's tucked in an alcove under a festive chain of tiny lamps. I feel very emotional as I lay here in this sanctuary listening to people in the streets enjoying their night. I'm jealous of their carefree and seemingly uncomplicated lives.

There was a time I had great faith in friendship and love, but this seems to diminish more and more with every disappointment. I'd hoped my bond with Ryan could withstand anything, but it hasn't. I'd expected to be loved for life, but it was a lie. Even the man I see for casual intercourse is unfaithful to someone he'd supposedly made a pledge to. I've little faith in humanity. I'm at odds with the world because it is at odds with me.

Tomorrow morning I'll ... actually, tomorrow morning I've no idea what's going to happen. I just know I can't go back to my folks for a third time. Not now. Not ever.

The Colonel is purring away, blissfully unaware of the damage he's done. My wrists are smarting from his aggression, but I'm mindful that it was the cage Thomas and I put him in that drove him to distraction and destruction. It wasn't his fault. That's why I still hug him and love him just the same. He's trying to settle in, but he's on guard. His eyes can't shut, and his ears are twitching with every new sound that this unfamiliar place carries. I fear for his tiny little life more than I do mine. I promise, my old friend, I'll look after you. I'm all you have. And you are all I have.

Saturday 1st May

Thank the lord for Ms Molasses Brown and her compassionate heart. She arrived at 7 a.m. to find me stuck in amongst the sagging cushions.

'Haven't you got a home to go to, boy?' she joked before catching sight of my baggage. 'Ah, what's happened?'

I told her everything.

'You can stay at a place I have down Leith Walk. It's not the kind of palace those hoity-toity queens have made you accustomed to, but it's cheap, and no one gives a damn what muck you drag home, providing you clean up after yourself.'

'But I have him,' I said, pointing to the Colonel.

'Look, I've recently lost a reliable tenant, so you're in luck. I also have a new house rule that says every new lodger should come with a cat.' She smiled reassuringly. I've never met a more maternal person than Molasses. It's a crime she doesn't have kids. She's so kind. 'No deposit necessary, as you work here. It's simple: you wreck the joint; you lose the roof over your head *and* your job. I'll deduct the rent directly from your wages.' *Kind, but firm, it seems.*

'Thanks,' I said, 'you're way too good to me.' And then I burst into tears.

She cupped my hand in hers and said, 'Look, I've been mighty down in the past, my boy. Judged, put-upon, shunned and excluded by people. And at the point when I thought of ending it all, an angel appeared before me and helped me find a new path. I know how deep life can drag you down. But you have to let go of the past. It's like a magnet that stops you in your tracks. It's time to give sentiment up and start living your life.'

She was right. I'd been clinging on to the ideals of my past. Fooling myself that I was moving on when, in fact, all I was doing was facing the wrong way. The tears stopped. She pulled me close to her and held me as delicately as any mother would a once lost child. And with that embrace, I finally let go of the past and accepted that it wasn't all that great.

'It's 323 Leith Walk,' she added as she squeezed me. 'Top floor flat. Just knock on the door after your shift. Sally will give you a tour and a key.'

I dried my eyes and blinked in surprise. 'Sally?'

'Hasn't she told you she rents from me?'

I hesitated for a few seconds and reluctantly said, 'No, but I'm sure it's going to be great!'

So I'll be sharing with a screwed-up party going waitress-cum-pole-dancer. Wait until my mother hears about this. She's going to need new kneecaps with all the prayers she'll be uttering for me.

Sunday 2nd May

323 Leith Walk.

The bedsits are on the top floor of a long row of tenements just above the Caprice restaurant. Sally was there, in a black and red silk housecoat and 7-inch heels – What else? – to show me around the room I've been given in Ms Molasses Brown's 'Land of Lost Souls', as my hostess put it. Room 4, my room, is next to Sally's (Room 3). There are four bedsits in total. The bathroom, with a shower over the bath, is shared between all. There's a payphone in the hall that rang a few times, but no one answered it; Sally ignored it throughout my tour. Later, when I answered it, there was just static at the end of the line. It sits on a mahogany telephone table that's laden with unopened mail from previous tenants. All-in-all, the hall is clean and functional. The carpet looks new but retro 70s, and the air has the fresh odour of Magnolia & Vanilla Shake n' Vac about it. I wanted to step back in time, and there I was. There's also a storage cupboard just to the right of my room that's locked.

Sally pushed open my door and hollered over the jazz music that bounced cheerily from her pad, 'Your chateau, Monsieur.' It's about twelve foot wide and around twenty foot long. As Sally flipped the switch, the bulb blew and threw the place into an eerie darkness. Dust tumbled in the moonbeams fighting their way through the dirty window panes at the farthest end. 'Don't worry about that,' she laughed, pointing at the defunct bulb, 'it happens all the time here.' She disappeared into her room for a second and reappeared with an oil lamp. She beckoned me in with repeated waving of her cigarette holder, casting trails of wispy smoke that carelessly filled my room.

I stepped in and looked around. I dropped my luggage, and my heart simultaneously hit the floor with a thud.

This is it? This is the hand I've been dealt? My life has been reduced to an ancient Hotpoint fridge/freezer, a Baby Belling stove and a single bed that should be in a museum. I've heard of downsizing, but this is ridiculous! The fridge/freezer I can deal with, but the single bed pretty much says that my sexual fun has ended. I was premature to think I'd slept under my last single duvet at my folks' place. The large sash window needs a deep clean, and the wallpaper has pretty much seen the rise and fall of the Berlin Wall.

Sally continued to grin insanely and move excitedly around the room. 'Isn't it super, darling?' she asked. She obviously couldn't see my pained expression through the greyness and the plumes of smoke pouring from her lungs. 'Outside that window is a New York-style fire escape. Classic, darling! You can climb all the way to the roof if so desired. Delightful views, I'm told. The electric is paid by a metre beside the fridge – £1 coins only – there's as much hot water as you want and you'll have extra heat from the boiler that's housed in the cupboard just here between the window and the fireplace.' She struggled to open the cupboard door as it caught on the thick blue carpet.

'But it's so ...'

'So cheap? Yes, I know, darling. All this for just £40 a week.'

Cheap wasn't the word I was looking for. Grim was the word I felt my throat swallow as I heard the astoundingly low cost of weekly residency in the *Land of Lost Souls*. I pushed my pride aside. 'No,' I muttered perfunctorily, 'it's ... it's ... perfect.' I felt my face smile on the outside and hoped it would work its way inwards. 'Well, I best get cleaning,' I added in an attempt to snap myself into some sort of positivity. I flipped open my scrubbing case.

'You travel with cleaning products?' she asked, a tad amused, flicking ash into the palm of her hand for the first time.

'Doesn't everyone?'

'Right, well. Good. Very good,' she said, looking at me strangely. 'I have a bottle of gin to finish next door and a few old-but-new-to-me LPs to listen to.' She edged towards the door, 'I'll leave you to it. But if you feel like christening your first night here, give me a knock, neighbour.'

She really does have her priorities in the wrong order. She could've enjoyed an evening bonding with me while we made windowpanes shine without a single streak instead of smearing her thick lipstick on crystal. People are weird.

Before she left, I asked, 'Who rented this before me?'

'Some part-timer. An oldie who would stay for short periods but paid full rent. They disappeared in December last year, and the room has been empty ever since. I think Molasses has been holding it open in the hope her old chum would turn up. We now assume she's left this planet.'

'Why do you assume that?'

'Because the rent payments stopped coming and occasionally, just occasionally, we can smell her perfume in this room. Just about there,' she cast a perfectly manicured fingernail towards a rocking chair that sat portentously in a corner by the window. I felt a shiver rattle down my spine. 'Oh, don't worry, sweetie, just think of it as an unpredictable yet pleasing plug-in air freshener.'

This was no comfort at all. Sally left the room just as the grim reaper shuffled in.

Almost Midnight. The room is as clean as I can make it in Victorian lighting. The bed I'm lying in is musty, and the metal frame creaks every time I make the slightest movement. I've avoided the rocking chair. There actually is an unnerving smell of perfume in that spot. The Colonel has been scatty and has decided to take umbrage under the bed since I let him out of his box. I've been edgy. I'm hiding under the sheets. Hopefully, by tomorrow evening, things will improve, and it'll start feeling a bit like home.

Monday 3rd May

11 a.m. I'm driving to IKEA, even though I'm bloody knackered as I woke every hour to check if the rocking chair was occupied by the spectre of an excessively perfumed pensioner. I need to invest in some new bedding and kitchen utensils. Honestly, how could anyone exist with just one bowl, one spoon and a cup without saucer? How could the fragrant deceased live with the grime I found on arrival? Why was an old lady living in a bedsit at her time of life anyway? Shall people remember me like her: a spinster who lived and died in one room?

2 p.m. I've just arranged a cheeky session with Alistair. We're having a brief meet in a cruising area (my standards have dropped drastically) as he's working late and I'm not comfortable taking him back to my bedsit with a shoddy single bed. Besides, what would my new neighbours think?

11.45 p.m. During our fun in the pouring rain, a guy breezed past and asked if he could join in. Surely there's some kind of etiquette to follow when cruising? Like, don't interrupt a guy mid-flow. Ruined my orgasm. Alistair chuckled about it on the way back to our suspiciously parked cars, which, now some time has passed, I admit I find it ridiculous and a bit funny too. The whole cruising for sex outdoors is risible and a little sad, especially once you've shot your load and the compulsion to copulate vanishes. Men of all ages pacing around in the night's rain like spunk volcanoes eager to erupt under the right stimulus. It's just ludicrous. There are better things to do with your time. But, at the same time, it is incredibly exciting. Maybe I'm enjoying the risk factor.

Just as Alistair jumped in his 4X4, he asked me, 'Have you ever done a three-way, Mr?'

A little shocked, I blurted out, 'Of course not! It took me three years of monogamy before I allowed Thomas to keep the lights on. And even then it was just a nightlight. Have you?'

He quickly replied, 'No. Well, not really,' before pulling the door shut and waving goodbye.

'Not really?' I asked myself quietly as he sloped off down the sodden lane. 'What exactly does *that* mean?'

11.55 p.m. I heard sobbing from some other room in the bedsits. It stopped the second I opened my door to investigate, so I can't be sure who the sad soul is. I suspect it's one of the neighbours I haven't met.

Tuesday 4th May

I popped into 21 Leith Street before work and attempted to get my deposit back, but was ridiculed by Tony's laughter as he slammed the door shut in my face. He really is the rudest man on the planet. I kicked their pot plant over in a temper.

'You'll pay for that!' I heard him call from inside. I imagined he was watching me through the spy-hole, so I stuck two fingers up at the door and poked my tongue out in a merry dance for a few enjoyable seconds.

'You're nothing but a tight-fisted arsehole, Tony,' I shouted.

'Excuse me,' came a short, sharp voice from my rear. It was Ryan. I tried to apologise and argue my case, but he pushed past me, and their door was slammed in my face once more. I blew a raspberry in frustration and continued to send angry V signs. It may not be the most adult thing to do, but at times like these, it is the most satisfying.

'I can still see you,' came Tony's voice through the wood.

I left mumbling expletives, just after I heard Ryan say to Tony, 'You know, I think he's losing it.'

He may be right.

Wednesday 5th May

10 a.m. Holy crap! The Colonel has escaped onto the roof and won't come back in! He somehow managed to climb through the small gap in the window and scurried up the rusty old fire escape. His distressed meows woke me. I fear I may have to call the fire brigade.

I've knocked on Sally's door to see if there's access to the loft as I'm most definitely not taking the external route – I have a massive fear of heights – but all I got in return was, 'Piss off whoever you are. I have a steel drum banging in my cranium and could have possibly damaged my liver for the rest of my short and meaningless life.'

I suspect the lady consumes too much.

11.20 a.m. A knock came at my door just as the emergency services lady cast a mocking laugh down the line. When I opened it, I found a stout sexagenarian male with a silvery beard (all pointy like a wizard's), and unbrushed hair tied back in a ponytail. His eyebrows, which are white as snow, are bushy and come to a point at either side of his dome-like forehead, exaggerating the wizard look.

'Whatcha, fellow citizen!' he said in a West Country accent. 'I'm Melvin, your friend and neighbour in Room 2, but you can call me Melve. I believe you require a bit of Melve magic to get a distraught cat off a wet slate roof?'

How did he know?

'Are you a magician?' I asked, dispelling my disbelief for a minute.

He chortled in a mad-professor way, 'Me, my boy?'

Please be a magician, please! I thought. *Please, and sort out my messy life with a wave of your wand. Please let this be Oz, Narnia or even Wheelie World!*

'No, sadly not,' he replied, dashing my hopes. He must've seen my disappointment as he tried to recover some interest. 'Well, a magician of sorts: psychologist, social worker, explorer, ukulele player, Munro bagger, cake baker, your live-in maintenance man and general jack of all trades, that's me. You don't get to my age without picking up a few talents on your travels.'

'Have you travelled?'

'Yes, lad! Extensively. Far and wide. Almost to Venus and back, if I could've.' He pointed at a battered rucksack that's seen better days, 'I have this ... for the cat?'

'Oh, my! The cat. Yes! The cat. Come in.'

Melve leant over the sink and squinted up at the roof, hairy bum-crack flashing to me from the brim of his safari shorts. His back-fat spilling over the edges. 'I see,' he said with some excitement. 'The little rascal has managed to scale up to the next level even though the dropdown ladder's stuck. Won't take a sec, I'll have the little bugger down in a jiffy.'

He leapt up on the sink and dug around the rucksack like a kid looking for a bag of Jelly Babies. When he unravelled a large bundle of knotted rope with a rusty hook at the end, I began to worry.

Surely he's not going to? No, he couldn't possibly? Oh, sweet Jesus! He is! I thought as he lay back on the sink and called to me, 'Push your hands against my feet, would you sonny?'

I looked at his sandals; they were tired and had sand stuck in the crevasses. I hoped it was sand and not dead skin cells from his dry, cracked heels. Was that sand in his toenails too? Oh, sweet Jesus! I squinted in the hope of some obscurity. He pushed against me, almost knocking me over, and before long he was stood on the rusty grate outside and swinging the hooked end of the rope like a man possessed.

'This is well dangerous! Come back in, and I'll call the fire brigade,' I pleaded to him.

'Danger, my boy? I piss in the face of it, prostate willing,' he yelled from outside the glass. 'Here goes nothing!' He rotated the hooked end of the rope with such skill and precision for an overweight man in his sixties that I was most impressed, stupid though his behaviour was, it gathered speed and began to make a whooshing noise as it cut through the damp air.

'Come back in,' I implored, 'I've only just met you, and I really don't want you to die.'

'Die, laddie? Me?' He thrust the rope into the air confidently. I heard the metal hook clunk and scrape on the platform above until it caught on something firm. 'Eureka! I'm not going to die, young man. I'm going to fly!'

With his words still ringing in my ears, his feet battered against the window panes, leaving sandal prints all over my thorough housework, and he was off, scaling up the side of the building as his lungs wheezing with every stride.

Nimble, for an oldie, I thought.

For what seemed like an age, I waited with my heart in my throat until I heard Melve's rasp growing in volume, until his 'Worzel' accent hollered, 'Open that window wider, me laddie, we have a passenger!'

The previously immobile ladder was now briskly screeched down to the level outside my window with a clatter under the weight of a globetrotting, ageing hippy. The Colonel peered sheepishly from the inside of Melve's rucksack. Melve carefully scooped him out and placed him on the sink. The wee bugger scarpered off under my rickety bed.

After I struggled to pull Melve and his beer belly back into safety, I slapped him on the shoulder for being so stupid and thanked him at the same time. My nerves were shot. He seemed to get a thrill out of the small drama as he gleefully coiled up his rescue rope, grinning from ear to ear.

'Wow! I haven't done the Spiderman thing in years. Nice to meet you, old chap.' He shook my hand vigorously. 'I've lubed the ladder, by the way, old chum, in case the cat hops up again, and you need to follow it. I'm off for a rest and a joint. Want to join?'

'No, thanks,' I said.

'Really? Couldn't encourage you? A joint shared is a problem bared.'

'No, I really don't do drugs. Well, apart from when surprised.'

'Righty-oh. I'll be off then. Not a word, by the way. I could claim it's medicinal, but I'm as fit as a butcher's dog. Oh, and stay away from that cupboard in the hall. Ciao.'

What a weird thing to say. I'm convinced he's a little bit bonkers. A nice man, but bonkers. I washed my hands immediately and a further three times over. I can't get his yellow toenails out of my mind.

Thursday 6th May

It's election day, and I've missed my chance to vote. My polling card will be unmarked in the damp church hall close to *Little Troll Cottage* as I haven't notified the council of my sudden departure.

Mum called to see if I'd voted. She always does. She likes to be sure we choose 'the right party'. Her election day bullying started when she dropped her guard, and Mrs Thatcher became Prime Minister. I remember her saying, 'Thatcher the Snatcher has no idea what hard graft is. She should be dragged from Number Ten, her lacquered waves crammed into a headscarf and she should be forced to pull on cows tits and shovel shit for a week, that'll learn her.'

The silence was deafening when she learnt I'd been disorganised with my political household as a result of three changes of address within five months. Her tirade began after a minute's pause. 'Do you know that women chained themselves to fences so that you could vote?'

'The Suffragette movement was, in fact, for the women's vote,' I reminded her.

'Don't split hairs, Andy. It was for all of us, I'm sure even the gays if they were around back then.' Does she think we were mass-produced and vacuum-packed for a special release back when disco hit the mainstream?

'Besides,' I wrangled, 'the Suffragettes chained themselves to railings and went on hunger strikes to give women a *choice* to vote. *A choice*, Mum.'

'Oh, you always become so pedantic when you're wrong ...' she snipped back before the inevitable happened and that enormous shiny penny that had been launched in the air towards Airdrie clattered at her feet on the kitchen linoleum. 'Hang on a cotton-picking minute here: did you say you've moved three times? You've moved Again?'

She proceeded to sigh throughout my whole explanation and gasped for breath after I mentioned the word 'bedsit'.

'Get your name on the council list,' I heard her shout as I pulled the phone away to hang up. 'No son of mine is going to live in a ruddy bedsit.'

So much for striving for the right to choose.

Friday 7th May

So, it's a hung parliament, but not a well-hung one, looking at the choice of party leaders. A coalition is like a consolation prize for M.P.s, but they continue to grin insanely in front of TV crews as they meet and greet for talks at their party headquarters. I can't see Gordon Brown being suited to any marriage with any other political leader/party. He would become the ugly, abusive husband that people would come to despise.

8 p.m. A text from my mother: 'If u had voted the country wouldn't be in this mess!'

Bollocks to that. As if one voice can make a difference. I've voted strategically several times during the Eurovision Song Contest, and the United Kingdom always comes close to last.

Saturday 8th May

Sally caught me peering into the gloom through the gap at the bottom of the hall cupboard door.

'What you doing, Mister?'

I remorsefully looked up to find her in nothing more than a pair of red heels, tan tights, denim hotpants and a man's shirt that was tied flirtatiously around the waist in a knot, exposing a pierced navel. I fibbed badly and said my last £2 coin had rolled under the door.

'Liar,' she grinned. She fought with the tiny pocket at her rear and freed a large, hefty key. She tutted and inspected some damage to her green nail varnish for a moment before pushing past me to get to the lock. 'You were being nosey, right?'

I couldn't deny it, Miss Marple had nothing on her, so I just nodded and said, 'Aye, that's about right. Curiosity killed that cat,' I joked, but my humour was met with a single disparaging glance as the key was slotted into the lock and turned until a thick clunk was heard. I waited, unsure of what I expected to see beyond the door, but an air of expectancy continued to hang for an age before she stepped briskly backwards, pulling the door wide and illuminated the mystery with one tug on the internal light switch.

Nothing but old furniture, lamps, wardrobes, bookcases, books, brass bed heads and other tat filled the space. The air was musty and congested, with a hint of something else. I couldn't put my finger on it, but there was definitely some kind of spice to it. My bloodhound nose wasn't given enough time to carefully define the scent as Sally popped her head in and said, 'See? Nothing. Nosey parker.' I was moved to the side by her gentle but persuasive hand, and the door was firmly locked.

'I'm sorry,' I said, a little embarrassed. I decided to change the subject, 'Were you okay the other night? I thought I heard crying.'

'Me, crying?' she dismissed my question with a laugh and wave of her hand, 'Sweetie, I haven't cried since I broke the heel off my favourite pair of stilettos in 1994.'

'Are you sure? And then I thought I heard something moving around in here just after the crying stopped.'

'Don't be silly,' she said as she walked towards her door. 'You probably heard my TV or something. I fell asleep watching an old black and white movie, one of those over-acted dramas from the 1950s, that's all. I'm just fine, darling.' She opened her door and, before shutting me out, she added, 'I'm always just fine.'

But you don't have a TV, I thought.

Sunday 9th May

How much longer are we going to be in talks before we get a government that can make decisions? How many working breakfasts, lunches and dinners will it take to form one cohesive coalition? I'm confident they're ordering more than your average 'Meal Deal' from Boots and spending my heavily taxed wages on regular deliveries from local takeaways. While watching the BBC news this evening, I spotted a stain on David Cameron's shirt that was a perfect colour match to Beef and Black Bean Sauce. It was the smallest of stains, but it's all the evidence I need that he'll bleed this country dry and lead us towards a sloppy, messy end.

Monday 10th May

11.20 a.m. A quick bedsit booty call with Alistair lasted beyond the usual half-hour. Postcoital, he surprised me by flipping me on my side for hugs and lethargic chat. It was a struggle to fit into my god-awful single bed (lust outweighs embarrassment; he has met my tiny room). We were squashed together like sticky boiled rice packed in a small takeaway tub.

'Are you going to be okay here?' came the concerned voice from behind my neck. His words felt as warm as his breath. 'It's a bit ...' he struggled for kinder words, '... old fashioned and scant.'

I stared up at the dated 70s orange and brown ceiling and sighed, 'It is a bit, but I like to think of it as vintage living.' His hand slid down my arm and then his fingers entwined with mine. 'I'll be fine. I'm happy in my own space, small though it is. It's not that bad, and the neighbours are friendly, a bit eccentric, but welcoming all the same.'

'What about your buddy? You'll miss living with him.'

'I will, but his boyfriend's septic, and that's rubbed off on him a little. They're like terrible twins. I don't want that in my life.'

Alistair hugged me tighter and wrapped a snug hunk of leg around the thinness of mine. He kissed the back of my head and said softly, 'I worry about you.'

The words hung in the room for a moment. I didn't know what to say. Could this guy actually have feelings for me? I shouldn't get my hopes up, I know that, but it feels so good to have him clutch me, comfort me and care. I plucked a phrase from Sally's book, 'I'll be fine. I'm always just fine.'

What I wanted to say was, *I'm always fine when you're around.*

Tuesday 11th May

Gordon Brown has resigned as Prime Minister. This marks the end of a thirteen year Labour government. Has it really been that long? It only seems like yesterday Tony Blair was dad-dancing his way through their election campaign to *Things Can Only Get Better*. Christ! Have I aged thirteen years already? Harold Wilson once said that a week is a long time in politics. It seems the opposite for me;

thirteen years is very little in my ever contracting life.

I spent the evening clipping my chest hair over the bathroom sink. I've counted at least fifteen grey hairs amongst the brown. I've chosen to remove the grey individually through plucking (hurts like hell around the nipples). I will not let age defeat me. I'm considering wet shaving the whole damn rug to give some kind of illusion that I'm youthful. Thirteen years of disappointment from the Labour government has taken its toll on the economy and my follicles.

Wednesday 12th May

A yellow post-it note appeared on the bathroom cabinet overnight. It said, in very boxy handwriting:

> 'Could whoever carelessly left their pubic hairs in the sink please remove them? This is DISGUSTING!!!!!!!!!'

Is there ever any need for nine exclamation marks? Pubic hairs indeed! It's chest hair, and I was damn careful to flush them all away. Who is this pube detective anyway? I'm pretty sure it's not the I-don't-give-a-shit-about-my-shit Sally or the Sasquatch that is Melve. I grudgingly used my kitchen spray to cleanse the sink thoroughly and tore the note down in a temper, which left a sticky residue on the mirror that I spent the next fifteen minutes trying to rub off, but only succeeded in sliding the sludge to the lowest corner of the cabinet door. This will disturb me every time I walk into the bathroom more than the 80s green porcelain.

7 p.m. I've invested in a microwave as it's impossible to cook a proper meal on or in a Baby Belling stove. My options are: two hot rings to heat two pots at the same time, or one small ring while I compress something into the tiny oven which has the depth, width and height of a single person's ready meal. I refuse to be pushed into this style of cooking. It's lazy and not very cost-effective. I'd prefer to cook a big batch of food and box it off in the freezer, creating my own stock of healthier ready meals.

Thursday 13th May

Cometh the hour, cometh the two public schoolboys: the Liberal Democrats emerged from a meeting with their Parliamentary Party and Federal Executive just after midnight to proclaim that a coalition deal had been "approved overwhelmingly", sealing a joint government with the Conservatives.

A marriage between the two seems impossible, but I guess there have been many handshakes and deals formed in sealed rooms around Westminster that we'll never know about. Not forgetting the copious amount of artisan pizza consumed at our expense.

Friday 14th May

Two visits from Alistair in one week. Do two meets in one week keep us in the casual fuck-buddy category? We lay in bed for over an hour after our fun. He held me in what is becoming the usual position, his chest against my back, and I lay there content enough to let the day slip away. The only reason the snugness ended was a sudden rush to an eleven o'clock meeting on his part. I had a full day off, so was well into a dreamy and chilled mode when I kissed him goodbye. I was just about to slip back into my bed and soak up the pheromones he'd left behind on my crumpled sheets when a knock came at my door.

Excited, I leapt up and called, 'Can't get enough, eh, big boy?' I got the shock of my life to find Mum and Dad stood in the hall. I couldn't hide my surprise and embarrassment as I feverishly reached for more than a pair of pants. 'Did you ring the doorbell?' I asked, guilt written all over my pink post-climax face.

'Some tall lad let us in on his way out,' she said, oblivious that the man she was talking about had just had his tongue wrapped around mine seconds before. 'Well? Let's see it then, this little palace you're staying in.'

She pushed past me and waited expectantly to be shown around my room, clutching her handbag tightly to her waist, straightened her jacket and pursing her lips, as if she was the Queen on a dreaded duty-bound tour of some needle exchange.

'Just a sec!' I said as I hurried past her and fixed the bed best I could to cover up a multitude of sins (my bottom sheet had become the sexual equivalent of the Turin shroud).

She wasn't impressed at all. 'Well, I never thought it'd come to this: a shoddy room in a dirty street with hardly a stick of furniture. And no washing machine. How will you wash your clothes?'

'By beating my clothes on a rock at the side of the Water of Leith,' I joked.

Dad laughed; she didn't.

I composed myself. 'There's a laundromat across the road,' I replied, soberly.

'What, with the ... *public?* You'll be washing your underwear where other people have washed their underwear? Just minutes before you in the same drum?' Her nostrils tightened as if she'd just fallen into a sewer.

'Well, they're not going to give me my own machine,' I quipped again. She snorted and looked at my crooked bedsheets. I blocked her path in case she attempted to straighten them. 'Look, it isn't all that bad,' I told her. 'I'm actually very happy here.'

Dad glanced around while nodding and smiling, 'Well, it's bigger than the berth I had to endure on the rigs. And I'd to share that with two other stinking lads. We shared a laundry basket too. It could be worse, Beth.'

Mum sighed, 'Well if you insist on staying in Little Beirut instead of coming home to us, I guess we should do something about it. Get your coat, Son. Charlie, get your wallet. We're off to IKEA.'

Dad hung his head in despair, 'And how much is this little excursion going to cost me?'

Mum was already making her way to the front door, 'About as much as an afternoon in the bookie's, I imagine. Don't argue.' Out she went, through the main door and off down the stair.

'You know, Son, I can see how much this appeals to you, living here on your tod, away from trouble, like your mother. Have they got a room I could rent?'

'Is she not getting any better?' I chuckled.

'Worse. Much worse!' replied Dad, grimly.

I now have a double bed with a fabulous comfy mattress, new chest of drawers, sofa-bed, rug, and two touch-lamps being delivered on Thursday next week. I've spent the evening scouring my new utensils and cutlery to remove any contamination from the great unwashed that seem compelled to finger every item on IKEA's shelves. Also, I now have such a mass of Tupperware I could freeze an entire cow, albeit in small sections. Mum insisted I invested in more as, 'You can never have too much Tupperware. Tupperware is the housewife's friend.'

I'm very thankful for their help. I'm also grateful they've gone.

They bickered in every aisle, and Mum kept saying, 'Suit yourself,' every time I turned my nose up at some ridiculous item she waved in front of my face.

'I've limited space,' I told her, 'and Dad has a limited wallet.'

'Andy, he's so tight-fisted he's become arthritic in both hands,' she moaned. 'Don't let him fool you. He's minted.' Again, her delusions of grandeur creep in.

Oh, and I've unpacked the Hornsea. It's beginning to feel a lot more homely.

Saturday 15th May

It seems Sally is back to 'normal' and we're back to being buddies again. We shared a long day's work together, and I was invited to catch up on all the recorded episodes of Dr Who I've missed over the past few weeks. She now has internet *and a* recordable TV, how can this be possible in a bedsit? I have no television as yet, so this was my first proper invite into the lioness' den.

Her room is twice the size of mine. The walls are adorned in purple leafy patterned wallpaper that compliments the magenta drapes around her four-poster bed. A white marble fireplace was full-bellied as flames licked the flume. A polar bear rug laid before the crackling fire as if it had just been run over by an ACME steam roller. A mahogany grandfather clock ticks away in the corner of the room. Oil lamps adorn the mantle, which Sally claims are safer than the electrics in the place. Her shoe collection is vast, carefully stacked and organised on display shelving. One pair, in particular, caught my eye: some ruby-red slippers, just like the ones worn by Dorothy in Oz. The whole room is quality. Fair to say, I'm jealous. The walls are laden with an assortment of ominous nude self-portraits, mostly with deep red paint splattered in random places over the naked flesh (I'm not jealous of these). When she caught me gawping at them, she said, 'Oh, that was during my artistic phase – a very tumultuous time of my life – now that I'm channelling my art in a mode that's more me, I'm more at harmony with the world.' I must've looked confused as she quickly added, 'The art of dance, darling. The art of dance.'

I'm pretty sure pole dancing is not heading to the Radio 2 Culture Show any time soon, I thought as I nodded and kept a fixed grin.

Next to the well-stocked drinks cabinet is Sally's pride and joy: a classic Masterwork portable record player, encapsulated in a light-blue case that is in remarkably outstanding condition. Her vinyl collection is strewn haphazardly around this area and consists mainly of tragic divas who died years ago. They're in chaos: not in historical, alphabetical or generic order.

'Don't you just love the sound of a needle dropping on a 78, darling?' she asked as she hovered the arm of the record player over a specific groove in the vinyl. 'Deee-vine!' she yelped as the static of vinyl and needle combined and produced the voice of Judy Garland singing *The Man Who Got Away*.

I began to tell her that this is one of my favourite live performances, but Sally hushed me and took my hand to dance slowly around the room. I say dance, but it felt as if this girl was more in need of a hug. Who am I to ration hugs when I get them free and plentiful from a bisexual married man?

We danced, drank, watched Dr Who and, in the small hours of the morning, we bounced around on an orange space hopper until a little bit of sick came up in my mouth. Oh, how we laughed when I fell off. Proper, side-splitting, head aching laughter. Adulthood never seemed so fun. After all, what's the point of being an adult if you can't be childish now and then?

I think I may be more than just a little tipsy.

Goodnight.

Sunday 16th May

That damn ash cloud is back, looming over Northern Ireland like an invisible force-field repelling all commuters. Their airspace has been closed again. The situation is described as 'fluid' and could cause problems for the south of England tomorrow. At least this time I'm not waiting for a compulsive liar to return to take home a frustrated cat from a Prada-clad cell.

Speaking of my cat, he seems to be quite content for now. He's taken to wandering around the hall as, when I'm home, I leave my door ajar for him to roam freely. In the early morning and evenings, after being fed, he tends to sit on the draining board and eye up the birds who chirp away in the huge Rowan tree that almost touches the fire escape. The poor things are blissfully unaware of the predator that's just moved into their neighbourhood. He rests well on the bed beside me at night, just in the nook behind the bend of my knees as I lay on my side. Most of all, he's stopped talking to me in my sleep, which either means he's settling in, or my imagination is calming down at last.

Monday 17th May

The veil has closed in on the U.K., the no-fly zone is back in place, and I've served several angry tourists today who haven't tipped as they're fast running out of patience and pounds sterling.

Tuesday 18th May

The U.K. is back to normal. Massive chunks of metal and steel filled with aviation fuel are travelling at high speed over our heads once more. Putting it that way, I'm not so sure that's such a good thing.

Wednesday 19th May

Someone has left lovely wet wipes in the loo today. I suspect Molasses is responsible for looking after my bum. She is the perfect landlady: never seen or heard, and yet keeps the place clean and manages to look after the small things in life, such as my sphincter.

Thursday 20th May

Tried to arrange a hookup with Alistair today but got knocked back. I'm feeling weird and emotional suddenly. What's wrong with me?

Friday 21st May

Serving in the café brings all kinds of unexpected delights. A stacked Spanish guy – mid-forties, dark brown hair and goatee beard (both with a sprinkling of grey), and killer biceps – cruised me for the whole of his Brown Stew Chicken before asking me out on a date. I would've said yes immediately, but felt a weird obligation to run it past Alistair before I accepted, even though we are most definitely not an item (but the lingering hugs and passionate kisses after sex are confusing me). After much consideration and sexual tennis, I did neither. Instead, I thanked the Spanish hunk and, as I slipped him his bill, said, 'Sorry, but I'm not looking for anything serious right now. Thanks.' A total lie.

When he left, Sally called me over and said, 'He must've liked you a lot, boyo. Just look at this tip; a whole twenty pounds. If you don't want him, I'll shag him!' she joked as she stuffed the brown note into the pocket of my pouch. I suspect she would, being an almost-prostitute already. The line she treads is as thin as a threadbare G-string.

Saturday 22nd May

Another post-it note, but this time attached to the cistern and typed in bold, declaring:

'Whoever has stolen my wet-wipes,
replace what you've used
by next week!!!!!!!!!!!'

Oops! That'll be me! Is this person serious? Do they actually expect me to know the exact quota I've used over the past few days? I feel the need to leave a note telling this idiot to stop using up all the exclamation marks. I mentioned it to Sally as we were getting ready for a night of cocktail-inspired merriment.

She cringed, 'Oh, that'll be Gwen from Room 3. Our uptight-never-been-kissed-never-mind-shagged-office-temp-and-unfriendly neighbour. Haven't you run into her yet? And I do mean to say, there will be a run-in when you meet her. She always has a face like a well-spanked ass.'

'No.'

'Oh, you are in for a memorable experience. She's severe, to say the least. The most cantankerous bitch I've met in my entire life. And you know me, I get on with everyone, sweet-cheeks.'

I nodded in agreement but found her last comment challenging to support with any conviction: if she could just work on being a tiny bit more empathetic to customers, my opinion would change. 'Great,' I sighed, 'I've pissed off probably the crabbiest person in the world.'

Sally adjusted the strategically placed locks of hair protruding from her purple beret in the sunburst mirror of the hall and laughed, 'Oh, don't give it a second thought, I've been using them too. That and her nail clippers.' She tightened the belt of her raincoat that hid a multitude of sins, 'Leave anything out in this place and it's a free-for-all, darling. She should've learned this small detail by now. She's been here for almost a year. A whole year I've had to listen to her playing that damn cello.'

'Cello? I thought you said she was an office temp.'

Sally laughed, checking her teeth in the mirror for any unwanted additions, 'She's a musician. Sorry, I should say, a struggling musician. Hasn't got a hope in hell. For performance, one really needs the ability to perform. She has all the creativity of a tin opener: stick blade in, twist, cut metal, open tin, slop out food.'

'I think I'll replace them, just to keep the peace.'

'Suit yourself, Andy-darling. But you know you're as soft and wet as those butt-wipes. You need to harden up. You won't get anywhere in life without being a cold and calculating bitch like me.'

'Seems like too much effort.'

'Well, when you need a mentor, I'm here.' She spun around and smiled at me excitedly, 'Okay, are we ready to cause a commotion uptown?'

We were off.

******

Our night on the town had one goal, and one goal alone: to get drunk. No, in fact, become so inebriated that we'd be glued to a stool in some bar that we'd randomly stumble on in the pissing rain. Within the hour, and several martinis later, we were well on the way to achieving our objective. I was drunk and more relaxed around my new neighbour, so I plucked up the courage to ask my drinking buddy, 'Have you ever been married, Ms Knowles?'

Enigmatically she replied, 'Does Sally Knowles look like the marrying kinda gal?' Then she whispered in my ear, 'I was once, but I killed him and buried him under a plum tree at the bottom of the garden. He gave me such lovely plums.' I must've looked stunned as Sally slapped me on the shoulder and added, 'Just kidding, darling.' And then, less reassuringly, 'It wasn't a plum tree; it was a pear tree.' Then she laughed and threw her head back. 'Bartender, more!' she cried. 'We want to become drunk and disorderly and have our arses felt by perfect strangers.'

She was joking, right? About the murder thing. I hoped so. Frivolous talk high on booze, I assured myself. The night moved on, and it all became a mess of alcohol, dancing feet and the Great Sally Show. But now I'm home, alone and slightly sober, I wonder if she really was joking.

Sunday 23rd May
Hangover number ... oh, who cares. I have a hangover. That's all.

Monday 24th May
A busy shift in the café was interrupted by a text from Alistair, 'Wanna meet? We don't have to have sex, if you don't want, a chat would be great.'

No, no, no! I don't want it to be anything other than sex. I want it to be plain and simple lust. Wham-bam-thank-you-man. Cum and go. That kinda thing. This is not good. That handsome stud spins my head. That handsome, sexy, kissable, oh-so-kind and huggable stud.

I haven't replied. Molasses caught me chanting in the cellar, 'He's attached, enough is enough.' Which, when she asked what I was doing, meant I had to cover my tracks by pretending I'd been in full, unabashed flow of *No More Tears (Enough is Enough)* by Barbra Streisand and Donna Summer. I continued to sing it, despite my best efforts, badly. The dancing wasn't necessary, but I couldn't stop once I'd started. I felt the more conviction I gave it, the more convincing it would become. Unfortunately, my vocal and cavorting capabilities lack confidence under a disbelieving, scrupulous eye. I felt a fool. Now I know how talentless hopefuls feel on the X-Factor.

Tuesday 25th May
A new post-it, this time on the lavvy lid for unavoidability:

'You have less than four days
to return the wet-wipes, thief!!!!'

This is way beyond anal.

Speaking of which, Alistair has been persistent with his requests for coffee and chat. However, work keeps me busy and distracted. I just can't. It's too soon after Thomas. Conversation is out. Sex is out. I can't even see him as a friend. God, I want him so bad! No! Stop it! Sweep him under the proverbial rug, ignore and move on, that's the answer.

11 p.m. I've just had a moment over Alistair's muscled, hairy, toned calves. I'm spent and disappointed in myself, but at least it's only between my right hand and me, and I'll sleep well.

Wednesday 26th May

8 p.m. Damn it! An evening off and 323 Leith Walk is a ghost town. Even the Colonel is ignoring me; he's stalking Sally's door ... traitor!

9.30 p.m. I've scoured the inside of the Baby Belling (disgusting), mustered up four ramekins of crème brûlée and put them in the very vocal fridge to cool. I've achieved what I thought was the impossible: home baking in a tiny electric stove, and yet I'm not satisfied.

10.10 p.m. I may be going stir crazy. Three of the ramekins are now empty, the contents of which are being attacked by the acid of my gut as I write. One remains for a special friend who may appreciate it.

10.33 p.m. I've plucked four hairs from the top of my right ear and four from the left (one thick and brown). I am now symmetrical in my ear hair growth and destined to become Chewbacca by the time I'm forty.

10.46 p.m. The carpet in here has a join, close to the far end of the room, just before the kitchen linoleum. I've never noticed this before. It's all of four inches in width. Why such a need? My room is smaller than the average roll of carpet. Funny the things you notice as you brush your teeth. Bedtime.

11.10 p.m. Can't sleep. I'll try relaxation therapy. I have a CD somewhere.

11.40 p.m. I can't find the damn relaxation CD and have become stressed trying to look for it. I've arranged my music collection alphabetically. Two of my ABBA cases are empty, lost in Thomas' car, I imagine. I remember taking them with us on a trip to Blackpool last summer. I'm irritated now and wide awake.

11.50 p.m. I've agreed to meet Alistair for a drink in Bar Boda. However, for the sake of judgement on my strength of character and determination, *he* texted *me,* and even then I lasted at least four whole minutes before my twitchy thumb bounced across the screen in reply. Yes, four full minutes! I would typically have only lasted four whole seconds. You can't say this boy isn't improving on this rules of dating malarkey. If I was dating, which I am most definitely not. It's just a beer with a fuck-buddy.

Thursday 27th May

9 a.m. Warm skin, why do you fool me so? Hugs, why do you saturate my flesh and nuzzle my soul, giving me hope? Kind words, why do you fall on my emotionally starved ears and nourish my malnourished heart? Alistair, you spoon me until dawn, and I ache not a jot. Not an arm or leg becomes numb. You hold me perfectly. Numbness. How could I possibly be numb to you?

Your wife is away. Convenient. Far too tempting for a boy who's always wondered what it would be like to share the sweet surrender of naked slumber with you. To wake with you and see your handsome face smile back at me was a moment of joy. I asked you to stay the night. My bad. I'd hoped you'd find some excuse and say no, and yet at the very same time, I'd hoped you'd say yes. These ambitions were one and the same, intertwined and at odds. But how can a man like you resist intimacy and a perfectly baked crème brûlée? Nothing good can come of this, I know that, but the second you said yes my mind was already in bed with yours. I love the sound of your voice close to my ear as we share the ticking of the clock, your breath on the back of my neck and the smell of you on my skin after you leave.

The bedsits are full, busy and noisy. And now, finally, I'm at peace.

Friday 28th May

Café Jamaica ran out of champagne by 9.30 p.m. due to a cartload of businessmen descending on us like a swarm of pinstriped beetles from a conference at the top floor of the Omni Centre. I was hurriedly sent to *Broughton Bin-ends* only to find it shut. No cheery Christina to chat to on my ten-minute skive. I used up the next thirty minutes trying to find a nearby shop that sold alcohol before licensing laws caught up with me.

I arrived back with a bag full of clanking bottles and sweat on my brow from what felt like a ten-mile hike. My hair had flopped in the rain and, as my luck would have it, the Spanish hunk from last week had arrived in my absence and taken up residence next to the bar. I became a complete fool, tripping over my words as I read the specials to him while clumsily attempting to lick and flick my hair back into some kind of style – as it turns out, a sachet of lube can be just as good as any hair gel for an emergency hair-do situation (Sally's idea).

'If you pull him, your head can double as a self-serving lube dispenser, sweetie,' cracked Sally.

Alas, my allure must be fading as my age flourishes. It's only the hair that's lubed tonight. Really though, why should I care? I don't really want a relationship. And besides, what I have with Alistair will do me just fine for now: a non-fuck-buddy-non-relationship.

Saturday 29th May

Mum called me up extremely upset late tonight with the vocal quiver she gets when in emotional turmoil. I assumed something was wrong with Dad immediately.

'Dennis Hopper has died of prostate cancer, Andy,' she vibrated down the line. 'He was the man that convinced me to jump on the back of your dad's old Harley back in 1969 thanks to *Easy Rider*. Burnt my high heels on his exhaust, but it was well worth it.'

Did she really think I knew or cared who Dennis Hopper was?

She continued, 'Your father used to look like him in the right light. At times I used to get him to wear the gear for me ...'

TMI! I grabbed some paper and crumpled it next to the microphone in an attempt to mimic static down the line and hung up. She tried to call back twice, but I ignored it. Why, in their sixties, do my parents feel the need to provide me with their sexual history?

'It's a sign that both of them are missing intimacy, and neither of your dysfunctional parents is willing to talk about it,' explained Sally, waitress and unqualified sex counsellor. She may be right.

In other news: I must decide on a regular day to do laundry. It's so unsightly having your socks spilling out in the same room you butter your crumpets. I must make the effort tomorrow and cart my mouldy clothes over the road to the laundrette. I'm not keen on the woman that runs the place; she looks like she's sucked lemons all her life and reeks of cheese and onion crisps. I've lost touch with my whiter-than-whites. The homemaker in me died the day my love-life crumbled to dust. How I miss seeing my dazzling sheets flapping around in the sunshine and the smell of *Spring Fresh* wafting through our kitchen door. These days it's a twenty-two-minute wash, fifteen-minute tumble-dry and a quick run up our stair with my linen haphazardly crammed into an IKEA bag. Oh, how far this Domestic God has fallen.

Sunday 30th May

I guess you could say I was pretty brave knocking on Gwen's door to hand over a gift-wrapped packet of ass-wipes and a bottle of wine. She's a woman who could be pretty, if she didn't have two strips of dark hair across her face: a moustache and a monobrow. This is exaggerated by the sleek scraping of hair into a firmly controlled bun, which has been dyed a shade of brown that's too dark for her pallid complexion. I felt like grabbing a Dulux colour chart and dishing out a few tips from the silk selection. Her pallor is best described as 'Funeral Home'. Her lips are thin to the point of nonexistent, exaggerating the little bits of biscuit in each corner, and her eyes are such a pale green that on any other face they'd be beautiful, but on her, they seem to give the impression she's not of this world. Her ice-like eyes darted down towards the wet-wipes and her neck flushed, showing some kind of humanoid characteristic that reassured me she wasn't entirely a malevolent alien.

'So, you're the culprit,' she snapped in a thick German accent. I think she's around 35, but it's hard to tell someone's age when their face falls naturally into a thunderclap.

I explained, 'I'm so sorry for using your lovely wipes – it wasn't just me I hasten to add – but in the spirit of goodwill, I've decided to return more than I've used with a nice bottle of wine. A fresh start?' My eyebrows twitched in anticipation.

Gwen sucked air through her teeth and stated plainly, 'I don't drink alcohol, Mr ...?'

'Andy. My friends call me, Andy,' I said, hand and olive branch extended.

'My friends call me Gwen, but to you, I'm Ms Graumann.' Olive branch firmly slapped back in my face. She swiped the wet wipes out of my hand.

'Look, I'm sorry we got off on the wrong foot. I want to make amends. We all have to get on here, I think,' I quickly added as she began to close the door.

'Not me, I keep myself to myself, and that's just fine. Now, if you don't mind, I have to be ready to leave here at ten-twenty, to catch my bus at ten-thirty-six, for a rehearsal at eleven-ten. Good day, Mr Angus. Don't bother me again, I'm much too busy for drum-hum small-talk.'

The door shut in my face.

'It's *hum*-drum. And you're doing nothing for the stereotype!' I yelled bravely. I looked at the bottle of wine and thought, *Och well, all is not lost, I'll share it with Sally tonight.*

Just then, the door swung open again, and the bottle was ripped from my hand with, 'On second thoughts, I'll take it. I could use cheap wine such as this for *cocking*.' The door slammed shut.

I feel as close to her as I would Eva Braun.

Monday 31st May

The first of June is almost upon us. Nearly halfway through the year. It doesn't seem that long ago I was monogamous, moral, balancing household bills and poisoning my Aunt at New Year. How things have changed. Today I shared a picnic with a married man and paid for nothing. He also bought my groceries on the way home and dropped me at my door. I can see how easy it is to slot into the category of 'The Other Woman'. I wonder if he is as generous to his wife?

This thought hit me just as I was picking my bags out of the boot of his car and, without thinking, I asked him, 'What's your wife's name?'

He looked guilty and said, 'Andy, my handsome man, don't make it any more complicated than it needs to be, eh?'

I shouldn't force it, I guess. Some secrets are best kept stuffed in the back of that closet he seems determined to hide in. However, today it's summer, and the air smells of nectar.

Tuesday 1st June

Okay, from now on, Tuesday is laundry day. I was up early enough to wash and dry three loads of smelly, fusty fabrics without a hitch. Although I felt a bit awkward when I caught a whiff of the assorted spunk rags I've used over the past few weeks as I stuffed them ashamedly into the drum. Cheese & Onion woman was hovering over my shoulder at the time, offering detailed instructions on the simple usage of a dryer named *Speed Queen* (no, really, it's an actual brand).

I must remember to use only white towels to mop up from now on and not what's close to hand: dark coloured tee-shirts do not hide the milkiness at all. I felt such a whore when I peeled them apart. I unravelled two towels, two tee-shirts and one pair of blue pants. What is wrong with me? I'm thirty-five, having sex regularly and yet masturbating more than a chorister at a Catholic cathedral. I could be on the sloppy road to sex addiction.

- *Note to Self:* buy magazines to drive away the tedium of a busy and yet uninspiring laundromat.
- *Other Note to Self:* NOT soft porn, i.e., Men's Health Magazine with all the topless, fit, pouting models.

Wednesday 2nd June

Who needs soft porn when Alistair is around? Mercy, mercy me!

Thursday 3rd June

Christina is back from a wine-tasting week in Brazil. How I've missed her Spanish charms. Walking into her shop is like stepping out on a glorious vista coated in lavender that relaxes the mind as palm trees gently sway in a calming breeze. Her free samples of wine help too, if I'm honest. I'll be seeing more of her these days, now that Molasses has elected her as our primary supplier of all things inebriating.

'I've offered her a special rate,' said Christina as I sipped on a New World red she was keen for me to taste.

'It's delicious,' I said, and before I knew it, she thrust a bottle into my hand.

'Take this for yourself, my friend. A special offer for a special man.'

I'm overawed. We've only shared a few brief moments, and already she thinks of me as a friend. I need a normal person in my life like her.

Friday 4th June

The Spanish hunk was back in Café Jamaica this evening. Great fortune this time that I wasn't burdened with liquids like a Middle Eastern donkey, nor was I drenched by persecuting rain clouds or sweating like a glass blower's arse. I find his looks captivating. I've always had a crush on dark-haired chaps with foreign accents.

He asked me in deep, sultry tones that made me drool, 'Would you like to come along to the opening of my new exhibit down Leith on Sunday?'

'Wow! You're an artist?' I said, a little taken aback by my apparent enthusiasm. However, I'm always impressed by any out of the ordinary career paths people take. It adds on 10% sex-factor for me. Far more interesting than a dentist or an accountant. 'Can I bring a friend?' I asked, in need of some moral support.

'Of course, you can, handsome.'

I blushed.

'It's at 8 p.m. Is that okay?'

'That's more than okay. It's super-duper-okey-dokey!' I said, making a fool of myself while having minor palpitations. He gave me his flyer and smiled kindly. I left his table with what can only be described as a 'chubby'. What is wrong with me? I'm a walking, talking tube of testosterone.

On my travels, I mentioned to Christina, 'I've a sort-of date with a handsome Spanish lad,' expecting some kind of enthusiasm.

But she said, 'Be careful, all men from my country are stunted emotionally, hung-up sexually and favour their mothers over anyone else. This is why I married a Brit.'

I laughed and said, 'I'm just looking for a bit of fun, nothing more. Besides, British men are well known for being slobs and reserved.'

'You mean you are going to have sex on the first date?' she asked, stunned.

I immediately felt guilty and lied, 'No, of course not,' and hurried out the shop as fast as possible when weighed down by two boxes of Malbec. I admire her strength in morals in this day and age. I'd admire them more if they didn't make me feel such a slut. Anyway, it's easy to have morals when you are monogamous and married.

Saturday 5th June

1 a.m. Awake, waiting on Sally returning from bruising her hips on metal fashioned into rods and wondering if I should just skip the gallery/Spanish guy scenario tomorrow. I feel this weird obligation towards Alistair. I know he hasn't mentioned commitment and he's most definitely not the most committed guy in the world, but boy, it feels like so much more when he holds me. Am I misreading pity hugs for romance? Or am I just, as Steve used to say, 'Dick-struck'?

2.25 a.m.

'Really? You're passing up the chance of a night in the company of interesting and artistic individuals, not to forget, darling, a handsome, creative guy, for a cheating, closeted married man who pops in and out of your life and uses your bed as casually as he uses a parking space in a multi-storey carpark?'

With Sally putting it like that, I'd no option but to agree it would be healthier to take a trip down Leith on Sunday than spend a whole day waiting on Alistair's call. 'You can be very cutting at times, Sally Knowles,' I nipped back, a little bruised by her directness.

'So would you be if you'd been pawed by lecherous hands for several hours as crisp £20 notes are stuffed down your G-string, all the while maintaining a happy, flirtatious air while risking paper-cuts in the most inconvenient of places. I feel like I've been raped by Sir Walter Scott repeatedly.'

'Ouch!'

'Yes, you should see the accident book at work, it makes for interesting reading, but I digress. I'll happily escort you on Sunday if you need a friend to lean on. Besides, it will maybe break this fascination you have for the married businessman.'

'Okay, decision made. Viewing several walls covered in artwork created by a very handsome Spaniard wins hands down against moping around my own sparse partitions listening to Tori Amos and wallowing in self-pity.' A smile spread across my face, 'And it's heartwarming to know that you have my best interests at heart.'

'Yes, I do, darling,' she said, patting me on the head. 'You did say there will be free wine, didn't you?'

Sunday 6th June

Jesus (no, that really is his name) is an accomplished artist with several thousand followers on Twitter and Facebook. His latest exhibit, *TORSiON*, deals with the conflicts of the metrosexual man in the modern-day and the suffering that's caused by society's expectation to man-up while being sensitive to their own – and others' – needs. *TORSiON* (lower case 'i' to represent the twisting of the spermatic cord on which a man's testicle is suspended and receives its blood supply from) represents the emotional barrier society's built, restricting the free flow of testosterone and the emasculation of men. Therefore limiting the surge of natural machismo that needs to be vented to ensure a happy, balanced life as a breadwinner, head of household or father. It's pretty bleak viewing if I'm honest. Full of large canvases filled with dark shapes and jagged edges that made no sense to me but seemed to mesmerise Sally. I spent most of the night trying to forget about any kind of distressing torsion and instead focussed on how big Jesus' balls might be (now there's a sentence I never thought I'd write as a Catholic schoolboy).

He was busy, but at the same time very attentive to my needs, topping my glass at every given moment and guiding me with supportive hugs as he introduced me to people who are way above my social standing. He's the perfect gentleman, even complimenting Sally on her good looks and charming personality several times, which she lapped up. I swear she was flirting with him more than was comfortable for anyone there. It was like watching a dragged-up Dick Emery the number of times she threw her head back in laughter and yelped, 'Oh, Jesus, you are awful!' while patting him on his powerful shoulders.

One posh lady asked me what my chosen career path was and, when I told her I waited on tables, she replied, 'How very noble of you to elect to do charity work. Is it in one of those soup-kitchens?' I immediately suspected she was a pensioned Yummy Mummy.

Sally butt in, 'No, it's a job we do to keep the wolf from the door of our charming bedsits. At Café Jamaica? Just next to the wine and sex shop off Broughton Street.' She then continued to clarify, in a somewhat drunken and frankly unnecessary fashion, 'That's not a wine *and* sex shop, you understand, my fair lady. The two establishments are very much separated by the café. A wine merchant, and a sex emporium, if you please.' She laughed loudly and continued with her rambling, 'However, a wine-slash-sex-shop could be highly successful. Who knows? It could be called *Vino Vibrators*.' More ostentatious laughter from she, more cringing from me, and then I swiftly swept Sally away from public view in a gentle, gracious motion towards a steaming mug of thick black coffee.

Despite this minor dent, a car crash was avoided. I'm seeing Jesus on Tuesday night for a few drinks in *The Street*. I'm anxious for a second date as, by my estimations, Jesus has a sizeable set of balls on him. They were positively parted and bulging down either side of the seam of his crotch every time he sat down.

I kissed him goodbye quickly and was all of a flutter as I poured a merry Sally and my chubby into a taxi just before pumpkin hour. Second date achieved, on which I plan to check for a torsion thoroughly. Sex on a second date does not equal slutty behaviour, surely? I won't tell Christina.

Monday 7th June

8 a.m. Woken by a text from Alistair:

'Howzit, buddy? U been behaving?
Fancy a fuck & hug?'

I ignored it. I don't want to lie.

11 p.m I've just shared the most uncomfortable spiral staircase ascent with Gwen as she carried a massive cello case on her back. Uncomfortable as in the conversation, not the cello case. I was lugging two bags of laundry as well (Monday is laundry day this week as Tuesday is now date night). I've had more natural conversations recently at the clap clinic, and wisdom teeth extracted with less blood and spit.

'Ah, you play the cello?' I panted as I caught up with her, aiming to start some friendly chat.

'No, I am carrying a gigantic machine gun, what do you think?' she snapped, looking rather flushed. Even low on oxygen and at the point of collapse she's bitter and sarcastic. I wanted to poke her in the shoulder with my finger and watch her topple from our landing until she crashed in a heap of wood, strings and grey polyester, but instead, I opened the door for her and let her pass without even a hint of a thank you on her part. I imagine her interpretation of any musical score will be as flat as the page it's written on. The cold, unfeeling, socially challenged bitch.

Tuesday 8th June

I was itching to finish my shift early this evening, but Sally was later than a Virgin train to Birmingham New Street. Her flimsy excuse was a medical appointment ran late. At 6.30 p.m.? Substitute *appointment* with *client* and I think I'd have a clearer picture.

Molasses' watchful eye kept me covering the wench's tables while she flounced around for a further ten minutes with her hair and makeup. Molasses' vision is very selective when it comes to Sally Knowles. That girl can get away with murder and leave the body decaying in the middle of the café for weeks, and she wouldn't raise an eyebrow. I enjoy Sally as a friend but struggle to enjoy the woman as a colleague.

Despite this unnecessary stress, it's 8.30 p.m., and I'm dressed and ready to meet Jesus for date night number two. Dressed to a point as I'm going commando. I want my balls to feel free and easy to grasp at any given moment. It feels quite thrilling and risky. What next? White water rafting?

Wednesday 9th June

Just once, *once*, I want to meet an available, handsome, single gent who isn't screwed up in some way. Oh, it was all going so well. We talked. He held my hand over the table. I learned more about him and liked what I heard. He seemed to like me. We edged closer. He kissed me with those fantastic, juicy lips. We edged closer still. He pressed his crotch against my thigh. We pretty much left the bar after four flexes of his shaft and were at his place after a ten-minute taxi ride.

The sex started halfway up the stairway to his flat. We were half-naked by the time we tumbled in his door. He threw me on the bed and stripped my lower half, thrilled to see I was going commando, which was very apparent once we were both completely bare.

But then something shifted in the universe, and his formerly proud manhood whimpered and died. After ten minutes of his flaccid willy flopping around the bed, he slumped onto his side and said, 'I'm so sorry, Andy.'

'Don't worry about it,' I said, in an attempt to comfort him, but in reality, I was desperate for him to get hard so that I could finish my night off with a bang.

'Maybe if I suck you, it'll help. I love doing that,' he assured me.

Not too much of a hardship, I joked to myself. He had the power of a Dyson vacuum cleaner, and I would've enjoyed the moment had I not glanced at his willy and found it was even less excited than ever. A button mushroom. What was so awful about me that he couldn't get it up? Did I smell? Have I really gained that much weight that it repulses event the most blue-balled of men once I'm naked? Is Tony right, am I lardy and unattractive?

'Is everything okay?' I asked, after a further five minutes of flaccidity.

'I'm sorry, Andy,' he apologised, almost in tears. 'I've been having problems ever since ... ever since ...' he was crying now.

Oh, God. Not the ugly crying sex thing!

'... ever since my mother died six months ago, I haven't been able to focus properly on anything.'

Six months? That takes us back to Christmas, I thought as I lay by his side and comforted Jesus with gentle strokes of his thick curly hair. It seems I wasn't the only person to have an awful festive period.

'I'm sorry to hear that. Was it sudden?' I asked.

'No, cancer. She was sick for months. She tried chemotherapy, but nothing worked. She was very ill. I miss her terribly. She was my mother and closest friend.'

I had no words. I felt judgemental. And the sex didn't really matter. I was beginning to understand the magnitude of his grief when he made it more transparent. 'I still have the nightdress she died in. I sleep with it under my pillow. It keeps her close to me and helps me rest.'

Okay, a little bit freaky! I felt my gaze purposefully avoid the pillows askew at the top of the bed.

'She wore it for a day or so. We didn't want to move her as she was in such pain. It still smells of her,' he continued. I was just dealing with this small detail when he reached under the pillow and, from beneath the case, pulled out a red cotton nightdress with yellow sunflowers dotted all over it. I began to freak out internally. I had to keep calm and treat him like he wasn't pulling the weirdest night of my life out of the bag, therefore, if he were crazy, I'd stand a chance of getting out in one piece. 'Sunflowers were her favourite,' he continued eulogising. 'She was a wonderful woman. Kind to everyone.' Then he did something that made even my stubbly pubes stand on end: he raised the dead woman's nightdress towards his face and inhaled deeply. 'I can still smell her on it as if she was in this room.'

'Okay, Jesus,' I croaked as I placed my hands gently on his forearms and lowered the nighty away from his face, afraid to defile the sacred shroud, 'I think we should tuck Mummy away, put on our clothes and have a nice cup of tea. Would you like that? Tea in the kitchen?' *Or maybe away from sharp objects, best make tea and head to the lounge.* 'Or the lounge? Yes, the comfy, warm, safe lounge. Maybe without boiling hot water. Maybe without the need to enter the kitchen at all. Perhaps a soda? Do you have a drinks cabinet in the lounge?' I stumbled over my words and made haste to get dressed.

The poor guy's obviously still in mourning. It was at least half an hour of counselling over warm tonic water before I called myself a cab and zipped out the door. I waited outside for it to arrive even though it was pouring down. I would've stood in the middle of Seafield sewage works if it meant I was waiting outside his flat.

I feel for him, I really do, but this has tarnished the relationship a little. Lack of erection aside, having your date's mother in bed with you as you fool around for the first time isn't an easy thing to get over. Would she be hanging around every time we had sex or settled down to sleep? Oh, God! I hope he doesn't wear the bloody thing every now and then. He could turn into a modern-day Norman Bates if he carries on with this ritual.

The taxi arrived, the driver checked my destination, and I said, '323 Leith Walk; home.' I never wanted my own bed or my own company so much. I slept naked, as I've gone off nightwear. I slept soundly with the Colonel's reassuring purr at my feet. I hadn't considered when Christina said Spanish men turn to their mother's regularly for reassurance, that it could go beyond the grave.

Thursday 10th June

'R u ok?' was the first text through this morning from Jesus. Ignore, swipe and delete. By late servings at Café Jamaica, I'd the same text, word-for-word, from Alistair. Ignore, swipe, delete. Regular meets with Alistair are becoming complicated, but then so are one night stands. I thought life was tricky back at Little Troll Cottage. How wrong I was. The most complicated part of my life back then was flossing.

Friday 11th June

'Burlesque, darling! Isn't it simply outrageous?' squeaked Sally as she hopped up and down at the bar, almost tipping a tray of Sour Sop. She was referring to an 'interview' she has on Tuesday at *Titty Ha-Ha's*, an exclusive Burlesque/Comedy club at The Shore in Leith.

I asked, 'What's involved at an interview at *Titty Ha-Ha's*?' Apparently, it's an actual 30-minute interview, a presentation on the history of Burlesque and a performance on stage to a song of Sally's choice. There's far more to stripping than I anticipated.

'I have three days to find a theme, costume, music and routine, and then I can finally leave that dive off Lothian Road once and for all. Maybe go professional and jack in waitressing too,' she said. 'Andy, sweetness, I need your help.'

I'm a sucker for a happy person. 'Of course, I'll help,' I said, unaware of what would be involved.

'Super,' she yelped. 'You can be my willing test audience-slash-victim.'

Oh, dear.

Saturday 12th June

5 a.m. My anxiety dream is back. I've just woken to the high-energy beats of *(I Lost My Heart to a) Starship Trooper* echoing through my head like an empty 70s disco hall. This time it showcased Sally, Jesus, the dentist and Alistair. Sally was executing a mad, fast-forwarded disco version of a burlesque strip, the boys were strutting their stuff on roller-skates and wafting silk caftans while orbiting her. I was serving drinks around the hall as I watched, enviously excluded from proceedings. A slave for the night.

As the song finished, Molasses took the mic and, catching sight of me, declared, 'Good Lord! Look at that boy. He thinks he can carry off a G-string with those sugar-lump hips!'

After which I looked down to see I was wearing a red sequinned thong and ruby-red slippers. Said hips were spilling out over the strained elastic. The audience pointed and laughed as I struggled to hide behind a velvet curtain, from which Tony appeared holding a ventriloquist dummy that was a twisted caricature of Ryan. 'Oh dear,' spat Tony. 'Look at the travesty that is Andy Angus, Sugar-lump Hips!'

The Ryan dummy mimicked this and chanted, 'Sugar-lump Hips! Sugar-lump Hips! Nobody loves a Sugar-lump Hips! Nobody ever could!' The crowd began to slow-clap, encouraged by Molasses, and chanted along with dummy Ryan.

All exits were blocked by people standing to clap a jeer. I closed my eyes and clicked my heels together. I sat bolt upright when I woke in a cold sweat, muttering the words, 'There's no place like home.'

What the hell does all of this nonsense mean?

11 a.m. I think I've trust issues regarding my newfound buddies, especially Alistair. A man committing infidelity isn't the most principled of people to be falling for. But why would Molasses be so cruel in my dream? She's the kindest person I've ever met. Maybe I fear her deception the most. She's become like a second mother to me. One that doesn't mind me staying out late at night and having sex with random men.

11.45 p.m. Home from work and a deluge of texts from Alistair. Ignore, swipe, delete. The truth is, I feel guilty, but I shouldn't feel guilty about going on a failed date with a mourning Spanish artist, should I? Especially as Alistair is married. Especially as the willy was flaccid. Especially as we haven't mentioned commitment. Is it possible to remotely court the notion of commitment when one half of the – whatever we are – is cheating on his wife? However, it would be great to know where we stand for safety and sanity issues. I'm an emotional yo-yo. I've cleaned my room top to bottom and organised my vast Doctor Who Magazine collection by issue number to try and tire myself out.

Sunday 13th June

Day one of dedication to shifting the blubber. Back at the gym determined to get a six-pack like Jason Statham. Even just one little ab like Jason Statham would keep me happy. Nash was there training some girl. I'm thoroughly disappointed that he's shaved his legs for a fitness model competition. They're so smooth and shiny I'd swear he's moisturising them too. Justin Bieber's bum has more hair. It's very off-putting, muscled though they still are.

I reluctantly asked Sally between serving greasy hangover cures at the café if she needed my help shopping for a costume, secretly hoping she'd say no. It's getting awfully close to interview day. She replied as she placed the wrong order at the wrong table and sauntered casually away, 'Oh, darling, I already have the gown. I only need you to rate my routine tomorrow.'

I hastily switched her miss-fired food to the correct table and half-heartedly said, 'Oh, good. I can't wait.'

I'd caught sight of her practising her routine in her camel-toed leotard in one of the dance studios at the gym. I'm now filled with dread. I'm not used to all this tit being flaunted. I once caught sight of my mother's wrinkled boobs; it put me right off the buttered crumpets I was having for breakfast. I'll be strong and insist that one performance will suffice, or else, by the end of the week, I'll be as sick of tit and fanny as a retired midwife.

Monday 14th June

Dress Rehearsal Day

The routine kicks off with Sally dressed as a 1950's housewife, in a floral housecoat, rollers and headscarf, as she parades around to *Whistle While You Work* and produces a collection of cleaning items from various nooks and crannies about her person. The final reveal is the lady clad in a homemade loin-cloth (made with J-cloths) and two oven scourers attached to her nipples in some way that defies gravity but may not defy chaffing. I was exposed to Performances A & B but was interrupted, to my relief, before Performance C by the clanging of the old doorbell.

I was amazed to see it was a somewhat fraught Alistair. 'Have you been ignoring my texts?' he asked pointedly.

I was flabbergasted he was so concerned, but even more so when Stripper Knowles popped her head around the door and said, 'Ah! Are you Andy's standby shag? Perfect, another willing victim.' She seized him by the arm and tossed him on her bed. 'Sit there and give me your thoughts on this little routine, darling.'

I could see Alistair's eyes light up as Sally ran through Performance C. I felt a pang of jealousy if I'm honest. Once over, I clapped and gave the thumbs-up enthusiastically to escape speedily, and shifted Alistair to the relative comfort of my own room.

'Interesting friend you have there. Are your other mates as fit as her?' he asked, a bit too keenly for my liking.

This stirred me to say, 'Alistair, I haven't been in touch because I went on a date last week.'

There was silence from his side of the room and then, 'Ah, okay. I suppose you're a free agent. I can't really lay any claim over you.' He appeared a little hurt. 'Is he nice?'

'He was, yes.' I didn't go into detail about the nightdress misadventure, I simply added, 'But I don't want to see him again.'

'Ah, good. I mean, you can if you want to. You can see anyone you like.' And then, annoyingly, he repeated, 'You're a free agent after all. My strapping rugger stud looked boyish and hesitant for the first time. I was too. This was uncharted territory for both of us. Alistair got off the sofa and moved towards the door. 'I'd best go.'

I stepped in front of him and pressed my hands against his chest, 'Look, mister, what are we doing? Should I be faithful to you? Is there more going on between us than just shagging? Are you happy how it is? I feel there's more going on than both of us want to admit.'

He stared at me with a heavy weight behind his eyes, searching for the right answer. 'Andy, we can't be nothing more than fuck-buddies. I'm married. Am I more gay than straight? I don't know. I don't know if I'll ever know. It's impossible. I'm holding you back.'

Something inside me wanted to scream, 'But I bloody adore you! Nothing is impossible!' But I knew that would've pushed him into a corner. I fully understand he's not ready yet. He has to experiment and grow if he's to be sure this life is for him. And for that to happen, I have to step aside.

So there I stood, my hand on his racing heart, feeling it beat firmly and passionately for the last time and hearing myself say, 'You're right.' We were more naked and vulnerable than we'd ever been before, right from our very bones. There was no song and dance, no shouting, no drama. He just stepped out the door and closed it slowly but firmly behind him. He'd given me his answer. That's what I wanted. So why hasn't it made everything right?

Tuesday 15th June

It's been a drab, dull laundry day. I spent the morning staring into the repetitive cycle of a Swan washing machine while the population of Edinburgh passed by the windows, seemingly having a ball. The cheese and onion woman had to remind me twice that my machines had stopped. Even the smell of the new fabric softener (Sunshine Meadow) on my clothes couldn't cheer me up. There's no sunshine on Leith. I'm thoroughly fed-up.

I met Sally on the way back to my room and tried to offer some encouragement for her interview this evening, but cynicism oozed from my heart into my lungs and stifled the passion for producing positive words. She knew I was low.

'Alistair?' she asked, seconds before she left with her costume in a small light-blue suitcase.

'Yup.' I kept the acknowledgement short, barely able to breathe the word. It took all my energy not to cry.

'The big shit! I could murder him right now. All the damage he's doing.' She slapped a cloche hat on her short locks and picked up her case. 'We'll talk later. I've got to go, darling. Wish me luck!'

'Break a leg!' I hollered as she scurried excitedly out the door. I returned to my dreary bedsit with two bags of fresh laundry and a shit-load of loneliness. The Colonel was curled up next to my pillow. I ignored the pile of ironing and curled up next to him. My furry friend. My constant companion. My therapy.

Wednesday 16th June

I guess it didn't go well for Sally, I heard her throw open the front door at 3 a.m. and drunkenly shout, 'Fuck you all, you untalented, short-sighted bastards!' It echoed down the stairwell. She somehow managed to trip her way into her room to sob her heart out. For a few minutes, I lay awake and considered getting out of bed to reassure her, but I was on the early shift and honestly have no idea how to console her when she hits the bottle in a rage. She quietened down somewhat, probably in a drunken doze, and I drifted off again but was woken half an hour later by thudding noises from the cupboard through the wall. *Is this what it's like to be haunted?* I wondered as I lay there, quivering under the duvet. *This place is filled to the rafters with tormented souls in the dead of night.* Silence fell once more, but I spent the next half hour with my ears twitching at the slightest of sounds. Eventually, tiredness won over, and I dozed off.

Thursday 17th June

Oscar-winning filmmaker Danny Boyle and director Stephen Daldry have been chosen to organise the London 2012 Olympic Games opening ceremony. This has to be a recipe for disaster, surely? A mixture of *Shallow Grave, Trainspotting* and *Extremely Loud & Incredibly Close* does not make for a jolly time. There will be limbs exploding, injecting drug users and freaky ceiling crawling babies on high wires above the spectators' heads. And I thought the Olympic logo was bad enough. Disaster!

Friday 18th June

Gwen rapped on my door this morning and woke me at some ungodly hour. She was already suited and booted, and about to leave for work in her usual grey tones. The norm, apart from something else, something weird. Was that compassion in her eyes?

'Can I help you?' I asked her in a confused, lethargic state, wrapped in my duvet.

'I just wanted to let you know that your mother called the payphone last night. She asked that you call her back for a chat.'

Jeez! How did she get the number? 'A chat? My mother never just wants "a chat", there's always an agenda,' I said.

'Okay.' Gwen turned to leave, but stopped and faced me once again with even more compassion in her gaze. 'Also, I'm sorry for your losses. This year has been tough on you. I'll try to be kinder.' She attempted to give me three comforting pats on the head that just felt like mild physical abuse and left.

My bloody gossip of a mother will talk to anyone about my troubles, it seems. I'll kill her! I'm not calling her back at all!

Saturday 19th June

9 a.m. A knock at my door moments ago. Sally. 'Watcha, brotherfucker! Ready for the penultimate episode of Season Five of Doctor Who tonight?' she asked as if the past few days of her absence and her 3 a.m. drunken-drama had never happened.

'Sure,' I hesitated, 'are you okay?'

She smiled and unsteady grin, 'I'm super, sweetie. Why wouldn't I be?'

'Because I heard you didn't get the gig.'

'Oh, that little inconsequential matter?' she laughed as if it'd been a small blip in a sparkling career. 'Nothing to get upset about. So, my place? 5 p.m.? We're both on early shifts so we can make a big night of it and hit the bars later. We simply have to get you out on the market again. No more Mr Alistair breaking your heart. Onwards and upwards! See you then. I'll order pizza. Ciao, darling!'

Away she went, off for her long soak in the tub that often delays my morning rituals, and back to normal, it seems. I'm convinced she's on the edge of mild schizophrenia.

Sunday 20th June

By club closing time we were drunk, both still single (although it's impossible for Sally to find a man parading around gay bars with me as her fag-bangle), and drowning a portion of chips in salt at Café Piccante as the heavy dance music blared from the speakers that hang above the Formica tables. We shared the room with a bunch of drunken, screeching girls I call 'Hooch Whores'. Each one of them was in desperate need of a make-*under*. If we were drunk, they were most definitely on another level that bordered on stomach pumps and intravenous fluids.

I asked Sally, 'Where are you from, originally?' But her reply was as obscure as ever.

'Oh, around, you know,' she announced, dramatically waving a chip in the air before swallowing it whole and sucking the grease from her emerald nails while keeping her lipstick perfectly intact. 'Here and there, like the Scarlet Pimpernel, you know. Although, I like to think of myself more a scarlet lady, my darling.'

I snatched another chip from the box and could see, despite my blurry vision, a white pebble-dashing of salt that would dry up the hardiest of camel humps. 'But where exactly? Where have you been all this time? You didn't just hatch out of an egg,' I said as I shook the chip briskly and, due to its length and mass, it snapped in half and landed perfectly on a particularly gobby Hooch Whore's shoulder. There was momentary relief on our eardrums as everything paused under a multitude of gasps. Then their cawing turned towards us. All six of these Jagermeister bombers got up from their kebabs and assumed the position of mouthy Hooch Whores in attack formation around our table. They squawked at us like midnight seagulls dive-bombing hungrily towards a freshly laid pool of vomit.

Sally, quick as a flash, grabbed my arm, I grabbed the chips, and we were up and out the door quicker than you can say 'Deep Fried Mars Bar'. 'Keep your bangs on, sisterfucker,' yelled Sally as we scarpered out the door. 'Anyone would think you had a chip on your shoulder.' Cue riotous laughter from the chip shop staff. Cue the Hooch Whores chasing after us.

We laughed and sprinted until we lost the teenage-tribe down an alleyway (which wasn't difficult as they're still learning to run in heels). We finished our chips in a quiet spot by some old garages and bins brimming with trade waste. Sufficiently stuffed, Sally pulled a hanky from her handbag, dabbed it on her tongue and rubbed it against my greasy chin. It was spontaneous and caring and took us both by surprise. She stopped for a second, looking sheepish, finished the job quickly and popped it back in her bag.

'So, the past. Do you want the potted history of Sally Knowles?' she asked.

'No, it's fine. I'm just nosey. Well, maybe a little detail.'

'I went to a private all girl's school in the highlands; I'm an only child; Mother and Father live in Washington D.C. and never visit as I'm a huge disappointment, they're originally from Glasgow; I've studied art, drama, music and dance and failed to graduate in all as

I've been bounced from every University that's accepted me for some misdemeanours that weren't totally my fault, darling; before I landed in Edinburgh I spent five years travelling, saw the pyramids in Egypt, sailed down the Congo and stayed with an Amazonian tribe for a year; I've had two significant loves in my life, one French, the other Mexican, but left them both behind to see the world; I came to Edinburgh in 2008 as part of a struggling and haphazardly cobbled together burlesque show during the Fringe, which ran and died on the stage at Café Jamaica for two very long weeks. I was left high and dry by the production and Molasses offered me a job, but I've fallen in love with Edinburgh and have decided to stay for a while and see where it'll take me. But Andy, the past is the past. What does it matter where I'm from and what I've done?' she whispered in the blue light of dawn. 'It's where I am right now that's paramount. Oh, I know I drink a little too much sometimes and miss having a warm, naked body by my side on the odd occasion, and I know I'm running from the past, but isn't everyone running from something? Inevitably, something will catch up with me. Age, probably.' She shook her head and grinned, 'but I'm loving it, darling. You've been a calming influence. You with your structure and rituals, thank you, you're saving me from a life on the edge.'

So I'm right, she is on the verge of some kind of breakdown. Teetering on the edge where many have fallen. I was just about to ask her if she'd committed some sort of crime, but she tugged me into her bosom and held me close, shivering as a stiff breeze permeated what little clothing she was wearing. She looked at me with sad, dark eyes and then tucked her head into my chest. I could sense she just wanted to be held. As we stood there, closer than ever before, I had a thought:

I'm not just holding her from the edge; we're holding on to each other in fear of what lies beneath.

Monday 21st June

I ran into Gwen as she came out of the bathroom tonight. She said, 'Hello, friend, how are you?'

'Oh, hello again,' I stammered as I forced a smile and we exchanged rooms. 'I'm fine, thanks.'

She gave me three clumsy pats on the head again and added,

'Well, I'm here if you would like to, how do you say? Wiggle chins? You British are so funny with your sayings, no?' and laughed.

'Okay. Thanks. Goodbye. I have to pee.' I locked the door hurriedly. Her behaviour is most unsettling. On the toilet cistern, I found a new pack of wet wipes with a post-it attached, saying, 'Feel free!' One exclamation and wet wipes? That's progress.

Tuesday 22nd June

Laundry day

Ryan walked in during the last five minutes of *Speed Queen's* drying cycle and dropped off two bags of washing. What the hell was he doing on my turf? He has a perfectly good washer/drier at home. I ducked behind a copy of *What Car Magazine*, but it proved far too small to cover my face and my TARDIS tee-shirt (an obvious giveaway). Realising this, I replaced the mag quickly and removed my load before the cycle ended, stuffing the steaming mass of damp cotton into my linen bag like a demented 1950s housewife that's been idle all day and realises the husband is coming home early. Unfortunately, the exit is next to the service desk, so I was forced to lug my bag onto my left shoulder to cover my flushed face and shuffled towards the door.

I could hear Ryan lecture the Cheese & Onion Woman, 'Be extremely careful with this couture, will you? It's mainly Armani, with some casual wear by Diesel and Fat Face. I don't want to find it can only fit an Action Man by the time I come to collect tomorrow. And please be sure to wash your hands, I saw you sucking the remnants of a sherbet dip off your fingers through the window ... Andy! I didn't know you used this place. What a coincidence.'

I cringed behind the heavy bag, which was more laden than usual due to the added volume of water still in the fibres and getting heavier by the second. My arm could take no more, and I dropped the pile before my shoulder dislocated. I stopped cringing and pulled my best surprise face. 'Ryan, I didn't see you there,' I lied – truth is it's hard to miss a guy with an electric blue Mohican (a new addition since we last argued). Struggling to find some common ground, I clutched at ever breaking straws and reluctantly asked him through a painted smile, 'So, how's the civil partnership coming along?'

'The wedding, you mean,' he corrected me dryly. He switched quickly to the familiar toothy grin. 'It's going well. Very well, in actual fact. Well, with a few hiccups here and there,' he added through gritted teeth. 'But nothing that can't be ironed out,' he hastened to add.

I could tell he was stressed, his left eye was twitching somewhat, and he crossed and uncrossed his arms several times until he stuffed his hands in his pockets to stop the habit, a telltale symptom that has never changed since we first met. The friend in me wanted to help instantly, but the bitch in me told me he'd made his own *civilly partnered* bed and he should lie in it. The bitch won. I conjured up an excuse to leave, 'I have to go. I have to take the Colonel to the vet.'

He moved desperately in my way and said, 'Oh, dear. I hope the little tiger is alright?'

Sure you are, I thought. *You didn't give a damn about the wee man the day you threw us out and left us combing through bins on Rose Street for potato peelings.*

'He'll be fine, I'm sure,' I hastily replied, tripping over my laundry bag as I squeezed it out the door. 'Have a good day!' were my parting words, but I really meant, *Have a nice life! I'm glad to be clear of the emotional firing-line between two terrible twins.*

******

Later, over cocktails at Harvey Nicks, Sally said, 'Good for you. You're best shot of him and his twisted, emotionally stunted boyfriend.' She downed the remainder of her cosmopolitan and tapped on the glass, 'Excuse me, handsome chap,' she called to the waiter. 'Another two of these, muchas gracias!' She shuffled on her stool, crossed her toned thighs and leaned on the bar gracefully to survey the scene. 'Stick with me, kiddo,' she said, perusing the talent in the room, 'I'll show you the highlights.' She turned her nose up at several men quickly and then turned it towards me, 'Now, we need to work on getting you back out there shagging. What trade websites do you use?'

'What? None. Why?' I mumbled supping on my cosmo, aware I was as public online as a knitting circle in the Outer Hebrides with dialup.

'None? Really?' she asked in disbelief. 'Then we have a lot of work to do.' She patted me hard on the thigh. 'Pop into my pad tomorrow evening after work. I have a list as long as my legs I could give you. We'll create some profiles, and then we'll show that married hound how much you care.'

If there's a website called *pimpmyfriend.com*, she'd use it. Is it wise to give a social butterfly who dances on the laps of men the publishing rights to your life? I may have to take the 'Child Lock' off my somewhat inexperienced mind and allow the floodgates to open.

'We'll have to get the right profile picture snapped, darling, in the right light, at the right angle, with the right age-defying filter. Tell me, have you ever considered a decent haircut?'

As I digested her last comment, I began to wonder if I had just replaced Ryan with a female version of Ryan.

Wednesday 23rd June

Post-shift and post-gym, I hauled myself reluctantly up the spiral staircase of 323 Leith Walk towards my online pimp. I was feeling flat and achy, so wasn't entirely in the mood to be prostituting my life on the world-wide-web, but nothing ventured, no chance getting laid.

'What sites have you heard of?' she asked me, a tad more excited than I expected any heterosexual woman to be over gay dating sites.

'Gaydar, Gay.com, Pink, I think?'

'What about Squirt? Recon? ManDate? Man-Mate? Mate-a-Man? Man-oh-Man and MAAAANN?' she asked, flipping open her already primed laptop.

'Never heard of them,' I replied.

'Jesus, sweetie,' she groaned. 'Where have you been living, under a rock?'

'No, just next to one out in the sticks, where the only cottaging going on involved wealthy townies looking for a weekend getaway.'

'I see we have a lot of work to do here. You can be my little project.' Again with the patronising.

After an hour or so, we had created my Gaydar online persona, *Fitgeek22*. '22' due to there being 21 *Fitgeeks* out there already. Where have they been hiding all this time, if they do actually exist? I haven't met a single fit geek since I became a singleton. Mind you, if they are in any way on a par with my fitness level, then they aren't really that fit after all (poetic licence, perhaps, or self-motivation to get fit soon-ish). Profile picture to be added later, when my body image catches up with my online ego.

Description, likes, interests, hobbies, some role-play and sexual preferences listed publicly (God I hope Mum doesn't read this by some twisted misadventure online), but penis size and status of CUT/UC left to the imagination. Sally was blasé regarding this particular piece of information, but I firmly believe friends should most definitely *not* know the size, girth and the extent of skin coverage of your member. Friendships do not involve cock.

Sally's been very generous and lent me her laptop for the time being. I'll steer the mouse away from any picture and video folders she has warned me against looking at rather suggestively. I'm sure it will be filled with smut which has been filmed shakily on a camera phone. Friends should most definitely *not* know the size, depth, girth and skin coverage of your vagina.

Thursday 24th June

Slight waking worry overnight regarding my online persona. *Fitgeek22* is more aware of his HIV status than I am. I lied to Sally as she hovered the mouse over his profile's HIV toolbar. I couldn't see a category listed as 'Undecided', 'Too gutless to have the test', or 'Stupidly still doesn't know status after all these months'. I quickly blurted out, 'Negative, of course,' followed by an uncomfortable chortle.

'When were you last tested?' she asked, her X-ray vision scanning my blackened, dishonest soul.

What's one more lie? In for a penny ..., I thought. 'A month ago. And three months before that.'

'Super!' she yelped and clicked away at the column, turning *Fitgeek22* into a responsible member of sexual society who updates his HIV status regularly, unlike me. This was the tipping point, I guess, when *Fitgeek22* became more online fiction than fact. The real me is disgusted with my other-self. But why should I be forced to take responsibility for another's reckless behaviour. I was in love with a man who convinced me I was all he needed. I can't be blamed for trusting him and letting the condoms expire. I know I'm way past the window period for exposure to the HIV virus (if I have been exposed to it at all), and now is the time my blood would start showing antibodies, but I just can't bring myself to get that damn test. It's already terrible being a single guy in his mid-thirties, to become an HIV positive single guy in his mid-thirties is the worst-case scenario.

What would Sally have said if I'd admitted my failing? Would someone of her background really have the right to lecture me? Is she really the kinda girl that would judge me on that? I don't think so. But still, I lied.

Friday 25th June

I think I'm going to have to get rid of my little car. I've abandoned her for weeks in some estate along Easter Road that has free off-street parking. A tax disk reminder arrived today. £130 for another six months is an expense I can't afford. Then I have the MOT a few weeks later, which she's sure to fail as she needs two new tyres, has a faulty number plate bulb, misfires at 50 mph, her breaks are grating when I apply them, and her handbrake needs tightening, or a new cable, whatever's best. And that's not taking into account those little hidden costs that mechanics always seem to discover, managing to whittle out another hundred-or-so-pounds from your wallet.

I know of no trustworthy mechanics that I haven't had sexual relations with. It's going to be expensive and a right royal pain in the arse. Mechanics are like Hollywood plastic surgeons: they have to come recommended by a friend.

To have her scrapped would amount to the same as the road tax, so that would be £130 in my pocket twice, I suppose. Also, I have to be realistic, I haven't used her in months. Am I hanging on to her because she's the last relic from my last chance at happiness? (She was my 29th birthday present from Thomas.)

'If you want to be better off, get rid of that money-pit and buy yourself a pushbike,' advised Molasses. 'You will save yourself many pennies and remove half the gut you keep sucking in every time you catch sight of yourself in that damn mirror.'

I looked at my reflection at the other end of the café and became aware that I had already, without realising it, tightened what I now laughingly call my abdominal muscles. Is it any wonder Thomas wanted to leave me? I am falling to bits and will soon need a zimmer frame to help me over that hill called 'middle-age'. It must be one hell of a steep hill as it leaves people bloody knackered for the rest of their lives.

Saturday 26th June

I am such a geek. I have watched every episode of Doctor Who since I was a child and still find it the most exciting show in the world. The season finale did not disappoint. Matt Smith is firmly the Doctor in our eyes now (Sally & me), and Karen Gillan is turning into a great companion. I thought I'd never get over David Tennant's departure, but I have. It shows how fickle we can be.

Sally saved the best 'till last. After the show ended she folded back a red velvet curtain to reveal shelves filled with classic Doctor Who DVDs. 'Shall we watch City of Death?' she asked, excitedly.

I am ashamed to say I clapped my hands together in glee, skipped on the spot and yelped, 'Yes! Yes! Yes!' akin to Meg Ryan in the Kat'z Deli scene of *When Harry Met Sally*. It was, what I term, a *Sticky Geeky Orgasm*.

Sunday 27th June

I found an invitation at the foot of my bedsit door today:

Dearest Andy,
You are invited to the Birthday of
Ms Molasses Brown
On Sunday the 4th of July
@10 p.m.
Location: Café Jamaica.
RSVP

Everyone has an invite, even Gwen, much to Sally's consternation. 'For the gods, Andy!' she moaned. 'I can understand Melve's invitation, I mean he can scrub up very well and has many fascinating and fabulous tales to tell, but Gwen? The woman who is bitter because a house fell on her sister in a land called Oz?' That girl has as much personality and individuality as a Starbucks mug and all the charm and elegance of a lawnmower.

'Do you think she'll go?' I asked.

'She'll go, just to spite me,' she chewed her lip for a moment in thought and then declared, 'Which means I have to go, just to spite her. Ha!'

This should be interesting.

Monday 28th June

Bloody hell! I've stolen someone else's blind date. Literally high-jacked a hot banker from HBOS and selfishly steered him away from his intended meet. I was waiting on Sally showing up at The Street – she was late as usual – minding my own business when I noticed this tall chap with strawberry-blond hair giving me the eye. Who couldn't, I ask you, resist a little flirtation back? Little did I know the guy he'd arranged a date with was a well-endowed doppelgänger he'd met online.

'You look better in the flesh,' he said, grinning as he approached me while I sipped on a pint and bashfully kicked at the bar.

'Thanks very much,' I blushed as I tried to figure out in what other way he'd seen me than in the flesh – I have no pictures on my Gaydar profile as of yet, and therefore no hits either.

He stuck out his hand and introduced himself as 'Dannyboy69, you're "13inchGAP" no?'

'Am I?' I asked, confusion lifting and realisation dawning. 'Yes. Yes, I am!' I straightened myself up and announced proudly for everyone at the bar to hear, '13inchGAP, that's me.' What was a boy to do? I wasn't going to admit to being anything less, and besides, I'd do anything for just five minutes having my ears licked by this hottie. From then on, my little fib snowballed, careering down a hill of untruths, collecting more lies as it plummeted faster and faster towards a valley littered with deception debris and broken promises.

One gifted drink later and I'd become Mike, a train driver and live-in-landlord that owns a rare breed of ginger poodle and donates his free time to a soup kitchen in the Grassmarket every Friday evening.

All this deceit I could handle if we left it at a wet lick of my earlobe, but I now have a date with Dannyboy69, which actually means sex, judging by the level of online chat reiterated by an excited Danny Boy (AKA: Josh). This is becoming ridiculous. I now have two online personas: one Sally and I created and another I have unexpectedly been asked to write the screenplay for.

I could kill Sally for being more than an hour late. I should not be allowed in bars to drink on my own with handsome men. I'm an irresponsible child stood too close to a full pick 'n' mix without a chaperone. When she finally did show up, Dannyboy69 and I had exchanged mobile numbers (necessary, as I claimed to no longer be using the web to find men, just to be sure the real 13inchGAP didn't get wind of the fact he'd been robbed of a perfectly lovely man). I excused myself, saying my *older* sister had arrived with a blocked fallopian tube and quickly ushered my new big sister out of the door. Sally chuckled at the tangled web I'd managed to weave in less than an hour. Friday is our night of passion. How the hell am I going to find all those extra inches by then? There really is stiff competition out there.

Tuesday 29th June

Laundry Day

Ryan appeared at the laundrette again today. He was actually *washing clothes in public!* How the mighty have fallen. Doing it all wrong, of course, mixing whites and colours in the same drum. This ignorance does not surprise me in the least, but his willingness to wash his dirty linen in public by his own Molton Brown moisturised hands does. My domestic daemon was chattering loudly on my shoulder by the time he had stupidly dispensed fabric softener into the detergent drawer, but I let that slide. However, when he tried to pour a bottle of thick bleach into the machine, I couldn't keep quiet any longer.

'Stop!' I snapped as I threw down a copy of SFX magazine I had found stuck on the top of the Speed Queen (finally quality reading matter in a public place). 'Move away from that industrial washer, you clueless queen. You're obviously a complete stranger to the care of casual clothing.'

Ryan acted surprised that I was there, but I saw him clock me the second he peeked through the window.

I felt the uncontrollable desire to educate this fabric philistine. 'Never wash you colours above 30; never wash your whites below 60 – they say you can get them whiter than white at 30, but it's a marketing ploy and total lie – most of all, never mix your load *and,* worst of all, add bleach to the mixed load on a boil wash!'

'Thanks,' said my old friend. 'I am completely useless at this. The laundry company we used online just went bust, and our washing machine is kaput.'

'It could've died ages ago, Ryan. You guys would never know as you never use it.'

Ryan laughed a little, 'Yes, you're probably right. Hey look,' he pointed at the dryer I found the SFX mag on, 'They actually have a dryer called "Speed Queen". '

It was heart-warming to learn I wasn't the only person in Leith that found this funny, 'Yes, I know, hilarious isn't it?' I chuckled. Just then, my machine beeped to remind me my load was done. It snapped me into a more sober mindset. 'That's me done,' I said awkwardly. 'I best get going; I have work.'

Ryan said, 'Sure, sure,' rather sorrowfully, I thought. 'Nice to see you, though. I hope the wee man is alright?'

'What? Oh, yes, the Colonel. Nothing keeps him down for long,' I replied.

The next few seconds were filled with an awkward silence, the thrashing of wet clothes against steel drums and the hearty munching of a small, dumpy laundry assistant feasting on a packet of cheese and onion crisps as she leant on the counter and stared vacantly out of the window towards the blazing summer sun. I actually didn't want to go. I watched him carry on with his new-found chores for a moment and anticipated striking up a full conversation, but the words just wouldn't come. The mental block was Tony and how unforgiving they'd been as a couple.

'Nice to see you too,' I agreed and left.

The truth is, despite everything, it really was.

Wednesday 30th June

'I'd like to purchase a penis pump that will give maximum results in minimal time. Do you have such an object?'

These are not ordinary words you'd expect to hear coming out of a friend's mouth when shopping, but then this is not what you expect to be shopping for in your lunch hour, and Sally Knowles is no ordinary friend. We were in *Heads Down, Bums Up* sex shop, next to Café Jamaica. I was too embarrassed to approach the young lad as he was handsome and I didn't want him to think of me as teeny-tiny. Sally did the talking.

'Aye,' the youth replied in a deep, manly tone, dropping me a wink as he reached under the counter with such a cheeky grin that caused me to blush, turn away quickly, and promptly knock over a stack of Tom of Finland books. 'We have this.' He pulled out a tall box with a naked hunk on the cover using the enclosed apparatus while lost in fake rapture. 'It's the most tried and tested on the market. Five stars.'

'A five-star pump, eh? Five-star and hopefully *not* unleaded,' I joked as I scooped up the books.

Silence from my friend and the assistant.

I coughed. Okay, I'll ... sorry, *she'll* take it.'

He dropped the box into a blue plastic bag and said, 'That'll be £80.'

I gave him my cashcard, blowing my cover instantly. 'Oh, it's not for me, it's a gift.'

The assistant joked, 'If I only had a pound for every time I've heard that one.'

Sally interrupted, 'Oh, and he'll need the tightest, smallest rubber cock-ring you have in this establishment.'

I kept my eyes fixed on the assistant and said through gnashing teeth, 'Thanks a lot, my dear, tactful friend.'

******

Later, with misgivings, after several horny texts from Dannyboy69, I knocked on Sally's door for reassurance. 'Look,' she simplified, 'it's just going to enhance what you have. Pump it, practice with it, and on the day, secure it with the cock-ring, and you'll have the most impressive piece of Angus beef this side of the city. All the best male strippers do it before a show.'

'Okay,' I said, a little more confident, but just a little. 'If it works for them.'

'You'll leave with your ego intact and your reputation enhanced, not to forget a fantastic night frolicking against a stacked frame. If you need a hand with the pump, darling, I'm here to help.'

'No, no, that won't be necessary.'

'Well, if you change your mind, I'm more than willing,' she winked.

I spent the following hour with my willy trapped in a vacuum stronger than space and my legs elevated on the wall as I lay on my back on the bed (the instructions claim this encourages blood flow and growth). I've noticed little change apart from my willy being a darker shade than usual. I have a headache too. This guy had better be worth it!

Thursday 1st July

11.45 p.m. More reassurance needed. I threw in a casual question amongst all the horny texts between Dannyboy69 and 13inchGap:

'R u a size queen?' I asked, contemplating coming clean.

The reply was a very firm, 'Yes, I am. I worship men like you. I can't wait to worship you tonight.'

Damn it! Trust me to stumble across an out-and-out size queen.

Pump Progress: One hour in the morning, and a further hour at night. Headache in both heads now, but my willy looks impressive once the blood flow is restricted by the rubber ring.

Friday 2nd July

Date Night!

Pump Progress: Three sessions today in assorted positions as desperation creeps in. Willy looks large and veiny when in the cock-ring, but is a slightly worrying shade of purple, and the ligament feels tender. I'm nowhere close to 13 inches, but am I a bigger and better version of myself? My packet does look obvious in my jeans, so there must be some kind of enhancement. However, it's very uncomfortable and slightly embarrassing as I now look permanently aroused, and Gwen's just shot me a weird look on my way back from the loo.

Saturday 3rd July

I was forced to come clean over dinner. I could see my date was a little disappointed when I broke the news that I'm just Mr Average.

'How far off thirteen inches are we talking here?' he asked, staring mournfully at the burrito that was spilling over his plate.

'Minus six, if the heating is on,' I winced in the hope that this would suffice.

'Ah.'

'But I am told it's the perfect girth and handsome, if that helps?' I continued to work some much-needed P.R. on my penis.

Dannyboy69 mulled over his predicament, sighed and said, 'Well, it's not the size, it's what you do with it that really counts, they say.'

An hour later, back at my bedsit, I had Dannyboy69 doing precisely what his online persona said he could, even if mine could've been taken to court under the Trade Descriptions Act. He seemed very happy with his lot until it came to penetration. It was then I realised all my intense pump exercises had caused some kind of damage that meant, even with the cock-ring on, my willy was not willing and had given up the ghost due to painful throbbing and possible dislocation. It was just weeks ago I was witness to someone else's no-show, and now, here I was, having similar complications.

I became aware Dannyboy69 was nowhere near as excited as he'd been when he assumed the position. 'Um, do you have a dildo?' he asked over my panting, confirming my manhood was no longer the star attraction.

'Eh? No, I don't, sorry!' I had to think of something penis shaped and big enough to satisfy his appetite. Appetite = food = my solution, 'I do have a cucumber in the fridge.'

'That'll have to do,' he dolefully said as if I was offering a staunch meat-eater a substandard vegan option.

Within minutes, Dannyboy69 was writhing around in sheer pleasure and enjoying the moment far too much for my liking. 'More! Give me more! Harder!' he cried.

Okay, I thought, *I'll damn-well give you more!* I felt cheated that I'd been replaced by a piece of vegetable matter from the gourd family, so I gave him what he wanted: harder, faster, firmer, more! His ass was resilient and seemed like a Brazilian wrestler on steroids.

'More! Keep going; you're gonna make me cum!' Which was great for him but, as I felt well out of the picture by now, I was as soggy, flaccid and cold as a used teabag. On the point of one very full, intense ejaculation, he thrust hard against my straining knuckles and the cucumber veered off into the darkness that exists somewhere between this universe and the next.

Call it guilt but, after an hour of vigorous searching, and after several unhygienic minutes of Dannyboy69 straining over my kitchen sink in ridiculous positions, I was sitting patiently with winos for company in A&E at the Edinburgh Royal Infirmary awaiting his fate.

By 2 a.m., he emerged from the ward walking with some degree of difficulty. He sat gingerly next to me and said, 'Firstly, you lied to me from the get-go. You obviously have size issues to create a fake profile to entice vulnerable guys like me.'

Vulnerable? I've never known anyone more capable! 'I'm sorry,' I said, which helped not a jot, judging by the small thundercloud erupting over his head. Think positive, I thought, 'Hey, at least they got it out.' I paused, 'They did find it, right?'

'Yes, they found it, but I've lost my dignity. Which brings me to my second point: never call me again.' As he left, he shot me one last piercing glance that told me he meant every word. To him, I'd acted like a 13-inch cock, but not the kind that turned him on.

When I got home, I logged on to Gaydar to delete my profile, but curiosity got the better of me. I entered the 'Hung' chat-room for a quick look-see. The same cold, black walls, the same revolving door, the same empty names. One, in particular, caught my eye: Dannyboy69, openly chatting in desperation for a big, fat juicy number without a hint of a bruised ego or anus. Back in the saddle once more. I took Fitgeek22 out of the room, relieved that the charade was over, but not before I checked my mail. My inbox remains gloriously empty for now. Good. I need the rest, in more ways than one. Unlike those hardened queens out there, I can't keep losing hours of my life to the online merry-go-round of great expectation and disappointment. Fantasy is always better than reality. I was dishonest, yes. I got my comeuppance. My penance will be my constant companion for the next few days. Ouch!

Sunday 4th July

'No birthday presents, please, just don't ask my age,' insisted Molasses.

The café was filled with a diverse buffet of humankind in taste, culture and class. Sally was buzzing, flitting around the room excitedly in a slinky cocktail dress studded in red sequins that made her shimmer with every turn of her tight frame. Men seemed to follow her around the room and, when she moved to a new group, they welcomed her with an inclusive sweep of their arms.

Gwen, on the other hand, was socially awkward. She said a quick hello and found her comfort zone: in the shadows between the busty fireplace and velvet curtains. She looked as if she'd rather be in Chernobyl at the height of its meltdown than at the party. Ten out of ten for effort though: she'd slipped into a two-piece navy suit, but combined with a blue and red chiffon scarf and her hair strapped into the usual steel bun, she looked just like a British Airways reject.

Enough! I thought. I bid her a quick hello and edged her out of the darkness towards Christina, another apparently lonely soul. Christina seemed uncharacteristically uptight, sadly. Some minutes of stilted conversation ensued. Then silence. Both ladies' eyes followed the scarlet butterfly fluttering around the room. I caught Christina and Gwen check their own attire in comparison, straightening their skirts and crossing their legs tightly away from one another.

Christina volunteered, 'I'm not very good at this kind of thing. I don't usually do big crowds. My husband, Nick, on the other hand, is a social chameleon. He can charm his way through a six-course dinner with the Lord Chancellor, or a simple burger at McDonald's with a bunch of teenagers. But he's away on business. I hate flying solo.'

She wasn't her usual bouncy self, for sure. Gwen was indifferent. I wasn't going to play social worker all night, so when I spotted a massive bowl of rum punch on the table, I delved in with three glasses and insisted we toasted friendship. Then love. Then alcohol.

Fast-forward two hours and several more glasses later, and the two of them began to loosen up. Sally even leaned over the back of the sofa and, hugging Gwen, said, 'You know, Gwen, you do have lovely thick hair. If you pop round to mine one night, we could work on a new look for you.' She stroked Gwen's impregnable barnet.

To my surprise, Gwen was happy to have her stroke away, in fact, her neck softened, and she reclined her head into Sally's ample cleavage. 'Yes, that would be super-fantastic,' she slurred while draining the last of her glass.

'Nick hasn't made love to me in months,' chirped in Christina.

Silence.

'Well, this is awkward,' I said.

Melve, who'd been deep in conversation with a citrus fruit drier about the unnatural risks of colour changing lemons, immediately cut their debate short when he heard Christina's declaration. 'There, there, you delicious specimen of womanhood,' he belched as he slithered next to her, almost knocking me from the sofa. 'The man is obviously a fool, blind, a zombie, or simply has no heart. I can't understand men who have no interest in carnal pleasures. You are the most beautiful woman in this room.' This would've been charming had he not slid his tongue across his lips at each pause.

'Thank you, you are very kind, but I don't want to have sex with you. You are lovely, but you look like a hairy King Edward potato,' said Christina.

Melve sighed and said, 'Fair enough,' as he tucked back into the pint of cider he'd almost poured over me on his descent. 'I've the droop of the brewer tonight anyway.'

'SAGA Magazine was delivered to my door this morning,' cried Molasses as she attempted to sit on a beanbag, failed miserably and drunkenly slid onto her side until she was prone and wide-legged on the floor. 'We all know what that stands for ... *Send All Grannies Away*. I'm not a dried up granny, I'm as sweet and juicy as a jackfruit at the height of summer.'

'I'm still a virgin at the age of thirty. Why is it so hard to meet a man, fall in love and get married? Why do they all want to get into my knickers first?' complained Gwen.

'Do they seriously want to do that while she's in them?' whispered Sally to me.

'She's only thirty?' I whispered back, dumbfounded.

'Well, as we're all sharing tragedies, I've a wealthy family that have totally disowned me, just because I refuse to live as lord of the manor in a stately home in deepest darkest Somerset and be restrained within the rotting walls of a loveless pre-arranged political marriage,' volunteered Melve.

Sally, with pound signs in her eyes, suddenly became interested in Melve and asked, 'How rich, dearest Melve? You know I've always wanted to go pick out a diamond with the right man at Tiffany's.'

Molasses barked, 'Down, girl!'

I figured as we were all unloading in the hope of rum-induced amnesia, I'd unburden my recent sexual misadventure: 'I spent Friday night at casualty with a guy I barely knew as doctors removed a cucumber I accidentally popped up his colon. When is sex going to become *normal* again?'

Stunned silence. Christina stopped blubbering, Molasses stopped inspecting her wrinkles in a tablespoon. Gwen's cheeks flushed. Melve took a large gulp of cider. Sally chewed on a cocktail cherry and glanced around expectantly.

'Wow,' said Gwen, 'you win!'

'Sweet, Lord!' laughed Molasses. 'Why on Earth did you take him to A&E? Why didn't you try to coax it out by wafting a ham sandwich under his anus?'

Fits of laughter ensued. Somehow we'd managed to make light of our shitty lives and maybe, dare I say it, bonded. I'm not saying we're great friends, but I think we're on a path to becoming something more than just sad, lonely individuals who have nothing but a café in common. Molasses' Rum Punch it's pure voodoo in a glass. I've slept the best I have in months and have no hangover.

Monday 5th July

My car is sick and requires a hospital appointment. The automatic transmission is struggling, and she makes a terrible clunking noise from under the bonnet when I push her hard up a hill. I barely made it into ASDA's carpark this afternoon. Infuriated and red-faced from being verbally abused by a bunch of frustrated boy-racers behind me in a Fiat Cinquecento, I dumped her in one of the many disabled spots and faked a limp all the way to the trollies.

On my way back, I forgot to limp and was accused, rightly so, of stealing a space by a below-knee amputee in his forties. I added a stroke to my act and slurred an incoherent protest. It's not easy slurring, limping and lugging six bags of messages into the back of a clapped-out Vauxhall Astra. I continued this lie as I returned the trolly, under the watchful eye of the cynical forty-something, only to trip on the gammy wheel and fall to the tarmac as safely as a stroke victim could. God knows how real disabled people cope.

'That poor schizophrenic man has fallen over,' I heard a woman cry. 'Get help.'

'I'm not schizophrenic!' I snapped without a hint of a speech impediment.

Wheelchairs are very uncomfortable, as it turns out. Wheelchairs and poorly laid tarmac are a lousy combination too. So are wheelchairs and taxi ramps, as I discovered when my act pulled in an audience and I was helped by caring, unsuspecting ASDA staff to get home swiftly. The crowd waved me off as I was driven slowly but surely out of the carpark. I waved goodbye with my good arm and faked a happy but stunted smile, until I clocked Ryan and Tony amongst the throng, gawping at me in disbelief. Just my bloody luck!

The taxi driver was caring and overbearing, helping me from the taxi all the way up the stairs to our hall. 'It's not a very disabled friendly flat,' he said, a little out of puff after lugging half a grown man's body up three flights of stairs. 'You should talk to social services. I'll put a word in. My son's in one of the Edinburgh offices.'

'It's okay, I'm agoraphobic, I don't usually go out,' I lied.

'Then what were you doing in a massive carpark?'

'I forgot.'

'You forgot you were agoraphobic?'

'Yes, yes,' I stammered, clutching for something. Anything! 'Because I have dementia.' Could I upset my karma any more?

'Poor lad. Dementia, eh? And only middle-aged,' he said, rubbing my limp shoulder. 'Dementia and a stroke on the third floor. I'll get my son to come have a look at you anyway. See if we can get you some support.'

'No, please don't. I like to be left alone. I actually don't like socialising with anyone, especially strangers.'

Just then Melve blundered out of his room and spotted me. 'What's up, old bean? Great party the other night, eh? You were in full swing. Oy! Oy! What's this? You brought home another bit of stuff, eh? You hound,' he growled suggestively.

'No, no, this is a taxi driver,' I protested.

'Saves on fares, you sly old thing. I understand,' said Melve as he tapped his bulbous nose. 'We've all prostituted ourselves in some fashion or another, whether it be for a lift home or a poke of chips.'

'No, you've got it all wrong, this poor lad's had a stroke,' interrupted the taxi driver.

'What? Today?' asked Melve. 'Well, we must get you to the hospital,' he said, taking me by my good arm and helped me towards the front door.

I shook myself free and said, 'Stop! Don't you know more and more people are turning up at accident and emergency units with unnecessary illnesses? Everyone needs to stop being so damn caring and autocratic and fuck off.' I pulled free from the taxi driver and gave him short thanks as I ushered him out the door, limping all the way. Melve went to speak, but I shushed him with a wave of my hand as I waited on the footsteps to fade and for the main door to shut. I headed back to ASDA faster than you can say 'Handicap Badge'.

By the time I'd returned to my car, it was the only one parked in the disabled bays and, more tragically, my Ben & Jerry's had melted into a sloppy milkshake and leaked through the carrier onto the back seat. Damn you, suffocate prevention safety holes. Damn you, bad karma. It's the last time I do a big shop out of town; it's not as convenient as they lead you to believe. I now have to return a wheelchair and begin Act Two of my performance.

Tuesday 6th July

Washday.

It's about average temperature for a Scottish summer, 21 degrees, but inside that laundrette, it feels about 200. I swear the guy next to me last had a wash back when *Snickers* were *Marathon*. I was just getting some light olfactory relief from a bottle of Ariel Colour & Style when Ryan swanked through the doors again.

'Oh, fancy meeting you here,' he exclaimed as he dropped his full bags on the patchy, worn linoleum.

I rolled my eyes. His charade was becoming pitiful, 'It's Tuesday, Ryan, it doesn't take Carol Vorderman to work out that it's seven days since my last weekly wash.'

He slumped himself down next to the man who had potatoes growing from his armpits and then swapped seats to one next to me with a very audible, 'Phew! Disgusting! Hey, were you drunk at ASDA yesterday, or just losing it?'

I chewed on a jelly baby, offered him one from the box and said, 'Neither. What do you want?'

He smiled at the red gelatine and gleefully popped it in his mouth, squishing it to nothing between his dazzling bleached molars. He nudged me on the shoulder playfully, 'To be friends again. I miss you.'

'I'm not sure if I can, Ryan. You said some very hurtful things and threw my cat and me out of your home when we needed a friend the most. If it hadn't been for Molasses, I'd be malnourished and have infected foot ulcers by now.'

'I'm sorry, I was distraught; your pet did ruin our wedding suits.' he stressed, reaching for another piece of confectionary.

I tucked the box behind my back and said, 'Sorry, but only the first one's free.'

'Don't be daft,' he laughed as he swiped the box out of my hand and mused over another victim. 'Please,' he pouted. 'I promise it'll be different now: we won't be your landlords, so there will be no added tension there, and I won't mention the wedding at all.'

I laughed. 'You just have.'

'Oh, all right, just a bit. But I'll tone it down for you.' He offered me one of my own jelly babies and added, 'I've been insensitive. You've just been through a breakup, and all I can talk about is love and marriage and horses and carriages. I'm so wrapped up in my own happy success I forgot you were adapting to a new life with no friends.'

'No friends? I have plenty now,' I assured him.

'Oh, have you?' His disappointment was obvious. This made me a tiny bit happy.

'Oh, alright,' I submitted, 'but you and Tony are on a trial period of two months. Any snash and I'm deleting you from my phone permanently.

'How's about I buy you a drink tomorrow night? A new start.'

I shuffled in my chair and looked through the condensation towards the silhouettes of passing strangers. 'I dunno.'

'Two drinks then?'

'It's hardly compensation for being thrown out, and no deposit returned.' I was milking it for more than it's worth, but the devil in me couldn't resist. I wanted him to squirm a little. I needed to learn how desperately he wanted our friendship back.

'As many drinks as you like. Cocktails even, at Harvey Nicks. You can't have the deposit back, it's gone on the wed ...' He clamped his mouth shut tightly.

I laughed. 'Done!' I reached out my hand, Ryan wiped off the sugary powder from his, and we shook on it.

'Thank fuck!' he said as he leapt from the chair and turned to the Cheese & Onion woman. 'Two bags of laundry to be done by tomorrow by three, thanks,' lugging them onto the counter.

She was non-pulsed. 'It'll be done by four, sonny, no earlier,' she growled.

'Three, or else I'll be speaking to your boss: he goes bowling with my mother every Wednesday, you know?' threatened Ryan.

'All right then, three,' she spat.

'Thank you very much, I knew you would see the light.' He gave a smarmy grin, took his ticket triumphantly and leant over to whisper in my ear, 'I'm so glad we can be friends again. I can't stand coming here to stalk you. Our machine at home was fixed two weeks ago.'

'The things a boy will do for his mates,' I joked.

'Yes, I'll see you tomorrow at eight. As it happens, the destruction of our suits was a godsend; we claimed on our insurance and, after posting our little tragedy on social media, we now have free limited editions sent specially from Prada. Oh, and keep the fact we were at ASDA yesterday to yourself, eh? We have a reputation to uphold.' He minced towards the exit, threw a repugnant look towards the stinky guy, and told him, 'It should be illegal for people like you to mix with society. Do you see those clothes in that machine there? They're being washed. Do you understand that? *Washed?* With an exotic item called *soap*. Ciao, Andy.'

The potato-pit guy sneered at me as Ryan left. I gave a nervous grin and said, 'I'm so sorry, he was born and raised in a London suburbia and doesn't know how to communicate without an interpreter in these foreign lands. He's actually very kind and giving.' It was then I realised my rediscovered friend had left with my box of jelly babies. Freeloader!

Wednesday 7th July

7.35 p.m. I'm plucked, showered, shaved, squirted and looking the best a guy in his mid-thirties can after a long day on his feet. I've a mental list of the things to get off my clipped chest. I'll lay down the law on the rules of our friendship and not cave-in when Ryan flutters his puppy-dog eyes. I'll be levelheaded and drink responsibly. I will certainly not be drunkenly coerced.

23-something p.m. Drunk, am I. Martini and vodka cocktails are best, they are, and make me squibbly. Friends can be for life and life is for friends ... ok, best stop writing as I now know I now talk in Yoda talk talk speech anyway. Night!

Thursday 8th July

My friendship with Ryan is back on track. Civil Partnership chat was kept at a bare minimum, I think. Only a light dusting over wedding cake flavour, but nothing too sickly, as far as I recall. We're old but new. We have to be. I have to accept that we'll never be able to go back to who we were before I left, before Steve died, when the friendship included three slightly different personalities. Why should we? Can't it be as good, if not better, than it was before? I'm less dependent on Ryan's friendship since I moved into the weird and wonderful *Land of Lost Souls*. I no longer reach out for his approval and shrug off any critical glance with ease. I'm more relaxed, and therefore we're more comfortable as friends.

'Just one thing?' I remember him asking before my memory went fuzzy and the barstool became wobbly. 'Could you be just that little bit more tolerant of Tony?'

I almost spat out my drink. 'Hey, boyo! I have been nothing but tolerant!'

'Please, it would mean so much if two of the most important men in my life got on. I've asked him to do the same for you.' And then that grin, with puppy-dog eyes for good measure, 'Please, do it for me?' Just until the wedding and then you can be as horrid as you like. He'll be well under my thumb by then.'

'Oh, alright,' I said, as I sank the last of my cocktail and rattled the ice cubes suggestively around the glass. 'Buy me another, and we'll work on a deal.' After that, the evening became very muddled. A deal was struck, but I'm hazy over the small print.

Friday 9th July

My car is screwed. It's the end of the line. The automatic transmission is pretty much jiggered, and it's going to cost far more than she's worth to have her fixed. Damn it! If only Alistair had stuck around, I could've got a free service and repair. I've viewed a few websites and have been given a quote of £110 if I take it to a scrapyard in Edinburgh, but if I drive her to Inverkeithing, I'll get £200. I'm driving to Inverkeithing tomorrow.

After Café Jamaica locked its doors, we all sat and bitched for an hour or so while sampling tequila. Even Gwen hung around and sipped on a small shot.

'Come on, get it down you, girlfriend,' hollered Sally, slapping Gwen so vigorously on her back her tight bun almost wobbled free.

'I've got to go soon anyway,' said Gwen as she passed on the last few sips and pushed the glass away to the other side of the bar. She stood up and slipped into her coat. As she did so, her thin lips muttered hesitantly, 'Um, do you think we could do that girlie night soon, Sally?' The music stopped at that exact moment, and we all waited for the unbelievable to happen. Could Gwen and Sally really be alone together in the same room and be friends? What could they possibly have in common? Surely the universe would implode?

'Sure thing, Gwen. I'd like that.' Sally scribbled on a napkin and stuffed it into Gwen's hand, holding it there as if they were planning to elope in secret. 'My number.'

As Gwen left and the universe began to take on its usual dimensions, Sally turned to me and said, 'So, kiddo. Inverkeithing tomorrow, is it? How are you getting back?'

'I thought I'd take the train.'

'Is the scrapyard close to the station?'

I pondered for a minute. This detail had escaped me, all I could think of was getting more bang for my buck, or rather, more buck for my old banger. 'I'm not sure.'

'I'll follow you up and give you a lift back. I've nothing to do until tomorrow night anyway.'

'You have transport?'

'My dear Andy, there are many more things to learn about the legend that is Sally Knowles.' She curled the black bobbed wig she was sporting around an emerald fingernail and grinned, 'Mr, I have horsepower that kicks like a mule.'

10 a.m. tomorrow I set off for the last time in my beloved old jalopy. I think my heart may break. I'm driving her to an automobile slaughterhouse. On my way home, I made a point of walking down the quiet street where she's parked and patted her on her rusty bonnet. If the cat that ran from under her nearside could understand English it may have heard a man's voice croak, 'There, there, old girl. I do love you. You were my escape when I needed you the most.' But talking to cars is silly, isn't it? Cars are just heaps of metal. But heaps of metal that do the family shop and take us to the

beach on long sunny drives. Cars are where brothers and sisters cower behind headrests as they watch the back of their parents heads dart angrily back and forth over misdirections on creased maps. It's where we share snacks, play Eye Spy, and fall asleep under rugs. And, if we're fortunate, they're where we hold hands with the one we love while enjoying the freedom of the open road and the glory of nature in search of something shared and new.

They're not just lumps of cold, heartless metal; they help us to achieve our dreams.

Saturday 10th July

Two firsts today:

I said goodbye to my old car. There was a lump in my throat as I watched her tail turn the corner amongst the threadbare and crushed carcasses of the motoring industry. I almost threw back the £200 the nice chap had given me along with her death certificate and chased after her to stop the cannibalisation of her parts. But within minutes, she was out of sight and out of my life. The tears that began to gush were halted by loud revs of a gutsy engine and the skid of two wheels on the gravel. As the dust clouds disseminated, a slender figure in red leathers and knee-high boots kicked down the bike rest and slid off the seat with all the sleekness of a trained dancer. I peered into the helmet but could see nothing other than my own puzzled expression.

'Hello, sweetie,' came a muffled voice from within. Then the helmet was lifted, and Sally Knowles shook her new lengthy locks free. 'How I loath helmet hair.' Sally fished a helmet out of the small compartment behind the seat of her bike and pressed it firmly onto my chest. 'No time for tears, big boy. Get on.'

Cue my second first: riding pillion passenger on a motorway with a skilled, edgy driver. I was shit-scared and yet loving every second. As we zoomed across the Forth Road Bridge, I let out a joyful howl as the absurd beauty of the moment hit me; glorious day, gorgeous view and a reckless friend saving me from the dark. Life would never have been like this had I stayed in Little Troll Cottage.

11.20 p.m. I've found myself flicking through pictures of motorbikes online, which randomly included motorcycles with hot topless men either riding them or sprawled seductively over them, which then led to me searching for more of such images. A shiny new world of sexual fantasy opened up before my eyes, and my mind spun. I'm pretty much spent now. Goodnight.

Sunday 11th July

I raved to Sally about her bike for the whole shift. I could see she was growing weary of me, but I had so much to ask her. How long has she been riding? Why did she never tell me? Where can I learn? How cheap are they to run? How *do* you cope with helmet hair? How dangerous are they?

In between the afternoon rush, she bullet-pointed off the answers quickly:

- Two years.
- It never came up.
- Cheaper than a car but more expensive than the bus.
- I always look fabulous, sweetie, haven't you learned that?
- Dangerous if you are going too fast and become careless. They don't call us 'Organ Donors' for nothing, kiddo.

You would think, having a fear of dying at any second, injury and illness, I would've been put off by the term 'Organ Donors', but I still want to give it a go.

'If you're still peachy-keen tomorrow, then pop round to 22D Comely Bank Row,' she said. 'I have a garage that I'll be tinkering in for the afternoon. I'll give you a bike to trial on, and we'll see if you're still keen.'

'Don't you worry, I'll still be keen,' I assured her.

Monday 12th July

There was my little grease monkey, dabbling away and looking like a modern-day Charlene from Neighbours in a red-spotted headscarf and blue dungarees. Two bikes sat in her garage: the mean sporty number I'd ridden pillion on, and a classic Honda, which had some of its inners dissected and laid neatly on a mat.

'Just a sec,' she grinned excitedly as she wiped her blackened, oily hands on the worn denim and disappeared into the rear of the lockup. From deep in the clutter I heard a clatter of metal and some cursing. Then repetitive squeaking which got louder and louder until it reached the courtyard beside me. I daren't look down because I just knew my hopes were going to be shat on if I did.

'Where is it then?' I peered beyond the two bikes I'd just admired, ignoring the spindly thin wheels I could see just out of the corner of my eye.

'It's here, darling.'

'No, that can't possibly be it,' I laughed, glimpsing at the rusty metal she was leaning on.

'Andy, this is your training bike.'

'But ... but ... it's a *bike*.'

'Yes?'

I leaned forward and whispered in her ear as not to offend the poor antique, 'A *pushbike*, not a *motorbike*.'

'Yeeeesss, I get that.'

'I thought you would be giving me a motorbike. You know, to get the feel of it. Have a cheeky wee jaunt around the courtyard by myself.'

'You must be joking, darling!' she scoffed. 'I'd be mad, not to mention irresponsible, to do that. No, this is the best way to learn. If you want to be safe, then you have to feel vulnerable, more vulnerable than you would in a city with an engine, so pedal-power is the best way to go about it. Then we'll talk motorbikes. Besides, this'll help you get fit too.'

'You're joshing me, aren't you?'

'When it comes to road safety, I'm deadly serious.' She sighed and scowled a little, 'Look, it's a Princess Sovereign with a traditional lugged and brazed hand built frame, five-speed gears and fully-enclosed hub brakes. It's a classic.'

The very name, *Princess*, made me squirm. I mean, if it'd been a sporty bike called MAXX I would've been less disillusioned, but a *Princess?* 'But I've ridden a bike before when I lived in the country,' I argued. 'I know how it feels.'

'Not in the city, over slippy cobbles, with rush hour traffic and nippy drivers, you haven't though. Then you'll know vulnerability.'

I knew my pal was trying to do me a favour, so I didn't have the heart to say no. 'Couldn't we at least remove the wicker basket?' I whimpered.

'But it's part of the style, sweetie.'

Thirty minutes later, this queen squeaked away from the comeliest part of this fairy-tale city with a Princess, wicker basket and all. I walked her all the way home; I was too embarrassed to ride her without a helmet to cover my blushes.

Tuesday 13th July

Drinks with Ryan *and* Tony at *Pricilla's* – the kind of bar that serves cheap drinks to the lower end of the gay scene.

'Why are we even here?' asked a prickly Ryan.

'Because it's cheap, Boo-Boo. We need every penny for our wedding, remember?' hollered Tony over the ear-shredding Europop blasting from the clapped-out speakers. Tony stretched a hollow, false smile towards me, which I repaid with an equal amount of fakery. We were on our best behaviour. Ryan had acted like NATO, drawing up conversational boundaries and safe zones for negotiations to continue over the Iron Curtain that divided our temperaments, while in a bar that resembled some rundown cabaret club in Moscow during the early 80s (very apt).

Some minutes later, I caught sight of a hunky David Beckham lookalike on his lonesome leaning against the bar, confidently cruising the crowd while sipping on a lager. 'Blimey! Who's that stunner?' I asked.

'That's Handsome Harry. Works part-time as a receptionist at Tony's G.P. surgery and part-time for Harvey Nichols. I must say, for a minimum wage earner, the man is minted,' divulged Ryan. 'Wears nothing but the best and newest designer everything, and even with staff discount, that isn't cheap. And he's a total stud in bed ...' Tony shot Ryan a glower as he quickly added, '... so I hear.'

'Then why is he drinking here? And why have you kept this hunk a secret?' I asked as I was distracted momentarily by a prematurely aged queen throwing a nicotine-stained fist into another's face. We slinked further away from the brawl in one well-choreographed move and continued.

'He lives one block down the road, in a flat that's akin to something out of *The Home Show* ...' interjected Tony as Ryan fired daggers back at him, '... so I hear!' he added, darting his lizard tongue in defiance at his husband-to-be.

I left them squabbling and made my move. I figured a guy who followed fashion so feverishly would be into any new blood on the scene, and I reckon, despite my age, I'm a born-again queer. My opening line was, 'Hey there, I'm new here. Know of anywhere a guy can go for a *quieter* drink?'

Handsome Harry looked delighted to see me as the nicotine fisted guy was launched past him towards the exit by a gaudy drag queen dressed as Little Bo-Peep. We looked on as the drag-handled upstart was grabbed by a shovel-handed bouncer and cast smoothly into the sun-bleached street. As the dust in the air swirled in the wake of the human meteor that'd just been sent into orbit, Handsome Harry threw back his drink and said in a thick cockney accent, 'I know just the place. One block away.'

I waved a jolly goodbye to the Terrible Twins and headed to Handsome Harry's super apartment. There followed one very intense bout of shagging.

Wednesday 14th July

This evening, after excellent comfort food at *Mum's* on Forrest Road, Sally, Ryan, Gwen (with a new and more effervescent coiffure – think Kelly Garrett of Charlie's Angels – thanks to a girly night at Sally's) and I did the inevitable post-mortem that occurs when one of your friends (Ryan) starts the conversation with a sly, 'So, about last night ...?'

'When you say *safe* I trust we are talking condoms here?' asked Gwen as she balanced precariously on a stool with her legs akimbo in the aptly named *Frisky*, a frozen yoghurt bar just two ticks down the road from *Mum's*.

'No, sweetie,' interposed Sally. 'Like I showed you. Like this.' Sally stood up from her stool and composed herself. She then seated herself elegantly and swept her hands down her perfectly balanced legs which were being caressed by a purple pencil skirt. She crossed them slowly, hugging each thigh tightly with the other. Sally's Pygmalion project nodded in agreement and adjusted her posture to mirror Sally's.

'Normally, yes, but this time, no,' I replied, 'This time it means so safe I could hardly move a hair on his head. In fact, I couldn't! When I grabbed the back of his neck for a heady snog, he muttered, "Don't touch my hair." '

Sally slammed down her tub, 'Oh, for fuck's sake! Are you sure?'

'Aye, said it twice,' I assured her.

'Well, I knew he liked to keep himself pristine, but that's one inch short of a loofa!' joked Ryan. 'I mean, we all like to look our best, but at times like this, it's great to let loose and become so hot and sweaty that your hair becomes matted and your makeup gets smeared all over your face. Your bodies slither and slide as one as you screw and screw until you fall into a tangled mass of hot sticky man-sex on the dirty bathroom floor.'

We gawped at Ryan, our expressions as frozen as our yoghurt. He surreptitiously scraped his little plastic spoon against the bottom of his tub. 'Okay, I'll admit it. Our wedding seems to be taking up all of our energy. We haven't had proper sex for months, and I could shag a greyhound in the middle of a race right now. I have needs, damn it!'

I smirked, content that it wasn't all flowers and fumbles for them. He swung a finger towards my nose, 'And if you so much as grin for one more second I'll slap your hair so out of shape you'll wish you were bald, my friend.'

'As if I care about my hair *that* much,' I joked.

'Hmmm, evidently so,' agreed Ryan, nibbling on his spoon with a cheeky grin.

'You wear makeup?' asked Gwen. 'How long have you worn makeup?'

Sally tapped Gwen's knee gently. 'Focus, Gwen. It's acceptable for men to wear makeup once again.'

'But I've only just started wearing makeup, and I'm in my thirties,' exclaimed Gwen.

Ryan shiftily moved his eyes from Gwen and turned to me, checking his foundation was still flawlessly applied by flipping open the camera on his phone 'So, you couldn't touch his hair. How the hell did you manage when you hit the sheets?'

I leaned in to whisper. The gang placed their cups on the table and edged forward. 'That's the thing, you see, he didn't get undressed. He wore his suit throughout with his bits just hanging from his fly. I think he got off on it. It was kinda horny.' I was almost ashamed to admit that I'd developed another fetish.

Sally hummed in agreement. Then she announced with much

aplomb, 'You know, at the club, I have a regular customer who's happy to have me dance around him, almost touching him, but tantalisingly not. He likes the closeness, to feel my breath on his skin, but never ever wants me to touch him.'

'What's that all about?' asked Ryan.

'I don't know. All I know is it turns him on. He pays double for it. One of my best clients. Normally I'm fighting to keep their hands off me – they have to pay a lot extra for that – but he prefers the "no contact rule". Maybe he feels he isn't cheating on his wife if I keep my distance. All I know is he's the hottest devil in there and, if I'm honest, I would love for him to touch me. But he doesn't and that in turn drives me wild. Go figure.'

Gwen flashed Sally a glance of disapproval and asked me, 'Are you going to see him again?'

'Fuck, Gwen. The work is "fuck": "Are you going to *fuck* him again?" ' corrected Sally.

'Sorry ... *fuck*.' With her German accent, she seemed to add more emphasis on the letter 'K', almost as if it was capitalised. The word seemed taboo coming from her mouth. I took a moment. I've never heard Gwen swear up until tonight. It was rude, and for a time, I became concerned for the type of woman she'd become under Sally's mentorship.

'You know,' I said. 'I think I will. Just to see how it goes.' I grinned as I sucked on my little spade. 'Maybe next time we can both be suited businessmen.'

'Just don't mess his hair!' joked Ryan.

'Quite!' I agreed.

Thursday 15th July

I've just come home from lazy sundowners in Holyrood Park with Ryan. I was often distracted from our conversation by the many talented joggers beating the path around Arthur's Seat. He eventually gave in and joined me in a spot of *Horny, Hitched or High-road*. It's not a challenging game. You inspect the passing talent and quickly judge if hypothetically they would be a quick fumble (Horny), someone you'd take home to your folks (Hitched) or you would rather they jogged on (High-road).

It's a fast-paced game, especially at lunchtime, necessitating quick decision making with only seconds to scan, process and decide: front/side/back/top to toe. There's no prize; it's just a bit of harmless fun. After several rounds of the game, I found a higher proportion of *Horny* suitors in comparison to Ryan's *Hitched* quota.

'I guess that just confirms that I'm the marrying kind,' he smugly announced, laying back on the warm grass.

'Either that or you're just a desperate old queen in need of companionship,' I quipped, splashing cold water on his boyishly smooth chest from the bottle of rather unremarkable spring water I had bought for a remarkable price.

'I'll show you who's old!' he said as he leapt up and ripped the bottle from my sluggish hands. The T-shirt I was wearing was drenched by the time he was done chasing me around the park. 'Oh, dear,' he said smugly, 'you're drenched. What a shame. Take it off and lay it on the grass. It'll dry in no time in this heat.'

'Are you kidding me? And expose my fat white bits to the masses? I don't do public ridicule. I've enough private ridicule every time I'm alone in front of the bathroom mirror,' I said between gasps for breath.

'Don't be silly, Andy,' he panted back. 'You have a lovely, natural build. I'd kill to have your chest.'

My already flushed cheeks became rosier still. It was nothing to do with the summer sun or the sudden bout of exercise between two almost middle-aged men, no this was because Ryan had struck a nerve. His flattery, his honest opinion of me, made me blush. Why do I care so much what he thinks when I told myself not to?

'Nah,' I tried to shrug it off, 'let's not even go there.'

'Aww, come on! You, Andy, are the best of the best! Most people are just custard, but you are crème brûlée. If I were single and you jogged by ...' just then his phone rang on the blanket we'd upset in our tussle. The Dallas theme tune blared in our small patch of the park, causing a few sun worshipers to come to life and look around in amusement. I was glad when he eventually answered the call. A short conversation filled with, 'Yes. Yes. Soon, Boo-Boo. Promise,' assured me it was Tony. When he hung up, it seemed he'd lost his train of thought. He stood there for a tick peering at me quizzically. I'm not sure if he saw the want in my eyes – his face showed no inclination – or if the call from Tony caused some kind of reality check.

Yes? If you were single and I jogged by, what? Would it be Horny or Hitched? I asked myself.

He shivered and croaked, 'It's getting cold. We're soaked. We should be getting back.'

If a T-shirt can dry quickly in this heat, then so can we, I thought. But there was little point arguing, Tony could herd in Ryan with a single word.

The walk home was general chat on whatever could fill the stifling air until we split at the end of London Road with an awkward hug. I was barely conscious of the traffic on Leith Walk and the rabble of people as I slid by, my shirt almost dry from the kindly breeze blowing towards me from Leith. I asked myself again, *What kind of jogger am I to Ryan? Horny, Hitched or High-road?*

Friday 16th July

I didn't sleep well last night. My thoughts were locked on what could've become of Ryan and me. One night, over several Scrumpy Jacks, a week or so after Steve died, we admitted some kind of mutual attraction while we watched the crowd boogie at CC Blooms. I was just about to throw caution to the wind and kiss Ryan when stupid Tony fell into him and sent him flying down the steps onto the dance floor. It's the only time a guy can be said to have fallen for Tony. I tried to help Ryan up, but Tony shoved me out of the way to save him from the stampede, and he's muscled in ever since. Before long, they were dancing lip-to-lip to *Yes, Sir, I Can Boogie,* and I was firmly reinstated to 'friend' status.

And now I feel really alone; therefore, I've arranged to meet Handsome Harry tonight after work. He's under strict instructions to be suited and booted for my arrival. It's safe to say, I have officially developed a fetish. I'd hoped it would take more than one encounter to lead me down a filthy path, but no, it seems I'm easily led.

Saturday 17th July

Why am I having no luck with sexual encounters these days? It ended abruptly when I accidentally spilt some of my seed on his designer suit. I told Harry he could send me the dry cleaning bill.

'Do you think I can really afford this suit?' he snapped.

'Can't you?'

'Of course I can't! I'm a weekend shop assistant and part-time receptionist, for fuck's sake! I was taking it for a ride: i.e., you. I have to return it unwashed and untainted if its to stand a chance of slipping on the rack unnoticed.'

'Isn't that a tad dishonest?' I asked

'Oh, holy Moses, Andy. I do it all the time. The scene piles so much pressure on me to look my best. I'm *Handsome Harry*, after all. I've a reputation to maintain. Do you know how many crisis loans from the DWP have kept me in face cream and couture over the years?'

This guy has mastered the art of deception. Handsome Harry is definitely all about appearance and nothing more. He has zero personality, the conversation is stilted, and it's impossible to touch his damn hair.

'My supervisor will know this has been used,' he said as he dabbed the leg of his unaffordable trousers with a wet wipe. 'She's been trained to spot the slightest hint of bobbling.'

I slowly but surely put my clothes back on, edging towards the door as I did so. 'I'm sorry. Send me the dry cleaning bill.'

He barked, 'And what shall I say the stains are to the dry cleaning staff, custard?'

I hesitated, almost agreeing, but I decided I was better than that. My clothes may not be designer, but they are within my budget, very me and honest. I went to leave, but before I did, I remembered something Ryan had said. I smiled and replied, 'No, not custard, Harry: Crème Brûlée; the best of the best. Which is what you've missed out on.' And then I shook my hand vigorously through his perfectly sculpted quiff, rocked it from its lacquered foundations and left it in a state of ruin. Most satisfying.

Sunday 18th July

Sex is becoming not only a joke but increasingly expensive: the drink you buy yourself before they arrive, the drinks you buy them, the meals, the breakup coffee, the dry cleaning bills. Perhaps celibacy is the answer to a balanced current account. I'd save on nights out searching for a lay and the taxi ride home when I wake in some random room on the other side of the city.

Monday 19th July

I decided, as the great weather will not last forever, I'd take the bike out for a ride. It's been tethered to the railings on our landing for the past week or so, and the guilt is gnawing away at me every time Sally asks if I've taken it for a spin. I'm doing my best not to lie, it's my summer resolution, but white lies are such a grey area. I tried in desperation to remove the bloody basket from the handlebars, but it appears to be welded in place by some technology developed by NASA.

One hour later, I was a bucket of nerves as I hit the confusion caused by the tram works at the top of Leith Walk. Where there used to be a delightful roundabout and ornamental clock, there's now the equivalent of spaghetti junction had it slipped off a plate and splattered on the kitchen floor. Not a single lane is clearly defined. Buses careered around either side of me dangerously close. At one point, I was sure I'd become a Lothian Transport sandwich, but luckily I was too slow to be caught in the tail end of these hunks of metal. Agitated cars beeped their horns at me. At one point, as my skinny legs began to quiver over the incline of Leith Street, I was overtaken by a Vicky Pollard lookalike pushing a baby buggy up the central divide. I hope the tram works are worth it.

I decided no more. Sweating, I returned home via Waterloo Place, ignoring the gay cruising area like a good boy, and headed towards Easter Road. On the side streets, between the two main strands of Leith Walk and Easter Road, I pedalled off-road and onto the tranquil safety of a public footpath. A momentary relief as two coppers popped up from nowhere. I swerved to avoid them, they dived for cover, the bike went crashing into a small fence, and I finished head first in a hedge, sustaining scratches to my face and minor bruising to my shins.

After a severe talking to, in which I was made fully aware of the highway code and the misuse of public paths – as clearly explained to me by a very dry but dishy police officer – my name and address was taken, and I was given a warning. I felt two inches tall by the time I walked away from the group of neds on trainer bikes and scooters that'd gathered to watch my impromptu roadside reprimand. A five-year-old boy judged me. Really, I could see it in his bloody eyes, he *judged me!* I even heard an audible tut as I pushed my bike away. Another asked his pal, 'Isn't that piece of shit a girls bike?'

This means the basket will be removed ASAP! It's been severely damaged by the argument with the fence anyway; a godsend. I'm sure Sally will have a blowtorch in her garage for such eventualities, or as part of her act.

Tuesday 20th July

Of all the G.P. surgeries, in all the world ...

I was there to pay for my embryonic fetish which had been aborted on Friday night. I counted the cash out purposefully at the reception window for Harry to see. I was hoping he'd sympathise with me, as I let yet another five-pound note slip through my fingers towards him, and change his mind.

One arid exchange of words, a small fortune later, and I was stomping down the stairs under a small thunder cloud. I was almost out the door when I heard hurried footsteps follow me on the serviceable grey carpet. Could it be Harry, conscience pricked and guilt-ridden, sprinting to give me a full refund, or at the very least an apology?

'Andy!'

I recognised that voice; I was afraid to turn around, I knew it was him. He who hugged and held me so close that I felt safe, safer than I have in a long time. The guy who blew my mind sexually, who'd only just begun his journey down the yellow brick road and yet knew exactly how to treat a man with one delicate flick of his tongue. I carried on walking, determined not to face what lingers in the back of the closet.

'Andy!' more anxious this time. I knew I only had to push open the door and walk into the street. The second I stepped on the pavement, the bustle of the city would pull me away from this moment and take me to something new, perhaps something more exciting than him. I could smell him now, as clearly as when my head nestled amongst the warmth of his chest hair. My foot went to fall on the tarmac below, but it hung there unable to move in the summer breeze as a bumblebee buzzed by, totally ignorant of the complications in life.

Once more, with desperation in his voice, *'Andy!'*

Reason said, don't turn around, but my heart had a greater need. I wanted to see him. I had to see, at the very least, that he was okay. I glanced round, trying to shield my fragility from him, but just long enough to catch a glimpse of something new, something I'd never seen before: pain behind his eyes. I could see it as clear as I could see the walls, the door, the windows and the thin grey carpet.

'I miss you,' he blurted.

I wanted to say I missed him too. I wanted to tell him I'd been stupid and we could work something out. That I missed this guy, who had danced in and out of my life like a bumblebee over vibrant summer flowers. The man I hardly knew and yet felt so safe around. It was exactly what I wanted to hear months before. But I knew, since that snowy night we met, the seasons had changed drastically, taking me with them. But for him, nothing had. He was still shifty. He crawled and cowered beneath his own skin, disguised by the straight man costume he wore every day.

'Don't, Alistair,' my voice echoing boldly up the sparse stairwell. This time more firmly, *'Don't.'*

Foot on tarmac, then the other, then again. Soon I was walking down the street, and that particular door had shut behind me. He didn't follow. I was glad of that. The traffic, the breeze, the drone of the city encompassed me in a haze, but it wasn't the Edinburgh I knew, it was an animated picture book flickering before my eyes. I was swallowed up and lost amongst the pages. The birds, the people, and even the buildings were indefinable. Like a Monet painting up close.

I found my way home to you, dear diary, in the hope that some clarity can be found amongst these words. If not today, then maybe when I look back upon this page in days to come.

So far, not so good.

Wednesday 21st July

'Spunk!'

'Pardon?' I asked Sally as she smoothed oil on Ryan's shoulders while we lazed in the debris of what had been a picnic in the park. She's decided to experiment in complementary therapies in the hope it will develop into a new sideline. I pray she doesn't include happy endings.

'Spunk, I said. Jizz, cum, semen, swimmers ...'

Gwen darted her eyes around in embarrassment, 'Please, Sally!' she muttered. 'There are children here.'

Sally raised her head gracefully over Ryan's glistening shoulders and slid her white sunglasses down her nose to take a look around Princes Street Gardens. 'Well, it's about time these noisy little brats learned they weren't conceived as immaculately as their parents would have them believe, so hush and eat your Yum-Yum.'

Gwen tutted, scowled at Sally and moved on, digging her ample teeth into the sticky, sugary dough.

I snatched one from the packet, but was careful to use a plate; I can't abide crumbs, even in a park. 'You have a point, Ms Knowles?' I asked, lip-smacking over the unhealthiest of Scottish snacks.

She glanced disapprovingly toward Gwen, 'My point is that spunk makes men desperate and stupid. Oestrogen and the biological clock makes women desperate and stupid. Adoration is born out of the need to release, procreate and stupidity. We're all just jars of hormones really.'

Gwen laughed, 'Oh, come on! If only it were that easy. There is no simple equation for love. If there were, we'd all be married and raising children by now.'

'Who said anything about love? I didn't,' I protested. 'This is sexual experimentation with some hugs thrown in. Or it was, rather.'

'Sure,' chipped in Ryan for good measure. 'Keep telling yourself that and it will be easier for you and all of us to deal with in the end.'

'If I have to listen to your so-called wedding plans, then you have to listen to my sad single life,' I affirmed.

Ryan nodded. 'Point taken.' But added, 'And it *is* a wedding.'

Sally kneaded Ryan's shoulders heavily, so deeply he flinched, 'Sorry, sweetie! Was that too hard?' she asked.

'A little bit,' he winced towards the rest of us and rolled his eyes. 'But it's okay, I hardly use my shoulders.'

Sally smiled and winked at me, 'Cool! Then I'll continue. Besides, my dear friends, it's listed in Maslow's Hierarchy of Needs.'

'What: Love and Belonging?' asked Gwen.

'Yes, otherwise known as spunk. Regular sex with our partners keeps them happy and close. This keeps us happy, protected and in love with someone we think understands us. And so spunk nurtures.'

'That's just bull! If Tony and I stopped having sex tomorrow, I'd still want to be with him. There's so much more to our relationship than just sex.'

'Yes, sweetie. And ask yourself how long before the gap between the two of you in bed widens until that closeness and intimacy slips off the edge and rolls under the mattress to be forgotten amongst the fluff and pizza crumbs. The less sex couples have, the wider the intimacy gap, scientific fact!' She squeezed Ryan hard on the shoulder blades with her thumbs, and he opened his mouth wide in pain.

'So you *are* saying Alistair wants me after all?' I asked, a little confused.

'No, I am saying he wants that intimacy, that closeness and feeling of belonging Maslow describes, in a way he can't get from his wife. Sex with you is a way to feel that. The urge to cum drives Alistair towards you, as yours does towards him until you are stuck together in as much of a gloopy mess as that Yum-Yum in Gwen's fingers.'

Gwen was about to devour the last chunk of her pudding but gagged on Sally's words and threw it down on the used paper plates I'd stacked neatly. They fell over, causing an incredible urge for me to tidy them away immediately into a plastic bag.

'The key, I imagine, is not to end up a couple of Yum-Yums,' joked Ryan.

'Yes, my point exactly: stop having sex with him,' she said firmly to me.

'Don't worry, I'm not going back there. Hell, no,' I assured them.

Every one of my friends raised a collective eyebrow and looked away.

'Come on! I'm not that gullible,' I laughed. They began to clear up our rubbish and clamped their lips shut, eyebrows still raised. 'Oh, come on. Give me some credit! It's not an issue.'

'Then why are we discussing it?' asked Gwen.

'Because you asked how my week was,' I argued, but I was aware she had a point; I'd obsessed over him since yesterday's collision.

Ryan, always the champion of true love and monogamy, popped his t-shirt back on (relieved, I imagine, that his torture was over) and cheered, 'Good for you! I know my Andy; he isn't a home-wrecker or dumb-dumb!'

I smiled. His support was graciously received, but I know I've already damaged Alistair's marriage in some small way.

Thursday 22nd July

Maybe it's the summer sun, nature becoming frivolous around us, or the want in my eyes, but I've picked up a guy without any online help. At the barber's, amongst the football pages of *The Sun* and testosterone-fuelled chat, I picked up an actual living, breathing man. Not some pretentious profile with a photo that's had every flaw filtered out. I clocked him in the mirror as soon as I sat on the mottled bench. As the barber clipped the back of his neck to a 0.5, I pricked up my ears. I picked up snippets of information about him while he chatted to the barber and I hid behind a battered solo copy of *Hello* magazine (the right magazine to send out the right signal; imagine the confusion if I was peering over a copy of *Nuts* magazine).

He's thirty-three, lives just around the corner on Albion Road, has a mother with MS, or who works at M&S (the hairdryer was turned on at this point), Welsh, has a mortgage that's crippling him, and travels up and down the country working full-time for a clothing retailer. I spent the next torturous and delightful ten minutes being cruised by him via the mirror. I was like Alice Through the Flirting Glass, slowly but surely being tempted into another, more colourful world of arousal.

Eyebrows trimmed, hair styled and waxed and it was time for him to leave. Once the cape was flapped off, it revealed a fit frame that suited the skinny jeans and tight chequered shirt he was sporting perfectly. His ass is like a peach. I was most disappointed when it left. I needed more than just the cheeky wink and a smile he gifted me as he swung out the door. I wanted to chase after him, but my barber was already calling me to the chair. As I sat down, my cutie's cologne enveloped me. I inhaled deeply until the barber swept the cloak around me and fastened it so tight my Adam's apple hid in shock.

Moments later, I was brushing the hair off my forehead with a coarse tissue as I leapt up the steps from the shop.

'Looking good, mister.' A familiar cologne danced under my nose as it dawned on me someone with a Welsh accent had just spoken not too far from my rear.

I smiled to myself before I turned to greet him. 'Cheers, I think it's too short. He always loses track of my do and cuts it within an inch of its life.'

'Oh, "do" is in again, is it?' He was teasing me, and I liked it.

'Yup, that and "bad", as in *good*,' I joked.

'Bad or good, you look great,' he grinned. I felt my neck flush. 'What do you think of mine?'

'Well, you would look good with any cut, with no hair even, or dreadlocks,' I stammered. What was I saying? *Shush, Andy!*

'God forbid!' he laughed. Then he offered his hand. 'I'm Chris.'

Chris Quiff, I thought. 'Randy ... Mandy ... I mean, *ANDY!*' I clasped his hand desperately, shaking it like a crazy man. 'Andy, that's my name. Not Mandy, because that would make me a girl, which I most definitely am not.' He looked at me, still smiling but saying nothing, as I continued to shake the life out of his wrist. I couldn't be sure if he was re-evaluating his decision to approach me and planning his escape. I thought, *About now would be an excellent time to stop talking, Andy!* But my mouth did the opposite, 'You see, I have a penis, therefore, not a Mandy. A little bit randy, maybe, but most definitely an Andy, because that's my name. Christened and everything ...'

He smiled and looked intrigued by the escaped mental patient he'd stumbled across. 'Are you nervous, Randy Andy who's not a Mandy?' he asked, breaking my ramblings and pausing my ridiculous handshaking with his other hand.

I felt like a schoolboy. 'Aye, just a bit.'

'No need,' he winked again, which didn't help! 'Hey, want to go out on a date, if dates are still cool?'

'Yes, they are, very much so. A date would be great!' I laughed nervously. 'I'm a poet, and I don't know it ... oooh, shut up now!' I said out loud. 'Me, not you!'

He laughed and reached into his back pocket. 'Here's my card. Call me.'

I shifted my head giddily from side to side and stupidly replied with, 'I fank ewe!'

'Call me tomorrow, Randy Andy.' He winked as he walked past me and smacked my ass. Really, he slapped me square and hard on the bum. The cheeky bugger. As he walked away, brazenly looking back every now and then, I flipped over the business card he had slid into my quaking hand and read the top line. It said: 'CHRIS BROWN – Window Dresser.'

I gazed after him in awe. Could it actually be? Nah! Surely not? The legend I'd heard about with the biggest willy in Edinburgh, possibly Scotland? I hoped so.

Friday 23rd July

'Mercy! Yes! Take it, use it, suck it, sit on it, dip it in chocolate and do it all again, sweetie!' This was Sally's answer to my possible date with Chris. In fact, it could be Sally's answer to anything, animal, vegetable or mineral (we were spoiling ourselves with lunch in The Tower restaurant at the top of the National Museum of Scotland). 'What are you afraid of?' she asked.

'I was in a relationship for ten years. I'm afraid of taking anything more than the average six-point-five inches.' I placed both my index fingers opposite each other to emphasise my point, 'Anything more than this and I'll struggle.'

'That's never six-point-five,' she interrupted.

'Yes, it is.'

She placed her hands side-by-side on the glass-topped table and slid them apart slowly, stopping short of the edges of her bamboo placemat. 'This is six-point-five inches.'

'Really?'

'Yes, my naïve friend. I've had enough flashed at me over the years; it's been a very extensive survey involving many nationalities.'

'All this time I was lead to believe that Thomas was "average". Shit! No wonder I'm crap at triptych picture hanging. I feel totally cheated. Like I've been forced into some kind of decade long diet.'

'You have, darling. It's a surprise you're not malnourished,' agreed Sally. 'It's an outrage. An outrage. It's time you got some healthy meat in you.'

10 p.m. Chris and I have a date tomorrow night at *The Dome* on George Street.

Saturday 24th July

8 p.m. I've become complacent and missed several washdays. I've had to slump for the only fresh t-shirt I have left. I only hope they don't turn me away at the doors of *The Dome*. Not everyone appreciates a t-shirt with the rescue protocol of every Windows user out there: 'ctrl, alt, delete', but in place of the delete there's a Cyberman's head. Neat, I think, but is it *The Dome*? At any rate, it'll be good for me to out myself as a Whovian on the first date. Saves many months of hiding it in the toy cupboard along with my childhood (and sometimes adult) desire to be Wonder Woman.

Sunday 25th July

Sundays are meant for days off and long lies. They're for wasted hours spent spooning a new squeeze in bed. They're for spells of sleepiness broken by fits of desire and unhurried bouts of sex until you fall dreamily back into the pheromones of the other. Sleep, wake, desire, and so it continues. Rinse and repeat. This is the perfect Sunday morning, but alas, not my Sunday. Not in my bed.

I'm a top, or a bottom, depending on the notion. I think I'm more top than bottom, so I'm not even sure I can fit into the 'Versatile' category if you are flicking through labels. My online 'role' would now say nothing. I figure it's best to keep it fluid as I'm still working that one out. Maybe I'm neither. Anal sex can be so overrated. The thing is, I'm the kind of guy that needs coaxing into anal access. A few kisses here, a lick or two there, a caress from behind. I'm not the kind of guy that opens up the second the bedroom door closes. I irrefutably detest a dry finger rammed up there within a second of unbuckling my belt. This does not make my head go light, and my legs fill with helium. But I was desperate for company, and did I mention? He's hung like a horse! So I persevered. Regrettably, he did too. From then on, it was an uphill struggle. He said we could just spoon and sleep, but then I was woken soon after by firm prodding and dry-humping. It could've been his lack of anal manners, or my quiet fear of anything bigger than a Chiquita banana, but my anus tightened to the point of becoming invisible. If this was meant to be a party, my arse became socially inept and hopped into the next taxi to Virgin Ville.

By 2 a.m., several retakes and empty condoms later, I was losing the will to live, and the single life became an attractive alternative. But he insisted he was a top and only a top as his many inches buckled under the resistance of my Olympic standard anus. He pressed on.

'You like that big fat cock, don't you?' he asked, sweat dripping from his brow.

Was I suddenly in a 90s porno? What's a boy to do? 'Yes,' I lied, 'yes I do.' I didn't want to have a bad review plastered all over the scene. For a second I lost focus, and my rectum gave way, allowing him full access, zooming up me faster than a drag queen on speed gunning for a dance floor filled with half-naked rugby players. 'Get it out! Get it out of me!' I screamed as I flipped him off my back and sent him crashing unceremoniously to the floor.

'You just had to say no, Andy.' Grunted Chris as he clutched his lower back. His quiff had collapsed into a sweaty pile of gloop, and he suddenly seemed less attractive.

Really? Surely the past two hours of this pantomime should've been some kind of hint, I thought. The next few hours were more uncomfortable than the previous, both of us too gentlemanly to do the right thing and call it a night. So there we were, sexually dysfunctional and at separate ends of the bed with the Colonel purring happily between us. I was glad of the fury bolster.

I prayed Molasses would call me into work as soon as dawn broke. She didn't. I decided to lie, 'Oh, dear, I forgot I was working today. I have to be at work by seven,' I said, rushing around the room in a pretend panic. 'You'll have to go.'

'Call me,' he said without intent.

'Sure,' I lied, as I finally shut him out. I lethargically staggered the short distance back to bed. The warmth of the duvet caressed me. *The things I do for company*, I thought. *Alone at last.*

Monday 26th July

'I have a haemorrhoid! I literally had minimal penetration, a night of prostration and sexual frustration, and all I get is an enormous haemorrhoid?' I complained.

'Oh, honey, if that had happened to me, there would have been a castration to finish off that little rhyme,' quipped Sally.

'I'm sure they could print that on a t-shirt: "I endured a night of frustration & all I got was this lousy haemorrhoid!"' blurted Ryan, laughing and almost sending the froth from his cappuccino across the table.

'Can we please not say *haemorrhoid* at the breakfast table? Especially as I have blueberries with my oats,' pleaded Gwen. She winced and camouflaged her berries by submerging them in the gloopy porridge.

'Oats! I didn't even sow my oats!' I cried. 'There may have been a reprieve if that had happened, but no, I was totally oat-less! We both were.'

Gwen, Ryan and Sally had joined me for a pre-work breakfast while Molasses was out of town visiting The London School of Coffee. It means two free breakfasts for me on top of the usual free dinners the café gifts me every double shift.

'Okay, we'll call them *blueberries* then,' I joked.

Gwen clattered her spoon onto the table. 'In what way is that helping?' she bit back.

Ryan piped up, 'Jeez! What's got into you? You've been grouchy since we met at the bus stop.'

'I'm sorry, I am practising a piece for a show in the Festival Fringe and time is marching on. My group is in a bit of untidiness, and we have only days left to get it right. If that is not bad enough, we are a tenor short in the choir because of pig flu. Most unfortunate.'

Sally pretended to look for her bag under the large, solid oak table and joked, 'Here, my purse is somewhere. Let me give you a loan of a tenner, sweetie.'

We groaned in unison.

Gwen drew breath and stared Sally down, 'Yes,' she let out a short mocking chuckle, 'go on, laugh. We'll see who will be laughing again when a certain someone at the table needs assistance to remove a strip of wax from her back.'

Sally gasped, 'You, bitch! That was an emergency, and you were sworn to secrecy.' Sally defended herself, 'I have a couple of light-blond, practically invisible to the naked eye, strands of hair just out of reach on my back.'

'All is fair in love and war,' smirked Gwen.

'Well, you'll know all about the latter and nothing about the former!' bit Sally as she took a smug draw on her cigarette and blew smoke in Gwen's face.

'Oh, great! Now we're dredging up old WWII submarines. Stop them, Andy,' pleaded Ryan.

'Blueberries!' I shouted so loud, Barry appeared from the kitchen.

'Aye? Do you want more?' he asked.

'No, thank you!' I replied, almost exasperated. Why do I put myself through these mass meetings? Barry disappeared back into his cave. I whispered, 'What can be done for this kind of thing?'

'This was bound to happen eventually, Andy,' said Ryan. 'You are thirty-five, after all. You're lucky to have got this far through life without a single pile. Nothing a trip to the chemist won't fix and a little patience. And, Gwen, I have a tenor that may suit. Matt is his name. Very pleasing on the eyes and ears.' My ears immediately and hopefully pricked up until Ryan added, 'And I'm sorry, Andy, he's straight, and you're out of action.'

'Oh, my God. You actually know some straight men?' I asked, clutching my chest in mock bewilderment.

'Yes, I do, and don't give me any lip, or I'll switch your Anusol for Deep Heat.'

'I'm Andy Angus, and I have a haemorrhoid,' I announced as if at an AA meeting.

'It's a fact of life. Everyone knows it's all downhill after thirty-five. This is just the beginning. Old age doesn't just come on its own.'

'Thank you for that stark reality, Ryan Leadbetter. Might I remind you that you're mere months behind me,' I said.

He mocked me with a single laugh. 'No, I'll be fine; I live in Tupperware and have plenty of money for surgery, my poor, poor ancient friend.'

Bitch!

Tuesday 27th July

Sally's finished my bike, and it looks fantastic. The basket's gone, there's storage compartments fitted to the rear, and it's been resprayed a sporty red and black.

'She looks so good I almost want to trade her in for my bike,' she said.

'Really?'

'Are you kidding? I have the beast of my dreams throbbing between my thighs. Enjoy.'

A butcher bike gives me more confidence on the roads for some reason. Nothing seemed to faze me on my return home from a trip to the chemist, not even my troubled anus. I passed Tony as he left work. I could've zipped past him with two fingers raised to the air, but opted for the more casual, 'Hello, Tony,' and continued onward thinking, *Eat my dust, sucker! The back blubber will be no more!*

Wednesday 28th July

Matt, the tenor, arrived at the bedsit early this afternoon. He's a dashing lad in his early twenties with ginger flicked hair that has natural highlights at every tip, and a sparrow-like chest that bulges and pushes the top of his preppy shirt open just wide enough to see an inviting mass of blond chest hair. He's built like a brick shit-house. I imagined his shirt popping every button from its threads as he inhaled deeply from the climb to the third floor. Why is he not gay?

I most definitely saw Gwen blush. She clumsily loosened off the blue elastic band that was strangling her hair and attempted to shake it free. She may have been aiming for 'sexy and sultry', but this is impossible for a woman who spent her formative years at the Ann Widdecombe School of allure. The clasp that held the heavily lacquered fringe in place became tangled amongst the wiry mess, which she spent the next few minutes hopelessly trying to pull free. Moments later, her head was thoroughly crocheted. She gave up and left the clasp somewhere in the disaster, looking like a crazy cat lady who has been abandoned by every cat she owns.

'Good to meet you, at last, Matt,' she said as she shook his hand so firmly, I saw him wince. 'I believe you are my tenor in shining armour,' she over-exaggerated a breathy laugh and tried to blow the fringe/clasp combo out of her eyes. 'Come in.' More breathy laughter and sexy Matt was swallowed up into the blackness of Gwen's lodgings.

I wish they'd finish. It's been two hours of repetitive tenor and cello antics interspersed with many mistakes, flirty giggles from Gwen and repeat performances of previous mistakes. It's putting me right off Countdown. If music be the food of love, then hit the crescendo and cum already!

8 p.m. It is not easy to treat your own afflicted bottom. I've spent a few minutes squatting over a small mirror to inspect the damage thoroughly. In my head, it was the size of an unshelled walnut and at bursting point, but on closer inspection, it's smaller than a petit pois pea. It throbs like someone's reverse parked a bloody Mini Metro up my butt. It's been an annoying distraction all day. God, I hope it's not chronic! Small though it is, it is not attractive in the slightest and will hamper any future pursuits in finding a man. Rimming and anal sex has been deleted unexpectedly from my jolly pastimes. And who the hell decided that a pointy plastic tube would be the best method for internal cream application? And why make it white? It hurts and disgusts me. I couldn't bear to look at it after I retrieved the offensive weapon from my already traumatised anus. I washed it with Dettol under a hot tap through squinted vision. I have this horror to endure at least twice a day and after every poop, which will disgust me further. Now I'm more irritated than ever. How can anyone be sociable with a haemorrhoid?

Thursday 29th July

'So, we've decided to go for a musical theme for the wedding,' announced Ryan as I swerved past him at the bar, balancing meals for two recently Civil Partnered lesbians and respective mothers-in-law.

'Oh, lovely. What composer? Beethoven? Handle?' I asked as I plopped the plates down.

'Not exactly,' he shifted awkwardly in his stool. 'More Chicago, Westside Story, Mama Mia with a tad of seventies disco thrown in.'

I laughed one of those spontaneous laughs that has a bit of catarrh behind it. 'You are joking, of course?'

'No, I'm MGM serious.'

'Seriously, you want your special day to become a homage to every camp movie ever made?'

'Well, Tony has always loved musicals, and I do love Chicago: it was our first trip to the theatre together.'

'You're having a laugh.'

'No.' he paused for a second. 'Oh, and we need dancers, so I've put you on the list.'

'Dancers? For what?'

'For the opening and closing of the show. I mean, our wedding.'

'You're winding me up, I know it.'

'Sally is doing the choreography, aren't you?'

Ms Knowles spun around elegantly, grinning from ear to ear as she passed with arms stacked with Potato Puddings, 'Yup! Chance of a lifetime for me. Director and choreographer of my own hit show. The DVD will look fabulous in my portfolio. It shall be spectacular, darling. The gayest wedding of gay weddings.' She blew Ryan a kiss and danced her way through the café.

I raised my finger to Ryan. 'No! I said no more wedding shenanigans.' He beamed at me with a wide Hollywood grin and then turning on the old sad eyes routine. 'Oh, very good. Almost Oscar-winning, buddy, but it's not going to wash with me. No chance!' I asserted. *This* is what comes of allowing your friends to mingle.

We start rehearsals once the Edinburgh Fringe is over and everyone involved is free of other commitments. I'll buy the leotard and leg-warmers at a later date if I prove to be a hit, which I say is most unlikely as I have infamous two left feet; I was the only munchkin in our school production of the Wizard of Oz who couldn't follow the yellow brick road. I fell off the stage and demolished Primary Five's papier-mâché depiction of Moses parting of the Red Sea. The audience gasped as I took out ten Israelites and their only hope of escaping the Egyptians. It did raise plenty of money for charity, however, as the video sold well and became the most popular release ever by Saint Dominic's Primary.

Haemorrhoid Watch: No smaller; just as painful. I apparently look deep in thought, according to Gwen, when, in actual fact, I'm distracted by the little blighter hanging off my bowels.

Friday 30th July

4.50 p.m. Bloody hell! It's survival of the fittest out there. It's as if the apocalypse has been announced and everyone's running around like crazy, bumbling buffoons. The buses are packed, the streets are full of tourists wandering in haphazard directions and unexpectedly stopping the flow of pedestrian traffic to point at some arbitrary view. Car horns are peeping at taxis aggressively, taxis are peeping at cyclists, cyclists are banging on the side of buses in sweaty fits of rage, adding to this belligerent concoction.

The natives, such as myself, head towards this turmoil with jolly expressions and comments like, 'Let's have some fun at the Festival,' and, 'Of course the kids will love it; bring the two push-chairs, honey,' but leave with concrete frowns, uttering, 'Let's never do this again,' between expletives. When I left this morning, I was a cheery soul desperate for culture, however, by two o'clock, I wanted to bludgeon every last idiot to death who got in my way.

I've returned to the safety of my bedsit with a ready meal, bottle of wine and a classic Doctor Who marathon planned until I:

a) Fall asleep on the couch.
b) Finish the wine and that bottle of Malibu I've stashed away for a rainy day and naturally pass-out on the couch in a pool of drool with a cat sleeping on my neck.
c) Cut out the middle man, turn my TV around to watch all fourteen episodes in bed with all I need to enjoy my evening stacked next to me on my bedside table, and then pass-out.

Option *C* it is!

8.45 p.m. Being alone and single isn't all that bad: I've managed to run a minibar with nibbles in the space that's formerly been occupied by Thomas. I'm uncharacteristically comfortable with my sloppiness, which means I'm already tipsy.

9.30 p.m. Being drunk and applying Anusol Cream to one's nether regions is not an easy trick. You need to be an experienced acrobat!

Saturday 31st July

10 a.m. One squinty-eyed gaze at my phone confirms how my evening panned out. A text or two from Sally and one request to join her after work with another bottle of wine explains why I woke up next to her in my bed. The main menu for *Pyramids of Mars* was still looping around on the telly. 'I bring Sutekh's gift of death to all humanity!' could be heard repeatedly through the tog of my duvet. *Oh, do you really?* I thought as I turned the box off, feeling slightly empowered by shutting the trap of an evil god. It didn't last long. I was back in bed as soon as I kicked Sally out.

1 p.m. I've lost my haemorrhoid. It's gone. Where the hell did it go? Is this normal? It's as if it's never been there. Did it drop off overnight? I did see the Colonel playing with something small in the corner of the room earlier. Or has it just nipped up my bum to lull me into a false sense of security, ready to rear its ugly head the second I'm in with a chance of sex? Am I back in action?

Sunday 1st August

The Festival Fringe officially begins today. This morning I found the guidebook laid by my door with corners folded marking the shows Sally's found of interest. She's circled many with comments like, 'This looks good,' and, 'This could be a riot.' Her choices are dance or drama related. I spent the morning flicking through the pages and noted some for myself.

When I made my way towards lunch with Ryan, I found another guide marked with thin posits by my door: Gwen. She's used highlighter pens to correspond with the following descriptions: Orange – really want to see; Green – could see if time; Yellow – if I miss it, I won't cry. Mainly jazz or free comedy. None tie-up with Sally's plans. Also, there's a request to help flier her own show at Old St Paul's, 'We could make a fun night of it!!!' it said. A soul-destroying evening stood in the warm Scottish rain attempting to be energetic and charming to tourists who, even if they do actually take a flier, will toss it aside quickly to become trodden into the glossy, wet cobbles is not my idea of 'fun'.

When I arrived at Bar Boda, Ryan was thumbing through his copy of the Festival Fringe Guide, 'So, what do you want to go see this year? Your first year back in the big city.' My heart should've soared, but all I could think about was my ever-decreasing bank balance. This is going to be an expensive month if I want to keep everyone happy. Nice to have friends, though. Not cheap, but nice.

Monday 2nd August

Christina dropped off six bottles of wine for each of us at the café. I felt as if I'd interrupted a heavy conversation between herself and Molasses as I wandered in. They stared at me for a second as if an alien was growing out of my forehead, then Christina waved the gift of wine under my nose.

'Thank you,' I said, giving her a squeeze. 'Why do I deserve this?'

'Oh, for being you. Always live in the moment,' she said as she nodded towards Molasses and left.

After she'd gone, I asked my boss, 'What's up?' Has Molasses been discussing my personal highs and lows with our wine merchant and she was feeling sorry for me?

'Fyah de a mus-mus tail, her tink a cool breeze,' she said.

'Eh?'

'It means nothing and none of your business,' she answered quickly. 'Potatoes to peel, lad. Put that lot in the back, and I'll get started on the butternuts. Oh, and make sure Sally doesn't catch a breeze of this. I'm hiding her bottles. It will take that girl only one night to kick the ass out of all of them.'

'Agreed.'

11.30 p.m. The end of a very long day and a text from my mother: 'You have forgotten two of your nephews' birthdays. I am disappointed in you. Visit soon! Mum, X.'

I'm in the bad books yet again. I'll make the dreaded trip on Sunday.

Tuesday 3rd August

As I peered around my door for an urgent dash to the lavvy in my protruding pyjamas at 5 a.m., I saw Matt cautiously leaving Gwen's room. Suspicious, as there wasn't a single note played all night. So why was he there? My Spidey-senses are tingling. Had she been keeping more than just his vocal cords warmed up?

Later, as I helped two yawning musicians flier the Grass Market, I asked, 'Late night last night?'

They both paused in unison and said in well-rehearsed rhythm, 'No, we were just up early to practice in the church hall this morning.' However, Matt stumbled over the location, saying, 'town' instead of 'church' before Gwen stepped in to correct both of them, 'The town church hall. At Pilrig.'

Well stick me in a red and blue leotard and call me Spiderman, I think they may be lying. Is it possible Gwen's finally met her sexually inexperienced match?

Wednesday 4th August

A phone call from Ryan, my well-read friend.

'I know it's a huge ask, but could you also do a reading at our wedding?'

'Ugh, can't you ask someone else?' I begged. 'I hate public speaking.'

'Please? Tony's suggestion is his friend Brenda, who hasn't seen a dentist since Sarah Greene left Blue Peter and is threatening to wear a sleeveless dress; we can't afford frame-by-frame photoshopping in the video.'

'Um ...'

'He's going to ask her this afternoon at work, but if I get you to say yes this morning, that cancels her out.

Silence from me.

'It's just one more favour.'

'Okay, I'm regretting this already, but I'll do it.'

'Deal! Oh, it's *A Tapestry of Love*, by Anon. I don't really know the author, we just found it in one of those marriage preparation books, and I love it. Got to go, I have a facial in five. Byeeee.'

I chuckled to myself after he hung up. 'That's "ANON" as in "Anonymous" you plonker. I'll tell him later. After the wedding.

Thursday 5th August

One lunch break used up shopping for the nephews' presents. I grudge getting them anything. I absolutely deserve some kind of compensation for being a single gay man with no children. I've no plans to have kids, even if I could I wouldn't want them, so I think I should balance an invoice and total it up for my fortieth birthday. It would be enough to afford a first-class ticket to New Zealand and back, I'm sure.

After an age of indecisiveness, I settled on two rather cute, funky t-shirts. One with a smiling dolphin reclining in a deckchair and the other with a meat-eating dinosaur chewing on a leaf, both with the caption 'Think Different' underneath. The shop didn't have them ready to go so I'll have to pick them up on my way on Sunday.

'Surely it doesn't take much time and effort to print two tiny tees?'

The Brummie guy with multiple piercings and as many tattoos (an art student I imagine) who looked dead from consecutive nights clubbing replied, 'It takes skill and a steady hand to make most prints, mate. The slightest movement and you'd think you was having a bad trip. Besides, the Festival's caused a rush on our Scottish range.'

This bloody Festival. It seems to be the excuse for late buses, bad attitudes and delayed pieces of cotton smeared in coloured paste. If the price is a reflection on the skill, I'll expect two masterpieces that my nephews can frame on their walls for years to come. I'm £50 lighter in the pocket.

Friday 6th August

Today I saw Sandi Toksvig's performance at the Gilded Balloon. Not a single buddy of mine was free at short notice, but I decided I couldn't miss my chance of seeing a childhood idol live. Sandy was great, of course. Perfectly timed wit. But I really did feel quite alone sat in that packed audience.

Today I really missed having a partner.

Saturday 7th August

Someone has nicked the seat off my bike right from under my very nose. I'd left her in the usual spot, tethered to the lamppost across from the sex shop, in a respectable part of a kindly city. Who would do such a thing? I discovered my robbery at closing. It was getting dark, but luckily I hadn't far to travel as I was going to a show at the Free Fringe, which was round the corner in the basement bar of The Phoenix. When I got there, Ryan and Tony (my Fringe dates for the night) were two drinks down already. My timing was rubbish as Biffo glanced at and swirled the dregs at the bottom of his glass, hinting he was dry. If he slammed that damn glass intentionally on the bar once, he slammed it a hundred times. I caved-in and bought my wealthy friends with a lavish city centre flat a drink each. Ryan went for the cheaper option (beer) but bloody Biffo wanted a cosmopolitan.

I made it clear I couldn't afford to make a night of it as I was totally skint. 'Aww,' said a disingenuous Biffo, 'I can't remember what it's like to be poor like you. It must be so time-consuming travelling to out-of-town discount clothing stores and rifling through poorly organised racks with nothing to guide you but harsh strip lighting.' A slap was on the cards for him, but he moved the night on within a blink of an eye. 'Could we move downstairs quickly, Boo-Boo? All these beer-stained sweatpants are making me nauseous.'

It hasn't stopped your damn thirst though, has it? I thought. Anyhow, I think the clientele in The Phoenix is a good mix, but I could see Ryan was out of his comfort zone, so I obliged. He's more at home sipping over-priced French plonk while standing in a 90's wine bar in a white linen suit and Panama hat.

The show was great, but the venue was tough to endure. The heat was as much a pain in the ass as the crappy plastic chair that tortured me throughout. My glass of gin was down like a shot and, without thinking, I was back at the bar getting yet another round. No offer from Biffo. This is why he's rich. I'll make damn sure I eat every scrap of food delicately laid in front of me at their reception and drink Champagne until my liver collapses. I walked home totally pissed off. So much for fun at the Festival.

Sunday 8th August

It may be summer, but I was right back in the bleak mid-winter at the cul-de-sac in Petersburn. Mum blew a chilly wind the second I walked through the door. 'Oh, it's just you,' she said dryly. 'I thought it was your sister who visits regularly and never disappoints.'

I tried to counteract this by faking some excitement, 'No, it's me. Surprise!'

'You'd better come in then. And don't bother your father, he's going through his quiet phase again. And take your shoes off, I'm not having you trail dirt all over our new carpets.'

Dad's depression comes to the forefront sometimes, which results in lengthy silences and faint replies. He's never been the same since he jumped to relative safety during the Piper Alpha disaster. He was in the living room watching some old reruns of Ground Force. I say *watching*, but it really was just a man staring at a screen. If you moved the telly, he probably wouldn't have noticed Charlie Dimmock's wobbly breasts disappear.

In came the kids like some circus show had begun, running riot within seconds, and not a single shoe removed, I might add. At the tail end appeared Marie, my very fertile sister. Fake-tanned to the extreme, under a weight of blond extensions, industrial-strength makeup and in nothing more than a tiny denim skirt, boob-tube and five-inch wedges. A papoose was strapped to her skinny frame with the latest failure in contraception bawling from within as loud as a foghorn.

'It's those two swinging on Dad's chair, in case you've forgotten who your own kin is, Bro,' she hollered over the tiny lungs sarcastically, skilfully slapping both troublemakers on the head while whipping out a veiny breast to feed the papoose. 'Beckham! Brooklyn! Get off Granddad, he's watching Ground Force – oooh, I'd like tits like hers, mine are going to be as saggy as two burst prunes by the time this hungry wee shit is done with me – besides, Granddad's sick this week.'

How can she put a time-limit on his illness? I gave my feral nephews their perfectly gift-wrapped t-shirts (I paid extra for the store to do a tidier, more time-efficient job than I could). Beckham and Brooklyn swiped them out of my hands and tore the paper to shreds without a thank you. They disappeared as they did so and returned moments later wearing, not two cute and funky children's teeshirts, but two oversized adult teeshirts instead. Very adult, in fact. Beckham seemed pleased with his *Flex for Sex* tee, but Brooklyn was less than happy about his *Gay Men Do It Harder, Faster & With More Spunk!*

'What's sp-u-nk?' he asked his mortified granny.

'Well, this is a very sick joke, Andrew Angus,' snapped Mum.

'Bloody hell!' I gawped. 'There must've been a mix-up at the shop.'

'What kind of life are you leading in that godforsaken city?' growled Mum as she tugged at the unruly boys to wrestle the offending items off.

'I think I've just pimped out my nephews,' I joked.

'This is no laughing matter ...' snarled Mum.

Riotous laughter came from the corner of the room where Dad had been watching the whole drama unfold. Red-faced, eyes watering, beer-belly heaving. 'Leave the boy alone, you daft cow,' he said as he got up and swiped the TV remote from her recliner. 'He's doing just fine. It's the best laugh I've had all year.' He winked at me and changed the channel. 'I think the footie's on. Better than this crap. Who wants a beer?'

'Daft cow?' repeated Mum, flabbergasted.

'Beth, I do love you, but you drive all of us bonkers at times. Stop being so pious,' he plopped a kiss on her forehead as he headed towards the fridge.

It was worth Mum's sour-puss for the next wee while as Dad quickly moved from the dark, murky waters of the North Sea into some kind of sunny lagoon. For now.

Monday 9th August

I'm amazed how moved I became over the small concert Gwen's team played tonight. It's a shame it's only a two day run as it deserves more. For such a tiny set of musicians to pull off what they did is a credit to them all. I think *Ode to Joy* may be my favourite piece of classical music henceforth. Sally, Ryan, Molasses, Melve and myself watched a girl who doesn't usually step into the limelight become engrossed in her passion and positively shine. It seemed we were all moved by the pieces played. I'd even go so far as to say I saw a tear in Sally's eye, but this would be highly unusual, right?

Applause! Yes! Applause! For they did well. And yet more praise for Matt taking Gwen's hand during the bowing and curtsying and then, more importantly, for the kiss he planted on the lips of her stunned face. A kiss that left us all smiling and wide-eyed. Matt never left her side for the rest of the evening. It seems the boy is besotted.

Tuesday 10th August

Major red face! While running an errand to Christina's wine shop, I saw some youth in a hoodie fiddling with my abandoned bike. I had them in a headlock as Ryan came stumbling out of the sex shop with a grey plastic bag poorly hidden in his tweed jacket. I urged him to call the cops as I kicked the back of the thief's knees, reducing him, rather impressively I thought, to a wreck on the ground.

'Get off him, you idiot!' screamed Ryan. 'That's Tony!'

My knee was now in the small of his back. 'What? Why is Tony robbing my bike?'

'I'm not, you tosser!' panted Tony from under me. 'I was fitting a new seat to your piece of shit.'

I looked down and to my embarrassment, next to Tony's shaking hands, were a couple of wrenches and a brand new seat. 'Why?' I asked.

'Because he's trying to be nice,' bit Ryan. 'It was supposed to be a surprise, but I guess that's pretty screwed now. Now get off my fiancé!'

I lifted my frame off his thin torso gingerly, pulled the shaken boy to his feet and apologised. Tony glower at me, turned his nose to the air and demanded, 'Take me home, Boo-Boo. I think I have internal bruising. I can feel my kidney's failing thanks to this bone-crushing hippo.'

Ryan slung his man's arm around his neck, and they staggered off. I offered to help, but all I got in reply from Ryan was, 'Ha! No, thank you very much.'

I looked back at the new bike seat (it was an expensive piece of kit) and felt terrible. Tony had tried to do something kind, and I'd ruined it. He must be ill, surely?

Wednesday 11th August

6 a.m. Damn it! The guilt of yesterday evening's fracas with Tony has kept me tossing and turning for most of the night. I loathe to admit it, but I'll have to pull something sickeningly nice out of the bag to repair the damage, even though I know there's no bruising or failing kidneys. I think Brothers Grimm would applaud Tony's storytelling. However, I do value Ryan's friendship, so needs must.

12 a.m. Flowers would be the answer. Tony limped away from the front door as he let me in, taking a sick-day due to supposed GBH. He flopped on the sofa and hardly acknowledged the bouquet I was waving under his snooty nose.

'As way of an apology,' I said.

He didn't take them. He looked at them as if I'd just handed him some shit in a burst carrier bag and turned his head towards the TV, 'I don't like lilies, they smell of pond water and ejaculate, drop so much muck around and stain your clothing,' he snarled. He let out a feeble sigh and stroked his forehead. 'Could you put them in water? I'm fearful if I reach under the sink, I'll burst another blood vessel.'

I wanted to smack him over the head repeatedly with the lilies until his wall was stained with a combination of pollen and blood. For a moment, I actually imagined it. Snapping myself back into reality, I found the vase, which wasn't difficult as I was probably the last person to tidy it away. I turned the tap on, and Biffo moaned, 'Even the gushing water hurts my ears,' as he pressed a cushion either side of his thick head. I turned the tap down to a trickle, slid the flowers in gently, and placed them on the windowsill closest to the couch.

'Not there,' he said, pushing my patience further, 'I won't be able to see my Boo-Boo coming home if they're there.' I imagined beating him repeatedly about the head with either pillow in a sweeping motion, rhapsodic laughter leaping from my insane grin until the stuffing flew from both pillows and his cranium. *No, I came here to make peace,* I told myself and plonked myself down next to him on the sofa just close enough to invade his precious personal space.

He peered over the cushions, acting like a frightened little boy. 'Don't beat me again,' he hammed-up.

'Oh, please!' I cried. 'Look, what would you like me to do? This truce obviously isn't working for either of us. And even if Ryan actually believes we're friends, it won't last forever as one of us is bound to explode in front of him. Something's got to give.'

Tony pulled the cushions away from his face and appeared almost human. He nodded, 'You're right. Ryan wants you at our wedding, so we do have to get on somehow. There's a finite period of tolerance before one of us kills the other. So I want you to do all that you can for Ryan, keep him happy, and then ...' he bared his shark-like incisors and concluded, '... leave Edinburgh.'

I shook my head, 'I can't do that.'

'Yes, you can.' He fanned out both hands to mimic explosions, 'Poof! Off you go in a cloud of pink smoke.'

I got off the sofa and made for the door. 'No-can-do, Tony. This is my home, my city and Ryan's my mate. Hell, I've even made new friends. So we're going to have to find our bonding moment soon.'

Biffo inspected his claws in such a way I expected him to preen them as keenly as the Colonel does. He sighed again, but this time, it had a steely resolve. 'Very well,' he said nasally. 'You leave me no alternative. Let the mud-slinging begin.'

'Blackmail?' I laughed. 'You'll find nothing on me.' I walked into the hall, past the bedroom where I spent weeks in torment under Tony's rule. I remembered how I looked forward to moving in with Ryan. I thought about how disappointed they made me feel. How much Biffo had ruined my stay. *He has nothing on me*, I thought as I stepped out.

'Everyone has something, Andy Angus,' I heard him say. 'It's just a matter of time before I find your decaying skeletons.' He let out a shrill cackle, 'I'll get you, my pretty, and your fat cat too!'

As I peddled my bike home, I began to feel uneasy. He seems so confident I wonder if he knows something already. Oh, how I detest him *and* his Dr Spock eyebrows.

Thursday 12th August

At the café today I helped a bus driver remove some Red Pea Soup from his shirt. He's a chunky lad in his thirties, but carries the weight well, not classically handsome but has a certain something. I don't think it's the uniform as I've never become aroused when boarding public transport.

'Better than Daz, you are,' he grinned, tapping the now damp but clean area I'd spent ten minutes rubbing with soda water. A tuft of thick hair popped out from between the buttons. 'Can I buy you a drink?'

I hesitated: my recent bad luck in the dating game ran through my mind.

'Come on,' he continued. 'I'll give you a free ride on the bus any time you like.'

'What route are you on?' I asked.

'Twenty-two.'

That's my main route through the city, if I'm not biking or hiking it, I thought. I could see Molasses' eyeballs twinkling over his shaved head. 'Well, I don't really date clients, but what the hell.'

I'm heading out tomorrow evening with bus driver Paul. Hope springs eternal. He left with pep in his step. It seems I've made his day. Molasses caught me as I went to change into my bike gear. ' "Don't usually date clients," ' she laughed. 'You've had more clients here than I've cooked hot dinners, young man.'

I couldn't help but feel a bit hurt. Is she right? Will the Slut-o-meter combust by 2011?

Friday 13th August

I can't believe I forgot what day it is. Of all the days to have a date. I'm not that superstitious, but with my recent luck, I need as little hindrance as possible. What disasters await me, I wonder? Shall he lean in to kiss me and I'll fall down a flight of stairs? Will I accidentally stab him with a cocktail stick in the back of the hand? Worse still, will he just stand me up? I'm off to Joseph Pearce pub to meet my next possible jinx.

Saturday 14th August

It was a brilliant date. I expected frogs to fall from the sky, or a vast interstellar starship to land on the top of Arthur's Seat because this kind of thing just doesn't happen to me. Paul's a perfect gent. He paid for everything, pulled out the chair for me to sit (which was the only mishap of the evening as I was unaware, missed it, and ended up sitting unceremoniously on the floor), topped-up my glass of wine when needed, insisted I walk to the inside of the road as we walked home to keep me safe from traffic, and even the kiss goodnight was spot-on. A simple goodnight with no pressure for a quick fumble.

'We're meeting again on Monday night,' I told Sally as I floated towards my room.

'Oh, so is it *lurve* then?' she asked while stirring a mojito with her index finger. She sounded most sarcastic in tone.

'Don't be silly, it's just date number one,' I said, feeling her attitude dragging my feet down towards the swirly carpet.

She grunted and looked me up and down, 'With you back dating, and Gwen blowing that tenor, it'll soon be just Melve and me living here.'

I felt guilt smother my joy, but I've no reason to feel guilty. I made no promise to pause my love-life when we became friends. Looking into Sally's room, I could clearly see that it's stuck in some bygone era. On pause. I realise now that this isn't a woman who loves everything retro; this is a woman who's afraid to walk into the uncertainty of the future. The past is clearcut and defined; the future, a chaotic mess.

'Good lord! Don't be so fatalistic. You were the one pimping me out not so long ago,' I said.

She reached over, stroked the side of my face and grinned, 'I know, my dear. Don't listen to me, I'm just jealous. I need to stop feeling like my world would end if your heart ever left me.' She slid around the door frame and looked into her room. Ella Fitzgerald was singing *I'll Never Fall In Love Again* beautifully through crackles of static as sapphire tip met shellac.

'Are you drunk, Sally?' I asked, concerned she may be on another downward spiral.

'Sweetie, sobriety is an inconvenience I suffer out of necessity, and today there's no need to conform.' She flashed me an enigmatic smile and straightened her back, seemingly growing a few inches taller. 'My good friend, Mr Isautier, insists inebriation is the order of the day and who am I to argue?' She bowed and slinked back into her room, her pink floral kimono fluttering as she went. 'I bid you goodnight, sweet Sir,' she waved and swung the door shut. Ella's voice increased in volume. I'm glad I didn't invite Paul in as I hate introducing Sally when she's in a state.

I checked my mobile as I shut my door and noticed a text from Ryan: 'Thnks 4 the flowers. Tony loves them. Pop round sometime soon, my friend! X'

It seems all's forgiven.

Sunday 15th August

Now I love Ella Fitzgerald as much as any gay man, but I've found I love her less if she sings until two in the morning. I was knackered, but I still headed out to the Free Fringe to waste two hours of my life that I'll never get back. Reason being:

A. It was a dreadful show, under-rehearsed and the comedy timing was so far off-beat it was practically an old piece of vinyl that had been scratched to buggery. But more importantly ...
B. I was forced to make small-talk with Biffo as he sat between Ryan and myself for the duration of this travesty, followed by more small-talk in the bar afterwards.

He's terrible when he's sticking the knife in, but worse when he's supposedly healing old wounds he inflicted. It's disconcerting. I felt that every friendly grin he passed was motivated by some smug idea he has some dirt on me. I made my excuses and left before the ice in my gin melted. If Tony continues to make my life this uncomfortable after they're civil partnered, I may have to dash from our friendship after all.

On the plus side, I got several excited texts from Paul about our next date on Tuesday. When I told him I'd just cycled home from the Grassmarket, he seemed to become enthralled. A pile of suggestive messages followed surrounded by goofy emojis with tongues poking out suggestively.

He called just as I was slipping under the duvet. 'Do you wear the gear? Like, the full gear? Cycling shorts and all?' he asked, sounding less a gentleman and more a heavy breather.

'I do, sometimes, aye,' I said, deepening my voice and trying to sound like I'd just stepped off a building site.

'Wear the shorts under your jeans on Monday, please?' He was panting now, so I knew there was more than just a mobile in his hands.

'If you want,' I said, conscious of the power that my words had over him. Finding his fetish fired me up and from then on we enjoyed an impromptu bout of phone sex. I may've been knackered, but where there's a willy, there's a way.

Monday 16th August

Woken at 1 a.m. by a text from Alistair:

'I miss you. Please, can we meet? A. x'

Go away, your timing is crap, I thought as I hit the off switch. I need to change my number ASAP if I'm ever to move on.

Tuesday 17th August

Last night, while wearing nothing but cycling shorts, I had my hands splayed against the steamy windows of a Number 15 bus as it sat idle in the depot. It was a scene reminiscent of the feature film *Titanic*, if Kate Winslet was an Edinburgh cyclist and Leonardo DiCaprio was a bus driver with a fetish for all things Lycra.

Paul's a gent during sex: thoughtful, caring and tender with every touch. Sure, it could've happened in a classier setting, but I'm not going to argue with biology. We were initially just popping in to pick up his payslip, but the setting, lateness of the night and the risk of getting caught inspired us, and before long, we were semi-naked and elated.

When I woke this morning, I had a cheeky grin on my face as I passed Sally on the payphone. 'Hey, brotherfucker!' she called after my tail. 'Still playing *On The Buses*?'

'Oh, yes!' I smugly replied. 'I'm tempted to remain unwashed and keep his sex all over my well-pawed body!' And then, I couldn't resist one more gloat, 'Oooh, yes, sister. Horny as!'

She looked astonished, as if she's the only person in the whole of creation licensed to enjoy a close encounter of the sluttish kind and to talk boldly about it, but what's good for the goose ...

Paul and I are meeting again on Friday, which seems intense, but I need to be proactive in the hunt. I need a life partner soon before I get too old to fumble with them in unusual settings.

Wednesday 18th August

I've bought more Lycra cycling shorts in assorted colours; one for each day of the week. I'm so easily led towards new fetishes. Maybe it should concern me, but I'm enjoying it. Besides, I'll never hook a man if I'm unwilling to try new things.

Thursday 19th August

A shiny new phone. An iPhone, no less! Yes, I'm up with the gadgets of the young dudes. Flash or what? Even being tied into a 24-month contract doesn't take that sheen off. Bye-bye, Pay-As-You-Go, and hello financial responsibility. With it comes a new number, new address book and, as a result, the deletion of any recent sexual encounters from my life. I've been fiddling with its features so much that I've developed tunnel vision. My thumb keeps swiping over the touch-screen to wipe off any offensive smudge that tarnishes its sparkly new look. I'm obsessed with checking it every few minutes, just in case someone has texted me, and I *need* to reply. I find myself handling it just for the sake of swiping it open and moving the icons around. I can feel the 'Apple Loop' winding its way around my needy soul. The only thing is, I need to sync it with my iTunes account, which is shared on Sally's computer. I guess I'd better make my peace with Ms Knowles. I'll take her a bottle of rum to lubricate the situation.

The first text to arrive was from Paul. He sent, 'Can't wait for dinner tomorrow,' followed by a pile of aubergine emojis. He's hinting that we're going to a vegetarian restaurant, I bet. Vegetarian food never fills me up. I don't want to be famished late at night, so I sent back a shrimp emoji in the hope it's at least a pescatarian restaurant, and I can get some form of real protein. He hasn't replied. I hope I haven't offended him if he's entirely vegetarian.

Friday 20th August

I think I've fallen in love. I'm in a new relationship. Today I woke and stroked my iPhone and asked him if he slept well. It's intoxicating. I keep picking him up. When I'm bored, I find myself flicking through web feeds and, for the first time in my life, I've joined a social network that doesn't involve dating men: Twitter.

At one point, during our non-vegetarian dinner (weird), Paul exaggerated a yawn and said, 'Andy, it's like you're spouting a sermon from a pulpit that has the Apple logo etched on it. I get it, you love your new phone, but we've had dessert, when are we getting round to some fun? Did you remember the cycling shorts?'

I hadn't.

Forty minutes later, we were back at mine, and I was given the virginal treat of a climax through Lycra by another's hand. Paul didn't stay the night, he's on the early shift tomorrow, but I didn't mind as I was itching to see the notifications that pinged during sex. So far I've four new followers, thanks to the hashtag #gaygeek and #doctorwho. This pleases me.

Saturday 21st August

10 a.m. Melve is back. I asked him how it went. He said gleefully, 'I've been sorted for E's and Wizz in a field in Hampshire for the past five days and transported umpteen ladies to multiple levels of ecstasy.'

Nobody with liver-spots should be taking drugs, especially E. It's for the young. Nobody with liver spots should be touching 'umpteen ladies' too. Drugs are dangerous: you may inadvertently have sexual intercourse with an ageing hippy who wears open-toe sandals in the fruit and veg aisle of the supermarket.

11 p.m. Some bastard has stolen the seat of my bike again! Why? I cycled home with my arse a few inches away from a metal pole that could've given me an unfortunate trip to A&E and several health professionals amusing anecdotes. Of course, of all the people to bump into, of all the bobbies on the beat, I had to slam into the very same officer who reprimanded me for cycling on Edinburgh's paths weeks ago. Stupid of me to cycle past Gayfield Police Station, but I was actually trying to avoid the main roads as much a possible. I attempted to explain my predicament to Officer 7469, but he was having none of it.

'Do it again, and you'll be fined, and the bike will be confiscated,' he said, hardly looking up from his notepad.

'But what about the asshole who nicked my seat twice already?' I asked.

He frowned and tucked his pen and pad away in his top pocket. 'All noted, now move along. *Don't* cycle.'

'Really?' I asked unconvinced.

'Aye, really. I've noted every detail of your very comprehensive and lengthy explanation. I'll be in touch if and when there are any developments. Now, off you go.'

I pushed my bike home. I've tried to be pissed off with him, but he is so devilishly handsome and authoritative that I find him very likeable in a masochistic kind of way. My mind wanders towards his shiny buttons, picturing them being undone by my cuffed hands, all the while he's telling me exactly how I should behave. Alas, I know in my heart that he's not gay. Oh, be still my beating hardon.

Sunday 22nd August

I've made peace with Sally. It didn't take much. I told her how strange Paul was with me today on the phone. I'd asked him if he was free any time soon, I was actually looking forward to it, but he was terse in tone and asked, 'Will you be bringing your beloved iPhone with you?'

'Why did he ask that, darling?' asked Sally as she applied a wax strip to the top lip of a rather tense Gwen who was clutching the sheets of Ms Knowles' bed in dread. It seems we're back on 'darling' and 'sweetie' terms too, a good sign that she's more content with the state of our friendship.

'He said, "You were more interested in that damn device than me, Andy. Every time I reached for your hand, you reached for your phone. You checked it more thoroughly than the menu." I don't need to look at the menu, I know the grub at Pizza Express like I do all of the Doctor's companions, in chronological order.'

'Poppycock!' she said as she ripped the adhered strip form Gwen's lip with such ferocity I felt our fruitfully follicled friend was going to punch her square in the face if she hadn't been clutching her own in pain. Apparently, Matt's developed a rash from pressing his face against hers. 'Pain, darling, it's the price we pay for men,' she assured Gwen. 'I should know. I've suffered more torture from men than a woman in a Japanese war camp.' She turned back to me, 'Maybe you're just not that into him.'

'What? No, it can't be that. He's great. I'll admit I've become a little obsessed over my new phone,' I said. 'Maybe I wasn't attentive enough. I've arranged a cinema date with him on Tuesday evening, where all mobiles have to be firmly switched off.' I think the threat of eviction from the Filmhouse should be enough to quash my so-called 'addiction'.

Thanks to Sally lending me her computer I've spent the past few hours downloading songs and syncing my iPhone. It's now 1.30 a.m. Where did the time go?

Monday 23rd August

2.15 a.m. I've found a few games apps that kept me amused until the battery died. Why doesn't my room have a socket close to the bed where I can charge the phone and settle under the duvet? Stupid old-fashioned wiring. It's charging on top of the fridge, the most inconvenient place *ever*.

11.45 p.m. Both Gwen and Matt have inflamed faces. I was right affronted when they arrived at tonight's showing of *Briefs* – an all-male drag/burlesque act that should've raised my blood pressure many times, if I wasn't distracted by Spotty and Spottier. Matt's face is scarlet around the chin, and hers is raw under the nose, tracking into both nostrils, thanks to Sally's bolshy attack on the poor woman's follicles and the lovers' lengthy snogging sessions. In daylight, they looked like bloody glue sniffers thanks to thick layers of Sudocrem. Embarrassed, I ushered them quickly into the tent. I figured the dim lighting would help, but the UV lighting illuminated Gwen's smearing, causing her to look like a female Hitler.

I skipped post-show drinks and made my excuses to leave. 'Ah, you have your handy with you,' said Gwen, as I whipped my phone out of my pocket. 'Take a picture of us.' They cuddled in close and smiled goofily like a couple of ridiculously painted comedy clowns.

I lied, 'Oh, sorry. My battery's just died.' Do they really want their first picture together looking like this? I think I'm doing them a favour. Coincidently, when they stand so close together, you can really see how far apart they are in years. They'll thank me for this.

I checked my mobile discreetly around the corner. There were two more followers on Twitter and a further three by the time I got home. It shouldn't matter, but it does.

Tuesday 24th August

Date night is firmly, most definitively, absolutely off! Leaving work, I became aware of two men wrestling with each other next to where I'd secured my bike. Well, I say wrestling, an accurate description would be one man being firmly taken in hand by another and having his arms twisted expertly behind his back until he was slammed against a brick wall. On closer inspection, my new bike seat was twisted as if it had been tampered with. The guy holding the other to the wall was in police uniform, and the wall kisser was in bus driver getup. Closer inspection revealed it was Paul being arrested by Constable 7469.

It transpires that Paul not only enjoys sexual intercourse with guys in cycling shorts but also has a fetish for the parts of bikes that touch cyclists' sweaty bottoms. He's a known thief and sexual deviant. The kind that would steal knickers off washing lines back in the 70s.

'Andy, is this your bike?' asked Paul from the open window of Constable 7469's car. I couldn't bring myself to answer him, I was so disgusted. It turns out there's been a spate of bike crimes in the area. They suspected a bunch of kids, not a middle-aged bus driver with an anarchic fetish, but once they matched up CCTV footage from several university bike racks, the evidence was insurmountable.

'Told you I was on it, Mr Angus,' said Constable 7469 smugly. 'I take *all* crimes seriously.' I was shamed into submission once again, and slightly aroused.

'You're not going to press charges are you, Andy?' stammered a troubled Paul, squirming to get a better view out of the car. My constable's counterpart closed the window as Paul called, 'But you enjoyed fun this way too. You like Lycra, don't you? You understand, surely?'

Constable 7469 raised his eyebrows, 'Do you know this man *intimately*?'

'Ignore him,' I chuckled uncomfortably and felt my face go crimson. I gave my side of the story to the handsome policeman, including the inescapable fact that Paul was, in fact, known to me and that he most certainly had a desire for everything pedal related. Sadly, through association, these details make me look like some kind of fetish-feeder, so definitely no chance of a date with Officer 7469 now, even if he is gay.

I binned all of my new cycling shorts as soon as I got home. I'm well shot of Paul. I've never been one for dressing up to turn a guy on. The closest I got with Thomas was leaving my thick thermal socks on in winter. It was so cold in that cottage sometimes we'd just have fun with my willy popped through the fly of my Doctor Who pyjamas ... reading that back, I see why he felt the need to have sex with every harlot in the Borders and ran off with the modern-day version of Nell Gwynn. Doctor Who Dalek pyjamas? This is not the kind of behaviour that makes a man tremble at the knees. What was I thinking?

Wednesday 25th August

The number of people being diagnosed with sexually transmitted infections in the U.K. has risen for the tenth year in a row, according to the Health Protection Agency, which is unnerving. I feel physically sick when those three little letters (HIV) rear their ugly head. The report was playing on the café's radio as we were setting up. I had to step outside for air. As I staggered out of the café, feeling faint and upsetting set tables as I went, I heard Molasses ask Sally, 'Is he okay? He's very sweaty.'

Once outside, the fresh air quickly revived me, and the bustle of the street began to act as some kind of antidote for my angst. I felt a chill at my sternum. I glanced down and found a substantial pool of salty water drenching my tee.

'Are you all right, sweetie?' asked Sally as she joined me on the step.

'I'll be okay,' I said. 'I just came over a bit unnecessary. Probably due to the stress of yesterday's shenanigans with the bus driver.'

This, of course, was a lie. I've no idea if I'll be okay. I know I'm far from it at times, but I can't bear the thought that my life would have to change dramatically forever. The chance of finding an understanding, loving relationship would be limited. Casual sex would become more complicated and less casual. There would be clinics and appointments, and my life would be dictated to by a drug regime. My blood samples would always carry a hazard label. People on the scene would stick warning labels on me the second I stepped on it. And Mum would hit the roof.

'Okay, but if you need to go home, Molasses and I can manage.'

'No, I'll be fine.'

'Okay,' Sally slapped me on the back and got up. 'Stop the drama then. You gays are all about the drama,' she joked as she rubbed my head, messing my hair playfully in the process, which was slightly annoying and comforting at the same time. She went back inside. I followed a few minutes later and found the news had moved on to another topic, and therefore, so could I. For now.

Thursday 26th August

I've called the police station and told them that I don't want to press charges. I figure Paul will have enough to deal with the likes of personality tests and being treated like a cat in Pavlov's house. When I asked if Constable 7469 was around for a chat, the officer at the end of the line (heavy smoker, judging by the gravel in her voice; in the job for too long, judging by the dissolution in tone) got snappish, 'He doesn't spend his days hanging around the station, don't you know? This isn't a social club, don't you know? There's a lot of crime out there, haven't you heard?'

I rounded off my call with a sarcastic, 'Thank you for your time. I have to go. I'm a very busy man, don't you know?' Adding, 'Bitch!' after I hung up.

In other news, I've received a copy of my reading for Ryan and Tony's civil partnership:

A Tapestry Of Love

Just as two very different threads woven in opposite directions can
form a beautiful tapestry,

So can your two lives merge together to form a beautiful marriage.
To make your marriage work will take love.
Love should be at the core of your marriage;
love is the reason you are here.
But it will also take trust – to know in your hearts you want the best for each other.
It will take dedication – to stay open to one another;
to learn and to grow together even when it is not easy to do.
It will take faith – to always go forward to tomorrow,
never really knowing what tomorrow will bring.
And it will take commitment – to hold true to a journey you both now will share together.

Anon.

I think I may choke on my own vomit while reading it. If not, I'll definitely struggle to swallow the champagne as we toast the happy couple.

Friday 27th August

Sally burst into my room first thing with our communal laptop in hand just as I was extracting three irritating grey hairs that've sneaked into my eyebrows without so much as a final bugle call to my youth. 'Have you seen this?' she asked as she made herself comfy on my freshly made bed. Of course, the Colonel immediately made himself snug on her lap, adding to my irritation.

I tucked the tweezers into my hand discreetly and sighed as I moved away from the magnifying mirror that seems to have the magical ability to see twenty years into my future. I cringed when I saw my pillows go askew as she shuffled upright. 'Seen what?' I asked, pulling her forward and fluffing them back up.

'This!' she flipped around the laptop for me to see. There was my previously picture-less Gaydar profile with a terrible selfie of me looking very flushed stood next to my bike. It was the worst picture ever: a bad case of helmet-head and sweat.

'When did you do this? How did you get into my profile?' I asked aghast.

'A month ago, sweetie,' she grinned. 'And, you should know there isn't a password in the country I can't crack. Anyway, focus, dear. Just look at all the hits you've had – are you even checking this?'

'I gave up online shenanigans after my first disappointment.' I was annoyed, to say the least, she'd taken my profile and not only added to it, but rejigged it. 'That's an awful picture of me, Sally,' I groaned.

'Others don't seem to think so. You have loads of mail too, some from very hot guys. One in particular.'

'Really? Give me that.' I said, snatching the computer from her hands.

I sat with her and scanned the pages. There are some awful looking guys out there with dreadful kinks. One, in particular, wants to have balloons burst on his naked body as I stand over him dressed as a clown. Another wants to go for a walk in the woods on our first date, which screams axe murderer to both of us. A few are into cycling gear, 'Best to avoid them, sweetie,' assured my pimp. But there are some cute guys. There's a guy called Chico4ManStud (Spanish, living in Edinburgh), who had asked to meet up last week. Sally claimed, 'That's you; a Man Stud.' I really don't think so. However, more interestingly, there was one guy with the tag TheBeatGoesOn. Could it be? No. Surely not? Yes! It was Constable 7469. My handsome-but-stern-policeman. He'd asked if the man in the picture was me.

'What do I say?' I asked Sally, my heart growing wings and fluttering excitedly around my ribcage.

'Yes, of course, you fool. To everything he says. He's hot.'

So, I wrote: 'Yes, it's me. The idiot with the bike. How are you?'

'Now, keep your options way open. Don't limit yourself. A man as divine as you should have the pickings of the fruit when it's ripe. You want to write to the Chico man too.'

I argued that I didn't want to complicate my life, but she'd already typed a reply: 'Hello, I'm very well, muchas gracias. And I'm very interested.'

She punched send. 'You're not exclusive until you have *the discussion*. And we'll cross that bridge when you actually meet and hold a guy down.'

'It'll be exclusive the day I actually meet someone who isn't a weirdo, which will be a miracle at this rate. There are no sane available men around my age in this city.'

Saturday 28th August

Hungover and serving alcoholic beverages while richly spiced food wafts warmly in your face is never a great combination. *But it's my job, and I love it,* I kept telling myself. Sally was obviously feeling last night's escapades too, insisting the only way she'd get through the day would be with massive doses of Co-codamol and Jackie Onassis sunglasses. She hardly moved her lips as she spoke, almost as if too much flexing of her facial muscles would cause her irreparable damage, 'I swear, if I so much as catch a glimpse of a bleached smile today I'll have to punch their lights out with one swift motion. Hangovers are a huge inconvenience in my life, as is work.'

We were all suffering after one last jolly out on the Fringe before it ended. I can't remember much about the show we eventually agreed to see after bickering over a sticky, ale-soaked table. I think it involved a stuffed giraffe, a very amateur comedian and songs from the Spice Girls. I suspect it was Melve and Tony's choice. Melve, because he's always had a soft spot for giraffes, and Tony's, because he's always wanted to be Baby Spice. The chances of that happening are as remote as me winning America's Next Top Model.

Just when my head was beginning to feel normal (after several glasses of Irn Bru), Gwen burst through the doors and grabbed me by the arm so tight I could believe she's a member of the DC Lady Arm Wrestler club. She pulled me to a quiet spot and hurriedly said, 'What I told you last night, mention nothing. Especially not to Sally. Unquestionably, absolutely, most certainly not ...' her boyfriend had just walked in the door. Gwen became all light and airy with a sprinkling of stress. '... Matt! How are you, my uber schon Freund?'

The musicians stayed for dinner. I orbited around Gwen every now and then in the hope of more information being slipped, as I have no clue what the hell she's talking about, but no titbits were thrown my way. What conversation did we have last night? I must've been wasted. They left arm and arm, as couples do when merry and drunk on nothing but mutual adoration, and I was none the wiser. Sally glancing over the top of her shades just enough to reveal bloodshot eyeballs and demanded, 'What's up, brotherfucker? Spill!'

I pressed the glasses back up her little button nose and answered honestly, 'Your guess is as good as mine.'

Sunday 29th August

Christina is closing the wine shop indefinitely. She's heading back to Spain for medical treatment.

'Why Spain? And what treatment?' I asked as I hoisted another box of Jamaican beers on to the trolly.

'I am confident in the health-care system at home. It has kept me safe and well for years,' she said as she dragged the café's usual order of spirits across the wineshop floor. 'The NHS is broken here. Nurses are kept from patients by a wall of paperwork. There are hardly enough domestics to clean the ever opening and closing wards. If I don't catch a super-bug, I will die of starvation while being taunted with plates of anaemic meat forgotten by exhausted nurses at the end of my bed.'

I thought this was a bit harsh, but decided an indecisive grunt was the best reply under the circumstances. 'What are you being treated for?'

'Ovarian cancer.' She took the usual cheque from Molasses out of my hand as if this was her only concern. I felt my spine flinch. She rang up the till and added, 'Ten years ago I came here fit, well and full of optimism, and now I have cancer. Forgive me for choosing the better option.'

I hope she doesn't think Scotland somehow gave her cancer. A pile of questions stacked in my mind. What would become of the shop? How long will the treatment take? Is it terminal? Will she be coming back? But all I could stupidly muster was, 'My mum's best friend had ovarian cancer.'

'And how is she?'

I became uncomfortable. 'Oh ... she's not so good. She's a little bit dead, actually.'

Awkward silence.

'Anyhoo! I'd best get a move on,' I said as I edged towards the door of the cancer sufferer's shop. 'If I'm any later, I'll be dead meat.'

'Someday I may let you know how that feels,' Christina added.

'Sorry. So Sorry. I'm an idiot.'

She shook her head and smiled, 'It's okay. I'll be fine. I wanted to tell you alone. You're a nice boy and someone I consider a friend.'

Why does she have to be so lovely? She doesn't deserve this, no one does, but she definitely doesn't. All I had to do was get the weekly order. Why do I have to put my foot in my mouth so often my toenails are becoming soft?

Monday 30th August

'Let's go to New York and get drunk in a speak-easy, darling.'

'But I can't afford to. And it's dangerous,' was my reply within a New York minute.

'Nonsense, Juliano's stamped out all that nastiness. They have such beautiful people there. Very sexy men, I believe,' she winked as if this would encourage me. 'The architecture is outstanding, all those skyscrapers, Central Park. Oh, and Soho, darling! So-ho!' She clasped her hands together, 'Oh! The Chrysler Building! The food is amazing! Anything you want at any time of the day. The parks! The chess hustlers! Hotdogs! Real New York hotdogs!' Sally kept banging on even though my mother was at the end of the line. 'At this moment they have art installations around the city playing bell noises to draw people to disused railway lines.'

'Disused railways? Bells probably installed by axe murderers,' I whispered, covering the phone.

She was reading some article in The Times Magazine from a reporter who'd just been to NYC and raved about it over three colour pages. 'Now stop littering my room with bloody exclamation marks.' I pushed her into the old rocking chair that the Colonel uses as a But & Ben when my bed is rather full, putting a stop to her hopping around like a hyperglycaemic child. 'Mum, what do you mean you're invited to the wedding, I mean, civil partnership?'

'I've had a beautiful invite from Ryan and his lovely *friend*, Tony.' 'Friend' is her usual turn of phrase as she's still not comfortable with the label 'boyfriend'. It's alien to hear the excitement in her voice. It only manifests on the birth of a grandchild or when she faffs over the young priest at her church. 'Tony even wrote me a little note saying it wouldn't be right if I weren't there as I'm the mother of their best friend. Of course, your father's invited too, if he can tear himself away from his precious fish for a day.'

'Of course,' I dead-panned.

'We'll come for the whole day, as it's only right to get my money's worth out of a new dress,' her words echoed from ear to ear as my mind was wandering to other matters.

Moments later, Mum hung up, but I was still stunned, and with my phone stuck to my ear, I asked Sally, 'Did you hear that?'

'Yes, sweetheart, I heard.' Sally continued to ogle pictures of Manhattan, unaware of the magnitude of the mind-fuck Biffo has instigated. 'Your folks are coming to Ryan and Tony's wedding, blah, blah, blah, no biggie.'

'It's a huge biggie!' I felt my precious iPhone become harder as my fist tightened around it. That bitch has invited her to ruin my day! I haven't even got an official invite yet, and he's invited Mum!'

'Oh, who's throwing exclamation marks around carelessly now?' she joked. It fell flat. Sally chucked the magazine on the draining board, came towards me to fix my fringe and said, 'I know sweetie, it is awful, parents always cramp their kid's style. But it isn't *your* day, it's Ryan and Tony's.' Then she smiled excitedly, eyes gleaming, 'That's why we should say, "Bugger that!" and jump on a plane to New York.' She started to sing *We'll Take Manhattan* with stage-worthy aplomb.

I collapsed on the bed face down. 'I can't. I can't afford it. Besides, flying bloats me, and I think I may have a period coming on. From now until December.'

Sally patted me on the back, 'There, there, my poor, bloated friend. We'll get you some frusemide and slap that bitch Tony back somehow, don't you worry. New York?'

'Maybe next year,' I said, aware that my fear of flying, or rather crashing, was the real reason I was knocking her back.

'I'll hold you to that.' She kissed my forehead and left.

I can't understand why anyone enjoys being hemmed in like a heard of sheep in a tin can that defies the law of gravity. Flying or this ceremony: which is the lesser evil, I wonder?

Tuesday 31st August

I found Molasses and Sally in a sea of wine bottles when I arrived at work. 'What's happened in here?' I asked. 'Have we over-ordered?

'No, it's stock from next door,' said an uneasy Sally.

I threw my jacket on the bar and dashed to Christina's. The shutters were down, and a sign was stuck to the door in laminated A4. In grey letters, it said:

SHOP CLOSED
INDEFINITELY
DUE TO ILL HEALTH.
WE THANK OUR
LOYAL CUSTOMERS.

I returned to the café at a laggard pace with my heart slumped in my stomach. Molasses and Sally were still busily coordinating the stacks of bottles and boxes around the room but paused as I opened the door and lamented, 'She's gone. I didn't even get a chance to say goodbye. When did she go?'

'Last night,' replied Molasses while counting a pile of Chilean red that was crowding the bar. 'She's left the keys with me. Asked me to help empty the stock. She was just too tired to continue. She insisted on taking less than half price for everything. Made me feel mighty bad.' She turned back to her spreadsheet.

'Do we have a number for her?' I asked, my voice struggling to keep going.

'Just for next door,' said Molasses. 'She said she'd call when she was able, but for now, she wants to rest and her family around her. Her husband will be dealing with things over here.'

I felt at a loss. 'After all this time we've known her is that all we have? A number for an empty shop? How can you be so ...?'

Molasses stopped scribbling on the invoice sheet and cut me a glare that could've set the very paper it was printed on alight. 'Cold? No, not cold, Andy: practical, just like Christina.' Then she smiled, 'You haven't learned yet that the only way to get through the shit life throws at you is to be practical, my boy. Poun a fret cyaa pay ounce a debt.' I could see her eyes were glistening more than usual, then they became hard as steel, 'She's gone for now, but she will be back better than ever.'

I needed that. That definitive reassurance. Molasses is the only person I know who could deliver it with conviction. I chose to be practical and helped clear the room. It felt nothing like work, more like therapy: shifting, quietly thinking, stacking and thinking some more.

Wednesday 1st September

While catching up on my late weekly wash, Sally burst through the laundromat doors in a tizzy, caressing our shared laptop.

'He's replied!' she cried unabashedly to the whole drab room.

My mind jarred, 'Who? Who has replied?'

'Your copper, who else?'

'There's a long list of guys,' I argued, aware that people were keenly listening through boredom.

'There's two,' she said dryly and jumped into the seat next to me as 'Bandage Calves' (a woman I've labelled due to her filthy bandages and ulcerated lower limbs) struggled to her swollen feet to empty the Speed Queen. 'Please, honey, if I'd not intervened, your life would amount to nothing more than a hamster in a cage. I need your hotspot.' I looked at her blankly. 'Your hotspot.' She sighed and held out her hand, 'Andy, I need to connect this laptop to the internet on your mobile telephone, do you understand the words that I am saying?'

'Not really, no,' I had to confess. It seems my phone can do much more than I anticipated. I must get round to reading the manual. I've no idea what she did, but there he was, TheBeatGoesOn (Constable 7469) in all his glory and with a new picture too.

'He's keen,' she added, clapping her hands together excitedly.

'You think?'

'Sweetie, just look at what he said.' I leaned in to see his reply to my previous message. 'See,' she pressed on the screen, and her fingernail distorted the display, 'he wants to meet you this week. Somewhere local, which could mean he wants sex later, and asks that you don't come by bike.' Sally frowned at the latter, 'Which I think is a joke, but let's hope it's not typical of his personality because that was garbage.'

I felt my heart beat faster and grasped the laptop from her. 'Saturday evening, that would be good, right?'

'No, darling, Saturday we have the first dance rehearsal for the wedding.'

'I'd forgotten about that. Or blanked it from my mind. Bugger. Okay, Saturday morning then. I don't start work until twelve, which gives me time to meet and quash my first and second impressions of him being an uptight, but very handsome, sadist. Hopefully, I'm wrong, and he actually has the kind of personality I wouldn't kick out of bed.'

'Well, book him in, chuck. I have to go. I have a total Kojaking booked within the hour.' She nodded suggestively towards her nether regions and then clip-clopped to the exit. As she pushed the door open, she stopped and addressed the room, 'By the way, I'm appearing at Madam Yo-Yo's this Friday night if any of you like a little something risqué and debonair.' She ruffled the hair of a stunned teenager who'd been reading some physics text, 'Student discount given with every performance. Bye, darlings.'

It seemed my wash cycle finished quicker than usual. I left with my clothing freshly laundered and my optimism too. Roll on Saturday morning!

Thursday 2nd September

I've spent the day gazing at Constable 7469's profile picture, which I've conveniently sent myself by email and stored to my iPhone. I'm slowly becoming besotted by his rugged looks and broad shoulders. As he smiles, the sun catches a set of perfectly lined white teeth. He also has the most wonderful dimple in the middle of his chin, which I imagine will jiggle with laughter when he discovers what a hoot I am. He actually looks friendly and quite approachable out of uniform and not at all like the rule-book flicking authoritarian he is at work. He even has one ear pierced. Please, please, please, let him be likeable, perhaps even loveable. I've playfully substituted the TARDIS wallpaper on my phone with his handsome face, just for today.

Friday 3rd September

'Can we meet tomorrow morning? I have something urgent I need to discuss with you,' asked Gwen before we entered Tony and Ryan's lounge, or as I like to call it, CPHQ (Civil Partnership Head Quarters), for the planning stages of their – I still can't believe I'm writing these words – opening dance number.

I explained to her, 'I can't. I've arranged two dates back-to-back in one already packed morning.' (Chico4Manstud is date number two.)

'Two?' she asked, surprised. 'Wow, that's ... impressive,' she faltered, trying to sound envious, but I know she was judging me.

Which made me ask myself, *Have I become a virtual whore, or am I just keeping my options open?*

The evening was dominated by Tony. It was all about the shows he'd like to feature and what he'd like his dancing puppets to perform. Two hours filled with useless, unfocused, mind-numbing chatter, and then I was pleased to leave with Melve.

'What a bore,' Melve whispered in my ear as the door closed behind us. I nodded in agreement. 'Oh, knock on my cave some time, old chap. I feel I've been neglecting you. Can't stop now, networking to do. I have a whisky waiting for me next to a new acquaintance. I'm hoping to wrangle the bugger into designing the dance costumes at a reduced price as a gift to the boys,' he added.

Costumes? When were they mentioned? I must've zoned out longer than I thought.

Saturday 4th September

I sat in Vittoria restaurant with waves of excitement flushing over me. But then my excitement transitioned into anxiety, then dissolution, despair and disappointment. *Never mind*, I thought to myself as I self-consciously paid the waiter for the cappuccino I'd been nursing for an hour, *Maybe Chico4ManStud will have more integrity than my absent constable.* I moved on to Embo café with my tail between my legs.

No, it seems the Spanish are a notoriously fickle bunch too. I left an hour later thoroughly down in the dumps, caffeinated to the max and hungry. That was two hours in total trying to keep my options open, and as it turns out, a reject like me really has no options. Not a single one. I dragged my ageing carcass towards home.

As I passed a *Big Issue* seller outside Tesco Express, he keenly asked me, 'Big Issue?'

'Yes, it is a big bloody issue, actually,' I ranted. 'If people don't keep their promises and leave a guy hanging and hangry on his morning off, I'd say it was a *humungous* issue. I'd like to meet one man, just *one man*, who's *normal* and isn't a sexual deviant that screws around. Who can cook, maybe. Who happens to like classic Who and the new series in equal measure. Who loves watching reruns of The Golden Girls. But most importantly, a man who will actually turn up when he says he will so that I can get a tiny glimpse of who he really is, not some silly typeface on a website that exists to satisfy the whims of men who just want to get their jollies off!'

Customers began to notice me as they came and went from the store. I could see their eyes fearfully shifting away from the ranting madman on the street. I realised I'd let a nine-month catalogue of pent up disappointment spill out on to the sodden pavement. The Big Issue seller rested both his hands on my shoulders to steady me and asked, 'Mate, you okay? You're going a wee bit raj.'

I was too hangry for sympathy. And suddenly, woozy. 'Excuse me,' I said, as I slipped out of his grasp and trembled my way into the shop. I was feeling a little light-headed and hypoglycaemic, but all I could see was frozen ready meals and stupid, useless veg. I believe I was irrationally trying to gnaw the plastic wrapper off a cucumber when I passed out.

I woke up on the storeroom floor with the shop manager and a till assistant peering over me, 'Do you think he's a druggy, Rab? He seemed on something,' I heard the manager whisper.

'I dunno, Dawn,' muttered Rab. 'Drug addicts don't care about their five a day, I'm sure of that. Besides, cucumbers are useless; they're ninety-six per cent water.'

'True,' agreed Dawn. 'Hey, methadone's green. He could be craving his next hit and disorientated.'

'Sssh, he's coming round. You all right, mate? You collapsed over a stack of discounted fruitcake with a cucumber stuck in your mouth.'

'Cheap fruitcake?' I asked, slowly sitting up. 'That sounds about right: it's probably where I felt most at home.'

Sunday 5th September

I found three messages waiting on me yesterday evening after our first dance rehearsal (which I was useless at!): two on Gaydar from the constable and a third slid under my door from Gwen. The constable *had* tried to reach me to say he couldn't make it, after being called in to cover a home game. Why did we not exchanged phone numbers? I was overly cautious, that's why. Being cautious is no way to find a man. And why didn't I check online beforehand? Because I'm an idiot. His second message arrived moments after I settled into bed, asking if I'd received his first. I didn't want to admit to waiting for him for over an hour, so I wrote, 'Yes, I saw it. Sorry I didn't reply. Been busy at work myself.' Nonchalance seemed the best way to play it. I attached my mobile number, my email, my postal address, our pay-phone number, Twitter tag and the number for Café Jamaica. That should do the trick.

Gwen's note was a little more to the point:

WE NEED TO MEET
ASAP!

Her words were almost carved into the A4 as if written by a Victorian lunatic scarred from been tortured in some asylum.

I selected a mellow blue ink fountain pen I use for special occasions, and wrote in the softest of strokes, 'I'm available any time for a dear friend.' That should calm and reassure her, I hope. If she really is headed for some kind of asylum, I don't want to be the person who pushed her through the rusty gates.

Monday 6th September

If you want to meet for a quiet chat, you don't arrange to meet at The Filmhouse Café during the afternoon. It's littered with film buffs, kids, yummy mummies and bleary-eyed students. I could hardly hear Gwen over the chatter.

'Sorry, you what?' I asked, my face flinching over the screams of a baby drooling with fresh puke. More inaudible chatter from a sheepish Gwen ensued. A toddler sprang free from a feeble mother and knocked headfirst into our table, spilling a few drops of my pint over the edge of the glass, which reinforced my desire for alcohol-fuelled fun over bedtime stories any night. I ignored the child's blood-curdling screams that followed and cradled what was left of my pint. 'What did you say?' I hollered.

I could see Gwen was becoming irritated as she filled her lungs and projected her voice as efficiently as Kiri Te Kanawa, 'I'm still a virgin.'

Of course, the room didn't fall silent. That would've been a miracle.

'Did you bring us here to re-enforce this issue?' I joked. 'Because right now, from where I'm sat, being a virgin is an excellent thing to be.'

We finally found a quieter side of the cafe to sit. Gwen composed herself and said, 'This is what I wanted to talk to you about: I think

Matt is becoming frustrated with me.'

'You haven't had sex yet?'

'Did you not hear my declaration? He has, in the past. I have been waiting for the right man.'

'Do you think he's the right man?'

'I don't know,' she looked pensive. 'Maybe. Maybe not. How do you know?'

I laughed, she was asking the wrong person, but I cast my mind back and said, 'Picture it: Airdrie, Autumn, 1990. Before smartphones and AOL. A spotty teenager with a greasy centre parting, yet to flourish into the handsome, successful prince you see before you today ...'

'What?'

'Sssh! My story; my artistic licence.'

'Oh, okay.'

'A virgin. Eager to experience the touch of another's lips and feel them all over his body. Keen to make love for the first time and feel something other than awkward, ugly and lanky. Imagining over and over again how wonderful it will be. Tender, everlasting, romantic.

'In reality, it was brash, over in a flash and left me short of cash. I arranged to meet a guy outside ASDA after finding his number on a cottage wall. My intention was a chat and maybe heavy petting, his was - I guess the devil is in the detail here, as I did mention his number was on a toilet wall - sex and sex alone. Within minutes of the meeting, I was kicked out of his Fiat Uno – for which I gave him ten pounds towards petrol – and stood in the chilly breeze of our local park dazed and red-faced over what we'd just done, and with my jeans barely fastened. I thought I stank of sex and immediately felt guilty. But the job was done, I could tick it off the list, and so I made my way home. I'd become "a man". But it didn't feel special.

'For days I thought everyone knew I'd popped my cherry, but really they'd no idea, and even the guy I'd shared that special moment with didn't know or seem to care. I never saw him again even though I wanted to. He was, after all, my only real contact to the gay world. But he never returned my calls. I think I came across as lazy and selfish in the sack, but really I was just stunned it actually was happening.'

'Oh, dear. That's awful. Why are you telling me this?'

'Because, if you do feel ready, then at least it's not with a random stranger in a leaky Fiat Uno.'

She thought for a moment and nodded, 'Yes, that's correct. I guess, if it does happen, it won't be as shallow and soulless as your first time. I'm lucky to be in some kind of relationship, at least.'

'Thank you, I feel very special now,' I said, sarcastically.

I checked my messages when we parted: finally, a text from the copper asking for a second chance. I've arranged for 3 p.m. on Thursday at Affogato. A guy needs to feel special somehow. And if he actually *is* a time-waster, I can drown my sorrows by diving headfirst into a carousel of tasty gelato.

Tuesday 7th September

I spoke to Ryan about my expected cabaret performance at his civil partnership, 'I think it'd be best if I don't dance at all.'

His reply was terse, to say the least. 'Well, thank you very much, Andy. It won't be just you up there, and it's only for a short period. Tony and I are the main attraction. Over the years I watched you vogue, do the robot, the hucklebuck, the running-man, the jiggy, and the macarena, all in public and barely tipsy. I'm sure you can manage less than four minutes of choreography a walrus could master. You simply cannot leave me high and dry now.'

His rant added years onto me. 'Have I lived through that many dance crazes?'

'Again, it's not all about you. I need you there,' he pleaded. And then he became steely-eyed, 'Don't let me down.'

'Okay. Sorry. Crisis over,' I assured him. I'll do the bride's bidding, but I refuse to wear any silly costumes. I have some integrity left.

And he compared me to a walrus! Rude!

Wednesday 8th September

I asked Melve tonight, 'Hey, could I have the key to the hall cupboard as I need to store some items that are cluttering my room?' (A total lie as I'd heard someone in there at 1 a.m. and wanted to get to the bottom of what entices them in there at weird times of the night.)

'Sorry, sunshine, I don't have it any more, Molasses has it. She said it was getting packed in there and she's planning a clear out, and besides, there are items of value housed within that she wants to protect, so it'll have to be under her supervision. Do you want me to ask for you?'

'No, no, it's fine. It's just some old CDs. I'm sure they'll slide neatly under my bed in the right storage box. Never you mind.'

Missed my chance. There's no way I'm asking Molasses. What does go on in there?

Thursday 9th September

Date Night No. 2.

Ruined by a no-show from my constable yet again. What's the bloody point? I waited half an hour and took my jaded heart to Ryan's with a sharing tub of gelato to bitch over. 'Not even a text!' I complained, discreetly scooping larger spoons of my favourite flavour of peanut-butter chocolate.

'Ditch him,' said Ryan. His tongue was bright green with the pistachio flavour I'd bought for him.

'We haven't had a date yet, so technically I can't ditch him,' I explained, reaching in for more of my treasured peanut-butter chocolate.

'True, I forget the rules of those first meets,' he nodded as he delved in to steal gelato from my side of the cup, which I'd surreptitiously turned closest to me. 'It's all a cloudy haze of kissing and clubbing to me – sorry, sweetie, do you mind if I take some of this?'

'No, not at all,' I said, grudgingly.

'Just a sec ...' Ryan skipped to the cutlery drawer and returned with a dessert spoon. 'I hate those flimsy wee shovels.' He proceeded to dig out a colossal hole in the previously skimmed surface.

'Oh, have you tried your mint pistachio? It's amazing too.'

'Yes, a bit, but this peanut-butter chocolate is delish.'

'I know,' I muttered as I watched an ever-widening crater begin to appear.

'Send him a text, let him know how you feel, you have nothing to lose,' he advised, taking more of my favourite. 'He's a police officer, no? Handsome, available gay police officers are hard to come by. I know, I watch Street Crime U.K. Is he handsome? Show me his picture.' I obliged as he scraped a thin layer off the pistachio. 'Oh, you're right, the peanut butter was good, but the pistachio is far superior.'

Was? There was nothing but after-goo where my coveted peanut butter had once sat. I envisioned sticking my little shovel in his eye as he swiped my mobile out of my hand.

'Oooooh, he's gorgeous. Forget texting him: call him.'

Against my better judgement and under the advice of a friend – which absolves any real responsibility – I called my double non-date. It went to answer-phone. I was on the verge of hanging up when Ryan flapped his arms and desperately whispered, 'What are you doing? Leave a message. He'll see you've called anyway.'

It's tough to be natural under peer pressure. I left a bungling message that rambled between prompts from the gelato thief. I tried to sound blasé about being stood up again and made it clear I was still available.

'I didn't sound desperate there, did I?' I asked Ryan.

'No, dear. Not at all. You kept your cool beautifully,' he exaggerated and delved in for another rampage over the gelato.

I impulsively lost all selflessness and countered his attack, gorging on it, scooping huge chunks into my mouth so fast it gave me brain-freeze. Ryan wasn't happy at all, which gave me some satisfaction. Steve used to say, 'Watch that one, Andy. Give him the moon, and he'll want the stars.' The older we become, the more I see it.

Friday 10th September

'I'm sorry! I got stuck at a major RTC on the bypass.
U must thnk me a total time-waster.
Give me one more chance?
Geoffrey.'

I showed the above text to the crew at the Café. 'Hell, boy! What is wrong with you?' asked Molasses as she slapped some sense into me. 'I'd commit murder just to be interrogated by that man for a few short, hot and sweaty seconds.'

'Agreed,' chirped in Sally.

'Hold on a sec,' said Ryan as he snatched the phone from my hand, 'why do you have his picture as your screensaver?'

'Oh, I think my phone got a virus and became corrupted in some way.'

‘Yeah, a virus called luuuurve,’ jibed Ryan.

‘Hardly! We haven’t even got past the first date. I haven’t really seen him yet,’ I assured him.

‘But you have,’ argued Ryan, ‘you’ve seen him more often on the street than any other man you’ve dated recently.’

‘Aye, well, technically I have *seen* him, but I haven’t seen the full *him*, as in a date-night scenario,’ I argued.

Ryan went into dreamy mode, ‘Sometimes that’s all it takes, a quick glance across a crowded room, just like me and …’

I quickly steamed some milk to drown the deluded boy out.

I have a date with Geoffrey on Monday night. One last attempt and then he’s deleted, just like all the rest.

Saturday 11th September

It was my worst nightmare realised at the dance rehearsal tonight, which went on far later than I’d hoped. The opening number is: *(I Lost My Heart To A) Starship Trooper!* Does Ryan not know about my anxiety dream? Have I not mentioned to him that this song has tormented me for more nights than I care to remember? Have I casually said it without realising Tony was within earshot, and he’s now using this moment to abuse me mentally every Saturday or Sunday until they’re civilly partnered?

Sally took us through some of our placement and steps in the wizen old church hall. Within minutes she became matriarch like. ‘Let me tell you, performing costs, and here’s where you start paying. In sweat,’ she announced to us all as she sat wide-legged on a chair decked in a black leotard and tights (her, not the chair, as that would be silly). ‘Anyone get the film reference?’

‘Yes,’ we said in irksome unity, ‘Fame!’

‘Oh. Okay, let’s move on then,’ she said. ‘Costumes!’

‘Please tell me there aren’t tight-fitting silver hot pants involved,’ I moaned.

‘Not at your age, Andy,’ joked Biffo. ‘We want people to stay for the ceremony, not leave with their eyes bleeding before we’ve even arrived.’

I left under a cloud. I grunted to Molasses that I could throttle Tony at times. She agreed, ‘I’ve been tempted to improve his looks by turning the cappuccino steamer full blast on his sour expression, my young friend, but society frowns on this. He simply ain't worth it. Besides, you don't want to inflate hot air with more hot air, he's a big enough gas-bag as it is.'

Sunday 12th September

Chico4ManStud found me online and asked to jump into a private chat-room. When in demand, pimp yourself out before it all dries up, I say. We chatted for a good twenty minutes. Still not a whiff of a profile pic. I asked why.

'I don't want to put myself out there, I'm old fashioned that way, but I'll send one just for you.'

Handsome! Handsome man! Thirty, dark hair, thick chest hair, strong legs due to afternoons running around Arthur's Seat, five-foot-eight, crewcut, dark brown eyes, seven inches uncut, lawyer. Yum! I'm interested. He apparently chickened-out of our last date as he figured he was punching above his level. I couldn't help but be flattered, but asserted, 'Some kind of message would've been nice.'

He was very apologetic. He thinks I'm the hottest guy he's ever seen and really wants to meet. If I'd give him one more shot, he'd be 'indebted' to me 'forever', apparently. Flattery seems to get an online profile anywhere as I've arranged to see him before I meet my copper tomorrow. I know, I could be setting myself up for a double whammy yet again. Don't judge me. I'm merely keeping my options open. He'll be wearing a light-blue Paul Smith shirt and looking nervous at 1 p.m. in the Caprice, the Italian pizzeria three floors below this very room. Hope springs eternal.

Monday 13th September

I arrived at the Caprice as planned. He was already there: over six feet of hunky man-meat, sharply dressed and handsomely presented. His hair, salt and pepper grey, his eyes, heavy and broody, his Paul Smith shirt stretched over the girth of his pecs, nipples protruding through the fine cloth. I knew those nipples well. My tongue had licked every inch of them into submission. His hands were fidgeting over a flat white, as well they should have. I felt anger well up inside me as it dawned on me I'd been set up. There was no Chico4ManStud; there had only ever been him. But, before I could allow myself the justification of scorning him in public, I noticed that he was on the verge of crying. Or had been crying. Either way, it softened me.

'Andy, I'm sorry,' he said like a boy, fingers fumbling with his silver cufflinks over and over again, thumbnails stained grey from oily engines. 'I had to see you, and this is the only way I could. My head's mince.'

I like to think I can be cold and merciless when I need to be. I try to channel Alexis Carrington at times, but today she just wasn't coming through. If I could've turned myself into a glacier, I would have, but I found it impossible seeing him so vulnerable and lost. I pulled up a chair and said, 'Okay, Alistair. This had better be bloody fantastic. I'll give you five minutes. Talk before I walk.'

He spoke about how much he missed me. How empty he felt. He admitted to having gay tendencies, always feeling this way, but hiding it from everyone, including himself. 'I'm tired of it, Andy. I left my wife months ago.' Emotional bombshell number one, a good bombshell, if there are such things. Was there hope after all? I smiled inside but immediately scorned myself for being so callous and fickle. *His poor wife*. 'Finding you online took some effort, I scoured the web for weeks,' he continued. 'I knew it was a risk creating a false profile. I'm sorry I bailed on the last date, I just got too nervous. I knew I'd missed my chance. A golden opportunity like you doesn't come along very often, and even if you don't want to see me again, I'll be happy just seeing you today. It's more than I deserve, I know you think that.' I sat in silence. He shuffled his chair forward and leant towards me with both of his elbows on the table. Those strong forearms were back in the room. Oh, boy, he smelt good. 'I may have lied to you about who I was, in the past ...'

'And online.'

'Aye, and online. I've been lying to myself, but I've always meant every single word I ever said to you. You are the most amazing guy I've ever met. Please, if you could just forgive me and give me one more shot.'

I'm not sure when I forgot about Constable 7469, but I woke around 11 p.m., and I realised I'd left him hanging just as he'd left me. That was bad. But this afternoon something came up. Something important. Someone exceptional. His place smelt of freshly painted walls and new fabrics; a truly fresh start. I felt his rugged hand drag across my torso, and his tenacious arm pull my body close against his. His hard cock pressed on my ass and twitched as he kissed the back of my neck tenderly. His cologne enveloped me in a comforting shroud of familiarity. Other people didn't matter. Nothing mattered. The world was busily turning, but it was just us and the moon and the stars. I lay awake for a while in his new bed, in his new flat, with the moonlight flooding through the bay window and felt at peace. It seemed as if the stars were shining brighter than ever before.

At midnight, Alistair begged me not to go, but I realised I hadn't fed the Colonel since breakfast. We kissed a passionate goodbye at his door (almost in public), and I bid him goodnight. A short visit to test the water, but not in over my head, not yet. So here I am, at home. I'm sat with my feline buddy scribbling in this diary. I can see the moon and stars through my window, and they're still shining just as bright as they did with him. The afterglow hasn't diminished.

Tuesday 14th September

Found on Gaydar this morning:

'All is fair in love and war, Andy. I guess you gave as good as you got.
But my reasons were valid, are yours? I don't really care. I don't do mind games.
GAME OVER. Geoffrey.'

The fact is, I stood Geoffrey up because something better came along. He has every right to be pissed off. I kept it simple and wrote back, 'Fair do's.' I deleted my Gaydar profile. I don't want it. I want Alistair. GAME OVER, Gaydar, I've got something much better that just doesn't exist online.

'He's smiling like a Cheshire cat that's just shagged the local moggie and devoured a bowl of extra-thick cream,' reported Sally as she whipped up the usual rum-laced cappuccino for Molasses. 'Spill the beans, brotherfucker!'

Molasses smacked Sally on the shoulder so hard it caused her to clatter the jug of molten froth against the steamer. 'Just you concentrate on coffee beans for a change and leave the boy alone.' Sally muttered expletives under steaming white clouds and obliged. Molasses winked at me, 'Keep whatever makes you happy to yourself. Once it's out, it's no longer just yours, so relish the moment and don't let others shit all over it.'

I grinned and stuck my tongue out at Sally when Molasses wasn't looking. She's right, I fear my friends may do just that, therefore I think I should keep what Alistair and I have between us neatly tucked between our bed sheets for the moment. Just until I'm sure it's not going to go tits up.

Sally slid slyly past me and whispered, 'I know you had sex with the copper last night. It's written all over your face.'

Little does she really know.

Wednesday 15th September

4 p.m. A text request from Alistair to come round tonight about eight. Of course, I said yes. Then a further request for me to be naked when I arrive at his door, which shouldn't be a problem as he's the only tenant in his newly developed block. I sent a request back for him to be naked too. The reply:

'Of course, Sir. & it would please me, if I may be so bold to say,
if you ordered me to to do so, instead of asking.
It would please me very much,
Sir! :-p'

I could be wrong, but judging by the sudden swelling just below my waist, I think I could be moving into a new and exciting sexual postcode.

Thursday 16th September

Getting out of the front door last night was like being on some kind of Japanese game-show with my needy mates as obstacles. Sally wanted to discuss any issues I was having with the dance routine. I flippantly told her, 'I've issues with the whole damn thing!' and moved towards the front door, at which point Melve emerged from his room and asked if he could borrow some instant coffee.

'But you don't do caffeine,' I snapped.

'Um ... It's not for me ... it's for a friend who's staying tonight,' he stammered. I swear he blushed.

Probably some sexually deprived granny; an easy and almost immobile target for him. Sparing myself from the sickening details, I turned about and got him the only jar I have left.

'There you go, Melve. I hope your "friend" enjoys it.'

A key rattled in the lock and in came Gwen. I tried to say a quick hello and goodbye, but she squeezed my arm and asked, 'Can we talk again? I feel I am ready to give Matt ...' she leant in and surreptitiously muttered, '... all of me.' Her nostrils flared, and her eyebrows jittered in nervous anticipation.

'Not now. I haven't got time. But after the all-important dance practice would be good,' I hollered up the staircase.

Just as I hit fresh air, I bumped into Ryan. He smiled excitedly and asked, 'Andy, darling. How goes the day?'

I'd had enough. 'I'm sorry, Ryan,' I blurted out. 'I'm horny. And desperate. And in what could be the twilight years of what limited sexual allure I have, for that matter. I'm off for a shag before my date goes off the boil.'

He pondered for a second and said, 'Go get him, tiger.' Then pulled me towards him before I could sprint, 'But give me all the dirty details after the ...'

'I know, I know, after the bloody dance rehearsal. I know!' I hollered as I picked up the pace.

Twenty minutes later, I'd arrived at the Shore, sweaty, fully charged and aggravated. Stripped and finally cooling down, I rang the doorbell. The door swung open, and there was one hunk of man-meat, bollock naked apart from a pair of Doc Martin boots and nice thick socks that perfectly complimented his muscular calves. He was standing to attention, pulsing and poised for action. I could see this was as much of a turn on for him as it was for me. 'Get out here,' I demanded in my most authoritative tone. 'Against the window ledge and spread.'

He followed my instructions immediately.

'Smack me, Sir, please,' he begged. His balls were hanging low, I could see them swaying between his ass cheeks as he steadied himself for the onslaught. I took hold of them, gripping them tightly as I gave him a firm but caring smack. He moaned a little. 'Harder please, Sir,' he invoked, muscled cheeks pushing back against my thigh. I felt something new, a sort of horny anger, and went in for a slap that was so hard it echoed along the corridor and stung the palm of my hand. He writhed, gasping and groaning with delight, thrusting against me more so as I gripped his balls tighter to restrain him.

I heard an authoritative voice pass from my lips, 'Don't even move.' Struggling to open a condom, I thought I may lose the red mist that'd appeared before my eyes, but the sight of my man bent over, desperate to be taken in hand by his Master, soon infused my scarlet haze. I pushed inside him with such confidence I became something much more self-assured than helpless, lost Andy Angus: I was a man in control. We had wild, brutish, intense sex in front of that window, with the Firth of Forth before us as I plundered his ass for all it was worth. The more Alistair relinquished his very being, the more I became a sexual predator. Together, we came hard and loud: him all over the gleaming pane of glass; me deep inside him. Then calmness. I lingered on him for a time, abdomen panting against the sloppiness of his lower back coated in a mixture of sweat, lube and testosterone.

When I chose to release him, he turned to me and said with a satisfied grin, 'That was amazing.'

'I didn't go too far, did I?' my voice soft and spent.

'No,' he kissed me, still grinning, 'not at all.' Adding, with a wink, '*Sir*.'

I have no idea where this beast has been hiding, but I loved every second of it.

Friday 17th September

I woke this morning alone in Alistair's bed with his crisp cotton sheets caressing me, but not as splendidly as he had. I could hear the city stirring outside; the windows had been left open to cool us after another hot session. Thick red curtains swayed gently in the breeze. The distinct smell of charred smoked bacon lured me out of bed. It was then it dawned on me, I'd no idea where the kitchen was. All I'd mapped was the bedroom, bathroom and hall, but not the kitchen or even the lounge. Still naked, I wrapped the sheet around me and investigated. I found a large lounge that could fit all four of our bedsits within, with two windows that opened onto a balcony view facing the Kingdom of Fife. Three burgundy Chesterton sofas sat around an oval glass-topped coffee table. The rest of the lounge was minimal, with no ornaments or pictures hung on the walls, it became evident to me that he'd chosen to leave everything of his former life behind. On further investigation, I came across a second bathroom with hot-tub; a study-come-library; a games room, complete with classic jukebox, mini basketball court and pool table; and two more bedrooms.

I finally found Alistair in the kitchen, hopping on the spot, shaking his hand and blowing on his fingertips, 'Sorry – bugger – you'd think at the age of forty-five I'd learn that grills get hot when under a bloomin' flame,' he joked before sucking on his thumb.

I pulled his hand from his mouth, which made a generous popping noise as the thumb came free, causing some merriment between us, and guided him mercifully to the copious sink. From then on, I was stumped. 'How do you work this tap? Is that a tap?' I asked, unsure if the shaft of glistening metal would spout water by uttering some weird incantation.

Alistair smiled and inflected definitively to some unseen entity, 'Fanny: water, cold, medium flow.' Water poured from the shard in an appealing criss-cross fashion, I moved his injury under the flow and admired the patterns it made between his thick fingers.

'That's very Star Trek,' I joked. 'Who's Fanny when she's at home?'

'Home exactly, she's the A.I.,' and then he whispered, 'she's a bit of a grumpy know-it-all at times, so I named her after Fanny Cradock. And yes, I've always wanted to be the captain of the USS Enterprise. Total geek here,' he said, raising his free hand and parting his fingers to make a V sign. 'Live long and prosper,' he said with mock gravitas.

He'd no knowledge of the enormity of his actions. My geeky heart leapt for joy, 'Do-do-do you like Star Trek?' I asked, playing down my hopes that this guy could possibly be as passionate about Star Trek as I was about Doctor Who.

He laughed again, it was free and playful. 'Eh, duh? Haven't you seen my DVD library?'

'No, I got a little lost and ran out of string. How big is this place?' Then I realised, if this guy has a vast place, he also has a vast collection. I fixed my eyes on him and said in all seriousness, 'Please tell me you have a geek-den filled with such gems.'

'Fanny: stop the flow,' he commanded. The water stopped.

'Powerful words. How many women up and down the country would ask for such a thing every month?' I joked. He pulled a fresh tea-towel from a drawer and dabbed my hands dry.

'Oh, Mr,' he said as he kissed me on the lips affectionately. 'Do I have a geek-den.' He took me by the hand and guided me towards a door that was so unassuming compared to the rest I expected to find nothing more than a mouldy old mop and dusty vacuum cleaner inside. He positioned me squarely in front and cupped his hands over my eyes, resting his chin against the side of my neck. 'Prepare to cum in your pants once more, big boy.' I heard the door swing open, and I was ushered inside. 'Fanny: lights up.'

His hands slipped away, and I opened my eyes to see the ultimate home cinema. Three rows of very comfortable reclining seats invited me to sit in a room glittering with pin-pricks of starlight. Glaucous walls curved to a point in the ceiling. The facing wall housed the most mammoth home cinema screen I've ever seen. The smell of popcorn drifted towards me as I spun around in amazement to find two machines that supplied such delightful, delicious delicacies. There was a coke fountain and, more importantly, a bar.

I stood agog, 'This is amazing. A couch potato's paradise.'

'Every movie you ever wanted to experience, every TV show you've ever wanted to watch, every book you've ever dreamt of reading, every piece of music you've wanted to listen to, it's here.'

'Really? Nah, you're joshing me.'

Alistair folded his arms and said confidently, 'Name something.'

I racked my brains for a few seconds: it had to be something rare, something impossible, unattainable: 'Doctor Who: The Web Of Fear. Episode Three.'

'Fanny, play Doctor Who, The Web of Fear, Episode Three,' he said confidently.

An older woman's voice, soft but a little cranky, echoed around the room through hidden speakers, 'Now playing: Doctor Who. The Web Of Fear. Episode Three.' I could feel my eyes bulging in disbelief as the burgundy curtains peeled back to expose the full scale of the screen. *Impossible, this episode has been lost for years*, I thought. But the sting of the theme tune filled the room, and the howl-around black and white titles pulled me towards them in disbelief. Sure enough, the episode title, 'Episode Three', appeared from the vortex.

'But that's unbelievable,' I whispered. I blinked several times to be sure I saw straight, but Episode Three was there. This man had somehow got hold of one of the most sought-after lost episodes of Doctor Who. I had to steady myself on the back of a chair, which promptly reclined and sent me crashing unceremoniously to the floor.

Alistair couldn't help but laugh. 'Are you okay?'

'I think I've been sucked into a time-space vortex where anything's possible,' I quipped as I gazed up at his handsome face surrounded by fake twinkling stars. 'How could you possibly have this? The masters were junked by the BBC ages ago.'

Alistair wrapped his arms around my waist and swung me to my feet. 'Ask no questions, and I shall tell no sci-fi-lie.' He pointed at me firmly and said, 'Sit! Stay! We'll have breakfast in here.'

When he left, I couldn't contain myself. I hopped from foot to foot in excitement. Could this really be happening? Could he really be this amazing? Do I deserve this?

After many minutes involving the London Underground, Patrick Troughton & roaring yetis, he lifted my empty plate from my lap and wrapped his arm around my shoulder. I sank into the chair and rested my head against his. I thought, *He really is that amazing. And yes, you do deserve this.*

The day drifted by. The sun sank over the Kingdom of Fife as we drank mojitos in the lounge. Later, after fun on a rug next to a roaring fire, I dropped somewhat tipsily into those comforting sheets once again. Once more enveloped in Alistair's massive frame. Once more spent from taking charge. Knowing he was peacefully sleeping next to me again satisfied my soul. I could see the darkness of the sky through the gap in the curtains. Every now and then I'd catch sight of the man in the moon. He was smiling at me for the first time in ages. I whispered to him, 'Where have you been?'

Alistair stirred. 'You talking to me?' he asked, drowsily.

'No, I was talking to the man in the moon.'

He kissed the back of my neck and said, 'Goodnight, crazy.'

I felt his head nod contentedly on the pillow we shared. It was a partial lie, because seconds later, I asked myself, *Yes, Alistair, where have you been?* But I didn't utter a word. Forgetting all that'd gone before, all the mistakes we'd made, in that little pocket of time, right there in the small space between our resting hearts, we were perfection.

Saturday 18th September

'Where have you been?' asked a pissed-off Sally. 'You're twenty minutes late. Everyone's been waiting for you.'

I glanced around the church hall to see my friends grudgingly greet me. On a direct flightpath – cutting a conversation short he'd been having with some old queen sporting a lavender beret and thick handlebar moustache – came Ryan, fizzing like Vesuvius, bridezilla mode turned up to the max. He raised his voice for dramatic effect, 'Just a second, Trenton, there's an irresponsible shit I have to deal with,' and stomped purposefully towards me with his hands on his hips. 'I'm glad you could make it. Whoever you were shagging had better been worth the delay,' he spat as he strutted past, dropping a death stare after his shoulder wilfully collided with mine.

The room fell silent and became tense. Molasses said nothing, as usual, the lioness observing her cubs as they spar. Gwen was the first to speak, 'Andy,' she started, 'this is ...'

The ageing queen with the beret leered towards me, swooping one arm flamboyantly to the ground as he swished into a bow. 'Trenton Tanner, retired costume designer for BBC Scotland and distinguished homosexual. You are at my service.' He stood upright slowly and grimaced. 'Oh, life's a bitch. Years of stooping low to raise seams have wrecked this back and ruined these knees. Well, that and one very late night in a leather bar in Berlin, but I'll save that for when we're better acquainted,' he joked as he stuck out his hand and wiggled his fingers excitedly before my unaffected eyes, which was no mean feat as he barely reached chest height, beret included.

I couldn't bring myself to touch his nicotine-stained fingers, so my hands stayed by my side, and my face remained limp and unimpressed. 'Costume? As in, costumes?' I asked. 'As in, dress-up and make-up and ...' I could hardly bring myself to say the word, ' ... camp couture?' Their special day was fast becoming everything I'd asked it not to be.

Trenton Tanner took my hand in both of his and shook it vigorously, practically raping it, and corrected me, 'No, dear. Costumes, as in, glamour, screen sirens, leading men, gay icons, and yours and every other gay man's historical right of passage, visually, stylistically and tunatically.'

'That's not even a real word,' I argued, snatching my hand back.

'Life would be dull if we didn't write our own lyrics. The sooner you do so, the quicker you'll fully discover your true self, cupcake. And the more you do, the less uptight you'll be. No one likes a frosty old queen, dear.'

'I'm not frosty,' I said firmly.

'Oh, get you, tiger,' Trenton mocked as he popped on a monocle and pranced around, inspecting me as a judge would a pedigree at Crufts. I'm sure if I had a tail, he would've lifted it and scrutinised my lower regions with much aplomb. 'Mind you, all the greats have had a little attitude. Yes, my little cherubs, this will do very nicely,' he nodded in agreement towards Ryan and Tony. 'I think we've found our leading man. He has all the poise of a Greek statue, if not the hips. Can he dance?'

'Leading? I don't want to be leading anything,' I groused.

Tony slid by on cue with the usual snide remark, 'Pu-lease, can he dance? He has all the moves and dexterity of a Stannah stairlift and even less charisma. It's totally fine, Andrew, if you think you're incapable, we can always ask Barry.'

Not to be outdone by bitchy Biffo, I took everyone in the room by surprise, saying clearly, 'Okay, I'll do it. For fu ... Ryan's sake.' It was my equivalent to spitting at Biffo's feet.

'Wonderful news, my little cherub,' grinned Trenton as he smacked me on the arse, which made me yelp in fright. 'Besides, the lead's costume is a rehash from an old Space 1999 episode and would sag on anyone else.' He dropped a tape measure from my head to the floor and then whipped it around my waist so quick I'd no time to pull my gut in. 'With a few tweaks around the waist,' he added, thoughtfully. I swiped his hand away as he dived in to check my inside leg. 'Never mind, sweet-cheeks. A bit shy, eh? I'll get that at a later date,' he winked.

Over my dead body, I thought.

'Super! A star is born. I'll widen the waist in preparation for your first fitting,' he concluded as he draped the tape measure around his neck and moved towards the corner of the room. As he went, I heard him pass an aside to Tony, 'I only hope there's enough fabric between the stitches.'

I do believe Trenton and I will not be close friends.

'Can we get on?' asked Melve. 'I've a lady booked in for eleven tonight, and I need plenty time for the Viagra to warm up.'

'Dear Lord!' cut in Sally. 'Okay, chop-chop! Let's get this done and get out of here before the hardest thing in the room is anything other than a Viennese Waltz.'

I spent the next hour bungling my way through my star turn as Sarah Brightman at a gayer-than-gay civil ceremony. I was terrible. We all were. Sally tried to give me some encouragement, 'We have to work on the old rolling of the hips, darling. I'll give you extra tuition this week.' Wrapping up, she announced, 'That's all for tonight.'

'Great!' I said, as exuberantly as a hitobashira maiden at the local Japanese town planning office.

******

Later, with my tardy timekeeping consigned to history, our jolly group enjoyed drinks at the rather rambunctious Café Habana. Sally yammered over the din of some cloned clichéd pop song, 'So why have I been feeding your cat two days on the trot, Andy Angus? Divulge.'

Such is the joy in my heart over the delectably lickable Alistair, I became desperate to blab all, just to tell someone, anyone, how wonderful he makes me feel. But I clamped my mouth shut and pondered the consequences. It's too early to say, not for me, but for him. He's not out yet. I'm sure it's only a matter of time, and that's what I should give him, as much time as he needs. I smiled and said, 'Oh, no one special.'

Sally looked up at me pitifully, popped out her saddest eyes and pouted so much I could've easily rested my shot glass on her lips, 'But we always tell each other everything, sweetie.'

'Do we?' I asked her purposefully. She talks and talks, and yet I really know very little about her. 'I'll spill if you do,' I nodded, knowing very well that not even a corner of her protective packaging would peel from its edges.

True to form, she didn't crack. 'You're right, darling. At our age, the here-and-now is all that matters. Let's not dwell on the past.' She downed her drink and announced to everyone she was getting the next round, much to their celebration.

Sunday 19th September

What's better: staying in bed all day with a sleepy hangover, or staying in bed all day with a sleepy hangover while being spooned by a lovely man who nibbles on your ears and finds that wee pocket of energy you didn't think you had? The latter. And that's exactly where I spent my snoozy Sunday.

Monday 20th September

'I really wanted to talk to you privately on Saturday night, Andy,' said Gwen as she fidgeted with her cutlery nervously in the café. She'd popped in for a solo lunch, something she never does, which told me she had something pressing to get off her now pert chest.

'Are you here again?' butt in Sally. 'Aren't you usually munching on a jar of pickled cabbage in some office stationery cupboard at this hour?'

'Rotkohl,' corrected Gwen.

'Bless you,' quipped Sally. 'Oh, to be as popular as you, Andy,' she called before vanishing into the kitchen.

Sally was in a particularly cutting mood today. I ignored her and asked Gwen, 'What's up?' She motioned for me to join her. I was relieved to sit and take the pressure off my aching calves borne out of repeated tensing during my two-hour edging session with Alistair last night.

'Where were you yesterday?' she asked me. 'You are usually around the bedsits most nights.'

I smiled to myself and thought, *How my world has changed. I must've been so predictable before, always at home if not at the café, watching any old crap on my tiny old telly to fill the emptiness of an almost-life. But now my life is brimming with sexual desire, fulfilment, experimentation and mutual respect, not to forget those lingering hugs. My cup is brimming over.*

'Andy!' I heard Gwen snap to spurn me out of my daydream.

'Gwen, dearest,' I said calmly, 'we don't clock in on shift here, so why on Earth should we be clocking in at home?'

'We will be, if you don't get your ass off that chair soon, boy!' hollered Molasses from the bar, moodily polishing a pint glass with such vigour I expected it to shatter at any moment.

'Be quick,' I said to Gwen, edging off the chair in anticipation of my manager's wrath.

'Matt,' Gwen whispered quickly, 'he's really pushing the intimacy. I feel pressurised. I want to wait until marriage, that's if it gets that far, but he wants to do it now, to be sure we are compatible. What should I do? I don't want to loose him.'

I fully appreciate the need to 'try before you buy', without it I would never have known what another erection feels like apart from my own. I can sympathise with the boy. His nights must be spent kissing, dry humping and aching all over, only to be left with blue balls on a chilly walk home. I'm sure, unintentionally, Gwen has become the world's biggest and most unlikely cock-tease, but I can't stand anyone who pressurises another into performing before they're ready. I know! I know! I've been dominating Alistair for the past few meets, but that's fully consensual role-play. He begs for it, so no harm there. With too much ground to cover, I said quickly, 'Come see me in the morning, I'll be home then. And it's *lose* not *loose*.'

'Thanks so much, Andy. You're a good friend.' She leant over her plate and patted me clumsily on the head again, a foreigner to sisterly affection, she looked as if she was patting a dog for good behaviour. What chance does she stand being natural and affectionate when naked?

I felt the tail end of Molasses' tea-towel catch me on the shoulder. I was off that chair quicker than you can say 'consensual sex' and back in the kitchen dropping off the next ticket.

Tuesday 21st September

I missed Gwen as I spent so long in Alistair's comforting arms. I had no time to shower. I ran up Leith Walk redolent of Alistair. I felt as if everyone I passed knew precisely where I'd been and what I'd been up to. Walk of shame? No, this was an Olympic sprint. And, to be honest, I felt very little shame. But still, I was too late. As I knocked on Gwen's door, frantic and sweatier than I'd been with my man, the silence confirmed the worst: I'd broken my promise. My dear friend needed me, and I was too wrapped up in my own rapture to give a shit.

'She's gone to work,' came a familiar voice from behind me. I turned to face Sally, sporting electric-blue hair, all curly and confusing, and the biggest, bluest false lashes I've ever seen. Her hands were on her hips, and her legs were semi-crossed as she leant on the door frame. I could tell for the first time in our friendship that she was judging me. 'She's temping in some god-awful shoebox of a call centre today.'

'How was she?' I asked, panting and holding on to my knees.

'She looked upset, Andrew.' Sally used my full name, which was foreign to me and made me a little discomposed. 'You do know that little shit is pressing on her cherry, desperate for it to pop?'

'How do you know that?' I asked, realising I'd stupidly confirmed a vague suspicion she'd had. I covered my mouth quickly in an attempt to withhold the cascade of secrets I'd sworn to keep.

'I'm sex-psychic,' she claimed. 'I can pick up on the deflowering of virgins and ...' she stepped forward and sniffed around me as intensely as a cat that's stumbled on some catnip, ' ... I can always, always, *always* tell when someone has just had sex.'

My bones rattled. 'Don't be daft, no one can do that,' I insisted. I told myself, *Sex is just sex to her, so why worry?* 'Okay, okay! I've had sex! It isn't a crime, although you would think so the way you're acting. God knows you've had plenty of action. Jeez! You have the nose of a bloodhound!'

'I entertain gentlemen privately in a club, that's different, and socially acceptable, darling,' she said. She sniffed again and nodded, stepping back from me with a look of smug satisfaction. As if her hypothesis had just been confirmed. 'Ultraviolet, definitely Ultraviolet,' she affirmed.

'Your hair?'

'No, but I have decided on a refurbishment, don't you just adore it?' she stroked her locks and smiled. Then she fixed a deathly stare on me, 'I meant the aftershave that you're soaked in. It's not your usual, but I have smelt it on you before. I just can't place who from. You don't wear it as it gives you a rash, if I remember.'

Her words hung in the air. I felt the ceiling bearing down on me. The 70s patterned wallpaper began to spin. I started to hope the carpet would suck my feet through its yellow and orange swirls and quickly gobble me up. It didn't. *Damn you, imagination, why aren't you over-active when I need you the most? Now is not the time to be average!*

Sally's eyes narrowed as she tilted her head to the side, cogs turning, slowly putting the pieces of the jigsaw together from the edge and working her way towards the centre. I hoped that my recent jaunt into promiscuity would leave her bamboozled. I saw her mouth fall open in slow-motion, gearing up to say something. Maybe Alistair's name? How to stop her reading my mind and ruining the joy of secret sex with the guy I'd previously been having secret sex with while his wife was around? This time it's different, there's no wife, and yet I feel guilty. Maybe I've overstepped the mark and walked all over the acceptable grace period for couples who've broken up. I didn't want to justify my actions to anyone, least of all a self-righteous stripper.

At that crucial point, Melve's door opened, and Trenton Tanner waltzed out, spinning around with his arms wide as if to bid a warm goodbye to a semi-naked Melve. Melve caught sight of us and, to Trenton's surprise and somewhat disappointment, he swiftly grasped one of the costume designer's hands and pulled it towards him, shaking it with such masculinity it made Trenton squeal and almost topple forward in the ambush.

'Cheers, mate,' bid Melve playfully, punching Trenton on the shoulder, which caused him to yelp like a doting pup who'd just had his paw stepped on. 'Thanks for measuring me up for the costume and coming all this way,' Melve skilfully pirouetted Trenton around and lead him towards the door, 'and for the cake,' he concluded, catapulting a bemused retired BBC employee into the stair. Melve swung the heavy door shut as an ever-shrinking Trenton vanished between the crack, unable to utter a fair goodbye, stammering in astonishment.

Sally was still frozen with her finger in the air, like a weeping angel caught in a mirror, agog at Melve's antics. I felt some relief. 'He brought cake, would you believe?' stated Melve, folding his arms in a fuddled attempt to cover his stark, greying moobs. 'Artists, eh?' he guffawed. Troubled by our bourgeoning curiosity, he exited stage right to the sanctuary of his clutter.

Sally and I faced each other with eyes wide.

'That's new!' I said.

'Yes, it most certainly is,' agreed Sally.

The window of opportunity dropped open before me, and I made no hesitation in clambering to my escape. 'Well, it's been great to catch up, but I'm going to be late for my shift, and we both know how hard Molasses can whip a boy who's timing is sloppier than Scots Porridge Oats,' I nodded and smiled a smile as phoney as Pamela Anderson's breasts.

'Hey, hey! Wait a minute. I haven't finished with you yet, brotherfucker!' yelled Sally. But it was too late, I was halfway down the stair and giving a shit less with every step, pulling the neck of my T-shirt up around my nose and deeply inhaling the safe scent of my man as I went.

I'll catch Gwen tomorrow morning. I'll crawl past Sally's door with all the skill of a SAS soldier. I'll knock on Gwen's door early, at a time when I'm sure Sally will be stupefied under a blanket of gin.

Wednesday 22nd September

Gwen didn't come home. I didn't sleep well at all. My ear lifted from the pillow every time I heard the slightest movement. I was woken by the Colonel pouncing at a seagull on the fire escape. It was dawn, and the sun was creeping over the rooftops of Leith. Like a worried parent, I made a pot of tea, popped on my housecoat, and sat in silence at the little secondhand Formica table I bought for a tenner last week. I watched the cool breeze from the open window accentuate the steam from the substandard instant coffee that was at odds with my treasured Hornsea love mug. There's a chill in the air, and the haar becomes sluggish with its feet on these late September mornings. I caught sight of myself in the mirror and was disgusted by the stooped, ageing geezer gawping at me. Oh, to be youthful once more. I thought about my sixteenth year, underage – as the law decreed then – skipping about Glasgow's gay scene, living the wild nights of a young queen without a care in the world. I thought of my restless parents waiting for me to come home. Often I didn't. I'd disappeared into the night. Today I gained insight into their woes.

Sure, Gwen's been out all night before, and it hasn't bothered me one jot, but that was before I knew the pressure she's under. Before I let her down. She may not be an inexperienced teenager, she's an adult and well-travelled, but she is naïve, vulnerable, and an amateur when it comes to love. God! Is she in love? I hope not as anything could've happened by now.

'Why do you care so much?' asked Alistair as he munched hungrily on the takeaway I'd brought for dinner (I even love how he dines: tearing off big chunks of nan bread like a caveman and slapping it unceremoniously on our plates).

I thought for a moment, wanting to be honest and entirely sure of my answer. 'I like to believe, even in these times where sex can be anonymous, casual and with as many people as you like, that there are people like Gwen out there who still believe intimacy is something to be cherished, cradled and protected. Kept safe until you're ready to give it to that special someone who, with all certainty, connects with you like no other.'

'Wow,' said Alistair, blinking in surprise and scooping a clump of basmati rice from the tub. 'Sometimes I think I know you, Andy Angus, and then you go and surprise me some more.'

'What do you mean?'

'I dunno ... I thought you were a playboy, in a way.'

I knew this was my time to say exactly how I felt, but I held back in terror that he'd run for the hills at the thought of a proper relationship with a man. I did, however, say, 'No, I'm in it for more than just sex.'

He said, 'Good. So am I,' and leant over to kiss me full on the lips with a big, greasy garlic-soaked kiss that made me groan in playful disgust. He growled and moved around the table towards me, pouting all the way. I tried to wriggle away, but he caught me and smothered me in big sloppy snogs, chuckling as he did so. He accidentally burped in my face, and we fell to the floor in fits of laughter. He wiped my chin with the palm of his hand and said, 'Sorry, Master. Sorry for taking liberties.' Becoming earnest, he added, 'I should be disciplined.'

Within the hour, I'd taught him a firm lesson and, for the first time, *he* fell asleep in *my* arms.

It's definitely more than just sex.

Thursday 23rd September

I was boiling mad by the time Gwen showed face. 'Where the hell have you been?' I asked as she stumbled from Sally's room, wearing nothing but the pole dancer's revealing robe and Jackie Onassis sunglasses. She mustered a grunt as she pushed past me like a blind, unbalanced woman and staggered towards the sanctuary of her room. She clung on to the door handle to gain some stability before pressing down with weary shoulders and slicking through the crack without a word.

'She's been biding with me,' said Sally triumphantly at my rear.

'It doesn't look as if she's had much sleep,' I said, concerned that Gwen was on a slippery slope towards the scree of Sally's debauchee lifestyle.

'Oh, a wee drinkie or two won't do the girl any harm,' she quipped, waving her hand dismissively.

'Is she okay?'

'Matt's finished it, so she's not so cheery, no,' she reported while admiring her nails. 'However, a few more alcohol-fuelled nights with torch-songs and some good, healthy bitching in my fabulous company, and she'll be peachy in no time.'

I should've been there for her, not this slightly immoral wannabe matriarch. A silence fell between us. Sally watched me with the same disconcerting stare Molasses has when she lords it over punters at the café.

Sally's tone softened, 'Don't worry, Sonny Jim. She didn't lose anything apart from the bus fare there and back. Our girl can still be forced into white robes, chained to a rock and sacrificed by some cult in honour of a virgin-hungry god.'

Relieved, I said, 'I guess they're a rarity these days,' and laughed.

'Tell me about it, poppet!'

'Anyway, thanks for the update,' I added, awkwardly. 'I best run and jump in the shower.'

'Off somewhere special?'

'As a matter of fact, aye, I am,' I said as I entered the bathroom.

'Darling,' she called after me. 'Do you fancy a trip on the bike? One last jolly before the dangers of autumn roads? It could be fun. Just you and me.'

To keep the peace, I agreed, but really I'd rather be taking a ride on the back of that bike with Alistair. Then bend him over the handlebars and take him over the warmth of the leather seat on some secluded country lane. Oh, my! I'm becoming quite comfortable in my 'Master' role.

'I'll be in touch,' she shouted through the door. 'But it has to be within the week, the weather is meant to turn the most unsavoury shade of grey over the next fortnight.'

'Okay. Sunday, as the roads will be quiet.'

Alistair is away on business from then until Friday. I'm going to be alone again, and that doesn't fill me with joy. Am I becoming too attached? I find myself reading over our text messages in moments of solitude and saying his name in quiet spaces just to conjure him up in some small way.

Friday 24th September

'Neglect!'

'What?' I asked the darkness as my head leapt from Alistair's snug pillow.

A hand cupped my shoulder, 'Are you okay?' Alistair's speech was lethargic but concerned. I turned to him. His beautiful head was nestled in the pit of two pillows, one leg was tucked on top of the duvet, as is his habit. His right arm was outstretched and trapped under my pillow, numb from cradling my neck for hours. This is how we sleep. I love it, but last night was not the best. I'd just been pricked awake by a dream I couldn't recall.

'Sorry, did you say something a moment ago?' I asked.

'Not that I know of,' he said, lifting his dead arm with the other and grimacing. 'Jeez! I think I may be getting bed-sores from all this spooning, Mr.'

'Sorry,' I said, rubbing it to get the circulation back. It was his first complaint on this subject. 'Maybe try hanging it over the side of the bed.'

Alistair rolled on his front and hung his arm towards the glossy floorboards. 'You just want to get me in a compromising position again,' he joked through a mass of feathers and cotton. It hadn't escaped me that the duvet was no longer covering his ample frame and his sweet ass was being kissed by moonlight. Firm, round, with just the right amount of hair shimmering away, it was an invitation to a party that I was happy to attend. 'Use me, Sir,' he pleaded. I didn't need to be asked twice. We were soon spent and had fallen asleep once more. The voice I'd heard was forgotten. I slept deep and short.

Far too quickly, time passed and work beckoned for Alistair. I was dropped off at 323 Leith Walk and very sad to say goodbye. 'Garages never really close, buddy,' he said when I questioned his gruelling work schedule.

All I could think was, *Buddy? Surely we're more than just buddies?* But it was too late. He was off.

I felt a pang of guilt as I caught sight of Gwen on her way to work. Luckily she'd missed Alistair's car melding with the morning rush hour. I decided to chase Gwen's tail up the Walk. I finally caught up with her on the corner of Albert Street. I was convinced she was wilfully gathering pace to get as far from me as possible. In fact, she was impatient to cross the road and didn't wait on the green man (something she never does).

I tapped her on the shoulder and tried a reassuring grin.

'Oh, I didn't see you there, Andy,' she claimed, continuing to walk towards Elm Row. I shouldn't have been surprised to find the old Gwen back: the plain, baggy clothing; the grey, thick tights; the washed-out pallor; the scowl; even the colour in her hair had dissolved. The make-up had been forgotten, and the smile that had developed slowly over the months she'd been falling for Matt was thin and weak.

I caught up with her again, 'Are you okay?' I panted. Nothing was wrong with her legs, apparently.

'I'm fine,' was the short reply.

'But Gwen, you look so pale,' I struggled to keep up with her. 'Girl, even your lips are white.'

She stopped. 'Good!' she snapped. 'I want them to be so pale they become nonexistent. What good are they to me now? If I never get to kiss his lips again, I don't want them! If my words can't pour into his ears, what is the point of them uttering one more syllable?'

A lump formed in my throat so resolutely I could hardly speak, but I managed a feeble, 'You'll move on and meet someone else. Someone better, who deserves and respects you.'

'No, Andy,' she cut me off. 'No, I won't. He was everything to me. I had never opened myself up to such joy before, and now I know what that feels like, I want all memory of it gone. But it stays with me like cancer, eating at my every thought, at every moment of my day, because it's worthless if I can't share it with him.'

I had nothing. What could I possibly have said that would've fixed this? She walked away, hunched and closed, more insecure and unsure than I've ever seen her. A shadow of her former self. But then she stopped. She didn't turn around. I could see her shoulders shaking, I knew she was crying, but I also knew I shouldn't take one more step. I heard her say, 'If I had slept with him, he'd probably still be with me. I have to lose it someday anyway. Isn't the possibility of being happy worth the risk?'

She walked away. I let her go. She was heading to a crappy call centre that would be as depressing as her personal life. As I watched her blend into the rest of humanity, I asked myself, 'What do you actually know, Andy Angus? Nothing. Absolutely bloody nothing.'

Saturday 25th September

Dance class is cancelled: both of the Terrible Twins are ill. What a relief!

I spent the whole day thinking of Alistair. His face was reflected in every bowl of soup I served, and every sentence I heard seemed to end in his name. I know what's happening. I know I shouldn't feel this way already, especially after the "buddy" comment yesterday, but I can't help it. I imagine my TARDIS pyjamas neatly folded alongside his Bjorn Borg boxers on *our* bed.

He picked me up just around the corner from the café, looking a little pensive, but he brushed this off with a quick kiss and a smile that I was almost willing to be fooled by. When he told me later, over a few bottles of ale at his flat, 'It's work shit. Don't worry about it,' I settled for this because it was getting late and any big conversation would seriously encroach on our snuggle time.

I'm keen for us to move on beyond the usual quiet night in and start living our shiny new life together in public. 'Why don't we eat out some night when you're back?' I asked, testing the waters.

Indecisive drumming of fingers on a beer bottle ensued, which I found myself subconsciously mirroring in anticipation. A long sigh and, 'I dunno, Andy. It's been a tough choice to try this kinda thing, you know? Us. And I just don't know where I lie with it all the now.' He concentrated on the label of his bottle and picked at it firmly with his thumb, unable to look at me. I couldn't look at anything but him. All I want is him.

Baby steps, I told myself, *that's all this man can make, is baby steps. Hell, we all do in the beginning. Be sympathetic, Andy, think of his needs.* I want him, without hangups, free and comfortable within our togetherness for the long run, but that won't come if he trips at the first hurdle and runs in the opposite direction.

'So, you don't really know if you are gay?' I asked, trying not to look as if I was desperate for him to admit to being just like me.

'Oh, boy!' he sighed. He took my hand firmly, 'Look, my man. I don't know what I am right now: gay, bi, or just a man who's into you. I don't know. And the thought of going public with any one of those options fills me with dread. I was born and bred in a small town, I'm still officially married to a woman, and one half of my family's steeped in Irish Catholic tradition. That's a lot of shit to deal with. Going public isn't an option for me right now.' He pulled me close, his kind eyes giving me some reassurance in the face of what seemed impossible. 'But I do know where I lie with you.' He squeezed my hand and stressed, 'When I lie with you, naked and shagged out, I'm more satisfied and the happiest that I've ever been with anyone in my entire life.'

I smiled. He may not have been singing the right lyrics, but he's undoubtedly got the right melody, and that'll do for now. Then a thought occurred to me, 'Hey, if not here, then how about somewhere else? How about a date-night in a different city altogether?' I asked. 'Say, Newcastle?'

Alistair laughed, 'You are incorrigible!'

'Safe ground. You won't know unless you try,' I grinned hopefully.

'All right, all right. Newcastle, here we come.' He pulled me close and kissed my cheek, 'Are you gonna be a pain in my ass all the way through this relationship?'

'Only in the best possible way,' I joked. *He said "relationship".*

'Show me.'

And I did, for as long as he needed to be shown. He's away tomorrow, and even though I'll have company, it'll be a very lonely day.

Sunday 26th September

Sally drove us to Aberlady beach just within the sound barrier. I forget how beautiful it can be out there. It's been a while since my rescue on the night Alistair reappeared in my life, and yet, today, even though I was physically back there, I was very much in a different place emotionally.

'Sun, sand, ham, cheese, and chocolate, what more could you ask for?' said Sally.

'Did you make all this?' I asked, amazed she'd been organised enough to fix a full lunch of bread, olives, cured meats and cheeses before setting off at eleven o'clock in the morning.

'Don't be silly, darling!' she replied, gulping on a bucks-fizz, 'I asked our adopted mother, Miss Molasses Brown, to provide this little packed-lunch.' Behind her jaunty bearing, I could feel a more probing route planned. I chose to ignore any reference to my absent nights and late arrivals and kept our coastal trip buoyant with small-talk and chit-chat, all the while, her expectant silences and raised eyebrows became more frequent.

'Hey, how's the internet dating coming along?' she asked.

'Oh, so-so. I think I'm pretty much taking a break from it as it hasn't been very fruitful.'

'I thought you had a date with that lovely copper a few weeks ago?'

'Oh, he turned out to be a complete asshole,' I lied.

'Why?'

'He hates classic Who and votes Tory,' I added to my fabrication.

'Ugh! One of those,' she flipped back on the thick tartan rug beside me and flicked her now long, purple locks over her bare shoulders. Her bikini was straining under the weight of her voluptuous boobs; I imagined I could hear the straps creaking as rigging does when a sailing ship billows in a stiff breeze. 'Better off without that sort of chap. He'll be dragging you around garden centres at weekends as a substitute for his inequalities sexually and forcing you to watch Newsnight while tucked up in bed of an evening. Very tragic, darling.'

Changing the subject, I asked, 'What's happening with Gwen?'

'Oh, now that is tragic. The last time I saw her was when she hoofed it out of my room without so much as a bye-or-leave after kicking the arse out of a bottle of gin ... on second thoughts, it was me who kicked the arse out of it after she left. She didn't even pay for the inconvenience of laundering my sheets.'

'You gals didn't ...?'

'Good God, no, darling. I think that would blow her quiet little mind and dainty little box apart; she vomited on my bed,' she laughed. 'She left with all sides of her virginity intact, you can be assured of that, and I think she will be staying that way for a very long time, the poor soul.'

'I just hope she doesn't do anything silly.'

'Like what?'

'I dunno, she seemed pretty upset the last time I saw her.'

'Don't you fret, my little gay friend. She'll do what Gwen does and retreat back into her cocoon. It's only natural when you've been betrayed by a man. And then, over time, she'll emerge as a beautiful butterfly and make him think again about treating any other woman that way.' Sally winked at me, reassuringly, 'I'll make sure of that.'

'Keep an eye on her, will you? She's not really up for chat with me at the moment.'

'Consider it done.' She laid back and moved closer to me. We shared the fluffy clouds for a time and turned them into something meaningful.

'That one looks like half-open corn on the cob,' I said.

'No dear, more like a badly circumcised penis.'

'You, always thinking of willies,' I joked.

Sally sat upright and scanned the beach, 'Speaking of sex, sweetie. I believe that gay men can be found frolicking in the dunes here if you look hard enough. Would you like to have a solo wander? I'll just lay here and fry for a while happily on my own.' Her eyes became expectant.

'No, thanks,' I felt a rush of excuses fill my mouth, 'I have helmet-hair, and besides, I don't feel comfortable in these old speedos. Laid here, it's possible I have a six-pack; when I sand up, it removes any doubt that I really am a fat bastard.'

'Up to you,' she said, kicking back again. 'But just so that you know, you look extraordinaire, Monsieur André.'

'Merci buckets.'

We stayed prone for some time. I figured she'd fallen asleep. I began to drift away myself, but was woken with the one question I'd been expecting, 'Where do you go at night, Andy-darling?'

I figured I could lie, run for the dunes after all, or just become hostile. Instead, I decided on the most straightforward and safest option: 'I spend my nights with a lovely man who keeps me safe and warm, and who makes me feel like the sexiest guy on the planet. He also makes me feel like I'm the wittiest, brightest, most amazing man he's ever met. That's all I want to tell you, for now, Sally-darling.' I moved my head closer to hers and whispered in her ear, 'Look, I love you dearly, but please respect my privacy, and I'll promise to respect yours.' I knew, with her closed book of secrets, Sally would find this impossible to argue with. Slightly underhand of me, but all's fair in love and friendship.

'As long as you're happy,' she replied, without opening an eyelid beneath her Jackie O' sunglasses. 'That's all I care about really, darling. There, that's the end of it,' she said, spreading one of her enigmatic smiles. 'But when you *are* ready, give me all the sordid details, please?'

I laughed. I felt the cloud of tension dissipate between us. 'Deal! Oh, a favour: could you feed the Colonel if I'm not around?'

'Deal!' she said warmly.

And, just as those little fluffy clouds floated by, so did the afternoon, lighter and more relaxed than it'd begun.

Monday 27th September

1 a.m. The evening, on the other hand, was restless. I text Alistair two hours before bed, expecting a relatively quick reply, but nothing came through. Maybe he was asleep. Perhaps he was busy with some businessmen doing what blokey businessmen do. Oh, God! What do blokey businessmen do when they entertain clients? Boozing in strip clubs? I've been fidgeting and kicking the duvet so feverishly the Colonel has chosen to sleep on the fire escape with his backside firmly turned towards me.

11.45 p.m. My perturbed night continued through my dreams. I woke, or so I thought, to a familiar voice from the past talking to me, 'Neglect!' it announced just loud enough to grab my attention. I peered into the grey to find the Colonel staring back at me.

'Decided to come in from your cold huff?' I said to him. I patted the mattress to encourage him to settle into his usual nook at the back of my knees, 'Come on, boy, let's get our heads down again.'

'Neglect, is a terrible inconvenience in anyone's life, even a cat's.'

I sat up, freaked that the voice of Noel Coward was somehow being transmitted through my moggy yet again. 'How are you doing that?' I asked. 'Is there some kind of vent in here that's causing all these crazy auditory manifestations?' I dipped over the edge of the bed and looked beneath it. 'Is it Melve having a laugh? Come on, Melve, stop arsing about!'

The Colonel sighed. 'When is it going to become self-evident that it is I, your cat, attempting to converse with you? Is that so inconceivable?'

'I'd rather it actually was Noel Coward. That would be somewhat easier to deal with.'

His eyes became like slits as he leered at me through the dim light. 'You are neglecting your friends when their need is greatest, my dear chum.'

My suddenly talkative subconscious had seriously lousy timing. 'But I'm happy, for the first time in ages, surely you can understand that?'

'Elucidate this relationship at this juncture to Ms Graumann, Ms Knowles, or Mr Leadbetter, and I'm sure they would agree it is nothing other than an affair. No matter the style and flare the rendezvous donates you, it is a gentleman's requisite to perpetuate what has been cultivated before this distracting flora bloomed.'

'I haven't given up on any of them,' I argued.

The Colonel flicked his tail from side to side and shook his head so vigorously it made the little bell on his collar tinkle. His back foot kicked up behind his left ear, and he gave it a good scuffing. 'Oh, the lies! The lies! They do cause my fur to itch so.'

'I'm not lying, I'm still here, supporting them to the best of my ability.'

'Good Lord! It's a future lie. You are slowly loosening your grip.'

'There's no such thing as a future lie.'

The Colonel stopped scratching, his back leg paused halfway up his saggy belly, and he said, 'Oh, my dear boy, we both know there are. When anyone makes a promise, and in the same moment they know they won't keep it, that's a future lie. You are cutting the bonds once so precious, like a rusty guillotine that moves painfully slow towards your chums' heads, you are moving on without them, severing their thoughts and extracting their hearts in the same instant.'

'Well, this is jolly,' I quipped.

Just then, a seagull came skidding to a stop by my window. 'Oh, a bird! How fabulous!' cried the Colonel, and with a hop and a scurry, he was out of the window and ascending to great heights to bite off most definitely more than he could chew.

Silence fell, and I'd like to say I woke in my usual spot, soaked in the usual sweat, in the middle of a tangled duvet, but I can't even recall waking or even falling back to sleep. Forgotten until I mulled over the reason for my lethargy with the suds in the shower.

Once ready, I knocked on Gwen's door: no reply. Then on Sally's: nothing. I tried to call Ryan on the way up the walk, but all I got was a quick, 'I'm sorry, honey. Can't talk. We're very ill. Call back tomorrow.'

I passed Christina's shop. It's looking pretty unkempt. The metal is beginning to rust on the shutters, and the sign that used to swing freely in the wind is hanging by a thread and spinning tortuously like my mind, propelled by the zephyr swirling through the city.

Maybe I am selfish. I knew nothing of Christina's illness until it was too late. And, many years before, I ditched my good friends within a month of meeting a man I barely knew and hightailed it to the Scottish Borders. And when message alerts stopped pinging, I didn't give them a second thought. Forgotten within the blink of an eye. I could possibly be the worst friend in the world, but the most attentive lover.

I asked Molasses, 'Is Sally running late again?'

She answered without looking up from the floor she was scrubbing, 'No, Sir. Not seen hide nor hair of the little shit – I'm never making strawberry daiquiris for anyone again; it's murder to scrape off this wood. She was working late at Madam Yo-Yo's, so I imagine she's either succumbed to alcohol and made her bed in a booth, or has been giving a Japanese businessman some extra attention.'

As if she'd some magical powers, just as she said 'businessman', my phone alerted me to a text from Alistair. I made my excuses and hopped into the toilet. A short text conversation followed:

'Sorry, been tied up with meetings & entertaining these guys. Call U

2night?'
'Yes, please! I'm missing U!'
'Miss U 2.'
'Look forward to it! xxxxxx'
'Me 2.'

That was it? I give him kisses, and he gives me nothing? Surely, if you receive kisses, you send some back? It's good manners.

It's almost midnight now, and Alistair hasn't called. If I've checked my mobile, I've checked it a thousand times. I've scoured the missed calls list and, just in case the texts are stuck in some kind of virtual holding bay, I've rebooted my phone five times. Just a simple word to say he's okay would make all the difference in the world. I know I have to shut down electronically and get some sleep, but emotionally, I'll be on standby all night. He has no idea the hold he has over me.

Tuesday 28th September

The newsreader on Radio 4 said that Britain isn't doing enough to take advantage of the opportunities that await in space. I mumbled to myself, 'Well, they're doing something; I know one Brit who seems to have been sent to outer-space and fallen into a black hole.'

'What did you say?' asked a highly speculative Sally as she spun around, balancing a tray of Fish Tea with all the elegance of a Russian Ballet dancer.

'Oh, nothing,' I fudged.

There was a crack just like a whip and Sally winced in pain, trying desperately to keep the tray steady. Molasses flicked a damp dishcloth over her shoulder with a look of satisfaction. 'Leave the boy alone,' she snapped. She reached for the radio and switched it off, 'And since when did we become so old we broke our hips and started listening to Radio 4?'

'It was old Andy's choice,' said Sally smugly as she plopped the four bowls down on the usual table we share pre-lunchtime covers.

'Itch-bay,' I growled.

'Now, children!' Interrupted Molasses. 'Let's have a peaceful brunch with no squabbling, please!' She grasped both of us by the shoulders and pushed us firmly into our seats as she bellowed to Barry in the kitchen.

'Jesus! I think the ships on the Firth of Forth heard that foghorn,' winced Sally. Molasses hushed her and slapped the back of her head, all be it gently. Barry joined us, and we ate in silence. The undertone of munching, slurping and breathing became so unbearable I was relieved when my phone rang.

'Hey, Mr! Sorry I didn't call,' pre-empted Alistair, 'but it's been mad down here in old London town. You okay?'

I quickly moved from a table brimming with suspicion towards the safety of the front door. 'Yes, yes. I'm fine. Just a sec, the reception's better at the front of the café,' I lied with my hand cupped around the mouthpiece. 'Been missing your hugs though.' All my anger was diluted by a big dose of relief.

'Well, how can I fix that?' he asked.

'I dunno.'

'I think I need to give Andy some hugs tonight.'

'Really?' Suddenly, all ill-thoughts were eliminated by joy and arousal.

'Aye, get ready, my man. I'm coming back early. I'll be home by ten.'

I could barely contain my excitement after I hung up and made my way back to the table. Everyone acted nonchalant as they slurped on their soup. 'That was Orange, my network, trying to sell me another tariff,' I said, lying through my teeth.

'I've never seen anyone so thrilled to get a cold-call,' quipped Sally, sipping on the fishy banana broth with narrowed eyes. 'Didn't you just take on a new contract?'

'Yes, I did,' I said slowly, trying to think of an excuse, 'but they want me to take on a second line, for business.'

'But you don't have a business,' counteracted Sally, as a wry smile slid across her cheeks, relishing every second of my torture.

'I may have, someday, and so they want to see if I want one. Just in case. It may get me a new handset.'

'But you just got a new ...' she continued.

'So what about those terrible trams, eh?' I yelped as I sat down uneasily and continued, 'When will they ever be ready?'

'It seems to me there's been a lot of wasted money and lies with those damn trams,' said Molasses.

'There's a lot of it going around. The lies, I mean,' added Sally, like a dog who had a ball clamped in its jaws and wouldn't let it go.

Molasses smacked her on the shoulder and instructed her to, 'Shut up and eat your broth.'

The ball was dropped unceremoniously and left aside, for now. I don't know how much longer I can keep him a secret and hide my fever over our relationship. This is getting tough.

Wednesday 29th September

The radio silence on his part was forgiven the second he kissed me. The energy expelled during our mammoth session inspired by the torturous days of being pulled apart had us hungrily eating chips 'n' cheese at one in the morning. Eating greasy food in bed is something I never do. It's unheard of for me to fall asleep without brushing my teeth, never mind leave a half-empty chippy box on the bedside table, oozing the smell of salt and sauce in my face. It took no time at all to drift off smothered in quiet elation as I found myself back in his arms once more. I find a healthy orgasm leaves you not caring a single jot about the debris and disarray left in its wake.

I'm learning that Alistair is not a cook as he's had two minor disasters over simple meals, today's being two English muffins, which he was absentmindedly cremating when I breezed into the kitchen in his used underpants, and one exploded egg dispersing in a pan of over-boiling water. 'Are you ready for my specially slaughtered Eggs Benedict?' he joked.

Keen to impress, I quickly seized my chance and took control of the culinary disaster with such gusto I could even convince Mrs Beeton I'd never fallen from the throne of Domestic God.

'You see,' I taught my slave tenderly as he peered over my shoulder at the now fresh pot of simmering water, clutching my waist as he nuzzled the back of my neck, 'you add just a drop of vinegar and cause a vortex, like so.' I swirled the water swiftly and slipped the contents of one freshly broken egg into the pot with ease. Fortunately, it spun and began to solidify into a neatly formed poached egg that Delia Smith would be proud enough to have on the cover of one of her books.

'Impressive!' he said. And then, more importantly, 'You're a dab-hand in the kitchen as well as the bedroom. You can stick around.'

'I aim to,' I said, deliberately focussing my attention on the all-important egg that suddenly held my future within its perfect little form.

'I love this,' he said.

'It's only poached eggs on a bit of dough with gloop on top, really.'

'No,' he tilted my head towards his and kissed me tenderly on the lips. My morning breath seemed not to matter. 'I love this. What we have. I love it, Andy.'

My full attention was now on Alistair, the egg could hard-boil for all I cared, and I found myself saying, 'I love us too.'

I know he didn't say he loved *me*, but he loves *this,* which really means *us*. That's progress.

I was dropped off around the corner from work with such a passionate parting kiss it had me joyfully smacking my lips. I drifted, two clouds above nine, towards the doors of Café Jamaica without a care in the world. *Such a contrast to a few days ago,* I thought. *It seems, if you play by the rules, you reap the rewards.* Barry White's *Love's Theme* played in my head. *Nothing can spoil this feeling today,* I assured myself as I walked through the doors to be greeted with ...

'She's only gone and done the most stupid of stupid things in the history of stupidity since the word stupid was first logged in the Oxford English Dictionary!' pounced Sally as I drifted towards the bar. 'She screwed Matt, even though they've broken up. And, you know what? He dumped her anyway.' She raised her hands to the ceiling like a pleading Jewish grandmother as if to ask God why.

The needle scratched across Barry White's vinyl so harshly I'm sure it'll be unplayable for the rest of my life. My face fell, 'Where is she?'

'She's in the staff room with Molasses. She's in pieces.'

'I'll go see her.'

'No, I think she's pretty cut-up, the poor thing, I don't think she'll thank you for that.'

I wanted so badly to talk to her. I could hear her sobbing from the bar. But I took comfort in knowing from personal experience that Gwen was in safe hands. Molasses knows how to take care of anyone in a crisis.

Sure enough, as it came closer to opening the café, the sobbing stopped, and soon after, an anaemic Gwen was escorted delicately out of the café and helped into a waiting cab. Molasses quietly ordered us to look after the shop for the day as she left. We nodded and continued setting up as if nothing out of the ordinary had happened. Until they were out of sight, at least.

'Oh, God, she looked awful,' I muttered to Sally.

'The silly mare probably thought giving in to that idiot would encourage him to stay. But we all know that men take what they want and leave you soiled and barren.'

'But you know that's not the same for every man,' I assured her.

She let out a deep, mocking laugh, 'Love it 95% friction and 5% fiction, sweetie. You of all people should know this. Ask a guy if he loves you before he ejaculates, and he'll convince you he does, hell, he might even convince himself, but once those little rugby balls have emptied, not a chance. Ipso facto. It's not your fault,' she added, giving me a pity-pout, 'you men are wired differently from us. The quicker us girls learn this, the quicker we'll lower our expectations and the less disenchanted we'll become.'

I scrubbed hard at the bar, intent on removing a stubborn beer stain that'd taken root in the varnish, and hopefully wiping her embittered beliefs away at the same time, 'You're so damaged,' I said through tight lips.

'Damaged, no. Realistic, yes,' she said, holding her head high.

'If we don't live for love, then what's the point?'

'Because, my dear chum, there's more to life than just love, like friendship, for example. A need that brought you here not so long ago. Or have you forgotten?'

She hightailed it down to the cellar to retrieve some stock. The conversation was over and shoved to the side as the first customers arrived. She carried on like the life and soul of the parade, entertaining the room in the same style she's learned from Molasses. I tried my best to do the same, but I'm not so well rehearsed in pretence. She's a consummate professional when it comes to this. I've seen this act so many times before. From the day I met her, she's pretended to be so much bigger than her tiny self. Why should today be any different? At the end of the day, our tips were down. My fault, I suspect, as my parade had stumbled through a torrential downpour, packed-up their colourful banners and chirpy instruments, and caught the depression bus home. My mind had stuck on Gwen, to what a fool she must feel, just from one moment of desperation. My thoughts shifted from Gwen towards Alistair and his wife. How had it ended for them? Did she feel used after years dedicated to him? Is she as confused as Gwen, unable to truly learn why the love had to stop? I don't even know her name, Alistair won't talk about her. Maybe there's too much pain there. Part of me hopes he does feel it, just a little, but not too much that he can't move on. Just enough to prove he's capable of caring if he's to care for me at all.

Thursday 30th September

September is shutting its door. The Indian summer glory days will soon depart. A new door, decked in crisp fallen leaves of amber and sienna, is about to open on the chilly winds of October, heralding the inevitability of darker nights and morning frosts. The British public will scowl, grumble in agreement and press on through the shortening days. But my selfish heart craves early dusk, the shiver in my spine, the jitter of my jaw and necessity for warmth, because this will draw me closer to that wonderful man, and he to me. For those sub-zero hugs will become more frequent, closer and snugger with every slump in the mercury.

******

Gwen popped her head round my door – I'm intentionally leaving a clear path for visitors in an attempt to prove to myself and my cat that I'm still accessible. She tapped timorously on the frame and asked, 'Can I come in?'

The sight of her made me smile. 'Sure!' I cleared the pile of fitness magazines that linger with intent on the unoccupied side of my sofa and encouraged her to join me with a spritely pat on the cushion. She sat down, silent and deep in thought for a few seconds.

With a sharp intake of breath, she said, 'I'm ...'

I knew she'd come to apologise. No need. 'Cake?' I asked, already off the sofa and taking the lid off the tin that hid my latest failure. I presented to her, 'One collapso chocolate espresso cake. Baking is a bitch in a Baby Belling oven,' I joked in an attempt to reassure her we were fine.

'You should put that on a T-shirt,' she laughed, taking a plate of half crumbly, half gloopy cake from my hand.

'I might just do that. I think I'll be more successful at T-shirt printing than baking.'

'Is this a new hobby?'

'Not really, I've baked for years but never found the right balance of ingredients, or the correct oven temperature, or been able to decide if it's actually cooked. Story of my life, I guess. I never really have been good at cooking either. I may have actually killed someone through salt poisoning at New Year. I never could keep a clean house too, even though I spent days scrubbing, dusting, hoovering, bleaching and sweeping. I had the picture-perfect home in my head, and yet, no matter how much I worked myself into the ground, I couldn't achieve it. I am, what I'd call, a failed domestic god, and I'm okay with that. But baking the perfect cake is a goal that I know is achievable for an underachiever like myself and keeps me distracted on a lonely day off.'

'You're lonely?'

I didn't want to admit to pacing around my mobile as a clingy puppy does outside her master's bedroom door when its shut and he's slumbering soundly inside. But I did want to be as honest as I could, so I said, 'Aye, I'm missing someone.'

Gwen raked at the soil on her pate. I couldn't decide if she was deep in thought or thoroughly grossed-out and hopeful of unearthing an edible crumb, 'I know how that feels.'

'Gwen, I need to ask you something. Did you sleep with him because you thought it'd change his mind?'

She nodded as her eyes glassed over with tears, 'I think I did.'

'But you need to know that it's okay to make mistakes.'

She looked at me, the green of her eyes had lost their shimmer, almost hollowed out with sorrow, 'It wasn't special. I hoped, somehow, it would change his mind. And that, to me, was worth it. At the time.'

'And now you know it didn't, what do you feel?'

'A fool.'

I shook my head, 'No, he's the fool. I bet he'd made up his mind before you slept with him. He took advantage. With men it's 95% fr...' I stopped myself, aware that I was about to reiterate Sally's cynicism. But I don't believe that. I'm a man, after all, and I crave love. I took a deep breath and concluded, 'You did nothing wrong.'

'I wish I believed that.'

'You won't, not right now, but you will with some distance. It's amazing what clarity comes from detachment and the passing of time.'

She nodded repeatedly. 'I'll try.'

'No, you don't need to try right now, but I want to tell you that you did nothing wrong and that you're still you, who we all love in our own weird, fucked-up ways.'

She laughed. 'This cake could be a metaphor for my life right now too. I'll eat the crust only if you don't mind?' she said, forking the doughy disaster around her plate cautiously.

'Yup, steer clear of anything half-baked from now on. Especially immature males,' I said with a smile.

She grinned back. 'Agreed.'

Friday 1st October

Finally, the call from Ryan that I was promised days ago. He's feeling almost better, 'Almost!' he stressed. 'I'm dragging myself out of my sickbed just because you said you were in desperate need.' He faked a weak cough. Did I actually say those words? I don't think so. The trouble with drama queens is they give off more spin than a ballerina.

We met for coffee at Lovecrumbs, a new place I spotted the other day while on a meander through the city. Cake and beverages are the only options there, but boy-oh-boy, do they do it right. Once seated, Ryan glanced around the place with the disdain of a Mother Superior at a brothel. He glared at the cakes on display as if they were the discarded pulsating placentas of evil dictators and then tore his eyes away, 'Oh, my. So much sugar,' he said, tugging the collar of his Prada shirt with one finger as if struggling for breath. 'I feel I'm gaining calories by inhalation alone. I suspect the walls are coated in it too. You really shouldn't be frequenting places like this at your age, Andy. Not unless you have a special clothing account set aside to fund your ever-expanding waistline.'

'My, my! One mild twenty-four-hour infection can make a right bitter queen of you, can't it?' I chastised.

'It was more than a mild infection; I'm on my second course of antibiotics, and the doctor tells me I should take it easier generally,' he said as if stress were something to be proud of. 'She believes the wedding, wonderful though it will be, is draining my immune system. If you'd seen me two days ago, you wouldn't have recognised me. I was a husk. Don't they cover the cakes here?'

I sighed. 'No.'

'What? They just leave them sitting on the shelves of that tatty old wardrobe for every passing student to cough on? Disgusting. I'll be lucky to make it to our big day at this rate.'

If he's feeling run down it's his own fault; this huge ceremony and all the sparkle and oomph that goes with it is their own doing. It doesn't have to be the biggest, boldest, all singing and dancing affair of the decade, but there's no telling this drama queen that. No one actually gives a shit if the colour of the ribbons tied to the chairs matches the dainty little ribbons on the favours exactly, or if one of their *unpaid* dancers is out of sync with the rest, or if butter icing is better than fondant. I'd be happy with a registry office and a small meal at Wannaburger. And as for this second course of antibiotics, Tony's probably badgered some young, wide-eyed G.P. at his work to supply them.

'Is this going to become a bitching session, or are we going to be friends?' I asked, sighing heavily and accidentally blowing a nut from my forkful of Coffee & Walnut cake.

Ryan pouted and became humble, 'Sorry, darling. It's all been a bit much. How are you?'

'I'm fine,' I said quickly, dodging the bouncing ball of my personal life. 'I really want to talk to you about Gwen. She needs a little support.'

'Continue,' he said as he pushed the fallen walnut away from himself with the corner of his napkin.

'I figure that, and it pains me to say this, you guys embody the closest thing to a stable relationship that the café crowd can muster, which is pretty worrying, to say the least.'

'Oh, I don't think I like that.'

'Well, it's true. You should be flattered.'

'No, not that, the "café crowd" thing. Terrible name. Is that what we're calling ourselves these days? I wish I'd been at the board meeting when that one was thrown across the table, I'd have squirted it with bleach and wiped it clean away.'

I became irritated, 'No, you enormous idiot hiding behind a fat ego. Besides, you've never seen a bottle of bleach, let alone touched one. Focus, please!' Ryan was about to argue, but we were disturbed by the server arriving with our drinks.

'I hope this green tea is worth the wait,' he said dryly to her. 'One could die of dehydration in this establishment. By the way, have you ever heard of air conditioning?'

'Middle-class Tourette's,' I explained apologetically to the server, who shrugged and left us. I said to Ryan, this time in a softer tone, 'Can you just – and I can't believe I'm about to say this – bring her closer into the realm of your sickeningly stable relationship?'

Ryan bobbed the skewered bag of leaves in and out of the steaming water, taking his time to reply. 'If you use kinder words, then I'll consider it.'

I'd forgotten, flattery was always how we swayed Ryan in the past, so I gulped down my pride to pitch it in a better way. 'You're the closest we have to a family. Gwen's in desperate need of some guidance and mothering, and I believe the two of you, especially you, would be a fantastic role model for her.'

'Well, not to be confused with being self-righteous, I think Tony and I are perfect role models, yes.' He couldn't have looked any more pious, but I let it slide. 'I'll talk to Tony later this evening, although it'll take some serious coaxing and sexual favours [I winced quietly inside]. She really is very drab and will clash with all of our furnishings. We may have to find a suitably depressing chair for her to sit on.'

'Be nice,' I stressed.

Ryan rolled his eyes, 'I'll call the German tomorrow. See what I can do. No promises.'

I thanked him. I need someone to be there during my absences, even if that person comes with a useless appendage such as Tony. It's the lesser evil. Hanging with Sally Knowles will hardly keep her on the steady path of righteousness. I'm mindful of that day she accidentally drugged me. And as for me, I'm busy shagging a man who's closeted and still legally married to a woman whom I've had little regard for, therefore, I think my judgement's a bit foggy.

Saturday 2nd October

Another night listening to the odd groan and creak of the bedsits while missing Alistair. He was enjoying a night out with various members of the board while I tossed and turned in my vacuous bed. He did, however, text me several times over the evening and into the night, which massaged my paranoia into submission and helped me drift off around 1 a.m.

Imagine my surprise in the morning when I turned the corner off Broughton to find Alistair stood on an old set of wooden stepladders and fiddling with the sign above Christina's shop, which was precariously hanging by a thread and threatening every passerby with a concussion. He was kissing the rusty chain with a pair of heavy bolt cutters. Just as he caught sight of me, he closed them tight and cut clean through the chain with little effort, bringing the sign crashing to the ground. It bounced towards me, shattered into shards and died on the pavement.

‘Hey, my handsome guy,’ he said, losing his cheeky grin momentarily as he missed a step on his descent. ‘I thought I’d get rid of this before it became a liability.’

I looked at what was left of the sign that had Christina’s blood, sweat and tears soaked in every groove and knot. It was irreparable. I began to pick up the pieces. I felt a little resentment towards Alistair as I believed he’d interfered in something precious I wasn’t willing to close the door on just yet. ‘Why the hell did you do that?’ I asked, regretting my words as soon as I saw the astonishment on his face.

‘Sorry, I was just trying to help. That thing was a damn health hazard. I couldn’t wave goodbye to you one more day while it took a closer swipe at your lovely head.’

‘Why?’

‘Uh, duh! Why do you think, you plonker? Because I care about you.’

‘Wait, say what?’ I said, sparse of breath.

He reached into the boot of his car and pulled out the very same shovel that’d helped rescue my old Astra from the snow when we first met. He followed my doting gaze to the tool and joked, ‘It will always be our shovel, you know?’

‘Don’t be silly,’ I said and smiled as I slapped him on the shoulder. I helped him sweep up the mess. I carefully placed the remains of Christina’s business into the café wheelie bin. It felt the right place to put it, not in some street-side trashcan that any drunk could piss in.

Deed done, all packed up and Alistair was ready for the off. ‘Got to go. But I’ll see you tonight?’ he asked.

‘Yes, please!’ I keenly replied. For a Master, I’m pliable putty in his hands. Practically fluid.

My slave hopped into his 4x4, grinning all the while, and added, ‘Of course I care about you, dafty. I don’t know what the hell I’d do without you.’ He winked through the passenger window and sped off to another day building his empire.

He doesn’t know what he’d do without me. Bliss!

Sunday 3rd October

If Melve and Trenton Tanner think no one suspects they’re up to no good in the midnight hour, they really should think again. It's as obvious to us as the Monroe affair was to President Kennedy's security team. Trenton came to the dance rehearsal this evening. Totally unnecessary. He stood out like an uncut cock at a Jewish nudist colony. He claimed he was there to observe the range of our movement to fully understand the strain laid on the costumes, but in reality, his bloodshot eyes were focussed on Melve and Melve alone.

He interrupted Sally's strict choreography during a particularly tricky segment, stopping everything with flapping arms and yelps of, 'No, dearie, this simply won't do.' He took Melve from behind by the arms, practically spooning him, and said, 'What you're doing is marvellous, scone – you have the strength of a lumberjack in those thighs, oh my! – but you need to accentuate the movement in your arms with a sprinkling of grace and finesse.' He subsequently took Melve in hand and guided the poor hippy through the already well-rehearsed segment three times over. They were in such close proximity, given half the chance (and a few more inches), he could've certainly swept Melve's chimney.

The repeated contact had the opposite effect on Melve. He became progressively ruffled after every mini-lesson and expressed movement with as much silkiness as a tank taking a shortcut through the Botanical Gardens. The close encounter of the third kind ended when Melve snapped, 'If you could just let Ms Knowles do her job, please, Trenton!'

'Excuse me, but I thought you enjoyed the musings of an artist in your life,' Trenton bit back. 'Or maybe I misheard you. Or misjudged you. Or maybe you are just a total cunt.' He stormily pulled on his ridiculous khaki Mackintosh coat with gold sequin sleeves and slapped on his matching beret (sequins included). He clattered hurried heels to the exit and just about took the door off its hinges.

It's never good to be almost outed during an argument.

'Right, my little dancing puppets, focus!' snapped Sally, thankfully. 'Again, from the top, and this time with more conviction. We only have a few more months until showtime.'

******

Later, on our way down Leith Walk, I asked Sally if she was actually looking forward to Ryan and Tony's ceremony. 'Hell, no, darling.

I'm looking forward to the show tunes, not the vomit-inducing lovey-dovey crap. It's sickening. I've been subjected to dozens of straight marriages, silver anniversaries, christenings, and even bar-mitzvahs. The gays were my sanctuary, but now that y'all are getting in on the act, it's ruining the party. Soon, cruising will become a family pastime on an actual boat, on an actual ocean, and they'll replace the darkrooms of leather bars with creches. Please, go have amazing casual sex with your mystery man and keep the gay scene semi-normal for the rest of us.' She didn't have to tell me twice; I was on my way to Alistair's anyway.

Monday 4th October

While reaching almost the edge of what must've been my 20th buildup, Alistair asked me with euphoria bulging in his eyes, 'Have you ever thought of doing that?'

We were watching a particularly horny orgy scene being performed by at least fifteen guys. I had to admit, although it turned me on, it'd never been something I thought I'd achieve before I drew my pension. And by then I most definitely would've missed my chance to enjoy it with such nubile lads. At that age the most stimulation I'll experience will be static from a nylon carpet as it reacts with my gliding zimmer frame.

'Do you want to do that?' I asked, hoping he didn't.

'Kinda,' he admitted, rapturous eyes pinned on the sweaty screen. 'But with you in charge. Having me submit to sucking guys of your choosing. Allowing them to do only what you want them to do to me. Humiliating me in public, like the dirty, worthless slave I am.'

I hate to admit it, as liberal as I've become (there was a time I couldn't even contemplate sex in the kitchen – buttocks on a food preparation area seemed wrong, but living in a bedsit, where the kitchen is just a few paces away from my bed, has almost eliminated that hangup), this is new and unsteady ground for me. It knocked me off-kilter. I can't imagine three-way with anyone; I believe it'd be like trying to make pralines and chop logs at the same time. Especially with a guy I may be falling for. I'm not ready for that kind of mind-fuck. But at the same time, we've not discussed exclusivity and commitment yet, so I can't blame him. I'm hoping he wants something close to my ideal, but I could be wrong. I felt my hardon deflate slightly and flop around in his hand. 'I'm not sure I could do that,' I said.

'Sure, you could. You're the Master after all. I hear there's places, like saunas, where we could arrange this.'

'If it's something you want to do, then we can try it,' I conceded. Unsure of where we were heading. Every path, at every turn, looked unsteady and uneasy now.

'We could just have people watch if that's easier for you?'

'I guess we could,' I agreed, still hesitant. He was as hard as a rock; I was as soft as a jelly roll, but he was ignorant of the pudding I'd become.

'Great, let's look into arranging it when we head to Newcastle. More discreet there.'

Can public sex ever be classed as *discreet*?

I continued to be jacked off, somehow managing to regain and maintain some form of stiffness, and eventually, against all the odds, I shot a glossy load that satisfying my jacker he'd done an excellent job.

'Enjoy that?' he asked, towelling down his own whitewash.

'Yeah, it was great' I lied. *It was great to a point,* I thought to myself. I wasn't expecting openness in our relationship already, but I guess voyeurism is just having sex without walls, right?

Tuesday 5th October

When I asked Ryan and Tony to take more interest in Gwen's life, I assumed it would be as good friends, offering some kind of template or guidance, not as the hired help.

'What?' asked a priggish Ryan. 'She needs work, and we need a cleaner twice a week: it'll be a perfectly symbiotic relationship. We'll be in perfect harmony from 9 'till 11 twice weekly, precisely.'

I'm aware that symbiosis can be many things: mutualism, amesalism, commensalism and *parasitism*. Having one amensalist and one parasite in your life does not create harmony. You can imagine which of the Terrible Twins is which. Neither should be allowed to cohabit.

'Yes,' added the parasite. 'Think of it as the gradual rehabilitation of a poor, sick mind via the cleansing of a tastefully furnished home and a chance for the poor girl to practice her challenging spoken word with someone who has actually studied English literature.'

I totally forgot Tony has a degree in English Lit, which begs the question, why is he wasting his life away behind the reception desk of a doctor's surgery where the dark shadows of pig flu and norovirus can be regular visitors? Actually, I know why: he loves to poke his nose into people's misfortune and revels in the knowledge that others are sicker than him. Not in mind, but in body.

'There's nothing wrong with the woman's English,' I argued.

'Please,' guffawed Tony. 'I had to describe to her what an AGA was and she miss-pronounced cushion as 'kushon' when she was Hoovering, or as she put it "hovering" the lounge this morning. I mean, get a clue!'

I'd no argument. I'd never met an AGA before I had the misfortune of cleaning theirs and have heard Gwen miss-pronounce cushion twice before. We don't have a 'Hover' at 323, but we do have a 'Die-soon', apparently. Maybe mingling with them will help her in many respects, but I can't help feel they'll take advantage of her, as they did with me when I lived in their oh-so-exclusive palace.

No fun tomorrow evening, Alistair's flying to France to develop his new business venture. An elderly millionaire wants to invest in the breakdown retrieval arm of his company, branching into Paris and extending into other parts of Europe. I'm on my own again, but I'll be otherwise engaged anyway as it'll be my mother's birthday. I dread the long days without him.

Wednesday 6th October

Today we looked like any other happy family celebrating a birthday. Mum yelped with over-enthusiasm when we jumped out of the darkness and surprised her at Chee Chee's Chinese restaurant. I suspect she already knew. She screamed and 'oohed' and 'ahhed' as if she was faking an orgasm. I bet the usually family informer (my sister) had let the cat out of the bag yet again.

The cheap wine flowed freely, which I noticed was being decanted – and I use that term very loosely – from an ASDA's own box by a crouching Mr Chee. He skulked behind the corner of the bar to hide this shameful practice, which was pointless as he neglected to cover the box when he placed every refilled carafe on the bar. Crouching

Chee, Not-so-hidden Grape Juice. Wine? From a box? In a restaurant? Unacceptable. It's the grape equivalent of battery chicken farming. The food, which hopefully saved Dad a few pounds, was of the Chinese buffet style: all monosodium glutamate and grease. There's a talent to turning chicken, beef and pork into the exact same flavour and texture, no matter which sauce it's hopefully been thoroughly cooked in. Nevertheless, I was starving by the time we ate (8 p.m.) and piled my plate full as if famine was about to hit Scotland.

The Birthday girl had plenty of gifts tossed her way by neighbours and family alike. I sat there wondering if a woman in her failing years really wants a speedboat ride over the Clyde, but my sister seems intent on killing off her very own babysitter and supplementary child support without a thought. Mum was discombobulated when she ripped off the Telly Tubby wrapping paper, which I had craftily pieced together from the scraps of previous nephews' birthdays, and squinted at *Fork to Fork*, by Monty Don. I feel it could help her both in the garden and kitchen, and God knows she needs it, I'm probably still digesting additives from the crispy pancakes she served us through the 1980s.

Mum threw me a lacklustre, 'Oh, thank you, Andy,' and thumbed through the pages with all the enthusiasm of a clapped-out racehorse walking through the rusty gates of the knacker's yard. After scanning a few colourful pictures of a beautiful English garden in full summertime bloom, she turned to Mrs White and said, 'It's a bit unrealistic. There's not a whirligig in sight.' She sat it on the table and leant over to give me an awkward hug. Later, I was very disappointed to find her using it as a coaster for the lipstick-stained glass of red she'd been draining faster than Crouching Chee's tap could pour. I decided to sneak away pretty soon after this and head for the train, passing Mr and Mrs Chee unashamedly squeezing every last drop of wine from the surgically removed inner wine bag on the surface of the bar. They must've assumed we were all too pissed to care, but I was sobering up fast and desperate to catch the last train home.

Mum came running after me into the dreary rain, almost slipping in her heels on the soaked pavement. Steam drifted from her sweaty brow as it hit the cold Airdrie air. She's like sonar, able to pick up

Russian subs and escaping homosexual sons with a single sweep of the grid, so I shouldn't have been surprised my careful exit was caught and pursued at warp speed. 'Off so soon?' she asked, teetering on her heels like a member of Riverdance having a mild seizure. I quickly explained I only had fifteen minutes to catch the train. She leaned forward, her breath reeked of stale smoke from her perennial hidden habit and hugged me. Well, I say hugged, more like clutched my clothes desperately to stay erect and rested her chin on my shoulder, gazing up at me with glassy eyes. 'I'm sorry I was never the mother you wanted,' she slurred.

'What?' I asked, supporting her like a puppeteer by her floppy arms. I felt the sudden need to reassure her and move on quickly, 'You were all I needed, Mum.'

'No, I was a shitty mother.' She steadied herself and pushed from me in an attempt to prove she could stand. She failed, and I half caught her as she buckled some poor sod's car bonnet with her barely covered arse. She sat on the glossy metal as the rain-soaked her sorry face and bounced off her thick foundation, the street lights reflecting every crack in her skin. Every stress and strain of parenthood and matrimony gazed back at me. 'I forgot you one time. When I went to get the messages. I left you outside the bakers on the avenue. It was only when I got home and saw your nappies hanging on the line, after I'd made myself a cup of tea and was rinsing out the mug at the kitchen window, I remembered I'd left that morning with a shopping list, a pram, and an Alsatian.' She wiped the rain from her nose and eyes and patted my now drenched head. 'Funny thing is, I remembered to collect the dog, he was right next to your pram, tied to the shutter, but I totally forgot you. When I realised, I ran, heart in my throat, all the way back. I would've hated myself if anything happened to you, but there you were, fast asleep and unaware what a neglectful mum you were unlucky enough to have.'

I was aware the train had left Queen Street by now, but I had to stay and listen.

She let out a loud, short laugh, 'That bloody yellow teddybear that hung on the hood of your pram glared at me all the way home. I told no one but our G.P. He said I was still in a daze after Luke's passing, but that didn't make sense to me as I should've been so overprotective I'd never have left you, but he said these things take time and can affect people in funny ways. I still wonder how long it'll take? I should've been there for him too that night. I wish I'd never tucked him in. Never said goodnight. You never think that last kiss goodnight will actually be the last, but it can be, remember that. Your dad and me, we can fight, we've had some riots over the years, but I never go to sleep angry. I always make sure I kiss him one last time. I'm stubborn, God knows I am, but by ten at night I can see that the clock is ticking and he'll take off his socks, tuck them neatly into themselves and make moves to get ready for bed, and I'm desperate to make up. That's the hardest lesson I've had to learn. But how long will it take to feel normal again?'

I'd no answers. I always feel uncomfortable when Luke's mentioned. He was her first. My big brother. He only lived a month before she found him still in his cot. He'd slipped away in his sleep, we hope. No distress. She's told this drunken tale many times, but each time I hear it, it gets harder to bear. As the years go on, I hope that she's forgiven herself. And as another year passes, and time moves on, I think she has, but she hasn't. In her mind, she often walks into that room and finds his little corpse.

God, I wish she'd forgive and forget. I want to take that horrible memory and bury it deep within the Earth. I'd dig a hole to the core if it would help. But memories aren't physical, they can't be put in a box, or burned, or buried. They live and grow with us as we grow, and we learn to live with them, like I thought I had with Steve. I hope she learns she wasn't a shitty mum. She was, and still is, bumbling through motherhood like any other. Sometimes getting it wrong, sometimes getting it right, but always, always, loving unconditionally. She may not be the kinda mum I wanted, but what you want and what you need are often poles apart. She wasn't a bad mother, either. She's my flesh and blood and nothing like me, and that's good, not shitty.

'Mum,' I said, aware of the extent of her need and the limitations of my time, 'you were the best. To all of us. And I mean all three of us. You look after our Marie and all those grandkids loads. She couldn't cope without you. You supported me wholeheartedly when I came out. And Dad always says how much you doted on Luke. It came from nowhere. He wasn't ill, he was asleep, and he simply slipped away.'

'I'm sorry I'm so hard on you.'

'He's a tough act to follow; he's never disappointed you.'

Mum laughed, and wiped the rain off her chin, 'Well, there is that.'

I glanced at my watch. I'd less than ten minutes to catch my train. 'I have to go, Mum.'

She nodded and quickly said, 'Come with me to visit him soon, please. It's just your father won't. He says it drags him down. And your sister's superstitious, she thinks it may jinx her.'

'I promise,' I said. 'Now get back inside and drink the next box dry.'

She snorted and stood upright, fixed her matted hair and wiped the rain from her weathered hands. 'How do I look?'

'Like a million bucks.'

'Liar,' she laughed. 'I look like a drunken old tart.' She kissed me on the forehead and turned me towards the station. 'Go!' she yelled, smacking me on the bum affectionately.

I ran like the clappers, turning my head to see her safely in as I crossed the road, but she was gone, back inside to cheers and laughter. The karaoke night with her mates was starting soon. I was relieved. They know how to look after her.

I caught the train just in time. I dried off my ears and pressed in some headphones as I sank back in the chair to settle into the twenty-minute journey to Queen Street to catch my connection. KT Tunstall crept up on me and sang *Through The Dark* as I gazed sleepily out of the window. The last time I heard this, it brought me to tears on a snowy hillside in January. I was pretty screwed up then. This time, the rhythm was slow and therapeutic, and it settled me in some more. I could make out familiar streets through the greyness of the rain and the remote amber hue of the street lamps. I began to test myself, how well did I know Airdrie and Coatbridge? Occasionally I'd lose my bearings, but I found them quick enough again, which impressed me. Small victories. But when the train passed a large patch of seemingly open land, I had to stop. I knew exactly where I was. Somewhere out there, in the sodden soil and blackness of the night, lay Aunt Moira and Luke. I turned away and quickly changed the song to something more upbeat. I'm still not there yet.

Before I settled for bed, I texted Alistair several kisses. He reciprocated immediately. I sent some more, and let go of the night.

Thursday 7th October

Gwen continues to look washed-out. She brooded around the cafe all evening, sucking the light out of every corner of the room as she dragged her unhappy carcass back and forth from the brightly coloured couch to the tropical bathroom, and back to the filament bulbs above the bar. Tonight she's been drinking brandy like a diabetic seeking out sugar on the verge of a hypoglycaemic attack. She only stopped when the bar ran out of Asbach. If Molasses hadn't pointed her way to the door, she would've moved on to something else, I'm sure. It pains me to see her this way. Sally volunteered to escort her home.

'She's heavier than she looks,' I said, as we dragged her inert frame onto the back of a Hackney. 'Do you think she's well on her way to alcohol dependence and depression?'

'If she is, I'll soon slap her out of that,' said an agitated Sally, stopping to inspect her leg. 'She's laddered my lovely tights. I'm not doing this kind of manual labour more than once. She's just been rejected by a man; it's nothing worth crying about for more than a day. It's time to get back up and get on with it. She's passed her grace period. Besides, I'm the only alcoholic, drug-taking, heartbroken diva allowed in this district, there's no room for another.'

As the taxi juddered away over the subsiding cobbles of Broughton I wondered, what exactly does *she* have to heartbroken about? *She* with the concrete heart.

Once my shift was finished, I checked for messages from Alistair. I was delighted to find at least three, but also a voicemail from Mum begging me, through a muffled line and abused vocal cords, not to mention our conversation in the rain. 'Your dad has no inkling I left you behind.'

I sent her a quick text, as I was well on my way to Alistair's in a cab and couldn't be bothered with the whole drama again, telling her ' "Mum" is the word'.

I think the pun was lost on her as she merely texted back, 'OK.'

Now that I've had time to consider it, I'm a little put-out that she walked all the way home with the dog and failed to remember her own flesh and blood stranded in small shopping hub. I guess I shouldn't be surprised; she cried for hours when the vet told her the dog would have to be put down. I'm not so sure she would hesitate so long over my life-support machine. She'd probably reach her decision quickly due to the NHS smoking ban. I can hear her now, 'Oh, switch him off, I'm dying for a fag, and the smoking shelter's half a mile away. I can't put up with this bloody torture any longer.'

Perhaps I should write a living will not to be switched off on the whim of an impatient addict, but to be kept alive until a responsible member of our family can be contacted. Such is the fickleness of her decision making: she once bought a pair of furry high-heeled flip-flops at the lowest temperature in winter and voted for Tony Blair just because he has nice teeth.

Friday 8th October

Another night of sordid passion and comforting squeezes from my slave. Being a former scout really does prepare you for anything life throws your way; the knots I learned to tie when I was covered in badges and wearing knee-high shorts came very much in hand last night. *If only Mr Knox, our asthmatic scout leader, could see me now*, I thought to myself as my guy groaned in pleasure as I pressed hard against his prostate with my index finger while he was fastened to every corner of the bed. I was surprised we weren't using rope, but my slave advised me that this can burn and leave questionable marks, so he had laid out long thin scarfs left by his almost-ex-wife during her speedy departure. I had to say, after our fun of course, that I was amazed he was so well-informed.

'I've been doing my online homework for my Master. I aim to please you,' he bantered with that cheeky grin I could kiss all the damn time.

It's nice to know he does his research to keep me happy. I'm really getting comfortable in my role, I thought. 'So, how was Paris?' I asked as I settled down to sleep within his massive frame.

'Oh, so-so. Business is stressful and boring to talk about. Life with my Andy is much more fun.' This made me smile blissfully, until he asked me, 'So, Newcastle next week?'

'Uh? Oh, let me check my shifts, and I'll get back to you.'

I'd hoped he'd forgotten all about the whole public sex

shenanigans or at least gone off the idea. I faked a deep sleep, the only time I've faked anything with him. Annoyingly, he was snoring within minutes. It took me ages to drift off as I didn't feel quite so in charge at that point.

Saturday 9th October

Kicked out of Alistair's flat early due to his cleaner's imminent arrival, I got back to 323 to find Gwen setting off to scrub the Terrible Twins' flat. I had to ask her, 'Are you happy cleaning up after two impetuous queens?'

'Not really,' she said, 'but the money is needed, and it stops me waiting for the phone to ring from the agency ... and Matt. Besides, I enjoy how their AGA gleams after I spend the afternoon scrubbing it outside-in.' I noticed her previously manicured nails were chipped and blackened underneath but chose to pass no comment.

'I can understand that,' I agreed. 'I get an amazing sense of accomplishment once I've cleaned my Baby Belling, even if it's nowhere near an AGA.'

'Well, I've always been the plain Cinderella stereotype,' she said bitterly. 'Maybe this is all I'm meant to be.'

'Even she got her prince in the end,' I assured her.

'No, I had my prince, and he turned out to be a genetically modified pumpkin which was tough to swallow and bitter to the taste.' She fastened her burgundy headscarf tighter and said, 'I have to go, I have a lot of Hovering to do.'

Hopelessly, I called after her down the stair, 'It's *Hoovering*.' How will she ever get a proper job if she can't tell the difference between a *hoo* and a *ho*?

Sunday 10th October

Oh, to be detached from the queens' wedding, but I regret I'm tied into every rehearsal until a merciful two-week break in November. November! I'm sure we would've mastered a simple four-minute dance routine by now, but every week some bright-spark (usually Tony) adds a new element to my nightmare. Today, he decided they want it as close to the awful 70's video as possible, but to switch the female roles to male, and male to female. I suspect this means my costume will be a lot tighter (silver Lycra, perhaps) and I'll have to cope with props too, i.e., torches and glitter. My pleads were met with indifference.

'We all have to suffer for art,' said Ryan.

'This isn't art; this is torture!' I argued. 'This body isn't made for Lycra.'

'Honey, that body isn't made for anything but thick Arran knitwear, we all understand that. Best get your work-shy tushie to the gym then, hadn't you?' interjected Tony, somewhat unnecessarily.

'That's rich coming from a man who's daily workout consists of pirouetting on a swivel chair between a telephone, computer, percolator and a bag of doughnuts,' I barked back.

'Now, now, children. Play nice,' said Trenton, purposefully standing between our venom. 'I'm sure I can come up with something equally classy and classic that will complement the whole segment. Here's my number, Andy, to arrange your first fitting.' Trenton handed me a business card that said, 'Trenton Tanner: Costume & Fashion That Reaches to the Stairs'. The word 'Stairs' had the letter 'i' scored out in blue ink. The cheap bugger's too tight-fisted to pay a few quid to have them re-hashed. He glanced over at Melve (who he'd been theatrically ignoring all day), leaned in close to me and whispered, just loud enough for Melve to hear, 'And we'll work on getting the fitting just right for your wonderful frame.' He paused and then said with several winks, 'Inside leg's not a problem, by the way. I can be very thorough, if you need me to be.'

'Thanks,' I yelped. 'Can we get on? Quickly?' I pleaded to the room. I've never been so desperate to dance in all my life.

Trenton mouthed to me, 'Call me.' It made me shiver.

What are the odds there'd be a typo in both of Trenton's phone numbers *and* his email address? I hope so.

Monday 11th October

I've been talked into a trip to Newcastle on Thursday morning. How did this happen? I'll tell you how: a night of edging, increased endorphins, several pornographic group compilations, an extended, slow release of my seed, and a heart stolen by a man who loves to experiment in spunky pleasures.

'The sauna doesn't open until eleven,' he told me as I chewed halfheartedly on the muesli he's purchased in an attempt to assist my sudden interest in all things slimming and Lycra. 'So I think, if we get there by one, it should be fairly full for a touch of PDSE.'

'PDSE?'

'Public Display of Sexual Expression,' he said as if I should've known.

'Is that a new thing?' I asked, disconcerted by his expanding knowledge.

'I dunno, I just heard someone say it in a chatroom the other night.'

'A "chatroom" ?'

'Aye, but don't worry, Master.' He patted me on the shoulder to bolster my tentative trust. 'It's only research for our fun. I wouldn't step out of line for fear of punishment, Sir.'

'Okay,' I said, striving to be firm and masterful in tone, which is tricky to do with a mouth full of muesli. I'd rather eat ten packets of dry muesli than go to this sauna. Maybe it's good to try something new now and again. Keeps it fresh. What's the worst that could happen? I'm certainly not going to lose my guy to a bunch of men who want nothing more than anonymous sex in a backstreet sauna, am I?

Tuesday 12th October

Luke's Birthday.

Less than a week and I was back in Airdrie. This time I was determined to keep my promise to Mum and, within an hour of arriving, we were tending to my big brother's grave. The grounds are well-tended, and the shrubs that map out the paths are bursting with life, even at this time of the year. Life feeding on death.

I asked myself, *What's the worth of a wee man like Luke to this place?* A single rose would've finished him off in one season, blooming over spring and summer and slowly withering away over autumn. But, unlike Luke, that rose bush can be reborn and be just as vibrant in the years to come. It really is a waste: his life, quiet and un-lived, in that place of death that bursts with colour and fragrance and fights for attention. It was screaming at me while he lay cold and silent. Was there anything of him left, really? Was Mum now placing a bouquet of lilies and tulips on nothing?

'Where's Aunt Moira?' I asked, squinting through the gravestones.

'Three rows back and six headstones to the left,' she said without tearing her eyes from Luke's stone. Mum knows this graveyard like the back of her hand. 'I know he's here. I've been here so many times to see your Auntie, but I just can't bring myself to stand over him on my own.' She bit back tears. 'He was a good baby. Never cried. I somehow wish he had, then I might've known something was wrong.' She clasped my hand and leant on my shoulder, hiding her tears. Too sober now to show them, but her stifled breathing told me so. I pulled her closer and tighter. Just then, I caught sight of Mrs Hammond tending to George's grave, just as before, in the same beaten coat, dustbuster in hand, hunched, worn, older.

Mum waved to our old neighbour. 'The poor dear. She's here more than the undertakers. Every afternoon, if the bingo isn't on at the Four Isles. Your children shouldn't go before you; it breaks your heart permanently. Let me say a wee prayer, Son. Then I'll let him be.'

We left quickly. Mum finds it difficult to go see Luke's grave, but she finds it even harder talking about him to anyone other than family, so we paid our respects to Moira, Gran and Grandpa Stewart, Gran and Grandpa Angus, and nodded a quick but respectful hello to Mrs Hammond before making our way home. It was the graveside equivalent of Supermarket Sweep.

After a dinner of tinned hamburgers in gravy, tinned new potatoes, and frozen broccoli, she walked me to the railway station. As we neared the station, she said, 'They want to pull this place down and build a new flashy estate, with proper play parks that aren't made of concrete and no local library.' I felt a pang of angst. They couldn't possibly tear my old scheme down. Our home. Our homes. Mum pulled a letter from her parka and unfolded it. She handed it to me and said, 'It's from the council, asking for a simple "Yes/No" vote. There's another leaflet offering all kinds of glimpses into a shiny-happy future sat in warm homes, with modern kitchens, spacious gardens and off-street parking. We'd get a good return on our house, but we'd have to move. We'd no longer be part of Mull.

'But there'd be nothing left of who we once were,' I said, scanning the letter anxiously.

'I know.'

'What does Dad say?'

Mum sighed, 'Your father hasn't seen it yet. I imagine he'll be as indifferent to it all as he is to me. He'll go along with it, I think. I've spent too many years beating his brow, and now I think I've crushed whatever fight he had left. A bit thick of me. I've made him less than half the man I married. Let that be a lesson to you: never allow your own ego to grind a good man down.'

'You should show him the letter. He's going to find out from one of his mates at the club anyway. There might be fight in the old dog yet.'

'I know, I'm delaying the bloody inevitable,' she said. 'Oh, here's your train.'

I sprinted the rest of the way. Catching my breath in a seat facing a blind woman with a young guide dog. The dog was panting as much as I was, with one of those inane smiles. I thought, *Maybe I've been blind. If they knock down Mull, that'll be every wall that I hid behind while playing Kick the Can, every tree I climbed, the quiet place I practiced snogging with Lisa McKenzie, the garden where Mum has always grown raspberries, and my teenage bedroom ripped from the land forever. They have to do something.*

Wednesday 13th October

I was caught by Melve as I skulked out of the bedsits tonight. He asked, 'Ahoy, there sailor! Where are you off to so late with such a gluttonous rucksack?'

I've tried to travel light, but I find the older I become, the more interventions I need to stop time. It's a constant battle to stay youthful. I say 'stay' but I know that ship sailed with the launch of the QE2. All I needed when I was young was a good scrub with Zest, a dollop of Dippity-Do and a spray of Insignia. I hushed him and whispered, 'If I tell you, you must promise not to tell anyone.'

Melve crossed his heart and did the old cub scout sign. I mouthed 'Newcastle' to him. He didn't get it. I exaggerated the silent word once again, which seemed to cause nothing but confusion.

Then, joy of joys, Gwen's door opened just as I carefully grunted, 'New-castle.'

'What's going on? What about a new castle?'

'No,' Melve corrected her, ignoring the finger I was slowly

dragging across my throat, 'He's going to *Newcastle*.'

'Who's going to Newcastle?' came that familiar voice behind me.

I sighed, knowing it was Sally in her usual spot. 'How do you do that?' I asked, turning to face her. 'You don't dress in camouflage typically. You're like a bloody Cheshire Cat.'

'Why Newcastle?' she asked.

'Sssssh,' said Melve, glancing shiftily around the hall, 'he doesn't want anyone to know.'

'Well, it's a bit late for that, Melvin,' I asserted. I had to come up with an excuse quickly. 'The shops are great there, and there's a little Vietnamese restaurant I'm keen to try. Top marks on Trip Advisor.' I was raking over the limited information I had on the city. I omitted the words 'gay' and 'sauna'.

They all nodded, but I could tell they weren't convinced. I quickly made my exit.

It wasn't until I got into bed with Alistair later, after discussing the option of using one of the many slings publicly, that I realised no one really knew where I was going. What if he crashes the car on the A1? Or if I slip on wet tiles at the Jacuzzi, fall in, bash my skull open and drown? Or worse, what if we have a fatal sling-like accident, would anyone ever find out I was dead? Dead in a gay sauna: would I want anyone to find that out?

I'll text Sally the address of the hotel we're staying at tomorrow. It couldn't hurt. She knows half the truth anyway. If I don't return, she'll search for me. I'd never forgive myself if Mum and Dad had to identify my body, fresh from some fridge, glistening with frozen scum from some (literally) seedy jacuzzi.

Thursday 14th October

1 p.m. Necessary cryptic text sent to Sally (God only knows what she'll make of it), and it's off to the sauna after breaking every speed limit possible on the way to Newcastle. The sudden jarring of brakes every time a speed camera was spotted began to get on my nerves, which could've lead to some kind of couple-like argument, if we were an actual couple. We're fuck-buddies who care for each other deeply, it seems, and in about 30 minutes we'll be showing our erect willies to random naked men who may, or may not, want to watch or join in. Oh, blimey! What if they do want to participate? What's the etiquette to kindly ask someone to piss off while you are all pink and vulnerable?

I'm trying to be masterful and slap myself out of this dread. *Keep focused, it's only sex in front of strangers, you've done this before in front of the telly during Question Time,* I've told myself repeatedly.

8 p.m. Back in our room. It's an undeniable fact that fantasy and reality can never share the same point in time and space. What you visualise, and what actually happens, are two very different things.

Once my slave had paid the thirty pounds entry fee, we were given two towels that could only be described as large white flannels. It was impossible for me not to think of Sharon Stone in *Basic Instinct* every time I sat down. The lockers, we were disappointed to find, were towel sized too. I folded my clothes neatly but ended up rolling them into one big ball and stuffing them in the pigeon hole they laughingly called a locker.

Alistair's a big man and also has more sense than his supposed Master. He reversed quickly and asked for a second locker, which the assistant (forties, scrawny, skin leathery brown from over-use of the sunbeds provided between the toilet and the drinks machine) was happy to provide. When I asked, I was shot a disdainful look and told there were no more lockers available. A total lie as the bloody sauna was practically empty when we ventured downstairs to the 'labyrinth'.

The labyrinth was nothing more than a massive space dimly lit by faulty spotlights, flimsy cabins for private use, some with barred windows for a free peepshow, and two large jail cells. The gates on these cells closed but didn't lock. I guess Health & Safety have judged a locked gate too risky in the event of a fire. Nice to see they care. Shame they didn't care so much about the layer of scum muting the gloss of the shower tiles. During our meanderings, we passed the dreaded sling that looked almost impossible to get out of without the help of a strong man, and found a large wooden cross in the next room, which I imagine is used to strap (if you had such utensils with you) your victim down for some tickling or torture. I guess that's the idea, to stay stuck and vulnerable until the tenth guy (if you're lucky) sets you free. And throughout, all I could think was, *All this wasted space and yet they have no room for large lockers.*

We caged the joint for at least an hour, taking showers, sitting in the jacuzzi, wrinkling up in the steam room, and almost becoming dehydrated in the sauna. The water fountain, I'm sure, was breeding Legionella, so I refused to use it. Alistair went to the bar to get his Master refreshments as I practically crawled out of the sauna with my blood pressure at my heels.

I loitered by a stained wall painted in arrows which pointed in directions that I couldn't care less about at that point. I downed a bottle of warm spring water and got my breath back, resting my head against the wall of arrows, when a large, varicose cock flopped its way through a hole in the wall, almost slapping me on the cheek and sending me scurrying in fright to the other side of the room. I heard Alistair laugh hysterically as I got lost in the void, not to be seen for at least fifteen minutes due to a wrong turn through a densely curtained darkroom. The techno music in that room was deafening to my Radio 2 tuned ears. I couldn't make out anything in the low light and the copious lines of black drapes. I stumbled into a few surprised torsos, made my apologies several times and promptly walked into a wall. *If this is the supposed anonymous sex we were in search of, then someone, please, get me a torch and a sizeable luminous name badge*, I thought.

Alistair managed to rescue me with the help of a young masseuse calling and waving a glow-in-the-dark dildo. I was thoroughly embarrassed, glad to be free and ready to give up, but my slave continued on the hunt.

After several hours of milling around and discussing possible voyeurs, we settled on a couple who'd only slightly caught our eyes when we arrived. Time dwindling and desperation rising, they seemed more attractive after a few hours of frustration. It was now or never. It was time to dry off our trench foot and take a tumble in a leather sling.

Alistair wriggled into the sling with all the grace of a hippo slipping into a canoe, but got comfortable quickly with his ass in the air, legs spread wide, and patiently waited to be shown who was boss. This was the only part of the fantasy that actually rang true. The rest of the scenario was clunky, to say the least. The earmarked semi-attractive couple became bored and wandered off in search of a new piece of teenage totty that'd breezed past them sporting nothing more than a smile and a stiff pole. Beauty before age, it seems, and our combined ages couldn't compete with such a lean body and a willy you can hang a kettle-bell on.

Hampered by older men (I'm talking coffin dodgers here) not understanding the unwritten code 'If the gate is shut, do not enter'. Or maybe they just didn't care. They had as much right to be there as we did; they had paid their fifteen pounds after all, albeit, with a pensioners' discount. Some came within inches of us, inspecting every detail of our 'act'. One even cupped my balls while I was engrossed in taking my slave down a peg or four. This could've really stopped everything, but my dominant side kicked in, and I kindly but firmly removed their hand with some authority from my nether regions. They got the message.

My slave seems to have enjoyed it far more than I, which really shouldn't be the case if he follows through with his role: humble and self-loathing. I should be the one feeling empowered and determined to push him further next time. But no, when I finally reached a half-hearted orgasm, after an eternity of self-consciousness in front of a dwindling audience (Alistair had cum some time before), I was glad it was over.

The typical walk of shame home after some frivolous night of fun is nothing compared to the age it takes post-coital in a sauna to mop up, shower, dry off, get dressed and get out of the premises. I left wrinkled in body and crumpled in soul. I need to review with Alistair later over dinner. I get the feeling he's deeply satisfied. He's napping soundly on the hotel bed. I'm still flushed, dehydrated and sipping on my fourth bottle of water from the minibar while sitting next to an open window. To passersby, I must look sad and lonely. They wouldn't be far wrong.

Friday 15th October

11 p.m. Our dinner was delicious, and he treated me like a king. I began to forget all about my anticlimax-climax. Typical human, one need trumps another, i.e., food over sex. Alistair looked at me with such warmth and longing I couldn't bring myself to slide our sauna escapades under the microscope. Instead, I suggested we hit the gay scene.

'What? The actual gay scene? As in actual public houses?' He winced over the word 'public'.

I nodded, 'Aye, maybe even a club as well, with an inebriated stop at a chippy on the way home.' *Come on,* I thought, *I did the damn sauna thing for you. This is the least you can do!*

He swigged on his beer thoughtfully, and then, to my surprise, he sniffed and said, 'Alright, in for a penny, in for a pink pound.' I had to double-check I'd heard him right, and my ear hadn't become clogged by jacuzzi water, but he confirmed it with, 'Well, why not? We're far enough from home. I'm sure no one knows me down here.'

I was rather hoping for something a bit more profound and liberating, but I guess it was a step in the right direction. Before he had time to finish his last Bia Hơi, we were walking down the gay strand and selecting the most comfortable bar to get slowly pissed in. We settled on The Bank, which was throwing a drag show with the entertainment dressed as nuns recreating the *I Will Follow Him* moment of *Sister Act.* Non-threatening, drag queens most definitely are not, but if my stud was going to hit the gay scene for the first time, he was going to have to go through that baptism of fire just like the rest of us. His nervousness showed as we stepped over the threshold, but with every passing second, he became more himself. Pretty soon, we moved closer together, drank, clapped and eventually kissed and hugged just like any other loving gay couple. Bliss!

The hangover this morning could have dragged me down, but I know nothing can take last night away from me. I was drunk, but I remember every single beautiful second of it. Alistair was grinning like a panting hyena when we hit the burger bar at 3 a.m. He thanked me for getting him out there for the first time. I thanked him for making his first giant leap. I quietly thanked God he got there, and maybe even said a little prayer that now, after all the secrecy, we can begin to move forward together.

This morning, we stopped for a late breakfast in Ponteland and continued up the A698, connecting on to the A68, and followed the road to Edinburgh. A lazier path than the A1, weaving through the beautiful Northumberland Forest and over the border to Scotland at its peak. The scenery, the idle chat and the intermittent handholding between gearstick shifts told me that something extraordinary happened overnight. Sure, it may've taken a misguided trip to a sauna, but I felt we'd moved up a level.

Alistair stared through the driving rain as we hit Jedburgh and said, 'You're a good man, Andy. Not many men would put up with me. Not many would've done what you did for me in that sauna.'

'Oh, you're welcome,' I said, shifting in my seat apprehensively.

'Listen, I know that kinda thing's not for us. I'm beginning to realise that living a fantasy isn't always as thrilling as playing with it in the mind. There's so much more to us than just sex.'

'Stick with me, buddy,' I said, 'I'll learn ya'.'

He turned his focus from the road to me and grinned. 'I will,' he said.

I smiled all the way to Café Jamaica. I kept smiling through my backshift, and not one single cantankerous customer could wipe it off my face. And that's why, in the end, I'm glad we tried the sauna. It's the long way round, but we're getting there.

Saturday 16th October

I don't see why we have to leave Alistair's flat so early just because his cleaner, Dominica, is coming at 9 a.m., but I found myself walking into 323 Leith Walk after the usual prostitute's wash over his bathroom sink. The Colonel's taken up residence on Sally's four-poster with not a hint of guilt on his content face as I walked in the door and caught him sprawled on her luxurious velvet sheets. Sally was caterwauling in the shower. I turned my nose up at the Colonel and made my way to my room. As I gently pushed my door open, Sally stopped singing *Single Ladies (Put A Ring On It)* and hollered, 'I've fed your pet, my gorgeous-but-cruddy-stop-out!'

'Thanks!' I called back, my eyes darting around looking for some kind of hidden CCTV. How does she know it's me? I quickly got ready for work. No time for a shower. Sally took ages, obviously washing off the remnants of some disgusting man. I smelt of Alistair all day. Delicious!

Later, at Café Jamaica, Sally nudged and winked at me, causing some spillage of beer on my tray, which irritates me as I challenge myself on every single order to keep my tray immaculate. As I plopped the pints down for a gay couple with a toddler strapped in a massive pram – they're most certainly not helping the campaign for gay and lesbian adoption by drinking through the day in the presence of a minor close to a window – and mopped up the spillage with a fresh cloth, she purred in my ear, 'I have news.'

'What? You've decided to give up stripping and will be running for the position of Conservative MSP for Edinburgh North and Leith?'

'And limit my wardrobe to one shade of blue and give up feather boas? Not a chance, darling! I'm a rainbow-coloured stick of rock, brimming with pride inside and out. It's in the job description of a fag hag,' she guffawed. She glanced around like a spy incognito, as if she was about to give me all the codes to the New York Central Bank, and said slyly, 'No, Gwen has a sister, and she's 180 degrees of our frowning Frau.'

'What, a total slut? That's a bit harsh considering the source of this information.'

Sally slapped me on the shoulder and quickly checked her nails. 'No, my delightfully bitchy friend, she's *young* and *beautiful*.'

'How do you know? Have you been rifling through her photo albums?'

'Not at all, I get enough of a kick glancing through yours when you're out with whomever it is you're too shy to tell me about. Nice selfies, by the way, but I must say that a man of your age shouldn't pout so much. It reminds me of Mick Jagger going through a midlife crisis.'

'Hey, those were potentials for the Gaydar profile,' I protested.

'And I wondered why things were so sparse,' she laughed, leaning on the bar and ignoring a customer who was desperately miming as if signing a cheque. 'No, Gwen introduced her. I might add, she was reluctant to do so, but I was my usual genteel, persuasive self and got the low-down.'

'You are about as genteel as a sledgehammer on the gonads, Ms Knowles,' I bitched while acknowledging the desperate customer's needs.

She smiled with a certain amount of pride and added, 'I aim to please, especially with my older, more submissive clients. Anyway, my dearest butt-hugger, she's staying with our dreary neighbour for a short time, checking out the city for a possible move, and I think it's just the distraction she and we need.'

'A beautiful sister?' I pondered.

'I know! I thought moustaches and monobrows were as

embedded in her DNA as limbs. How wrong I was.'

Sunday 17th October

Sally was not wrong. Gwen's sister is stunning, but she has the character of white wine vinegar. We met her proper as she escorted her sister along to our dance rehearsal. With long sweeping legs that could rival any supermodel, glossy, perfectly coloured hair and juicy lips that any man would love to hang from, she cast a shadow over every other woman in the room. She's a modern-day version of Botticelli's Venus (only with clothes on).

Everyone, even the, 'Hey everything's cool, man,' Melve was agog when she entered the church hall. He stumbled over his words, not only to her but to the rest of the cast members. Trenton jibed him, 'Focus, man! You don't like anything fem, remember?'

I introduced myself and immediately put my foot in it, 'Hello, Gwen. Is this your little sister?' Taking her sister by the hand and shaking it delicately.

'No, I'm her older sister, Natascha. The years haven't been kind to my little sis, but there's nothing surgery can't fix.' There was just a hint of a German accent. On the whole, you would think she was British, practically cockney. 'Might I add, you are a very handsome man.' I warmed to her even more. 'If you looked after your skin a little more, that is.' And subsequently cooled a little too.

Natascha works in PR, employed in London for the past ten years, dealing with clients such as Alesha Dixon and Hugh Grant. 'I took over his image not long after that awful incident with that coloured hooker.' She seemed clueless or not to give a shit about political correctness, and barged onward, 'It took some doing, but I made roadside blow-jobs popular. I've thought about branding the term "Dogging", but it's too late now. Everyone's using it, and just as many are doing it.'

'Her mother must be so proud,' Sally uttered to me. The competition had begun already; I could hear a referee's whistle blow.

'I hope you're going to scrub my sister up for this wedding,' Natascha projected to Trenton. 'She's had minimal experience in the art of makeup and even less opportunity in life to wear any, despite my constructive criticism.' Gwen's gaze was fixed at her feet, quietly watching her ego slope out of the room. 'My darling sister wouldn't know one end of a hairbrush from the other,' she laughed hysterically. Natascha was ignorant of the sudden shift in vibe from welcome to awkward.

'I'd like to show Natascha the right end of a hairbrush: the spiky end, right across her bare backside,' muttered Sally, moving forward to start a tirade of insults.

Molasses grabbed Sally by the arm and spun her back on the spot, 'Wise monkey know wha tree fi climb,' she said through gritted teeth. 'Down, girl.' Sally sulked in her kennel.

The boys arrived twenty minutes late, which I feel is totally hypocritical in retrospect of the abuse I received for being only a few minutes late a week-or-so ago, but my protests were drowned out by girly screams that shredded my eardrums as Natascha and Tony skipped towards each other in joy.

'Natascha! Darling!' screeched Tony, pelting across the room to embrace her, causing every roll of fat (highly visible through his white stretched-to-the-limit polo shirt) to judder independently of his frame. They admired each other like long-lost siblings just reunited by Cilla Black. 'How long has it been?'

'Too long, and you haven't aged a day, my little Schätzchen.' She was blatantly lying; Tony's aged quicker than a teabag that's been used fifty times over in one day.

It turns out they met in London and shared the same temporary accommodation just a few months before he and Ryan met. Tony had travelled from South Africa to consider living there full-time, Natascha had journeyed from Hamburg to contemplate the same. Tony only lasted a few weeks, claiming Londoners were too rushed and unfriendly, but I imagine it was he that was too slow and nasty. He chose Edinburgh as his next stop, sadly. Natascha stayed, married a wealthy London landlord and has spent most of his cash on surgery, by the look of it. Tony settled down, stole my friendship and tainted my life. The two of them never met again and were totally unaware they had Gwen in common, until now.

'It's amazing,' declared Tony to the room still holding Natascha's hands, 'I had no idea your surname was Graumann, Gwen. Isn't Edinburgh so small?'

'Too small,' I muttered to Sally.

At the end, we didn't even stay for the lovely Almond cake Molasses had baked as a reward for our hard graft. Natascha, of course, refused a slice, 'No thank you, I'm allergic to nuts, and besides, I didn't get this figure,' she fanned her fingers down her long torso, 'by eating second-rate baked lard.'

Molasses' fixed smile faltered for just a millisecond.

Tony clapped his hands in excitement, 'Oh, that's something else we have in common, I have a nut allergy too! You simply must come to the wedding, Natascha.'

I became nauseous and left with Sally.

'Why am I not surprised they're friends?' I asked Sally on our path home.

'Because you know as well as I do, every super-bitch needs her bitch, who will bitch and appreciate the super-bitch as much as the super-bitch appreciates herself, darling.'

I sighed, 'Oh, dear, I feel one hell of a bitch-storm coming our way.'

Monday 18th October

'That bitch!' said Sally as she stormed into my room, interrupting my joy of catching BBC weatherman Tomasz Schafernaker for the first time between the morning bulletins.

She stood in front of the telly and blocked his cheeky, handsome face. I peered around her from the sofa. 'Can't you knock?'

'It's an emergency. Look!' Sally held out her hand. She was holding a small number of makeup products. 'Frau Face-ache, Natascha, has blatantly crept into my room while I was away waxing my fanny in the lav and "borrowed" some of my products. She had the gall to admit as much when I caught her, red-handed and red rouged, slapping it on her puss in the hall mirror.'

She threw the lot in the bin with a clatter. I leaned the other way; for a petite girl, she was suddenly massive. 'Guess you better start locking your door again,' I said, fanning my own naturally rouged cheeks. 'Is it warm in here?'

Sally frowned and said, 'No, it's not.' She slumped down on the sofa. 'What are you watching? Ooooh, who's this?' she cooed. 'He's dishy. And, no, I won't start locking my door, sweetie. Why should I limit the circulation of air due to a petty thief living in our midst?'

‘It’s Tomasz Schafernaker. And the fresh air you’re talking about must be supplied by Benson and Hedges, judging by the stink from my bath towel ... must you smoke after every shower?’

‘Yes, I must. Listen, I’ve not lived as a fag hag for years without learning how to fashion my nails to be gentle on the most delicate of flowers, or, when needed, to pluck the mouldiest of petals. If that banshee wants to take liberties, then the next one will be her last.’

Tomasz smiled and said a cheery goodbye. The screen switched to some young female news presenter. ‘Aww,’ we whimpered in unison.

‘I think I may be in love,’ I said, leaning dreamily on her shoulder and savouring the image of the sexiest weather guy on the planet.

‘I think you may be in lust,’ cracked Sally. She slipped off the sofa as I sank face first into the pillow, imagining it was Tomasz’s stubbled face and kissed it several times. ‘Besides, I thought you were avoiding anyone called Tomasz, or Thomas, or Tom, or even Tom-Toms for that matter after your disastrous failure of a non-marriage to one.’

‘Thanks for the kind reminder,’ I said, looking up at her lazily from the sofa. ‘Besides, this particular Tomasz is unattainable and therefore safe.’

She chuckled, ‘Any time. I won’t stay for tea, I have to get to class by eleven. Oh, and don’t be masturbating over Tom-Tom for too long, my horny little friend. Leave that mystery man of yours something to rub.’

‘Class? What kind of class does a lady of the pole need to take at eleven in the morning? I didn’t realise they offered courses in anal at Edinburgh Uni these days,’ was my bon mot.

‘I’ll book you in,’ she retorted. ‘From what I’ve heard through our party wall, your rhythm is totally off, and as for your dismount, utterly ridiculous. Bye, darling.’

I waited for the next weather report, but Tomasz must’ve gone off shift as some older, less attractive chap took to the air and made everything seem dull and dreary.

11 p.m. Just under an hour ago, I watched Melve smuggle Trenton Tanner into his room (the benefits of being opposite the main door and no longer having a key in your lock). I was alerted by Trenton’s squeal – a squeal I’d know anywhere – as he caught sight of a large spider that's been cohabiting in our hall for the past fortnight. The spider has now been evicted by myself, however, as far as my ear can discern, Trenton has not.

11.45 p.m. Now I've just seen the two Germans arrive. Neither in a good mood. Natascha was chewing the ear off Gwen for some reason. Damn it! I failed German in secondary solely because my teacher repelled me with such awful halitosis that could melt the rubber end of a pencil. I refused to ask for help with difficulties and suffered the lowest marks in the class.

11.56 p.m. Once again, through the keyhole, I saw the pink fleshy edge of Trenton's buttocks enter the bathroom. They're obviously back having their wicked way with each other. Thank goodness I couldn't see anything more as this would have scarred me mentally for life.

Tuesday 19th October

'Good morn ... wha' da hell happen to your eye, my boy?' asked Molasses as I arrived at work.

'I think I have a case of Pink-eye and I've no idea why,' I lied. 'I'm cautious not to rub my eyes in case of infection or premature wrinkles.' That bloody lock has some kind of infectious bacteria from outer space that has blown into my perving eyeball and caused me to look somewhat puffy and droopy on the right lid. This will teach me to run my own solitary branch of a Neighbourhood Watch.

Molasses tutted loudly and leaned towards me. She grabbed my head firmly, as a cat does with her kittens, and scrutinised it. 'Jesus, you look like Quasimodo. This won't do.'

I spent the rest of the shift stumbling around in Sally's Jacky-O sunglasses and, by three o'clock, my sight was limited due to some weird puss-like fluid that would come and go over my eyeball. I was sent to the chemist immediately upon revealing this horrid sight to my colleagues. If I'd passed a fancy dress shop on the way, I would've bought an entire pirate's costume just for the eyepatch.

At the chemist, I hammed it up in a bid to secure the most potent treatment for my affliction. I lied about the length of my illness (over two weeks) and begged for a cure. I needn't have bothered as, when I removed the sunglasses, the chemist recoiled in disgust at the alien entity living on my face.

'Thank you,' she said, gulping down some bile. 'You can put your sunglasses back on now. Right now. Before anything else gets in it,' she grimaced. What she actually meant was, 'Before you scare off the customers with your disgusting face.'

Minutes later, I had a bag of drops in hand and was off home. All I had to to do was get to 323 and keep my head low for a few days, but every lie has its own penance, and my penance came in the form of Tony. He just about passed me on the street, I had my head as low as possible to avoid him, but my Jacki-O disguise hadn't fooled him.

He grabbed hold of my arm and declared, 'Andy, it is you, isn't it? Why are you wearing those ridiculous ...?' Too late, he was scrutinising my bashful face now, peering behind the dark rims. And then, the inevitable. His vicious smile widened. 'What the hell has happened to your eye?' he asked with a tone of smug curiosity.

I'm wearing huge sunglasses, damn it! Trust him to have bloody Xray vision!

'You're red all around the socket, I can see. Oh, dear, that's ... ugly.'

Where was the compassion? Where was the sympathy? Come to think of it, where was that bloody pirate's outfit now? *Eyepatch. Must remember to carry an eyepatch and mace for future encounters with this brat.* After ten minutes of torture, and the offer of a brown paper bag from an ogre less-worthy to be canny over another's appearance, I tore myself away from his goading with the parting words, 'I'm glad I can brighten your day in some way, Tony. I hope to return the favour soon. Very soon, in fact.' I heard his screechy laughter fade in the distance as I gathered pace. Once I turned the corner, I paused, removed the sunglasses, blinked up to God and muttered some expletives as I shook my fist to the heavens. Just then, as luck would have it, a seagull shat in my good eye.

10 p.m. I've told Alistair I'm suffering from a highly contagious cold. I'm not telling him I have a disgusting eyeball: he'd never kiss me again. He was very understanding and reassured me he'd be waiting eagerly for my return to health. The next few days were meant to be spent happily back in his arms, but I guess I'll compensate by smothering myself in Doctor Who DVDs, ice-cream and Erythromycin ointment, which I've applied to both eyes just to counteract the bird flu that's probably mutating in the one good portal of sight I have left.

Wednesday 20th October

How long does it take for the inflammation to go away? If this is a glimpse into the future, droopy eyelids and bloodshot sclera with more marbling than a stately home's fireplace, I don't think I want to live beyond fifty. I'm glad I cancelled my time with Alistair. Why would anyone want to look at me? *I* don't even want to look at me.

Sally descended on me armed with lavender joss sticks, a multipack of Tetley and a collection of classic Doctor Who DVDs. 'I figured you needed some geeky time with your sister from another Mr and a hot tea-bagging session. Don't look so worried, sweetie, the kind of teabags you soak in boiled water ... although, I do know a man who loves a roasting hot flannel on his ... '

'I'll pop the kettle on!'

Within the hour, fragrant wisps of incense altered the vibe of my room as they danced in the evening sun. I lay on the sofa with my head cupped in her hands as she bathed my eye with all the skill and care of an experienced nurse, finishing off by gently applying a perfectly warmed teabag. At one point, I looked up into her doting eyes, still caked in crusty eyeliner from the night before, and I thought I saw a glimpse of something other than Sally Knowles. A woman I'd never seen before. I saw some motherly person who was capable of more than just bravado and glitter, more than just fleeting friendships and casual encounters with men. And just for a millisecond, somewhere in the blackness of her eyes, I saw the possibility that she was actually capable of love.

'Do you know, darling,' she said as her eyelashes flapped away the depth of her gaze, 'I had a client just the other day ask me to sound his unwashed penis with a fresh cigarette and the antique cigarette holder I use in my act. The audacity of it all!'

I accepted her dissolve into the entertaining Ms Sally Knowles and asked, 'Did you do it?'

'No dear! No contact. And besides, smoking may kill, but it must never, ever give you communicable diseases.'

I had to ask, 'Sorry, what is "Sounding" ?'

'Oh, that's when you take a long object and pass it down the urethra. Some men find it a big turn on ...'

'Okay, stop. There are some things I just don't need to know,' I insisted.

'You'll thank me for this knowledge in the future when someone asks to perform it on you.'

After the experiences I've had, she may be right, although I'm confident for now that Alistair will never push things too far. No more saunas or public sex for us. We're moving into a more robust and intimate stage of our relationship.

Time moved on from teabagging and sounding, and it wasn't long before the gin martinis added an extra dimension to Doctor Who's 1970's time-tunnel effect. At some point during *The Green Death,* I dozed off, waking much later alone by candlelight, warm under Sally's patchwork quilt with the Colonel purring happily in his nook at the back of my knees. Rested, settled, cared for. Try as I might to ignore it, but this place feels more and more like home.

Thursday 21st October

Okay, maybe I've been wrong, and the girl has healing hands: the wonderful Ms Knowles has managed to reduce the inflammation overnight! I'm not cured, but I'm well on my way to recovery. Either that or the antibiotics have administered their medicine quicker than an over-worked house doctor in a remarkably well scored NHS hospital, which I find very hard to believe. I like to think the care of a good friend can beat any bug into submission, even cancer. Oh, Christina, where are you now? I hope you're getting better.

I heard Gwen playing her cello after slaving away at Ryan and Tony's. She hit a melancholy that left me unable to move for some time. At that moment, nothing could pull me away. No mobile phone. No lover's call. If an earthquake rumbled around me and caused the fabric of the building to fall to pieces, I would have waited to the last note. It was bliss to allow myself to surrender to it.

I felt the need to tell her, and so I found myself knocking at her door, whereupon she appeared cautiously between the crack. 'I'm sorry for the noise,' she said. I could see she'd been crying.

'Noise? No, that was a beautiful companion on a lonely day. Thank you. It's just what I needed to hear. You played with such … meaning.'

'Pain inspires me, it vexes me to say. Is your eye sore?'

'It's getting better, thanks to the kindness of friends.' At the risk of spoiling her inspiration, I suggested we escaped the bedsits for a while and catch a movie. Within the hour we were hiding in the dark, clutching a carb-fest to our chest and feasting on the black and white thrills of Hitchcock's *Psycho* at the Filmhouse cinema. It's so graphic and brutal and still scares the living daylights out of me. I won't rest well tonight, but it was well worth it for the time with Gwen.

'Thank you, Andy,' she said as we bid each other goodnight, 'that cheered me up.'

'Really? I think that may be the first time any Hitchcock horror has had that effect.'

'Yes. Matt may have been a total, how do you say, tozzer?'

I nodded in agreement, not wanting to ruin the moment by correcting her pronunciation, 'Close enough.'

'But he never tried to stab me to death in the shower.'

'Every cloud.' I joked. 'I'm no expert, Gwen, but you may want to aim just a little bit higher than being brutally sliced to death at the hands of an unbalanced lover.'

'Let's make that a deal between the two of us then: no crazy lovers from now on.'

'Agreed,' I said, tempted to tell her I already have a man in my life who is anything but crazy, but I didn't.

Friday 22nd October

Infection, crustiness and the droopiness of a deflated eyelid couldn't keep me at home last night. Alfred Hitchcock and my overactive imagination saw to that. I was due some loving. Alistair has now seen me at my worst (so far). He laughed at my 'cold' cover story. 'So, on the bright side, we can snog?' he asked.

I didn't think I could allow myself to take authority over him as I imagined I looked ridiculous. 'Okay, we're having sex tonight, for sure,' I said. 'I'm horny. It's been *days*. But, just for a change, let's do it a little differently. Have you cum since we last met?'

'No, Master.'

This satisfied me. We haven't discussed exclusivity, but reading between the lines, this man is already saving himself for me. So, as his Master said, the tables were to turn, ever so slightly. I was blindfolded, which gave me confidence as this covered my contagion. I was then tied to the bed and allowed myself to surrender to the firm touch of his strong paws and the delicateness of his cocksure tongue. Unable to take control, this went on for what could've been hours, I'm not sure as I was now outside of time. I allowed myself to ebb and flow to his every whim. At times I became so high it felt transcendental. All the while, as a single digit did the work, he kissed me gently up and down my thighs, brushing my bristling hair with the warmth of his lips, adding to my rapture until I could hold it no more. Feeling my warmth splash all over my, by now, ridiculously sensitive and convulsing body, it was without a single touch of my manhood. It's the first prostate inspired climax I've had in my life and the most surprising. This man is for me. He reads my body like a book, studies it eagerly and takes me to places I never thought I was capable of going.

Saturday 23rd October

What's a boy to do when he has all this pent up excitement regarding his newfound lover? I told Sally all about last night while serving hangover breakfasts to the usual crowd. Everything, except his name.

'You lucky homosexual,' she said dreamily. 'If prostates were available on the NHS I'd be first in line. I've always wanted to know how it feels to have one tickled. Maybe I should go the extra mile and go private. After all, something like that should be quality. I'll suggest they flog them at Harvey Nichols on a glittery shelf, next to other items of calibre, such as Manolo Blahniks and rare 45s of Gershwin.'

Molasses pinned a poster to the community notice board and interrupted, 'Missy, they'd be sick of you at the returns desk; you'd wear many out before their warranty was up.'

'I'll ignore that snide remark,' said Sally as she scrutinised the freshly hung advert. It read:

EDINBURGH'S FIRST

MISS FAG HAG PAGEANT:
A CELEBRATION OF AN
UNSUNG HERO
OF THE
LGBTQ COMMUNITY.
In Aid of Waverley Care
Saturday 6th Nov. 2010
Café Jamaica, Broughton.

'I think I've found my next glitzy role,' grinned Sally, fanning herself with a menu haughtily.

Natascha appeared over our shoulders as pleased as punch. 'There's more than one star in the night sky, darling,' she said. 'Isn't that right, Tony.'

'Natascha. Tony. Oh, what a treat,' I said without a hint of joy.

'You?' asked Sally in disgust. 'But you've only been here five minutes, *I've* lived in this city for years. It's about *our* community.'

'I think you'll find it says "LGBTQ Community", which I'm very much a part of in London, and I'm a very close friend of Tony's, who's lived here for many more years than you.'

Sally tutted. 'Who you've known for what, five seconds?'

'Ladies – and I use that term very loosely – please refrain from a cat-fight in my establishment,' interrupted Molasses, hand twitching over the damp tea towel on her shoulder, locked and loaded for a quick flick the second any earrings were removed. 'The competition is open to any female who has supported or been supported by a homosexual man. Friendship mileage nonessential information. Geographical status is not exclusive to Edinburgh. Remember, the main objective is to raise a sizeable bundle of cash in good spirits.'

'Game on, it seems, sister,' announced Natascha, as she poked her tongue in her cheek and high-fived Tony on their way out.

'Don't call me sister!' warned Sally, but Natascha was indifferent. 'There's nothing in my genes that could be related to something as poisonous as you.'

'Are high-fives cool again?' I asked.

'High-five, my ass!' growled Sally. 'I'll high-five her forehead with my foot next time I see that self-important bitch. There's only room for one diva in this town, and that diva is ...'

CRACK!

Molasses' patience had worn thin and, with a cheeky smile, she had just whipped Sally's firm ass with taut, damp linen. Sally scowled at her adopted mother. Molasses widened her eyes in innocence and said, 'What? You said, "High-five my ass," and that's what I did, in my preferred modus operandi.'

Eye Update: Eyelid almost normal, but still looks like the wizen grandparent of the other.

Sunday 24th October

In the words of RuPaul, 'You better work!' And that, it seems, is what I'm expected to do for the next few weeks. Sally's asked for help with the pageant. She's determined to get in on the action more than a chubby chaser at a Weight Watchers meeting. With only two weeks to spare, there's a lot to get on with. The rules state artistic support from your nominated fag bangle is required at some point in your performance. I'm now Sally's hesitant fag bangle. There are five categories in all: evening-wear; the talent contest; a question & answer session; down a pint and a cocktail consecutively in one; and most worryingly for me, presenting your fag bangle in a swimsuit. Again, emotional blackmail was applied thicker than a drag queen's makeup when I murmured mild protest.

'Andrew, sweetie, darling, cupcake, this is very important to me. Any self-respecting homosexual would do this for their adored fag hag,' Sally pleaded. We were sitting waiting patiently for the others to turn up for the dance rehearsal on the old stage with our legs swinging to the rhythm of Donna Summer's *Bad Girls*, so she had plenty time to bat her eyelashes and grind me down.

Ryan and Tony arrived, with Gwen and Natascha in tow, and I felt my shoulders instinctively pull back, and my spine straighten in preparation for a bitchathon. Natascha and Tony smirked when they saw us. 'What's she doing here?' I asked Sally. 'She's like Jabba the Hut's evil little friend.'

'Yes, and we're the rebel alliance. Bags I'm Princess Leia. Do you want Jabba over there to win? Because you know he'll see it as another victory. She's my opposition, which makes Biffo yours.'

I mulled this over. I couldn't let Biffo thrash me again; he's won so many times already: stealing Ryan from me; finding my fat naked hips glued to their sacred bathtub; having me thrown out of their place; catching me on a girlie bike in broad daylight; and last week's infected eye derision. No, the balance had to be redressed.'Okay, Princess Leia,' I confidently said, 'let's do it!'

Leia leapt down from the stage, landing graciously in her 6-inch heels, and added, 'Super! Better get back to the gym too, sweetie. No one wants to be the flabby friend of a fag hag. It is swimwear after all.'

'Oh, God!' I said. 'I'll have to share a stage with a practically naked Tony. What if they choose Jabba over Han? I couldn't handle that. First thing in the morning I'm getting pumped!'

'That's my dedicated little fag bangle.'

Monday 25th October

'Glasgow?'

'Yup, big boy. I've booked us a five-star hotel on your next Saturday off.' Alistair's keen to head out on the scene once more. Even though it isn't quite our home turf, it's moving closer to it. I was beginning to get excited about it, but then I realised my next Saturday off is the weekend of that damn pageant! 'Aww, cancel the pageant, or pull a sickie. It's rare we get a chance like this,' he moaned.

'Kinda rich coming from a businessman who's frivolous lifestyle is maintained by the reliability of loyal staff,' I joked. 'I'd love to run away with you, but I can't.'

'But you're not at work. It's just for charity, so no commitment there,' he said, fixing his chosen tie for the day in the large bedroom mirror that we enjoy having sex in front of.

'Aye, this is true, but they're my friends. And it kinda does involve work. Café Jamaica wants to support the LGBTQ community. Molasses has always intended the café to be a mishmash of all that's good and great about diversity, so I do have some kind of duty. They may need another pair of hands that knows the lay of the land,' I argued, zipping up my hoody next to him. We looked like the oddest of odd couples.

'It's your choice, big man. I'll leave the booking open for now.'

My choice? We only have two options: the freedom and anonymity of any other city apart from Edinburgh; or staying at home in the biggest, swankiest, but darkest closet in Scotland.

******

I tried my hardest to go to the gym. I even packed a bag and got to the sheeny-shiny sliding doors of the promised land of a healthier and happier life, but the sight of all those slim, fit, muscled and perky individuals traipsing in sickened me. I looked down at my thin, pale Scottish legs after a pair of tanned, muscled calves strode confidently through the doors and regretted being stupid enough to think I'd look semi-normal in public. I turned my knobbly knees towards the exit and left. It's futile. I'm a lost cause. There's nothing that can turn this bulging cargo ship around within a fortnight. I can't afford surgery either.

I have only two weeks! Shiiiiiiiiiiiiit!!!!

Tuesday 26th October

Mum called. She's shown Dad the letter at last. She had to, keeping him out of the loop was bankrupting her; she's been taking Dad on trips here, there and everywhere to keep him away from the club, she's even invested in a year's membership to Historic Scotland.

'It was the truth or our marriage,' she told me, 'but all your father can see is pound notes. I swear, Son, if he chooses to sell to the bulldozers and banks, we'll be dividing that profit in court at our divorce hearing.'

She can't be serious, they've been together for years and have a joint membership to Mecca Bingo (and now Historic Scotland). And to divide a house filled to the rafters with tatty bingo winnings will not be an easy task.

Eye Update: No discharge but still wrinkled and a bit saggy. More tea-bagging tonight.

Wednesday 27th October

Eye Update: Last day of eyedrops. Suspicious eye is not yet fully recovered. I keep eyeballing it, literally, in mirrors through the day. Surely I should be getting better faster than this. Is this due to a lowered immune system caused by some untreated virus?

I bumped into Melve on the number 22 bus tonight. He looked totally out of place sat back and centre in his massive magenta kaftan with added Celtic frills and navvy boots. I was most embarrassed and tried to avoid eye contact as I moved to sit far from him in a seat reserved for the elderly, but he attracted much attention by yodelling my name down the aisle like some mountain goat herder. I know I should support equality and acceptance, but really, people do try your patience. I would've much rather sat next to a jakie in a shell-suit with a centre-parting than that.

He was on his way home from some wealthy Marchmont lady's taught-at-home-class on tantric sex for the over-fifties and those of limited mobility. This information caused me some degree of gastric reflux that took some time to settle.

'Tantric sex, or Neotantra, if we're proper here, is a lot of hugging and heavy breathing with charming, eccentric ladies, dear boy,' he bombastically informed me.

'Lucky ladies of Edinburgh to have you to hold,' I wisecracked.

My jokey jibe was lost on him as he agreed wholeheartedly and smiled, 'Yes, quite.' And then he became most serious and growled, 'I've yet to have some form of orgasm, you know, but it has worked wonders with the blood flow to my testicles.'

'Lucky ladies of Edinburgh,' I said with my nose turned towards the open window. 'You really are a keeper.'

'Have you ever thought of mastering the art of Neotantra, old boy?'

'I'm almost at the end of my 35th year and just mastering the art of physical intercourse, I think anything more nebulous is a long way off,' I assured him. Are you planning on using these new techniques on any recently aquatinted friends in our circle?'

'Like who?' he asked as if he didn't know.

'Trenton Tanner?'

'I have no idea what you mean. Trenton and I are just good friends who share a love of real ale.' He shifted uncomfortably in his seat.

I nodded knowingly and said, 'Sure.' They've been spotted in The Regent (which is a gay bar that, by coincidence, serves real ale) by Ryan on no less than five occasions. Usually lurking in the shadows, at the back, stroking each other tenderly with not a pint glass in sight. I think the jury can come in and cast its verdict.

Thursday 28th October

I found a note stuck to the handlebars of my bike.
It read:

Use this, not the bus,
my plump little gay.
Ms Knowles.
X

I guess peer-pressure is building to look as good as any ageing homosexual possibly can in less than a fortnight for this pageant. Anyone would think it was the annual Mr Gay U.K. contest! I looked at my poor lonely bike, snubbed for months and idle, leaning forlornly against the bannister of the main stair. A spider was busy making a home in the rear wheel arch. The insect led me to think of the arthropod-like Tony and his constant mocking. I immediately about-turned and picked up my helmet from the umbrella stand.

Gwen popped out from her morning ablutions and asked, 'Where are you going with that?'

'I'm heading to work, but more importantly, I'm proving a point to my biggest critic: myself.' I strapped the helmet on and added, 'It ain't over until the fat homo slims.'

I unchained my bike with great purpose and set off down the stairs with a fanfare playing in my head that could accompany a great army's charge into battle in some war movie, all crashing symbols and rising strings.

By the time I'd struggled with the pedals to the top of Broughton Street I was out of puff, my thighs were on fire, my forearms ached, and my symphony was reduced to just a single flute that was dishearteningly losing momentum. I wobbled off the saddle and decided to walk the rest of the way. There was a fat lady at the corner of Broughton Street and York Place singing for spare change amongst the early morning commuters. I assured her, 'It's not over! Not by a long chalk, Aida! I'll get there. Just you wait and see.'

11 p.m. Time for a session with my slave down Leith. He's off all day tomorrow, as am I. Much moistness awaits. I'm taking the bike, not the bus, as testosterone elevates my stamina.

Friday 29th October

Love inspires my ambitions to flow in one direction and one alone. Bouts of fervent exertion, exhaustion and moments of lengthy recuperation enveloped in another's lethargic appreciation stimulate waves that irrigate further desire. My only need is for sexual intercourse with him. The hours have slipped by me, and yet I feel every minute, nay every second, has been quality. He's a wonderful lover. I call him this in the quiet recesses of my mind. The unthinking, irrational part of it that questions nothing and is instinctive. The sheer pleasure of watching his naked body rise and fall stirs up a passion in me that could leap to an open window and call to the world, 'He is mine!'

But not yet.

Saturday 30th October

I've been parading around for the best part of an hour in a selection of underwear that has gone from briefs to very brief! My critics, Sally, Gwen and Melve, were typically candid in their opinions. I'm a sensitive thirty-five-year-old who's holding onto his youth by a hair's breadth. My looks are fading faster than my mind can adjust to this unfortunate atrophy. They should be more sensitive than a heckling crowd at the Free Fringe. I drew the line at the Man-kini (which can never be taken seriously) and the one-legged bikini bottom.

'You do have a perfect bubble-butt, Andy,' enthused Gwen uncharacteristically. Surely not a racy compliment?

'Yes, very much so. Like a peach!' encouraged Sally.

'Ah, to bite such a juicy peach would persuade anyone to have more than just the recommended five a day,' added Melve. Also out of character for a closeted-homo-cum-hetero-hippy.

I've ignored my butt entirely over the past few months, focussing instead on the ever bulging hips, but it seems that fat has some positives despite the minuses of clogged arteries, difficulty breathing and the financial cost of mobility scooters. Today I've become obsessed with peering at my ass in the mirror in ass-orted (pun intended) poses. My preferred pose is the jaunty side angle look over the shoulder with a cheeky glance back at the audience. It has the added benefit of making my tummy appear firm and tight. I'll employ this look as much as my allotted slot will allow. A red aussieBum Boosterjock has won this particular contest, and Sally assures me it will win us the pageant. The rest of the garments will either be binned or kept for a special occasion with a certain silver fox of mine. The jockstrap is earmarked for tomorrow night.

The evening of girly giggling was interrupted by disapproving tuts from Natascha, who pulled her sister from the sparkling wine and canopies laid out by a frivolous Sally. 'It's time you put down the wine and stop playing with the competition, Sister,' she cut in without so much as a hello. 'You know how silly you get on alcohol. You should support your family. After all, we're the ones who have nurtured and supported you all your life. Not these no-hopers.'

Gwen, who roared with laughter moments before, followed her sister like a mouse. 'Nurtured, my sweaty ass!' spat Sally. 'Oppressed is more like it.'

'Agreed,' added a disgruntled Melve. 'Even a rose in the most fertile soil needs the sun to shine for it to bloom, or else it dies.'

'Natascha seems to think the only sun that matters is the one shining out of her own ass,' grumbled Sally before necking the last of a bottle.

Sunday 31st October

All Hallows' Eve

Final week of dance classes with the gang and then a break for a while. I'm glad of it if Natascha and Tony keep appearing as some vindictive double-act. Ryan's lost some of his sparkle, which is understandable as he seems to have been swept aside by the overbearing duo. When Gwen suggested wearing plimsoles for comfort during the performance, Ryan didn't bat an eyelid. His indifference is out of character.

Sally suggested, as it's Halloween, we warm up to Michael Jackson's *Thriller*, which I quite enjoyed. We all had to act like zombies. This is much harder than it looks. 'Perfect, Gwen!' called a pleased Sally. 'You're doing the perfect impression of the living dead. Everyone, can you please watch and learn from Gwen? It's vital you know how to get into character quickly.'

Natascha was terribly cruel to her sibling, 'Yes, the lines of reality are blurring; you've been method-acting this role for the entirety of your life, it seems. It's often been hard to discern if she's alive or dead at times.' How Tony and his fag hag roared with laughter.

If she'd insulted any other female in that room, there would've been some kind of stiletto slaughter, but Gwen just shrivelled up into a social husk (which added to the zombie effect) and faded into the shadows without so much as a grunt of dissent. I made it my mission to step on Natascha's toes at least once tonight. I managed it twice, even though she isn't actively involved, which pleased me no end and caused Gwen to smile from behind her hands.

How can one individual cause so much grief? It's as if someone invited the grim reaper to a birthday party and he ate all the cake before the candles were lit, popped every balloon, sacked the DJ and stuck around to watch the fallout from his actions.

Monday 1st November

All Saints Day

1.35 a.m. Strange things can happen on a moonlit night. My mooning ass was aligned perfectly with my man's face and caused much celebration for both of us. The bareness of my butt in the jockstrap may have proved too risqué to model on stage, but anything goes when two men are so deeply into one another.

8 p.m. On our morning drive to our respective jobs, Alistair brought up the subject of skipping merrily off on Saturday to a Glasgow sauna for fun and frolics. Perhaps he thought I'd be more game after treating me to a fantastic experience last night. Or maybe he assumed I'd be so knackered from lack of sleep I'd relent easily.

'A better, more upmarket sauna may be more fun, Master.'

'I thought you didn't want to do the public sex thing again?'

'I don't, but they may have great toys we can play with.'

'Upmarket doesn't necessarily mean more fun: I once spent a dreadful night at Hadrian's Brasserie with a surly waiter and a pot of poorly cooked mussels,' I assured him.

'Come on, live a little.'

I immediately wanted to sit on his face for a second time, only for the pleasure of shutting him up. I thought, *Why can't you see I'm just happy being with you? Why can't we just keep it between the two of us?* But I'm a coward. I'm scared of losing him if I don't claim to enjoy every aspect of our sexual experimentation fully. Maybe this is where I went wrong with Thomas; if I'd experimented more, he might never have been sucked over to the dark side. Alistair is, after all, the only eligible man I've met this year that isn't weird or unhinged in some way. And he's devastatingly handsome. *And* I get the impression he cares for me more and more every day.

'Let me think about it,' I lied. Maybe time will pass, and other priorities will take this obsession's place.

I leant back through the open passenger door to give him a kiss, but Molasses reared her hawklike eyes as she popped up the specials board just outside the café. Alistair grunted a quick 'Go! Go! Go!' as his usually affectionate hand turned on me and pressed hard against my face, thrusting it out of the car into the open air. He drove off in a jiffy, only remembering to shut the car door halfway down the street.

'Good morning,' said Molasses as I scooped up my dignity from the pavement. 'A late night, my boy?'

'Sort of,' I said as I kept a low profile and scuttled on by. I'm pretty sure she couldn't see who was at the helm as Alistair's 4x4 is covered in tinted windows.

Tuesday 2nd November

9 p.m. Just caught Melve kissing Trenton goodbye at the front door. Yes, I was peering through my keyhole again. It's risky business being the local busybody as my door wasn't firmly on the latch, and so, when Melve shut the front door on a cheery Trenton, it caused a draught that briskly pushed my door open, whacking me on the forehead. Melve heard me yelp and, after I kicked the door shut in a temper, I glanced again and caught sight of his crotch as he gave me a knock. I rushed to the sofa and casually said, 'Come in,' and pretended to be engrossed in a magazine.

'I guess you saw that,' he said.

'Saw what?'

'Me kissing Trenton goodbye, or rather, he kissing me goodbye.'

I gave a nonchalant shrug. The Colonel drew me a disparaging glare and then buried his face in his tummy to ignore my lies. Melve sat on the bed next to him and stroked his back tenderly. The Colonel purred loudly in approval. Melve explained that he really has the best of times with Trenton. The sex is fantastic, apparently (I asked him to skip over the more exceptional details of such antics as I was midway through a blueberry yoghurt). They have a passion for ballet. Share the same taste in classical music. 'Hell, the boy has even read the same books as I,' he affirmed. 'When I'm alone with him, I'm free and easy, old chum. But when we're together in public, he's always pawing me, sitting way too close to me, or sniffing the back of my neck.'

The man deserves a medal if he does that, I thought.

'Oh, I know what you're thinking, dear boy.' *Did he?* 'You think this stallion sat before you has had many transient sexual experiences with both the male and female form, many at the same time, so no problemo.'

'Well, I wasn't thinking those exact words.'

Melve continued undeterred, 'But all of these have been in group situations with men who chop logs or can find their way around a Bedford engine. I just can't be seen to be with an effeminate male, not in public, not even amongst friends.'

'If you really do like him ...'

'I do,' he interjected.

'... then you're going to have to suck it up and learn to love it.'

'Could you?'

'Of course, I could. And you should. Who cares what other people think? Most people won't bat an eyelid.'

'Maybe you're right.'

I hope I convinced him; I know I didn't convince myself. All of the men that have attracted me have been on the butch side. A whiff of effeminate behaviour and they're off the dating list and straight on the effeminate friend list, no matter how gorgeous they are. Perhaps that's why Ryan and I never ventured down the path of romantic entanglement. I was attracted to him the moment I saw him, but as I got to know him, it lessened. I still find him a stunning man, but apparently not enough to get over my secret hangup. So I should just stop bitching about their civil partnership and get on with it. Ryan's found his perfect match. They share a mutual love for the flamboyant. This spectacular day they're planning proves that. I just have to suck it up.

Wednesday 3rd November

'Why are we here?' I asked. It wasn't a profound, philosophical question; Ryan and I were standing in the jumble of clothing that is TK Maxx. He knows I hate shopping with a passion and had chosen the only slot we could actually spend time together alone – the first time in months – in a place that was the equivalent to having an aching tooth pulled anaesthetic-free by a dentist with severe Parkinson's.

'Well, I can't be expected to throw money away on clothing that may have to brush against some hellhole's cheap stained decor, or maybe vomited on by some local chav – although, why a chav would be there I've no idea, as I know no such degrades – or worse, torn from me and stuffed in a bin while I'm cuffed to a lamppost in Granton, or some similar godforsaken place. Although, the last is not an option and if you do this to me, I will personally pluck out your eyeballs with a corkscrew.'

'What are you talking about?' I asked, picking up a pair of paint-stained jeans.

He shook his head at the jeans and said, 'No, dear. They're hideous. My stag do?'

I stared blankly.

'In less than two weeks?'

I smiled nervously. I could feel his expectancy.

'That I asked you to arrange?' He looked at me with steely eyes.

'Ah, the stag do. Just kidding,' I laughed through deep breaths. 'You didn't think I'd forget my best friend's last night of freedom, did you?' I paused to rack my brains. When did I become the bloody stag planner? 'Oh, the things we have in store for you, my boy. Prepare to be astounded. And a little bit worried. And amazed. It's going to be one hell of a night!' I punched him playfully on the shoulder.

Ryan's eyes narrowed, but thankfully he still has some misguided faith in me as he turned his attention to flicking through jeans on a rack that was labelled '32/34, M' and said, 'Super. But don't invite that bitch Audrey from my work; she's fifty-eight and doesn't wear a bra.' He shook his head at the racks of clothing and said, 'Oh-dear-oh-dear, this just won't do. This is pure fiction; there are no thirty-two waistlines here. It's just for the fatties. You might find something suitable, though. Shall we switch sides?'

I was happy to move, despite his cheek, and breathed a quiet sigh of relief as I pretended to examine the pile of denim thoroughly, but in reality, the tiny mouse had fallen off the wheel inside my head and was darting around my skull in panic.

'I do hope that you have kept to my guidelines, Andy?'

Guidelines? Great! There are rules. Frickin stag do rules! Of course, there are rules: this is Ryan I'm supposedly planning a party for. I tapped my nose knowingly and told him 'Don't worry, it's all been arranged under your strict guidance.'

'Good.' He threw a pile of rejected jeans into the arms of a passing assistant and said to her, 'I now see why there are two Xs in TK Maxx; everything here is cut for the XX-Large straight portion of the population. Don't you have anything for a slim and youthful homosexual?'

When I got home, after I spent further laborious hours in NEXT with Ryan casting judgement over the 'cheaper side of fashion' with a critical eye that would rival any dragon from *Dragons' Den*, I consulted my living Filofax: Gwen. She was preoccupied in the bathroom. Her nerves must be shot to shit living with that brute of a sister, I distinctly heard her vomiting, even though she pulled the chain in time with her convulsions. When she emerged, she looked very pasty.

'Of course, it's Friday the 12th,' she said, gulping hard and struggling to get her breath. 'You agreed to it during the lock-in at Café Jamaica months ago.'

'Friday the 12th? But that's next week!'

'Yes, is that a problem?'

'No,' I lied. I didn't want to tell her as she, being their cleaner, may let it slip while scrubbing their parquet flooring. I must've been very drunk at that lock-in. I changed the subject to relieve my panic, 'Are you okay?'

Gwen looked embarrassed and pushed her way towards her room, saying, 'Yah, yah. I am fine. I have just eaten something rotten that made me vomit, please don't fuss.'

So, the 12th of November is the night. That's my birthday, but that's okay, I was planning on skipping it this year anyway. Ryan's stag gives me the perfect excuse. I won't be turning 36, I'll be staying young(er) at 35.

Note to self: Buy face pack. Several face packs.

Thursday 4th November

Disaster has struck! Sally lost her balance on stage last night during a particularly rowdy gig in Madam Yo-Yo's and toppled face-first into her colleague's muff, whose legs were poised in a Y formation on the lower stage, ready to pop chestnuts from her opening (must be a seasonal thing). Sally's snapped two ligaments in her right ankle and can barely make it to her drinks cabinet (a sure sign it's serious).

'How unfortunate, you poor thing,' consoled Ryan as he stroked her purple hair as she sprawled on her chaise longue sipping a large brandy. 'I toppled once from a podium in CC Blooms and came round to find my head was wedged between the sweaty bosom of a rotund bingo caller.' He held his hand to his chest, sickening himself as he relived the trauma of that forgotten memory, but revelling in being the boy who survived to tell the tale. 'I almost suffocated, you know. She was drunk and had passed out in the collision. If I hadn't vomited profusely, causing the woman to waken and recoil in disgust, I could have died.' He nodded at each of us in the hope of sympathy and praise.

'Anyway,' interrupted a slightly testy Sally, 'back to *me* and *my* problem, sweetie. I can't do the Fag Hag Pageant like this now, can I?'

Ryan patted her on the head and stood to leave, 'Yes, yes, you are right,' he squished up his face and attempted a look of pity (he needs to work on this). 'Best you stay rested for the next week or so. We want you to be fit for the dress rehearsal for our wedding, don't we?' He left. Apparently Tony is getting a mild addiction to *Deal or No Deal*, and he wanted to get back before he got sucked into a three-hour binge marathon.

'So that's that,' I sighed. 'No more pageant. Gone is the wonderful moment when we'd slap Biffo and Natascha back into their cages ...' or so I thought.

Enter Gwen, 'I'll do it.'

'Do what?' asked Sally, digging a bottle from beneath the cushions that supported her back and pouring another generous splash of brandy in her glass.

Gwen sat close to Sally and eagerly said, 'I'll take your place in the pageant.'

Sally laughed, 'Are you kidding me, kiddo?'

'No, I want to prove to my sister that I am not just some trail of cat sick that she chooses to scrape off the bottom of her shoe.'

It took several minutes before Sally and I moved. This was far better than we could've imagined. Sally downed her brandy and winced. 'Bloody hell,' she said, struggling against the fire in her throat. 'Sisters doing it for themselves, but head-to-head? Now that will be interesting.'

'Are you sure?' I asked her. 'I mean, I'm doing it, but all I have to do is strut around with some confidence in some scant underwear.'

'Yah, I am sure,' she said. 'I've slept on the floor since she arrived. I've given up my bed, my pride, my self-respect, but not any more.'

'Are you sure, sure?' I asked again. 'There'd be a shit-load of work to do, and we have less than three days to get you primed and ready.'

'But it can be done. I've seen the least confident of performers turn it around in two days, darlings,' insisted Sally. She poured another shot and offered it to Gwen. Gwen declined, but I snatched it for Dutch courage. This could go so wrong or be the biggest slap in the history of slapped faces for Tony and Natascha. Sally rubbed her swollen ankle, admiring it as if it were a trophy, and said, 'Every cloud, sweeties. Gwen, you are our secret weapon.'

Friday 5th November

Neither of us will be going to Glasgow on Saturday. I'm very relieved about this. Alistair will be working all day, which means all talk of sauna sex is off, for the time being. This also means he'll be unable to watch what could be the most humiliating ten minutes of my life at the 'Parade Your Poof' part of the pageant (try saying that without spitting on your stilettos). I'm relieved he can't, or won't, come as I'm pretty sure it will be a disaster for our team. Gwen is absolutely lovely for stepping into the skyscraper-heels of Sally Knowles, but I just don't think there are enough hours of rehearsal left to have a recently deflowered virgin learn the art of sexual allure while entwining herself around a makeshift pole. It takes 'strength, flexibility and endurance', according to Sally. She isn't wrong. I tried to raise myself vertically from the ground on such a pole at Madam Yo-Yo's while Sally collected her wages. I only managed to flip one ankle from the ground and passed two accidental bottom burps. Humiliation ended my not-so glittering career as a male stripper. Besides, who knows what disgusting communicable diseases cling to a pole that has been polished by many muffs.

Speaking of the risk of communicable diseases, I asked Alistair if he was okay with Saturday being a sexually sober affair for both of us. 'Not a problem, boyo. Covering Fife will knacker me, but the boys need their holidays. I enjoy the drive anyway.' His words were at odds with his tone. His voice was flat, and he hardly looked at me over breakfast.

I've purposefully left my toothbrush next to his on the bathroom shelf. A small statement of intent. Next week I'll leave a razor, shaving gel and some night cream. The week after, day cream. Then I'll tuck some of my spare underwear in the drawer cosily next to his. I'm not going to mention the word relationship again until he does. I don't want to scare him off. Subtlety is the word of the month.

Almost Midnight: Just back from watching the Meadowbank fireworks display with Alistair from the top of Calton Hill. It's cheap and easy from there if you can withstand a nippy November breeze and dress appropriately. I hadn't, but he kept me warm by tucking me inside the front of his thick overcoat in a lovely bear hug, which pleased me very much. I ensured he stayed warm by sharing a hefty dose of whisky from the flask Steve got me for my 21st birthday. Alistair inspected the inscription on the face of the flask under the colourful explosions. 'Who's Steve?' he asked, squinting to make out my dead friend's sentiment. 'An ex-shag?'

'No,' I lied, 'just a friend.' It's a can of worms I've been keeping the lid on for years, I don't intend to rush to the cutlery drawer to find the tin opener for something that only happened twice and was never spoken of again. It didn't affect the friendship. Much.

He squinted at the flask some more. 'It says, "With Much Love".'

'He was a good friend, that's all. Died about ten years ago. Hey, look at that!' Fireworks are a pleasant distraction, thankfully.

I enjoyed Alistair's reactions to the pyrotechnics thoroughly. The burden of business lifted from his shoulders and, for a time, he became the biggest kid, cooing at every eruption over the glistening Firth of Forth as he pulled me deeper into his coat, so close I could feel the steady thudding of his heart against my back. His hands cupped mine and I felt myself fall for him a little bit more. And then he asked, 'Hey, isn't this the place where you gays come to have fun?'

I stammered for a while, stuck on the 'you gays' part. Surely he sees himself as one of us by now and has no interest in the local habits of the average cruising man? Surely this kind of information is unnecessary to a soul whose aim in life is to serve his Master wholeheartedly and remain loyal to his lover? I was about to ask him as much but some adults, well over their fortieth years, exploded a banger in some close-by dog poo, causing everyone to scarper.

'You don't get this kind of shit if you pay for a ticket,' joked Alistair as we ducked behind a shrub for cover. He was breathy and giggling, and he pulled me close for a kiss inside his hefty collar. Then he gripped me by the shoulder and catapulted me into some bushes. I was dumbstruck and watched as some guy approached Alistair with three kids and a disgruntled wife in tow.

I checked my forehead. No blood, just a tiny lump caused by a stubborn branch whacking me on the way into the shrubbery. I waited patiently until their brief conversation was over. I knew Alistair wouldn't just throw me into a dark space for no good reason. When the chat finished, which seemed to last an eternity, Alistair fished me out and apologised profusely. It was his business partner, Johnny. I understood. We left soon after and took a cab home.

I had to handle an uneasy Alistair for the rest of the night as a mini-egg slowly hatching on the side of my skull. Give him his due, he tended to the swelling with a gentle application of a bag of frozen peas wrapped in a tea-towel and soft kisses. Guilt perhaps. Can you actually be bush-whacked if it was you that hit the bush? Does the bush believe it's been manhandled? More importantly, will Alistair ever come out of the damn closet? I'm bursting here with adoration for the man, and yet he seems content to keep it all bubble wrapped and boxed off. I'm an emotional yo-yo. It's driving me a tiny bit crazy.

Saturday 6th November

What was I thinking? I may chicken out of the whole evening. Why have I agreed to do this for a bunch of people I'm only now starting to get to know? A few facts I have to share with you and you alone, dear diary: I'm teetering on the wrong side of thirty; I'm living in a bedsit with three other individuals who are stuck in the status quo; I have little drive or money to change my status quo; last night, after we'd just got back from the fireworks display, I was so desperate to get to Alistair's loo that a trickle of wee came out just as I locked the bathroom door. Am I'm officially over the hill and gradually gathering pace, nay, plummeting towards forty and mild incontinence? Will the crowd ridicule and heckle me off stage?

I relayed a small amount of these woes to Sally, who said, 'Andrew darling, it's not your pageant. You're only a small part of it. It isn't about you, my poor deluded friend, it's about raising funds for a worthwhile cause while making damn sure other individuals lose dramatically. In other words: suck it up, buster.'

There's nothing quite like a brutally honest friend to put you back in your place. I'm the insignificant gay guy on stage in nothing but his underwear, it seems.

Pressing matters:

- Ryan's stag: I have done nothing.
- The 'exclusivity' chat with Alistair.
- Shave back, sack and crack in case I get exposed by a rowdy spectator in front of the whole café.
- Do some press-ups in the hope I can inflate my flabby chest within the next few hours.
- Return to the gym within the month or insist on cancelling my membership, contract or no contract. They're making a bloody fortune out of me, and I haven't as much as rested my arse on a fitness ball recently.

Sunday 7th November

Natascha is a self-important, talentless bitch with as much charisma as a packet of plain rice crackers. Her choice of evening wear was an Eeyore onesie, of *Winnie The Pooh* fame. She emerged on stage to the Benny Hill theme, dancing and cavorting with an inane grin like an idiotic mime artist. I think this was an attempt to show her playful side, akin to the playful side of Sadam Hussain, I imagine. It bombed like a weapon of mass destruction. She just looked plain silly prancing around as other, more refined hags, looked on in disbelief. She wasn't a patch on Gwen, who'd chosen a slate grey strapless A-line ball gown with beaded sash, which complimented her new, slimmer, post-breakup figure. She'd been keeping the dress for that special gig she's always dreamt of at the Usher Hall. As she showed it to me earlier today, she said, 'I might as well wear it tonight as I know that ship has sailed.' This saddened me.

Sally bellowed to me over the applause, 'You know, it's not too late, I could spike the wicked witch and her familiar's drinks before they hit their mark and stop them in her tracks with a nice dose of diarrhoea. I'm reading the most wonderful book on herbal remedies from the 1920s that tells you what is best and what is best left well alone. It's a fascinating read. Some nasty stuff could be crushed into a nice mojito and never be traced.'

I told her, 'We really need to have a chat soon about your morals, Sally Knowles. No, if Gwen's going to win this, she's going to win it fair and square.'

Anyone would have found the talent section gruelling, I imagine, as it was closely preceded by the 'Down A Pint & Cocktail' section. Natascha's choice of Guinness followed by a large dram was ill-advised, but down the hatch they slid, and within minutes, her eyelids began to twitch, and her speech began to slur.

'Oh, dear,' whispered Sally into my ear, 'I do hope there hasn't been a dreadful mistake, and that isn't the 100% proof fiery bottle of whisky that Molasses keeps for special occasions.'

'You should know, you were in charge of the drinks.'

'Yes, that is true, but I can't be held responsible. The lighting in here is very dim, and it's difficult to see through these thick eyelashes,' she said through a pitiful attempt to stifle a malevolent grin.

Natascha's fifteen minutes had begun. Her performance piece involved her reading a self-penned poem, *My Fag Bangle Simply Sparkles On Me*. It was mercifully short. I include the stained script here for posterity:

What's that you see?
It's my fag bangle on me.
On my dresser at night,
It's so plain, nothing special to see,
But my fag bangle on me?
It simply sparkles, you see?

Why can this be?
This fag bangle on me.
I'm nothing, very plain as can be.
Invisible to see,
But with this fag bangle on me,
I simply sparkle, you see?

Without each other, we can't be,
My fag bangle nor me,
I can choose no other,
I am nothing without my brother,
We are nothing without each other,
But together we glisten, you see.

My fag bangle simply sparkles on me.
And me for he ...

Biffo had joined her on stage. He appeared in a flesh-coloured sequinned catsuit spinning a golden hula hoop which, I think, was supposed to rotate in unison with her words. He repeatedly dropped the hoop, to the amusement of the audience.

I whispered, 'This is terrible, Sally. I mean, I wanted it to be below par, but this is painful to watch.'

'I know, sweetie. And I thought all gay men were experienced with hoops,' she joked. 'Don't worry, something tells me it's going to end in the same way Milli Vanilli's career did: with much ridicule.'

A few, much more rehearsed contestants later, and it was Gwen's turn. Gwen had proved a poor pole dancer during rehearsals, and Plan C had to be hatched. 'She simply doesn't have the strength and flexibility as I, darling,' said a smug Sally. And so, when our girl took to the stage, we were blessed with a sombre revamp of *Thank You For Being A Friend*, the theme from *The Golden Girls*, played with gravity on her aged cello. It could've been a risky choice, but amongst the throng who have Blanche, Dorothy, Rose and Sofia's lines etched into their minds, it was a huge hit. And when our girl left the cello alone to sing a cappella in the most astounding soprano voice with pitch-perfect precision, it blew all of us away.

'Did you know she could sing?' I asked Sally.

Sally shook her head with teary pride in her eyes, 'Not at all, sweetie. Wasn't that divine? Unexpected and divine!'

And then it was my turn to hit the stage with a bunch of younger, much fitter gay men. As we lined up behind the curtain, I could see they all looked tanned, buff and were bulging in the right places. Everyone apart from me. I was plain, pasty, plump and shrivelling up in fright. The lineup was announced by Molasses and went on confidently to the beats of *It's Raining Men*, but I remained petrified behind the curtain.

'What's wrong?' asked a tense Sally.

'They're all so ... beautiful.'

'Yes, yes. And so are you. Get a move on, kiddo, or we'll be disqualified.'

'But I'm in my pants.'

'Look, just think of it as a big swimming pool, and you're in your swimming trunks, that's all. A busy swimming pool, maybe the gayest swimming pool you've ever dived into, I'll give you that, but nothing you haven't done before.' I felt her hand stroke my shoulder reassuringly and then, rather bluntly, shove me out into the spotlight. My late and yet sudden arrival caused some laughter and jeering, but pretty soon, as I started to dance while shaking in my boots, I was celebrated by the crowd just as much as the other men and being pawed by a greasy octopus in the front row. I wasn't a total flop, I guess. At my age, I'll be thankful for that. So I'll take the few pleasurable comments thrown from the audience and put the rest down to poor central heating on a cold November night. My moment in the spotlight was over. No biggie, as it turned out. I can't be that hideous after all.

Molasses stuck a microphone in front of Gwen's nose and asked, 'So, Gwendoline, what elevates you above all other fag hags here?'

Gwen chewed her lip in uncertainty. The room fell silent. I heard Sally grunt, 'Come on,' as her eyes bulged eagerly through the gap in the curtains. She turned to me and said, 'I have no idea what she's going to say.'

Gwen stared at her feet for several seconds. The microphone screeched with feedback. I could see her catch sight of a vinegar-faced Natascha, still pressing her overbearing thumb on her from across the room. The octopus woman began to heckle our girl, which seemed to push Gwen to gently clear her throat and say:

'Well, I don't really think I deserve this award. I want to win it for my friend, Andy. Before I met him, and other people like him ... in fact, all of you people who have learned to live as who you are with pride, I was just ... existing. I wasn't living. In fact, I recently fell in love. I got lucky for a while. But I got, how do you say, dumped? Yes, dumped, by a guy who wasn't worth playing a note for. And boy did I play, but he had his own agenda. And when the you-know-what hit the fan, my friend was there by my side, not only to lean on but to hold me up in a tight embrace. He was persistent when I was stubborn. Loving when I was harsh. Constant when I have been inconsistent. He's taught me that even though someone walks all over you, you don't have to stay down and let every other person do the same. And if I am honest, I can't imagine I've been that supportive of him, but if I have been just a fraction of the friend he has been to me, then I know I'm good. I know I will be there for him, for all of my new friends, because this is my family now.' She turned her whole body towards her sister. 'You know, we confuse the saying "blood is thicker than water", believing that it means family is closer than friends, but we have this wrong. I know the true meaning of those words. The blood of the covenant is thicker than the water of the womb, Natascha. These people you almost tolerate are my friends, my family, my soldiers at the frontline, at my side in this battle we call life. They are my covenant, not you.'

Sally, now at the foot of the stage, started clapping enthusiastically. I joined her. Melve and Trenton followed, and before long, a ripple effect washed through the cafe until the place was a cacophony of sound. The crowd settled down to vote as Molasses rocked an outstanding take on Tina Turner's *Proud Mary*.

Gwen was crowned in a cheap, tacky tiara that most definitely would cause some scalp irritation if left on too long, but the girl wearing it sparkled like a diamond. Natascha left soon after without a word of goodbye. Tony was hot on her heels on his invisible leash. Sadly, Ryan was barked at and had to follow, but as he went, he whispered to our table, 'I just want you to know, I voted for Gwen. She really was the only choice.'

Sally glowed with pride for Gwen for the rest of the night, and at one point I leaned into Sally's ear and said, 'You know, under that Brillo pad of an exterior you hide a spongy softness that could almost be described as maternal, Sally Knowles.'

'Maternal?' Sally turned her nose to the air. 'Please don't swear at me, Andy. There has yet to be a maternal ovum hatched in these clapped-out old tubes, and if it ever does, may it never be fertilised. Barren is my womb, and that is how it shall stay. Life is less complicated that way.'

Money Raised: £1432 (not bad for a quirky café with eclectic patrons).

Question: Can we not find a better term than *fag hag*? It perpetuates the notion that it's still acceptable to call us *Fags*.

Monday 8th November

A bunch of birthday cards fell through our door. Five in total. They were postmarked from Airdrie. All of them were addressed with my mother's handwriting. She continues to oversee the birthdays in our family and therefore removes any shred of sentiment from the cards as they're all written by her and stuck under family members' noses to be signed. My sister has habitually not given a shit over the years, even though I've sent cards and gifts at every birthday, christening or Holy Communion to her ungrateful bunch. I know the cards have all been procured from the discount shop that used to be the old MFI store, knowing Mum's retail habits and the paper-thin quality of the contents. 'Card' is a very loose term, it seems. Some are so thin I can see the good wishes on the inside before I open the envelope. The usual warning was scribbled on the back of all, 'Don't open until your birthday!' Apart from one, which said, 'You can open this one.' It was a note:

> 'We've sent these cards as a goodwill gesture, even though you've forgotten many key dates over the past year. The word "family" seems not to matter in these days of Jeremy Kyle and Facebook – it hasn't gone unnoticed you've refused my friend request twice, by the way. What selfies could you possibly have to hide from your own mother?!
>
> The neighbours, if you can call them that, seem only too happy to sell up and move on. I would fight for the community, if there was one to fight for, but community spirit only shows face when the pint glasses are full at the Thursday night darts match, so I think I'll just get pissed with the rest of them and stick two fingers up to the council building next time I pay the tax. Martha Renton is working

there and is pregnant to some lad from Chapelhall who rides a motorbike and has the most terrible rhinitis. Not a good combination if you wear a motorcycle helmet. I heard last week he had a sneezing fit that upset the queue at the post office. It was pension day, and the over-eighties decided it was too hazardous to stay, fearful of infection this close to Christmas, they cleared out as fast as they could, walking sticks and hips clicking all the way: it was like a mini special Olympics. Even with the provision of a winter fuel allowance and free health care, they're not willing to take the risk. I ask myself why the Renton woman has such airs and graces if she's lumbered with a man like that. Not a handkerchief in sight. You would have splashed alcohol sanitiser everywhere. I don't know where you get your fastidiousness from, Liz Chatterley's son is gay, and his house is a tip.

Anyway, Happy Birthday when it comes. 36 isn't a special one, so don't expect much. I imagine you won't visit as you've just been. That's OK. I've sent a parcel. If it doesn't arrive by Thursday, let me know. I'm lucky enough to have insider knowledge being a part-timer for the Royal Mail.

Love, Mum. X

P.S. You dad's bought three pirañas. If we do have to flit, I think the removal men won't shift them as they probably aren't insured against flesh-eating fish.

P.P.S. I hope you've kept yourself clean over there and seen hide nor pubic hair of a sex clinic. I hear random sex with strangers is all the rage in cities with massive retail parks.

She must be 'friending' the wrong Andy Angus on Facebook. I pity the poor man. I've tucked the 'cards' away. I haven't opened them as I do believe (probably as a result of having it drummed into me by my folks at every birthday, Easter and Christmas) that they should only ever be opened on the day, after a proper night's sleep. I was shocked at the age of fourteen when I discovered my parents were total hypocrites, catching them opening their gifts before midnight on Christmas Eve. First, the awful revelation on Santa, and then that. This was when I began to mistrust them.

To-Do List:

- Book a classy venue at short notice for Ryan's stag.
- Book a male stripper (hopefully, Sally has contacts).
- Book flashy transport of some sort.
- Ask Molasses if she can cater at short notice.
- If no classy place free, ask Molasses if the café can be the venue (less flashy, but more realistic).
- Establish guest list & send invites ASAP (probably by text message).
- Discreetly borrow Ryan's phone for guest details to send invites.
- Head to fancy dress shop & find a suitable costume for Ryan & theme for others.
- ~~Purchase good quality handcuffs.~~
- Borrow handcuffs from Alistair's drawer.
- Book pampering session as preemptive compensation for poor stag.
- Work out how much all this costs.
- Spread the cost amongst guests.
- Don't stress, even though I have less than seven days.
- Find an appropriate wall to bang head against that won't cause too much damage internally or externally.

Tuesday 9th November

Natascha has packed her bags and moved on to some other sap in some other city willing to listen to her drivel. Probably back to London. There are a lot of gullible people down there, I know, I've seen many episodes of *Cowboy Builders*. According to Ryan, she and Tony had a blazing row after the Fag Hag Pageant – she was disgusted by Tony's performance and put her coming last squarely on his shoulders.

'She didn't even say goodbye,' said Gwen, rubbing an aching tummy (her stomach has been troublesome since Saturday night's drinking during the competition). 'I didn't expect her to jump for joy when I won, but I like to think, because we shared the same womb at some point, she would find it within her heart to replenish the food in my cupboards she has been fortunate enough to digest over the past few weeks.' She unzipped the worn beige cardigan she wears while lolling around her room and revealed her prized. It's a T-shirt identifying her as 'The Ultimate Fag Hag' printed in pink. She sighed and pulled the T-shirt tight for me to read clearly, 'But I guess it was worth it, just for this. Oh, and to see the back of the bitch,' she grinned.

It seems our shy neighbour is finally growing a pair.

11.50 p.m. One hour of general chat; two hours of edging; thirty seconds of intense orgasm; zero hours spent talking over the public sex issue with my man. I'm so easily distracted by amazing sex, it's disgusting

Wednesday 10th November

Things are getting desperate. I can't find a venue that is both classy and free for the stag on Friday. Ryan will kill me. I've fallen on the mercy of Molasses yet again. She's willing to close Café Jamaica early on the promise I can get a minimum of forty people to come to the party. I assured her I already had forty guaranteed while vowing mentally to copy Ryan's contacts somehow from his phone.

When I asked cheekily if she could cater as well, she sighed and said, 'I suppose you want me to bake a "Wave Goodbye To Your Freedom" cake too?' I put on my best smile and nodded. 'Oh, okay, but we have to make a good return. I'll tell chef Barry to put extra salt in the food to give them such a drouth they'd drink Lake Superior dry.'

So classy is out and rustic Jamaican is in. What's not to love?

******

Later, I begged Sally to find a male stripper, and I'd meet the expense. 'Any expense, as long as they can be there on the night to deliver the goods for thirty minutes at least.' I stressed, 'I do *not* want the average "straight-guy-next-door" type.'

'Hmmm ... muscled doesn't seem to be his thing,' she mused.

'No, but I don't think a Tony doppelgänger would go down well with the crowd, do you?'

Sally pondered this and nodded her agreement. 'Don't you worry, my frantic little friend, leave it to the great Ms Knowles. I know just the chap looking for extra cash. He's straight, possibly, and doesn't mind a little man-on-man contact. And as for the pampering session, look no further, I've been educating myself on the art of relaxing massage via Youtube. I'm sure I can set up a makeshift therapy room here.'

I thanked her, although I'm aware she has the delicate touch of a navvy, but I've little choice as I need to be frugal. She'll do. He'll have to like it or lump it, and if my previous massage from Sally is anything to go by, he'll have plenty lumps by the end of it to lump it with. But the relief I felt was short-lived when I contemplated the lateness of the hour and my inability to catch Ryan before he headed to the ballet with his husband-to-be. I confessed to Sally I was desperate to gain access to Ryan's mobile to botch together some kind of guest list by tomorrow afternoon.

'Oh, honey, that's the easy part,' assured Sally. 'The lad has a smartphone and spends most of his time downloading *this* song and *that* app, always pressing keys to purchase from the ever-growing iTunes store. Keys to very private codes and passwords. And, being a creature of habit, he seems to have the recall for only three passwords in total. And if someone with a photographic memory can gain the occasional glance while his keypad is in action, someone like a subtle waitress, then these details could easily be popped into another's computer, and all that delightful information could be downloaded from their Facebook page.' She dropped the needle on her record player with such smugness you would think she had just discovered the cure for cancer. As Barbara Streisand crackled into existence and began to sing *The Man I Love,* I was willing to believe she could've done as much (the curing cancer; she's incapable of loving any man – Sally, not Barbra).

I couldn't stop grinning. 'And do you know of such a waitress?'

She flipped open our shared device and cracked her fingers in anticipation. 'Watch and learn, kiddo. Watch and learn.' Within the hour we'd sent invites to at least sixty of Ryan's nearest and dearest. Sally poured herself a glass of bourbon and drew heavily on a cigarette. She exhaled, clasped the cigarette between gritted teeth, and said, 'I love it when a plan comes together.'

'How's the ankle?' I asked, noticing she was striding around in heels once more.

'Bliss, darling! I have the most irresistible supply of Tramadol provided by the newsagent on the corner. On the hush-hush, you understand. I can barely feel the pain, and it gives me the most wonderful tingling sensation on my lips.' Her eyes widened, and she smirked, '*Both* sets.'

I thanked her and bid her a hasty goodnight.

Thursday 11th November

I had trouble locating my toothbrush in Alistair's bathroom last night. The glass I'd placed it in last week was empty apart from some toothpaste and floss. After some raking through cupboards, I found it tucked inside a brown leather toilet bag at the back of the cabinet under the sink. I assume Dominica must've tucked my brush away in this bag believing it to be Alistair's travel toothbrush. I'd like to enlighten her soon, but it's not my place to talk to the staff as of yet. Instead, I settled for a small visual statement and placed it back in the aforementioned glass in plain view. She'll get the message eventually. I've little respect for her anyway. I've noticed, after she 'cleans' his place, the loo brush is dry, and the porcelain below the water level of his toilet is grey from a week's worth of use. And as for her ability to wipe down a dirty skirting, I'm beginning to wonder if she has limbs at all. Things will change when I move in. She may have to go if she can't come up to my standards.

I also found a small bottle of essential oils, which might have gone off. I'm not sure what scent they were as there's no label on the little brown bottle, but they stank to high heaven and made my pulse race when I sniffed them. I was tempted to throw them away, but I screwed the lid on tightly and popped them back in the bag. I hope Alister never treats me to a massage with this or I'll stink like a cat's litter tray all week!

8p.m. I now have a complete guest list of forty-two people, evenly divided between males and females. I know none of them, bar the usual crowd from weekly dance torture. Ryan popped into the café to check on my progress. I told him the bulk of it's organised.

'The bulk? What is there left to organise?' he fussed.

'Don't you worry,' I said. 'It'll be the biggest event of the LGBTQ community this year.'

'LGBTQ?' he asked.

I was astounded I had to explain to one of the most entrenched members of the gay scene what every single letter stood for. That pink bubble they live inside is thicker than I imagined. 'How could you not know this?' I asked, almost dropping a tray of Jackfruit Casserole on his Prada shoes. 'You are the epitome of a seasoned dancing queen. ABBA wrote that song preempting your teenage years. You have a rainbow flag hanging in your hallway. You did drag at the age of eighteen and have joined the community on their float at every Pride march since. How can it be you don't know what LGBTQ stands for?'

Ryan smoothed every crease out of his clothes and fixed his hair as he usually does when feeling uneasy. 'Well, it's never come up until now. Thank you very much for making me feel like an ignorant savage,' he said, adjusting his shirt collar that was already perfectly crisp and pointy. 'Besides, I may be gay, but I don't have to become a bore and join every political movement. Stonewalk was years ago.'

'Stone-wall,' I stressed.

'Walk, wall, mall, who gives a shit?' he raised his arms dramatically and flapped his hands at me as if I was an annoying wasp. 'And you're wrong, Andy Angus. The biggest event of the *gay* community this year will be *my* wedding. I'll see you at four tomorrow when I hope you will be less argumentative.'

He left under a thunderous cloud.

'A civil partnership, not a wedding, which the LGBTQ community and others tirelessly fought for, you ungrateful ignoramus,' I called once he was well out of earshot.

Friday 12th November

My Birthday.

It's never a good sign when the first person to wish you a happy birthday is your cat. It's not as if I've advertised the fact I'm now thirty-six years old (even older if you count the nine months in my mother's now discarded uterus) and want the attention, it's just a little disconcerting when your cat continues to neb in on your life and pass the occasional remark, or worse, monologue. One more year towards becoming that crazy cat lady, I guess. I thanked him anyway, just before my head raised from the cushion on the sofa and he scurried up the fire escape to catch some rat with wings.

I'd fallen asleep while watching *Torchwood* – an excellent spin-off from *Doctor Who*. Being the wrong side of thirty means this nodding off in front of the box is becoming a habit. I usually manage to catch the end credits, but this was new: a full night on the couch. It's pretty tragic as I live in a bedsit, and my bed is less than two meters away.

I got up, made myself a coffee and opened the cards from Mum, which were manly cards depicting sporting activities (football, race cars, etc.) except one. It said 'To My Gay Son', which made my heart melt. Inside it read, 'Enjoy Being Queen For The Day!' Which impressed me less. One of my nephews has heavy-handedly drawn a large '6' in purple crayon next to the number three on a card obviously for a three-year-old. Again, there's a picture of some footballer with a mullet and a strip that was in season over fifteen years ago. He's tackling the ball and is mid-pirouette as if Rudolf Nureyev has stumbled into the wrong performance.

The parcel Mum sent has almost arrived. An 'attempted' delivery note was found crumpled between the inner and outer flaps of our letterbox at 5 p.m. I've been in all afternoon. This is a downright lie. The buzzer and doorbell are fully functional. The postman/woman/person obviously can't be bothered carrying such a, what I imagine to be, large parcel up the three flights of stairs, and would rather take time out of *my* busy day and have me walk all the way to *their* depot. When Mum called to wish me a happy birthday, in amongst the stockpile of grievances she reported about living with Dad, I told her my present had failed to materialise. 'I suspect it's never left the sorting office,' I bitched.

'Don't be so damn silly, Andy,' she bit back. 'Your telly was probably up too loud. The Royal Mail is one of the best postal services in the world. I've no idea where you get this suspicious nature from.'

That's rich coming from the woman who doesn't trust the bagless vacuum cleaner. She puts Dyson, and the such, down to the rise in asthmatics in the U.K. Smoking twenty fags a day in front of your grandchildren on the hush-hush at your daughter's house is, of course, just fine and entirely harmless.

'I have to wait 48 hours before my gift is ready to be collected, which, as Sunday is looming, will be Monday morning before I can see what it is. I wonder how many more crumpled notices I'll find around Christmas and what tremendous journeys your Royal Mail will be sending me on. I wonder how many children up and down the U.K. will learn that Santa is actually a sadist in a red van.'

Silence from my mum. Then, 'You're fast becoming a grumpy old man, Andrew Angus.' She hung up.

Anyway, birthday aside, today is about Ryan's stag, and I should focus on that. I've invited Alistair again but, judging by his groan and the sudden tension in his skull (his ears pull tightly in towards the back of his neck when he's stressed), I shouldn't hold my breath. I think I have everything in place. Better get my slap on.

Saturday 13th November

11 a.m. The day after the night before.

Stag nights are more tricky than I imagined. Massaged to the point of becoming a tender piece of loin, I helped Ryan to dress in his lovely (but cheaper) clothes for a night of fun and frolics, totally free of charge and at the expense of his closest friends. He winced as I helped tuck his arm into the sleeve of a D&G shirt I could only dream of affording as a unique feature in my wardrobe, let alone a cheap substitute, and said, 'I hope this isn't a sign of what disappointments are to come, Andy. That woman has the paws of a hippo and the talons of Dolly Parton. How she wipes her own arse, I've no idea. The most chilled thing in that room was your cat, not me.' I quickly thrust a cosmo in his hand and spirited him out of the door before Sally got an inkling of his aggravation. I made him drink it just outside the main entrance to be sure his bitching didn't resonate up the stairs.

Our lift to the café was thirty minutes late, which amused him less as we were now caught in a freak downpour. Sally joined us and confidently popped up a golfing umbrella that garishly advertised Madam Yo-Yo's. Ryan looked up and grimaced at the silhouette of the club branding and the topless go-go girl. 'And what is this travesty?'

'It's from the club, darling. A clever piece of marketing and very handy in Scotland; businessmen who get their balls out on the golf course need to know they can get their balls out at ours too, as they're the bread and butter of pole dancers up and down the country.'

Ryan moved out from under the brolly and chose to stand several feet away from us in the rain. Thankfully, we were in the pink limo within a minute. I figured my dripping wet stag was stony-faced due to the deluge, but I was wrong, he was pissed-off because of the chosen mode of transport. 'You know I *detest* anything pink,' he finally volunteered after supping on cava with his nostrils pulsating like a pug's. 'In what crazy parallel universe did you think I would enjoy a ride around town in a car with a sunroof from which partying slags usually flash their tits?'

I said nothing, neither did Sally, we sat and 'admired' the decor. Suddenly the flashing lights, little mirror-balls, pink furry seats and Donna Summer's *Bad Girls* seemed totally tacky. When we picked up Gwen from her temp job at Baillie Gifford's, things became more ridiculous as she was dressed in full Princess Fiona costume, top-to-toe in green *Shrek* body paint.

'What the hell are you wearing?' I said under my breath as I handed her a glass of warm cava and ushered her into the car.

'What? You said gay icons, did you not? She is a gay icon, no?'

'No, she's not. Jesus, you could've chosen Madonna, or anything else close to normality.'

'Oh, great,' said Ryan, smiling through gritted teeth, 'it's fancy dress too. Sheer bliss.'

For a guy who hates pink limousines so venomously he took an age to get out of the car when we arrived at Café Jamaica. 'This is it?' he said dryly from the car window. 'For my stag, you have brought me to a place I use practically every day for a caffeine shot?' We smiled and nodded keenly into the car. He sank back into the fur and slid the tinted window up in denial.

Sally banged on the window, rattling her rings on the pane so hard it caused some concern on the driver's part that she may chip the glass. The window was dropped again by the anxious chauffeur. Sally leaned into the car, 'Now look, you ungrateful shit, there's a pile of poofs and the such in there waiting to celebrate your last night of freedom, which may end prematurely if you piss me off further and I'm forced to remove both of your balls and tiny cock as well.'

Ryan pouted, 'It's not "tiny".' He let out a resigned sigh and got out of the car. 'And what have you come as, Sally? A moody bitch?'

'No dear, that's you,' she chirped back. She placed her hands on her hips and announced proudly, 'I've come as myself. I'm already a gay icon in these parts. You simply can't improve on perfection.'

'The jury's still out, darling,' said Ryan. 'Okay, let's get this disaster over with as quickly as possible.

The place erupted when he stepped in, and Ryan played the part by smiling, nodding and hugging in demure appreciation. He turned to me and whispered, 'Who are half of these people?' As it turned out, I'd inadvertently invited a bunch of freeloaders who were only friends of his friends on Facebook. He occasionally stalks these random people online, just for the sheer nosiness of it, and had no intention of letting them in on his real life. Serves the nosey bugger right!

It took six shots of tequila, and a piece of 'special cake' baked by Molasses before the boy's puss turned from curdled milk to creamy satisfaction. By the time Sally's stripper arrived, Ryan, or rather 'Dusty Springfield' as he had been transformed into at this point, was having a ball and impersonating her perfectly as *You Don't Have To Say You Love Me* played on the old jukebox. My job was done. At last Ryan had defrosted and didn't give a damn.

He needed sparse encouragement to lay on the floor and have the well-stacked 'fireman' bow his shiny helmet over him. Even less persuasion to lick aerosol cream from the tanned skinned man's perky nipples. By the time our fireman took off his helmet, to protect his manhood from our eager gaze as he yanked off his bulging thong, the stag was a sloppy, creamy mess of excitement and inappropriate touching. I began to wonder if Ryan could actually be faithful to a poorly sealed bottle of acidity like Tony. The stripper fought to pull Ryan's hands away as he tried to pry them into the cavity of the helmet now acting as a codpiece. Ryan grunted and squealed on the floor. He was a cross between a greedy ape and an excited adolescent. It was then, with the helmet off and our stripper facing us, that I realised exactly who he was. Everything seemed to stop when we clocked one another.

'Andy?' exclaimed our entertainer in a thick Irish accent.

I blinked in disbelief, 'Nash?'

Ryan's perseverance was rewarded when the shiny gold helmet was easily torn from our stunned stripper's grip and flung to the jeering crowd. Nash's meat flopped either side of his bulging thighs coated in that lovely thick, dark hair, shading every striation of muscle as beautifully as the contours on an ordinance survey map. Nash smiled at me with such cockiness it rekindled the lust I had for him with one wink from his Irish eyes. Molasses, who was ready in the wings with a white terry-towelling housecoat, covered the lad up and announced the show was over. She looked down at a hysterical Ryan and joked, 'Please, dear. Go clean up. It looks as if you have been raped by a sperm whale.'

I tried my best to clamber through the throng to catch my former gym trainer, but he'd already taken his money and run. Sally's words from Wednesday hung in my ears, 'I know just the chap looking for extra cash. He's straight, probably, and doesn't mind a little man-on-man contact.'

The night rolled on, and we had no need for handcuffs to restrain the bride-to-be as she was so wasted by midnight she couldn't move from her perch, half sitting, half bowed over the arm of the sofa. 'Is he okay?' asked Gwen, wide-eyed as if she'd never seen anyone so intoxicated before, 'He is very, very drunk.'

'No, dear,' said Molasses, 'he's, what we call, *glued.*'

Collectively we made the decision to return Ryan to Tony in one piece, be it with added beehive and heels. I used my last tenner to deliver my floppy friend to his husband-to-be and, as neither Gwen nor I had any cash left, we chose to walk home from there (Sally had been held back to help Molasses clear up). We'd just got to Elm Row when a red Mini pulled up alongside, and a cheery Irish voice called, 'Do any of you girls want a lift?'

'Hey, Nash,' I said, trying to keep my cool, removing my stetson and spinning it clumsily on one finger as I rested my hand on the side of his car. 'Aye, that sounds great.'

'Why? We only live nine minutes walk from here,' complained Gwen.

'Gwen, you look like the Incredible Hulk's wife. We'll take it!' I chirped.

Sitting next to the lad in the car was sheer joy and torture all rolled into one. It hadn't escaped my attention that he was buffer than ever. However, Gwen spent those precious few minutes of our journey with her green head chattering away between the headrests. I wished she wasn't quite so drunk and sociable any more. I could feel Nash's forearm brushing my right leg every time he changed gear. I was a wreck by the time we arrived at 323.

'Well, Nash. I'm sure there's nothing more you'd like for us to do but sit and chat a bit longer,' presumed Gwen (Us? It'd mostly been her!), 'but this lad has had a very full day and needs his beauty sleep.'

'No, no, I'm fine,' I protested, feeling my chance of one night admiring this Adonis slipping away from me.

'Yes, that's what you say just now, but you'll thank me in the morning,' she insisted, pulling the car door open for me and tugging me out by my arm with all the strength of a lumberjack.

'No, no, I won't,' I whined.

'Yes, you will. You were just saying the other day how restless your nights have been. Bye, Nash, you handsome devil. And thanks again.'

Nash looked bemused and amused, 'No bother. Hope to see you again soon,' he said, smiling broadly at me with a nod.

'Yes, thank you. Bye!' Gwen said at the same time she shut the car door.

I was frogmarched into the stair with very little time to see Nash's tail lights drive away.

'Gwen, I think you may have just given me blue balls,' I sighed as we made our way up the stair.

'What's that?'

'I'll explain when you're older and wiser, but for now, I'll let you know it's very, very painful.'

4.15 p.m. I've come to realise that I'm not just an emotional yo-yo right now, but I'm also a sexual yo-yo too. I shouldn't be craving sex with an Irish PT/stripper while I'm having fantastic sex with a Scottish mechanic/businessman. I have to focus on one man. The man that gives me all those reassuring hugs at night. Not a sometimes smoothed leg hunk. Yes, that's it! Nash's sometimes smooth, yet muscular, womanly legs. I'll focus on that.

Birthday Sex: zero.
Productivity: zero, spent the day on the sofa immersed in 1960s Doctor Who.
Cold pizza from the previous night consumed: three slices.
Late Birthday Sex: on it; heading to Alistair's now.

I'm so lazy, fat and fickle.

Sunday 14th November

'Thank you, very much, Andy!' came the pithy voice down the line as I woke in the arms of my slave. 'Tony is really pissed-off with those disgusting pictures pasted all over Facebook.' I slid up on the pillows in an attempt to rouse my bleary head. Everything, including myself, was askew after a night of passion brought on by a horny subservient in desperate need of satisfaction. I'd no idea what Ryan was nagging about. 'Why don't you check them out?' he said. 'They've been posted publicly by my supposed "carefully selected friends" *you* invited.'

'I'm sorry, Ryan. I'd no idea,' I said, trying to calm him down.

'Have a look, then maybe you'd understand the implications of how far this kind of tagging can spread. Tony's grandmother, whom I love and respect, is in a state-of-the-art care home and has an iPad attached to her headboard. There wasn't enough Trazodone liquid in her *As Required* bottle to calm her into a peaceful slumber last night. She spent the entire time trying to escape from the home to catch the first flight to Edinburgh. If she breaks her hip, Tony's holding you personally responsible, thank you very much.'

I bit my tongue and apologised again. I explained the problems involved in arranging a stag do at such short notice. 'I did the best I could.'

'Not good enough, Andy. You had months! Half the people were strangers, and now there's an online furore from the real friends you failed to invite. Congratulations, you may have managed to ruin not only my stag but my wedding too.'

'Surely you mean to say, *our* wedding?' I corrected him. 'It's Tony's day as well.'

Alistair stirred next to me, stuffed his face into the pillow, and said without care, 'Oh, for fuck's sake, hang up on the spoilt wee shit! I have to get to the garage by nine this morning, and I'm still cuffed to this bed.'

I covered the phone with my hand and shushed him. He rattled the handcuffs and nodded towards them. His left wrist was creased and red from a night spent under my control.

There was a pause at the end of the line. Then, in a low lone, 'Who the blazes was that?'

I made my excuses and hung up, but I'm sure I heard Ryan say, 'Is that who I think it is, Andy?'

I freed my slave willingly after the cat may or may not have been released from the bag. I've given Ryan's postcode a total body-swerve today.

Monday 15th November

I picked up my gift from the post office this afternoon after an eternity waiting for the chap on the deserted service desk to show face. I rang the buzzer that was loosely sellotaped to the counter so many times I had to apply alcohol gel thoroughly to my index finger on the way out (if iPads can be supplied to pensioners, why can't the Post Office provide a properly installed buzzer?).

'Sorry,' said the breathless but cheery chap. 'I thought you were someone else.'

'What, another valued customer, perhaps?' I said dryly.

He checked my driving licence and chuckled.

I explained, 'I had a skin infection when it was taken, which left me inflamed for weeks and necessitated the application of topical antibiotics four times a day to my lower lip and chin.'

'You look just like my wee kid after he's been suckin' on a raspberry jubilee.' He laughed and coughed sharply in succession, then swallowed hard and composed himself before he reached hypoxia. He disappeared for a few seconds and returned more breathless than before. He must be ill, he wasn't away long enough to use a stepladder, not even a small stool on wheels.

When he slid the package towards me, I couldn't help but notice it was disappointingly book-shaped. I was disgusted. 'I'm no expert,' I said tersely, 'but I can imagine this would slide through my letterbox with ease.'

'Seems not. Your postie would only return it if he had trouble.'

'What trouble? Did he try to post it face forward?'

'Perhaps yer flap is heavily spring-loaded, they've a load of issues with health and safety regarding stubborn letterboxes and won't take the risk. We cannae afford to insure every single finger, you see. No on our wages.'

I trudged to work, but not before I turned towards the depot and showed them my fully-functioning digit. It was rather unfortunate a shocked priest had just got out of his car and assumed my minor protest was directed towards him.

******

I opened the package in the café. It is a hardback by Professor Brian Cox: *Wonders of the Universe*. On the first page, was written, 'To my wee boy, who used to dream of the stars. Love, Mum.'

I bit back tears.

Sally popped up from the kitchen grinning. 'Did you see those fantastic pictures of Ryan on Facebook? Outrageous!' she revelled. She noticed my gift as she tied her money pouch around her waist. 'What's that, kiddo?'

I slid the book towards her, 'It's a gift from my mum. She may be a hard cow at times, but she cares, I suppose. I used to dream about the vastness of the universe. I would lay down the glen next to our scheme with my best friend –she had skint knees, was called Lisa and peed in my paddling pool once, but that's beside the point. We would stay out late just to watch the stars. We'd hide from our mothers' calls to come in and freeze our backs to the ground in winter in the hope of seeing a falling star.

'We'd imagine where we'd go if we could escape the daily drudgery of school, concrete and Crispy Pancakes. We'd dream about what was out there, make up stories of other planets with weird aliens, certain, because Hubble told us so, that there were far more stars and planets out there than we could ever imagine. More to life than just kicking around a council scheme.'

Sally checked in at the till and asked me, 'Have you been on the sauce, sweetie?'

'No, I'm sober as a judge.'

'Honey, that isn't saying much; I know a few judges. Besides, aliens. Ha! There's no such thing.'

'But you must think there's more to life than this?'

'I don't care for stargazing,' she dismissed with a flick of her locks. 'Here-and-now is all that matters. I couldn't give a damn what's happening on other planets circling a star billions of lightyears away in a corner of the universe I'll never see. I have enough on my plate. Don't be daft, Andy. No one gives a shit about that stuff; it's all selfies, hashtags and celebrities nowadays.'

She's wrong. I called Mum tonight and thanked her.

11 p.m. WTF?! I had no idea Pluto had been downgraded to 'dwarf planet' status. When did this happen? It's an outrage!

Tuesday 16th November

I think I may be obsessed with the BBC weatherman Tomasz Schafernaker. I rushed to the telly every time I heard his tones rattling through the bleak weather forecast on News 24. I did a quick Google search and found that he has appeared in *Gay Times* in nothing more than a pair of black shorts. And, glory be! He is *buff!* It quite distracted me from my bran flakes. It wouldn't be so bad if he didn't deliver the forecast with such a cheeky grin at every patch of fog or frost predicted in the U.K. He cycles to work, according to the *Gay Times*, and likes to eat healthily. I figure he does more than that to get such a fit body. I caught sight of my own sad form in the mirror. The legs and butt are doing fine, better than fine actually, but the rest of me is rather toneless and goes south from the waist up. That's 50% of me classed as undesirable. I called the gym and arranged a 'Return To Fitness' training session tomorrow. Who knows, I may even be trained by someone from the Irish Republic.

I was late for work due to the careless clarity of the BBC Breakfast News presenters. 'In a few moments, we'll be hearing from Tomasz Schafernaker with the weather ...'

Moments? How long is a moment? Is it worth sticking around for the next ten minutes? You are useless, Bill Turnbull. Fifteen minutes is not 'a few moments', it's cocking ages!

11 p.m. I've just had the most aggressive session with Alistair yet. I fear I may have left him a little battered and bruised. He seems to be proud of the pain I've inflicted and carries his lashed buttocks like a badge of honour. He said, 'I'll feel you every time I sit down.' I think of him all the time. I want him to do the same for me, not just when he pulls up a chair.

I adore the man and the passion he stirs in me, but I'm not sure where these scenarios will take us, or what they're turning me into. When I catch a fit man bent over in public, I get the most unacceptable notion to smack his backside hard as I pass. My mind is becoming a belligerent version of a *Carryon* film. I've taken to sliding my hands into my pockets to act as a small form of restraint.

Wednesday 17th November

Just watched the full ITN interview of Prince William and Kate Middleton discussing their engagement. I was excited until they talked about the rock on her finger. William has given Kate his mother's engagement ring. An uneasy feeling washed over me and stayed with me for the rest of their optimistic chat. I wouldn't be happy wearing that. How could you feel confident in having a long and joyous life together wearing the ring of a divorced princess who was hounded by the paparazzi to her death in a French tunnel? I would be hard pushed to say yes, no matter how lovely William is in speedos, how many glistening solitaire diamonds there are, or how blue the sapphire is. The Queen will look at it every time, and her mouth will flinch in that awkward royal way, as it so often does when she is forced to meet the likes of Freddie Star in the line up of a Royal Command Performance.

In non-engagement related news: Alistair is becoming obsessed with group scenes on the big screen of his home cinema (almost as obsessed as I am to BBC weather reports). We spent part of the evening mutually masturbating between a 'cumpilation' of men in various cuts of porn movies, all involving three-ways or four-gys. I enjoy it to a point (I must do, I'm erect throughout), even his breathy plans of what parties we could arrange and what we could do to our male guests, as well as what they could do to us, turn me on. But this is fantasy and, as we know from previous experience, fantasy and reality don't sleep in the same bed. He says as much afterwards, but I can't help feeling he's checking my reaction and pushing the envelope each time. I wonder if I agreed to what may be inevitable, what could be the worst to happen? No, monogamy is what I want, with him. But it's tough to argue your point when you have a former rugby player sat behind you, his thick thighs pressed against yours, licking your ears and stroking both nipples at the same time. I gave in, climaxed and settled into his nook for the rest of the night. I'll make him want me and me alone.

Thursday 18th November

Alistair brought up the subject of age difference in relationships over our usual healthy breakfast (orange juice; grapefruit segments; low-fat yoghurt; and boring bran). I said the classic, 'Age is just a number.'

'Is it though, Andy? I'm not as young as that Tomasz guy off the weather you keep banging on about,' he said, a little sourly.

I came up behind him and tickled his ribs, jibing him with, 'Oooooh, is this jealousy I see in your eyes for the first time?'

He pulled my hands off him and moved away to rinse his bowl, 'You know, sometimes when you talk about TV shows on BBC Three, I have no clue what you're on about.' Then he nodded to his groin and added, 'And I have no idea how much longer this little soldier will keep charging forward.' He has nothing to worry about there; he has the libido of a Playboy Mansion pool boy.

I asked him, 'Well, how old was your wife?'

He replied, 'Forty-three. We both like The Archers on Radio Four and love trolling around garden centres on Sundays.'

Like? Love? Surely he meant this in the past tense? He zoned me out for a time and looked deep in thought, which did nothing for my anxiety over losing him. I left with my stomach churning like a washing machine thrashing a bowl of decaying fruit in clotted cream. How can I compete with his misspent but obviously happier past? And surely he knows the wonderful Tomasz Schafernaker is blissfully unaware of my lust for him and totally unattainable, delicious though he is.

11p.m. Back at Alistair's apartment.

I decided to tell Alistair about my recently muted birthday in the hope that adding another year to my physical and mental being will calm his woes. It may have done just that as he said, 'Och, you shouldn't listen to me. I'm just feeling a bit lost today. I've no idea where I'm heading.' Which means, as a result, I have no idea where *we* are heading either. 'Why didn't you tell me it was your birthday, you plonker?' he asked, wrapping his arms tightly around my shoulders.

'Thirty-six isn't a special birthday,' I said.

'Nonsense, every birthday you have is special.' He turned me around and kissed me on the forehead. 'This deserves a wee night out. Just you and me. Leave it with me, eh?'

I smiled and nodded but was thinking at the same time, *How could it be anyone else but just you and me? You're still hiding in the closet.* Anyway, I shouldn't grumble. It gives me some hope that he may even feel as strongly as I do. 'What you got in mind?' I asked.

'A surprise or two. As I said: leave it with me.' He kissed the back of my head hard and patted me on the shoulders. He stank of manliness as he hadn't showered since today's shift, all oil, grease and sweat. I became slightly aroused by both his mechanic stench and his devotion to making me happy. He was going to shower, but I wanted him to stay filthy and paw me with his dirty, calloused hands until I was just as soiled.

He got the message.

Friday 19th November

Home from drinks at The Dome with Ryan, Tony, Sally and Gwen. It ended on a downer for me. While peeing at the urinal, Tony appeared next to me and said, 'Don't worry, your secret's safe with me.'

I glanced over and tried hard not to catch sight of his – as I imagine – ugly penis, and asked, 'What are you blabbing on about?'

'You and Alistair, and all the naughty things you're up to.' I looked at him in shock, keeping my eyes level with his. He was grinning with delight. 'Don't worry, I won't breathe a word to anyone.' He shook his willy, and I heard his fly being pulled up with the confidence of a tennis player who'd just won their last match. He washed his hands painfully slow. I stayed rooted to the spot, unable to move or continue peeing. He dried his hands briskly with a swagger. I watched his back from the corner of my eye. I felt my face get hotter with every puff of air from the machine as my willy shrivelled up. It'd practically disappeared when Tony walked up behind me and peered over my shoulder. He tutted, 'Oh, dear,

Andrew. I expected more from you. You say you have your hands full, and yet, you've nothing to show for it. You're a very busy boy, and no one really knows why. Except me.' He laughed. It echoed off the tiles. He slapped my shoulder, which made me jump, and said, 'So let's be friends from now on, eh? You keep the peace, do as I say and agree to whatever my husband-to-be wants for our wedding, cut out all the moaning at rehearsals, and I'll keep it all nice a quiet.

'You're asking a lot,' I croaked.

'Oh, Andrew. Nothing's impossible. Ryan would be so disappointed to learn you were messing around with that married man again. You'd lose him. You know how *moral* he is on such matters. I know that you're pretty much here to stay, god knows why Ryan fawns over you, but I figure I may as well use it to my advantage while you're around. On this one occasion.' He turned on his heels. His shoes squeaked on the floor as he made for the exit. 'Do the right thing, even if you are screwing up someone else's life, stop screwing up ours.' I heard the door bang and looked around. He was gone. I finished peeing and left without saying goodnight.

I haven't gone to Alistair's. I'm back at 323. I don't feel like sex tonight. Not at all. How can the bitch possibly know?

Saturday 20th November

8.30 a.m.

That vicious little gnome of a boyfriend of his has blabbed all, I know it. Ryan called and asked, 'Can we meet? I need to talk to you as soon as possible. It's urgent.'

'What's this about?' I asked with a lump in my throat.

'I'm not willing to discuss it on the phone.'

He never calls so early on a Saturday. They're rarely up before 11 a.m. I guess Tony just couldn't wait to stick his filthy claws into my hairy back.

11.45 a.m. I met Ryan in the top floor café of John Lewis. If he was about to air my dirty linen in public, I wanted it as far away from friends and gossipy queens as possible. The place was filled by cloned elderly women; all short, permed and grey, and hopefully too deaf to eavesdrop on a good friend ditching his best mate due to his loose morals regarding the sanctity of marriage.

Ryan was tucked behind an advert for the John Lewis Wedding Registry. *Very apt*, I thought, as my buttocks clenched and my anus cork-screwed tighter. His face was as ashen and stone-like as a soldier from the terracotta army of Emperor Qin, so I figured I was in for a rough ride.

How to approach a polar breeze? I always feel a casual 'Hey!' works best. This was met by the same frosty tone as before. My next question regarding food was met with, 'No thanks, I had a small raspberry yoghurt an hour ago, and now I have heartburn.'

Dodgy ground prevailed with an equally hesitant silence between the two of us. Ryan took deep inhales of breath as if he was about to say something, but couldn't.

'Maybe I'll just get a coffee,' I said as I stood and rattled the change in my pocket.

Ryan grabbed my hand, tugged it gently and blurted, 'No, please stay a second. I need to say this. If I don't, I think I may haemorrhage all over this table, or attack the next woman who coughs uncontrollably for another ten minutes over their breakfast.' A pensioner wearing a purple Alice-band at the next table coughed and fought to hold in loose-fitting dentures. 'For Christ's sake, woman,' snapped Ryan, 'who on Earth tackles a fruit and nut flapjack over the age of seventy? Do you have a death-wish?'

I apologised, calmed him and moved him to a quieter spot, away from octogenarians and infants, towards a view of our much loved Calton Hill. Sitting him down gently, I took a deep breath and asked, 'Okay, what's wrong? Have I pissed you off?'

'What? No, dear. It's not you. It may have taken me a while, but I've totally forgiven you for the stag disaster. I never hold a grudge, especially if the intentions were good, if not a little misguided. I'm not a monster, Andy.'

I sank back in the chair, relieved. 'Then what is it?'

Tears filled Ryan's eyes. Could it be that he had finally realised he absolutely and positively does not want to marry a man with as much taste and charisma as a cucumber? Had he discovered Tony had been having an affair with the postie? Or, had Prada gone bust? 'It's this wedding, you see,' he said between gasps for air.

'Yes?' I said, eager in the hope of a late cancellation. My part in their dreadful dance show was being erased in my mind's eye already.

'It's just getting too big for me.'

Oh, that. Is that all? I thought.

He continued, laying out a pile of anxieties, mounting them up one on top of the other, 'I feel like I'm living in someone else's timetable. Running to catch it up, actually. There are questions I hadn't even thought of. I mean, the wedding planner at the hotel asked me if we wanted to feed the band. I hadn't given it a thought. Should we? Is that etiquette? And then there's the cake. Tony wants to save some money, so he's asked Mum to transport the cake across town as it costs one pound per mile to have it moved by the baker. I mean, how little could that be on top of a considerable budget already? It's an exact reproduction of the Taj Mahal and very delicate ...'

'Why the Taj Mahal?' I found myself interrupting.

'It's where I proposed to him? When we were on holiday two years ago to the day?' He said this as if I should've known. 'It won't stand the journey in the back of a Smart Car at the hands of a nervous pensioner. There's only so many speed-bumps and sudden stops marzipan can take.'

I heard myself say, 'I'll pay for the transport of India's most loved jewel, don't worry.' What was I thinking? I'm just recovering from the wedding list fiasco.

He continued as if this was just the tip of his ever-approaching iceberg, 'And then there are the shoes. I totally forgot to get shoes. I haven't even looked at the blessed things. *Me,* forgetting about *shoes!* Shoes are my thing. I'm obviously not well. This shows the subliminal strain I've been under. And the licence in the hotel is until midnight, but the band is only booked to play until eleven. We still have to get gifts for the whole wedding party, and how do you buy for a mother-in-law who can buy anything she wants and is allergic to gold, silver, pollen, gluten, alcohol, dairy, nuts, perfume and seaweed?'

Now I know where Tony gets his fussiness from, I thought. 'Gift her a medical dictionary,' I joked.

Ryan remained ashen-faced. 'That is not amusing,' he said through quivering lips.

I straightened my face and apologised. He continued.

'What if the transport is late? What if yet another of the many couples invited break-up and ruin our already re, re, re and re-rearranged seating plan? What if the tracks don't play for the dances? Say I fall down the steps on the way to the ceremony? What if Tony doesn't want to marry me at all?'

'Okay, you need to calm down,' I told him. Ryan was beginning to hyperventilate. 'This is getting out of hand. There is an infinite number of things that could go wrong. Are you going to stress yourself into a crumpled heap in the corner of your lavish hotel room by the time the day actually arrives?'

Ryan held onto his mouth in an attempt to control his breathing and shook his head. Then I remembered something Steve would say when Ryan was charged with worry, 'Someone needs to stick a bag over that boy's head to get him to shut the fuck up.' I remembered, ever since my collapse in Tesco, that I was carrying a large paper bag. I produced it from my rucksack and covered Ryan's crimson and confused expression entirely.

Ryan remained motionless, stunned into sedation by his friend's irrational behaviour. 'I get the principle,' he mumbled from beneath the crumpled paper. 'A little unorthodox, however, suffocating me into serenity.'

'No, sensory deprivation,' I replied smugly. It seemed to be working already. Ryan lifted the bag over his chin, protesting that he looked silly and should take it off. 'Oh, no you don't! Not until I've told you a few facts.' He let go, and the bag fell back into place. 'Are you listening?' The bag nodded. 'Good, now listen to me. Are you really listening?' Mr Bag Head nodded again. 'It's all going to be okay. You have a truck-load of family and friends who'll be there to support you both and will walk over hot coals to be sure you marry this ... lovely man.' I mumbled the last two words as quickly as I could so that I could ignore the fact they fell from my own lips. 'And if small things do go wrong, so what! It's about the two of you being madly in love and celebrating that fact with loving friends and family. You don't need to do anything you don't want to. No one expects a song and dance, even though you've promised one or two, you just need to be there for each other on the day and tie the knot.'

Mr Bag Head crumpled forward several times in agreement and asked, 'Can I come out now? It's getting hot in here, and I fear my hair is asphyxiating on its lacquer.'

'No,' I said firmly – taking on a master's roll seems to encourage my assertiveness no end. 'There's something else I need to say.' Ryan was pleasantly quiet for the first time in weeks, probably knackered from the release of months of mental, drip-fed wedding torture. I seized my chance. I wasn't going to let my life be ruled by Biffo the Bear. If emotional honesty was what he was serving for breakfast, then I had my own slice to plop on the plate. 'I'm having a closeted affair with the closeted ex-rugby payer again.'

It was finally out there.

Mr Bag Head remained perfectly still. His chest rising and falling slowly as the only indication I hadn't actually smothered him. I became scared he was forming some kind of righteous opinion, but I thought, *In for a penny, in for a pink pound,* and continued, 'But he's single now and has been for months, so that's not so bad. And I think we may actually be becoming good for each other.'

'Okay,' he said cautiously.

'Also, I think I may be in love with him. So, I really need you to support me in this, because if it all goes tits-up, which it may do as I'm not sure he feels the same way, I'm going to need you to be there and listen, and not tell me you told me so. Because I get the feeling, this is bigger than I can handle right now.'

'Are you ready for something so soon after Thomas?'

'I don't know. That's the problem, you see. All I know is there's no one I can talk to about the good and bad involved other than you. I need a friend that isn't jaded by love, and you're it, I'm afraid.'

The bag nodded. Slowly at first. But then more enthusiastically. 'Okay, tell me all about this man of mystery. But with this ridiculous thing off my hairdo.'

I leant over and slipped the bag off his head. Ryan immediately picked up his mobile and turned the selfie camera on to checked his hair was still good to go in public. Once he was satisfied there had been no irreversible damage, he said, 'Okay, friend. I'm listening.'

I told the story of Alistair and Andy so far, and even though I'd been backed into a corner by Tony, it felt good to say his name out loud to someone who cared. Ryan listened intently, or at least seemed to, it could've just been light relief from his own woes. I don't care. It's out there now, only a fraction, but that fraction equals a considerable pile of comfort to me. Tony can say what he wants now. With every private detail I unveiled, every single word I uttered, his threat became weaker.

I'll help with their wedding as much as I can. I'll go that extra mile. I'll help my dear friend have the best day of his life. He may be getting hitched to an arsehole, but it's Ryan's special day too, and I won't crap all over that. I'll dance the merry dance without care or complaint. But this time I'm dancing to my own tune, not Tony's. I've asked Ryan to keep it to himself. He doesn't know that Tony thinks he has me over a barrel. I want to keep the twisted little shit guessing for a while.

A minor victory, but a victory no less.

Sunday 21st November

I attended dance class and didn't grumble once. I smiled and nodded politely, particularly at Tony, ignoring his acerbic comments. When I was encouraged to 'court more flamboyance' in my movements, or criticised for my lack of stability, I agreed and got on with it. I ignored the fact that Gwen selfishly ate practically half of Molasses' apple pie, leaving a tiny slither for me by the time I got to it. I ignored the 'secret' affair between Trenton and Melve; affairs are the business of those participating in the affair and no one else, I appreciate that.

Tony was quietly enjoying my subversive behaviour, until I told Ryan, 'Oh, I can't make drinks at your place tomorrow evening as I have one hell of a steamy date.'

'That's okay,' said my friend with a knowing wink, 'enjoy!'

Tony's lips curl inwards as he said, 'You know, I don't think Ryan appreciates being stood up for a random shag.'

But Ryan shushed him, 'Don't be silly, Pookie. Everyone needs their fun. You enjoy yourself.'

Poor bewildered Biffo.

Monday 22nd November

I returned to the gym for a short, breathless, sweaty session only, and surrendered myself to the jacuzzi. Chilling in it should've been relaxing, but not when a certain PT/stripper slides into the tub next to you in nothing more than a tight pair of speedos. Where's a boy to look other than the obvious? I became a bundle of nerves.

I could only manage a quick sideways glance and nod when he shot me an ebullient smiled and said, 'Good afternoon.' The next ten minutes were hormonal torture. If I made a sharp exit, I'd appear rude; if I soaked too long and remained tongue-tied, it'd seem I was ignorant. Nervous and aroused, I had no escape. The torment was maximised when the sound of the motors stopped, and the bubbles ceased. Silence is not golden. Why wasn't he leaving? God damn it! The bubbles had done their job. He obviously wasn't feeling an ounce of tension. We were now just sitting in a pool of warm water. This was getting silly, and I was pulsing all over.

There was only one thing for it. I had to leave first. I slipped my hand in the pocket of my shorts to tame my unruly stiffy and tried to launch myself out of the water as fast as my sluggish muscles would allow. I reached for the seat next to me to gain some leverage to push myself up with my free hand, but where I expected the feel of the smooth plastic tub, I felt the hair and skin of Nash's resting calf. I let go immediately and slipped under the water. Panic-stricken, I splashed around a bit, trying to gain some self-respect, and after inhaling and choking on some recycled water, mustered a quick, 'I'm sorry, goodbye,' before exiting bent over and whipping my towel hastily from the hook. Or so I thought. I looked such a fool drying off with some child's *Thomas the Tank Engine* towel.

What the hell is going on? I have Alistair now. I don't want anyone else. Wonderful, handsome, thick-thighed spooner Alistair. He's taking me out on a loving birthday date tonight. He is mostly perfect, but my silly willy seems to think very differently when it comes to the solidity of our relationship and the solidity of Nash's legs.

Tuesday 23rd November

The most unexpected development of the night was not the surprise sumptuous meal I experienced at Prestonfield House. It was not the copious volumes of cocktails we consumed at 1 a.m. in an exclusive private member's club on Princes Street. It was not the romantic walk home, holding hands without a care while taking the scenic route along Regent Road. No, the most interesting development of the night was the quick jaunt into the bushes not very far from

Regent Terrace. Alistair was horny, and I was pretty much swaying in the cold breeze due to several margaritas. He said he owed me some birthday fun and I was more malleable than dough at that point.

It was a bit frosty, but Alistair said it would be nostalgia for us. The only parts of me that stayed warm were my ankles, as my jeans were around them within minutes of staggering onto the darkened path. I soon experienced that nostalgic feeling of my knob chilling against the crisp breeze, and then the warmth of Alistair's mouth swallowing the lot, shocking me with his cockiness in a public space.

If I was unprepared for this, then I was even less prepared for the warm hand that appeared from nowhere and smoothed the erect hairs of my goose-pimpled ass. I jumped forward in shock, knocking Alistair on the forehead with my belly, which made him snigger and say, 'Will you calm down? The lad just wants to give us a hand.'

I remember turning and seeing the smiling face of a stranger. A personable, friendly face. Not what I expected in such a desperate part of the scene. I always thought it would be bustling with wrinkled pensioners, staggering to keep their zimmer frames upright on the uneven ground, demented with lust. But this was unexpected. A horny young man. Caressing me, adoring me, of all people.

Moments later, after much grunting and vapours of breath, we'd relieved one another and had barely the time or the inclination to bask in the afterglow. The street lights, the chilly night air, the passing cars, all that had added to the excitement, suddenly shamed me into reality. I pulled up my jeans in a shot and wanted so desperately to get as far away from that path as quickly as possible.

'Cheers, guys,' said the stranger as he carefully fastened the belt that had brazenly been chinking on the ground seconds before. 'It's crazy, eh? What we do for fun. I mean, we walk miles and miles in Baltic air for a quick release. What's that all about?' He gave a cheeky laugh as he patted me on my now well-covered bum and said, 'Great arse, by the way.' I thanked him, but his adoration just seemed cheap and nasty at that point. He nodded and went on his merry way. Deeply satisfied, I imagine.

Alistair seemed to have a spring in his step as we moved towards London Road. There was most definitely no pep in my step as it felt like the worst walk of shame of my life. Even though I was still obviously physically drunk, I was quietly sober in thought. A cab took us home to bed, and I remember thinking, as Alistair scooped me closer into his nook, that the stranger was right, it *was* crazy. And now, in the warm light of day, it seems even crazier. And I can't help feeling I was led astray when I was at my weakest point: drunk and desperate for someone ... for him to love me.

Wednesday 24th November

You would think we'd never been closer. Alistair bounced around the kitchen like a happy bunny while prepping breakfast, and at one point, as our butter knives crossed in the Lurpak, he looked up from the dish and said, 'I love this, Andy. I love what we have. I love you.'

It was what I'd been waiting for all this time, but those words, instead of flipping around my starved heart, fell flat. Those beautiful words should've meant so much more. But having three-way sex so early on our path does not lay solid foundations for a monogamous pairing. If I'd wanted a relationship where I could 'play' with others, I'd have stayed in the Borders with Thomas. But then, that wouldn't really have worked for me either.

I dug deep and tried to excavate the joy that was buried somewhere next to my optimism and smiled as I said, 'I love you too,' with as much conviction as I could muster. I meant it, yesterday, I really did. I've wanted to tell him all this time. It's well-rehearsed in my mind, but it just isn't how I imagined it, with the taste of another's mouth still on my tongue and the taste of another's cock on his.

He wrapped his arms around me, and we made love officially for the first time on the kitchen floor. Alistair looked intensely into my eyes, but I found it difficult to let him in, so I flipped him over and did what all great masters do to their hungry slaves: I fucked him hard, harder than before, against the punishing floor, because I wanted him to pay for the other night. I wanted him to pay for leading me up a path that he knew was cruised heavily by men. I wanted him to know who was in charge. But more so, I wanted to prove to myself that we could still be as close in our own unique way. But when we were spent and laid on the cold hard floor, the cold hard facts were all too real in my mind: I hadn't made love to him; I'd just fucked him. The man I've loved all this time, I'd treated like dirt and hadn't given a damn. I was so angry. And that's pretty fucked in itself.

And all the way up the road, towards my usual drop-off point around the corner from work, I could feel it happening: that slow, painful fracturing of my heart. A small unseen fault, but definitely there, just waiting to tear right through and break it in half.

Thursday 25th November

I set up an emergency meeting with Ryan to discuss my recent foray into three-way sex. I choked on a piece of asparagus when he excitedly said, 'Three-way? How exciting! Tell me, what were the dynamics? Who took charge? Is it someone both of you know or was it a total stranger? Was there any awkwardness?'

I assure him that the awkwardness came seconds later after expelling a load that is probably still frozen to a gravelly path close to Calton Hill. I chastised him for his enthusiasm. 'I thought you of all people would be against openness in any relationship.'

'There's nothing wrong with a bit of frivolous fun, if that's all it is, within the boundaries negotiated and agreed between the couple involved. If it's between two, three, four, or more parties, then clear rules should be drawn up and reviewed regularly.' Ryan was treating relationships like NATO countries, allowing free passage between their borders under certain conditions and perks.

'So you agree with couples having open relationships?'

'Yes.'

'But you're getting married.'

'Yes, that is true, but you know as well as I do that we have had, and still do have, mutual friends who have perfectly loving open relationships which have stood the test of time. Some may say it solidifies their love.'

I was astounded. I found my self repeating, 'But you're getting married.'

'Yes, we are. And playing with another team is not for us, but we have fantasised about it. Well, more so Tony than me. It does get him fired up during sex. I just go along with it until he's relieved. Then we hug and fall asleep, and it's put to bed along with us, until maybe a month or so later. Then we talk dirty again and get it out of his system. You know, sometimes I take our double-ended dildo and ...'

I covered my bleeding ears, cutting him off mid-sentence, 'That's enough, thank you. Doesn't it concern you that this fantasy talk may lead to reality?'

'Oh, cupcake, I also indulge myself in the dream of having my own interior design show on Channel 4 with Phil Spencer, but we both know that isn't going to happen either.' Ryan dismissed it with a flap of his hand, 'It's just mere flighty fantasy, my anxious little friend, nothing more. He's happy, and I'm happy.'

'You see,' I said, 'the problem is, I indulge myself in the fantasy of having a loving and monogamous relationship with Alistair, but have indulged myself in *his* fantasy of three-way just to impress him.'

'Oh, that's a bit of a bugger.'

'And now he says he loves me after we shared some stranger, so what can that mean? Does he love me more for my supposed openness, my "anything goes" attitude, which was actually my "I'm pretty inebriated, actually, and may not fully understand the implications of this, as of yet," attitude.'

To be honest, I expected more of Ryan than just 'bugger' and 'shiiiiit', which was all he could offer for the rest of my exposé. And his parting pat on the back and reassurance to 'play it by ear' was just rubbish. He left in a rush as he was ten minutes late for a kilt fitting for his happy monogamous life with Tony. His final inspirational comment was, 'Chin up, chappie, it may never happen.' If someone's chin is scuffing on the ground, it most certainly has already happened.

******

In other news, I think Gwen may be bulimic. Last night, she stopped off at Café Jamaica for a chat, allegedly, but then hoovered up every scrap of leftovers from the kitchen. She delayed lock-up by spending the next fifteen minutes in the downstairs lavvy. Then, this morning, I distinctly heard her vomiting in the bathroom moments after I overheard a spoon come to rest in a breakfast bowl through her bedroom door. I was passing to pick up the mail and got distracted. The fact that her room is nowhere near the front door is neither here nor there.

I passed on my concerns to Sally. She said, 'Rejection and the monotonous ticking of a woman's biological clock can cause females to do the most extreme shit to appeal to men after being tossed into the slops bucket of life. Her body image may be distorted by Matt dropping her like a German hot potato. She looks tired and drawn all the time, sweetie, and let's face it, you couldn't sew the fat on her if you tried, even before the dumpage. It took half a tube of costly foundation and warm lighting to convince anyone she was actually three-dimensional at that beauty pageant.'

A bit harsh, I think, but we've both resolved to keep a close eye on her.

Friday 26th November

Nash was at the gym again today, well, actually leaving the showers on his way to the sauna. It took all my willpower not to follow him, especially as he dropped me the heaviest 'follow me' look that has ever been passed between cruising men. If he's the Pied Piper, I'm most definitely a dirty rat in this respect. I shouldn't have these desires at all. I think I'm pretty messed up. Oh, Alistair, why did we do that?

I promised myself the distraction of a hefty slice of millionaire shortbread in the gym cafe as my reward for walking slowly but surely in the opposite direction. Instead of cheating on my man, I cheated on my healthy living promise and devoured the thick slice of shortbread drenched in chocolate and caramel as passionately as I would Nash's ass. I washed it down with a grande mocha smothered in whipped cream and left the café feeling a right filthy bitch. At this rate, my aspiring washboard stomach will most certainly be a bulky twin tub. I may even eat myself into a situation where I'll become so fat I will be unattractive to all, apart from those crazy 'feeders' you see on daytime talk shows.

Perhaps I wouldn't feel so tempted to bounce on a personal trainer if I fully understood Alistair's intentions. He loves me, I know he does. You don't hold a guy all night long without that. But concrete facts are what I need. If he wants commitment, I'll give it 100%; if he wants to play the field ... um, I'll have to think about my reaction to that one. I guess Ryan's right, I'll have to play it by ear.

11.15 p.m. As if to assure me of the risks involved in playing around, Radio 4 reported tonight that more than a quarter of people living in the U.K. who have HIV don't know they have the virus.

11.30 p.m. Again, insomnia sets in. I'm staring at my ceiling as I lay alone in bed. Through the murky darkness, in the shadowy recesses of my mind, hidden amongst the cruddy clutter of life's distractions, I'm aware I still don't know my HIV status. I tell myself, *Surely by now, you'd be ill or show some kind of symptoms*. They say early diagnosis is the key to living a long life. How late am I if this is the case? Too late?

Enough scribbling. Get some sleep before paranoia sets in.

11.40 p.m. You have been feeling a little run down recently, was a recent thought. The curtains billowed inwards and parted as if some fleeing entity had just found refuge. A chill rattled my core. I got up and slammed the window shut. The bare, twisted limbs of the trees contorted frantically in the gale and, for the second time since I moved here, the room seemed unwelcoming and bitter. I text Alistair, 'R u up?'

Nothing back.

11.50 p.m. I've pulled open the door of the cupboard that houses the water heater, to let residual heat out, and turned my radiator up to max. It's creaking and clanking into life as water somehow manages to flow through its prehistoric veins. The gale continues to batter the old sash window, which is now rattling as if a poltergeist is trying to get in. I've thrown a thick blanket over my duvet and settled down with the Colonel curled between my arm and chest as tight as a ball of string. His eyes almost rest and then open wide, peering into the tumultuous night between the gap in the curtains that heave and wheeze slowly back and forth in the draught as wearisome as a lifelong smoker's lungs. His tail flicks in spasms, and he moans and sighs intermittently. I know this cat well. He knows it's more than just a gale outside; winter's on its way. The last time he reacted like this, we were approaching January: a month that was merciless and gruelling.

Saturday 27th November

Snow has rested all over the city, covering the streets in a thin duvet of white crystals. I slipped and slid my way to Alistair's in eager anticipation that he was home safe.

'Sorry, I was out. Pub crawl! Hungover today. Mind if I skip tonight?' was his late reply to my anxious texts that came through just as I entered his building via the services buzzer.

His apartment door opened to reveal an exhausted-looking man.

'Didn't you get my text?' he asked, a little testy. No kiss.

'Oh, aye! Here's your text, I must've missed it,' I lied as I bullied my way in. 'I was worried,' which was the truth. I *was* worried. Worried he'd gone off me.

He edgily glanced around his apartment as if he had something to hide, but I could see nothing out of place. As usual, it was as pristine as a show-home. Everything was as it should be. Except for my toothbrush, which was nowhere to be seen again. Alistair agreed with my suspicions, 'Dominica must've thrown it out, the idiot. She's a bit suspicious of anything out of the ordinary – communism does that to people – I'll buy you a new one.' He kissed me at last. A bit dry and fleeting, but still a kiss.

I hope she's thrown out that noisome essential oil too, I thought.

'Hey, I went shopping in Buchanan Street yesterday,' he said, changing the subject with the subtly of a sledgehammer.

'You were in Glasgow?' I said, the words sticking in my throat.

'Yeah, with the boys, remember? I told you last week.'

'I must've forgotten,' I said, but I honestly couldn't recall him saying anything about Glasgow. I would have remembered that, surely?

He plopped a box from a designer boutique on the kitchen table. Inside was a sharp leather jacket that was way too young for a man of his age. 'I got this while I was there,' he grinned. 'Cost a small fortune, but I figure I can afford it.' He put it on. 'What do you think? Am I ready for the gay scene now?'

I lied, 'Aye, looks really *trendy*.'

'Here, try it on,' he said. He spun me around and helped me into it. It hung on me like a sack of potatoes. I suddenly felt tiny and meek. He squinted at me and concluded, 'Hmmm, a wee bit too big. Never mind.'

I flapped the copious sleeves that hung limply over my knuckles playfully and sighed, 'Och, I've never been able to share clothing with a boyfriend. Nothing new here then.'

Alistair frowned and helped me out of the jacket, which was easy as it was sliding off my rawboned shoulders anyway. 'I'm too old to be called your boyfriend,' he said, broodily.

'What then?'

'Buddy works best for now,' he replied as he left the kitchen with his new purchase.

So we're buddies? But you love me. I felt even smaller than before, but reluctantly agreed, 'Alright, buddies it is then.'

Sunday 28th November

The cat is out of the bag, and I'm not talking about the Colonel for once.

After I bullied my way into Alistair's apartment, I bullied my way into his bed. If he was hesitant to become my boyfriend, he could damn well act like one overnight, I'd make sure of it. I contrived every kiss, every hug, every second of sex with him to convince him we're right for each other. 'This is the most comfortable I've ever been with any man,' I said expectantly as he began to doze. He nodded and kissed the back of my head. I lay awake as he slept soundly for over half an hour, then I drifted off.

I continued my campaign through breakfast until he dropped me off just around the corner from Café Jamaica. I leaned in for one final kiss, slipped on a patch of icy snow, and the Trebor Extra Strong Mint I'd been sucking on promptly leapt off my over-zealous tongue, flipped past my uvula, down my oesophagus and rested somewhere necessary for inhalation. You don't appreciate air until you find you lack it, then it's all you can think about. Between turning, what was later described to me as, 'assorted shades of cyanosed that a Dulux colour chart would be proud of,' I was ushered into the café by Alistair while desperately clutching my throat and ad-libbing as much creative sign language as it was possible to say, 'Help, I'm choking to death here.'

A panicked Alistair signalled for help from my friends. It seemed like a lifetime before I felt four heavy slaps on my haunched and heaving back. And again, only harder. And then a fist was thrust into the delicate area between my ribs and my diaphragm. I was losing it. Everybody moved in slow-motion, and I could hear a whooshing sound punctuated by my own pulse. The din of the room, the concerned voices and the reggae all echoed and muffled into some kind of auditory soup.

I heard, in a Jamaican droll, 'Come on, Mr, she needs you. Don't you dare choke to death.' The firm fists were now beating the shit out of my ribcage. And just when I could stand no more and death seemed a comfortable option, out flew the offending mint. It jettisoned across the room and smacked Sally in the eye.

'Ouch! You bitch!' she yelped cupping her face.

Molasses rested me in a chair. As light returned to the world, I caught sight of Sally's killer heels. One was tapping in frustration, waiting on me coming round. 'So, *this* is the guy you've been seeing? I should've guessed.' I looked up. Her face was laden with disappointment. Alistair's was glossed in fake indifference. 'You really do like to complicate your life, don't you?' she added.

I looked around. Molasses, Sally, Ryan, Melve and Gwen were there too. Was I dreaming? Disorientated by the lack of oxygen, perhaps? No, they were real. Just my luck! The whole gang. I took a deep breath, mustered up some courage and announced proudly, 'Yes, everyone, this is my boyfriend, Alistair.'

I couldn't be sure if collective looks of disapproval were being cast our way, or if they were just uncomfortable glances, I was too fuzzy to see anything clearly. Their reaction at that point didn't concern me. What did was Alistair's parting words as he slipped into his car.

'Why did you say that?'

'Say what?' I asked.

'Say I was your boyfriend.'

'Because you are, aren't you?'

'I'm not sure what I am, Andy.'

He gave me a cursory kiss and sped off down the road.

My shift was awkward, to say the least. Fed-up with Sally's evil daggers by dinner time, I asked her, 'What is your problem? You were happy for me to see him months ago. What's changed?'

She smiled bitterly and said, 'You, Andy, that's what's changed. You've become so sad and desperate, you've stooped to this, a married man who may never leave his wife.'

‘That’s rich, coming from a woman who almost risks chronic sciatica to stoop low enough to pick up filthy cash from the laps of married men. At least Alistair and his wife are separated.’

‘Are they?’

‘Aye!’

‘And what of his poor wife? Does she know the real reason they broke up, if he’s so far back in the closet he’s in Narnia, or has he left her hanging? Or fed her some kind of bullshit that, comfortably for him, won’t stick too long? You forget, Andy, I know his type. They’re ten-a-penny in my lowly circles.’

‘What do you know of real relationships? A woman who’s so scared of commitment she spends her evenings drinking herself into a lonely stupor and her nights running from one nameless man’s bed to another’s.’

We were nose to nose, challenging the other to take back what was said, but neither of us backed down, snarling at each other like two territorial mongrels. Molasses separated us with a jet of soda water. Soaked, I was sent home to simmer down while Sally was kept safely out of harm’s way at the café.

I’m home now, but I won’t be staying long. I’m heading to Alistair’s as soon as he gets back. I’m not waiting around for more mud to be slung my way. I’ve sent a text of apology to Ryan telling him, due to stress, I’ll be skipping the old dance practice tonight. He’s disappointed but understands. Sally’s attitude will do nothing but push me away from her and closer to my man.

Monday 29th November

When I got to Alistair’s last night, our conversation took up where he had sped off. I asked him what his issue is with being my boyfriend. It’s just a silly label, anyway. If he really does love me, this shouldn’t be such a huge hurdle.

‘If it’s just a silly label, then drop it, Andy,’ he snapped.

That hurt.

‘Sorry,’ he said, ‘I shouldn’t shout at you, the one guy who keeps me sane. Thing is, I can say I love you. That’s easy. You’ve been my rock through all of this crap. You’re my first thought when I wake and my last at night. I depend on you. Everything else is so complicated at the moment, but you’re the most uncomplicated part of my life. Being with you's easy. I admire how comfortable you are in your own skin.' He paused and added, 'But I'm not sure yet if I'm gay or just a guy who really enjoys sex with men. I'm far from being comfortable with that, and you deserve so much more.' He looked close to tears.

I felt everything could slip away if, at that moment, I agreed and gave in to what he seems to think is inevitable. That fractured slither of my heart was holding on, but only just. I had to get us back to where we were before. Before it got messy. 'You're wrong,' I said, smiling to reassure him, 'it'll all be okay.' I kissed him. 'We'll get through this, no problem.' I kissed him again. 'And you'll see how easy it is to be comfortable in your own skin too. I love you.'

He looked through me deep in thought. It was ages until he answered. 'I hope so,' he said and kissed me back.

******

It turned out last night's dance class was a washout. Sally was a no-show and, despite Trenton taking charge of the rehearsal, it ended in chaos, backbiting and confusion. The final push happened when Melve snapped at Trenton as he escorted him closely through some problematic steps. Melve's chakras got in a knot, and he barked viciously at his not-so-secret lover, 'Would you please stop pawing me? You're always pushing me this way, pulling me that, grabbing my hand, chirping at me and swooping in for kisses like a demented bat.'

'I'm sorry, darling. What would you prefer? Should we just go on pretending we don't share the same eiderdown at least twice a week and I'll keep sneaking in and out under cover of darkness like some criminal?'

'No,' bit Melve. 'Let's not. Let's just call it quits, eh?'

Trenton rushed from the room in floods of tears, according to Ryan. Melve shook his fingers through his hair and brought it back to the usual mess it was before he started seeing Trenton.

'There, that's better, wouldn't you agree? Back to the freer, happier Melve.'

No one agreed, and the night ended there.

In other frosty news:

This whole country has been muted by a thick blanket of snow.

Hundreds of people are trapped in cars and lorries on the worst-hit roads in Scotland. Edinburgh's transport network is struggling. We were told by a frustrated bus driver that we'd have to get off at the end of Princes Street, as Leith Walk was impossible because 'bloody council workers can't get out of bed early enough to sprinkle a little grit on tarmac.'

I asked him, 'Why? Snow falls and settles every year, it's hardly a revelation, and yet councils and transport providers act as if they've never seen so much as a flake before. Are their headquarters based in the Sahara desert? You know, in Iceland they have over six months of snowfall in the year. Up to 54 inches at its worst. And yet they manage to travel with minimal difficulty.'

He pulled his collar closer around his neck and shivered. 'Yeah, well this ain't bloody Greenland, and I ain't a bloody Eskimo, so tough-titties.'

I attempted to correct him, 'The indigenous term is Inuit, not Eskimo,' but he whipped the doors shut as I spoke and sped off down Leith Street with such recklessness I was actually glad to be off his bus.

Abandoned opposite Ryan's flat, I caught sight of him staring blankly out of the lounge window. He looked thoroughly fed-up. I waved to him. He eventually saw me and beckoned for me to join him.

'Why, oh why did we decide to get married in December?' he asked, rhetorically. 'We didn't think snow would fall so soon and cripple the U.K. This could either make or break us, Andy.'

I got behind him and rubbed his shoulders reassuringly, all the while thinking, *Please let it break the two of you up*. I asked him, 'Paper bag time again?'

'Yes, please.'

We spent the next ten minutes in silence. I took his place at the condensation coated window and mulled over my relationship with Alistair. Then I thought about how right the Colonel had been about the harshness of this winter. Crazy. He's just a pet with zero psychic powers, and he can't really talk. It's all in my head, which is a little worrying as I may be heading for a total mental breakdown. Ryan stayed inside his quiet space long enough for me to draw a broken heart on the pane with my finger: two friends, one drawing out the torture from the inside; the other shutting his out.

The silence was broken by my paper bag friend saying, 'I don't judge you, by the way. Regarding Alistair.'

'Thanks, I appreciate that.'

'But Tony does.'

'At least he's consistent,' I said, deadpan. My real mates seem to be anything but. Ryan and Sally's reactions are poles apart and not what I'd expected at all. My world is upside down, and I'm being pulled inside-out.

Tuesday 30th November

Today's weather report on BBC Radio4 was concise: 'The U.K. weather forecast for the next few days is fairly straightforward: we're all going to get some snow.' No shit, Sherlock! People are still struggling to work. Everyone has the same pissed-off expression as they wade knee-deep through the city.

By 7 p.m., Molasses decided to shut up shop as there had only been two customers supping on the same bowl of soup for the past hour and a half. Judging by the matting of their hair and the whiff, they sleep rough. Molasses gave them an extra cup of soup and a half-empty bottle of whisky as compensation for sending them on their way.

So, with little planned for the rest of the evening, I asked Alistair if he wanted to go to the flicks. 'With me,' I felt the need to add. 'Kinda like a date?'

He agreed to be seen with me in public, but added, 'I'll have to put my phone on vibrate, just in case someone's stuck in snow on a country lane or something.'

I couldn't argue with that, it is his livelihood after all, but the glare of his phone was an irritating distraction in-between Colin Firth's spluttering and stuttering in *The King's Speech*. The rightful mutterings of disapproval from the small audience ended when we were asked to leave by a scrawny teenage member of staff.

'It's been reported that you may be filming this release on your mobile; I must ask you to leave due to possible infringement of copyright law,' said the attendant, quaking in his plimsoles.

I argued that the actual quality of video on a mobile phone was laughable and would limit any market for piracy drastically, and besides, they were obviously desperate for trade as I'd counted only ten heads, including ours, in the theatre.

'Yes, the snow's probably encouraged people to stay at home and watch a poor quality copy of this movie on an illegal site. The same site that may be in your browser history,' he added.

'Okay, well best go then,' said Alistair. 'I have to get back to work, anyway. The film ain't doing it for me, and there's a caravan stuck on Sheriffhall roundabout. I'll go help. All of the other lads are stretched as it is. Stay and enjoy the movie.' He patted me on the back and paced quickly towards the exit. I didn't feel like watching the rest of the film. We hadn't even skimmed the top layer off our extra-large box of date-night salty popcorn.

Feeling very unwelcome, I left soon after and wandering into the carpark, just in case he was still navigating his way out, and I could catch a lift. No luck. I took the bus (limited-stop, part route and acerbic driver, of course) with my extra-large date-night salty popcorn to Leith Street and was welcomed into Ryan's flat with open arms. My timing was perfect, apparently, as Tony had skipped off to bed while Ryan sat up watching an old Hammer Horror film and had begun to contemplate scouring the local store for something savoury.

I conceded to a failed first almost-date and gave him the entire box. 'I'm glad it's of some use to someone,' I said, a little depressed. 'I suspect he only bought it as camouflage as he kept sliding down his chair and sank further behind the damn box every time someone walked by.'

Ryan, barely aware of anyone else in the room except for Peter Cushing and Christopher Lee, munched on the crispy corn ravenously as if he'd been snowed in for days without supplies. Another claw-full of salty polystyrene was shovelled into the pink spinning drum of his mouth and was washed down with a large slug of Pilsner. Crumbs began to litter their sofa. He was unconcerned. Gwen will have that mess to clear up, I bet. Had he forgotten I was there? He took a breather between gulps and the case of tunnel vision he'd developed while watching the film ended long enough to say, 'Well, cupcake, you can kick the man out of the closet, but you can't make him mince.'

'I don't want him to mince,' I sighed. 'To sit together in public in daylight would be quite nice. Maybe even do some handholding, if the opportunity arose.'

Ryan nodded blankly. He was back in the movie. Living it. A damsel was in distress as Dracula hovered over her neck, ready to suck the life out of her. She screamed an ear-shattering scream. Ryan screamed and jumped, popcorn flew everywhere, which made me yelp. Then, just as Dracula entered his tomb, Tony, a real-life blood-sucker, showed face. Makeup free and bitter in tone – he'd be perfectly placed in that tomb – he moaned about the lateness of the hour and lack of beauty sleep. The fun, for what there was, had ended. I left.

I'm now in bed. My bed. The only text from Alistair was a short, 'I'm busy, sorry!' The Colonel's with me. I knocked on Sally's door as I felt the need to build some bridge to get back to the sunny side of our friendship. She's not in. The snow is persistent outside my window. I've pulled the curtains wide. I'm watching the clumps spin and fall heavier and faster from the hazy purple sky. My window is frosty inside and out. This time, I drew two hearts on the glass. One of them bled and became disfigured.

Wednesday 1st December

I've just had a blazing row with Sally in Heads Down, Bums Up next to the café. I caught her sneaking into the establishment as I took out the recycling. She'd called in sick, but looked remarkably chipper for someone allegedly suffering from a bout of diarrhoea and vomiting. The only person I've heard vomiting at home is Gwen (musicians can only vomit in *Fortissimo*, it seems). I dumped the trash, followed her, cornered her between the harnesses and dildos and challenged her on her supposed illness and sudden ethical stance on relationships.

'I *am* actually suffering from nausea induced by the copious buckets of verbal diarrhoea you're spouting, Andy,' she said spitefully. 'I can't sit by and listen to you make excuses for that man any longer. He's bullshitting you, and you're such a doormat that you're willing to ignore the signs because you're scared of being alone. It makes me gag.'

'Say how you feel, why don't you, Sally? It's not as if you've held back on anything else, is it?'

'What's that supposed to mean?'

'Well, who are you really? I'm getting vertigo from the mountain of dross I've had to climb just to get to know you the little I have. Don't judge me when you can hardly muster the energy to open your door just a fraction to let the people closest to you peer in. We take you at face value because that's all you ever offer: a grown woman who drinks as much as a twenty-year-old on a binge, who can only make enough cash stripping to live in a crappy bedsit and piss the rest up the wall. A woman who's so bitter about love she can't cope with anyone else being happy.'

'Who mentioned love?'

'Alistair has, despite it all, he says he loves me. And, you know what? I love him too. Why is that so hard to accept?'

Sally slid open a box containing a rather large dildo and acted irritatingly nonchalant. She admired its form and stroked the shaft slowly. She chuckled to herself and continued to gaze at the rubbery reproduction. 'Then you're in more trouble than I imagined, darling,' she said. She thrust the sexual aid below my nose and added, 'Alistair is as genuine as this piece of craftsmanship. Sure, it will give you all the right sensations in all the right places, it may even give you the best sex you've ever had in your limited experience, but that's as far as it goes. It won't make love to you, just as Alistair is as incapable of doing so.'

'You don't know him. You don't know how good he is to me. How can someone so incapable of love understand? Why am I wasting my time on you? An emotional cripple. What kind of friend are you really?' I was done. We were over for sure. I'd leave the bedsit tonight and never go back. I'd move in with Alistair and find a job elsewhere. Something better than a crummy café.

The sales guy called to us from the front of the shop, 'Hey, are you okay?'

'Yup, everything's just fine,' I said as I turned to leave, but Sally held me back and pushed me against a pile of vintage Jeff Striker DVDs.

She beat the dildo on my chest and punctuated every word:

'The - kind - of - friend - who - cares - about - you - deeply - The - kind - that - doesn't - want - to - see - you - get - hurt - The - kind - who - has - been - protecting - you - from - the - truth - because - she - knows - the - truth - really - fucking - hurts!'

I pushed her away. She fell hard against a display filled with metal cock-rings. Some tumbled to the floor and clattered towards the checkout. The sales assistant shouted at us, 'Right, you two! I like a bit of S&M, but this is not the time or place. You'll drive my customers away.'

I said, 'We are in a *sex shop*, for heaven's sake. Anything goes, surely?'

'Not this kinda shit,' he said. 'Come on, bud, time to go and leave the lady alone.'

Sally was out of breath. Panting against the jingling metal on the wall. My heart was pounding, and adrenaline was seething through every pore of my body. I could feel every cell on fire, sensitive to the slightest touch, gunning for a fight. But I decided to walk away, my body buzzing, disappointed with the resolution and struggling to contain the energy that was being released.

'He loves me. Deal with it,' I asserted.

Sally pushed up from the wall with one swift kick of her heel and came towards me. I thought she was aiming for one more hit. I'm ashamed to say, I ducked like a coward, but not a blow was thrown.

Just the breathless words, 'I know men like him. I sit on their laps every day and dance their merry dance. Check his phone. Check his browser history. Check his garbage folder. Check the receipts tucked away in the pocket of his wallet that he keeps for expenses, and then tell me I'm wrong.'

I walked out of the shop and slammed the door shut on our friendship. I cancelled the rest of my shift. Already short-staffed, Molasses wasn't happy, but I couldn't give a shit. When I got back home, I texted Alistair and packed as much as I could into my rucksack. I then played the usual waiting game: my expectant heart, contracting quickly with every random text from others who pale in significance. By the time he replied, I was about to have a coronary. I called him as soon as I knew he had his phone in his hand and slopped my heart out down the line. Then, mercifully, I was with him within the hour.

I told him I couldn't go back, not to 323, not to work. I told him Sally and I had a such a big bust-up it would be impossible to continue being friends. I wanted his pity and love. I told him nothing of her advice to check his belongings because it's nonsense. He held me close until I came down from the ceiling and rested beside him on the sofa. The warmth of his being, the rise and fall of his chest as my head finally rests upon it and the heartening redolence of his cologne suffice. He's assured me I can stay as long as I need. That will be indefinitely. He loves me. I know it. Why else would he ask me to move in? I don't need to check his phone, or any other device, his kindness is all the reassurance I need.

Thursday 2nd December

Snow and ice continue to cause problems up and down the country; schools are closed, airports are in turmoil, rail networks are struggling and, most importantly, it really is hampering my attempts to move my bloody stuff from 323 Leith Walk! I've managed only one rucksack full, risking life and limb with several near-misses and one collision with an unusually jolly undertaker. I'm not risking my Hornsea collection in these conditions.

Despite our fallout, Sally must still be feeding the Colonel. There was a fresh bowl of half-eaten Felix laid on his mat, and his little box of treats had been moved from the cupboard and laid on top of my fridge. I'm not confusing this with a reprieve; I know she cares for that cat more than me.

I asked Alistair if the Colonel could move in with us. Where I go, he goes. 'Ah, therein lies a problem, my man. I'm allergic to cats. I flare up and can't catch my breath if I so much as see a whisker,' he said. 'I've had to take tons of antihistamines just to stay a few hours in your bedsit.'

Bugger! Why has he never mentioned this before? Surely he knew life with me would entail scraping the bottom of a litter tray and never being able to wear shorts at home without the risk of lacerations every time the doorbell rings? I'm ashamed to admit it, but I contemplated leaving the Colonel behind, just for a minute, but I know I can't. We've been through far too much. I'll go to the chemist tomorrow and pick up some allergy pills. If he really does love me, he'll take them and try to cope.

11.30 p.m.
Alistair's Pad.
I'm all alone in this palatial mansion. Alistair's out on the roads again. I spend the hours worrying he's safe and well. Last night, I dreamt his truck had skidded off a cliff. I woke with a jolt. *What the hell would I do without him?* I managed to doze, but the damn clock held my subconscious at ransom. At 2 a.m., I heard the door shut and his boots falling to the finely polished wooden flooring. And then, joy of joys, his warm naked body slid into our bed and pulled me close. Everything was right and good once more.

Friday 3rd December
Molasses called me at 7.30 a.m., 'I need you back at the front of the café within the next hour, Sonny Jim,' she demanded.

'Hell will have to freeze over before I work in the same place as that Knowles woman.'

'Boy, have you looked out of your window today? It has.'

'Either she goes, or I go. Do you know, she almost bludgeoned me to death with a large rubber cock? Of the non-farmyard variety.'

'There are just three pieces of information I want to make clear to you, my dear.' I imagined her brimming with authority, aloof with her tall stack of hair almost touching the ceiling, drumming one row of perfectly manicured nails rhythmically on a beer pump as she does when her patience is being tested. 'I don't expect gratitude, but I do expect loyalty amongst friends and staff, especially staff who I regard as friends. Sally has taken a sabbatical, maybe indefinitely, we will see; so you can forget about playing the wounded party, stop sulking and get on with the job I so graciously gave to you. And finally, and most importantly: your mother is here.'

It was as if someone had just clashed large cymbals on either side of my head. Mum, at the café? Alistair was busy reading the usual emails on his phone when I got this dreadful news. He cocked his head slightly but stayed focussed on the screen when I told him, 'My mother's in town. I don't know how long I'll be away for,' and gave him a quick goodbye kiss on the cheek.

'Oh, okay,' he said, suddenly back in the room as I was leaving, 'let me know when you'll be back, bud.'

It took me an extra thirty minutes to walk to Café Jamaica. I was knackered after wading through the snow with exaggerated bent knees like a leggy flamingo. What I couldn't wade, I was forced to slide on. Every single step involved a minor risk assessment. When I got there, Mum was sitting laughing herself silly and sharing a long vodka with Molasses on the same sofa I'd roughed it on months before. Beside her were two bulging leather suitcases and a hatbox. I glanced around for Dad. Molasses and Mum stopped laughing when they caught sight of me. Then burst into fits of giggles as if I'd just confirmed some outrageous secret that I wasn't privy to.

'See, I told you,' yelped Mum between gulps of air. She looked different. Same parka, same hair, same makeup, for sure, but she appeared, dare I say it, happy.

'Where's Dad?' I asked, expectantly.

'With his precious tropical collection, I imagine.' She said and chuckled.

Molasses, noting the glare in my eyes, fought with the sofa to find her feet. 'I'm getting a bit old for mixing vodka with this kind of soft furnishing,' she said. 'Stay as long as you need, Mrs Angus. Everyone's welcome in the Land of Lost Souls.'

'Please, Mo, call me Beth,' she grinned. She saw I was most certainly not amused and pretended to sober her expression.

'What does she mean? Why do you need to stay anywhere?' I

asked, fearing the worst.

'Andy, Son,' I knew trouble was ahead, she only calls me Son when there's something difficult to tell me. 'I've left your father.'

Boom! It was like a kick in the gut. I crossed my arms to hold myself together. I could feel my whole body tighten. 'Explain.'

'He seems happy to sit there in that bloody recliner while the walls are pulled down around us. That man has no drive. He won't fight the council, he won't fight the bulldozers, he won't even fight with me. Last night, while watching *Desperate Housewives*, I thought to myself, I don't like the nagging bitch I've turned into, so I packed my bags when he was in the club and got the first train here.' She stood up as if she was a magician's assistant who'd just stepped from a magical cabinet, stretched her arms wide and warbled, 'Tadaaah!'

'Where the hell are you going to stay?'

'You're allowed one temporary house guest, apparently,' she said, cheerily. She nodded towards Molasses, who uncharacteristically kept her head low and pretended to look for something under the bar, then exited stage right to the basement.

'I've only got a double bed,' I made clear.

'You've that lovely bed settee I bought you, remember?'

Damn it! It's as if she's planned this all along.

Molasses waved a tenner at me and, after a prolonged, arduous ride in a cab, I was throwing my mum's hastily packed cases on my bed. I had to get back to work, but I'd prefer to keep a close eye on her. I told her not to go through my stuff, checked that my diary was still in my rucksack, and kissed her on the cheek. She laughed and asked me, 'Are you still writing in that thing? Your Aunt Moira would be pleased.'

Before I left, I felt an uncanny bout of concern. 'Will you be okay?' I asked, cautious about leaving this small-town woman in a tiny bedsit in the big smoke.

'Don't worry about me,' she said, flopping onto the sofa that will be her bed for hopefully one night only. 'It's bloody liberating, Andy. No screaming grandchildren, no housework, no weeds to pluck, no drunk man scraping at the lock with his key at two in the morning.' She turned on the TV and kicked off her furry boots. As she curled up, she added, 'Oh, and Andy. Don't call your father, there's a good lad.'

I nodded and left. I made my way dutifully back to work and most definitely did not call Dad. I may have texted him instead. *He* called *me* back immediately, so no promise broken there.

'What the hell is she doing there?' he asked.

'I don't know. She seems to think this will solve all her problems. Let me tell you, it doesn't. Living in a bedsit in this city just gives you more. I should know.'

'Don't tell me, tell her, Andy,' he said. I heard some anger in his voice for the first time in ages. 'Is it about this damn demolition? I knew she was in one of her moods, has been for days, but I didn't expect her to run out on her husband and grandkids for something as silly as this.'

I became irritated. Maybe I was on her side after all. 'It's not *silly*, not to her, or others who've built their lives around that scheme.'

'So says the boy who packed his bags as soon as he got a Young Scots Card.' There was a pause. 'I've one foot in the grave, Andy, I haven't got the energy for this. I know how to plumb in a Hotpoint washing machine, but I have no idea how to set the bloody-bollocking thing for a colour wash. That's what a lifetime with an overbearing wife does for you; they make themselves indispensable and then leave you high and dry whenever their eggs stop popping.' My dad, the chauvinist, then hung up.

******

Later, I got home to find only the indentation of my mother's hips in the sofa. The TV was on, and *The Good Wife* was playing, ironically. The Colonel was sitting in the middle of the room, looking at me expectantly with his 'WTF?' face. My nose enticed me across the hall, towards the familiar waft of her usual brand of high tar which seemed to be heaviest around the door of a certain ageing hippy. I put my ear to the wood and heard girly giggles of the flirtatious persuasion, which could've fooled me into thinking Melve had a young lady biding, but there was a hint of my mother's smoke-induced huskiness. It was the rattly cough that confirmed my fears. I gave the door three hard, impatient knocks and Melve answered wearing one of his favourite kaftans. I could see my mother over his shoulder, perched on a beanbag, legs akimbo, waving at me and beckoning me to come in. I glared at Melve. I glared at her. I glared at his rumpled bedsheets. I glared back at Melve. She was drunk, and he may have taken advantage of her already.

'Now, old bean,' he stammered. 'Don't be taking this the wrong way. Your mother is a delightful lady. She was a bit lonely, and I suggested we sampled some of the cheeky homely remedies I've brewed.'

I pushed past the outrageous flirt, hauled the giggling ball of mess to her feet and ushered her out of the spider's web. Before we left, holding Mum up by her wobbly elbows, I advised Melve, 'Make up your mind which team you're batting for. For all our sakes, eh?'

Gwen popped her head out of her door, curious about the commotion. 'Who's that?' she asked, peering fearfully at the drunken old soak I was supporting.

I replied, dryly, 'My mother. Don't have kids, Gwen, you'll only let them down at some point.'

'Kids? Don't be silly,' she laughed and snorted. 'I have to purchase myself a man first.'

'Don't bother,' I said as I heckled Mum into my room, 'men are an even bigger disappointment, trust me.'

Mum hiccuped and asked, 'Who was that old frump with the white sport socks and swollen ankles?' before passing out on the sofa.

Almost Midnight. Mum is snoring and grunting on her front as the bed settee creaks and groans under the degenerating bones of a post-menopausal floozy. I'm thirty-six years old, I should be in control of my own destiny, not bending it to another's beck and call. I should be the protagonist here. I called Alistair from under my duvet to let him know the latest drama. 'I'm sure she won't be staying long, but I best keep my head down while she's here. She'll have a fit if she finds out I've been bonking a man who's still married, even though he's separated, it's still a no-no for Mum,' I whispered.

'Och, well. We'll just have to cope,' he said. And then, unhelpfully, 'Her timing is crap; I'm horny as hell.'

This is a nightmare. I can't leave him hanging with Sally's words still ringing in my ears. The more I learn how randy he is, the less I trust him when there's bugger-all I can do about it. I assured my man I'd get away for at least an hour of fun tomorrow and cursed having a mother brought up on archaic Catholic values. I wish she'd live by them herself and hang in there with Dad. All this snow, which has been compacted and turned into thick ice, has caused massive travel disruption, and yet my bloody mother manages to get through without hindrance.

Saturday 4th December

Mum has selfishly used my only available clean bath towel – I like a fresh towel every day, but spending so much time flitting between two places is taking its toll on my housekeeping. Also, I noticed my semi-jokey sign that says 'Non-smoking Compartment' in the style of the old British Rail signage had either miraculously fallen down on to the draining board, or – more than likely – had been ripped down by a certain flame-haired smoker while I was out. I hooked it back on the wall and reminded her that, since I left home, I've hardly had a chest infection.

She saluted me from the sofa and said, 'Andy, I've never met a non-smoker who isn't sickeningly passionate about being a non-smoker.'

I left her doing the usual: tea, telly and gossip mags. She may have left my father, moved to the big city (temporarily, I hope), and might be facing the biggest tragedy of her married life, but she's found her comfort-zone with remarkable ease.

I showered at Alistair's, which was irritating as this ate into our sexy time before my shift; we only had half an hour in total to wash and get it on. In the end, it was rushed, felt like a format and his phone pinged and jingled with message alerts throughout that drove me to distraction. I was tempted to knock the damn thing down the lavvy. When he left the room to get dressed, I sidled up to his phone and surreptitiously pressed the home button. The keypad was locked and coded, but I could see a small list of notifications from a bunch of emails and apps. No detail of content was available. Probably set that way for a good reason, after all, he has only recently left his wife. Imagine the hullabaloo if she found a message from me, for instance. My heart was racing by the time I heard his heavy footsteps coming back down the hall. I placed it carefully in the same spot and continued to apply some Molton Brown body lotion as casually as my nerves would allow. He brushed past me with a kiss and picked up his mobile. The screen was smudged from my greasy hands. He polished it against his shirt and left the room while unlocking the phone. I peered around the door to catch a glimpse of the now fully-functioning screen, but he was too far away for me to see any detail. I curse Sally for planting this seed.

'Best get a move on, Master,' he called jovially from the lounge.

'I'll be ready in a jiffy,' I replied, reaching for my new toothbrush. It wasn't in its usual place. It was tucked at the back of the lotions and potions. Still handy at the sink, within sight to remind anyone to put it back in place if the need arose, but discreet enough to go unnoticed.

'It's just Dominica will be here any second.'

'Okay, coming!' I said, getting irritated. Then it dawned on me, if Dominica was coming for her weekly clean and I'd placed this very toothbrush next to his in the glass just a few days ago, then who else had tucked it away it? Why would there be a need?

I began to wish I'd more time in his apartment alone.

Midnight. Mum turned up at Café Jamaica, swinging on Melve's arm. Melve, uncharacteristically, was wearing a dinner jacket and had slicked his hair into a braided ponytail. He may've been the image of a smart gentleman, but underneath his costume, I knew his intentions were as greasy as the slop bucket in our kitchen. Mum was wearing a tight black evening dress that showed far too much of her wrinkled underarms (women at her age should have the public decency to cover up any skin that resembles an undercooked pork sausage). Her hair, however, was bouncy and had a vitality about it I haven't seen since my sister's wedding. And there was a new shade to it too.

'Hello, my pious son,' she said. 'Two cosmo-politicians, please.' Both of them were grinning like maniacs. Oh, and drunk yet again.

'I think you've both had enough,' I said dryly.

Mum snorted a laugh and said, 'I don't think so. I've been wined and dined by this lovely gent, and the night is young.' She kissed Melve on the cheek, leaving a sticky residue of her purple lipstick behind, which she wiped off affectionately with her thumb. 'I've danced in a speak-easy to jazz and ate chips 'n' cheese on the grounds of a private garden; took some effort to climb the bloody gate and I nearly tore my knickers, but it was worth it for the laugh,' she glanced around and whispered the last sentence to me as if it was the crime of the century. Then she shouted, 'But I'm part-retired and still fucking managed it!'

'Have you given her drugs?' I asked Melve. I've *never* heard my mother say the F-word.

'Yes, sonny,' he said, 'I've given her the best drug going: life.'

I wanted her to fall over and pass-out just like last night. What harm could two days in a row do to a woman of her experience? Decades bevvying on cheap vodka in a working mans' club provides some kind of immunity to the alcohol-related brain damage, I bet. She didn't topple over. I was forced to be nice and serve them drinks, as our job description states we must have unconditional positive regard, despite Sally's general irreverent customer service. I sat both of them in the corner of the room, out of harm's way in an alcove, but within ear-shot. If Melve slipped her a tongue, I'd be there with a rusty old kitchen knife to cut it off. But he was the perfect gent, which was reassuring and disappointing at the same time. I wanted a firm excuse to keep them apart. He treated her like a queen, but I've learned a lot about the modern man this past year: they want it hard and fast; Melve is no different.

The only smacker was a parting kiss on the back of her hand as they said goodnight back at 323. I noticed Mum was still wearing her engagement, wedding and eternity rings, so there's still hope.

I text dad: 'Get over here ASAP. I'm sure she still loves you.'

He replied: 'I hope so, I'm getting sick of Chinese takeaways, and the sink is full of dirty plates.'

Sadly, I can see how my mother thinks the flickering flame of love has been extinguished by a man with the romantic sensibility of a brick. He'd be as well sticking to fingers up to her before spitting on them and using them to snuff out the last flicker of hope from love's flame.

Sunday 5th December

At around 2 a.m., while hidden under my duvet from my mother's twitching eyelids, I texted Alistair. I was desperate to call him as my mind was running riot, but this was the next best thing. My text went unanswered, the silence gave me a kick up the arse, and I switched to another means of communication: WhatsApp. This didn't help at all. I could see he was online, but as soon as I sent a message, he went offline.

I spent the next few minutes searching the App Store for gay dating apps (I use the word dating very loosely here, as most are definitely for shagging): I found Scruff (for the rougher man), Jack'd, GROWLr (for bears), Gaydar, MISTER, PlanetRomeo, Recon (S&M/Fetish/Leather) and My Mini Gay Boyfriend (some kind of Sim-like game, I assume). It seems sex is available everywhere, in all forms, on and offline, at every minute, of every day, at any pin-point on the planet! I began to wonder, if all these apps have been created and become so successful, have we become addicted to anonymous sex? Are we so desperate to be adored and quickly satisfied that the art of getting to know someone in a bar has died a death with the Nokia 3310?

Then, when I scrolled up the page again in disbelief at the amount of 'as required sex' available, I noticed something that should've been obvious to me. That little icon, the one with the yellow mask in the centre of a black background, I'd seen somewhere before. It'd been in the corner of my eye so often it had become as plain and unremarkable as chipboard in the 1980s. I'd seen it as recently as yesterday, in amongst all the other junk on Alistair's phone. It's always been there, lost in the crowd of apps on his screen. It'd flashed in the cinema. It'd shown its ugly face as we settled down for the night and even as we woke in the morning. It was there when he swiped a little too far to the right. It was tucked away in the last page, inside a folder, barely visible in the minutiae of detail. But I know that little yellow mask, that recent addition to gay life that Ryan had mentioned was pulling the guys away from the scene: it was Grindr.

I got up, unable to sleep, wracked with anxiety. What should I do? I pulled my jeans over my shorts. Mum was sound as a pound. I knew where I had to go. Who I needed to talk to. I knocked on Sally's door and stood there hoping she'd appear in her usual state, emerald nails jarring with her makeup, another 'trial wig' perfectly fitted to her head and a flimsy nightdress unbuttoned to the cleft of her breasts. All enhanced by that faint mix of Chanel Coco Mademoiselle, Nagchampa, cigarettes and gin that effuse from her like an olfactory aura.

I waited expectantly. I wanted to say I was sorry and she was right, but once those words were spoken to another, it would all become so real, and there'd be no going back. I stood for some time, unsure of what I should do. I sat down at the telephone desk. A pair of old green wellington boots, which had been sat their idol for as long as I could remember, flopped towards my jittering knee. They reminded me of the old pair Aunt Moira used to wear when she was doing the garden or going on a country walk with us kids. 'Country walks are good for this creaky old heart,' she would say. I thought back to the safety of my old life, down at Little Troll Cottage, with Thomas. To last Christmas, when I was deluded but happy. It was a lie. Moira's dead, Mum and Dad have split, and Thomas was nothing but a big fat liar. It was happening again, the lies. I put the boots on. A familiar waft of stale air hit me when each foot slid into the rubbery darkness. I followed my aunt's advice. I went for a walk. *It's supposed to be good for a creaky old heart*, I thought to myself as I padded down the stairs.

******

It was still dark by the time I reached the top of Calton Hill. I'd left my phone and all of its problems in my bed. I chose the back way up the hill as I couldn't face the steps and all those guys grunting and pawing each other. I needed to see my favourite view of the city that's always reassured me.

I sat still in the frozen landscape, frozen in the heart of winter and with the heart's choices. Even so, I wasn't going to let the polar chill spoil the decluttering of my thoughts. The sky was clear and flawless. It was still and quiet and felt like it was just the universe and me. The coast of Fife was out there, just visible, spread flat like a lounging grey cat, basking in the warm glow of Edinburgh's lights, as it would a flickering hearth. My eyes followed the steady stream of traffic lights that illuminated Leith Walk towards the shore. Down there was Alistair, with all his lies, resting peacefully and totally unaware of the torment he was inflicting on me. 'Oh, I'm so bloody angry, I could scream,' I said out loud.

'Then, why don't you?'

I whipped around. There she was, the one who was going to tell me, 'I told you so.'

I turned away, relieved she was there, but I wasn't going to show that. Not yet. 'Not your usual footwear,' I said, snidely. She was wearing a pair of oversized walking boots.

'Yes, well, sweetie, a girl has to adapt. I've been staying with a friend of mine who enjoys a bit of hill walking.'

'Back to being "sweetie" am I?' I sniffed.

Sally sighed and fanned out the ridiculously huge overcoat she'd obviously borrowed from the man too and threw her butt heavily on the bench next to me, causing some bounce. She jovially hopped up and down on it a few more times, trying to push a reaction from me. I inspected her new-found clothes and said bitterly, 'Grey is not usually your colour, dear. I'm sure they have red or even green overcoats: red for scarlet and green for envy.'

She sighed again, 'Oh, please! Is that the best you can do? I beat you multiple times with a huge dildo, and this is all you've got? I expected more from a gay man who's already several miles down the road to Bitchville.'

I pulled a thin smile. 'How did you know I was here?'

'I followed you.'

'How did you know I was up?'

'You were on WhatsApp, and besides, I have my spies.'

I shook my head and laughed. 'You always have to keep up the pretence, don't you? The great mysterious Sally Knowles, eh? I'm sure, if that veneer ever cracks, there will just be a scared little girl underneath.'

She bit back quickly, 'I'm sure there's a scared little boy here on this bench right now, so let's deal with that first, shall we?'

I nodded. She'd come all that way in the blistering cold to be sure I was okay, after all. 'I've found something, just like you predicted, on his phone. A sex app.'

Her dark glistening eyes showed no hint of surprised; they stayed fixed on me. 'Did you read any of his messages?'

'No, I didn't get the chance. His phone's always locked. I don't know where to go from here. I really have no proof. But I know a guy doesn't have shit like that on his phone without intent.'

Sally stroked my head in reassurance. I tried to keep it together. I've missed her. She said softly, 'Look, darling. I can't be around just now. I'm ... not well. I'm not able to cope with life at full steam for the moment. Crap going on up here, you see,' she added, tapping her forehead with her cigarette packet.

'Are you okay?'

'Yes, yes, I'm fine. I will be fine. Just a blip,' she shook her head and patted my knee. 'Let's focus on you. I need a distraction. I can be there for you in some way, so here's what we're going to do.' She gave a cunning grin, 'Sweetie, are you familiar with the wonderful singer Kate Bush and her song *Babushka*?'

'Of course,' I said, 'What gay man of a certain age isn't?'

'Then let's see if virtual honey is as sweet and viscous as the real stuff.'

And so we hatched a plan.

******

Later today, one very tired Andy joined the rest of the throng for the penultimate dance class. It hit several bumps as we tripped over the many egos in the room. I have to say, without the dominatrix shadow of Sally looming over everyone, there's little focus. Trenton's doing his best, bless him. I've nothing but compassion for a fellow who's been jilted just because of who he is and, tonight, he discovered he's been replaced by a part-retired postmistress acting like a teenybopper during the summer of love. As Melve playfully ran his fingers through my mother's rejuvenated locks, Trenton rubbernecked wistfully towards them while calling out instructions. Ryan was remarkably calm. Lorazepam, I suspect. Tony's been known to slip him some before long trips on East Coast trains and visits to South Africa to see the in-laws.

Melve suggested to the gang (with his back firmly turned to Trenton),'I say, lovies, while Sally is away, why don't we get the beautiful Beth to stand-in. If she doesn't come back, we'll have a fully trained understudy on the day.'

Trenton laughed and said, 'I don't think so. Our insurance doesn't cover octogenarians.'

I should've defended Mum, but I know she'd become more entrenched in my life if she were granted a part. Mum's mouth was hanging open, ready to argue, but I leapt in and insisted, 'Mum, you can't. Sally's part is incredibly taxing on the joints and would play havoc on your housemaid's knee.' I dropped a heavy look to Melve, hoping he'd get the hint to behave. 'Besides, Sally will be back. She's a professional, after all.'

'Who is this ever-elusive, Sally Knowles? Did she train at the Royal Ballet?' asked Mum, sarcastically.

'No, she's one of the best strippers in town,' interjected Gwen as she munched on a third cupcake offered by Tony (shop-bought, naturally). He pushed one towards me as he flaunted the plate around the room, which made me dubious. I smiled politely and refused without even touching the frosting, fearing it was sprinkled with cyanide.

'Wow, a professional slut, you must feel so privileged,' bitched Mum.

I found myself defending the woman I'd privately labelled as a tart not so long ago, 'Mum, she's a good friend, so leave her well alone.' Then I purposefully added, 'By the way, Mum, have you got round to telling Dad you're here?'

'You know very well I've not, Andrew. And that's the way it is going to stay, do you hear me?'

I nodded in agreement. Little does she know her husband is on his way to sweep her off her feet and show her exactly how much he loves her. He has to for his own sake: there are very few takeaways in Petersburn, and they have no space for a dishwasher.

11.30 p.m. 'Why are you locking the bloody bedroom door?' Mum asked after I turned the key.

'Because I don't believe Melve's intentions are entirely honourable,' I explained.

I was more than a little troubled by her reply, 'I hope not; mine certainly aren't.'

Is no one faithful these days?

Speaking of faithful, Sally's suggested I keep up the pretence with Alistair. I've sent several texts telling him I love him, that I'm missing him and that I'm desperate to see him. I can't be sure he actually is screwing around, and therefore can't be sure I don't still love him. What if he's only having virtual sex? Is this cheating? Am I capable of loving a man who enjoys virtual-reality fun?

He texted back quickly, 'I love u 2. Get down here ASAP! I'm horny as F.'

Romantic, and yet slightly disappointing.

Monday 6th December

Still no sign of Dad. The situation is getting desperate as Melve is taking my mother to the Gallery of Modern Art and then swimming. *Swimming!* For heaven's sake! People their age shouldn't be seen frolicking almost naked in public. Why doesn't he ask her to go skinny dipping and be done with it? I'm hoping, once he catches sight of Mum's wrinkly cleavage, and she of his hairless, veiny legs, the notion to lick anywhere close to these parts will drop faster than a seven-year-old child down a flume.

I text Dad, 'Where r u?'

Hours later I got this reply, 'At the Workman's Club, steering clear of the twisted form of womankind, drowning my sorrows with the rest of my brothers.'

I reminded him that the term 'Workman's Club' was obsolete as women have been allowed through the doors for decades. Some, horror of horrors, can even be seen flagrantly drinking pints. He said, in such poorly written text it took me a few minutes to decode the meaning, 'We don't need their kind in here. It's our sanctuary.' His reaction is similar to that of gay men when a hen night enters CC Blooms and dares to set foot on the sacred dance floor.

8 p.m. Mum got back to her temporary home with Melve cupping her close to his belly. I could've kicked him in the balls there and then. I'd ensure irreversible damage to render all stirrings extinct. At first, I thought they were tipsy, but sadly they were just high on life.

'By God, it's just dawned on me, I've a gay son and haven't so much as stuck my nose in a gay bar. Let's go to a gay bar!' yelped Mum. She jumped up and down excitedly and kissed Melve a few times on the cheek. Disgusting! She's having a riot while my father is on a single lane carriageway towards a town called Suicide.

Why haven't you stepped into a gay bar with your gay son? Because your gay son finds the idea cringeworthy, that's why, I thought. However, the notion of having another evening playing cosy families with my mother in a confined space is worse. So here we are, gay son and estranged mother, heading out to raise merry hell on the pink triangle. I feel more nervous tonight than on my first wander into a gay bar in the early 90s. I need a human shield to hide behind. I called Ryan and insisted he was my chaperone. I reminded him of my unwavering support for his big day and that he owed me a favour. Luckily, he's already out drinking with Tony, and it's just a matter of meeting them in the right bar. Melve has his group meditation session scheduled soon, so he's out of the picture. Phew! He wouldn't recognise Mum anyway; she's applied more makeup than a pantomime dame. I believe her face will melt in the poorly air-conditioned basement of CC Blooms and slip to her cleavage by 11 p.m.

I called Alistair quickly from our bathroom (the only private room I have now). The reception was crap at both ends. I asked if he was okay about my unscheduled bounce around the gay scene. He was too supportive, actually, 'That's not a problem,' he said cheerily. 'If you do pick anyone up, feel free to bring them down here for a horny three-way session.' He laughed.

'You are joking, right?' I said.

He cleared his throat and chuckled, 'Of course I'm joking, idiot. Have fun.' The line crackled and went dead, but I swear I heard metallic clanking as the connection was cut.

Tuesday 7th December

Sadly, Melve appeared on the scene after his meditation, gliding in chilled mode across the dance floor as my mother danced on a podium, sweating out buckets of Aftershock at one in the morning – a time when all mothers should have their rollers in and be sleeping soundly after thumbing through a good Catherine Cookson. Edinburgh's answer to Tom Jones joined her on the podium with a handful of colourful shots that I'm sure should only be enjoyed by underagers. Melve stuck out like a sore thumb, what with his sandals and purple striped kaftan, and he soon attracted some judgemental glances from gyrating neighbours. His moves, which date from every era apart from now, looked ridiculous. But there's no accounting for taste, and soon the fickle crowd (who at first mocked his archaic running man, twist and robot) became entranced by this nostalgia and, before long, were mirroring his movements. Melve fever swept the building. By the third set, he was cheered and applauded and stood on the main stage with his arms wide in appreciation like some disco dancing messiah.

I hid at the bar away from the hysteria with Ryan and Tony, but pretty soon Ryan faked a yawn, hugged me and whispered in my ear, 'I'm sorry, honey, we have to go; it's a school night, and your mother's cramping our style.'

Alone on the dance floor, drunk and fed up, it dawned on me that if Alistair was playing the field, then why couldn't I? I was, after all, standing in a lively pitch. It was time to see if I could still score. I scanned the seething mass of wetness and pheromones: mostly too young, too drunk, or too old. The old were leering at the young, the young were blissfully ignorant of the old, and everyone seemed too boisterous and vociferous for me. But there was a guy who stood out. It was the T-shirt that really grabbed my attention. It was tight-fitting, straining against one hell of a set of pecs, but that wasn't the most arousing factor, it was the large print of a blue box floating within a swirly time vortex that really caught my eye. It was the TARDIS. Could I have found a geek in Edinburgh that was handsome and buff too? The ultimate, perhaps? He was hard to make out at first, shaking his butt and spinning to Alicia Dixon's *The Boy Does Nothing* with a buddy (I hoped, only a friend). I got closer to his back and could see a nicely trimmed crop of black hair that had the impressive duck's arse I adore on a man.

'Great T-shirt!' I shouted over the din, brimming with confidence for once. Months of training in the art of taking control had led me to this moment. I could totally be the protagonist for once. *I can pull off assertive, wherever and whenever I want,* I assured myself. Adrenaline seething through my body, the Master was ready to pounce on his unwary prey. No reply. This needed a firm hand, so I swung mine towards his right buttock and gripped it tightly, saying, in my most butch, resounding voice, 'One hell of a great T-shirt and arse you have there, mate!' As his glistening, sweaty neck spun around to catch sight of just who this cocky bugger was, and as my confidence was at its peak, it quickly scurried off and got lost somewhere between the DJ box and a crowd of lipstick lesbians. I imagine, a short time later, it got pulverised under some drag queen's platforms.

'Oh, it's you,' said Constable 7469, as if he was expecting Cher only to meet Katy Price.

I was lost for words. It was the guy who'd stood me up months ago, for valid reasons, and in turn, who I'd stood up, for little reason other than I have a fickle, indigent heart. I hadn't given the guy a shot in the dark and was beginning to regret my mistake. Retribution isn't always swift, but it soon gathers pace and kicks like a mule when it catches sight of your retreating butt. I couldn't remember his name. I was suddenly speechless. I tucked the offending hand behind my back to hide the incriminating evidence (he is a policeman after all). I could feel a different kind of adrenaline release, the type that's fearful and meant to slow everything down. I'm sure it should've given me time to think, but the whole place seemed to be hurtling past me in that moment.

I pointed at the Police Box on his chest again, opened up my arms in that 'Wow!' fashion and mustered up the words, 'I'd no idea you were a Whovian. This is amazing. I am too.' I pointed to my T-shirt. He stared at me blankly. I looked down and realised I was wearing a checkered shirt instead of the Dalek Tee I'd planned on wearing and then stuffed back into the dirty laundry bag in disappointment. 'Oh, that should've been a Dalek, I'm a Whovian too.' I grinned again but began to feel the corners of my mouth falter and quiver. Nothing. He and his tall friend stared at me in disgust. I also think I said 'dude', which is totally naff.

His expression was drier than a Ryvita that had spent the day in an oven at 200° Celsius. He looked me up and down, glanced at his mate and said, 'There's loads about me you couldn't be arsed to find out, Andy Angus.'

It annoyed me that he remembered my full name and yet I couldn't remember a single letter of his. I rattled off vowel sounds in my head, trying desperately to grasp hold of the damn handle that was attached to a firmly closed door in my mind, behind which laid his name badge in a discarded pile of failed recipes and expired wifi codes.

He kept his eyes on me and spoke to his lanky friend, 'Markus, this is the guy who left me waiting in a coffee house for over an hour. You know, the payback kid?'

Markus looked as if he'd just smelt a fart with a Brussel sprout attached and, still swaying his rectangular hips slowly to the beat as if I was a momentary blip on his glorious night out, said, 'Oh, *that* loser.'

Constable 7469 swigged on his beer and said, 'Come on, mate. This place has taken a dive. Chips and cheese?'

Markus dropped me one last dirty look as he followed his beautiful policeman friend into the shadows of the crowd. They may have left, I have no idea, all I could think was: *He waited for over an hour for me, he must've really liked me*; and, *Bugger, I could really go some chips and cheese now, with him;* and then, *I need a drink!*

******

I woke with my mother's hair in my mouth. I jumped from the bed and landed with a thud on the floor. The loose change in my back pocket jarred into my arse-cheek. I winced in pain and peered over the edge of the bed towards my snoozing mother. The room was dark. It was 5.35 a.m., enough time to sleep, but not enough time to sober up. Mum was comatose. A dead cigarette clung to her smeared lips.

Muttering emanated from behind me. I heard my mother's name being mentioned, followed closely by Trenton's. I crawled towards the arm of the sofa, aware now that my trainers were still on my feet, and peered over the top. It was Melve, sleeping like a big ugly baby. His kaftan was twisted around his floppy body, strangling his chunky waist and exposing so much thigh it was edging towards indecent. *At least I had the sense to keep the lovebirds apart,* I thought.

I got to my feet. My head was pounding from dehydration, and my ears were still ringing from the shrill dance music. I tripped over Melve's jettisoned sandals on my way to the sink. I filled a fresh glass and looked around for pain killers in my drug store (a Tupperware box). Zero. Then I noticed a blister pack sticking out of Melve's tatty brown leather wallet. I needed something to kill the cacophony in my cranium. I reached for the little foil wrapped strip. Said wallet was in the firm grasp of Melve's fist. Years of sleeping in tents at festivals with all-sorts of opportunistic thieves and lax security has trained his hand to become a claw. Then I noticed a good reason to back-off. The pills were blue. I looked closer. Blue and oval. I smacked Melve on the shoulder and said, 'Wake up!'

'What's that, Eartha?' he said as he sat up and struggled against the kaftan strangling his waist. 'Oh, it's you, Andy, dear boy.' He flopped back down on the sofa, massaging his temples. 'Oh, what vehicle drove over my head last night?' he groaned.

'Haven't you got a bed to go to?' I firmly said.

Once he was gone, I pulled the dead cigarette from my mother's twitching lips and flipped over the cushions of the sofa to lay down on relative freshness. I settled down to sleep again, but not before I text Dad:

'Dad, get over here. There's a man here who's sweeping her off her feet. He isn't a looker, but he has charisma, little inhibition and several Viagra, and he's not afraid to use them. A pretty noxious concoction.'

When I woke again, I checked my almost dead phone. Two texts from Alistair asking when I would be free for a frolic and, more importantly, one from my Dad. It said, 'I'm on my way.' I am, to say the least, relieved. Melve may be a free spirit with the same weird magnetism over women as the sixty-six-year-old Michael Douglas, but he's no match for a working man who can impersonate Elvis perfectly and knows how to kill the ladies with a smooth foxtrot.

******

Later, I challenged Mum over the extinct fag I found on her lips. I stressed how much I detest smoking, especially in bed. Especially in my bed. 'It kills people and soft furnishings,' I barked.

She said, without justified snappishness, I thought, 'Andy, I was inebriated for the third night in a row, I can't remember anything past midnight. I'm past giving a shit.' She pulled out her packet of Lamber & Butler and fumbled in her housecoat pocket for a green disposable lighter some queen had given her at the club. She waved both objects in the air and added, 'For the first time in my life, I'm free. No grandchildren to stain my clothing, no dinner to make by six-thirty, no garden path to sweep. Now, I'm nipping down to the street, like a good guest, and going to damn well enjoy at least two fags before I come back up.'

'But you're in your housecoat!'

'What do you think I'm going to do, flash my tits at the next passing taxi driver?'

'Anything's possible the mood you're in these days,' I grunted.

She left. I could've throttled something, but instead, I filled the sink and washed the pile of dishes that she's so ignorant of, which gave me some kind of satisfaction. When she returned, the suds were fizzing down the plughole, and I was ready to leave. I went to Alistair's. If she can do what she likes, so can I. I know I shouldn't have, but I needed to ignore all the crap going on, even the stuff I suspected he's into, and within thirty minutes I was in his arms, naked and warm, the nostalgia of what we had been soothing my frayed nerves.

When we were recovering on the hall floor, he asked me if I had time for a few hugs in bed. I wanted to, but I had to leave before I sank into the comforting pillow of his chest and fell for the rhythm of his heart once more. Nostalgia can be a trap. I claimed I had to get back to work and let him hold me one more time before I left. He looked bemused. Almost hurt.

If Sally's wrong and we've misjudged him, I'll make it up to him somehow, but for now, I have to be number one. I tried to convince him we're okay. I stuck to the plan. 'Keep him sweet,' she said. But I know I'm playing games, and I hate that.

Wednesday 8th December

With no sign of Dad by midnight, I tried to call him, but his phone was either off or dead. I've been on edge the whole day. Gwen popped into the café, and I introduced her reluctantly to my mother, who'd been idle there waiting on a call from Melve. I ushered Gwen into the cleaning cupboard and explained the situation with Mum, Melve and my absent father.

'She's lazy, uh?' she mused. 'You need to make her life miserable. She's in your house now, not hers. The orchestra does not play well with a torpid violinist or a listless drummer.'

She was right. What was I so afraid of? Why should she be comfortable? Buying me a sofa-bed does not buy her the right to lounge over the rest of my life. 'Hey, maybe she could be forced into working here, God knows we need the cover while Sally is AWOL,' I said.

'Good idea,' grinned Gwen. 'No one has the nerve to say no to Molasses. She'd have to take the position. She couldn't keep the pace. She'll be half-dead and buying a one-way ticket home by this evening.'

Molasses passed by with her arms full of steaming plates, reversed carefully, and eyeballed us through the crack in the door. 'What are you two children up to?' she asked as she balanced on one leg and tugged open the door with her knee.

We shushed her and beckoned her in. Again, I explained how miserable my mother was making me. 'She's really cramping my style, if you get my drift?'

Molasses raised her eyebrows, and her eyes bulged through the darkness. 'Aaaah, I'm so sorry, my boy,' she whispered. 'I assumed you would welcome the company, but nothing should get in the way of an active sex-life, eh?' She winked.

'Do you think you could offer her a job and make her life hell?' I asked.

Molasses pulled her neck in and looked offended, 'And what are you trying to say, my boy?'

'Oh, I love it here,' I insisted, aware how quick I'd changed my tune, 'but I know she'd find it tough. She's no grafter. She'd hate it and leave pronto.'

Molasses smiled and said, 'Well, we could all do with a little help, no matter how little that help is.' She peered around the open doorway towards Mum. We followed suit. Molasses tutted and added, 'Besides, she's beginning to drag this establishment down. Would you look at that?' Mum was licking the left-over froth from her cappuccino from the inside of the mug while twisting it around her face. Molasses let out a 'Mmmm-hmmm!' then added, 'It's time for a little job interview, don't you think?'

Within twenty minutes, Mum was fully employed, washing dishes, serving drinks and being a general dogsbody. Within the hour she looked harassed, haggard and in desperate need of a smoke.

Thursday 9th December

My sister called. 'Dad's missing and no one's able to contact him,' she cried, 'This is a living nightmare, I've lost two babysitters now. I've got an eyebrow threading booked in tomorrow. I can't have our kids there during; I'll be scowling so much I'll end up looking like Dr Spock. I refuse to have Star Trek eyebrows, Andy. If mum doesn't come home, I'm dropping the kids at yours.' I assured her an actual living nightmare was sharing a small room with a six-foot chain-smoker who sheds clumps of long, curly red hairs in every plug hole and sleeps in until lunchtime. She needn't be taking the easy option and dropping her baggage at my door. She yapped, 'I'm no' taking the easy option. I never have. The easy option would've been having cesarian sections. I chose to tear my vagina apart at each and every birth. That's love. That's commitment.'

I felt a sharp pain in the crotch and imagined barn doors flapping in the wind. Why is it whenever women mention their vaginas to me they're described in painful of disgusting prose? Is it any wonder I'm a Gold Star Gay?

My sister added, 'I have a spray tan booked in this afternoon and my nails afterwards. You come round and see how hard it is to be a working mum and find the energy to keep a man remotely interested in you after nine o'clock at night.'

I told her that selling door-to-door from a Betterware catalogue does not constitute a full-time job and to lay off the tanning; if she gets any oranger, we'll lose her in family photographs. Last time I saw her, it took me ten minutes to realise she was sitting on the lounge floor as she blended so well into Mum and Dad's teak sideboard.

******

All Mum did on the slip and slide home from work was criticise the menu choice in the café, 'I mean, Andy. Who the hell wants Jerk this and Callaloo that? What's wrong with good old mince and tatties? It's mucking up my digestive system.' She kicked off her shoes, flopped on my bed and asked me to rub her feet.

I declined, saying, 'I have to go to the laundrette as I've double the amount of washing. You could help by doing the dishes.'

She said, 'I'm too clapped out. If my hands touch another drop of detergent they'll crack in half: just look at how chipped my nails are from scrubbing plates in that pokey kitchen.'

I packed up the washing and left in a mood. Her parting words echoed in my head as I watched the suds slosh around her support pants, 'Get something nice for dinner that won't give me ring-sting for a week. Also, get me some Sudocrem or, if you can't find that, chapstick.'

I arrived back with two Fray Bentos pies and a tin of carrots. We ate in silence at the foldout table by the kitchen sink until Mum's heavy nasal breathing and munching drove me to suggest, 'Let's watch the telly, eh?'

The news was on, covering the blizzard on the M8. Piles of cars smothered in snow were backed-up into the blackness of the flurry. Headlights on most of the vehicles were either dead or a lacklustre yellow glow. A local STV reporter was interviewing a man wearing a bunnet, duffle coat and Celtic F.C. scarf. The reporter described the scene, 'Drivers have been stranded along the central belt overnight. Harthill Services is acting as a refuge for the cold and hungry. The Scottish transport minister has been criticised for not doing enough to cope with the bad weather over the past few days. I'm here with a Mr Angus. Mr Angus, how are you coping?'

'I'm doing okay, Mike. We've got a bunch of us sleeping close in the back of a truck with a couple of people who don't have British passports, if you know what I mean?' Dad winked at the camera. 'They don't speak much English, but they know how to play rummy, so that's passing the time. But it's getting desperate now, we've almost kicked the arse out of the bottle of whisky I packed to keep warm, and there's only so much man-made fibres can do. Although, there's nothing that can beat a grand Celtic scarf. Quality players and quality scarf.' Dad pulled the tail end of his scarf out from the neck of his jacket and pointed at it for effect. I glanced at Mum nervously, who was staring at the screen with her fork paused in front of her mouth.

'The government's advising against travelling, so why have you come this far?' asked the reporter, rosy-cheeked and blinking against the arctic wind.

'I was heading to Edinburgh to get my wife. She's ran away 'coz our scheme is gonna be pulled down, and she seems to think that I don't care, but that's no' true. You see, Mike, you'll understand, I'm a working man from the West, we don't show emotion like these funny metrosexuals, it's not in our nature. But showing passion for our rights, that's a different matter. Miners' strikes and closure of shipyards, that we know about. I was in Piper Alpha when it went down. It took a long time to get an honest answer out of the oil companies back then, and I guess I've not had any steam since. If you're listening, Beth, I promise to show you a wee bit more emotion and fight tooth and nail for our wee house and every house in the scheme. Hell, Mike, I might even help with the cooking and all that, if that's what it takes. I'll even get some more pills to help other things. There's a guy down the club who can get you a few wee blue ones on the cheap, if you know what I mean?' Dad laughed, dipped his eyes towards Mike's crotch and nudged him with his elbow.

Mike turned to face the camera, blocking out Dad with his voluminous red puffer jacket as best he could and struggled through chuckles, 'Thanks, Mr Angus, and now back to the studio.'

Mum slammed down her fork and snapped, 'You told!'

I picked up my plate, held my head high and said, 'Aye, I did. He's on his way, and there's nothing you can do about it. You have nowhere to run.' I moved to the sofa and munched on the greasy pastry with a smug grin (there's very little space to argue in a bedsit, I find).

'You think?' Mum left her pie and headed out the door.

Her intent dawned on me. I called after her, 'Don't think of knocking on that randy hippie's door.' But it was too late; I could hear a Somerset accent and then a door close. She's been there for hours now. I've taken a glass to the bathroom during my caffeinated-fuelled trips to the loo. Every other wall in this place is so thin you could hear a midgie fart, but the bathroom is built to withstand the H-bomb, damn it! I can't make out if it's heavy counselling or passionate love-making. It's ten at night. I'm done with it now. I'm off to bed to listen to Roberta Flack and ignore what may or may not be happening down the hall.

11.30 p.m. I've sent four text messages to Alistair, and yet there's nothing back. Is he playing hard to get, or is he just getting hard over someone else? I hate playing games; they're useless if the other person doesn't give a toss.

Friday 10th December

2 a.m. In between restless sleep, I was woken by gentle knocking. I found our 'shared laptop' laid at the foot of the door with a yellow post-it stuck to it. *Sally*, I thought. I looked around for her but not hide nor hair. I carried the laptop to my bed. The Colonel was purring, happy that Mum had taken leave, and some degree of normality had crept back into our lives. I peeled off the note, shaking my head to wake myself just enough to read it:

'Pull To Open.'

I did so, and the laptop sprung to life. A reminder popped up in the top right-hand corner of the screen. It said, 'Dearest Andy ...' I opened it. It continued, 'Click on Gaydar and let the recent chat page with "RuggerFCK4U" open. You'll see from the pictures, even with the gimp mask, that this is your man. He's wearing the same watch and has the same tattoo as you described. The fetishes fit too. He has the same profile name and images on Grindr, I've found. I'm sorry, my darling. I know this is heartbreaking, and you were hoping for a very different outcome, but the truth needs to come out sooner or later. I know that. I also know I can only do so much as this is very upsetting for me too. You'll have to provide the honey, my honey. It hurts, I know, but be brave. I've always got your back.'

Unable to cope, I snapped the laptop shut and slid it under my bed. I grabbed the Colonel and pulled him closer. He's nuzzled me for half an hour (a record). Such a tiny life, but so massive to me.

11 a.m. Four firm knocks at my door. I knew it was Gwen. She's always given four firm knocks in the same rhythm. Maybe it's natural for musicians to follow a familiar score. She had her mobile in her hand, the screen was alight under her furrowed brow.

'Have you seen Twitter?' she asked, excitedly.

'What? No, I gave it up. I just do Facebook. And recently a new thing called Instagram; prettier and less of a social-political-minefield.'

Gwen tutted and said, 'Like I care about that. Anyway, Twitter: your father is trending.' She walked into the room and clicked on the hashtag *#jiltedontheM8*. I could see all kinds of comments from strangers who had some sort of opinion or advice for my folks. Some supportive and nice; others were just plain rude. One person, tagged as 'Divorcee45' (probably the number of times she's been divorced), advised Dad to jack it all in and move to Quebec to be with her. She would show him 'true love and proper winter clothing.' There was a picture of her bare feet attached. A total foot-fetish slapper, judging by her choice of nail varnish colour and cheap ankle bracelet. And most definitely not house-proud, as the stains on the moth-eaten carpet declared.

'This is ridiculous!' I said.

Gwen nodded and said, 'Yes, social media usually is, but it can do great things. Just look.' She flipped to her 'retweets' and pulled up a post from the *Coatbridge & Airdrie Advertiser*. It asked, 'Does anyone know what happened to *#jiltedontheM8*? If so, contact us.'

'Your dad is fast becoming a celebrity,' she said, smiling so broadly it was as if a spotlight had just been shone on a set of piano keys.

When I caught Mum, she was already up, showered and heading to work with full slap on. I blocked her walk of shame form Melve's room, but she dared to have a cheery bounce in her step. I asked no questions. I didn't want to know the in's and out's of their behaviour last night. Her face turned to stone, and she quickly murmured, 'Good morning,' making her way purposefully to the front door with my hand tugging the sleeve of her Burberry coat. She barely looked at me as she declared, 'I don't have time to chat, Andrew. I have to be at that hell-hole of a café by one o'clock, as my own son is intent of working his poor mother to death just to prove a bloody point. Besides, I'd rather be as far away from here as possible when your father turns up. I've nothing to say to that man that I haven't said before.' She lifted her nose to the air and turned her head away from me when I held the door shut.

I thrust my phone in her face and demanded, 'You'll want to see this.'

I like to think it was the masses supporting their relationship over the web that softened her hard shell, but little changed in her expression until she hit upon the tweet from the *Airdrie & Coatbridge Advertiser*. And when she yelled, 'The BBC want to interview us?' I knew she had an ulterior motive. And when Dad appeared huffing and puffing at the door, blue with the cold and coated in fresh flakes of snow declaring his undying love and devotion, she burst into tears and threw herself into his arms saying, 'Charlie! Oh, my Charlie! How could I have been so stupid? It's been awful. I got stuck here. I've missed you. I never want to leave you again,' I knew that fickle mantra was chanting in her mind over and over again: *Celebrity! Celebrity! Celebrity!* Already, she was picturing herself on the cover of those trashy gossip magazines she worships.

She's gone. Now I have the space to sort out my own troubles, and all I can wish for is that another distraction will come along and delay the inevitable.

11.45 p.m. At 9 p.m., I was hiding in the shadows of the tenements across from Alistair's flat. I waited until my feet lost all feeling and the breath in my lungs had acclimatise to the frosty air, but his place remained dark and still. I walked home with salty tears drying on ever-thickening skin. He'd lied again. An afternoon text had told me he couldn't have me around as he was busy at his apartment entertaining his parents, but he wasn't at home after all.

The laptop was still breathing under my bed. Melve popped his head in the door, I suspect looking for Mum, but I quickly made some excuses and hastened his departure. With my door closed and firmly locked, I flipped open my Pandora's box. The battery was on the edge of dying, but I was determined. Powering up and sat on my reclaimed sofa, I was ready to continue the conversation between Sally's 'Babooshka' and RuggerFCK4U. I tracked back to get the gist of the language she'd used, the tone, the content and maybe the reason she couldn't go any further. There had been the initial greetings, the obvious confirmation that both were horny, the exchange of photographs – Sally's were fakes stolen from the web; Alistair's were shots of himself tied to a bed and then a door. Just another guy in a gimp mask, faceless and unrecognisable to many, but I know every inch of that body. And then the keen enquiry on Alistair's part for a quick hook-up within the hour. This was where Sally had made her excuses and ran with cold feet towards my door. *Why did she find this so difficult?*

Then a chat bubble popped up with a 'Hey!' He was online. 'Still horny?'

I could've signed off and ran a mile. Horny? I was anything but, but I did my best and faked it: 'Yeah, horny as!'

'Wanna come round and beat my ass?'

My fingers froze over the keys. The blood gushed in my ears so much that it felt as if my skull had softened and was visibly pulsating before me in the mirror. I pondered for a few minutes ... could I do this? It felt cruel to both of us. Here was a man lost in some kind of no man's land between the gays and the straights. He's confused. A foreigner, ignorant of the lay of the land. A stranger teetering on the edge of a new world, with no guidance, no role-models, just his own stupefaction coupled with a rampant sexual desire for the male form.

But then, who am I? I'm equally as lost and confused. That's the only thing I can be sure of. I know I need clarity. 'Yes,' I replied, stumbling over the keyboard, 'what's the address?' The address matched the one etched into my mind. He was now home and obviously alone. Final confirmation. My heart broke and shattered into so many tiny pieces, it would be impossible to put back together the same way. And with it came anger, not tears, just sheer bloody anger. He laid out exactly how he wanted it to play: the main entry door would be wedged open; his apartment door would be unlocked; he'd be waiting there, naked in the dark, blindfolded on his bed, expecting the riskiest ride of his life. It was so well-rehearsed, it was sickening.

'Wanna come round and beat my ass?'

Oh, Alistair, you have no idea.

Saturday 11th December

A List of Lies

- The slave is faithful and dedicated to his Master.
- Alistair is a sexual novice and cautious when it comes to putting himself out there, finding his feet with baby steps.
- We were going to build a life together, as soon as he got past his issues.
- Alistair loves me.

A List of Truths

- The slave is not only unfaithful to his Master, but he interacts in extracurricular activities with a host of Masters, some of whom may have been present when I walked in on his shameful act last night.
- He's confident and established as a sexual player and the only feet to be found were his very own, flipped into the air as he lay joyously on his back, engorged in a sloppy, sweaty soup of meat and bodily fluids stirred by three other men.

- There are more sexual than sexuality issues and, judging by the euphoria in his eyes, he is very comfortable dealing with them in the hear-and-now of sexual arousal. There's not a drug neat enough to provide such a rush of endorphins. I could slice myself into bite-sized portions, and it would not be enough to sedate his appetite.
- He's incapable of building anything other than a playroom of leather slings, assorted torture devices and shackles to each and every wall.
- Most importantly: Alistair does not love me.

2 p.m. The bride-to-be turned up at my door not so long ago in a rage.

'Andy, I'm sorely disappointed in you,' he said without sitting down. 'I can't believe you've been lying to me all this time. I thought we were good friends.'

I was at a loss and trying to keep my aching heart in. I shrugged and said, 'I have been completely honest with you ...'

'No you have not: you've been on Instagram for weeks, as it turns out, and never once enlightened me or asked to follow me, thank you very much!'

I burst into tears.

Ryan was taken aback. 'Oh, I'm sorry, cupcake. It's not that important. I didn't mean to be such a bitch, it's just you know ...'

'The wedding, I know,' I said between gasps of breath. 'It's not Instagram; it's Alistair.'

Are you okay? You look like you haven't moisturised for a month.'

I let it all go, all the hurt, all the hope, all the dreams I'd banked on and sobbed so much I almost swallowed my tongue during a fit of convulsive, unstoppable gasps for air. Snot dripped from my nose as my eyes gushed. There was drool. It wasn't pretty. But to give my finicky friend his due, he didn't recoil in disgust, he caught me in my free fall and held me tight, resting my now Vesuvius-like face on the shoulder of his precious Prada shirt. I let go enough to be rid of the despair, but not enough to remove the hurt. I need to hold on to that. I need to remember the damage Alistair's done. It'll ensure that I'll never wander into his hall of distorted mirrors ever again.

11 p.m. I was woken from my reclusive slumber by a barrage of ridiculously excited texts from Mum, Dad, my sister, her husband and Mrs White next door to my folks (I'd like to know who the hell gave some random neighbour my mobile number) to the fact Mum and Dad were going to be on the late-night STV news. I watched my folks feature as the weekend 'Dead Donkey'. My parents were interviewed by local reporter Bob McTavish sat at home in their favoured leather recliners, which had been pushed conspicuously close together for them to hold hands and gaze lovingly into each other's eyes. The lounge looked weird on widescreen and my parents more so.

'I'll be honest with you, Bob,' Mum said to the reporter in the fake plummy voice she usually keeps for conversations with important people, like her doctor or Father O'Brien, 'its a shame it's taken the threatened demolition of our quiet community for us to realise how much we love each other.' This was followed by perfectly timed batting eyelashes towards my blushing and rather awkward-looking father. 'But it's the kick up the backside we needed. We just hope that our neighbours will rise up and sign our petition to show us, and every single member of this community – and it is a community – how much they love this wee part of Airdrie. We may be small and insignificant to the local council, but we're stronger than the concrete that binds us together.' Then she rattled through her usual minors' strike/raising three kids/childbirth on kitchen linoleum tale. To me, it had more saccharin than a diabetic chocolate cake. Dad just sat and nodded between manic smiles into the camera. He looked terrified. I wondered how much of it was stage-fright or wife-fright.

Immediately after, a text dropped into my lap from Alistair asking, 'Was that your folks on the telly?' A Pitiful excuse for desperate interaction. I ignored this. Moments later he sent, 'R u ok?'

Now you're concerned, Alistair. You've picked an excellent time to grow a conscience, I thought. I wrote back, 'How do I make this clear? Never call, text or touch my life in any way ever again. What I saw the other night sickened me.' I think the big streak of piss should get the message. My phone and TV are switched off from all this insanity.

Sunday 12th December

My morning routine was hijacked by protestations from Melve that his intentions towards Mum were nothing but honourable. 'I was just flexing my straight muscles, my dear boy. I had to after all those shenanigans with Trenton.'

The poor man got the brunt of my anger. I tore into him as savagely as a cheetah would a baby wildebeest. 'Honour? Don't talk to me about honour,' I ranted, 'if you had one honourable bone in your body you would've walked tall next to Trenton, not hid ten paces behind him. If you're willing to play with the man, you should have the balls to walk the walk hand and hand. You have as much honour as Hitler and an equal amount of sex-appeal; you were lucky even to catch Trenton's eye. Now bugger off!' I slammed the door in his startled face.

Feeling guilty about my outburst, and too embarrassed to offer an apology, I escaped quickly for work but dragged my sorry arse towards Café Jamaica with as much enthusiasm as a gay man heading to a baby shower. Winter is still loitering, and it bites. Another text from Alistair piled on the grey: 'Please, forgive me. I'm lost without you. I'll never screw this up again.' The day was certainly starting on a low and pessimism was settling itself into that comfy chair in my mind, ready for a day's worth of self-criticism.

Or so I thought. For sat on the sofa, minus all of her hair and a few stones lighter, was the slight form of Christina, animated and in mid-conversational-flow with Molasses. I had to look twice, but it was definitely her. I felt a lump come to my throat. It was so good to see her in her usual spot screeching with laughter. If cancer has taken its toll on her body, it certainly hasn't quashed her spirit.

'You're back?' I asked, struggling with reality.

'Andy, mi hermoso chico! It's wonderful to see you.' She pushed up from the sofa, straining a little on her now thinner legs, and splayed underfed hands that beaconed me for a hug. I wrapped my arms around her and became aware of every bone in her vertebrae. I eased the pressure a bit, frightened I'd damage this delicate package sent all the way from Valencia, and gently stroked her protruding scapulas.

She filled me in at super-Spanish-speed. 'I'm just staying for a few weeks, taking it easy before I join all of you for the boys' wedding.

The treatment has been tough, as I'm sure my little bag of bones will tell you – all surgery, chemo and radiotherapy, boring stuff like that – but I've been given the go-ahead to travel, and here I am.'

I grinned at her, but then I felt a burst of emotion and had to bite back the tears that'd overcome my joy. 'I'm sorry,' I said, 'it's just a shock seeing you like this.'

'It's okay, Andy. I feel the same every time I look in the mirror. I have to remind myself that this isn't me, I've just been put on pause while the treatment did the job of killing all that nasty stuff inside. But I've already hit the PLAY button, and I will soon be up to full speed.' She smiled and added, 'Andy, it's all looking good so far.'

'But your lovely thick hair ...'

'Oh, I got over that months ago. It'll grow back,' she smiled.

'And in the meantime, I have quite a collection of daring wigs that she can test before the wedding, darling,' interjected Sally as she casually materialised carrying a crate of beer from the cellar as if she'd never vanished.

'You're back too?' I asked, astounded.

'Well, either that or someone has a lot of cash and an amazing plastic surgeon; it costs a shit-load to imitate a body as fit as mine,' she quipped as she tossed the crate on the bar and proceeded to cup her hands around her bulging breasts and shimmied her shoulders. 'The bitch is back. Did you miss me?'

Safe to say, I did. The gang is coming back together, and suddenly everything feels like it's going to be okay. I didn't say as much to Sally, though. She's not that sentimental. I gave her a dig instead, 'Oh, the great performer returns in the nick of time for her spotlight at the wedding.'

'Oh, that's right. It's the dress rehearsal tonight. I totally forgot about that,' she faked.

I gave an apathetic cheer and said, 'I wish I had. I'm not looking forward to recreating the role of Sarah Brightman.'

11.45 p.m. How much more stress can this body take? I was crammed into a box under a stage and made to enter via a trap door as the first few bars of the song *Starship Trooper* rattled through the ballroom of the hotel. A buggery-bollocking trap door! In all these weeks this is the first time it's been mentioned. 'It's a last-minute addition which will add a little flourish to the performance,' smiled Tony with malevolent blackness in his eyes. If I was stuffed in there once, I was stuffed in there a hundred times. The air inside my space helmet became extremely stale and clammy, the glass steamed up so much I'd difficulty seeing my mark and any stage directions barked from Sally were incomprehensible. It's as if Tony knows my worst fears and has condensed them into four minutes and nineteen seconds of disco torture.

'This is why we have dress rehearsals, darling,' consoled Trenton as we packed up for the evening. 'It's to iron out the finer details and remove the glitches. I should know, I spent two months on the set of the original Crossroads – I rest my case.'

'Now that would've been torture,' Melve said in agreement, insinuating himself into the conversation, but neither Trenton nor I were in the mood.

Trenton turned to chase after the Terrible Twins as they left hand and hand. He boomed, purposefully for Melve's benefit I imagine, 'Boys! Lovies! Would it be fine with you if I bring a plus-one on Saturday? I've just met the most marvellous muscular man ...'

Melve looked crestfallen. I gave him a body-swerve (as I'm unable to deal with someone else's emotional shit when my own cerebral lavvy is currently clogged full with the stuff) and followed Sally to say, 'A little bird with a big mouth – Ryan – tells me you're putting on a couple of solo spots at this camp extravaganza on Saturday.'

Sally glanced around to see if anyone was in earshot, 'Yes, sweetie, that may be the case.'

'Then why haven't I seen some sort of rehearsal?'

'Because, my budding-spaceman-slash-disco-diva, I'm a professional and don't want my shining performance to starstruck the amateurs, present company excluded, of course. Besides, it's a surprise.' She quickly changed the subject, 'Speaking of surprises, or lack of really, how are you coping after being shat on from a great height by the not-so-lovely Alistair?'

'Oh, don't worry, I'm getting by. I had a good cry on Ryan's shoulder the other day.'

'Oh, Ryan?' I could feel the bruising of an ego. 'Why him?'

'Because he was there,' I replied, aware my words may jar. Sally looked wounded. 'Well, you've been busy,' I added, apologetically.

She agreed, 'True, true. Anyway, I'm back now and won't be going anywhere. So just remember that I'm all ears when you need me. Well, that and I have breasts the size of basketballs to rest your tired, distressed head on too. Much more comfortable than some drama queen's boney excuse for shoulders.'

******

In other news, a pile of texts from Mum: 'Just booed Simon Cowell at the X Factor final. Bit of a thrill. His head looks even funnier from the back. It's out of proportion to the rest of his body. He looks like a life-sized Bobblehead.'

'Tomorrow, me and your dad will be on Loose Women. Watch it! Your dad's always liked the Nolans, so he's peeing his pants about meeting one of them.'

'We've stayed in two hotels so far, and I'm getting quite a collection of individually wrapped teabags and face cloths. The toilet paper is a rough as sandpaper, your father says, but I'm taking that too. Needs must! IBS! TTFN!'

TMI!

How can she possibly be helping the campaign? Undoubtedly the most important place to be when the cameras are rolling is standing in the scheme they're supposedly trying to save, not grabbing every celebrity freebie going. She's totally milking it. She wants to be careful with her sudden rise to fame as the Scots can react badly to such ignorance: I still remember Sheena Easton's on stage pelting after her return to Glasgow from years promoting herself in the U.S.

Monday 13th December

Ryan asked me to spend my only day off tying up loose ends for Saturday. This involved my most loathed pastime: shopping. In particular, shopping for others. Shopping for others I hardly know or have never met, i.e., the key family members at the ceremony. Boring!

Ryan has a love/hate relationship with his favourite pastime: he loves to shop, but he hates shop assistants. 'This is half the price just around the corner, I think you should be offering the same,' he lied to the poor shop assistant at Jenners who stood not a jot of a chance of making a hefty commission today. The boy knows what he wants and how to get it. He beat even the most adept salesperson into submission. He's carefully mastered the art of being interested and suspicious of a piece at the same time, examining the goods with the critical eye of an experienced antique dealer at a bric-a-brac sale. Every gift idea I suggested was blown to the wind with one dismissive swish of his hand. I questioned why I was there – internally only, as only a fool would get in the path of this retail locomotive – and became quietly grumpy and hypoglycaemic between the chain stores on Princes Street and the boutiques of George Street. By the time we reached John Lewis, I was ecstatic when he waved a voucher for a cuppa with cake. I snatched it like it was Willy Wonka's Golden Ticket and made a mad dash for the lift that would take me to the sugar and caffeine sanctuary on the top floor. The ten bags of shopping I'd been lumbered with (as Ryan is struggling with a supposed ingrown toenail) did not hamper.

As we were hoisted towards the café, we heard what seemed like prisoners under some kind of terrible mass torture. The doors opened to reveal a kindergarten on crack. Screaming toddlers and irritated parents seemed to be clashing like a pile-up on the M6. Ryan took a deep breath and said bravely, 'Okay, let's go in, but don't let any child with sticky, jammy fingers touch my very expensive Gucci trousers.'

'Okay, the same goes for me.'

Ryan scrutinised me from top to toe and said, 'I don't think you have anything to worry about; is Littlewoods somehow still afloat amidst this terrible recession?'

'It isn't,' I replied. 'It closed its doors in 2005.'

'Did it?' he said in wonder. He looked me up and down again and added, 'We really need to update your wardrobe ASAP!' He patted me on my tired shoulders and added, 'That's one thing I admire about you, Andy; your ability to dress down at any occasion and not give two hoots. I wish I had the balls to care so little about what others think, but unfortunately, I've been afflicted with the worst of diseases: an ego.' We stepped into the slobbering canteen of kids. 'I often wonder how many hours of my life have been lost desperately choosing the perfect outfit for the perfect occasion. It's tough for Tony and me being the gay scene's equivalent of Posh and Becks.'

Was this a constructive criticism sandwich without the encouraging layers? The sight of my salvation and salivation – cake

– over the minefield of sugarcoated exploding toddlers distracted my misgivings on his sincerity, and we soon joined two students on a couple of sofas struggling to look content and communicate over the din.

'We received the vouchers for choosing to have our wedding list here, you know? I would've shared them with Tony, but he's become allergic to nuts, cocoa, caffeine, gluten, wheat and sugar,' he said slicing off a delicate slither of caramel shortcake and popping it in his mouth with one pinky raised.

'Sugar? Is he diabetic?' I asked.

'No,' he replied as if it was a silly question. 'Have you bought anything for us yet? The wedding list is online.'

I was confident he knew I hadn't, therefore, honesty was the best policy. 'Not yet,' I said, shovelling a considerable amount of carrot cake in my mouth and attempting to look blasé.

'Well, you'd better get a move on, there's hardly anything left that hasn't been snapped up by more organised friends,' he dropped sarcastically. 'It's so nice to see people support us. It's reassuring to know that, in our thirties, we're still a popular couple on and off the scene.'

Ryan obviously equates the strength of a friendship by how many Royal Doulton saucers each friend 'gifts' them. By the time I got home, I was clapped out. The soles of my shoes had been worn to nothing by some queen who doesn't understand the urgency of a thirty-six-year-old bladder. I downloaded their gift list as soon as I emptied the bulging water balloon just behind my groin. I had Ryan's last words ringing in my ears as I scrolled down in desperation, 'We have vouchers as an option, but vouchers are for people who have given zero thought to what we really need. The gifts are what we'd really like.' I mulled over the words 'need' and 'like' as I scrolled back up. They didn't 'need' anything; they 'liked' *a lot*. I scrolled down the commodious catalogue again. The only thing left to buy was one of those fancy-schmancy Kitchen Aid mixers at £379! Neither of them bake. Surely it's a total waste of money if your husband is allergic to nuts, cocoa, caffeine, gluten, wheat and sugar? What's left to bake, fruit? It'll be on 'display', and the blades will never touch the silky divineness of a chocolate brownie mix, or make the egg whites of a pavlova glisten with sugary peaks. Anyway, it will rarely be seen under the mountains of takeaway boxes that pile up on their counters until poor Gwen works her marigold mitten-covered magic.

I wistfully looked over at my little Baby Belling stove which is pretty much useless at toasting bread evenly. Not its fault. It's pretty old. I was a useless domestic god, and I won't be becoming one any time soon, so its no great hardship. But a Kitchen Aid mixer? The ultimate in bakeware? Yes, I'm jealous.

I checked my bank account: I had £523 left until the next pay just before Christmas. In only a few clicks my account was down to £144. I have to feed myself, a cat and buy Christmas presents for my family and friends with that. I would've been as well tossing the £379 in the back of a bin lorry. Their wedding breakfast had better be good. I'm eating everything and drinking every last drop of free booze as compensation.

7 p.m. Just eaten three slices of toast with cheese and beans for my dinner. I used to love this. It was a special laid-back dinner Mum would make for us kids on the odd Saturday, which would have us leaping in the air with excitement, mainly because it gave us a reprieve from tinned veg and the cheap, chewy meat she would buy from Fine Fare. I was four forks in when I thought, *This is crap.* I cried over the plate as I took another mouthful, sat on my big empty sofa with only the TV news reporter for company. Salty tears dripped onto the beans and mixed with the sauce. I watched them dissolve for a time, sighed and then forced myself to eat the rest. Not a colossal bawling session, just a wee blip, so that's progress. Is this really what my life has come to? I'm the sad, lonely bean eater who lives in a bedsit. How long before I forego the trimmings and eat from the cold, jagged can with unwashed hands? Oh, it's not the immediate cashflow problem that's made me blue. I've been broke before. It's the loneliness and, therefore, everything else seems so desperately sad. It's palpable. It sleeps next to me at night.

Alistair, why did you have to be so screwed up?

Tuesday 14th December

Oh, joy of fucking joys! I have a discharge from my penis. I'd wondered why I needed to pee so much yesterday. By seven this morning, during a brief inspection, I found the opening to my urethra was not only inflamed, but it was freely dripping a white discharge.

I was caught by Sally as I scurried to the loo with a small glass in hand to inspect my urine for thready floaters. 'Good morning, sexy,' she said cheekily. And then more inquisitively, 'Why the guilty face?'

'No reason,' I lied, feeling my face flush.

'Come on, what have you been up to, you naughty boy?'

'Nothing,' I said, hiding the glass. 'Oh, what's the point? I don't feel that sexy this morning, and I do know what I've been up to, but what I'd really like to know is what someone else has been up to. Alistair in particular. I'd like to know which dirty pole or hole he's been at to give me a small delivery of milkiness this morning.'

Sally looked befuddled.

'I think I have ... no, I know I have a discharge coming from the most irritating of places,' I explained, showing her the glass. 'I was just about to check my pee for further evidence.'

'Ah, just a sec, darling,' she said as she nipped in her room. She rummaged in the base of the large wooden trunk at the bottom of her bed and pulled out a black tub with a colour-coded chart on the side. She rattled the contents delicately and grinned.

'If that's a pile of pills to solve my problem, I'll take all of them in an instant,' I said.

'No, sorry sweetie, it's not. But it will diagnose, or rather I will.' She tossed the container into my hand. 'Just dip one of the test strips in your pee and bring it back to the expert.'

Expert? I pondered as I aimed my fiery pee at the glass. *I guess being a professional shagger, you quickly learn how to diagnose and treat your problems. Your livelihood is at stake, after all, STIs are bad for business.*

'Yes, yes,' said Sally as she scrutinised the thin test strip and matched it up it to the colour chart. 'You see this little dark green rectangle here?'

'Yes?' I nodded, examining closely with her.

'That's protein. A lot of protein.' She pointed to another dark green rectangle and said, 'This is blood. A lot of blood.'

'Oh,' I started to feel a little queasy.

'Oh, and do you see this lovely lavender one at the top?'

'Aye, it's kinda pretty.'

'That's piles of leukocytes, and therefore not so pretty.'

'What does that mean?'

'Basically, you can't have sex until you get diagnosed, treated and get the all-clear. You likely have an infection.'

'Oh, what kind?'

'I have no idea, sadly, my poor infected friend,' she said casually dropping the strip of contaminated colours into a ziplock bag and disposing of it. 'That's why you need to head to Chalmers Street as fast as your chaffed cock will allow you.'

'What's on Chalmers Street?' I asked.

'Oh, you really are quite delightfully naive, aren't you, darling? It's where you'll find your friendly neighbourhood clap clinic.'

Square one, here I come, I thought. 'Well, I've been meaning to take an HIV test. When I say "meaning", I really mean "putting it off", if I'm honest.'

'Well, maybe this infection will inspire you,' she said dryly. 'How long has it been? Six months?'

'Give or take ten years, aye.'

'You mean when you met Thomas?'

'Yes,' I said coyly.

'The plumber who was fiddling with every drain and tap in the Borders?'

'Um, yes,' I whispered, that dry feeling returning to my throat.

Sally looked deathly serious and asked me, 'Do you think you've been at risk?'

I thought for a minute. Why was it so hard to say I could've been. It wasn't foolish to trust a long-term partner totally and have unprotected sex from the get-go, was it?

'You don't need to answer that, I can tell by your face, sweetie. Oh, my dear, why haven't we talked about this before?'

'I think I'm scared. I think I could have it, but if I ignore it, push it as far away from me as possible, then I'll lose sight of it and can continue as normal.'

'Honey, you have the right to be healthy and live a full and exciting life. But most importantly, you have to take control. Don't deny yourself that.'

I slumped down on her bed, 'I've been finding excuses not to go.'

'Life is full of excuses. There's always going to be a special event like Christmas, or a wedding to contend with, or a breakup, but there always comes a time when you need to know. Trust me, no matter how far you run, and how much time passes, you can never escape the past.'

'I know you're right.'

'Listen, sweetie. I lost someone very dear to me through HIV. I want to help.'

And there it was. The past. Her past. A fleeting glimpse of Sally Knowles from yesteryear. It came from nowhere. She'd been avoiding her story for so long I expected we'd never get there. A slither so similar to my own. She slid on her shaggy purple coat and fixed her – for today – bouffant hair. 'Come on then,' she said with great urgency.

'Come on where?'

'To Chalmers Street, silly,' she said, doing final checks in the large ornate mirror that leans against the wall of her crowded room. 'I'll chum you.'

'Are you sure?'

'No time like the present,' she smiled.

I tried to swallow, but couldn't. It was time to take the test I'd been dreading. Now I'd learn if the blood racing through my battered heart was positive or negative.

******

The slut-o-meter was back clanging in my ear as I explained to the nurse exactly why I was there. I had to leave the supportive tones of Sally behind in the waiting room, and suddenly the confidence I was oozing on the way in the cab depleted drastically. I slowed to a verbal standstill as I confided that two of my previous partners might have put me at risk. If it hadn't been for the fantastic support from the nurse, I think I may have backed out. But the reassurance from him that HIV no longer was a death sentence, treatments are now available that may have no side effects at all, and those that do are manageable. Also, some studies have shown that the viral load carried in the blood by an infected person can be as little as zero, cutting the risk of infecting another person considerably. That, combined with safer sex, could mean a long-term relationship is still on the cards, with a very active sex-life to boot. This all depends on early diagnosis, monitoring and treatment, of course. A fact that keeps popping up, and yet I've still been terrified to take the test.

Once I'd thought about all the pros for testing, and the fact I couldn't and wouldn't disappoint my friend who'd given up her whole morning to act as my sexual health escort, I figured there was little else left to do but dispense with my hang-ups and my blood. I usually look in the opposite direction when a needle is unsheathed, but I found myself unable to tear my eyes away from the little blue vein in the nook of my left arm as the metal shard pressed its way into my circulation and began to drain a trickle of the raspberry-red life-force within. As my nurse labelled the little tubes that held my future delicately in their sealed plastic walls, I could've changed my mind, snatched them from him and disposed of them in the sharps box beside me, but that would've been crazy. I accepted that the deed was done relatively quickly and almost painlessly.

I walked slowly but surely back to Sally while clutching a week's worth of antibiotics and coping with a familiar feeling of sluggish stomach cramps having just swallowed a pile of pills that could sink a German U-boat. She was casually sprawled out on her back over three chairs while reading a well-thumbed copy of *Hello*. The waiting room was empty apart from a single receptionist who was failing to eat a ham and cheese roll discreetly behind the service counter.

'I think next year I'll try some Botox,' she announced from behind the pages. 'I'm getting to the age where Instagram filters just aren't cutting it. The celebrity competition out there is fierce.'

'No,' I said, 'you're perfect just as you are.'

She dropped the magazine to her chest and looked at me, 'Now, sweetie, we both know that just isn't true. And don't get sentimental; you're not dying. Deed done?'

'Aye, and treatment has already begun,' I pointed at the box of Doxycycline jutting out of my top pocket. 'Chlamydia: no sex until the all-clear in a week or so and try not to shit myself within the next two hours.'

'And when do you get the results for the *other* thing?'

'Well, with the wedding on the horizon and the festive season approaching, and what with work and all that, it won't be until the thirtieth,' I confessed. They had offered me the twenty-four-hour testing option, but I'd knocked that on the head instantly.

'What? Why so long?' protested Sally.

'Look the deed's done, that's enough for me right now,' I argued, holding her back as she lunged towards the munching receptionist to bully her into an earlier date. 'It was my choice. If it is bad news, I'd like just one more Christmas in the season of ignorant bliss. You must understand that?'

She did. We left and put the conversation out of our heads. I thanked her and headed to my shift a little later than scheduled. Before I got to Café Jamaica, I sent a text to Alistair that said, 'Better get your busy throat up to the clinic; you've given me the clap.' And then, without hesitation, I blocked his number.

Wednesday 15th December

- Day two of treatment: four antibiotics taken; stomach talking to me all day but not on a rollercoaster; discharge now a clear, sticky fluid; willy still red and not a happy chappy.
- One appearance by Mum and Dad on This Morning; zero reference of me, several references regarding my sister, their 'adorable' grandchildren, their long, loving marriage and the plight of the scheme. Seems I'm pretty insignificant. Surely the fact I'm their only homosexual son gives me extra appeal? Mum touched Philip Schofield on the thigh four times, which I think is totally inappropriate for a married woman on daytime television. Philip did not reciprocate. His early years working at the BBC has taught him some decorum, thankfully.

Thursday 16th December

7 a.m. Woke with morning glory. I stared down at my fully engorged and somewhat chaffed willy in disgust. *How dare you,* I thought as I got out of bed and turned my thoughts to less arousing matters. I took my morning dose of pills with freezing water from our winter-chilled pipes. I contemplated dousing my relentless stiffy in the remnants of the glass over my kitchen sink. Does my willy not have the common decency to realise that it's sick and should rest? It's as if it's saying, 'Hello, you may not want to talk to me right now, but we've shared many good times that can't be ignored. Call me!'

8.20 a.m. Overheard Sally and Gwen chatting in the hall as I had my morning ablutions. Sally whispered, 'The clinic can be busy at that time, but I'm always happy to help and be there for a friend, darling.'

Well, that must be a record; two days and she's blabbed the whole sorry details of our trip to GUM. That woman cannot hold her own water. Every time I foolishly put my trust in her, she lets me down. She's really ripped my knitting this time! It's just a ball of wool!

11 p.m. I was short with Sally at work. By five o'clock, she asked me, 'What's the matter with you? You've had a face like someone's handed you a shit in a spring-loaded box since we opened.'

'Maybe I have,' I said, polishing a glass as if the stubborn stain inside was the most important obstacle in my life. 'Maybe there's a lot of shit that should be kept sealed in boxes.'

'What are you talking about, darling?' she asked. Then she whispered, 'Are those antibiotics screwing with your mind?'

'Perhaps yes, perhaps not, and even if that is or isn't the case, I'd rather keep it to myself than have some loudmouth jabber to all and sundry,' I sulked into the glass.

Sally shook her head in bemusement, 'You baffle me some times, Andy Angus.'

'Oh, aye?' I said, throwing the towel in a temper on the bar. 'Well, here's some more food for thought. You can forget drinks at the Regent. I'm washing my hair tonight.'

'Oh dear, it's going to be a long night for you then Andrew. How long does a cheap barbers' cut actually take to cleanse and condition? Five minutes, perhaps?' butted in Biffo, who'd just appeared in the café.

I was gunning for an argument now, so I snapped, 'Why don't you just go f...' at this point, Molasses and Ryan arrived laden with bags glistening with designer logos, so I quickly adjusted my tone and finished my sentence with a dissatisfying, '...ind yourselves a comfy seat and I'll bring you the menu.'

'No need,' gleamed Biffo, revelling in the moment, 'I know what we want: three cosmopolitans, garçon, and be quick about it. Chop! Chop!' He clapped his hands briskly in front of my face. I could've grabbed them and slapped them all over his head, but I promised Ryan I'd be good. I figured venting my frustration over Sally's lack of confidentiality on Tony (no matter how satisfying that would be) would be selfish. I did my duty and fixed their drinks. A cocktail shaker can be a good channel for one's bile. I shook it, banged it and threw it stridently on the beat of every overdramatic declaration of love and excitement Biffo barfed regarding their pending nuptials. I purposefully made his stronger than the rest, using less ice and cranberry and adding a triple of absolute vodka. I watched him like a hawk when he finally brought the glass to his sour lips. He took a sip. Would he cough and choke over the brutal drink I'd made him? Would he leap out of his chair and accuse me of attempting to poison him? Nope. Nothing. He has no feelings at all, inside or out, and this proves it. I squeezed two extra quarters of lime into that cocktail too. Can nothing beat this man?

Day Three of Treatment:
- Four antibiotics taken as usual.
- Discharge remains, but less cloudy and more watery.
- Still have weird pee flow when I first go in the morning and also some stickage to sheets.
- Tip of willy less inflamed, but flakey, dry skin noted.
- Four random erections today: one first thing; another on the bus (bloody cobbles); another standing in the line at the post office (someone was wearing Issey Miyake, I think I was aroused by association); and lastly, when I was taking out the bins at the end of my shift (I ask you!)

Midnight. I've just assisted a very drunk Ms Knowles into bed. She knocked at my door and announced on wobbly heels, 'If Mohamed won't come to the bar, the bar must come to him.' She produced a claggy cocktail glass from the depths of her shaggy coat. 'Oh,' she said as she inspected the inside of the glass and tipped it upside down, disbelieving it was uninhabited by liquor. She shook it and then tossed it over her shoulder. It didn't shatter, thankfully, but bounced on the hall carpet and rolled into the toilet. She clung on to the lapels of my housecoat and slurred, 'I must've sp ... sp ... split it.

There must be a trail in the snow. Come on, let's go find it. I've never had a frozen martini before, have you?'

I tried to push her off, almost knocking her through the wall, and found myself still giving a damn, grabbing hold of her and assuming the customary position of a supportive friend. 'I think the lady has had enough for one night,' I asserted.

'Aww, you're no fun these days, sweetie,' she jollied as she pressed my nose with her index finger. 'You're not the first person to get a sore willy, you know, Andy.'

While she'd brought up the subject, 'Why did you tell Gwen about our trip to the clinic?' She looked at me blankly. I explained some more, 'I overheard you mention the GUM clinic to her this morning.'

Sally pulled back in disbelief, wide of mouth and even wider of eyes, 'I never said a thing, I assure you, darling. Scouts honour. Cross my knackered heart.' She attempted to do so but missed.

'That's your knackered liver,' I pointed out. 'Come on, time for beddy-byes.' I helped her into her room. The door swung open and banged against her cream dresser. Several items fell onto the floor: assorted hairbrushes, jewellery boxes, condoms, etc.

'Five!' she declared as I peeled off her heels and placed them carefully back in the correct spot amongst her collection of footwear, conscious that many things said and done may be forgotten by the morning, but the sacrilege of tossing her precious shoes casually on the floor would not. I flipped her legs up on the thick mattress. 'Five!' she said again, throwing up her arms from inside the duvet and giggling.

'Why do you keep saying that?' I asked.

She leant on one elbow and tried to focus on me, eyes squinting through the boozy fog, 'Because that's the number you come up with when you put two and two together every time, my dear.'

I shook my head, 'More cryptic nonsense.' I started to pick up the shit we'd spilt as we clattered through the door.

She continued to babble. 'Don't worry, Andy, my love, your secrets are safe with me.' I scooped up the scree of condoms and put them back in their bowl. 'It wasn't you I was helping this time,' she continued. I carefully arranged the fine necklaces back on the clay bust that'd gone awry. Sally flopped back onto her copious pile of pillows and said, 'It was Gwen.' I picked up a wooden box that had fallen open and was face down on the carpet. The familiar melody of *Something In The Way He Moves* started tinkling away slowly from inside. I flipped it upright and began returning the items it'd housed, carefully popping them inside: pre-decimalisation coppers; foreign notes; two leather bracelets; a colourful brooch in the shape of an exotic bird; a small black jewellery box ... 'She has something that has given her pause,' continued Sally. 'A *pregnant* pause, you might say.'

'What?' I asked as I spun around and snapped the lid of the box shut, cutting off the romantic melody.

'Our friend is pregnant and in need of my help,' she added as she closed her eyes and began to drift off.

I scurried over to her and shook her by the shoulders. It was useless; she'd passed out, damn it! I left her to sleep and approached Gwen's door, raising my fist to knock and ... I dunno ... offer support? Would she want that? She hadn't confided in me, she'd chosen Sally, and as misguided as I believed that choice was, I'd no right to barge in and say so. I didn't knock. I walked away. It's late. I'm in bed now. So many secrets within these walls. What right do I have to go stomping in with my size eleven feet when I've done nothing but protect my own?

Friday 17th December

I didn't see hide nor hair of Gwen or Sally until the dress rehearsal. With no time to chat, I waited under the stage for my moment of glory as a Starship Trooper, while Sally gleefully paced out her routine with much aplomb above. Remarkably, the whole show went off without a hitch. I was winched up at great speed on the right beat and gave an 'outstanding performance,' according to Trenton and Sally.

As Ms Knowles and I packed the bulky spacesuits into Trenton's large trunk, I took my chance in the eves to ask, 'Do you remember the last thing you said to me before passing out yesterday?'

A contrite Sally said, 'Yes, I do. Honestly, someone should stitch up my lips when I'm tipsy, darling.' She edged towards me in desperation, 'You mustn't say a word to anyone, especially Gwen. She wants to pretend that none of this has happened.'

I laughed, 'Well that's going to become pretty impossible over the next few months.'

'Why?'

'Because there will be a little screaming pink package delivered, surely?' Sally's silence was a sign she and Gwen had other plans. 'Oh, my God. She's getting rid of it, isn't she?' My voice echoed across the stage.

Sally shushed me and poked her head out of the curtains. Everyone seemed to be going about their business as usual. She raised a finger towards me, 'Please, keep it down,' she whispered. 'She's booked into the clinic on Tuesday. We had the consultation today. I'll escort her. End of.'

I couldn't believe my ears, 'You're helping her?'

'I'm helping resolve the problem of being impregnated by an asshole, yes,' she uttered.

'I assume the asshole is Matt. How does he feel about this?' I hissed back.

'He's too young and irresponsible to know one end of a rubber from the other, what makes you think he'll be any better with diapers? Besides, he's been AWOL for months. Maybe you need a reality check here, Andrew dearest: the girl lives in a bedsit, for goodness sake, her music career is stagnant, and she's temping in offices to rub two pennies together. What makes you think she's even remotely ready to start a family? Case closed!' She slammed down the lid of the trunk with dramatic effect.

I was having none of it. I lifted the lid again and stuffed my helmet in, 'No, case open! She needs to tell him. He has a right to know. It may just be the kick up the arse this boy needs.'

'She can't find him,' insisted Sally.

'You're lying, there's social media, mobile phones, landlines, snail mail, all kinds of ways we could reach him. We have to try.'

'So says the boy who hid in the woods for ten years. Now drop it. Her mind's made up, and I support her fully. Besides, he'd probably pull an Andy Angus, and that just leads to more hurt.'

'What do you mean, "an Andy Angus"?'

When someone finds the slightest flaw as an excuse to move on quickly and blanks you for the rest of your life.'

'What? The guys I dated weren't relationship material, that's all.'

‘Oh, good lord! Andy, when are you going to admit to yourself that you just aren’t ready for another relationship? You want one, but you aren’t ready. Thomas broke your heart, we get that, but when are *you* going to understand that it hasn’t even started to mend yet? This guy Alistair that you were seeing, deep down you knew in your disillusioned heart he was unattainable and a safe bet.’

‘Don’t be ridiculous.’

‘No, having faith that a closeted married man who can’t even admit to himself that he’s anything other than straight is going to lead to a happy ever after, now *that’s* being ridiculous! He has more issues than the rest of us put together.’

‘How did this suddenly become about me, anyway?’ I exclaimed.

‘Isn’t it always?’

‘Fuck you!’ is not the wittiest of repartees, but it was all I could muster as I slammed the trunk shut and stormed off stage left. A wedding tomorrow and I’m definitely not feeling the love. I’m off for a walk to get lost in the shadows of this city.

Day Four of Treatment:

- Four pills taken.
- Moisturiser applied to a very unattractive penis that looks as if it should be attached to a dried-up husk.
- Four impromptu and inconvenient unintentionals, one during the argument with Sally (disturbing).

Saturday 18th December

1 a.m. (Or thereabout.) A walk is supposed to clear the mind, but all I found in my path was confusion and trepidation. I wandered past the Balmoral Hotel, knowing Ryan was staying there overnight to keep the tradition of the bride and groom not laying eyes on one another until they meet at the alter the next day (or rather, registrars podium, in this case). I looked up at the hotel and wondered where Ryan was tucked away in amongst the sandstone Victorian facade and the warm, inviting glow that spilt out from occupied rooms. As if by magic, my phone vibrated and I found Ryan at the end of the line.

‘Fancy popping up to the hotel? I’m a bit lonely and in need of a drinking buddy,’ he said. Serendipity had played its hand.

'I'll be right up,' I said with a smile.

'Nervous?' I asked Ryan when he opened the door carrying two full glasses of a golden liquid. The air had a heavy, peaty smokiness about it. He'd obviously had a few already; his cheeks were glowing like embers.

'No, not at all, just lonely and contemplating the future. Ardbeg?' He thrust a glass without hesitation into my hand.

'Just a small one,' I joked, 'and then it's to bed with you. You've to be plucked, shaved, scrubbed, manicured, pedicured, polished, styled, dressed and in the car by eleven in the morning – by the way, why do we have a car for you if the whole day is at this hotel?'

'I'd like to arrive in style. Besides, I want one more jaunt around this city as a single man in a Rolls-Royce.'

'Understood. A bit frivolous, but understood.'

Towards the bottom of our glasses, the conversation turned to our friendship, the gap years, and what could've been in between. I began to sense where it was all heading and, becoming uncomfortable, I decided I'd better leave. I faked a yawn, stretched and started to tie up my boots. Ryan knelt down and placed his hand on top of mine. He said, 'But I need to ask you, did you ever ... you know ... fancy me?'

'Don't be silly.' I laughed nervously.

'Come on, you can tell me now. I'm getting wed tomorrow, so it'll all be academic by the time one o'clock comes. You must've had some kind of urge. You made the first move, out of all those young guys in the club that night, you hunted me down.'

He was right, I'd been attracted to him and desperately wanted to take him home and do wonderful things to him, but I'd chickened out. Ryan was a player back then. He was good-looking and knew it. Steve described him as, '... higher maintenance than the Forth Bridge,' and, '... a cock tease.' Ryan enjoyed the chase, especially as he was always the one being pursued. I was too unsure of myself to be confident I'd be fit enough to catch him. Time moved on, and Ryan became more of a brother to me, so thoughts of anything else between us dwindled. Steve died, Ryan met Tony, and I moved to the Borders with Thomas. The rest is history.

'Okay ...' I began but stopped.

'Okay, what?' he asked, looking up at me with those damn puppy-dog eyes.

'Okay. I admit I wanted you bad that night, but there have been many more nights that haven't ended with my knickers in a twist over you.'

'Ha!' he bellowed. 'I knew it.' He looked at me tenderly and whispered, 'Kiss me.'

I sat back in the chair, 'What? No. Don't be silly.'

'Haven't you ever wondered what we missed?'

'Frankly, yes, but that's beside the point: you're getting hitched tomorrow. Ryan, would you kindly take your hands off my thighs?' I may have rushed up to his suite earlier, desperate to see him, but now all I could think about was hightailing it down the most convenient fire escape. Too late, he leant towards me, his lips locked with mine, his tongue brushed against my clenched teeth, and the warmth of his affection softened my resolve. For the first time since we met, I allowed myself to fall into him and get a glimpse of what'd be like to be with him intimately.

It wasn't bad at all. Very tasty. Passionate to a point, but it didn't send sparks flying from my crotch or put stars in my eyes.

He pulled himself away and withdrew to the other side of the room. I smacked my lips in contemplation. He paced back and forth, muttering to himself and wiping his mouth frantically with the sleeve of his housecoat saying, 'Oh, dear, oh dear. I'm so sorry. I didn't invite you up for that.'

'No,' I said, 'I hope not.'

'But, for my information, what did you think?'

I mulled my reply over carefully. 'Well, you know that there's butter, and then there's that stuff called "I Can't Believe It's Not Butter".'

'Yes?'

'Well, that was like "I Can't Believe It's Not Butter", all the look and feel of butter, but not the wonderful tingling sensation you get from a big salty dollop of creamy fattiness that's melted into the warm dough of an English muffin just as it touches your tongue.'

'Oh,' he said, sounding disappointed.

'For you?'

'The same, I guess.'

‘So, now we know. We’re friends – gay brothers – but we’re most definitely never going to be anything other.’ I finished tying my laces and swung my jacket on. ‘You’re right, it had to be done. Thanks for taking the plunge, so to speak.’ I hesitated to say the next part but figured I’d nothing to lose now, ‘You know, for a long time I resented Tony for taking away my chance of being with you, but now I know that we’re in a very different place, I’m really okay with it.’ I laughed. ‘It was nice. Comforting. Great technique and just the right amount of moisture and pressure, but it didn’t do what kissing usually does to me.’

‘What’s that?’

‘Cause a stirring in my budgie smugglers, my dear friend. And that’s saying something as I’m bloody horny and been coping with random hardons all day!’

Ryan smiled, ‘Yes, same here. On the kissing, not the erections. I’m too stressed for those.’

It was a relief that a question that’d hung over us for ages had been answered. Ryan and I were never meant to be lovers, but we will always be friends, and that is excellent.

‘I’m going to go now,’ I said. ‘Mainly because you have a big day tomorrow, but also because I want to be awake enough to see my dear friend marry the man of his dreams, flawed though he is, but that’s okay. I know, for me, no one’s ever going to be good enough for my best friend.’

Ryan nodded in agreement, ‘You’re right. God! You’re not going to say anything to Tony, are you?’

‘Ryan, please, it’s me you’re talking to. Of course not. It’s probably just pre-civil partnership jitters anyway.’ I kissed him on the forehead (a much more comfortable kiss) and said the words Mum and Dad would say to us kids to signal it was time for bed, ‘Teeth, toilet, bed.’

‘Okay,’ he said, ‘but one thing.’

‘Aye?’

‘Could you stop calling it a civil partnership? It’s our *wedding day*. It may say something different on the documentation, it may not legally be an actual wedding, but to us, this is our wedding day.’

I nodded in agreement. ‘Yes. Sorry. I should move on with that too. It’s your wedding day.’

I bid him goodnight. *Case closed.*

Or so I thought.

******

On my way home, I took a little jaunt up Calton Hill for a spot of stargazing and contemplation with no sordid intentions. With the occasional jabbing reminder that I'm recovering from a somewhat sticky infection and rocky relationship, star gazing and solace were really the only things planned. I sat on the usual bench, close to the path at the top of the hill, with my favourite view of the Firth of Forth, and soaked up the relative peace. So much traffic was in my head, and I desperately needed to switch off. The freezing temperatures had left the place barren of sexual activity, thankfully, and I was able to enjoy a good ten-minute reboot. I dug my hands deep in the pockets of my jacket to avoid the biting wind and felt something flat and smooth through the semi-numbness of my fingertips. It was a piece of creased paper, just in the corner of the right pocket. I pulled it out and managed to read the rough handwriting in the night's blue hue:

'I love you, my man!

Yours, Thomas. X'

I'd never seen it before. He must've tucked it in my pocket as a little surprise last winter; the last time I wore that particular jacket. Another lie. I hated him again, right there and then. It'd been in there all year. If anything was going to jinx a fresh start, it would be this. I tore it in half, and again, and again, until my fingers ached. Until every word, every single letter, was destroyed and indecipherable, and launched it off the hillside towards the steps below.

'Back where you belong, you lying, cheating bastard,' I called as I watched the poison confetti fade into the darkness, somewhere amongst the dirt and the frozen rubbers.

The moon disappeared behind a dark cloud and stayed there as I made my way back down to planet Earth. On my way around the back of the hill, I passed a grunting bush (a place many guys use when discretion is a must). *Oh, great, just what I need: another reminder that men will risk anything, even frostbite on their knobs, just to get laid,* I thought as I neared the two boys in the throes of passion. I hurried past and made my way to the light at the top of the stairs, close to civilisation. And then I saw, plain as day under the lamplight, Tony taking a breather at the top of the steps, just feet away from me. He was at a fork in the road, undecided whether to go left or right. I slid into the shadows and watched him nervously. What the hell was he doing there the night before his wedding? Hell, I know exactly what he was doing there! He headed in the opposite direction and vanished into the murk of one of Edinburgh's biggest cruising areas.

I hastened away and reached the comparative sanity of the streets. Hackney cabs zoomed along Waterloo Place, Leith Street was bustling with people enjoying a good night out, and Leith Walk was permeated by the smell of hot cooking oil billowing from the vents of chip shops as they served the drunken, hungry masses. But this normality couldn't shake me out of my cloud. I was disorientated and intoxicated with woes and forebodings. Too many people in my way on the streets. Too many people in my way in my head. I just needed to get home to some silence. To some clarity. To you, dear diary.

How the hell am I going to break it to Ryan that the man he loves is cheating on him? It's the night before their wedding, for fuck's sake! No ... it's their wedding *day!* Jesus! It's already their wedding day. Tony, your timing's crap! I finally have you by the balls, just when I was ready to move on. What the hell am I going to do? This will break my best friend's heart.

Ryan & Tony's Wedding Day.
9.30 a.m. I've hardly slept a wink and need to think clearly. I have to stop Ryan making the biggest mistake of his life. I have to stop Gwen making an even bigger mistake too. How does one man pull the curtain down on the biggest show of the year before it's even begun? How does any man have the right to tell a woman what she can and can't do with her body? Do I stop everything in the opening number, or do I slash the tyres of the wedding car before Ryan can return to the Balmoral? Do I reason with Tony to do the right thing and tell him?

Ryan & Tony's Wedding Day (Supplemental).

Just after 11 a.m., I was standing in Tony's room at the Balmoral. The ceremony was less than an hour away, and I was almost entirely cocooned as an astronaut, apart from the overbearing helmet, which I dreaded clamping to my suit as I was already short of breath having run up three flights of stairs that seem to have been designed by Salvador Dali. Tony was sitting at a dressing table attempting to soften his sour complexion with some makeup. His parents, Trudy and Jim, had given us some space and headed down to ensure the flowers were present and perfect. In the corner of the room sat a rack of costumes that would be his quick changes for the most ridiculous performance of the year. I gazed out of the window of the plush suite that Tony was fortunate to have for the day before spending the night as a lying, cheating husband at some secret location. He'd chosen a room with a birds-eye view over the main entrance. Despite the fresh fall of snow, guests were arriving in droves. The unknown faces were punctuated by a couple of very well-knowns to me: Gordon Bennett (the laughing dentist) and Jesus (the artist). I eyed Biffo suspiciously. Had he invited these people just to scare me off? *Of course not, that would be silly, and you should stop being so paranoid,* I told myself.

'What do you want, Andy?' he asked, without a hint of guilt, brushing the foundation crumbs off his face with the pompous attitude of a stuck-up duchess.

'For you to stop this farce of a wedding, that's what,' I demanded, drawing my attention away from the guests below.

Tony chuckled to himself and asked, 'Why would I do that, Andy dearest?'

I leaned over his shoulder to look at him directly in the mirror and caught sight of myself; I was pale and tired, but my cheeks were raging in anger. 'We both know what you were up to last night, Tony. I saw you up the hill.' He seemed irritatingly relaxed and continued to apply some perfume to every pulse point three times over. 'Have you no morals?' I goaded.

Biffo, unfazed, got up and slithered towards a charcoal tweed jacket that was hanging on the front of the wardrobe and casually adjusted the corsage. It was a yellow rose, Ryan's favourite, set amongst a small spray of white buds. A delicate symbol of friendship and here I was trying to do the best I could for a friend without annihilating his trust in love. 'And how and why would I call off the wedding?' he asked.

'By telling him, you don't love him.'

He laughed again, this time louder, his calmness irritating me beyond belief. 'You mean, lie?'

'It wouldn't be a lie. You don't love him.'

'But I do, Andy. Sex has nothing to do with love, not casual sex. You should know that by now.' He unhooked the jacket and rested it carefully on the rack next to the other costumes. The ceremony was getting close. I had little time left.

'You're immoral. He deserves better. I bought a bloody Kitchen Aid mixer for you. I'm eating nothing but beans and bananas for the next fortnight because of you. Have you any idea how much roughage that is?' I spat.

'No, do tell,' he said, dryly.

I stammered, unsure of my facts, 'Well, a bloody lot more than the recommended daily allowance, I'm sure.'

'Then we'd best make sure this wedding happens, hadn't we? Otherwise, there will be no top nosh for you later, eh?'

'Don't you dare take the piss, you of all people who have concocted this bloody farce just to wind me up. And for what? Revenge? Fear of my friendship with Ryan, is that it?'

'What do you mean, concocted this farce?'

'The bloody dance. The show. Fucking Sarah Brightman. I know you planned that addition to spite me. It's too random to be an accident. You might love Star Wars, but Ryan hates science fiction, and therefore would never agree to this unless you really pushed for it.'

'Oh, that. Yes, sorry about that, Andy dearest, but you would leave your thoughts carelessly lying around and your bedroom door wide open. What's a landlord to do but check the credibility of his new tenant? Your life made for dull reading, mostly, apart from what you laughingly call your love life.'

'What?' It dawned on me who exactly I was seeing at the time I was renting from this tosser. 'I have nothing to be ashamed of.'

Tony pouted. 'Oh, Andy Pandy. Poor deluded boy. You have the loosest morals of us all. All that hot, steamy sex, all those men, and a preference for the unattainable.' He gazed out of the window.

Something grabbed his attention, and he grinned smugly. 'Oh, look, Andrew. Some old friends are arriving who I believe you know very well. Look.' He slipped behind me and grabbed me by the shoulders. There was a reprieve in the weight of the spacesuit for a moment as he shoved me towards the window to get a better view.

It was then an unstoppable force was put upon me, and I was crushed.

'Take a look down there,' he pointed over my shoulder at a silver 4x4 that'd just pulled up outside. 'It's poor, frail Christina. Remember her? Your dear friend who's gone through hell with cancer?' Christina struggled to shut the door of the car, unable to gain momentum from her frail frame and the useless traction of her heels in the snow. The driver's door opened, and Tony added with relish, 'Yes, your dear friend and her husband. But then, you always knew deep down inside your dark, dingy soul, that Alistair could never leave his wife, didn't you? Or, as she and the rest of the straight world know him, Nick. Edinburgh can be so big, and yet so small.'

I couldn't believe my eyes as I watched Alistair hurry around the boot of the car to help Christina, his wife, close the stubborn door. *Christina, his wife. Alistair's Wife. Nick's wife, Christina.* It played over and over in my mind. He took her tenderly by the arm and pulled her close, kissing her full on the lips as he did so. She looked so happy, supported by her big, strong, steadfast man. 'This is impossible,' I said, blinking desperately to fix this discrepancy and hoping it was just a couple who looked a lot like Christina and Alistair. 'How?'

'Well, I do have access to privileged information, working closely with patients in need of care at the surgery. She's under Dr Wilson, a very nice man who's seen her and her husband – and I do stress, husband – come and go, from the U.K. to Spain for private treatment.' His words became fainter as my blood ran cold, and my heart plummeted. 'He loves her very much,' he whispered close to my ear. 'I've known for some time. And you've been at it for some time. So don't talk to me about morals, big boy. You've fucked Christina over real good, just as hard and fast as you fucked him.'

Tony was being unnecessarily cruel. 'But I didn't know. He told me he left his wife.'

'Did you really know that? Did you ever really check? Did you really want to know that? What would the commitment-phobe have done? You're pretty mentally screwed, Andy, and I doubt there's any hope of fixing you.'

I was seething with anger, 'You're just like him. What you're doing to Ryan is no better.'

Tony slipped on some cream robes and admired himself in the mirror. I was frozen to the spot. Why did he hate me so much? 'Do you really want to know what I was doing up the hill last night?' he asked, cockily.

I didn't reply. I watched their silver 4x4 be driven off by the concierge. I could see Alistair and Christina at the top of the stairs as they made their way towards the foyer of the hotel. Any second now they'd be right below me. Soon I'd be on stage in front of them: my friend, the cancer patient, and Alistair, a consummate liar.

'Lost for words?' continued Biffo. 'Finally!' He patted his greased hair in place. 'I was on the hill looking for Ryan. My husband-to-be. It wouldn't be the first time I've found him behind a bush, or worse, between another's legs. But that's usually when he's stressed or depressed, which was mainly when we first met, when you were both out painting the town red during your glory days. Mainly.'

'You're lying,' I said, hoping that my friend, who'd been my touchstone for love, would never screw it up for a casual ride with another.

Tony turned to me, deadly serious, and said, 'In the early days, it took me a while to see the discrepancies in the timings between your nights out and his, and, against all hope, I prayed it was you that was getting it wrong or covering up some misdemeanours. But there would be the dirt on his shoes, the taste of rubber on his cock, or the smell of another on his chest. At the end of a night out, no matter how much he loved me, he just couldn't pass up the thrilling chance of anonymous sex. God knows I hate the fact ... ' Tony's voice had begun to waver, but he kept it together, shook his head and sniffed back some composure, '... but I love him. Just when we'd got it cracked through years of therapy, you pop up from nowhere and bring that fear back with your drinking, dancing and late nights, just as it was before. The glory days are back, and I'm so sad about that.

'Inevitably, there was that same dirt on his shoes, that suspicious taste on his cock, and the familiar scent of deception on his lips. Oh, I could've died the day he asked you to move in. No, sooner, when you wrote to him saying you'd love to join us for our wedding. We never did figure out who sent you that invite, by the way.'

'What do you mean? It was Ryan.'

'No, he was as bewildered as I was when you messaged him and thanked him for the invitation. I'm sorry to say it, Andy, but you were long forgotten until that day.'

'No, you're lying,' I whimpered. 'He's my friend.'

He laughed in disbelief, 'I made the rent so high and yet you still moved in! Fortuitous that your moggie moved in soon after, though. All it took was a bit of teasing here, and a squirt of catnip there, to push the poor demented creature over the edge. It was worth the damage to our suits and Ryan's tears to get you out of our home.'

'You bastard,' I said through steely teeth.

'Look, Andy, if I've tried to get rid of you, my only motive has been to protect Ryan.' His words became weaker and shakier, 'Now, I love that man more than you'll ever know and I'm going to marry him. And you'll take a step back because I don't need someone with your track record influencing him any more.'

A solitary tear rolled down his cheek. It scared the shit out of me.

'Where's Ryan? I need to speak to him,' I said, pushing past him to get to the door.

'Leave him alone,' Tony barred my path and wiped the tear away, gazing at the clear fluid in his hand as if it was a foreign object. 'He'll kill me if he knows I told you. Believe me, it's the truth.'

I didn't want to believe it. I refused to accept it until Ryan admitted it. 'No, I need to see him.' One more determined push and he was out of my way.

I nearly fell over Trudy as I left. 'The flowers look perfect,' she announced.

'Great,' I lied. This was too much. I felt as if I was going to vomit. I felt like the biggest bastard in the whole of creation. How could I judge Tony or Ryan – whoever's cheating – when I'd been doing something worse to Christina? Poor, sick, almost at death's door, Christina? And where did Alistair stand in all of this mess? Had he known we'd become somewhat friends and played both of us for his own satisfaction?

I wanted to run as far away as possible, away from these lies, but Sally's right: the past catches up with you no matter what. I had to stop and hide when I caught sight of Alistair and Christina on the stairs, so I jumped along a corridor a floor above and was met by the entire modern-day version of Hot Gossip. 'I'll be glad to slip out of this bloody armour,' grumbled Melve, slogging towards me as if he was fighting gravity three times Earth's norm. He saw me. It was too late. 'Hello, old bean,' he said, 'we've to get downstairs ASAP; curtain-call in ten minutes.'

'I don't think I can do this,' I protested.

Sally's glittery face popped up from behind Melve. She scowled at me and barked, 'If you leave us high and dry right now, today of all days, I'll ram this damn helmet up your asshole, you prima donna. Gwen isn't feeling all that hot, but she's here, all the same, aren't you sweetie?'

Gwen waved at me apathetically from the back of the group. She looked pale and clammy. How could I say no? She was struggling with morning sickness and the trauma of an imminent abortion and was still willing to carry on. We took the back steps towards the stage. This was it; we were actually going live. I was about to perform a recurring nightmare I'd been having for months, Alistair would be watching with his wife, and I had to stop this bloody wedding somehow without hurting anyone. What I'd done to Christina was terrible, no argument there, but it was over. What Tony had said, I couldn't believe, but then, I'd never seen him cry over anything. I just had to delay the wedding, perhaps, long enough to speak to Ryan and find a path through the mess.

As I stepped onto the small platform that would toss me on stage in minutes, Trenton was helping me get my act together. 'Are you okay, sunshine? You look like you've seen a ghost.'

I gazed at my reflection in the visor of my helmet. I looked like a 3D version of *The Scream* by Edvard Munch. Beads of sweat trickled down my forehead and flowed like tiny rivers along the discernible lines on my face. 'Oh, Trenton, love turns all of us into old fools,' I said.

'Oh, darling boy, you aren't old,' he assured me. 'Just you wait until you get to my age. I'm ancient. I shouldn't be standing here; they should be excavating my mummified corpse from beneath the dirty, beer-soaked floorboards of Fire Island.' He lifted the dreaded helmet above my head and asked, 'Ready?' I took a deep breath, closed my eyes tight and nodded. I heard the disconcerting fastening of two metal clamps as it was secured into place. My breathing became amplified, and the creaking of the wooden platform that had been stressing under the fat of a 36-year-old idiot in a 40-pound orange launch suit fell silent. I could hear Trenton continue to talk as he knocked on the glass, 'Are we okay in there, boy?' I could see he was shouting and yet his voice was thready.

'Yes,' I shouted back, almost deafening myself in the process.

'Good,' he said, over exaggerating every word to be clear. 'You shouldn't have any problems, there's a vent in the back, just relax and breath slowly. Remember, the helmet can be removed easily by pushing on the lower part of the clamps. Thumb is best through the gloves.' He accompanied this with some flamboyant gestures with his hands.

I felt heavy vibration from above; my fellow space explorers were getting into position. Trenton was counting down with his fingers from ten to one. And then, most of all, I heard the dramatic opening of *(I Lost My Heart To A) Starship Trooper* kick in and took one last gulp for breath before I was boosted faster than a rocket onto the stage by some unseen stagehand with gorilla arms. I was now centre-stage, beamed down from some imaginary spacecraft amongst dry ice and flashing lights, in front of an expectant audience of over two-hundred people, including one closeted man and his clueless wife. For now, the spacesuit would act as the perfect disguise, but pretty soon the veil would be lifted by Storm Troopers One and Two (AKA: Melve and Gwen, respectively) and I'd have nowhere to run. I could just about make out Ryan, standing at the other end of the hall, poised for his glorious entrance, ready to fall on the lips of the man he supposedly loves. Too far out of reach.

I literally went through the motions. It was easy to remember the steps. It's astounding the clarity that comes before an impending crisis. Melve and Gwen took their positions beside me. Two clunks and I was able to breathe freely and see clearly. I hoped Alistair had got lost in the bar or even decided weddings weren't really his thing. I could see Mum and Dad in the second row, both having had some kind of makeover and looking like dashing caricatures of their former selves. Mum smiled and waved excitedly; it couldn't get more surreal.

A flash lit up the crowd, and there he was, brighter than a pulsar, his silver hair reflecting the brilliance faster than the speed of light. I could see nothing else but Alistair now. I felt Melve bump into me. 'Move, you pillock,' he muttered. 'You have to move to dance,' he added as he swayed in time with Gwen and I ricochet between them. But still, I couldn't take my eyes off Alistair. What was he thinking? Did he know all this time Christina was close to me? Hadn't I mentioned her to him? Surely I had. She owns a shop next to the Café; impossible for him not to know, surely? And why come to this wedding? Hadn't I mentioned Ryan and Tony to him? He's bound to have made the connection. But then, if he had, he should've made his excuses and not come. He's good at lying, I know that. When I mentioned them, had I just labelled them as *the Terrible Twins,* as I so often do?

And then there was a moment between us, just a glimpse, a hint of recognition, and he turned his eyes towards the floor and didn't look back. Was that shock? Shame? Guilt?

'Bloody move or I'll swear I'll reach up there and, spacesuit or no spacesuit, I'll grip your balls so tight *you'll* feel the Force, Luke!' came Sally's voice from under the prompter. I continued to dance. I found my rhythm and somehow fell back into sync with the rest of the group. The plight of Sarah Brightman and her star-crossed lover continued. I danced and ignored the silver-haired elephant in the room, as he did me, and soon enough I could see Ryan stage left trembling on the arm of his mother, Margo, as he worked up the courage to climb into the eaves.

I had to stop everything. This was the right thing to do. I made a resolve there and then to be the cliché that stood up at the 'any lawful impediment' part and tell the truth. And just as I made that vow, Storm Trooper Two collapsed in a crashing heap on to the boards and didn't get back up.

I slid on broken shards of white plastic, the plastic from Gwen's helmet, and glanced downward to find her writhing on the ground clutching her stomach. Seconds later, Sally was on the stage yelling, 'Call 999!' Moments later, we were in the wings, and Gwen was stripped from her cumbersome suit and sat clutching her abdomen in her underwear. I noticed spots of blood on her knickers. I began to panic.

Trenton grabbed me by the shoulders and shook me. 'Panicking won't get us anywhere, boy,' he told me sternly and then proceeded to hop around and stammer after catching sight of the haemorrhage.

The space opera continued to play, and a cheap replica of Apollo 13 descended towards the stage as Molasses and Melve winged it as best they could by doing the job of five dancers. Tony, temporarily dressed as Luke Skywalker, strutted down the aisle in time to the music to meet his groom accompanied by R2D2 and C3PO. Apollo 13 bumped onto the stage, and the lid to the capsule opened as blinding white lights flashed vigorously from within. Ryan emerged dressed as Han Solo, ready to marry Luke.

The show doesn't have to go on, I thought, *especially if a close friend is laid in the wings miscarrying*. As I made for the stage, Sally grabbed me by the arm and said, 'The Ambulance is here.'

I hesitated. This was my one and only excuse to stop this disaster without hurting anyone. Ryan was delightfully oblivious to Gwen's troubles. I was sure he'd postpone everything if he knew. I could enlighten him, and everything would have to stop. But then I heard Gwen's crushed voice calling for me. I turned to her and saw the agony in her eyes. We had to go.

******

Sally and I travelled with Gwen as the paramedic attached all kind of wires to her heaving chest. He listened to the noises coming from her tummy with a stethoscope and frowned. I waited for some confirmation that all would be well, but it never came. Speed bump after speed bump, we careered along the road towards the Royal Infirmary, blue lights and sirens blazing, disrupting the peace of the winter wonderland outside. Gwen cupped a shaky hand over her oxygen mask. Her fingers were blue at the tips. She was in a really bad way and clutched at my spacesuit frantically. I suddenly felt responsible. She pulled the mask away from her face and said, 'Andy, I need to tell you something ...'

I placed the mask back over her mouth and flaring nostrils, 'It's okay, I know. Don't worry, breath deep.' I figured she needed the oxygen more than a confession.

She shook her head and pulled the mask off again, 'No, listen. I wanted to be rid of it, but now it's all I can do to hold on to it. You have to believe me, no matter what happens to me, make sure it's safe.'

I placed the oxygen mask over her purple lips. I nodded and assured her, 'Don't worry. I will. I promise. And you're going to be okay.'

'And to think they will never get to see my wonderful mash-up of Cabaret and Single Ladies,' announced Sally from the far end of the ambulance. I scowled at her. She was wrapped in her fake fur coat, legs crossed and gazing offhandedly into a compact mirror as she adjusted her hair. As if she was on a taxi ride towards a merry night out. 'It's a tragedy, don't you think?' she asked with self-importance.

I felt frustration bubble from a cauldron of bile in my stomach and thought of my brother, and the turmoil Mum's gone through all these years over his death. I realised now why I cared so much. I hissed under my breath to Sally, 'Why, when it really matters, can't you drop the act and show some compassion?'

'Don't confuse being calm with not giving a shit, Andy,' she countered. She looked down at her feet and boorishly continued, 'I think I chose the wrong pair for today, don't you, Mr Ambulance Man? These will clash terribly with theatre blues.'

Sunday 19th December

2 a.m. It's the wee small hours and yesterday is done. I'm home alone. Sally waited in the ward just long enough to learn the fate of Gwen and her baby and then buggered off as fast as her heels could carry her from an awkward conversation in a sterile environment. I expect she was on a mad dash back to the wedding to prove she's actually the star of the show. I'm sure she performed well, she usually does. She's not at home tonight. Probably plumped for some male refuge. Who knows where she is? I'm done caring.

Ryan and Tony will be bound by law to one another, and there's nothing I can do about that. They're well on their way to a secret honeymoon location. It's too late. I guess I would've made a right spectacle of myself and I'm sure Ryan wouldn't have thanked me for that. I'm so confused over the two of them. Who's telling the truth? Time will tell.

Christina will be at home now with her husband. I've no idea how the hell I'm going to handle this while she's around. I can't be her friend having knifed her in the back several times over, albeit without full intention. Hopefully, I'll have a small accident and be knocked on the head just enough to cause amnesia over the entire episode and then, at the very least, I could keep my composure. If Alistair/Nick can box off his life, then so must I. If I could tuck him away in the hall cupboard in a cardboard box and tape down the lid to leave him in a dark corner forever, I would. I have to find the strength to do this or else I'll go mad.

More importantly, not everything I did yesterday was in vain: Gwen and her baby are doing fine. Panic over, but she's being kept in for surgery tomorrow. A young Irish doctor told her that her cervix is prematurely dilated, not a lot, but she needs a procedure called a cerclage to close the gap.

'They say I have an incompetent cervix,' she told me. Her colour had returned somewhat, but she was, as Mum would say, jiggered. 'I guess it's a miracle,' she said as she pulled the crisp, white hospital sheet around her shoulders, eyes filling with sleep and drifting, 'with an incompetent cervix and a useless boyfriend, who couldn't find the right opening or angle, I'm surprised I fell pregnant at all. It would have been easier to put a ship in a bottle.' This made me smile as I think it's the first joke I've ever heard Gwen crack. After she fell asleep, which was within the next few minutes, I stayed a further half-hour and listened to her breathing settle. Then, somewhat reluctantly, I caught the bus home.

And now Melve's just tumbled through the door. He was scratching at the lock with his key for several minutes. He *would* be the last to leave the party, even if the place were burning down, he'd continue to drink, smoke and dance his cares away. He'll be off his face. Trenton's public display of affection for his new, younger and – curiously – handsome man has wounded the old hippy deeply.

10 a.m. Mum and Dad have returned to Airdrie. They were interviewed by Lanarkshire Radio during the breakfast show. The local councillor, Fred Payne – who is the type of man that hides the grease on his collar under a roll of neck fat that resembles two large bratwurst sausages fused together – was present to give full backing for the bulldozing of Petersburn. He's been their local councillor for six years and is a well-known womaniser, which is astounding if you ask me as he's spray-tanned to the extreme, obese and can't shut his wet lips due to abnormally long gnashers that could eat an apple through a picket fence. He looks like the result of a one night stand between Janet Street-Porter and Donald Trump. But he's well-rehearsed in public speaking and is determined to undermine the Save Our Scheme Campaign by throwing jargon at the fidgeting feet of my folks.

After quoting many legal excuses, bamboozling not only my mother, but the radio presenter too, his droll tone became more upbeat as he said, 'We plan to keep the two primary schools, which have had consistently good grades from the inspectors, and also the playing fields, which will host next year's local summer sports day that I'll be officially opening, naturally. We'll be upgrading them too.' He voice became Churchill like as he added, 'But Petersburn has become an impractical slab of cracked concrete. The draughty single glazing alone would cost the taxpayer heavily to replace. The whole place is the epitome of 1960's brutalist architecture at it's worst and is best deleted from the landscape and rebuilt.'

'How do you feel about this statement, Mrs Anus ... sorry, I mean, Angus?' asked Jolly Johnny, a quick-witted breakfast DJ but otherwise useless political correspondent.

My mother cleared her throat and fumbled with a prepared piece of script that crunched powerfully into the microphone. After much hacking, Mum finally removed a troublesome chunk of tar induced matter from her throat and swallowed hard before saying, 'I think Counsellor Payne forgets the years he spent at the aforementioned primary schools, the games he played as a child on those fields, and the community spirit that raised him to become counsellor for Petersburn and Craigneuk. It seems he's forgotten the many hiding places a child can make within the labyrinth of concrete walls and the hours of fun a family can have at the play parks dotted around the scheme. Has he no pride and community spirit?'

'I do, Mrs Angus,' Councillor Payne assured her. 'But I'm sixty-two years old and grew up on a farm outside Melrose, several years before the blueprints for this scheme were drawn up by its banal architect. And those play parks you are so proud of have slides made of the coarsest mix of concrete known to man and have become a liability. Surely you can appreciate the risk involved when a soft-boned child glides down a slab of cemented aggregate – if that's even possible – that has become so tired and frayed it could sever every budding artery within that delicate child's body. Monkland's Hospital has had twenty-five head injuries come through its doors in the past year from play-related incidents in this scheme alone, and I say, no more!'

Mum's chair creaked audibly in the awkward silence. Research is vital if you want to take on your enemy. All she could muster was a faint, 'Well, it didn't do my kids any harm.'

She's a liar. My sister broke both her arms falling from a monkey pole, and I needed two stitches at the back of my head as a result of an overzealous, and I might add, unsupervised launch down such a slide. These incidents would have injury lawyers rubbing their hands with glee in today's blame culture.

'Did I also mention we're planning on refurbishing and extending the Four Isles Community Centre? With an added beer garden and barbecue,' slipped in the greasy counsellor before the interview drew to a close.

I heard Dad spurt out an inquisitive, 'Oh?' before the familiar jingle of my mother's Argos bracelet was heard, ending in a whip-like crack.

Mum called me moments after the interview. I lied and told her she did brilliantly, and I'm sure the Save Our Scheme Campaign is safe in her hands. She said Fred Payne disgusted her, 'He was wearing a shirt that was so ill-fitting it parted at his bloated naval every time he leant forward to speak into the microphone, which was drenched from his spit by the end. He's got untrustworthy, beady eyes and a yellow tongue. It put me right off my Typhoo, Son.' She segued, 'By the way, who was that girl on stage with you yesterday?'

I said, 'You know it was Gwen, right? The one who almost lost her baby? The reason I had to go?'

'No, not her, although I hope she's okay – I know what it's like to lose a baby, God bless her,' she said, a little melancholia. 'No, the other one who left with you two in the ambulance. I know her face.'

I said, 'That's Sally Knowles. You've probably met her before, as she works at the café and lives here.'

'No, I'd remember another one of them working there.'

'Another one of them what?' I asked.

'A coloured person,' she answered carelessly, ignorant of the fact she'd just dug up a word that should remain buried next to many more from bygone days of segregation and prejudice.

'Mum, you can't say that kind of thing these days. Actually, there was no excuse for it back then either.'

'Sorry,' she said, backtracking quickly, 'I meant *black*.'

This angry poof hung up the phone.

******

Gwen is post-op and in recovery. I had no time to visit as I was tied up at the café all afternoon, but gave the ward a quick tinkle. The nurse said she was doing fine. Baby is stable too. I began to relax until I heard she had a visitor: Sally was by her side. How dare she interfere! She couldn't give a shit about mother or baby a few days ago, and now she's all over them like a rash. I'll be having a word once she's home.

11 p.m. Sally's finally home. I stopped her on her heels as she edged through the hall.

'I hear you visited Gwen.'

'Yes, darling. She's doing remarkably well. I am pleased.' She slipped the key into her lock.

'I bet you're not really,' I said with intent, moving towards her.

'What could you possibly mean, sweetie?'

'A few days ago, you were sure getting rid of the baby was the best thing since curling tongs, and now you expect me to believe you're not whispering in her ear to carry on with plan A?'

'I want what she wants. A few days ago, she wanted an abortion; today, she doesn't. Simple. Life changes. I support her without any preconceptions, do you? '

'What's that supposed to mean?' I asked, hot on her tail.

She put out her hand, signalling for me to stop at her threshold, and said, 'I think you've allowed your family's past tragedy to cloud your judgement. Goodnight, Monsieur.' She slammed the door shut.

Can she mean little Luke? How can she know about his sudden death? I think I need to find a new place to hide this diary as under the mattress just isn't cutting it. I never dreamt, when I started scribbling in these pages, other people would be so nosey.

Day Six of Treatment:

- Four pills popped, four to go.
- Infection gone and Clinique face cream doing its magic on my poor willy.
- Five unintentionals: one morning glory; one walking to work; one walking from work (which amazes me in these low temperatures); a penultimate one signing for a package over the Parcelforce guy's tight-fitting trousers that revealed a rather large packet; final one (to date) while getting changed in the gym locker room (put clothes on in shame and left immediately).

Monday 20th December

I've subjected myself to the swarming festive panic-buying public, even though financially I know I'm pushing it. The combination of baked beans and antibiotics caused a buildup of wind that became problematic in the BHS café, but I was luckily stood next to a woman eating an egg and cress sandwich when I accidentally passed an emission, which hopefully overpowered the cloud.

I quickly moved into Rose Street, where the winter breeze would disperse any further issues. A brass band made up of posh-looking youths started playing Jingle Bells, but the spirit of goodwill is difficult to muster when your best friend has run off with a possible liar and a Kitchen Aid mixer. Or, your best friend is the cheat and he's been gifted a Kitchen Aid mixer in the belief that he's actually in love and plans on being faithful to one man for the rest of his life. Either way, they're milking it.

While in Topman, I heard familiar voices. When I turned around from the festive sock display, I saw Alistair (Nick, I need to keep reminding myself of his real name) and Christina going about their merry business arm in arm, laughing at the displays of Christmas briefs with not a care in the world. Panic-stricken, I picked up a fat woolly jumper and used it as camouflage as I sunk into the shadows, or so I thought. Escalators can be very sharp around the edges, as I discovered on my quick tumble down one in that instant. If it hadn't been for my many layers of sensible winter clothing and my ever-reliable parka, I could've suffered major lacerations, broken bones, concussion, or all of the above. Yes, I wished for amnesia days ago, but it's a painful job getting it. The sensor at the top of the escalator alerted the staff to the theft of one big woolly jumper, and I was speedily pounced on by security as the unforgiving metal steps spun me around on my back like an ant being flipped over repeatedly by a sadistic schoolboy with a stick. Humiliation always outweighs pain, and I left within minutes of the emergency stop button being pressed, thankful that neither Christina or Alistair (Nick!) had seen me.

Feeling glum, I limped my way through the rest of the day's turmoil and was glad to finally be finished with my Christmas list firmly ticked at every bullet point. I passed Ryan and Tony's place on my way home. Bedraggled by the unyielding crowds (there's supposed to be a recession on, for goodness sake!) and frustrated with my pithy budget (£10 per person), I took a breather and pondered my future. A cloud formed above my thoughts, and I found it hard to move. A Salvation Army band started playing the Christmas Carol *Oh Come All Ye Faithful* in the distance, just outside the financially endangered HMV store at the entrance of the Saint James Centre. I peered into my Protect Ur Pennies carrier bags: one cheap bottle of perfume for Mum; one cheap bottle of aftershave for Dad; two scented candles for my sister; assorted action figures – who aren't famous despite their dedication to fight for good – for my nephews; assorted D list dolls for my nieces; bubble bath for Sally, Molasses and Gwen (all different, powerful scents and weird fluorescent colours that could strip the skin off a crocodile, but needs must); tartan slippers for Melve (I'm sick of seeing his poorly maintained toenails); and a small fluffy teddy bear for Gwen's baby (a bit premature, I know, but I was feeling optimistic when I bought it as it was my first purchase).

I looked up at the Terrible Twins' empty flat. I could see boxes piled high at their lounge windows. I haven't bought them a gift for

Christmas; I believe they've more than they need for now, including my Christmas cheer. I looked down at my budget bags again. *This is shit!* I thought. *What crap I've bought. I have fragrances that have probably been tested on, and killed, many animals; two probable fire risks; soldiers who look like malnourished Action Men; disappointing bath-times; slippers for a man who never wears slippers; and cheap, sluttily looking pram-faced dolls who are destined for the bargain bin equivalent of a toy reality TV series. I'm sure, if I look hard enough, I'll find a matching Jeremy Kyle doll with flimsy cardboard set and a miniature DNA testing kit.*

When I got home, I dumped my bags on my perfectly made bed, moved them to the sofa and straightened the bed out again, fed a rather demanding cat, zapped a ready meal from Iceland and ate it from the container it came in (fish pie, £1.50). I've no washing-up liquid left and will have to use hand soap on my dishes until payday (Christmas Eve). I reluctantly popped a further £2 into the greedy electric meter (the dial barely moved above red), watched ten minutes of *Come Dine With Me*, turned off the telly once I noticed the meter was spinning like a 747's turbines (reality TV is no longer within my budget), put jacket, boots, scarf and gloves on again, snapped bootlace, adjusted the lace and tied the smallest knot in the world (boot laces are out until Christmas Eve too), picked up the £3 I'd set aside for the No. 36 bus, contemplated cycling out there but changed my mind when I saw chunky flakes of snow falling outside my window, and headed to the Royal Infirmary. Depressing.

******

Gwen was pleased to see me, a little tender around the nether regions, but pleased. She was laid on her side in bed with an RIE branded pillow stuffed between her legs. The plastic coating that protects NHS bedding from bodily fluids crunched every time she adjusted herself. 'It's the only way I can be comfortable,' she said, wincing as I moved the head of the bed up with the electronic control that had some form of sticky residue attached. I quickly expunged the offensive matter with an alcohol wipe from the multipack I carry in my rucksack and pushed thoughts of MRSA and Norovirus swiftly out of my mind. 'This baby had better be worth it,' she added, as I sterilised my hands with alcohol gel and dropped some into hers too. 'I feel as if someone has shovelled a cone-shaped cheese grater up there.'

'*Shoved*,' I corrected her.

'Yes, that would be right. *Shoved*. Although a shovel would also be a possibility too,' she laughed, then winced.

I moaned about Christmas and how dreary it's all become. Molasses has invited us to Christmas dinner at the café. I told Gwen, 'I'm not sure I actually want to celebrate anything this year. Last year was a disaster, this year hasn't been much of an improvement, and the next is already casting a dark shadow. I think I'd best keep my head down and watch the telly from under the duvet.'

'That's a shame. I hope to be home by then, and I had really hoped you would join us. You are my best friend, and it will be our last Christmas without a baby attached to my nipples.'

I felt touched that she held me in such high esteem. I sighed and smiled, 'Okay. 3.30 p.m., Christmas day, I'll be there, waiting to pull a cracker with you.'

'Super. Sally and Melve are coming too.'

'Ah, I'm not getting on very well with those two right now,' I confessed.

'I think you should move past that; it is the season of goodwill after all. Sally was just supporting me. I thought it was the best choice for me at that point, and you don't have a problem with me.'

'That's different,' I said, munching on grapes I found on top of her bedside locker. 'These are a bit off,' I winced as I struggled to cope with the three pieces of sweet, squishy mush in my mouth.

'Oh, they're not mine,' she said casually. 'I think they were left by the previous occupant. The nurses don't have the time to wipe their own anuses here, never mind ours. And domestics are few and far between.' I immediately spat them into a paper bag that was overflowing with used tissues and secured by surgical tape on the side of her locker. Then she asked, irritated, 'Why is it different? Because I changed my mind, because I'm ill, or both?'

I couldn't answer that. Perhaps it's different because she's ill and has decided to keep that little life inside her until it's ready to explode into the world, all pink, wriggly and lungs puffed with air, ready to make itself heard amongst the cacophony of planet Earth. Maybe Sally was right, perhaps I'm biased due to our family's loss.

Perhaps I'm a condescending arsehole. Do I only harbour friends who agree with me and discard the ones who challenge me? Am I that impatient?

'Look,' she continued, 'Sally was helping me then and is helping me now, nothing has changed there. You've been where Melve is right now, confused and scared of a relationship, painting over the truth with bright, colourful lies. Don't judge them.'

There was my answer. I am judgemental. I resolve to mend some bridges. It's the season of goodwill, what better time to start? Before I left, I asked her, 'Do you want me to track down Matt?'

'No, most definitely not! I can only look after one child at a time. I'm one-hundred per cent sure that even trying to form a relationship with him would be a mistake. Do you know he still collects Pokemon cards?'

I could've argued, but that would have involved me forcing my beliefs onto a vulnerable person. I left her with a warm hug and a packet of alcohol wipes. As I walked past the nurses' station, two nurses waved goodbye with bloodshot eyes and fixed grins. I could hardly see them for piles of paperwork. The phones were ringing incessantly. Just as I stepped into the lift, I heard a nurse with bedraggled, soulless hair and an equally soulless tone say into a telephone, 'Germany, aye ... No, she insists there's no father. Yip, yet another single mother, destined for the benefits office and a life of misery.'

As the lift door closed, I thought, *You're wrong. That won't happen. She's stronger than you think. And we, her friends, won't let it.*

Day Seven of Treatment:

- All antibiotics completed.
- Willy still a little chaffed.
- One panic about my pending HIV test result while wrapping gifts.
- Many negative thoughts on being positive.

Tuesday 21st December

Christina popped into work. I couldn't give her the time of day. Hell, I couldn't even look her in the eye. She must've chatted to Sally and Molasses for over an hour about their plans over Christmas and New

Year, 'Blah, blah, blah, a small family Christmas, blah, blah, blah, big Boxing Day party, blah, blah, blah, Hogmanay concert at the Usher Hall and then dinner with friends. Blah!'

It was hell. My thoughts turned to her husband, my erstwhile lover, formerly known as Alistair. I felt I could've walked up to her and dragged the man kicking and screaming out of the closet through sheer bitterness, but I know I would only have made fools of all parties involved, so I kept my trap shut and my hands busy. As usual, she insisted on a hearty hug goodbye. I could smell him on her. Her kindly embrace took me right to the hair of his chest and the beating of his heart. I felt very ill and confused. My arms, although wrapped around her tiny waist, were rigid with fear. I daren't have moved in case I nudged the knife I planted months ago further into her back.

******

Gwen will be home tomorrow evening. 'It turns out I am very resilient down there,' she said, sitting up in the bed. 'The wound is healing like sugary, fatty skin forming on cooling custard.' I tried to ignore the analogy. Cold custard and vaginas should never be mentioned in the same sentence around festive trifle time. She's being turfed out quicker than a Jehovah's witness at an atheist's funeral. The doctors claim it's better for her to be at home, in this age of superbugs. There's nothing like three flights of a spiral staircase to test the endurance of a reconstructed cervix.

Wednesday 22nd December

A text from the Bahamas:

'Hello, all the way from the Old Bahama Bay Resort! I hope all is well with poor Gwen. We were shocked to see her so frail and ill. Had I not been dressed head-to-toe in finest quality silk and satin (didn't I look amazing?!), I could've helped. Tell her to take this week off – we're away anyway – but if she could be back the week after and have the place tip-top for our return, that would be super. Ciao, Ryan. X.'

So much for looking after Gwen's needs, his only concerned is for his own to be met before they return home from their five star stay in the Bahamas. I know it's five star; I Googled it. It did nothing to lubricate the bitter little pill I'm swallowing from now until payday.

A life scavenging on the streets is only a month's pay-packet away for us on the breadline.

******

Mum called. Her inappropriate language at the close of our last conversation was conveniently forgotten. Apparently, Councillor Payne will be unveiling the plans for the new-improved Petersburn at Airdrie town hall tomorrow, some distance away from the scheme.

'If he thinks that holding this at the other side of town is going to stop us marching in there and giving our tuppence worth, he's got another thing coming,' she snapped. 'He'll be hoping we don't have the drive to gatecrash his little talk.'

I stressed, 'Mum, the town hall has been the source of many planning reveals over the years, you've chosen to live in Petersburn, it's not Councillor Payne's fault you live over two miles away.'

'You'd think, but you know what? The council have conveniently forgotten to grit all of the roads around the scheme to be sure we can't make it out. It'll take more than two miles and six inches of snow to hold me back. Being born in a coal-shed prepares you for this kind of nonsense. The scheme is rallying together. Your father and I own this place, I know, but we didn't think we'd have to up sticks in our retirement. We've heard the new houses will be fewer and don't even have bin cupboards. Everyone's up in arms. Where are half of us meant to live? And wheelie bins will congest every pavement. There's not enough Leylandii coated bin covers to hide that bloody disgrace!'

Not the bloody coal shed story again, I thought.

'Did you just sigh?' she asked, pointedly.

'No,' I lied, kicking myself for not covering the handset in time, 'I was holding in a sneeze.'

'I hope so. I expect your full support on this. Are you coming?'

I had no intention of going. Being trapped in the council chambers with a bunch of whining, post-menopausal woman is not my idea of a grand day out. 'Can't, I have the flu, hence the sneezing,' I fibbed, adding in a few croaks for effect. 'I'll be over to drop off presents sometime after Boxing Day.'

'Why on God's Earth are you outside then? You should be in bed with a mug of chicken soup.'

'That's why I'm out. I'm off to buy several cartons now,' I fabricated as I approached the familiar ting of the bell above Café Jamaica's door, pausing just as the door made contact with its brass lip. Unfortunately, a customer was trying to get out, which caused some momentary tug-of-war, which I won.

Mum sighed, 'It doesn't matter, we have over one hundred and fifty protestors. Besides, why change a tradition? You're always late with Christmas presents. Your nephews and nieces think Santa does a second visit on his way back to the North Pole, after a mini-break in the Caribbean.'

I'm *always* late? I could've saved so much cash over the years by buying gifts in the January sales!

******

Gwen's back at 323 safely – thanks to an uncharacteristically cautious drive home with Sally at the helm of her classic mini – and has been told to take it easy for the next few weeks. I conveniently forgot to pass on the message from Ryan; the boys can do their own dirty work. Molasses has been mollycoddling Gwen to the point of becoming an overbearing, expectant grandmother. She's stocked up Gwen's larder to the point of bursting. I was positively drooling over the homemade microwavable meals she's portioned out for the recovering mother-to-be. When she warmed up Gwen's lunch, it smelt and looked so damn good I produced an accidental jet of saliva from the back of my throat which shot across her mantlepiece. This phenomenon had never happened to me before and took me by surprise. It startled everyone else too.

Gwen asked me, 'Did you just spit on my statue of the Virgin Mary?'

I peered at the small figurine on her mantle, it did look a bit moist, but I denied all knowledge and left at warp speed. Great! I now look like I'm possessed.

Back in my room, I devoured my last few slices of plain bread with butter after the mould was picked carefully from the crust. I now have no butter and no bread. I have a half bag of old muesli, which looks suspiciously like wood shavings to me. I have no milk to put in the muesli. I can't bear the thought of eating it with water. Also, I haven't had chocolate in days, and I'm becoming envious of every customer as they tuck into their grub at the café. Hell, even the slop bin is beginning to look enticing. We don't get fed there unless we're doing a long day and I've been on half shifts all week. Things are getting desperate. Yesterday, I contemplated stealing a half-eaten Cadbury's Cream Egg from a toddler's sticky fist.

'Payday soon!' is the mantra of the moment.

Thursday 23rd December

Mum was arrested and thrown in the cells today. Dad bailed her out late this evening. I would've been sorely tempted to leave her in there until her case came to court. She's been charged with assault. The Save Our Scheme march broke into a brawl. Security couldn't cope with the sudden rise of emotion of over a hundred Airdrieonians hellbent on taking to the podium en mass to protest their case in a very Scottish way. After a particularly volatile exchange, mainly on my mother's part, Mum bopped Councillor Payne on the head with a leg of lamb she's planning on basting for Christmas dinner – some Save Our Scheme supporters met at the local butcher's, conveniently picking up their messages on the way.

Mum's only been released as she's not thought to be a threat to the general public. I beg to differ. 'Assault covers several pigeon holes in Scotland,' I told her. 'You could be accused of assault for simply leaping over a public bar in a threatening manner. God knows what they'll do to you for smacking a prominent – if hated – councillor on his sweaty head in full view of the local press.'

'It's all good publicity,' she said airily. 'I think I may have the most famous leg of lamb in the country sat in our fridge, Andy. He's just lucky I didn't choose a frozen supermarket turkey this year. But then, who wants a frozen supermarket turkey at any time of the year? Such bad quality compared to those dyke butchers down the road.' Again, such tact. Such diplomacy.

She'll be up in court in the New Year. My dad and sister are proud of her. I'm ashamed. My mother's now seen as a criminal. This could affect my prospects for future suitors, employment and adoption. She's behaving like an irresponsible teenager. 'I've made the front page of the local paper again,' she added with self-importance. 'I must say they've caught my good side. Payne looks like a frightened boar.' Mum paused before announcing the headline: ' "LIZ'S LAMB MEETS OLD MUTTON CHOPS WITH NO MINCING ABOUT." '

Oh, dear, God! Is there no end to this madness?

Friday 24th December

Christmas Eve.

Payday! (Thank the dilated Virgin Mary and her son's engaged head!)

9.30 a.m. I figured I should make some kind of effort and contribute in some small way to our Christmas meal. It's been quite some time since I delved into the world of baking: Chocolate Guinness Cake, take two! I have free run of the café's kitchen after closing to do it right this time.

11.45 p.m. One full day at the café, one hearty Jamaican meal eaten, and one cake baked, cooling and waiting to be iced tomorrow. A delicious and well-balanced cake, I may add. I chose to walk home with Sally at the end of our shift to kickstart the season of goodwill and save any awkwardness at the dinner table. It helped that both of us were a little tipsy on Molasses' mulled wine and copious cubes of chocolate liquors. I pointed out the most obvious constellation in the sky: Orion. It seemed to be fizzing with energy. Sally was curious at first. I could've sworn I saw some child-like wonder in her eyes as I described in detail the stars that make up the constellation: Betelgeuse, Rigel, etc.

But her amazement was as fleeting as a shooting star, and before long she let out a hearty yawn and interrupted, 'Hey, have I told you I'm seeing this new customer at the moment? He's some politician-or-other that enjoys having his ball-sack rubbed with sandpaper while he's bound entirely in linen, just like a mummy, with nothing exposed but his genitals. It's the most strange but delightfully easy job I've had in a long time, darling, because he then begs to be cocooned inside an Egyptian sarcophagus for the rest of the hour while I verbally abuse him, which gives me time to re-gloss my nails, etcetera. I do wonder where these unusual fetishes come from. I felt a little silly at first, but he pays well, and I guess if you have a sarcophagus in your spare room, you may as well make use of it.' She inspected her hands, 'The sandpaper acts as a wonderful exfoliator too.'

My stargazing bubble had burst. I'll never watch *Pyramids of Mars* again with the same innocence. As Sarah Jane and the Doctor creep around a sarcophagus in fear of Sutekh's release from his prison, I'll be imagining a horny politician sweating profusely inside in deep anticipation of Sarah taking a quick trip down to B&Q for assorted tools of torture.

I got back home to find a perfectly wrapped box, TARDIS blue in colour, sat in the hall by my door. 'Is this from you?' I asked Sally.

'No, dear, you should know I'm an old-fashioned girl that puts her tree up on Christmas Eve, not a day before, and that only opens her presents after she wakes on Christmas morning. I wouldn't be giving anything to anyone before Santa had the chance to empty his sack down my flume,' she added, suggestively.

'I'll open it tomorrow then,' I lied, quickly kissing her on the cheek and swooping the parcel inside. 'Sleep tight.'

I read the label, plopped the parcel on my bed and distance myself from it. I spent the next five minutes pacing around the room like a lion trapped in a cage. It was addressed to me, but that wasn't what had unnerved me, it was the familiar handwriting. I knew who it was from. I must've spent a further fifteen minutes staring at it. The Colonel watched me, perched on the arm of the sofa, blinking back and forth between the parcel and me as if to say, 'Well, aren't you going to open it?'

'What do you think?' I asked him. He remained silent. 'Great! You spend all this time chatting to me when I'm desperate for a good night's sleep, and now, when I'm asking for help, you just turn around and lick your arse!'

I leapt forward, placed the box on the floor and tore at the packaging. I recognised the contents immediately: an 18 inch Voice Recognition Dalek. Just what I wanted. Here it was, the embodiment of evil, staring at me, eyestalk waiting to be illuminated by one flick of a switch. The fanboy in me leapt for joy, but the jaded adult within remained grounded and sank lower still when I read the note attached to the box:

'Forgive me!'

I rummaged in the kitchen drawer and located the rolling pin that was last swung by my mother in an attempt to unblock Aunt Moira's airway. Without thinking any more about it, I pounced on the Dalek and thrashed it within an inch of its battery-operated life. I aimed for the eyestalk first and, once it was blind, I attacked every other part of it, venting my frustration until it was not only blind, but deaf, dumb, weaponless, crippled and every shred of malevolence was removed.

Within minutes the Dalek and I were in pieces on the floor.

It's too damn hard to start again if the past is lurking around every corner, waiting to exterminate your faith in humanity. Alistair/Nick isn't the neat and tidy end to my year I'd hoped for. I wish I could find the strength to find some closure.

Saturday 25th December

Christmas Day.

10 a.m. I could just stay in bed and ignore every bauble, twinkling star and Yuletide tune. I could wallow in my own self-pity and bury my head in the pillow to cancel out the bouncy melodic voices of Ella Fitzgerald, Nina Simone and Judy Garland singing jazzy carols in Sally's room. I could even veto Sally's jolly efforts to sing along and resist the temptation to do so myself. I could ignore the fact that Gwen's knocked on my door twice and demanded I get up and finish icing the cake. I could pay no mind to this day, our first Christmas together.

But then there's delicious home cooking carefully crafted by Molasses' loving hands, a table decorated in the glistening hope of light through the dreary darkness of winter, crackers to pull and so much booze it could sink a cargo ship in the calmest of seas. I'd be a fool to remove any chance of a happy day over some man who's having the falsest of Christmases with his poor, ignorant wife.

No, I shall get up and make the most of what I have, which to many may be very little – thirty-six years old, in a bedsit, with a cat as my therapist, single, surrounded by other dysfunctional-but-very-nice people and in a low-paid job that makes my feet ache – but to me I feel more alive than I have in years. I have hope and faith in the future. This is where I'm at, and next year doesn't seem as daunting as the this one. 2010 is almost over & I feel myself turning a corner. *That* alone is reason enough to get out of bed and celebrate.

Around Midnight (I think). All I said before is absolute guff! I may be drunk, I may be angry, but I see things clearer than I have in a long time. I'm sorely disappointed in humankind. They're swindlers and thieves, all! I trust no one. Life is shit! This is the worst Christmas ever. I'm stuck in a bedsit, slowly transmogrifying into a crazy cat lady, alone, in a dead-end job that barely meets my needs, with a charlatan of a friend who's whole life is a carefully crafted embroidery of colourful lies, the threads of which began to unravel just as my cursed Chocolate Guinness Cake was being cut. I've been played. Taken for a ride. I'm thirty-bloody-six years old, for Christ's sake, I should be the protagonist of my life, not others'. Ho! Ho! Ho! Merry fucking Christmas!

Sunday 26th December

Boxing Day.

I woke with one hell of a hangover brought on by too many cheap shots from random unnamed bars. I was alone. I had been all night. My room was still, apart from the familiar purring of the Colonel and the sound of an empty fridge struggling against the block of ice that now fills the freezer compartment through months of neglect. I rolled over to catch the time. Just after ten. As I did so, a small white envelope slid from the duvet and plopped to the floor. My name was scrawled elegantly on it. I peeled it open and adjusted the carefully folded paper to catch the light. A refreshing waft of Nag Champa lingered below my nose as my eyes focussed on the words:

'Dearest Andy.

I'm so sorry I lied. I'm trying to protect myself from self-loathing and, to do that, I'm running again. You want so desperately to recapture your youth, and yet, all my energy is spent trying to escape mine. You almost convinced me it was possible to be comfortable in my old skin. Thank you for that; I'm sorry I blew it. I should have confided in you.

Goodbye.
Love, Sally.'

I'd hoped yesterday was a dream, but this was proof it wasn't. Mum and Dad had nipped along the M8 to surprise us at our little Christmas party. We were full of joyous frivolity, turkey with all the trimmings and high on a toxic mix of wine, rum and tequila when they swung through Café Jamaica's doors. My parents cared enough to travel forty-five minutes to wish us well on Christmas Day when I shamefully hadn't given them a second of mine. I was delighted to see them, but that joy came crashing down within a few seconds.

'If Mohamed won't come to the ... Andrew Angus, what the hell are you doing with that lying, cheating cow?' asked Mum, smile gone and disgust evident from every furrow in her brow. Our awkward laughter took several seconds to fade. Surely she hadn't just said what we thought she'd said?

Melve turned to me and asked, 'What's she blithering on about, old boy?'

I followed my mother's daggers. She lifted a finger and pointed towards my friend, Sally Knowles. 'That thing there, that left George as soon as his body was cold,' growled Mum.

The room fell silent.

It was then, and only then, I saw the person beneath the layers of makeup, extravagant wigs and larger than life personality. Her face fell and with it her last mask too. Sally Knowles was ... is Lisa McKenzie, my childhood friend who I last saw twenty-two years ago. How could I not have seen her before? She lied to me. She played me like a fool. It all makes sense now why she'd disappear every time Mum and Dad materialised: they're too close to her recent history. I, on the other hand, am a distant childhood memory that ended at puberty.

Sally looked terrified, but not of Mum; her fear seemed to come from deep within as she cradled her stomach and took off without looking back, leaving me with nothing but questions. And now, thanks to Thomas, Alistair *and* her, I'm more disappointed and disillusioned than ever.

9.10 p.m. It took me only an hour to find their home. I was on a mission. I'd had enough of liars and, hangover or no hangover, I was about to root out the most substantial chunk of dishonesty in my life. I needed to scrub the slate clean.

Their bungalow was dripping in the joy of Christmas, in competition with other houses in their street. Children played on shiny new bikes on a road that was uncharacteristically quiet thanks to the holiday season. Every home tried its best to look different from the next, each one with individual family needs catered for and ever hopeful of a better, more appealing designer life than the previous. Redbrick, sandstone, pebbledash, flat roof, pitched roof, red door, black door, Victorian style, 80's convenience, extension after extension, and yet they all looked dull and samey. All firmly ticking assorted boxes of 'Safe', 'Retired', 'White British', '2.4 children', *'Straight in Suburbia'*.

Nestled amongst this pile of beige was their little haven. It was surprisingly easy to track him down. I'd headed in the general direction his car often took when leaving me at 323 and walked while watching his Grindr location fluctuate from far, to near, to far, to closer yet still, until it reduced from miles to mere meters. After hours on determined foot, I'd followed the GPS of his profile more or less to their street. It was only a matter of finding the right car after this point. He was stupid enough to keep the same profile name, perhaps through fear of losing his link to his true self and the only support he now has: his fuck-buddies. He's terminally incapable of giving it up.

The 4x4 sitting in their drive confirmed I'd found his home and screamed to me, 'dogger'. And yet, to any casual passerby, it would look perfectly innocent amongst every other family car in the estate, like a cold metal chameleon. Gleaming and freshly scrubbed of the, I imagined, incriminating mud that's often collected by drives down tight country roads, leading to salacious, anonymous excitement in woods, over car bonnets or on the squeaky clean upholstery.

A huge tree, well-nourished and glittering with carefully draped tinsel, silver baubles and delicate twinkling lights, filled one of two bay windows. Both windows were framed with outdoor lights, stretching around the front of their bungalow and into the garden. Everything was bright and transparent. No colour here. Why would there be? Nick's kingdom would, of course, have no hint of a rainbow. He can hide comfortably amongst the uniformness of the estate and bury his true self in layers of decking and Laura Ashley.

Christina, now in remission, is blissfully unaware of the quiet cancer eating away at her life.

It was the right house. The right home. I'd found the truth at last. But what the hell was I going to do next? I hadn't banked on actually finding him, so I hadn't planned the next step. I was driven by anger and disappointment, and a deep desire to right some wrongs inflicted on me, but now? The sound of laughter and music came from within their cosy corner of planet Earth; a Boxing Day party in full swing. The sun disappeared behind a cloud, and the reflection of the estate faded from the window. I could see clearly through the glass now. An abundance of guests picked at a buffet laid on especially for friends and family: the elite. I assumed there would be family there. *A brother or a sister? Parents? Their kids?! Please don't let them have children,* I thought. It's no surprise I know nothing about the man, but suddenly it became unbearably real how gullible I'd been. What I did know had been titbits he'd thrown me in passing and, like a faithful dog, I'd gobbled them up and waited patiently for more. Probably fiction. The only gospel truth I knew, I'd uncovered myself.

Two more guests appeared at their gate and wished me a happy Christmas as they turned up the drive. I suddenly felt ashamed and gazed towards something and nothing in the distance as I grunted salutations back at them. They nodded and headed towards the house. I caught them glancing back at me momentarily and then, thankfully, they ignored me and carried on towards the front door. When they rang the bell, I panicked and ducked behind a hedge.

I'd finally rooted out his other life and what jarred more than anything was, no matter how distant he'd been emotionally, he'd always been physically close. Too close for comfort now. Just ten minutes drive. Ten minutes to shake off one life and warm to another. Ten minutes from our dirty, invisible sex. Ten minutes from Christina's love to mine. So seamless it sickened me.

I heard the door open, and his familiar tone filled the air, warm and jovial and with not a hint of regret. His guests reciprocated, and the door closed. I stuck my head up and saw them being met in the front room by a buoyant Christina. She looked miles better. She's on the mend, but what for? The delicious smell of cooked ham wafted through the shrubbery and took me back to Sunday lunches at Gran

Angus' with Mum, Dad and Sis. It conjured up the image of the perfect family. At that moment, all I wanted to do was leap into that bungalow that was stuffed with family, food and lies and shake everyone out of their illusion. I wanted to wail that it was a deception, and their valuable time was being wasted.

I heard the boot of the 4x4 slam shut. I peered over the hedge. He was carrying a bag bursting with belated Christmas gifts when he saw me. His mouth fell open, struck dumb with fear. He turned to face me and seemed to make himself grow wider in an attempt to block his little secret from encroached on the perfection of his other life, frozen to the frosty gravel beneath his cosy slippered feet. We didn't move, just for a moment, both of us unsure of what was going to happen next. Was I really there to reveal all to his poor spouse? Could I be that cruel? Did I care for her so little to make her universe implode? Did I have that right? Was I really that hellbent on revenge? Could I do that to him? Where does all that once pure, all-consuming, unwavering love go? Can it diminish so easily?

'Hello, Nick. That is your real name, right?'

He grimaced. I walked toward him in full view of the house. He looked terrified. I asked him quietly, my words wavering, my lips trembling, 'Did you know I was friendly with your wife?'

He whispered quickly, 'No, not at first. Not until I was in too deep. I knew that you worked in the café next door, I knew she supplied your wine, but I didn't know you'd become friends until much later. I know it was fucked up, but I just couldn't give you up. I was trying so desperately to keep you both and keep you apart.'

'Why did you come to the boys' wedding then?'

'Look,' he said, moving further behind his car out of sight from the party, 'this isn't the time or the place. Can I meet you tomorrow?'

'Just tell me!' I shouted.

He put up his hand to pacify me and said, 'Okay, okay. I just went to a wedding that my wife'd suddenly been invited to. I'd no idea it was the Terrible Twins' civil partnership. There was no official invite. I assumed it was a real wedding between a man and a woman, not a civil partnership. It only began to dawn on me when I sat in that hall and saw the stage set with all that paraphernalia that you'd described to me after your rehearsal nights. I'm so damn busy all the time, she arranges the social side of life, and I just go along with it. But yes, I did know you were becoming mates and worried for a time. But once she travelled to Spain to get her treatment, I worried less, bounced between countries and enjoyed your company more while I was here. Selfish of me.'

'And this was when you conveniently told me you'd left your wife. Jesus! You even hired an apartment to convince me!'

'Ah, no. Not really. That's the company apartment for putting up international clients and senior board members.'

'You're nothing but a piece of shit, Alist ... Nick.'

'I know.'

'Do you love her?' I asked, my lips tight in an attempt to keep the tremors at bay. It took all my strength to speak, so stunted by the emotion inside. I felt, if I lost control, the shakes would resonate through my entire body and within seconds I'd end up a contorted wreck on the gravel. But luckily, those lips that once embraced his so eagerly remained constricted, carefully holding this mess together.

His eyes immediately filled with tears and his face flushed, 'Aye. Aye, I do. With all my heart.' He turned his face away toward the ground.

'Did you ever really love me?'

'I think I did,' he said as he moved almost inside the shrubbery. I stayed exactly where I was. I'd meet his honesty head-on, no matter the consequences.

'Please, Andy,' he pleaded with me. 'This is my whole life.'

He *thought* he did. That wasn't good enough for me. I was only willing to risk it all if he actually *did*. As it turned out, he wasn't worth it in the end. I'd wasted enough time and labour over him. It indeed wasn't worth ruining a marriage and a friendship over such precarious sentiments. In the end, there would only be pain and despair, and what for? An incalculable future with a promiscuous man who's still hedging his bets. No, he should love me, unconditionally. He should ache for me, as I did for him. He should be sure, at the very least, we're worth all the pain and turmoil we'd cause. He should love me without question. I, at the very least, deserve that.

'Then, you have two choices.' I said. 'Give it all up and live your life with her, as you promised all those years ago, and never mess around again, or take the risk and show her who you really are: live with honesty and integrity and allow her the autonomy to choose the life she wants.'

By now, he was super shifty. Nodding in remorseful agreement but agitated all the same. Eager for me to disappear. 'Don't worry, I'm not staying for the buffet. This is where I get off. I'm done with this screwed up mess. Don't ever contact me again and I'll promise you this, I'll continue to be her friend as long as she needs me, even though it'll kill me every time I see her or she mentions your name, and I'll keep all that you really are locked away more tightly than you have yourself. But you need to know this: if you think that beautiful, bright woman in there has no idea, you have another thing coming. Slowly, but surely, she's figuring you out.'

I heard Christina calling cheerily, 'Niiiiiick, where are you? The glasses need refilling,' from somewhere inside their house. I moved back to the camouflage of the hedge, for Christina's sake only. He couldn't move an inch until I was gone. He needn't have worried, I was off. Our final breakup. And for the first time, there were no tears. Not from me, at least. All I felt was relief as I was honest with myself at long last. It could have never have worked, Alistair and me, or rather the man I thought was Alistair. And Sally was right: I'm not ready yet; I should've known this. But what I didn't expect, given time, after eleven long years, I'd find my single self again, be alone, and be okay with that.

Monday 27th December

This evening, I found myself standing in Sally's room. It's so full of her life and yet echoes the emptiness of a tormented soul. All of her stuff's still here, her dusty old vinyl, her flirtatious housecoat that leaves very little to the imagination, the lotions and potions she insists keep her young and vibrant, piles of incense sticks, and that wall of shoes, neatly stacked as ever. But one pair is missing, obvious in their absence as they're her most prized possession: her ruby-red slippers. Confirmation that my friend of Dorothy has returned to Oz.

I'd been in there for some time, I guess hoping for some clue or explanation as to why she'd lied, or that she'd turn up in her usual blasé manner and elaborate on the where, when, how and why. I needed more, damn it, not just a room filled with camouflage. But nope. She's definitely gone. I could feel it, just like that feeling you get when you step into somebody's home for the first time since they died. That familiarity, that expectation that they'll pop out of the kitchen with a mug of tea in their hand and say a cheery hello, and then that awful silence and final confirmation that you will never, ever see them again. The last time I felt this way was in Aunt Moira's place. The time before, at Steve's. It was too familiar.

I opened the brown wooden box that'd fallen to the floor weeks ago. There were the usual trinkets held within that she rotated with every outfit, a sizeable amount of £50 notes, a mishmash of buttons and foreign coins, and that little hummingbird brooch, just like Aunt Moira used to wear. It brought that feeling of finality, of death, right back to me again. I shivered and noticed something buried amongst the jumble: a tiny black box I hadn't paid much attention to before. I was examining the contents of the box when Melve arrived.

'Do you think she'll be back?' he asked, pensively.

'Oh, I don't think so. I think she's been running for a very long time and is well practised at making a clean and swift exit, only taking the essentials. She's probably on a flight over the Bermuda Triangle as we speak,' I joked, freeing a single white gold ring from its slot. It shimmered in the soft yellow glow of her inner sanctum, glistening with magic and mystery.

'What's that you have there, young man?' asked Melve.

I slid the ring onto my wedding finger, but it wouldn't go further than my bony knuckle. I switched it to my pinky, and it fitted perfectly. It was untainted; not a scratch. 'This is where it all went wrong for Sally – I mean, Lisa – this is Lisa's wedding ring. It has their initials inscribed inside. It's so plain looking; Sally Knowles would never have picked this, but homemaker Lisa would have. They must've been so in love, don't you think? To get married. Her husband, George was his name, killed himself, you know?'

'Best leave alone,' he said, closing the trinket box. 'If she comes back and finds you rummaging through her stuff, she'll give you a rather swift scalping.'

'If she came back right now, I'd be the one doing the scalping,' I scathed.

'Don't be angry, my boy. All of us have difficult secrets, it's just some are too massive and all-consuming to deal with in one lifetime.' He placed the wooden box gently back on the shelf.

'I want mine tidied up neatly before I die,' I said.

'Life just doesn't run like that, Andy.'

'I guess not. But what pushed her to such extremes?' I slid off the ring and snapped the small black box shut, placing it purposefully back inside the wooden box.

'Death affects people in weird ways, my brother,' said Melve as he ushered me out of her room. 'When my father died, my mother went on her first Club 18 to 30 Holiday.'

I tucked the unseen ring into the back pocket of my jeans quickly and said, 'Oh, I'm sorry, did your dad die young?'

'What's that, old chap? Oh, no, no. If he had, we would have been a very happy family. No, he clung on until the bitter end, the controlling bastard. Mother was in her seventies when she took that trip. She paid twice the price to get the ticket and apparently laughed her head off at the thought of Father's disgust as she dived headfirst into a foam party brimming with half-naked, nubile young lads. She was a pensioner on acid, totally spaced out, with said bastard incapable of saying or doing a damn thing about it.' Melve dropped the chub on Sally's door and closed it firmly. 'Best let sleeping dogs lie, eh, my little cherub? No point in distressing yourself. Snooping in other people's clutter can drive a man batty. I should know, I helped clear out Warhol's townhouse in New York after he died at the hands of those unscrupulous surgeons. Now that was a warped can of Campbell's worms. Wait and see what the sands of time bring you, eh?' He patted me firmly on the back and merrily asked, 'Drink?' as if that would cure all.

Even though I was still feeling delicate, I agreed to a small tipple, 'I could do with a bit of hair of the dog,' I lied. What I really needed was the company. He pulled me closer with one arm and shook me so fiercely I could feel my fillings rattle. 'That's the Dunkirk spirit, my boy! Come on, I'll pour you a stiff one. Did I ever tell you about the time I was caught rummaging in the depths of an Egyptian queen's freshly unearthed tomb?'

I slipped onto the beanbag Mum had drunkenly settled in weeks before and nursed a rather large dram. Melve recited nights under the stars on the great Congo and the Nile, the colourful tribes he lived with for a month in search of the lost caves of the Amazon rain forest, tall adventures and great escapes, and all the while I was aware that some of it was truth and some pure fiction. I was also aware that Sally had plagiarised some of Melve's yarns and adapted them for her cover story. But Melve's invention is comforting escapism. Like a good book, it's safe. Steve always said, 'Never let the truth get in the way of a good story,' and I believe equally the listener should never let their scepticism get in the way of good storytelling.

The sky darkened and the wind, which had battered the old sash windows earlier, died down into a lull of gentle, reassuring respirations through the tiny gaps of the ill-fitting sills. Melve continued to chat while swinging rhythmically in his hammock. His arm swooshing here and there as his whisky slopped from the glass and formed tiny puddles on the bare floorboards beneath his undulations. Then he began to drift, the conversation slurred, stopped and started, and eventually, with the glass now empty and resting on his thigh, the hammock settled, and he fell silent. Nothing but the slow wheezing of the breeze in time with a kind hippie's somnolent breathing. I sat for a minute in reflection thinking about Sally and Lisa, her husband George and the rich tapestry she'd created, my own life and the tangled web of lies that'd been woven around it. How many times had I lied, even to myself, to protect myself from a shit-storm? Plenty. I gently removed the glass from Melve's hand, delicately covered him with a blanket, kissed the drowsy hippy on the forehead and took myself to my room.

I opened the drawer of my bedside table that I tuck my diary in now, the only drawer with a working lock, and pulled Lisa's ring from my pocket. So small and yet so important. I scraped around the back of the drawer and pulled out my own black box. I cautiously opened it and looked inside. It looked as bright and optimistic as the day I carefully chose it. I pulled the ring from the slot and resisted placing it on my finger. That would've been too much. It's almost a year since I last had the nerve to look at it. I carefully returned my lost hope to its slot, sat Lisa's ring next to it, closed the lid tight, kissed it and locked it inside my own little box of secrets.

It seems we aren't so different after all.

Tuesday 28th December

I was back on shift at 7 a.m. By the time Trenton popped in for lunch, I was in a right strop. He was his usual cheery, ostentatious self, which really pissed me off.

'How are you, young man?' he asked when I dragged my tired bones over to clear his dirty plates. 'You look as if someone's stolen your delicious mojo.'

'I'm tired of men and all that comes with them. I'm fed up with all this dating, shagging and putting myself out there. It's so damn hard to be gay in this day and age, with hook-up apps like Grindr in the palm of every man's hand, just to squeeze in sex between work and home. Men will have sex on a postage stamp if they have the urge. And when did everyone get so damn pretty and perfect? Every guy on Instagram is muscled, ripped, tanned, plucked and dazzling in the teeth department too. Whatever happened to Mr Average? I mean, we can't all walk around with a perfect 3D filter and always have the benefit of good lighting. And then there's all this civil partnership crap too. Why *do* we want to be like the straights?'

Trenton's lips tightened as he became tetchy, 'We're not yet, are we? Not really. No, you're entirely right: it's so hard these days, I mean, I had it easy, didn't I? All us old queens did, didn't we? Being gay when it was illegal. Being threatened daily for refusing to hide who we were, beaten even, and not a bobby on the beat would turn our way to help. Secret parties in fear of the police knocking on the door and arresting us, or worse, taking a pop at us. Being told that the person you loved was a minor, just because the law denied us equality. Feeling powerless when your friends were slowly ravaged by an untreatable virus that was labelled as "the Gay Plague" and to be told we deserved it because being gay was against nature and it was God's will. To be told we were sick and filthy and didn't belong, and to have no right to visit the one person you've loved and cherished more than anyone else in the world when they're painfully dying of that nasty disease. Unable to be by his side when he slipped away, unable to say a last goodbye as they slid that beautiful body you caressed for so long into the ground. You'd sell your soul just to have one more chance to hold him and tell him everything would be alright. Yes, my boy, it's so damn hard to be gay today. Don't kid yourself, it's a wonderland with free lucky bags filled with hope, rights, opportunity and glittery rainbows compared to where I've come from.'

He was right, of course, and I was being a self-centred twat. 'I'm sorry, Trenton. I'd no idea. You must think I'm an ignorant knob.'

He got out of his chair and hugged me, actually hugged me, and said, 'Yes, I do, a little bit. And you're a massive bit ageist too: that, you really have to work on as there's no escaping old Father Time. Before you know it, you'll become some old queen who craves the days he could turn heads without even trying. Some of us are outrageous because outrageous is all we have left, sweetheart.' I bowed my head in shame. Trenton placed a finger under my chin, lifted it and looked deep into my eyes, and for the first time, I really saw his. They weren't the broken, bloodshot eyes of an old man as I'd assumed; they were clear and bright, young and full of hope. 'Look, it's never easy for anyone,' he said softly. 'But there's far more of the good stuff than the bad these days, it's just we rarely notice the constant good; the catastrophic bad is always headline news. I guess I'm here to tell you, you're not special, honey: you'll just have to muddle through like the rest of us.'

He's right, of course, and my D-Day to muddle through is fast approaching.

Wednesday 29th December

Gwen spent the morning on and off the payphone in the hall. She was either poised next to it waiting for a call, on it, or heading to it or from it. I asked her what was so urgent – she practically hurdled over the umbrella stand during one burst of ringing, which I'm sure didn't help her granulating fanny. She panted, 'I've heard there's a blank spot for a cellist at the Hogmanay concert in the Usher Hall. The regular has become very regular with diarrhoea, the sub has come down with the same, and the sub-sub is at another concert in Berlin. I've been trying to track down the conductor through a friend of a friend who works on their PR team. It's the Usher Hall, Andy. This could be my last chance before I am buried in used diapers.'

'Any luck?' I asked.

'Not yet.'

'Are you sure you're fit enough to play? The stress may be too much. You don't want any more damage internally.'

She looked at me with certainty in her eyes, 'Andrew, I want this. This is not stress, this is joy.'

The phone rang, and we both stared at it with nervous excitement. She snatched it off the receiver and gulped before saying a desperate, 'Hello? Gwen here!' And then, disappointedly, 'Oh, hello again. Yes, he's here.' She pushed the receiver into my chest, saying, 'It's just your mother,' before walking away.

'Why are you not answering your mobile? Are you still hanging with that liar?' asked Mum.

'Which one?' I asked. 'There's been that many charlatans in my life this year. If you mean Sally, then yes, I am,' I said, irritated. 'Well, I would be if she were around. She's run off, thanks to you,' I grimaced and regretted that reveal the second I blurted it out.

'Now *there's* a surprise,' shrieked Mum self-righteously down the line. 'Old habits die hard. And her name is *Lisa*, not this silly persona she's concocted. Whoever heard of anyone called *Sally Knowles?* I mean, really!'

'I have, and anyone who cares about her has. And no matter who she was, she's still a friend,' I bawled back, a little surprised how much I was willing to defend the absentee.

'Well, you're old enough to make your own mistakes,' sighed Mum.

'You would think, yeah,' I said, sarcastically.

'But if she does come back, I know someone who will have a few choice words for her ...'

I cut her off, 'How's the campaign coming along?'

Silence. A pause at last. And then, 'Oh, it's gathering pace. Didn't you see the spread in the Daily Record?' I confessed I hadn't and prepared to listen to a long gloat. 'Oh, didn't I tell you? A lovely reporter came to the house on Christmas Eve to interview me. He brought along a nice photographer who took pictures of me preparing the leg of lamb I'd clobbered that slimy councillor with. Both Catholic boys. Nice boys. They admired your gran's statue of The Sacred Heart that's in the living room.

'Well, they said they'd put a lovely spin on me clouting him, not that I need it, and assured me they were passionate about the campaign. And they did. Lovely article. And they caught my good side, although the gravy stains on my apron bug me, but that's to be expected of a woman cooking for a big family, isn't it? Oh, and Mr Borkowski's shop is booming now that he's been interviewed too. He's the heart of the community, after all. With that and that young lass working for him – she's up for young local entrepreneur of the year, by the way; upped his sales through social media posts – he's bought the old taxi office next door and is expanding into house and garden items too. Bought all my veg from him for Christmas dinner – it's vital to support the local community. The dinner was a total success, but the way, your dad said it was the best I've ever done. The lamb was nice and tender,' she laughed. 'Anyway, I just wanted to call because I know you'd want to offer me some goodwill for tomorrow as I'm talking on Radio Scotland about the whole campaign and the infamous lamb incident.'

'Good luck,' I said half-heartedly.

'Thanks, Son. Got to go, I have Marion coming round for a black pudding buttie. I got some free from the butcher girls as a reward for doing their business no end of good – I name-dropped them in the paper. Bye! Bye! Byeee!'

She hung up without asking how I was, which isn't unusual, but I wanted to tell her about tomorrow. I wanted to say that I'd be quaking in some plastic chair in a busy sexual health clinic waiting on life-changing results. I needed my mum to wish me good luck. Not just good luck, but great luck, the luckiest of luck. But she wouldn't understand anyway. She'd just have a rant about my sexual antics and shame me down the line. It's not her fault, she's never known anyone with HIV personally, let alone taken a test herself, so how could she possibly understand? Her whole life has been spent in a cul-de-sac.

Right now, how I wish mine had.

Thursday 30th December

5 a.m. I dreamt a redbreast robin was trapped in my room and fluttering desperately against the top of the window. The Colonel was on the kitchen linoleum watching in bemusement. The bird was battering her fragile head against the glass in the hope of escape. I shot out of bed to release her, pulling the top panel open, but my tiny friend just fluttered downward, unaware of her escape route.

'Come on little thing, it's easy, just fly up. Head towards the fresh air,' I said.

The voice of Noel Coward said, 'This pitiable life is endeavouring to inhale. Frantic to move on, but on pause, marginally. Offer your hand, you oaf. Don't judge her incapacities. She's lost, she's perturbed, so guide her.'

I raised my hands, fearful of the desperation that was tearing away before me, scared I may break her fragile wings, and gently cupped them around her little breast, closing them and calming her. Her tiny heart tapped away in my hands as fast as my own. I held her to the opening and let go. She flew out, over the bare rowan tree and disappeared beyond. I could hear her chirping for a time, thankful and relieved it seemed, and then she was gone. Silence. Peace, for both of us. I turned to the Colonel and said, 'Thanks. I know what to do.'

7 a.m. Unable to sleep. They say it's not a death sentence any more, but for me, it is in a way: a huge piece of me will die if the result is positive. My life will change forever. I'll always be careful when I cut myself so as not to infect others. A common cold will not just be something to shrug off with a hot toddy and rest. People will probably never be able to kiss me again without taking a fleeting risk assessment. And what affects me the most, is the fact that I'll continuously be seeking approval from my family and friends, future lovers and people on the gay scene who, even though they don't want to admit it, harbour some kind of prejudice inspired by fear of catching it themselves.

I could just not go and never hear those words and live a short but mostly happy life. But that's been the norm for the past year, and that just isn't healthy. This year is hurtling towards its end. I need to close the door, shut this diary, and lay 2010 to rest. With it, those doubts and fears need to be dealt with, new ones will take their place, but at least the stock will be cleared, and the old crap will be unable to fester.

11.35 p.m.

'Just take a seat,' said the receptionist, casually. Had he said, 'Just take a seat and try to stop your heart leaping into your mouth every time a solemn-looking nurse appears and calls out the name of their next patient, who then disappears with said solemn nurse into the depths of the clinic, never to be seen again,' that would've been more appropriate.

Nurses came and went, some familiar, some newbies, all with caring, professional faces. I wondered which one would be the nurse to break the news to me. Did they know my result already? I started reading a magazine – *Bella* – but it was useless, I was stuck on the same page, the same paragraph, the same damn line, as I had been psychologically all year. I glanced up every time staff appeared and became fidgety, crossing and uncrossing my legs, flapping the magazine anxiously, crossing and uncrossing my legs some more, until I kicked the coffee table and sent a stack of magazines to the floor, falling between other patients' legs.

They were running late. *Surely they know not to keep people waiting who have come for this kind of result. This is a bad sign,* I thought to myself as I hobbled about and scooped up the magazines from the floor. Not a soul helped. All too wrapped up in their own worries, no doubt. *Was this a clinic just for HIV results? Was it a clinic specialising in bad HIV results?* My rational mind was in a boxing match with my insecurities, and it was losing. Picking up the mags from the floor was a good distraction: *What Car?* was scooped up from between Brown Tatty Kickers; *OK* was plucked from Blue Furry Boots; *National Geographic* was rescued from the heel of Black Calf Length With S&M-like Buckles; *SFX* was tugged from the toes of a pair of perfectly placed ruby-red slippers; I tried to discreetly pull *Scotland in Trust* from the clutches of an ignorant pair of cherry red Doc Martin's, but the boot-wearer was unaware, engrossed in a book.

Hang about, I thought, *ruby-red slippers? Who the hell wears ruby-red slippers to a clap clinic?* I turned back to look at Ruby-red. Yes, definitely ruby-red and most definitely there. The right slipper was now curled upward at the heel and resting on its tip. A hand reached down to help me pull the spine of *Scotland in Trust* free. A well-manicured hand, with glossy emerald nails. *Scotland in Trust* slipped free after the green glossed hand slapped the thigh of Cherry

Reds briskly and said, 'Move it, buster!' Cherry Reds lifted both boots clear off the floor in shock. We clung on to the corners of the mag as Ruby-red and I got to our feet.

'Need a hand, sweetie?' asked Sally, batting her long false eyelashes with not a twitch of self-doubt. She smiled, her lips exhibiting a chorus of dazzling teeth, and I could swear I heard angels singing. 'A promise is a promise, after all, no matter the complications,' she winked as she added *Scotland in Trust* to the stack and patted the magazines into a neat pile.

I was dumbfounded. How did she have the gall to come back? Who am I kidding? Of course, she had the gall! How could I ever doubt it? 'But ... but ... you left. Like, really left.'

'Yes, I did, darling. But that was pretty much due to my head being wedged in-between my own rather pert buttocks.'

'But you ... you're Lisa McKenzie. From Petersburn. You peed in my paddling pool!' I slapped her on the shoulder. She didn't expect that. She looked shocked.

'Was that for the paddling pool incident, which I regret, or my more recent inadequacies? Which I regret more so.'

'Both,' I said, firmly.

'That's more like it, brotherfucker. A bit of gumption at last,' she laughed as she rubbed the patch of skin that was now turning pink.

It was all getting too much, my heart was bounding all over my ribcage. 'Oh, Sally, I mean Lisa, I mean Sally ... I don't know if we can move on from this. I don't think I can take more of your nonsense.'

'Then let's get through today, right now, and I promise we'll get through a world of tomorrows,' she pleaded. Her eyes were full of certainty as if she had a shit-load of clutter she was determined to clear from her life too, and her brow was no longer its usual breezy self, but hardened, careful and determined. 'I'm begging you, Andy. Help me, help you, help me.'

'Andrew Anus?' called a redhead nurse who was heavily pregnant and yawning. We turned to her and said, 'It's *Angus!*'

'Sorry, my mistake,' apologised the redhead. Adding, just to be sure she'd got the right patient, '*Andrew Angus?*'

'That's me,' I confirmed. I held out my hand and felt Sally grip it firmly. I asked her, 'It's going to be alright, isn't it?' I needed one more lie, especially from someone who could do it with conviction.

'Yes, darling,' she softly said as she stroked my cheek, 'it's all going to be just fine.'

******

On our way back home, everything was technicolour. The frost had melted, and the dampness on the streets seemed to make everything glisten, reflecting the beauty of this breathtaking city. The trees, even though stripped of their greenery and patiently waiting on spring, appeared to burst with life. Strangers seemed jolly and approachable, perhaps even huggable. The late morning sky was so clear and blue it was as if heavenly angels had blown the clouds away with trumpet calls and thrown a faint moon up onto the canvas to befriend the sun, to reassure us that the darkness would never return and the current state of azure would become the norm. Not only that, but every sound seemed clearer, crisper, more tuneful than before, like a beautiful melody being heard for the first time, from the distant bagpiper playing on the cobbles of the Royal Mile, to the pips of the traffic lights at the Scotsman building, it was a symphony. As we walked along North Bridge and I caught sight of Edinburgh Castle, that ancient fortress upon volcanic rock, I felt as if I was fully entitled to be crowned King just for one day.

'Are you relieved, my friend?' asked Sally.

'Relieved? Blimey! If I didn't have some grip on reality, I'd be skipping down the street wearing your ruby-reds singing *We're Off To See The Wizard*.'

Sally hit the breaks and challenged me, 'Trade you!' as she nodded to my weatherbeaten boots and grinned.

I'm sure we looked insane, me in poorly fitting Dorothy slippers and Sally in my size elevens, singing at the top of our voices and skipping arm and arm down Leith Walk, pausing in fits of laughter part of the way and catching our breath as age caught up with us, but it was damn liberating. People smiled and laughed at us on our journey, and that was okay. Not a single disparaging comment was made. We seemed to be making their day brighter too.

I know it won't last, this feeling of euphoria, this harmony with the universe and every particle of it, but just for today, it's a new beginning. I can genuinely say to the world: I am HIV *negative*. And to me, with a year of petrification caused by fear, and doubt eating away at my core, I know I'm entitled to this day – this glorious, newborn day – to hold it, keep it, and say, 'Thank you for this second chance. I promise I won't screw it up.'

******

At midday, Gwen pounded on Sally's door as we negotiated our way through brewing tea and settling back into our friendship. The pounding was feverish. Her eyes were wide when she burst in. 'Is it the baby again, dearest?' asked Sally, cupping Gwen's slightly pregnant belly.

'Oh, good, you're back, whoever you are ... like I care about that really,' she panted. 'No, no, we're totally fine. Better than fine, actually. We're super-fantastic! I've got the cellist position for the Hogmanay concert at the Usher Hall! Can you believe that? Against all the odds, I got it!' She was now hopping up and down.

'Careful, darling, or you'll split the pod,' said Sally, clinging on to Gwen's stomach under some delusional theory that this would hold everything perfectly in place.

'That's fantastic news,' I said. 'Please be careful, though. You shouldn't exert yourself, remember?'

Gwen continued to hop. Sally, who was scared to restrain her, had to bounce in unison while supporting her. 'Don't worry, I'm getting preferential treatment as they are so desperate,' assured Gwen. 'But what a break it could be, me as part of the line up at the Usher Hall! Who knows where it will lead? Got to go, I have rehearsal right now and have to get used to the cello they insist I use, as mine will be too much for me and my pod to carry. Auf Wiedersehen!'

She hugged both of us and was off. Sally shrugged her shoulders and said to me, 'Who knows, maybe 2011 is going to be stuffed full of big changes for all of us. It's started already as I think that may be the first time I've ever known Gwen to hug anyone.'

Time was short, I had to be on shift within the hour, so I supped down my tea and bid her goodbye. I also warned her not to run off. She laughed. 'As if, darling. What do you take me for, some kind of erratic teenager?'

'Aye! Can we talk later about Lisa?'

She moaned, 'Today is about you, my negative friend; tomorrow, I promise, is reserved for Lisa. Just give me one more day to thaw her out, please?'

'Alright, but there's a time limit: before midnight on Hogmanay, and I promise I'll never mention her again.'

She smiled and said, 'Deal!' shaking my hand in a firm, businesslike way.

I bid her au revoir. The truth is, I like Sally Knowles. She's wild, irrational, messy, 20% tipsy 30% of the time, forthright and plain rude when the world does or doesn't need it. She doesn't crave love and isn't needy for it either. She's been the opposite of me. What's not to like? I don't really know if there's room for Lisa McKenzie in our lives. If she's been consumed by the incarnation of Ms Knowles, why should she be regurgitated? Through her own design, Lisa's become something else. Maybe something better. The events of the past, whatever they may be, have pushed her far from the woman she once was, but she's had the balls to chose her character, her life, her story and become who she wants. She's had the guts to walk away and start again from scratch. I've done nothing more than cling on to the past and my idealistic dream of love, to my own detriment. Maybe she deserves to be herself more than any of us.

******

When I got back, I respected her wishes and left her to her own devices. I can hear her now, pottering around with her old 78s, occasionally accompanied by the rigorous, rhythmic agitation of a cocktail shaker and the customary sound of her window sliding open to puff on a cigarette. I'm happy she's stuck around. I can hear Gwen's cello playing late into the night, the strings surely glowing as hot as newly fashioned steel from the friction. Practice is punctuated only by the whistling of her stovetop kettle. But now there's more, there's a tiny life sharing her room with her, being nurtured by the notes she plays, growing stronger every day. She's no longer alone. And then there's a hummingbird chanting a mantra as our resident hippy, Melve, realigns his chakras and clears the clutter from his mind. Maybe he'll find his own path through his confused sexuality towards love *and* pride. But, closer than any other is the Colonel: a content, purring creature of habit who has adapted to the changes in his master's life with little upset, but for a few slashes at a couple of designer wedding suits (not his fault in the end), the odd needling of a carpet and daily escapes to solitude on our roof. I wish I'd coped as well.

All of these melodies are reassuring. They're the rhythms of 323 Leith Walk. My friends living their lives, already part of mine.
This is home.

Friday 31st December
New Year's Eve.
9 a.m.
Well, I made it to the end of the year, physically intact, mentally ...? Yup, I think I'm okay. I'm still here.

Losses

- One part-time job.
- One cottage.
- One giddy aunt.
- One longterm relationship.
- One part-time lover.
- The respect of my mother. (But what's new?)
- My faith in humanity.

Gains

- One stone of sugar-induced fat.
- One pole dancing waitress (and former childhood buddy).
- One full-time job.
- One caring boss and landlady.
- The Terrible Twins (one of which is a possible sex addict).
- One bedsit.
- One German neighbour, soon to be single-parent by choice.
- One semi-retired globetrotting hippy neighbour.
- Edinburgh.
- My faith in humanity.

Since the great Nigella's book *How to Become A Domestic Goddess* was published, I've tried desperately to become a *Domestic God*, and I'm not sure if I've ever come close, but I've learned that getting your soufflé to rise and trying desperately to impress your other half and his tiny group of friends is not the be-all-and-end-all. There's more to life than moulding yourself for the approval of others. Just being yourself is enough.

Tonight is a party for all the crap we've been through. It's a celebration that our hearts are still beating and that they are, against all the odds, still capable of love. Tonight, Molasses is breaking down the walls that have separated us for too long; throwing a long overdue house warming here at 323. We'll eat, drink and share our hopes and fears for the new year. There will be no escape. No hiding ourselves from the celebration. No hiding ourselves from each other. It will be down to the last man, or woman, standing. But there's one thing I need to do before the firewater starts flowing. Someone I need to see. A bridge to mend in the hope that someday he may find his way back to it and harness the courage to cross it by himself.

4 p.m. I was surprised he came after the verbal beating I gave him. I was strangely calm; he was nervous, clumsy even. His tall frame came striding in, crashing into tables as he swept towards me, overcoat catching on the backs of chairs, and finally, once seated, spilling coffee and ineptly mopping it up with an impractically thin napkin, hopelessly spreading it around the table and all the while apologising profusely. That could so easily have been me months ago. Hell, weeks ago. But life's become more comfortable since I gave him up.

For a moment, I stared deep into his eyes. Allowed myself to bask in their affection. Despite it all, they still caressed me. I could tell he still wanted me. Needed me, perhaps. But how did I feel? That desperate hunger for his love has definitely gone, but nothing comes and goes without a trace, and all that energy is not expended for nought. It miraculously, despite the odds, leaves an impression: I still care.

I told him, 'Nick, I need to tell you, I don't blame you for a single thing. Not for one single hug, one adoring look, or one uttering of love from you. The sleeping around, the lies, the false hope you gave me, I don't blame you for that either. It's a baptism of fire out there. We all go through it. But how you're going about it is wrong. Taking your sexual antics out of the equation, this double life is damaging Christina and yourself. I'm just a stranger you met along the way, that's all. It could so easily have been some other guy. I'm not important, and that's okay.'

'You've no idea how important you are,' he softly said.

I ignored that. It had to become white noise. 'You need to talk to someone, someone who's been in your shoes, someone who isn't me, and find a way out of this. But I can't help you. I think in some warped way we helped each other, for a short time: I gave you something more than just anonymous sex, and you gave a helpless boy some control in his life when he was really lost. I guess I should thank you for that. But I want you to get proper help before you die inside forever.

'But, most importantly, I need you to know, I don't blame you. When you're able to say who you really are, call me, but only then. And don't think that means I'm waiting for you. I'll be your friend when you're ready, but I can't be anything else. But please remember, there's always hope.'

I got up to leave. His eyes didn't look up from the pool of coffee that was staining the grain of the tabletop. I could see his face reflected in the milky liquid. He turned away from his reflection and stared at the floor. He couldn't look at himself any more than he could me.

'Will I ever see you again?' he asked from behind the thick collar of his coat.

'I honestly don't know.'

To walk away at that moment, I had to imagine that he'd be okay, that he'd find his way to honesty and, even though it would be tough as hell for a time, he'd finally be happy. But this was my jumping-off point, and jump I did. Like a passing thought, I was gone.

******

10.45 p.m. The fireworks are primed and ready around the castle, Princes Street is closed to traffic, the streets are filled with cheery revellers intent on the best of nights. Every door is open in the flat, and the whole atmosphere has changed. Cocktails are merrily being shaken by Melve, who's expecting a first-footing from Trenton – perhaps reconciliation is on the cards – Sally has tried on her millionth dress, and in the hall, a large table has been erected and is groaning under the sweet-smelling casseroles prepared by Ms Molasses Brown. We're all set for a brand-new year. A new hope.

And as I reach the last few empty lines of 2010, I play *Through The Dark* once more, allowing KT Tunstall to sing it entirely. I'm testing myself. I even turn it up and listen actively to the words.

They are, of course, always the same; it's me that's changed. Yes, I'm still feeling my way through the dark, but most importantly, despite it all, I'm still capable of feeling.

Saturday 1st January, 2011

New Year's Day.

It's 10 a.m., the first day of 2011, and curiously I have no hangover. It was a fabulous party, which traditionally means I've soaked myself in booze to the point that I start to morph into a bottle of Tequila, but this time I paced myself. Thank goodness! What unfolded indeed required a stable gait.

Fifteen minutes before the bells, Sally decided to follow the Colonel's usual beaten path and straddled out of my window, heels and legs akimbo, sequinned dress hoisted so far up it revealed an almost nonexistent thong. Despite my calls to 'come back down right this minute' (sounding just like my very own mother), off she went, striding up the fire escape in the hope of gaining a superb view of the fireworks.

'Come on, darling, Calton Hill will be jam-packed with silly tourists. Let's not go there tonight. Oooooh, the view from here is amazing!' she hollered. 'I can't believe you've never been up here.'

'Really? I can!' I shouted upwards. I looked into the blackness of the garden below. Mercifully, I couldn't determine the distance my body could fall and crumple into a twisted, bloody heap if I lost my footing. That was a positive, not entirely reassuring, but a positive. I could see people across the way in neighbouring flats bopping around to indecipherable beats and hugging excitedly, enjoying the last few minutes of 2010 as one jubilant entity. I could've headed back inside, but the lesser of two evils really was the rooftop as Melve was tipsy and locked tongue to tongue to Trenton on my very own TARDIS throw – besides, I was pretty sure I'd just heard the distinct clunking of a golden disco belt as it was set free by an eager hand. I couldn't bring myself to look back. I'd promised Sally that she wouldn't be alone at the bells, after all. Mind you, a treacherous climb onto a slippery roof was not in the contract, so she was pushing my loyalty a tad. A deep breath and up I went. What's the worst that could happen, right?

Once I got to the top, I found Ms Knowles perched on the flat section, above the frosty tiles of the pitched slope, just next to a saffron glowing skylight. How the hell she got up there without sliding to her death in those heels is a mystery to me. I had slight issues reaching her, but with the help of a soft, steady arm, I was soon freezing my butt off next to her on the chilly felt. Sally plunged her hand into the depths of her cleavage and produced a red, leather-bound hip-flask. 'Isle of Jura, darling?' she asked, shaking the flask to entice me. 'For courage?' She unscrewed the little lid and handed it to me.

I imagined the sweet warmth from within the cold metal. I gulped back a throat-full, coughing a little as I handed it back. We took in the view and sat in silence for a time. The sky, though meant to be overcast, was so clear it was as if the Hubble telescope had photographed the entire universe for us and projected a glittery collage above our heads. I asked her, 'Do you remember when we used to lose ourselves to stargazing? Flat on our backs down the Glen. We'd be out way beyond our curfews, and our mothers would form a small search party with hands firmly fixed like spatulas, ready to clip us around the ears within a millisecond of the relief of finding us.'

Sally's smile fell, and her face became as fixed as the crisp moss that clung to the tiles around us. 'Yes. Yes, I do,' she said halfheartedly.

Silence.

A roar echoed around the courtyard below. A party in full swing was gaining momentum. It was heartening to me that this tumultuous year was almost at an end. I sighed contentedly, perched, however precariously, next to the safety of my childhood buddy. My past, not rediscovered by me, but gifted to me somehow.

'I can't go back,' she said.

'Nonsense, you made it up here quicker than my cat, surely you can make it back. Just take off your heels.'

'No, I mean, I can't go back to being her, Lisa McKenzie. I hate her. I hate every stupid, gullible, needy particle of her ...' she said, almost crying in anger, spitting every word out as if it was poison. She bolted a 'sweetie' onto the end some seconds later to be sure she was still Sally Knowles amid her rage. The party mood had ended, even though the carnival was happening everywhere, there was a definite jamboree vacuum in our vicinity. For the first time in our friendship, old or new, she cried in front of me. It was as familiar to me as her gaudy laugh. The very same sobs I've heard time and again in the middle of the night through my wall.

The clock was ticking; almost five to twelve. Only minutes left to throw the baggage of 2010 off that roof. She needed to move on. Hell, I needed her to move on! And I needed to understand, maybe not all of it, but some of the facts. I had to ask, 'Sally, what happened to you and George?'

She looked at me. Her mascara was nothing more than molten sludge sliding down her cheeks. And her eyes, her poor, heartbroken, beautiful big eyes, seemed to carry the weight of the world upon them, appearing to concave into nothing but blackness.

'The truth?' she asked.

'The truth.' I assured her, 'Don't worry, I'm here.' I pulled her close to me.

'The truth is, I married a man who was leading a double life.' She sighed, whimpered and pulled a hanky from the other cup of her bra, blowing her nose on it so loudly it ricochet off the walls of the courtyard. 'George was gay, or bisexual, but mostly gay.'

My blood ran cold as Nick came to mind immediately. This was going to be too close for comfort, but she'd been patient and listened to my tales over the past few months. Very patient, indeed. I urged her to continue.

'George killed himself, and I had no idea why. I thought maybe I'd pushed him too hard. I wanted kids, you see, he didn't. I'd nag him to the point where he'd disappear some evenings, just jump in his car and drive off. Then he started working late and leaving early in the mornings so that we'd never have a chance to talk. Eventually, the sex became less and less, to the point of maybe once a month, and I nagged him about that. Then I suggested counselling as I knew we had problems. That went down a storm. He flew into a rage that day and every time I mentioned it afterwards. So I stopped suggesting it. The fun dried up. I had nothing to say, nothing to celebrate, because all I could think about was how great we'd be as parents. I couldn't understand why he didn't see it the same way. Pretty soon, the conversation dried up. He'd grunt, and I'd grunt. We'd become caveman and cavewoman. If we could just communicate we'd get unstuck, I told myself. It was that simple, I thought. If only it could've been.

'When I heard he'd killed himself, I was on a day shift at the Monklands. I got a visit from the police at exactly 15:10hrs. I know the exact time as we had a three o'clock round and I'd just taken a patient's sputum sample from her bedside and was just recording the amount, consistency and colour – Betty Forfar, 72, Chronic Obstructive Pulmonary Disease, single, no kids, heavy smoker, 30 mL, green/brown in colour, third course of antibiotics and steroids in a fortnight, 200 mL of highly concentrated urine in her catheter, poor liver function, not hopeful – funny the things you remember. Sorry, you'd forgotten I was a nurse, hadn't you?'

'Ah, now it makes sense, the urine testing kit, the caring bedside manner over my infected eye and the push to get tested, I should've guessed. But how the hell did you become a pole dancer? The two careers are ...'

'Poles apart? Oh, dear Andy, that's such a bad pun,' she jibed.

'Aye, I know,' I cringed. 'Sorry.'

'I always was a good dancer, even at school, remember? I took some pole dancing classes as a fitness kick when I escaped to New York. I excelled at these, so much so, the tutor asked if I'd consider taking it up as a career. Besides, there's less documentation and less chance of being disciplined over tedious regulations.'

'I suppose so. Sorry, I got sidetracked. Continue.'

'My world caved in right there and then. My husband had thrown himself off a bridge because I refused to let things lie. That was my immediate thought. I'd pushed him over that edge. I dropped the little specimen cup, and the sputum glued itself to the office carpet. I remember thinking, *Carpets in any part of the hospital should be banned, it's not hygienic*, as I scrubbed at the gloopy mess with wet paper towels. The PCs, confused by my behaviour after such earth-shattering news, were unsure what to do next. I remember the charge nurse pulling me away from the floor, almost dragged me across the room to a quiet spot, as the tears flowed and my heart broke.

'The rest of the week was a blur. I couldn't bring myself to go see him, so it fell to his own mother to identify the mess he'd become. She'd lost part of her husband a year previous to a stroke, and now here she was looking at the remnants of her son, pieced together as best they could in such a short space of time. I felt bad about that. I loved that man, I loved her, and yet I didn't have the courage to take some of her pain away and do it for her. I hated him for putting us in that position, and then I felt terrible for hating him, and so the cycle continued.'

She sighed, her words becoming clearer and more confident. 'And so the week was spent not under a dark cloud, but lost in a thick, grey fog. I don't know how I navigated the constant stream of mourners, well-wishers and his family without feeling the overwhelming loss, but I did. I arranged the funeral and the wake. Keeping busy seemed the only option. I don't think I could help myself in any other way. Crying just wasn't getting things done. Besides, it takes up so much energy. I drifted in that fog with little guidance, autonomy or feeling. Comfortably numb, I suppose. I had to be. "Poor old, kind and gentle George," they'd say. All the while I'd think, *What about me? What about all of us who are left behind? He's left us in a right mess*. I felt even worse for thinking that. A loving wife shouldn't think that way. A widow should mourn and love what she once had, but I was so bitter about the hand I'd been thrown that I began to regret the past few years. I felt I'd wasted them.

'I couldn't visit him, once he was buried, I couldn't even drive over the bridge that would forever be George's. I'd avoid it at all costs.' She laughed, 'Hell, I even did a speedy U-turn one afternoon when it dawned on me I was just seconds from crossing that damn bridge, almost crashing into a truck. It wasn't confined only to the bridge, the whole town had changed to me. I would be forever known as the widow of the baker who threw himself off the Old Monklands Bridge. Pretty soon, I began to dream of escaping.

'It was two weeks after the funeral when I got the push I needed. I'd been clearing out the useless junk we'd chucked in the depths of our garage and found an old mobile plugged into the wall, just tucked behind the Flymo and a crate of empty ginger bottles. I'd never seen it before, but here it was fully charged. *How curious,* I thought. I picked it up and typed in his date of birth. No luck. It wasn't his usual passkey. It took me all evening to think of what it could possibly be. It turned out it was Nat King Cole. He loved him singing *Mona Lisa* and would play it to me often when we first dated: released in 1950. Four digits and it sprung into life. Little did I know what I'd find. I'd unzipped a network of sexual encounters dotted around the country, from Inverness to Birmingham, and a plethora of indecent images that would make even the most seasoned of strippers hair extensions curl. I then went on the hunt to uncover the truth. I checked his laptop: more evidence. I checked the wallet he carried around with him stuffed with receipts: further confirmation. I even found lube, poppers and condoms tucked in a shoebox in the back of his wardrobe: case closed.

'Fast forward three weeks later, and I'm in the clap clinic getting my results and lo-and-behold, I'm clean ... apart from the small complication of being HIV positive.'

Just then, it seemed all the bells, in every clock, in the entire city chimed midnight. Partygoers cheered a unified roar for the birth of 2011. Fireworks exploded over the skyline, and the smell of sulphur filled the air. And yet I was still stuck in a tiny bubble of time, five seconds to two-thousand-and-eleven with Lisa McKenzie.

'Oh, my God,' I said.

'Yes, I know, darling. Isn't it beautiful? Just look at the colours.'

'Oh, my God!' I said again. I really was stuck.

'I know, but do try to keep up, sweetie. It's a new year. We can start again.'

'Fuck me, was he positive? Did he infect you?'

'As I said, dear, do try to keep up.' She tore her eyes away from the cacophony above and said to me calmly, 'Yes. Yes, he did.'

The celebration around us seemed relentless.

'Look, Andy, I know you think I'm pretty much a Class A slut, but I've only ever been with one man, my husband, and I may be at the end of my career, but I've got through it without so much as a hand-job. I'm good at my job, and it makes me feel like the most adored woman in the world at times, during and for some time after. The other girls offer extras, but I'm in total control of my clients, and the no touching policy is something I hold dear to my heart. Hell, I haven't even kissed a guy since I found out my status. I'm terrified of talking about it, having to reveal the broken part of me to a man who may overreact and make a sharp exit. And rightly so, they have every right to live untainted, darling. As much as people are afraid of being infected, I'm just as fearful of infecting them. What's happened to me, I can handle, but I can't deal with forcing another human being to make the same adjustments I've had to make.'

I was amazed by how deep she'd buried the turmoil. That took a lot of energy. She'd listened to my woes over Alistair/Nick and kept it all in. She'd encouraged me to get tested, even escorted me right to the needle without a hint of trepidation. She's been there for me as much as her past could allow, and she had every right to shut everyone out when it became too difficult for her. Little insight I had into her personal hell. How judgemental I was and how suspicious of her I've been. She was opening up slowly and carefully, trying not to go completely mad, protecting me and trying desperately to get through life herself.

Lisa was the girl who stood up for me, fought the bullies off, encouraged me to be brave and climb trees and steep hills, and to swing from threadbare ropes over gushing rivers. She was the courageous one; I was timid. Nothing much has changed, she's still encouraging me to climb massive, scary trees because being stuck on the ground just isn't exciting enough. It isn't feeling. It isn't living. Today she looks very different from that tomboy I knew back then: she's mature, strong, sexy, intelligent: phenomenal. She's confident and vivacious, but she's still almost childlike at times. She's no longer Lisa McKenzie, she's become Sally Knowles, and maybe she never really was comfortable being Lisa, maybe Lisa was just a stepping stone to this person that I'm beginning to love. Are we who we were a year, a month, a week or even a day ago? I know I'm not. She deserves better than being trapped in her past.

I thought I was free of HIV. I thought I'd run from it. But here it is again, in my life, in a fully grown ass-kicking woman. Not in a man, like the last time. Steve didn't die of cancer. If only he'd gone and got tested sooner, but one year later was way too late. That's why I ran from this city. That's why I settled down so quickly. Self-preservation. Monogamy. Safety in fewer numbers. I had the fear of God put in me. I still have that fear. Ryan too. We never really *talk* about Steve. We never said HIV when he was dying because he didn't want to be known as the promiscuous guy on the scene that got his 'just deserts'. Out of respect for him, we don't say it, not even to each other. He was one of the few that couldn't tolerate the treatment, he had terrible side effects, and he really had left it far too late, hence my catch 22. It was too much for us to live with, so we ran our separate ways. Here they are again, those terrible letters, and I refuse to run this time. I wanted to find my past and start again. Sally really is my past, more than she knows, more than I could've ever imagined. She's the part of me that I could never live with. But Sally's the walking, talking proof that it doesn't have to be the end, that testing and treatment has come on leaps and bounds. She, and others like her, are proof of a happy ever after.

I mentioned none of this to her, I just said, 'I still have issues with it. It scares me to death.'

'Maybe that's a good thing,' she said, 'the fear of it may stop you being careless someday. Never lose the fear, but don't make room for prejudice.'

'Agreed,' I said. 'Thanks for being honest.'

'To be frank, darling, it's a bloody relief. It's a chore to be a diva and a torch song singer all at once; it's like having two jobs. And I already have two jobs!'

We laughed.

She paused. 'I had to know if I could trust you, there are still many people at home that want my blood, fools that they are. I'm sorry for not telling you sooner.'

'That's very much okay.'

'I don't want to run any more. I want to stay here with you and all the other crazy people who live here. To build something solid and look toward the future.'

I gazed over the rooftops. The stars were beginning to peek through the canopy of smoke as it dispersed throughout the burgh. We were but two people within a city of over five hundred thousand souls, all looking towards a new year, a 'new me', but I believed that no one needed a new start more than us. Then I remembered I'd been carrying something in my jeans. 'Oh, I almost forgot,' I said, dipping into my pocket. 'I stole something from your room, sorry about that.' I showed her the wedding ring.

'Oh, Andy, I can't,' she said regrettably.

'No, you see, I have the same problem. I can't let go of mine, see?' I delved in my other pocket and showed her the ring I'd planned on proposing to Thomas with a year ago to this day. 'But maybe these rings weren't meant for those relationships. Maybe they're meant for us.'

'What do you mean?'

'Look, I need to move on and so do you, so let's do it together. I want my friend back for good.' I got on one knee and showed her both rings. 'See, they're almost identical. That's too much of a coincidence for the universe not to be telling us something. Sally Knowles, would you do me the greatest honour and be my life-long buddy?'

She hesitated, pondered a while as she looked at the rings cautiously. Then she smiled, downed the last of her whisky and said, 'Why the hell not, brotherfucker?'

I slid my ring on the only finger that it would fit on her right hand: her thumb. She grinned with excitement as she admired it. 'Nice. Perfect choice,' she said.

She stood up and took her ring from the palm of my hand and said, 'There's no way I'm getting on one knee, not in this dress. Besides, I'm done with crawling, remember?' Then she instinctively slid the shiny palladium on my right pinky.

'Perfect,' I said. 'I think it's high time the pinky ring made a comeback.' I grinned.

We sat on the roof again and held our hands up to the sky, admiring our exchange. I asked, 'What do you wish for in 2011, Sally Knowles?'

She smiled, lit up a cigarette and took a long, deep draw in contemplation. The paper crackled, and the embers glowed. Her eyes lit up as if suddenly seeing a bright future. She exhaled slowly with her head held high, crouching with her knees close to her chin and said, 'To be fearless.'

I nodded in agreement, 'Me too. So let's start right here, right now. I need help with something.'

'What?'

I pulled her closer to me, cupped her face in my hands, and kissed her deeply, lovingly, without fear or condition. Sally, hesitant at first, pulled back slightly, but then she pressed hard against my lips, falling into the warmth of my mouth, as I did into hers. It was thirty seconds tops before we unlocked. A mixture of man, woman and smoke. I couldn't help but smile. A thousand kisses may have passed these lips, but this one meant more than any that've gone before. We were two friends, on a rooftop, saying goodbye to the angst of the past and opening ourselves up to the boldness of the future. One

HIV positive woman, afraid to kiss someone who's negative, who was afraid to kiss someone with HIV. It was an open door that both of us could leap through, and leap we did.

'There, that's got that out of the way,' I said, feeling a little cheeky and kiddish. 'Now we can get on with 2011, don't you think?'

She touched her lips, then covered them bashfully with both palms. Her eyes crinkled up at the edges. 'Darling! Our second kiss. Very naughty of you to use tongue.' She giggled quietly, which grew into a soft laugh, which caused me to do the same, which drew us into howling and caterwauling over the rooftops. The pain had been kissed away, and the wounds were beginning to heal. We could start again. We could regenerate.

Gwen called to us from below, 'Hey, are you two going to be up there all night, or are we going to have to come up and join you, pregnant or not? The concert was a total success, by the way.'

Sally shushed me with her finger against her lips, taming her laughter with tears in her eyes as smoke wisps curled from her lips. She called to Gwen, 'Sorry, darling. We'll be down in a jiffy.' Then she turned to pick something up at her side and said to me, 'Oh, I almost forgot to give you this, darling.'

She handed me a large, leather-bound book. 'What's this?'

'It's a bible.' She held back a chuckle with a snort. 'No, you klutz, it's a new diary.'

I became tearful, 'Thank you.'

'It's bigger than your last, but as that one's proved, your life is too big for the condensed version, especially with me in it. 2011 will be wonderfully Technicolor and in Cinemascope, darling! And I expect it to remain as detailed and uncensored as the last, not that I'm going to read it, of course.'

'Of course, you wouldn't,' I mocked. I opened it to the front page and found an inscription:

'For Andy, my friend.
Live without fear.
Dance like a diva.
Write like no one is reading.
Here's to a more honest year.
With love, Sally. X'

I pressed my forehead against hers, closed my eyes and whispered, 'Thank you.'

'Oft! It's bloody freezing up here now. Brrrrrr!' she said, crossing her arms and rubbing them with vigour. 'Anyway, sweetie. Let's not get too soppy. I'm running short on mascara.'

'Now *that* I don't believe,' I jibed.

She stood up, waved her cigarette in the air dramatically and declared, 'Come on, honey. Let's go see our friends and then hit the town.' She paused and gripped me by the shoulders excitedly, 'Oh! Oh! Let's find a policeman. Let's find two!'

'What? Why?'

'Because everyone knows you have to kiss a policeman at New Year. It's classic, and we are, after all, classy and classic. Besides, I'm on a kissing roll now. Come on, it'll be fun. No strings attached. Well, just one: I'll pick yours, and you can pick mine. Maybe that's two strings? Anyhow! No fear?'

I nodded in agreement and mimicked as if reading a theatre sign buzzing in dazzling lights, 'Andy Angus and Sally Knowles: Fearless!'

She dropped her cigarette on the roof and stamped it out.

'Careful,' I said, 'you'll ruin your Jimmy Choos; those are vintage, no?'

'Ha! And he claims he knows nothing about fashion. Nice to see I've had an influence at last. Besides, that may've been my last cigarette; I may give them up as a New Year's resolution.'

'Nah, I don't believe in resolutions; a waste of bloody time. Perfection is overrated. It's a new year. We made it! Let's celebrate that, let's not look for faults; they'll find us soon enough,' I said as we made our way to the warmth of our friends. As we made our way home.

******

2010 is done. I'm putting it to bed along with this battered old diary, the cover of which has become worn, and the pages are rippled from the pressure of my thoughts. Even when it's shut, I can see my life is bursting from between the lines. Our lives. Things change, we change, and nothing can stay the same, no matter how hard the control freak inside of us tries to bolt them down. But it's time to close this book and let it gather dust. Someday, in the distant future,

I'll take you down, old friend, dust you off and peek inside. A fleeting glimpse from inside the vortex, if you will, that will take the fear from the uncertainty of the days to come. The solidity of the past will reassure me that life is littered with moments that can seem insurmountable, but the world will still turn, people will come and go, some may die, but every single one of them will never be forgotten by those they touched. Somewhere in the vastness of space is us, and we are much more significant than we can ever allow ourselves to imagine.

Printed by Amazon Italia Logistica S.r.l.
Torrazza Piemonte (TO), Italy